BLADE & ROSE

BLADE AND ROSE SERIES BOOK 1

MIRANDA HONFLEUR

Cover art by Mirela Barbu

Map by Rela "Kellerica" Similä

Editing by Dominion Editorial

Proofreading by Roxana Mihai

Paperback ISBN: 978-0-9994854-1-5

http://www.mirandahonfleur.com/

ALSO BY MIRANDA HONFLEUR

Witch of the Lake: The Complete Trilogy

To my husband, Tony,
for being in my corner while I pursue my dream.
You inspire me, motivate me, and make every day better.

1

*O*ut the fifth-story window, or not at all.

It was her only chance to sneak out unnoticed. Rielle sprang from the bed and grabbed a coat, white wool with the master mage's four-bar chevron, and fastened the double rows of buttons from neck to hip.

Gloves next. No glow of spellcasting to give her away. She slipped her hands into the wool-lined leather and flexed her fingers. A new pair. The heat of her pyromancy last mission had ruined the previous set.

With a flick of her wrist, she extinguished the fireplace and every candle in the room, willing the flames away until only darkness and the faint glow of the gibbous moon remained.

She tossed her braid over her shoulder and opened the window latch. Her boot perched on the sill, she peered at the ground. Dark. Quiet. Empty.

Farther from the Tower, torches illuminated the walls of the inner bailey, dotted the outer bailey and the gates. Beyond them, white pines challenged the midnight sky, their peaks silvered by the moon. The forest— that was her destination.

If a guard on wall duty looked at the Tower of Magic instead of out at the gates and the surrounding wilds... Well, a mage jumping out her fifth-story window would not go unreported.

And yet, Olivia's silence—and the capital's—went ignored. On her desk was Olivia's latest letter, which she'd read a dozen times already and replied to three weeks ago.

No response.

She'd told the Tower's Proctor, asked about the capital... Nothing. Either no one knew, or no one cared. She curled a fist.

Tonight, she'd get her answer.

She tapped the window frame.

An early autumn wind riffled her coat. She shivered, eyeing the five-story drop as she climbed onto the sill.

If she got caught, she'd be punished into the next life, and Brennan—well, a werewolf was the kind of monster thought to exist only in fairy tales. The kind of monster that incited mobs bearing torches and pitchforks. And yet—

With a curl of her index and middle fingers, she called an updraft strong enough to catch her and held it. *This better work.*

She jumped.

The spelled wind pushed against her boots, her coat, *her,* as she descended, the force strong enough to keep her from breaking upon the rough white-marble courtyard.

Suspended just above the ground, she uncurled her fingers, dispelling the aeromancy.

Her boots clicked upon the courtyard's flagstones. She caught her breath. Divine be praised.

Briefly closing her eyes, she chanced an inward glance. Her anima's inner luminosity remained bright. As long as she kept her spellcasting limited to her innate elemental magic, she probably wouldn't need to find another mage for resonance later.

In the shadows, she crept to the eastern edge of the white stone inner wall, watching for patrolling guards on the battlements. Thankfully, they guarded against intruders and not escapees, but tonight, they were nowhere to be seen. Slacking off?

She shrugged. No matter. If they weren't here, her escape would be all the easier. In the cover of the inner wall, she sidled against it until she reached a stack of hay bales.

Scanning the battlements for patrols, she climbed over the sweet-smelling hay, prickly even through her gloves. Near the top, she stilled, holding her breath.

Not a single guard.

Something wasn't right.

She listened for something, anything, but heard only her own heavy breaths. Perhaps she'd see something from a vantage point on the wall.

With a grunt, she dragged herself onto a crenel, waited for any sound, and hearing none, emerged from between the merlons. Crouched, she scanned the length of the stone wall in both directions.

No one. There should have been at least two guards here, two more near the corner on the southern inner wall, but she couldn't see any.

A distant shout. She darted to the nearest merlon on the wall's outer face.

About five hundred feet away, just inside the outer bailey by the western gate, spells lit the darkness. Flashes of brilliant color popped in disarray. A skirmish.

A small group clustered around a single armored intruder. Torchlight glinted off his blade as he dueled a mage guard, evading, defending, attacking.

Her eyes widened.

Wildfire. He moved like wildfire.

Armor of massive plate—sage tinted. She knew it. Arcanir.

He had to be a warrior-priest of the Order of Terra. A paladin.

What was one of *them* doing here?

She counted the guards—six. All of them? No one left to even sound the alarm? They engaged the paladin at the western gate. Rainier Valentin fired a purple blur of conjured daggers while the paladin fought another mage wielding a massive scythe.

No, not another mage—another Rainier. All six of them were Rainier. He'd created five apparitions of himself, all of them attacking with ethereal weapons, distracting the whirling paladin. Every strike with the arcanir sword dispelled a conjured blade.

The five other mage guards lay afield, already defeated. Only Rainier and his apparitions remained to protect the Tower.

She spelled her eyes with earthsight. The fallen guards still glowed with threads of bright anima, were still breathing. She dispelled it. If he'd left them alive, the paladin wouldn't kill Rainier either.

Across the outer bailey by the eastern gate, two small forms crept in the faint torchlight—children? Tower novices, nothing separating them from the intruder but the length of a cobblestone path. Fiery red hair... and a shaved head. Jacqui and Luc. What were they doing out at this hour?

She curled her fingers into a fist. Would he see them as mere children? Or only more mages to fight?

Being mere children hadn't kept her or her brothers and sisters safe in Laurentine nine years ago. When the pirates had—

No, that's in the past. She took a deep, cleansing breath.

Rainier would keep him busy until someone from the Tower took notice. After all, they fought in the outer bailey of the Emaurrian Tower of Magic... Over a hundred mages lived here, including a wild mage and a magister.

One paladin. The odds spoke for themselves.

And if no one emerged, well... His luck would run out. As much as she needed answers about Olivia, Jacqui and Luc's safety came first. If the Proctor reprimanded her for sneaking out, so be it. She could handle another round of his discipline.

The paladin struck Rainier in the face with the pommel of his sword. No, an apparition of Rainier. Violet smoke puffed, rose. Dispelled.

"I mean you no harm!" the paladin bellowed. Barely a breath later, he breezed through three more apparitions. In a veil of smoke, he elbowed another in the abdomen hard enough to make him splutter and fall. Dematerialized on the ground. Another apparition.

The smoke cleared, and with an arc of golden light, Rainier conjured a fiery blade. No apparitions. Just him. He never did turn away from a fight.

"Let me pass!" The paladin raised the visor on his helm.

Rainier didn't move. "By order of the Divinity, you are to submit to questioning, paladin."

They were a little past questioning now. The paladin forged ahead toward the eastern gate.

She grimaced. Rainier's conjured blade wouldn't stop a paladin; while he was in his arcanir armor, no direct magic could affect him.

But with the conjured blade, Rainier set upon him anyway.

The paladin parried, his arcanir sword dispelling the conjured weapon, and coupled it with an armored uppercut to Rainier's jaw with his knuckle dusters.

She winced. Where were the other mages? She needed to get to Brennan. A backward glimpse of the Tower's doors revealed no activity. She looked back at Luc and Jacqui, huddled across the outer bailey, and then at the fight.

Divine's flaming fire. She pressed her lips in a tight line.

Rainier fell to the ground but pushed against it with his hands.

The paladin elbowed him in the back. "Stay down."

He did.

The paladin made for the eastern gate—and for Jacqui and Luc, who cowered together by the portcullis but assumed a battle stance. No. They had no chance of stopping him. But now they were definitely targets.

Magic coursing through her, Rielle focused on the paladin's path and formed a circle with her hands, straining to cast five hundred feet away. Anima flowed from inside her, powering her spell.

Beneath the paladin, the ground cracked into a web thirty feet in diameter. He wouldn't be able to jump clear of it in a full suit of armor.

He glanced down, then ran.

It was too late.

A great rumbling filled the air as the ground broke and collapsed, leaving the downed, injured mages gasping and coughing in the dust cloud.

Her spell transmuted the soil to stone, some twenty feet deep—she hoped.

She cast an updraft and jumped from the battlements. After landing on the soft grass, she cast candlelight, summoning a small flame to her palm to light the way through the darkness.

Ahead of her lay the pit she'd created, and within it, the man of the hour.

His little invasion would cost her information on Olivia tonight, and no doubt punishment from the Proctor. Besides the unquestionable fun of cleaning garderobes and scouring pots and pans, punishment meant having to stay in the Tower instead of going on mission. She'd enlisted with the Divinity to do some good in this world, not to play chambermaid.

All for some paladin's whim. She huffed and shook her head.

Well, her last chance to avoid—she sighed—*minimize* her punishment was to handle this impeccably.

Paladins considered themselves mankind's last defense against the so-called perils of magic. It had been centuries since there had been an *official* clash between the mages of the Divinity of Magic and the paladins of the Order of Terra. However, their relations had never been friendly.

But five years ago, during a mission in Signy, she'd healed a young paladin on the brink of death. They clung to honor. She could use that.

She approached the pit and knelt, crumbling dirt in from the rim and the freshness of earth into the air.

The paladin grunted. She poked her head over the edge to watch his futile attempt to scale the sides, his face contorted with the effort through his helm's open visor. He kicked out, pounded his armored foot onto the stone bottom, his hands clenched into fists.

Without help, he'd be going nowhere. When she held the flame out, he glared up at her and planted his hands on his hips.

"I demand that you free me." A deep, authoritative rumble of a voice.

She met his gaze squarely. "And *I* demand that you surrender."

He snorted and looked away, scanning the confines of his prison. "Surrender? What about 'no quarter'?"

No quarter. Yes, on missions, the Divinity required that mages give no quarter—take no prisoners.

"This isn't a mission. You will not be harmed if you comply. But if you are so eager to die, that can yet be arranged." When he didn't look her way, she shrugged: a waiting game would end only in her favor. "Suit yourself. I can wait. I'm not the one trapped in a hole."

The paladin pressed his lips together, still and staring into the shadows. His gaze meandered back to hers. "This has nothing to do with the Tower. I'm just passing through on my way to Monas Ver on the Order's business."

Perhaps his words would have had an effect where the Order held sway, but not here. "That means nothing to me."

He should have submitted at the western gate. The guards let nearly everyone through without so much as a question, and they would've even let a paladin through after questioning. An hour or two, and he could've been on his way. Everyone knew. If he didn't like it, he could've gone farther south around the Tainn Mountains through the duchy of Maerleth Tainn and its pass. But two hours lost beat several days.

The paladin exhaled a harsh breath. "Terms."

At last, a practical response. "If you harm no one, you have my word that I will allow no harm to come to you. You agree to meet the Proctor of this Tower of Magic and submit to his questioning."

He paced the dark pit for a moment and then paused. "I accept." Although he didn't seem pleased, the word of a paladin was renowned as ironclad. "I am your prisoner."

"Wise choice."

The paladin raised his head. "Well?"

"Sit." Geomancy leveling spells were not known for their smoothness, and she didn't want him unconscious.

He grimaced. When she simply waited, he heaved a sigh and sat on the bedrock with a clatter of armor.

She acknowledged his cooperation with a contented shrug. "Brace yourself."

She took a few steps back before dismissing her candlelight spell. Calling upon her magic once more, she formed a circle with her hands, tying her gesture to the invisible threads of anima in the earth.

When she raised her arms, the ground beneath her feet shook. Dust rose from the ground, shimmering in distant torchlight. A deafening rumble filled the air.

Off to the side, Jacqui and Luc struggled to remain standing.

The bottom of the pit rose, bedrock turning to loose earth and churning upward, raising the paladin with it.

At last, he was at her level, and she completed the spell. He scrutinized the ground beneath him with a frown.

He was a tower of a man, about six-and-a-half feet tall, and the full arcanir plate armor made him massive. It was rare that, at her own significant height, she felt so small.

"Luc, Jacqui," she called. The two novices shuffled over. She inspected the paladin's weapons belt; he carried a sword and a dagger. "Disarm."

He didn't move.

"I can't allow you to enter the Tower, much less the Proctor's quarters, armed." Although she preferred his compliance, her fingers tingled, ready to cast should he refuse.

"If I wanted to kill you, I wouldn't need weapons."

A threat. She grinned. "Then you should have no objection to handing them over."

After a ponderous silence, he threw off his sheathed sword, dagger, and sword belt.

"Luc." She cocked her head toward the weapons, her fingers still ready to cast. If the paladin dared attack Luc, she'd spell every stone in the outer bailey's walls to crush him.

Luc collected the weapons, gaping at them as though he held magic itself; it had to be his first encounter with arcanir. He moved behind her once more.

"And the armor," she ordered.

The paladin narrowed his eyes. "I will not relinquish my armor. It's not a weapon and poses no danger."

No danger? She raised an eyebrow. She'd seen him punch Rainier with his knuckle-dusters. The conjurer was still out cold.

His armor, shimmering a faint sage green over steel gray, showed some wear but appeared well maintained. It had seen a significant amount of combat.

But the paladin's armor wouldn't save him if he attacked her or the Proctor. There were plenty of surroundings to funnel into a whirlwind to crush him. And the Proctor, a force-magic magister, could do far worse to him.

"Come." She inclined her head toward the Tower.

His face hard, the paladin moved in the direction she indicated. From his shoulders hung a long, heavy woolen cloak of pure white—not unlike her own meticulously maintained immaculate mage coat—with the Order's moon-shaped coat of arms adorning its back.

A crowd of mages hurried toward them, voices raised in commotion. She grimaced. So *now* they came, when the work was nearly done? She held up her hand.

One stopped directly in her path.

Of course it was Kieran Atterley—a master singular elementalist, a hydromancer, and her bitter rival.

She cut around the paladin and faced Kieran. With his tall lean build, wavy copper locks, and bright sapphire eyes, he was the oft-cited hand-somest master in the Emaurrian Tower.

But that handsome face masked ruthlessness. He'd been a thorn in her side ever since she'd won the coveted apprenticeship to Magister Leigh Galvan seven years ago. Four years after that, when she was nineteen, Kieran had reported her to Magehold for master–apprentice misconduct, with nothing to gain but the satisfaction of ruining her master's life and hers. And last year, he'd pushed her down the spiral stone stairs from the Tower's second floor.

His ire seemed insatiable.

He sneered down at her. "I'll take it all from here."

Now, seeing a possible commendation in the capture of a trespasser, he wanted to *take it all from here*?

She leaned in toward him, narrowed her eyes. "You can take one thing. A knee to the jewels. You want it?"

He huffed a sharp breath.

"Then get out of my way."

He spat. "You—"

Before he could touch her, she gestured a flame cloak over her entire body. It flared to life, wreathing her in protective fire, ready for battle. She wasn't exactly the notorious Flame of the Crag Company, but she'd more than earned her four-bar master chevron. If he wanted a fight, she was ready. And he'd lose.

She strode into his path, her shoulder colliding with his. His black mage coat caught fire there, and he beat at the flames. She looked over her shoulder at the paladin. "Follow. Luc, Jacqui, you, too."

Taut as a harp string, Kieran stood aside as the paladin, Luc, and Jacqui moved past.

Luc outran them to the open Tower doors, and spilled the light from within. At the entrance, she dispelled her flame cloak.

When the paladin raised his hands, her muscles contracted, but he only removed his helmet.

The light of the Tower's sconces revealed a handsome visage: mid to late twenties, a few years older than she. Close-cropped brown hair and eyes a familiar blue, the color of the Shining Sea in a storm. A scar slashed through his left eyebrow. And like all paladins, he was clean shaven, but his lack of facial hair did nothing to diminish him; it only complemented a decidedly masculine jaw.

She turned away. He might have a handsome face, but she'd seen handsome faces before. Falling for their appeal rarely ended well. Especially when they belonged to unattainable men who'd sworn a vow of celibacy.

In her periphery, he scrubbed a hand through his hair and then rubbed his neck.

Low on the right side below his jaw, there was a scar about the width of a blade. Another just behind his ear—an exit wound. Healed, but poorly.

It couldn't be.

No, it was *him*. From five years ago.

2

*I*t *was* him. The paladin from five years ago. There was no doubt about it.

Trying to stay calm, Rielle instructed Luc to deliver the weapons to her quarters. The paladin's gaze trailed after them.

Perhaps he didn't recognize her. He had been, after all, on the brink of death.

Five years ago, she'd assisted the paladins in the Viscounty of Signy. One of them had died saving her and the hostages—Sir Bastien Proulx.

And she'd never forget the young paladin who'd fought Sir Bastien's killer and nearly died in the attempt. Blood pouring, red and frothy. Gurgling. Eyes like the Shining Sea pleading for life. He would die. She'd known he would die. But she'd had to attempt healing, although she'd never successfully healed anyone before. She'd hummed "Winter Wren," somehow lowered her inner barriers, whispered the incantation... Healed him. Healed the gaping wound in his neck. But she'd lacked the skill to fade the scar.

The same scar before her now. He definitely didn't recognize her.

His eyes met hers. Caught staring, she briskly ushered him to the Tower's center and ascended the spiral steps to the top floor, where the Proctor's quarters were located. Eight floors.

Eight *long* floors.

The man himself hardly ever left his quarters, but everyone else in the Tower had to make the climb.

Panting, she emerged on the Proctor's level and checked on her captive. The paladin stood calmly, unhampered by the several flights of stairs he'd just climbed—in full armor. He didn't bother hiding a smile. A dimple played at the corner of his mouth.

"Do you need a rest?" His eyes danced.

Smug brute. He dared taunt her, his captor? Was she wearing a sign today that said, *Try me?* She squared her shoulders. "The Proctor's quarters are just ahead."

"What's he like?" he asked, his voice deep, smooth, yet with a subtle roughness like lindenwood bark.

"Powerful." Cruel. Unyielding. A massive, sanctimonious pain.

The massive doors opened, and she came face to face with the Proctor's apprentice, Bernadette Dufort. The daughter of a Courdevallan baker, the dun-haired Berny had traded her chores for Rielle's kitchen duty from time to time. Berny averted her tear-streaked gaze.

"What's wrong?" Rielle reached for her, but Berny twisted away.

"It's the cap—" Berny shook her head and held back a sob. "I can't. I'm sorry." She ran toward the stairwell and disappeared in a hasty shuffle of steps.

"Berny—" Rielle called out, but to no avail. She furrowed her brow. Bernadette Dufort was one of the most composed mages—and people in general—she had ever met. It would take something catastrophic to unsettle her. What had affected her? She'd have followed, but not with a captive in tow.

All the more reason to deliver him to the Proctor. With a deep breath, she led the paladin into the foyer toward another set of doors. She knocked hesitantly.

"Enter," came the gruff reply.

Her shoulders slumped. Perfect. In a wonderful mood already.

The Proctor's receiving room was warmer than the Tower's cool stone walls allowed at the beginning of autumn. The sconces were enchanted with not just light spells but warming spells. The old man must have been feeling the cold at the ripe age of seventy-two.

Exotic Sonbaharan rugs woven in priceless Zeharan red, ultramarine, kermes, and other invaluable dyes covered the cool white-marble floors. The furniture, made of rare and exquisite purple heartwood, only graced the rooms of the Grand Divinus, monarchs, and Proctors.

Bookcases lined every available wall, some double stacked and stretching fifteen feet to the domed ceiling. There, a fresco included all eleven schools of accepted magic—elemental, illusion, force, transmutation, spirit, conjury, healing, cantus, lucency, shadowmancy, and augury, as well as the three schools of forbidden magic, sangremancy, necromancy, and mentalism—all engaged in war against one another.

The Dark Age of Magic. It was what the Divinity called the ancient time of the Archons, who had ruled covens of witches fighting one another for territory and dominance, before the unity of the Divine bound all mages together under the Grand Divinus and the Divinity of Magic.

This representation of the Dark Age of Magic graced the Proctor's quarters of every Tower of Magic, an ever-present reminder of the Divinity's importance. If only that reminder had taken.

She sighed inwardly. Rather than remaining united and focusing on making a difference, most of the Tower's master mages spent their time deadlocked over which feuding faction's tenets had the most merit.

Perhaps they needed more than a fresco to remind them. Maybe a look outside at all the people who needed mages to help them.

Or a song. A really catchy song.

Finishing up some scrawling in a book, the Proctor leaned over a table with his back to them, then turned. Authoritative in his heavy black mage coat bearing the illustrious five-bar chevron of a magister, he boasted a head full of gray hair and a mouth framed by lines and a well-kept beard. Tonight, he wore an unequivocal frown, the expression he usually wore in her presence. He held a piece of parchment before him.

"My lord?" the paladin asked.

No! Don't annoy him. She elbowed the paladin without a hint of subtlety, a move she regretted as tremors radiated up her arm at the collision with his armor.

The Proctor laughed. He actually laughed. A chill snaked up her spine. When had she last updated her will?

"Six," the Proctor said in a lofty tone. "You defeated six of my subordinates tonight, Sodalis." He used the Old Emaurrian address for paladins. "Your training has served you well."

She knew better than to trust that tone. At least the paladin had the good sense to remain silent.

The Proctor turned a frown on her. "And you, Magos? What were you doing outside?"

Divine's flaming fire. It would've helped to come up with an alibi.

Who'd been out there? Luc, Jacqui, Kieran, Rainier—

Rainier. She'd completed missions with him in the past, and they'd obliged each other with resonance from time to time. She chose her words with care. "I went out to see Rainier, but no one was guarding the

inner gate. When I looked out, I saw a skirmish, and I went to help."
Simple.

At the soft metal clink, she gritted her teeth and eyed the paladin peripherally. He'd tilted his head toward her.

Don't ruin this for me.

The paladin remained quiet, a mere twitching in his clenched jaw.

The Proctor waved the parchment. "Are you certain? Is that the reason for your midnight jaunt, Magos?" When she nodded, he heaved a sigh. "And yet, Rainier isn't often on the night shift. What is the reason for your jaunts on those nights?"

Deny, deny, deny. "I haven't the slightest—"

"Save your excuses. You've finally been caught." He didn't look at her.

She swallowed. He knew about Brennan? Did he know what Brennan was? What she did every month in that forest?

No, give him nothing. "I am confused, my lord."

The Proctor peered at the parchment, then regarded her and the paladin with narrowed eyes. "Do you not know each other?"

She opened her mouth, but no words came out. Five years ago, she and Leigh had mentioned in their report that she'd saved a paladin in the field, but she hadn't known his name. She still didn't.

Did the Proctor guess this was he? Imply she'd been meeting with this paladin?

For what purpose? She peeked at her alleged accomplice.

Accomplice to what? Why would she be meeting *him* in the forest?

After a brief hesitation, the paladin met her gaze. He looked her over before correcting himself, then turned away.

Young, handsome, forbidden.

The Proctor thinks this man is my lover. An illicit romance.

Another illicit romance.

Given her past, the motive fit. *Damn it, damn it, damn it!*

"No." She frowned. "If I knew him, my lord, why wouldn't I have let him defeat the guards and escape?" Her shoulders tightened.

The Proctor creased his brow and shook the parchment. Did he hold the report from Signy five years ago?

Before she could say anything more, the paladin took a slow step forward. "My lord, I swear to you this woman and I do not know each other. In any fashion." He cleared his throat. "If I may speak further, my lord, I believe I can clarify this situation."

The Proctor nodded. She, too, was interested in what he had to say.

The paladin stood to attention, firelight playing in the reflective surface of his armor. "I am Sir Jonathan Ver." The name designated him as an orphan raised at Monas Ver, one of several Order of Terra monasteries in Emaurria. "Since I took my vows at eighteen, I have been a Sodalis of the Order of Terra and followed the Code of the Paladin. Normally, like all men of my order, I give the Tower of Magic a wide berth, but I received a message from the High Priest of Monas Ver. In my haste to return there, I was careless and disrespectful. With utmost sincerity and deference, I apologize for my reckless actions." He lowered his head.

"A message?" The Proctor echoed her own curiosity.

"Forgive me, but it is private."

"I can respect that," the Proctor replied, much to her surprise and disappointment. "And why didn't you submit to questioning at the gate?"

The paladin's face tightened. "I needed to get from Villecourt to Monas Ver. Quickly. There was no time for questioning."

Quickly... He'd had to cross the Tainn Mountains. The next pass was at Maerleth Tainn, several days' detour. The quickest route was through the Tower's pass, but the paladin had gotten greedy, trying to avoid questioning.

The Proctor canted his head. "Did it not occur to you, Sodalis, that we would catch you?"

Ha! She grinned, but when the Proctor's gaze turned on her, she covered her mouth and coughed quietly.

"Forgive me for saying this, Proctor"—the paladin relaxed—"but I saw no reason why I wouldn't be able to fight my way through. The mages have forgotten who we are. What we can do. And cutting through the Tower's gate was the fastest available route to Monas Ver." He scowled pointedly at her.

She stifled a half-laugh. He would have made it through... until she'd spoiled his plans.

"Monas Ver," the Proctor repeated slowly. "Tell me, Sir Jonathan, is Derric Lazare still the High Priest of Monas Ver?"

He knew a High Priest of the Order of Terra by name? She closed her gaping mouth.

The paladin's bearing broke for a moment. "Yes," he answered. "May I ask how you know Father Derric, my lord?"

Because a respectable High Priest would never deign to associate with a hedonistic mage, even a venerable Proctor?

The paladin turned to her briefly. Had she snarled aloud?

"We grew up together." The Proctor stared in reverie for a moment. "I will contact him shortly. Have a seat." He gestured to the chairs studding his table and disappeared into another room.

Have a seat? The Proctor left prisoners standing. This paladin had transformed from prisoner to guest with the mention of one High Priest's name? What, did knowing this "Derric" suddenly excuse this paladin breaking through the gate and thrashing six mages?

She exhaled sharply. The night was full of surprises. She eyed the paladin, and he her, before she turned away. She removed her gloves, then flattened an imaginary wrinkle in her white mage coat.

"Contact? How can that be?" The paladin broke the silence.

There was one way, at least. "By aerarius, a magical communication brazier made of recondite. Does your High Priest have anything like that?"

A user could light it, whisper an incantation and the name of an intended partner who also possessed an aerarius, and it would enable a line of communication between them. Made from the scarce magical metal recondite, aerarii were created long before the Divinity and the Towers, in the Dark Age of Magic.

The paladin creased his brow for a moment but nodded.

So the High Priest of Monas Ver was in possession of an aerarius.

"I never knew it was... Derric didn't reveal much about his life before the priesthood."

"You know him well?"

"He raised me." He offered her a smile and then frowned. "Forgive me, but I don't know your name."

"Favrielle," she said too soon, her mouth acting before her mind could; she didn't like being called by her given name. She offered her hand.

He took her hand in his and, much to her surprise, brushed his lips over her knuckles in a whisper of contact.

She raised an eyebrow. It was the greeting of a nobleman, not an orphaned commoner—clearly courtesy of his former paladin-master, no doubt a noble. But he seemed sincere.

No. Since she'd deprived him of his sword and dagger, he resorted to unconventional weapons. Charisma. A tower full of mages was too much direct resistance for any one paladin, even given his impressive display at the gate.

"Well met, Favrielle." A brief but charming smile. He released her hand, but his touch still ghosted across her skin.

She covered her misbehaving hand with the other.

"Call me Rielle," she corrected gruffly.

The paladin furrowed his brow. She remembered too late that the only polite answer to familiarity was familiarity.

"Jon."

"Well, Jon," she said, his name falling uncomfortably from her lips, "it seems we're in for a long night."

There was no telling how long the Proctor's conversation would be, and that would hardly conclude their dealings.

Jon approached the table and pulled out a chair for her. *Don't fall for his flattery.* She wavered. *But don't give away that you know.* She took the seat and thanked him while he unfastened his cloak and carefully slung it over another chair. When he sat next to her, the scar on his neck caught her eye again.

But perhaps it wasn't him. Maybe it was a different man, with a different scar, caused by a different person.

"How did you get that?" she blurted, indicating the scar with a nod.

A wry smile tugged the corner of his mouth. "Perhaps by asking probing questions."

So much for etiquette. She stared at the scar, her curiosity overpowering her caution. "A healer could fade that for you."

"No."

"Why not?"

His hand went to where his sword pommel would be—but slowly—a contemplative gesture. With the sword absent, he curled his fingers before resting his hands in his lap. "It's a reminder of someone who died, and someone I have yet to hold to account."

She swallowed. The Code of the Paladin forbade vengeance. Paladins swore to uphold the Code and, above all, the four Sacred Vows of the Paladin: piety, poverty, sobriety, and celibacy. Priests and paladins of the Order were always denying themselves everything to please their goddess, Terra. "I thought the Order forbade vengeance."

"It does."

Whom did he seek vengeance on? If it had to do with that scar, perhaps it was against the man who'd caused it. Evrard Gilles, of the Crag Company.

An apprentice entered, bearing two cups. Her lips pursed, she served them. Tendrils of steam undulated and curled off the black surface, intertwined with heat and sweet spice.

Luxurious Kamerish black tea.

Rielle fought a grimace. If the Proctor had wanted to be polite to Jon, he would have dismissed her. The only reason she was still here was because the Proctor wanted something from her.

So much for her plans to go back on mission.

What torturous task would he ask of her? No matter what he required, her position meant she had to accept. While she was under contract with the Divinity, the king couldn't make her comply with her arranged marriage contract—to the man who'd humiliated her three years ago and been horrible ever since. Brennan Karandis Marcel. The werewolf.

She wouldn't be free of her arranged marriage until she turned twenty-three... in eleven and a half months. Eleven and a half long, long, *long* months.

Mages could refuse missions, but if she did, she'd get on the Proctor's bad side, and if she got on his bad side, well, he might look for reasons to give her demerits. And with enough demerits—

No, she couldn't risk dismissal from the Divinity, and the Proctor knew it. He'd been using her as his left hand for years.

The Proctor returned. "I spoke with Derric."

Jon's expressionless face betrayed nothing.

The Proctor sat at the head of the table. "Derric insists that instead of coming to Monas Ver, you go straight to Monas Amar for further proceedings. He has asked that I send with you an escort until you are reunited with the other paladins."

Jon raised his head. "Forgive the impropriety, but how can I know these orders are genuine?"

Her hand jerked, and she steadied her cup of tea before it could make a mess. Well, more of a mess than scalding her fingers.

The Proctor leaned back in his chair and observed Jon for a pensive moment. "He told me that you are no longer of the Order, Jonathan Ver, and that if you are here, you well know it."

She turned toward the paladin. The *forsworn* paladin.

He sat still, silent, his smoldering gaze locked with the Proctor's. The questions were myriad and unspeakable, at least in the Proctor's presence.

Which of the four Sacred Vows had he broken, and how? Was it the vow of piety—because he sought vengeance? Or was it celibacy, perhaps? She suppressed the curious smile threatening to show itself on her face.

Regardless, if an escort was required, the Order wanted him punished, debriefed, or just wanted to make sure he returned his arcanir.

But what had he done to get himself discharged?

The Proctor regarded Jon expectantly.

"I am a man of honor," Jon said, his voice firm. "I have broken none of the four Sacred Vows."

"Why you were discharged from your order is not my concern, but an old friend of mine has asked a favor, and I am inclined to grant it." The Proctor turned his attention to her. "And your mission is to escort this man to Monas Amar."

An escort. Fantastic. He could obviously take care of himself and didn't need her protection; she could be helping those who did. Wrangling a stubborn paladin all the way to Monas Amar would be a waste of her skills and a headache. A month-long headache. She cringed, looking at the tea. It was an unfit inducement.

Instead of helping those who needed it, a month spent with a man who hated mages and the Divinity. She hesitated. "Isn't there someone else available... whose abilities better suit this particular mission?"

"I don't need an escort—or a guard," Jon insisted. "If Derric wants me to go to Monas Amar, I'll go. On my own. I need no help from mages."

"I agreed to assign you a capable escort," the Proctor said sternly, "and so have I done."

She sighed inwardly. That was that.

At least she could possibly, with *exemplary* service, earn a commendation and advance one step closer to the magister's mantle. That tenure would mean inclusion in the Magisterium, the advisory body that helped the Grand Divinus determine worthy causes for the Divinity to pursue, among other matters. It would also mean permanent insulation from her arranged marriage. She hid a hopeful smile.

Only two more commendations, and she'd get a chance to test for magister. With her luck, her sponsor would hate her and the promotions board would ignore her achievements to focus on scandal. But a *chance*— even a slim chance—was more than she'd ever had.

Jon stared at the Proctor for a tense moment but finally nodded.

"Good," the Proctor replied, "because you leave at dawn."

"Who's my partner on this?" she asked. Mages worked in pairs.

The Proctor glowered at her. "No partner."

Off the books.

"I trust you to prioritize completion of this mission—"

No detours.

"—and return to the Tower for your reward."

Or you're excommunicated and left without protection from your arranged marriage contract. Got it. "Understood."

"You will travel to Monas Amar with stops at the cities of Bournand and Melain and no others. Make camp in the wilds, if you must."

No other cities? The Proctor wouldn't forbid a stop unless it was unsafe, but why would it be unsafe to stop anywhere else?

"Proctor—"

"No questions." The Proctor grabbed a sheet of parchment and scribbled a note, then rolled it up. "Bernadette will have supplies delivered to your quarters." He turned to Jon. "Please accept our hospitality tonight."

Jon inclined his head, his posture stiff. "Thank you, my lord."

He, too, had no options.

The Proctor turned to her. "Magos, I'm awarding you a commendation for your performance tonight."

She raised her eyebrows, trying but failing to engage her paralyzed tongue. A commendation... Only one more—one—and she could test for magister. And all that stood in her way was an in-person hearing, a thorough evaluation of her history, winning over her unknown sponsor, lucking out with the selection of three magisters who didn't hate her for the promotions board, an exam failed by the vast majority of candidates—

Her spine threatened to turn to jelly, but she stiffened. There was time enough to worry about all that later. For now, she had to carry out this escort mission in exemplary fashion. No pressure.

She manipulated her uncooperative body into a bow. "Thank you, Proctor." Now that he was in a good mood, perhaps he'd finally tell her what he knew of Olivia? "Proctor, if I may, about Olivia—"

"Please escort Sir Jonathan to your vacant apprentice quarters for the night." The etched lines of his face left no room to argue.

She sighed. The protest died on her lips. After this mission, she'd go to Courdeval and check on Olivia herself. It was less than a day's ride from Monas Amar.

The air at the Tower was becoming scarce, but soon, grapes might ripen on the willows. Snow might fall in the summer. The sun might rise in the west. And she might become a magister.

A slim chance, but a chance nonetheless. No more dirty work. No more arranged marriage. No more fear of fureur.

But this mission first.

She nodded. "Yes, Proctor."

3

*J*on trudged down the spiral stairway behind Rielle. Why had Derric asked for a mage to escort him? Derric had raised him from infancy, true enough, but was it really fatherly concern about his disobedience?

How patronizing. If Derric had but spoken to him, even by way of that brazier device—aerarius, was it?—Jon would have heeded his commands.

But no, instead, here he was, following a mage to quarters for the night, the first of many together on the way to Monas Amar.

Moving up alongside her, he studied her. Long, straw-blond locks tamed into a thick braid; a stubborn chin; full lips; and eyes the color of a summer sky. A worried frown, unwanted storm cloud, creased her brow. No more pleased by the mission than he was.

She glanced his way briefly and stiffened, then her face tightened in a smile. Forced smile. She moved ahead and descended three floors on the spiral steps, then entered a sconce-lit hall. Circular, windowless.

They stopped at a door, like all the others; wrought-iron long-strap hinges, scrolling decoratively, bound the sturdy oaken boards. She unlocked it and beckoned him to follow her into the dark.

"This way." With a gesture of her fingers, she cast a spell—a glowing light, tiny like a candle's flame—and guided them through an antechamber with two doors, one of them open. The candle's flame illuminated the small room, its austere stone walls softened with massive tapestries, its cold floor cushioned with a heavy-pile off-white rug with an ornate pattern. A vase of white roses graced a round table with four chairs, and beyond it, just below a window, a long table bore a line of clear vessels containing a variety of clippings—flowers, twigs, all in varying stages of growth.

So she liked plants. *A lot.*

A soft clatter came from farther in. Rielle ambled through a doorway to an open window in the bedchamber. The flowing white lace curtains flared around her as she latched it. The room was larger than the antechamber, but despite squinting in the dimness, he couldn't make out much beyond a large hearth awaiting flame, more plants silhouetted against the darkness, a double bed, shoes lying about the room, and books stacked on every available surface.

Clearly, she hadn't planned on guests.

His pack—thank Terra—rested on the floor next to the desk, and upon it—

Faithkeeper and his dagger. Since taking his vows eight years ago, Faithkeeper had always been within reach. Until tonight.

Terra have mercy, he'd prayed these mages hadn't taken off with his weapons to... study the arcanir, or whatever they did with something they so rarely got their hands on. He stared at his weapons belt. If only wishing for it to be in his possession could make it so.

But he'd never broken his word, and he wouldn't begin now.

She approached the desk, unclipped Faithkeeper from the belt, and held it out to him.

Frozen, he gawked at her. "You trust me?"

"Sword or no sword, I can handle you." She cracked a smile. "So there's no harm in returning it." The dagger, however, she left clipped to the sword belt.

The room's space was lacking, greedily claimed by furnishings. No swordsman in his right mind would attempt to use a long sword in such close quarters. She must have known that much.

He accepted Faithkeeper, a peace offering, and once the fine-grain leather of the sheath was back in his hands, he exhaled his relief. Terra help him, he'd never surrender his weapons again. "Thank you, mage."

"You're welcome. Gather your pack." Once he shouldered the bag, she led him back to the antechamber and pushed open the adjoining door to a dark room. "You'll be staying here tonight."

As he tried to make out the furnishings in the light of her spell, she gestured a flame with her other hand and flung it at the hearth.

A roaring fire sparked to life.

She opened the window, then flitted to the washbasin, where she conjured water to fill it.

All these things that took so much time to do every day, she did with simple gestures. He shook his head.

She repeated the feat over the water carafe and the tub, which even steamed. Hot water. His muscles practically melted at the thought.

When he caught her gaze, she smirked. Full of herself, no doubt. He narrowed his eyes. "Magic, even for such simple things?"

Her smirk vanished.

Good. Mages could learn a touch of humility. They were, in ways, superior, special, but while the priests and paladins of the Order of Terra remained humble, mages constantly elevated themselves. It was only a matter of time before they became as dangerously supremacist as the heretics they hunted.

He dropped the pack on the floor and unfastened his cloak.

In the light of the hearth, the room was extravagant, furnished in blackwood furniture—a four-poster double bed, two tall nightstands, a desk, an upholstered chair, vanity, and two armchairs—and jewel-toned brocades. A tapestry hung on the wall against the cold, and a thick rug added warmth to the marble floor.

The Divinity wasted coin on these luxuries, when there were children who starved in nearby towns and villages? The Grand Divinus claimed the Divinity of Magic was a "religion." If mages worshipped anything, it seemed to be coin.

At the monastery, he and his brothers all slept on simple straw mattresses with rough-spun bedding, enough to be serviceable, with furniture made by the paladins and priests themselves from the white-pine Ver Forest.

He laid his cloak over the desk's chair. "The room's... lavish."

She frowned.

Perhaps it was simple to her. Normal. Leaning against a bedpost, he unfastened the straps on his gauntlets.

"We leave an hour after sunrise," she said.

He could still try to make a run for it—break down the door, attempt to escape down the spiral stairwell and dispatch any mages who dared get in his way. Or he could leave with her tomorrow, and then lose her in the woods. He didn't need a nanny.

But orders... Derric had given him an order. The Proctor's knowledge of the discharge message had confirmed it.

I'm going to Monas Amar with this mage.

"Can't wait," he said flatly.

"Fine. Goodnight." Her pretty face slack, she left the room and shut the door.

He straightened. Had he upset her? He crept to the door, rested a palm on it. She'd captured him, true enough, but had only done her duty; otherwise, she'd been professional and hospitable... and he'd been rude and judgmental.

Was it too late to apologize? Too awkward?

The lock turned, and he took a step back.

Too late. Definitely too late.

Tomorrow would be better. He'd make an effort.

Heaving a sigh, he let his gaze settle on the bath. The steaming-hot bath. *Yes.*

He removed the rest of his armor and undressed, then sank into the blessedly hot water. Terra have mercy, there was nothing better on earth.

She'd spelled it so simply—he held a hand over the water and wriggled his fingers as she had hers—and it had been so, with her long, tapered fingers. Elegant. Smooth, uncallused skin. Soft, he recalled, as he'd kissed her hand. Slender, delicate wrists...

He rested his head on the rim of the tub and hissed. At the Proctor's insinuation that they were lovers, his mind had illustrated the notion. Vividly. Meeting the surly mage, glittering in her ferocity, for a moonlit tryst in the surrounding forest, eye to eye, face to face, body to body. A woman who didn't shrink away from challenge. His gaze had roved over her domineering sky-blue eyes, her stately posture, her—Terra help him— shapely figure, and he'd tasted that distant reality, right there in the Proctor's quarters, for one excruciating moment before he'd pulled back, hard, and remembered who he was.

Sodalis of the Order of Terra, eighth rank, Monas Ver First Company. Regardless of what some paper said.

The mage was beautiful but, to him, an unwanted distraction. It would never happen. He held to the Sacred Vows.

He forced his mind where he always did: the five-foot serpentine blade of a flambard. A crown strike, a block, an advance matched step for step, bound blades, disengage. A mirrored stance, sure feet, each step aware and stable. Blinded by rage, he'd once stumbled, but never again. In his mind, ever he surveyed that field of battle. No rage. Cold calculation and the sword. Only the sword. One last duel, an arrest, and he'd go home to visit Bastien's grave with justice in hand.

He washed quickly, dried off, then pulled clean braies from his pack and dressed for bed. From among his armor, he retrieved his belt pouch and the familiar tiny, corked round glass vial inside.

A cluster of golden yellow blossoms filled the vessel. Immortelle. It bloomed the better part of the year all around Monas Ver, fields of sunshine gold surrounding the monastery. Surrounding home. Derric grew it for medicine, but it had become the essence of home.

He took Faithkeeper in hand, left it nearby, accessible, and then slipped into the bed's soft, warm embrace. Tension fled his aching muscles. Terra's troth, it was comfortable.

Maybe he'd have to reevaluate the mages' extravagance.

He uncorked the vial of immortelle and inhaled the scent, so like autumnal maple leaves but spicier; it took him back to long days in the sun, training with his brothers, ever surrounded by bright immortelle. It bloomed in early summer and remained all year until the first frost, and once cut, immortelle dried almost perfectly preserved and kept for many months. He'd cut this cluster four months ago and hoped to be home again before its gold faded.

Would he still be welcome? Discharged paladins never came back to the monasteries. Would he be one of them? Nothing left in the monastery of him but a ghost while he made his way laboring for anyone hiring extra hands?

He corked the vial.

First things first: he'd go to Monas Amar, Sacred Vows unbroken, and petition for reinstatement. Either he'd find a way, or he'd make one. When he would finally return to Monas Ver, it would be as a brother, not a ghost.

As orders dictated, he would just have to allow the mage in the next room to take him.

4

*W*hen someone knocked at her door, Rielle jumped out of bed, flushed, heart racing. It was still dark. Jon should be sleeping —what could he want at this hour?

Divine, just like her dream. She laid a palm over her chest, willing her pulse to slow. It was the Proctor's fault. He'd planted the thought in her mind with his baseless accusation that Jon was her lover.

Blood rushed to her face. If only the Order of Terra mandated the mutual exclusivity of celibacy and attractiveness.

Perhaps it hadn't been a knock. An illusion of the night, and no more...

She took a deep, calming breath. Her anima sought resonance; that was it. Yes, that was all. That deep, replenishing connection with another mage, which somehow made the sum greater than its parts, the greatest coming from complementary mage pairs. Yet practical need to brighten anima wasn't the only draw to resonance. Greater than any other, it was pleasure, a spiritual sensation unlike anything else.

Like others of her kind, she needed a fellow mage from time to time.

But Jon was no mage.

It was an urge, no more, like hunger or thirst, and she could control it. If she had to, she could live off crumbs of brightening and just meditate for a few days instead of resonance.

Another soft knock. She lit a candle at her desk with a flick of her wrist. A simple spell, it barely dimmed her anima.

She darted to the washbasin, splashed her face to freshen up. For modesty's sake, she grabbed her silk nightgown's matching robe. No need to taunt the poor man. Her heart raced like a gust spell, and she covered her chest with a palm, willing it to slow.

What did he want? She headed for the door and stopped in front of it, taking a few breaths.

The knock sounded again. Farther away. It wasn't from the adjoining door but from the hallway. Not Jon.

She stilled, blinking too fast, and pressed her lips together. *Idiot.* She blew out a breath. Someone was at the *hall* door.

Eyebrow raised, she went to it. At least whoever was in the hallway hadn't featured in her latest dreamy insanity, and wasn't looking to escape. She gathered her wits about her and opened it.

Leigh Galvan stood in the doorway—a tall, slender wild mage in his early thirties and her former master. His black almond-shaped eyes, a gift of his mother's Kamerish heritage, contrasted sharply with his platinum-white hair, the mark of a survivor and master of wild magic.

Heredity wasn't the only door to magic. Harnessing the wild magic of the land from a Vein was usually fatal, but rarely, an exceptional person could control the massive primal force and come away a mage, and a strong one at that.

Someone like Leigh.

When she'd been his apprentice, she'd gotten to know him better than any apprentice should ever know a master, but she'd never learned why he'd taken such a risk.

He leaned against the doorjamb, disheveled. So he'd spent the evening and most of the night up to no good, like most nights. His black mage coat and a crimson brocade waistcoat hung open, his white shirt unfastened well past his smooth ivory-colored chest.

"What are you doing here?"

He grinned coyly, half-shutting his eyes. "What? Can't I visit a former apprentice?"

"Not this one, and you well know it," she grumbled, leaning out to search the hallway. If anyone saw him here—

"Oh, relax." The smell of alcohol blew past her. She rolled her eyes and took a step back.

He sauntered into the antechamber and drew the door shut behind him, ignoring her frown. "Everyone knows our time is done."

For the last three years, she'd kept a reputation beyond reproach, avoiding even a single catastrophic misstep. Such as letting into her quarters the man the Divinity expressly forbade her from fraternizing with.

He leaned against the door, eyeing her darkly, then winked. She kept her frown in place.

"All right, then. Frowny face it is. On to business." He proceeded into her bedchamber, pulled the chair away from her desk, and plopped into it. "I heard that you took a prisoner," he said, with a playful lilt to his smooth, melodious voice.

"I did." More of a charge now. Was that what had brought him here? Didn't seem worth his time.

Gazing past her toward the bed, he remarked, "I came to see for myself."

She followed his line of sight and sighed her annoyance. "Really? The bed? Perhaps that's where *you* keep *your* charges, but I'd say that's an... uncommon... preference."

He shrugged. His lips pursed, he looked unsatisfied by the inspection. "I can't help but wonder what you do out in that forest on your... midnight jaunts."

Midnight jaunts. The same words the Proctor had used. Exactly the same.

As much as she had wanted to tell him about her sangremancy bond with Brennan, how their monthly offerings helped him control his Wolf, Brennan had sworn her to secrecy.

If word got out, it would end with his werewolf head on a spike. As much as she hated him, she didn't wish for his death.

From under his pale lashes, Leigh stared up at her with a wry grin and swayed in his chair. "I thought 'lover,' but no, too simple. You don't love anymore, and you've been sneaking out for so long, since before you and I were involved, and you would never have betrayed me when we were..."

No, she wouldn't have.

"But you're no purist, either," he continued, "so no dancing under the moon, honoring the Dark Age of Magic. And you being an elementalist and all makes it quite a challenge for anyone to follow you."

For an elementalist, it was easy enough to magically cultivate a thicket here, open a hole in the ground there. It may not have been good fun for the tails the Proctor sent after her, but it certainly kept them busy.

"Tell me."

The days when Leigh's interest could rove into any facet of her life were long gone. "Not your concern."

With a sigh, he leaned back in the chair and scowled at her. In her days as his apprentice, he'd always managed to arduously work any defiance out of her, but no longer.

They had both changed since then.

"You will always be my concern."

She withdrew to the window and pulled the drapes and curtains aside, finding the surrounding land still dark. There were more important concerns. Perhaps she could divert his attention to those.

Her eyes darted to the crystal goblet on her desk again, and Olivia's old letters beneath it. "Any news of Olivia?"

Another of Leigh's former apprentices—although, granted, not nearly as... *close* as Rielle had been—Olivia had recently achieved the most coveted court position for a mage in all of Emaurria: Archmage, one of the Grands on King Marcus's High Council, and adviser on all things magic.

A crooked grin displaced Leigh's frown. "None. Or anything from Courdeval, for that matter. Don't change the subject."

"Nothing from Courdeval at all?" No correspondence from the capital? Unlikely. "In how long?"

"It depends. What do you do out in the forest every month?" His gaze followed her as she made her bed.

Maybe then he'd stop staring at it as if it were some sort of invitation.

"Just tell me," she said, pulling the sheet tight.

"Days," he answered.

Days? What could cease all correspondence from the capital for days? She wandered back to the desk, moved the crystal goblet to the edge, and opened Olivia's letter again. Perhaps there was some clue as to what might have happened at the capital. Why hadn't the Proctor just used the aerarius to reach out to Courdeval? Or allowed her to? It didn't add up.

Her back to Leigh, she reread the letter. Nothing.

"You can tell me what you do out there," he said, his voice warm and near. "I'll keep your confidence."

She forced out an exasperated sigh. What would it take for him to leave her alone about it? "I tear my clothes off, rub mud all over myself, and scream up at the dead gods," she hissed, slamming the letter down on the desk. "I sacrifice animals, deflower virgins, and dance under the moon, cackling."

His half-laugh misted on her neck, and she froze. He slipped her robe from her shoulders. It dropped to the floor, silk feathering against her legs to her feet. A whisper of fingertips caressed her bare arm from wrist to shoulder; a frisson rippled her ready flesh. His nearness felt so familiar, so comfortable. She closed her eyes.

His arm glided under hers to wrap around her waist, his palm pressing to her belly in the firm way she'd always liked. His lips brushed against her skin where her jaw met her ear, sending a tendril of need through her body. "Tell me. Perhaps our interests are aligned."

"And what is it you're interested in?"

"Right now?" His hand descended from her belly at the painstaking pace that had always driven her mad with desire, gathering the fabric of her nightgown. "This."

These were the steps to a dance they both knew well, but the music had stopped years ago.

She grabbed his wrist. "We shouldn't."

The words left her mouth against all indications from her body. Allowing this would be a mistake, toying with their rank and position in the Tower—and for what? A meaningless romp? They could each get that elsewhere.

"Shouldn't..." His lips kissed their way down her receptive neck in negotiation. "Very different from 'I don't want to.' "

A part of her wanted to, and he happened to be convenient, but that part didn't get to decide.

Once, nothing short of the Divinity of Magic itself could have kept them apart, but she didn't love him like that anymore. Years ago, after the Divinity's official ruling, he'd done everything possible to extinguish her love. He'd jumped from bed to bed, turning aloof, derisive even. And he'd succeeded.

At first, she'd thought he'd wanted to create the semblance of distance between them. At nineteen, she hadn't understood. She'd fought him, and worried, and cried, and scolded, and threatened, but he'd made plain his goal wasn't the *semblance* of distance between them but *actual* distance.

So much had changed between them. They were... something more than friends, but not lovers. And their relationship, such as it was, meant a lot to her. One night like this could destroy three years of progress.

"It's not worth the risk." She pulled his hand away from her clothes.

"What risk?" he whispered.

"To our positions, our relationship—" She turned to face him. Her elbow collided with the crystal goblet. With a clink, it toppled onto the desk and rolled.

Frantic, she grabbed for it, but it fell to the floor and shattered.

"Leigh!" she exclaimed. He could've done something other than stand there. Great Divine, he was an enforcer! He could've used his magic to catch it.

"What?" he shot back, staring at the mess.

A loud crash—the adjoining door smashed onto the floor.

Jon's eyes found her immediately. Half-dressed, he leveled his massive sword at Leigh. "Move away from—"

Leigh threw a force-magic spell at Jon, a blur that flew from his hand to Jon's chest.

It dissipated upon contact. Paladin sigil tattoos protected against magic.

She raised her hands. "Both of you, just—"

Leigh's gaze darted to the crystal shards. It would be simple enough for him to throw them with magic—

But he couldn't kill a charge of the Divinity, and he knew it.

He magically threw a book.

Jon raised his sword, slashing it in half. The blade caught on the bedpost.

When Leigh spelled a chair to fly at him, Jon dropped his sword and rolled. He closed the distance and grabbed Leigh's collar.

"Stop it!" One of them would be hurt if this continued.

Jon threw Leigh to the ground, hissing as books, shoes, more shoes, and other items from all around the room hit him.

"He attacked you," Jon snarled. His merciless voice matched his expression as he pinned Leigh and grabbed his hands.

"Control your prisoner." Leigh thrashed beneath him, spelling a jagged shard of the crystal goblet to poise above Jon. With a simple gesture, it would fly directly into his back.

She gestured a gust spell and sent the shard flying into the wall.

Twitching, Leigh eyed it. He could spell it free again if he wanted. Trapped beneath Jon, he looked back to her, the desire to do just that plain in his wild eyes.

With a frown, she shook her head. *Don't you dare.* Carefully, she approached the two men, avoiding the remaining shards of crystal before her bare feet.

Jon grabbed Leigh's hands, crushing them in the grip of one palm, and then seized the mage's neck.

Leigh's gaze remained unflinching. Only a mage of his caliber could maintain his control while pinned to the ground by a paladin.

Jon stared at Leigh without deviation. "I heard you—"

"That's not what happened." She knelt before Jon and, when he didn't react, reached out to touch his cheek, a spark of sensation humming at their point of contact. Strange.

He jerked his face up to hers, all fight.

"The goblet shattered by accident."

He didn't react.

She remained still, and slowly, his expression relaxed. He peered down at Leigh, who regarded him with no small amount of annoyance.

He released Leigh and rose. He held out his hand and, when Leigh took it, pulled him to his feet. As Leigh made a show of dusting off his clothes, he shot Jon a peripheral scowl.

"It's time for you to leave." She placed a hand on her hip and glared at Leigh.

Leigh nodded until he looked in her direction. He raised an eyebrow and pointed at himself in utter shock. "Me?"

"You." She tipped her head toward the hall.

At least Jon had taken the difficulty out of turning down her former master and the all-too-tempting surrender he'd offered. Perhaps even Leigh would think the better of it when he sobered.

He threw up his hands and strode toward the door, but then he turned and narrowed his eyes at Jon, tugged at the cuffs of his sleeves, and without another word, left.

Shaking her head, she tried to settle on what she'd say to Jon. *Are you all right?* Or *How much did you hear?* Or the all-important, *Would you be so kind as to keep this between us?*

Staring at the mess on the floor, he stood where she'd left him, barefoot and bare chested, firelight casting its glow on his tattooed skin. Power bulged and rippled beneath, animating the winding designs.

Before she could stop herself, her eyes feasted on the many battle scars on his body, devoured the labyrinthine pattern of his paladin sigil tattoos. They began on his back, continued over his shoulders and arms, across his chest, down over his abs and along his hips, teasing into the waistband of his braies.

She shouldn't have stared, but the view was excellent. As a grin claimed her face, she tried to shake it off and cleared her throat. *Propriety. Professionalism. Poise.*

Jon turned to her, hesitation slowing his movement and matching the uncertainty in his eyes. At last, he raked his fingers through his short hair and sighed. "Forgive me."

She glanced at the adjoining door, rent from its hinges upon the floor, and suppressed a smile. She'd seen many things, but never a man break down a door. "Try knocking with a little less force next time."

A brief smile flashed across his face, teasing a dimple at the corner of his mouth. He shook his head. "If I interrupted anything—"

"You didn't." When he gave her a doubting look, she added, "Leigh and I aren't involved."

He drew his eyebrows together. "No?"

"No." She approached him and bent to retrieve his sword, which lay between them, then paused. "He was about to leave."

"Was he?" He narrowed his eyes.

The implication was clear, and she couldn't fault him for his assumption. Leigh would never try to force himself on her, but Jon certainly didn't know that.

By the Divine, why did he care about her a whit? She hadn't given him a single reason to. He was a paladin, and she a mage. Their orders were diametrically opposed, and so were they.

And yet...

Forsworn paladin. A paladin no longer.

When she raised her chin, her breath caught as he eyed her, starting at her bare feet, traveling up her legs and to her face. A chill rippled its way up her lower back, and a whisper of silk breezed against her wrist; she was still in her nightgown, in her bedchamber, with a half-naked man.

As he closed the distance between them, she didn't dare move but to swallow. His eyes intense, scrutinizing, he leaned in, close enough for her to feel the warmth radiating off his skin. It was so quiet that she could hear his every slowing breath.

Silence, heat, and nearness wrapped her tight, and Divine help her, she'd forgotten to breathe. A ragged exhalation trembled from her lips. His scrutiny continued, but now, his heavy-lidded eyes asked a different question, darkened from stormy blue to midnight.

She held out his sword between them. His fingertips grazing hers, he accepted it, that same curious spark humming between them. He cast his gaze downward—down her nightgown—then corrected himself and looked away. Anywhere and everywhere else.

That was for the best.

He found her robe on the floor behind him, picked it up, and held it out to her.

She hastily threw it on. "So... do you eavesdrop regularly," she asked, "or am I special?"

He exhaled a laugh, raised his scarred eyebrow, and then righted the chair Leigh had sent flying. "The walls didn't keep much out."

"Neither did the door," she joked, as he gathered some of the shoes on the floor.

Holding an armful of shoes, he grinned as he tried to add to the lot he held. "Terra have mercy, mage... how many shoes do you need?"

"Always more than I have," she murmured, and they shared a laugh. She crouched to help with the shoes, and the laugh faded slowly. Pleasantly.

When had she last laughed like that? With Leigh, maybe. Long ago, before the scorn and coldness that had parted them. And before that... With her parents.

The cool, salty breeze from the shores of Laurentine stirred the meadows of her memory. Papa laughing as he played with her and her brothers and sisters in the courtyard, big and loud and raucous... and Mama's soft smile, quickly hidden with a bowing of her bashful face. Small memories. Painful memories. All she had of them.

It's in the past.

Together, she and Jon collected the books and everything but the shattered goblet. It remained, broken. "I appreciate what you tried to do."

He took the books she'd gathered, stacked them with his own, then placed them atop the desk. Among them was her now two-piece copy of *Immortal Creatures of Legend.*

He surveyed the damage. "I hate to see a book so wronged."

She shrugged. "It couldn't be helped."

In the silence, she couldn't look away from his scarred eyebrow. When he caught her looking, she asked, "How did you get that?"

He glanced out the window. "Broken bottle. Apparently the usual greeting when faced with meddling paladins."

"Are they ever anything else?"

"Says the mage interrogating me."

She pursed her lips. If he considered this an interrogation, what would he think of what happens in the Tower's dungeon?

He turned away from the window. "There are still a couple hours before dawn." His voice, smooth and deep, resonated within her, a sultry echo of notes that melted away her composure.

He headed back toward the apprentice quarters but paused and gave her a quick once-over. "Get some rest, mage."

"You, too." At dawn, their mission would begin, leaving behind broken doors, numerous shoes, torn tomes, and a shattered goblet.

He picked up what remained of the door and brought it to its proper place in the doorway. With a faint smile, he disappeared through it with the soft knock of wood rested gently against wood.

After putting out the light, she snatched Olivia's last letter from her desk, backed up and, when her thighs hit the bed, fell back into it. She stared at the canopy above. While there was still time before dawn, there was no way she would be able to sleep now.

She gripped the letter tightly. *Days...* Just what had happened in Courdeval? Was Olivia all right?

I'll find out. No matter what, I'll find out.

5

*R*ielle took in the musk of damp earth and fallen leaves. A comfortable breeze met them on the road. A perfect day for riding.

She nodded. All too often, her autumn missions came with matching autumn storms, smothering everything with a shroud of cold and damp. Not today.

She'd dressed warmly nonetheless: her immaculate winter master coat in her chosen color, white. Full length and hooded, it was made of the finest wool, but with velvet flowing around the stand collar and down the front, a single row of piping along the edges, and the master mage's four-bar gold chevron on each sleeve.

Fully armed, armored but for his helm, and cloaked, Jon looked as he had the night before but for a certain sportive gleam in his eyes.

Trouble. He was either in trouble or trouble himself.

Paladins often traveled alone. Why did Jonathan Ver require protection? His trespassing meant he didn't follow orders well enough, and perhaps his High Priest hadn't trusted him to go to Monas Amar. Nanny duty, for one paladin?

And why had the Proctor approved stops in only two cities? Bournand and Melain?

She chewed her lip. The smaller towns and villages along the way didn't have Temples of the Divine, with adepts and masters cloistered there to offer protection and resonance. But Bournand did.

And there was, of course, Gran in Melain, who would provide shelter and warriors if needed. Staying with Gran would be safe.

So Bournand and Melain offered them support, which meant the Proctor might have anticipated resistance. And limiting the stops to those two—with the temple and Gran—meant he might have anticipated threats in settlements lacking an allied presence.

Something—or someone—threatened Jon. But what? And why? The Proctor ripping her from the Tower on a mission like this while offering no answers warranted some digging.

Through the mountains, they passed steep, rocky cliff faces, bare but for shrubs dotting the rock, and ibex carefully navigating the terrain. The tree-lined road was quiet but for a couple merchants bound for the Tower and a few Broadsteel mercenaries on patrol for the Divinity. The area saw some outlaw activity from time to time, for which the Divinity retained Broadsteel.

Most passersby cast curious looks at her and Jon—a mage and paladin pair was indeed unusual—but only one look lingered. Launce, a swaggering Broadsteel mercenary and sometimes-lover. She hadn't seen him since his contract with Broadsteel to secure the Tower village had ended four months ago. He'd reenlisted, then. Shooting her a loaded gaze from beneath wind-tousled dirty-blond hair, Launce stroked his stubbled chin. Not much for conversation, but the man knew his way around a woman's body.

And it was as she needed it to be: physically satisfying, with no risk of developing an attachment to someone she could lose. Whose loss could trigger the catastrophe of fureur.

Launce tilted his head to greet her, a mischievous glint in his eye. She knew what it meant: *Find me when you return.*

Flushed, she nodded and turned away, only to catch a smug glance from Jon.

"Friend of yours?" he teased.

She pulled her shoulders back, raised her chin, and focused on the road ahead between her horse's ears. If his intention was to embarrass her, then he'd be sorely disappointed.

Bells tinkled as a pair of goat-herders shepherded their animals across toward the herb-rich meadows. So much grew here. She'd picked violet rocky thyme there, and intense-blue gentian flowers, rosy pink clusters of catchfly, mauve trumpets of pimpernel willowherb, and sweet-smelling mead wort. Plants whose cuttings she'd carefully rooted in water and then potted to keep her company in the long cold of winter.

Hopefully Jacqui would mind them as she'd promised.

In the dull stretch from the mountains, the questions about Jon only tempted her more. The Proctor had offered precious little explanation about her charge's situation. She looked over her shoulder at the Emaurrian Tower of Magic, the solitary white turret tearing into the azure sky over the Marcellan Peaks.

"Missing your hocus-pocus already, witch?" A smile played on his face.

"Witch?" she cut. "I thought even the least educated of our people would know the difference between a witch and a mage. But I suppose you can't be blamed for the lackluster education provided by the Order."

His mouth fell open.

Good.

He closed it and collected himself. "I did learn the difference. Mages learn magic at the Divinity's Towers, while hedge witches are sole practitioners outside of the Divinity's influence... All magic practitioners were once witches," he said. "But it seems the Tower doesn't teach the art of a good insult, does it, witch?"

She narrowed her eyes. Even if all practitioners of magic were once called *witches*, before the civilization, order, and wisdom of the Divinity had sophisticated them, as a mage it still rankled to be called such, and few dared.

Especially if they preferred their backsides unburnt.

She forced a grin. "Who needs insults when I have all the 'hocus-pocus' I need to handle you—and then some."

His lips twitched in a mocking almost-smile. "If you're plotting to kill me, at least try to hide it. It's bad form to taunt your victim."

She shot him a scowl, but he didn't seem to notice. "Feeling a bit insecure, are you? Even with all that shiny arcanir?"

He scoffed, but no retort came. Before the silence could reclaim their ride, she said, "I have a question."

"Don't you mages use a crystal ball for that kind of thing?"

She heaved a sigh and shook her head. "Right, yes... I forgot mine at the Tower, along with my cauldron and broomstick, so why don't you indulge me?" She flashed him a brief, pert grin. "Tell me... although I'm bound to heed the Proctor, what binds you to your High Priest's commands, now that you're no longer a paladin?"

He stiffened, tightening his grasp on the reins, then looked at her. The humor in his eyes faded, and he contemplated his navel. "I was aware of what I was sacrificing, and I swore vows to Most Holy Terra. That commitment and that sacrifice don't just disappear with a piece of paper." A muscle twitched in his clenched jaw. "Monas Amar is where discharge proceedings are finalized. Where discharged paladins"—he paused— "return their arcanir, their new status processed. But when I arrive, I hope to persuade the Paladin Grand Cordon to reverse the decision."

"You want to return to being a paladin?"

Members of the Order had so little freedom; she couldn't fathom wanting to adhere to such a lifestyle. To her eye, Jon looked about twenty-six or twenty-seven, yet had lived so little for himself. The Sacred Vows of piety, poverty, sobriety, and celibacy made for a modest life.

"It is all I've ever known." His voice slumped, deep and low. "And it is all that I am, even now."

There were some mages at the Tower who had been born there and had rarely set foot outside its property, nor desired to. Sometimes a person grew so comfortable in his box that he no longer dared pursue what lay beyond.

He'd provided one answer, at least: a troublesome man wouldn't want that life. So what kind of trouble was Jon in, or what trouble awaited them out there?

"So why this mission?" She drew her eyebrows together. "Why did the High Priest ask to have you escorted to Monas Amar?"

Lost in a wistful stare, he took hold of a gloved finger, where his Sodalis ring had been the night before. "Derric raised me from infancy. He knows that if I could, I'd come see him immediately and demand answers instead of traveling to Monas Amar."

"So he requires a mage to shepherd you?" Something didn't fit. "Do you know what you're accused of?"

He let out a deep breath. "I intend to find out more at the monastery."

That was no answer. What was he not telling her? A plethora of possibilities flew through her mind. Had he turned away from a paladin's duties? Failed to dispense justice? Deserted? Harmed an innocent?

No, he didn't seem the type. Had he broken one of the four Sacred Vows? Had he drunk ale, wine, mead...? Acquired a treasured trinket? Turned to a different religion? Spent the night in the arms of a lover?

She stole a glimpse. When she'd first seen him five years ago, healed him, he'd been handsome enough—not that she'd had time to study him as he'd lain dying—but all the time since then had given his pleasing features a hard edge, lent a certain rugged appeal. He was probably no stranger to women's attention, and could he resist indefinitely?

Still, in the Proctor's quarters the night before, Jon had vehemently denied breaking any of his vows. Perhaps the discharge was unfounded after all. She weighed the odds but didn't ask him outright. The silence between them grew and remained until the daylight dwindled.

They sated their hunger on the road with bread, cheese, and cured meat from their packs and some greens she'd picked—dandelion greens and the young leaves of lady's mantle. At dusk, they made camp among the fragrant silver spruces and Emaurrian larches of the Tainn Forest. As Jon built a fire, she set up a geomancy ward around the perimeter to warn her if anything large crossed into the vicinity of their campsite. Then she tended to the horses while he pitched their tent.

At least he helped. Her days as Leigh's apprentice had seen her setting up camp by herself while her master had sat at the campfire she'd built.

When a quiet settled, she looked around in the dark, her fingers twitching a moment. At home in the Tower, she would have been watering her plants now, tending them. Hopefully Jacqui wouldn't over-water them, especially her peace lilies and bellina orchids. The bellinas were particularly temperamental.

A tent stood in the light of the campfire while he rummaged through their packs and pulled out two bedrolls.

He set them down and disarmed for the night. Once finished, he hesitated a moment—she ducked behind her horse—and then he entered the tent.

A cold autumn wind made her shiver. She focused on the nearby shrubs, staring at the ripened purplish-red fruit of the common spindle, its lobes split open to reveal its bright orange seeds. Bold. Brave. Forthcoming.

With a deep breath, she checked the horses and the perimeter ward a final time, and when it started to rain, she spelled the fire to protect it and headed for the tent. A pause before the entrance to gather her composure, and she pulled the flap aside.

In the light of an oil lamp, he unrolled a bedroll, the other still bound and off to the side. When she came in, his gaze darted to hers for a moment, and then he resumed his task.

She sat and pulled off her boots. After picking up the remaining bound bedroll, he headed for the tent's opening.

"Goodnight." He went outside.

Sleeping out there, in the cold and damp? The tent was large enough to sleep three. Was he really so wary?

Shaking her head, she changed out of her clothes, which smelled strongly of horse, and into a roomy tunic and soft breeches.

Rain pattered overhead. Wind battered the canvas tent, and she shivered.

If she was chilly in the tent, Jon must be freezing.

She tossed and turned to her side as the rain pelted the canvas, as the cold bit.

"Divine's flaming fire," she grumbled under her breath. With a heavy sigh, she rose, then pulled aside the flap.

Soaking wet, he sat on his bedroll before her spelled fire.

"It's cold tonight. Too cold to sleep outside."

His stormy eyes met hers, and she returned inside. There. She'd said it. If he wanted to be stubborn and unreasonable and act like his virtue was threatened, he could ignore her comment. But she'd rather he didn't sleep out there and catch cold.

She bedded down again and settled, closing her eyes. Silence stretched toward sleep until a soft swishing interrupted. Jon must have entered and fastened the flap against the wind.

A loud flutter and a breeze—shaking out the other bedroll?—and then a rustling as he laid it opposite hers and slipped into it.

He'd seen reason, then.

She could feel him looking at her. Unmistakably.

He braced himself on his elbow, close enough that she could feel his warmth. "I didn't mean to insult you. If I did, I'm sorry. Please accept my apology."

Breathing fast, she nodded. He cared what she thought?

He lingered, as if ready to say more, then shifted. The light rose, flickered; he'd picked up the lamp. "Sleep well."

"You, too," she managed, squirming her way deeper into the bedroll. As he blew out the light, the tiny, delicate hairs on her skin stood to attention.

6

Nine years ago
The Emaurrian Tower of Magic, Divinity of Magic

The trembling started at her fingers. Rielle clenched her hands, wishing the tremors away. *Please, not now. Please.*

Trying to gather all the maturity of her thirteen years, she paced the Tower kitchen stiffly, waiting for whomever had come to see her.

She breathed slowly, trying to ease her troubled mind. Only a few night owls haunted the dining hall, perched over books and papers with what meager offerings she and the other two novices on kitchen duty had been able to prepare. She moved to the larder, empty of people, but the cluttered shelves didn't ease her nerves. At least her fellow novices on kitchen duty had given her privacy to meet with her unnamed visitor.

Behind her eyelids, flames licked stone walls and rafted ceilings. A rancid smell suffocated, burning—burning flesh. Screams, choked, hoarse... Cries for help...

Murderer. Demon.

No, that's not me. Not anymore.

Maybe the king's knights had come to take her away. Maybe they knew what she'd done.

No, no. It was in the past. That's what Magister Galvan had told her. It was in the past, and she needed to look ahead.

The Tower was the safest place for her to be. The only safe place. The

Tower would be her home now. Forever. Here, Magister Galvan would keep teaching her how to control her power. Here, stone walls kept her away from the surviving people she loved. Kept them alive. And they'd be safe from her. She swallowed.

The door flew open.

Brennan rushed toward her and gathered her in his arms. She melted into him, let him sweep her off her feet, breathed in the familiar spice of his scent, cinnamon and cypress. The eighteen-year-old noble was tall, handsome, her betrothed. And a werewolf—secret from everyone. Everyone but her.

After it all, she'd longed to see him more than anyone, and here he was at last. He'd come to her. He would understand, and with his love and support, she might live to stop hating herself someday.

"Rielle," he breathed into her ear. "Praise the Great Wolf, you're alive." His arms tightened, just a little, his warmth radiating through her novice mage robes. "I felt your anguish, and I ran to you—but when I arrived in Laurentine, it was—and I couldn't find you anymore, so it wasn't until my father received word from the king that—Before, I thought you were—" His voice broke.

The fire, Mama and Papa, her brothers and sisters—everything came rushing back. She buried her face in his shoulder. Magister Galvan had used an arcanir ring on her on their way to the Tower. It had nullified her magic, but it had also disrupted her bond with Brennan until Magister Galvan had removed the item.

Brennan brushed her curls with gentle fingers. "I'm sorry I couldn't come sooner." When she drew back to look at him, he cupped her face in his hands. "I thought I'd lost you." His usually jovial hazel eyes were dull and bloodshot.

Tears streaked wet trails down her cheeks.

He pulled her back into his embrace. "I can't imagine what you've been through and what they've made you suffer in this place. But I'm here to take you home."

She breathed in his soothing scent—but the word *home* jarred. "Home...?"

"Maerleth Tainn, Rielle," he replied, rubbing the back of her neck. "So you can be with those who love you."

Those who love me. Slowly, she drew away from him, and his hands slipped down her arms to hers.

"I can't." Their parents had planned their marriage ceremony for next year, to be consummated within four years. But the fire had changed everything. She couldn't risk anyone else. Not now. Perhaps never again.

If she loved, she could lose. And if she lost, she'd go into fureur and destroy everything and everyone.

It's in the past. It's in the past.

He glanced down at their joined hands; the tremors had started in her fingers again. The tremors... *No battle fury, please.* Battle fury, like a gateway, opened into full fureur—destruction incarnate.

"I need to learn to control my magic." To move where non-mages lived before mastering her power would invite only more tragedy. The trembling spread up her arms.

Brennan's brow creased. "My father can afford the best tutors for you. You can learn to control your magic at home."

No. Not there. Not at another castle that could burn and burn and burn, with no one to stop it.

"Everyone's a mage here," she tried to explain. "It's different."

"You won't hurt anyone," he said. "I promise. I'll be with you. Our bond will keep you calm."

But he couldn't be with her all the time. He just couldn't. She slipped her hands free of his, then turned away and wrapped her arms around herself. Only here could her violence be kept inside. "Magister Galvan said I won't have to worry about hurting anyone if I stay in the Tower."

"Rielle, wouldn't you rather be with me than here, among strangers?"

"Of course." Given a choice, she would always choose to be with him.

But it wasn't just that. If she couldn't control her magic and burned down the castle, he'd die with it, werewolf or not. And so would his family. That was no choice at all. Until she earned her mastery and could be confident in her own control, their marriage could wait. "But they said I could become a master in a few years, if I work hard. I'd feel better if I knew for certain that others were safe around me."

He shook his head. "The Proctor here said you're a quaternary elementalist, Rielle. Do you know how rare that is? They'll say anything to keep you here, to pull you into the Divinity. My father said they want you, your fortune, your lands—"

"No one's asking me for anything here, Brennan." Since the moment Magister Galvan had taken custody of her, no one from the Divinity had done anything but offer her aid. But what he said about quaternary elementalists, it was true. She'd read about them, how valuable they were to a bloodline. How valuable *she* was to a bloodline. "Perhaps it's you who wants something."

He squeezed her shoulder. "How can you say that?" he asked, his voice raw.

Perhaps she'd spoken too harshly.

"We Marcels have fortune and land in abundance. I want nothing but what's best for you." From behind, he wrapped his arms around her shoulders.

"*Here* is what's best for me. Only for a couple years. You can come visit whenever you want. I hope you do."

He went rigid. "You're far too trusting of these mages. Ingratiating themselves to a girl in a vulnerable state is a manipulative tactic."

Manipulative...? What was he talking about? Everyone had been kind to her, had made no demands, had treated her well even if she didn't deserve it.

"They do it to gain your trust, and once they have it, you won't even realize when they take what they want from you. My father's had dealings with Magehold. The Divinity's willing to submit to much without asking the mages—all for its own goals, its own ends." He tightened his hold on her.

What was the Divinity willing to submit to? Brennan's father sought something from the Divinity? All of this talk had begun to tangle. Why couldn't Brennan just understand that she needed to be here?

"You might be too young to see it," he whispered in her ear, his voice breaking, "but I do, and I can't let them take advantage of you."

He wanted to protect her?

With his hands clasped around her, she reached up to play with his fingers. She loved Brennan and someday would marry him, but she needed to stay at the Tower and master her magic; he was being overprotective and unreasonable.

"It's only a few years," she replied. "I'm only staying here until I earn my Mastery, and then we'll be married, just like our parents want." She swallowed. "Wanted."

He grabbed her shoulders and turned her around, stared down at her tempestuously. His hands traveled from her shoulders to her face, and his fingers stroked her cheek.

"Come home with me, Rielle," he whispered. "To the hedge maze, and the hazel trees, the mountains, and all that was promised." Slowly, he walked her backward until she hit the cupboard.

"After what I did to my family, I—" She squeezed her eyes shut for a moment, trying to keep the tears in.

His eyes widened.

Yes. This was who she was. If he hadn't suspected she'd been responsible, he knew now.

He cupped her cheek, and she melted into his touch. His arms claimed hers once more, locking her in his embrace. Even through the simple novice robes she wore, his touch made her shiver.

All that was promised. They were friends now, had been since she was five, but someday, they'd be more.

But they'd have to live to see that day first.

"Brennan," she said, breaking their embrace.

At the hurt rising in his eyes, she froze.

"Please, come home," he said, his voice raw. "The marriage will just be words on a paper for a few years, but if we marry, the king will have no choice but to revoke the Divinity's dominion over you and, until you're of age, to put you in my custody as your husband—"

"No." She wheezed in a breath. "I need to do this. I've made my choice."

"Are you refusing me?"

No, she wanted to marry him, but she needed to be here for now. "Brennan, I only need to master my magic. If you could just please try to understand—"

The soft whisper of slippers came from the kitchen.

"No," he replied, taking her hand in his. "*You* need to understand. You're too vulnerable to think for yourself right now, but I know where you belong. They'll try to keep us apart, Rielle. You're too valuable to them. And you either trust me or you don't. You either love me or you don't. It's either me or this place."

Her lungs constricted. There wasn't enough air. She couldn't breathe.

He wanted her to choose between being with him someday and keeping him and his family alive? Between his comfort and her ability to live with herself? She clamped one hand over her mouth, tears dripping from her face.

"Please," she gasped, "don't ask me to—"

"Me or this place," he repeated, his bright eyes fixed on her with unshakable focus.

Divine help her, she couldn't breathe. Sobs rent through her as he stared at her expectantly. She had to answer.

"This place," she mumbled.

His lower lip twitched. "Tell me you don't want a life with me someday, Rielle. You know you can't. Tell me you don't want me in your life."

A life with him was *everything* she wanted in the future. But after she was safe to be around. Why couldn't he just see it?

"Brennan, please, I beg you—" She wanted to raise her hand to her eyes, but his brows knitted together, he grasped it, holding it tighter and tighter until it hurt. Her eyes stung with tears, burning, burning, and she tried to close them, but it didn't help.

"Answer me."

Why did he have to make this so hard? Why couldn't he just trust her? She only needed to learn control, and then they could be together. Why did it have to be his way or none?

"Please," she cried, but her wrist hurt.

"Tell me now or leave with me."

It hurt, it hurt, it hurt.

"Tell me!"

"I don't want you! I want to stay in the Tower! I want to learn magic!" Her hands blazed.

He leaped away, unharmed, and her hands faded, but her heart had torn open.

"There are more important things right now than marrying you! You don't understand!"

He froze. Behind him, the entire kitchen staff and mages from the adjoining dining hall had gathered, exchanging concerned looks and whispering to one another.

When he looked back at them, his face reddened.

She had publicly rejected Brennan Karandis Marcel, heir to the dukedom of Maerleth Tainn and all its holdings, and everyone in the Tower would know of it before the night was out.

His eyes hardened.

Too far. She had gone too far.

She retreated into herself, wishing in vain she could take back those hateful words. An apology trembled on the tip of her tongue, but no—it wouldn't be sincere. She couldn't leave. Wouldn't.

He swept his sleeve across his eyes and raised his chin, staring her down with imperious coldness. "You've made your choice. Enjoy being a slave for the Divinity. Goodbye, Rielle."

No, no, no. This wasn't it. This wasn't goodbye.

But he'd already left.

She collapsed. Hugged her knees. Rocked.

Although the crowd huddled and spoke, she knew nothing but the screams, rancidity, smoke, the all-consuming fire and death and pain, and

Mama, Papa, Liam, Dominique, Dorian, everyone—gone. Gone, by her hands.

Warm arms closed around her. She inhaled lavender. Olivia. Olivia, who'd taken care of her for days when she'd been no more than a sobbing mess. At the look on Olivia's face, the tears only flowed faster.

Olivia held her closer, cried with her, and Rielle was shaking. Had been. And couldn't stop. Her heart had been torn asunder, but in the circle of Olivia's arms, she was safe. And so was everyone else.

BRENNAN STORMED through the Tower's dining hall, striding through mages who didn't step aside fast enough, not caring whom he toppled. He'd thought her dead. Dead! His heart had stopped, his life shattered. For the eight years he'd known Rielle, he'd loved her—as a friend, a confidant, as her future husband. He'd wanted nothing more than to protect her, to make her smile, to share his life with her.

When he'd no longer felt her through the bond—when he had thought her dead, he'd wanted to die. He'd planned to. Without her, there was no controlling the Wolf. He would have become a monster, a danger to all, and heartbroken.

But when the news had come she lived, was safe at the Tower, how he'd rejoiced. Great Wolf, he'd breathed in life in his relief. She was alive. And she was aggrieved, alone among strangers. Needing love. Needing consolation. Needing him.

He pushed aside the mages in the hallway and burst through the Tower's front doors, wild eyes scanning the drive for his carriage.

Already gone, at the carriage house.

Hearts pounded around him, voices whispered, and he looked at the faces surrounding him in the cold evening air. Already rumor spread like frost, touching all the loose tongues in the Tower with its chill.

A girl had refused Brennan Karandis Marcel.

His fiancée had repudiated him. *He,* Brennan Karandis Marcel, the heir to the dukedom of Maerleth Tainn, Marquis of Tregarde, Baron of Calterre, and the son of Faolan Auvray Marcel, had been brought to tears and humiliation by a mere thirteen-year-old orphan.

His face tightened, every muscle in his body hardening to painful rigidity, and his fingernails bit into his palms, spikes of pain blooming the wetness of blood. Rip their tongues out. He wanted to rip their flapping tongues out.

He could rip apart the entire Tower right now. Immune to magic, he could kill anyone who got in his way and take Rielle home, where she belonged.

Pain radiated from his clenched jaw. Some of the mages surrounding him receded.

Kill everyone and take Rielle home... And then what? Wait for the torches and pitchforks and the hunt for the beast that he was, feel the grain of the wood on the chopping block, taste the bite of the executioner's axe?

He slowed his breaths, looked past the meddlesome mages to the pines. There, in the pines, he could be himself, infuriated man or beastly wolf, and he didn't know which he needed to be right now. He stalked toward the sanctuary of the forest, and the crowd split to let him through. Each step away from the Tower became heavier, harder, anguished, but the pines didn't turn away his fury, didn't withdraw their welcome, and he offered himself into their embrace.

Great Wolf, he'd said everything, done everything he could to convince her. He'd come to her in sincerity, met her uncertainty with affection, and in the face of her wavering, he'd reminded her of the promise of their future. Husband and wife. Duke and duchess. He and she, they were intended for more, intended for each other, for their love to mature into the kind that sustained marriage, an eternal bond.

An eternal bond, and she rejected it for a life among strangers. Rejected him, all they'd shared and would share, for the affectations of a faith that wielded magic to influence the world. Wielding mages. Like her.

She had tossed aside someone who had always loved her, who had wanted the best for her, in order to become a tool. She'd deemed him worthless.

Pressure pushed at the back of his eyes, and he picked up the pace, ran through the ordeal of pine needles and abrasive branches, allowing their cuts, their castigation. Worthless. Was that it?

He couldn't breathe, needed to shed that black mantle that bound him, that crushing estimation of hers, and he clawed at his clothes, sending buttons flying, ripping the stitches apart, and at last, he called to the Wolf, uncaged him, Changed.

Fingernails became claws, hands paws, black fur bursting from his skin, and the agony claimed the rest of him as man gave way to wolf, muscles morphing, bones reshaping, metamorphosis. The pads of his paws cushioned into the cold forest floor, and relief rippled through him, but he ran, bounding through the forest, tasting the chill with his wolfish tongue, inhaling the myriad scents of the dogwood and white pines and Emaurrian larches, the rabbits, squirrels, and sparrows, the lingering spice of old magic.

It was the essence of her flowing through him that allowed him this control. Her blood. And he'd be forced to see her before the next full moon. A soft whine escaped him, but he stifled it.

He couldn't meet her so lowered, humiliated. And it would only get worse. Word would spread until every courtier would snicker behind his back. Rielle would have to acquiesce, publicly, else he'd never regain his standing. Or he'd have to humiliate her more than she had him somehow. But hurting her—

Hurting her.

He slowed his pace, swallowing, and flicked his tail. Did she even understand what she'd done to him, how deeply she'd hurt him?

No, how could she? A child of thirteen years? She wasn't even a woman yet. What could she know of this?

Make her understand.

Could he... make her understand? She'd tossed him away, but did she realize what she'd done, understand what she'd lost? If she understood, would she take back her repudiating words?

If he apologized to her, she'd stay with the Divinity, and he'd never reclaim his position among the Houses. She'd learn nothing, remain in the clutches of those who would manipulate her, and he wouldn't be a man worth inheriting his father's legacy or marrying the heiress to Laurentine. He needed power, influence, the ability to instill fear in the hearts of his fellow nobles, so that they always remembered he had teeth and, as long as they didn't displease him, chose not to bite.

His Companion, Liliane, had taught him the ways of court, the ways of women and seduction. And he would go out and use them. Rielle would understand what she'd lost when the rumors reached her at last, and she'd suffer them as penance, return to him, hurt by his philandering, jealous and heartsick. She will have learned her lesson, understood what she'd done to him, felt pain like he had, humiliation like he had, and she would want to reconcile and reclaim what was hers. Her place at his side.

Then they would unite and face the world together instead of against each other.

He leaped over a rock with a quiet yip. Yes, that was his path, his only path. It would be dark, unpleasant, and painful, but he'd emerge with his fiancée by his side. He'd save her from the Divinity, a life of loneliness, and from herself. And all would be as had been intended.

7

*S*tirring awake, Rielle tensed as a wave of magic surged through her, rippling up her ribcage. She lifted her head from the bedroll, canvas clutched in her fists, and checked the tent's flap. Still fastened.

Something had crossed the ward. No—the sensation was strong. Something large. *Someone.*

Enemy?

No. Werewolf?

Either way, she'd be going alone. Jon would remain here. Safe. She waited until his breath slowed, until she was certain he was no longer awake. He shifted in his sleep and rolled closer, close enough that she could feel his warm breath on her face. He rested a palm on her hip. Stunned, she didn't move.

But she had to go. She eased out of her bedroll. When she pulled her legs free, he stirred and blinked at her drowsily. "Mage?" he rasped.

"Privy," she whispered.

He gave a sleepy nod and rolled away.

Stay safe. She grabbed her mage coat and boots, then slinked out of the tent, scanning their camp. Nothing. No one.

Her heart skipped a beat. The tiny hairs on the back of her neck rose. A pull on the blood bond. Brennan had arrived.

She laid a fresh ward around the tent; it would blow a heavy wind inward and ripple her anima if something crossed. She placed it far enough to give Jon fair warning of any intruder. And she would come running.

Pulling up the hood of her white coat, she stalked into the woods. The trees tore into the dark sky, pine cones littering the ground beneath. Low shrubs hunched with withering foliage that would soon lose its weakening grasp.

None of the forest creatures stirred. Even the predators fled when they scented werewolf. If only she could do the same.

Through the prickly pine needles and reluctant branches, she made her way to a small clearing. It was as good a meeting place as any, far enough away that Jon wouldn't hear. She stepped into the silvery light of the waxing gibbous moon. It would be full in a few days.

She clasped her hands in wait, shrugging deeper into her coat as the wind blew past.

Within moments, two golden orbs materialized in the darkness, accompanied by a low, rumbling growl that infused the air with menace. Impossibly white teeth flashed into a snarling smile, and with a swirl of shadows, he lowered to his knee, half man and half wolf. The forest was eerily silent; not a single animal dared incur his wrath.

Brennan always knew how to make an entrance.

She drew the small, red-handled *al-dhammé* from her boot, and pressed the tip of the thin, tapered blade to her palm, just enough. A small, red drop bloomed there.

She wiped the al-dhammé on her boot's wool lining, sheathed it and, as always, held out her hand to him. The offering. He pressed his muzzle to it, sweeping his tongue slowly over her palm, and exhaled loudly, slowly, pleased. Amber eyes fixed on her from beneath a menacing scowl, grotesque on his wolfish countenance.

"I've needed your blood for days now." He snarled, his clawed fingers digging into the soil and clenching it in fists. "The moon's full soon. You kept me waiting."

Such arrogance. But every time the moon approached full, she knew an urgency burned in him. The Wolf's demands became fierce and did not abate until he was at her heel, reunited with his master.

Reunited with her.

Eleven years ago, the otherworldly cries of an animal in pain had spirited her from her bed in Laurentine. Her bare feet had taken her to the rocky beach outside the castle, where a wolf-like animal had lain in suffering. Injured all over, he must have fallen off the cliffs overlooking the Shining Sea. Despite his form, the look in his eyes had belonged to Brennan. There had been no mistaking it. She'd known those eyes for as long as she could remember. Brennan, the boy she had been betrothed to since age five. His pitiful groans had rung in her ears, lamenting the pain and begging for death. Sympathy had guided her hand to his wounded muzzle. He'd shifted nervously and nicked her with a tooth. Their blood had mingled.

She peered at him among the forest's shrubs. He wasn't the same boy. And she wasn't eleven years old anymore. "Perhaps I shouldn't have come at all?"

He changed from half-wolf to man. Unabashed in his nakedness, he took her hand in his and brought it to his lips, and then he raised it to his forehead in a firm contact he held in mock reverence. Even kneeling, when he looked up at her, his eyes were intense, imperious, the eyes of a lord, a king, an emperor. "Perish the thought. I'd have to hunt you then, and take my control in a less... pleasant manner."

Let him try. It would be the last thing he ever did.

As he rubbed his face against the back of her hand, a shiver ran up her arm at the coarseness, a day's growth of dark facial hair. She hated when he touched her; perhaps that was why he did.

Despite his cruelty and coldness, he was attractive, with bronze skin, hazel eyes, strong but fine features, a powerful body, and an effortless air of studied nonchalance. Many a woman had gotten lost in him. Too many.

"Hold your tongue," she said. "I haven't missed a month in eleven years. I could have left you to go mad."

Although Brennan had always been rebellious, his initial resistance to their offerings had dwindled as it drowned in the pleasure of that offering. As much as she hated to admit it, the offering pleased her, too. The bond was both bliss and torture: possessive like a chain, and yet, for briefly high moments, euphoric.

Just as he couldn't resist the urge to meet her before every full moon, neither could she. Every month, the bond rattled her until she saw him.

When she had rejected his ultimatum at the Tower nine years ago, he'd been quick to seduce a succession of women, adding notches to his belt—publicly—a clear message that her loss meant little to him, or perhaps an indication of what he thought of their continuing betrothal.

But she had resolved not to be petty or angry. It had been she, after all, who'd hurt him, and if he wanted to strike back, that was his choice. For three years, a long, cruel silence had ensued at their monthly offerings.

She'd resolved to live her life and move on. But when she'd given her virginity to Leigh, opened her heart to him, Brennan had curled an upper lip at their monthly offering in the Tower forest, his coldness turning icy. And when her affair had turned public, linking his fiancée and a foreign commoner—even one as illustrious as Leigh—the iciness became outright animosity.

Yet the bond continued unbroken. She would never be free of it, nor of him.

Brennan smirked, his hair catching the moonlight like glass. "Your behavior still leaves much to be desired, fiancée mine."

"You're one to talk. And don't call me that." It was tiresome and frustrating, ever a reminder of his family's selfishness. And his. His ultimatum at the Tower nine years ago, so confusing then, made sense when she learned that contracting with the Divinity interrupted the Emaurrian king's dominion over a mage, including the ability to enforce marriage contracts. As long as she contracted with the Divinity, she had the power to deny him her hand in marriage, and she only had to hold out one more year, until age twenty-three.

One more year, and she would be free of the betrothal.

She was the last of her line, Favrielle Amadour Lothaire, Marquise of Laurentine, an unmarried Emaurrian noble. Papa's line couldn't end with her, but she couldn't marry while the contract with the Marcels remained in effect. Just the thought of wedding her snarling monster of a fiancé sickened her, but privilege entailed responsibility. And she was bound to him, the contract unbreakable until the king or Duke Faolan, Brennan's father, could be persuaded; she or Brennan lost their titles or fortunes; she bore a child out of wedlock to another man; or she turned twenty-three.

The sooner, the better.

He rumbled a proud laugh. "No one makes me wait. Especially not you. And we both know how I react when you displease me."

Brazen beast. "You forget your place."

"Ever and always above yours. But then, you remember that well, don't you?" A rictus grin accompanied his answer. He drew near and sniffed. Breathed deep. "There's a man's scent on you."

She looked away from him, but no matter—he crouched and snorted a breath. His nostrils flaring, he picked her over with an amused gaze. "His scent is *all* over you."

"Keep your nose to yourself."

He laughed, a monstrous rumble deep in his throat.

She'd wanted to meet him days ago. Perhaps he had answers the Proctor and Leigh didn't. "What news of the capital?"

"You mistake me for a town crier."

"Please," she said, swallowing. The last thing she wanted to do was beg him for anything, but it was for Olivia. "It's important."

His eyes gleamed, but his smirk faded. "I... don't rightly know. I've been hunting a lot and haven't kept up with the news. Why?"

She shook her head. "A bad feeling." If he didn't know, she'd find answers in Bournand.

His body contorting, he dropped to all fours as black fur spiked from his skin and covered his body. Changed from man-beast to full wolf—massive, the size of a man. With a last glance in her direction, he melted into the forest's darkness.

She glared at the brush. She'd allowed the wolf back in once, at nineteen, the wound in her heart fresh after being parted from Leigh. And he'd gotten his revenge. For three years since, he'd been flaunting his upper hand, a bulwark of outward arrogance to shield his still-bruised ego.

After the fire had consumed home nine years ago, perhaps it had been her destiny to be ruined by every person she loved and to ruin them in return. It was for the best that she'd resolved to never love again. There would be no one who could cause her fureur, and no one she might kill with it.

It's in the past.

Only Olivia had been spared, and now, even that was uncertain. It had been a long time since she'd heard from her best friend. Too long. They had plans for Midwinter; after escorting Jon to Monas Amar, she could make the day's ride to the capital and intrude upon Olivia early.

Seeing no more movement, she made her way back to camp, Brennan's revenge heavy on her heart. She needed to find some leverage, something to force him into persuading his father to break the contract. She didn't want even a single day more of it looming over her. Of *him* looming over her.

A dark thought cast its shadow over her mind. She could threaten to reveal he was a werewolf.

But even as the thought formed, she dismissed it. No one would ever believe her. And, if by some miracle they did, she was more likely to be accused of cursing him herself.

With a dejected sigh, she kicked a pile of leaves. What kept Brennan awake late at night? What mattered more to him than breaking the curse? Did anything?

8

*J*on lay awake, staring at the darkness above him. His fingers moved to his Sodalis ring, as they always did when his thoughts lingered too long in the deep. The symbol of his vows, his commitment to the life of a Sodalis and the Order of Terra, it always offered him comfort. Always. But not tonight.

She's been gone too long. Perhaps she'd run into trouble in the woods? Wolves? A boar? Wild dogs?

She can handle herself.

He would wait a few minutes more, and if she didn't return, he would go after her.

The mage—no, the woman—would give him no peace. He could look at her for days. Bewitching, fey. Long haired, light footed, wild eyed.

Wild eyed. He closed his eyes and saw the wilderness in hers—fire, water, earth, wind. The elements in that sky-blue gaze, in her hands, in her body. The way she pursed her lips, the way she scowled, the way she challenged him, it made him fume—but it also made him smile. And her scent... He took a deep breath. Somehow, in the tent, beyond the overpowering scent of horse, the sweet aroma of roses and *her* had prevailed. It, too, was a spell, an enchantment willing his arms around her, his nose in her hair, his lips against the crown of her head. One he would defeat.

Terra have mercy, but he'd forgotten how women smelled up close. Vivid memories of bright mid-spring days, the verdant hedge maze at Maerleth Tainn, and the giggles of young women spun in his mind, mercilessly circling his repressed desire. He'd been a squire then, accompanying Tor to his brother's duchy.

No stranger to temptation, Jon had staved off that need with resolve and distance—and plenty of it.

And that's all this is—temptation. He shifted in his bedroll.

No, he hadn't wished to withdraw from the tent earlier for her weakness, but for his own. Terra have mercy, she had power over him, more than she knew. He huffed an amused breath. As much as he pushed her away, it might take no more than close quarters, some show of interest from her, and a moment of weakness to undo a lifetime of denial.

Some show of interest...

He sighed and relaxed deeper into his bedroll. Her surreptitious glances in his direction hadn't been as stealthy as she'd perhaps hoped. But they pleased him, pleased him in ways glances from other women rarely had.

Her curious study of him had straightened his spine, tensed his arms, expanded his chest, raised his chin... He wanted her to look. And he wanted her to like what she saw. Terra have mercy, but he actually enjoyed it.

And she...

He grabbed a fistful of canvas and pulled it off to cool his heated skin. He had fancied women before, and his vows had withstood the temptation.

And so they would again.

No woman would keep him from being a paladin once more, especially not a mage. Tor had warned him about searching for the apprentice healer who'd saved his life in Signy, about the temptation of women—and mage-women besides.

And he refused dishonor for the sake of this elementalist, this stranger, a woman. Paladins were above earthly temptations, and at Monas Amar, at Terra's holy monastery, among his brothers, this torture would end.

Until then, however, he would need some other measure to ensure temperance.

In the absence of physical distance, he would have to think of something else.

Soft footsteps crunched through the autumn grass outside the tent— hers. He stifled a relieved sigh, closed his eyes, and lay still, controlling his breathing. She didn't need to know he'd stayed awake to wait for her.

She slipped in, what little noise she made relaying her every move: the swish of a tent flap closing, the rasp of her shed coat, the rustle of her descent to her bedroll, the whisper of boots removed, the soft thump of them on the ground. She whished into the bedroll, shifted to her side, and a lock of her curls feathered the back of his neck.

A shiver shook him.

She went still. "Jon?"

Pretending would be useless. "Hm?" he replied as groggily as he could manage.

"Sorry if I woke you," she whispered.

He wanted to tease her, but there was a sad and lonely hollowness to her voice, a rasp. Had she been crying? He opened his eyes.

"Paladins sleep light," he offered by way of explanation. It was true enough; heavy sleepers didn't survive as paladins-errant, considering they often worked alone. "Something on your mind?"

She hesitated. "What does your faith say about forgiveness?"

A Divinist interested in Terran theology was a rare occurrence. "What about the Divine?"

She shrugged. "The Divine isn't like your Eternan deities—not a man, not a woman, not like a person at all. More like a power, inhabiting all life and all else, mankind and gods and our world, everything that was, everything that is, and everything that ever will be. We serve by keeping life thriving, by cultivating magic and mages, by brightening and deepening anima. Grudges and forgiveness are inconsequential personal matters." A troubled breath quivered free of her. "Confusing personal matters that perhaps your goddess may shed some wisdom on."

Let the heavens fall upon my head if I defend not the innocent, help not the weak, redeem not the suffering. "The Holy Mother bids us forgive each eve and rise without malice in our hearts." He hadn't lived up to those words, but they inspired. He rolled onto his side to face her. "What troubles you?"

Only tell me, and I'll see it remedied.

She curled up tighter in her bedroll, drawing her knees in toward her chest, slender arms holding together what threatened to fall apart.

He resisted the inclination to lend a comforting touch. Terrans had unburdened themselves to him over the years by the hundreds, seeking guidance when shadows lengthened in their hearts. He had listened, guided when asked, and had strictly kept each one's confidence.

"If you don't wish to tell me, you needn't, but I'm here for you." He bit his tongue, but it was too late. His mouth had already gone too far.

She sniffed bitterly. "For a Divinist?"

"Unless it's about the black arts. That's between you and the rest of the hags that dance under the moon."

She gasped and shoved him, a burst of laughter escaping her lips. He retaliated with a nudge.

Happy silence passed between them. He stared into the dark, touching the fading grin on his lips. Terra have mercy, but he was actually enjoying this. He cleared his throat. *Who keeps his tongue keeps himself from trouble.*

"Thank you," she said, by all signs earnest. "Perhaps someday, I will take you up on your offer."

He looked over his shoulder. "It's no more than I would offer anyone else." A prevarication, but he needed to make up for his earlier misstep. In such close quarters, his usual measure against temptation—physical distance—was unavailable, but he could use a different kind of distance. Callousness. He turned away once more. "No, on second thought, you're right. Your idle musings aren't my concern. Why don't you keep them to yourself next time so I can get some sleep?"

Too far. He immediately regretted the words.

"By all means," she snapped. "I wouldn't presume to keep you."

An apology would have been proper, but he thought the better of it. Rudeness would serve his vows, even if it disappointed etiquette. Overcompensating rudeness.

He mulled over the notion. Surliness pushed her away, provided him with the space to preserve his vows. In the absence of physical distance, perhaps it could accomplish what he needed.

Yes, this would be his winning strategy. He lay back and tried to sleep.

But it didn't sit right. If she was troubled, he wanted to stay up as long as it took to assuage her unrest. It had nothing to do with temptation; it was about relieving another's burdens.

Would it bring them closer?

If so, as much he disliked refusing to help, he couldn't risk it. Monas Amar was still a long journey away, and his resolve had already begun to weaken. He couldn't risk getting any closer to this woman.

She hates me. A woman with pride like hers wouldn't forgive the insult. Any man who derided her would find himself quickly cast away. And rightly so. Any man who derided her didn't deserve the pleasure of her company.

He'd insulted her, she'd snapped at him, and somehow he respected her for it?

Distance. Distance, Terra's troth, save me from this madness.

"I forgive you," she blurted out.

He raised his head. "Hm?"

"I'm trying to go to sleep without malice in my heart," she said, with a cynical edge. "I forgive you for being such a bastard. Goodnight." With that, she faced away from him and went silent.

He let his head rest on the bedroll once more, and although he didn't reply, a grin lingered on his face. He traced it with a finger and frowned.

Madness is already upon me.

He needed his restraint to hold. A man without restraint was a city without walls. He would keep his walls, or he'd need to remove the reason for them. The thought shrouded his tired mind until sleep took him.

9

*B*rennan raced through the forest's dense undergrowth in the shadow of the Tainn Mountains, covering more ground on four paws than he ever could on two legs. The freshness of damp earth filled his nostrils, along with the mustiness of old fallen foliage and the almost sweet scent of pine.

He could close his eyes and nearly forget her—but the honeyed notes of late-blooming honeysuckle bordering the woods invaded his keen nose, conjuring up images of Laurentine, honeysuckle vines on its coat-of-arms, and there she was again.

He bared his teeth and ran faster, willing each stride to distance him from thoughts of her. What he needed was to get home and come up with a plan to handle his rebellious betrothed. Time had already dwindled to less than twelve months, and soon it would disappear altogether.

He forced out an angry exhalation. The last Lothaire of Laurentine, his snarling little she-wolf, had few options if she wanted to honor her family. And she did want to. Desperately. He curled his upper lip.

She wouldn't die unmarried and childless, shirking duty and leaving her entire family in shame. Not Rielle. She'd been waiting him out, perhaps planning to marry some lowly baron—or what dregs remained of the Houses beyond the nobility already betrothed since childhood. Or perhaps she planned to take a new commoner plaything to bed, bear a son out of wedlock, a bastard ostracized by the Houses but able to inherit all the wealth of Laurentine and carry on her bloodline.

He snarled. Never. No Marcel had ever countenanced such a slight. He wouldn't be the first.

For years, he'd been waiting her out, and in eleven months, it would all be for naught? Every day that passed was another day closer to the end of the betrothal's term, her twenty-third birthday, and every day passing without her bearing him a child was another day she could die. Another risk.

A blood curse like theirs could be ended by a joining of the master and thrall bloodlines. By a joining of *their* bloodlines. By the conception of a *child* between them.

She'd have to agree; she couldn't hold out forever.

His throat tightened, along with the rest of him.

He needed a solution soon. His life in his own hands again, not at the mercy of a girl's whims. That day in the Tower nine years ago, he'd known the Divinity's power to shield its mages from the king's influence; he'd played every card in his hand to entice his young fiancée into a quick marriage and had left with nothing. *Less* than nothing. A reputation for being refused by a thirteen-year-old orphan in favor of scouring pots and pans and learning a few spells.

He, a Marcel, most faithful of Nox, the Great Wolf, the Dark God, the Unseen One, Life-Taker, Death-Eater, He-Who-Carries-Away-All. His family had not made offerings for centuries to be rewarded with such low regard.

Even if she hated him, he'd seen the way she eyed him sometimes. He could get her into bed. It might only take once to get what he needed. He swished his tail in pleasant rumination.

If his seduction failed, he could spread word of her every common relationship and shame her into eventual submission, as long as she never learned the source of the rumors. Marriage to him would restore her instantly; no one would dare speak ill of a Marcel's wife lest they desired humiliation, pain, or death. Her fatal attractions with scandal—the affair with that wild mage, and her glorious degradation at Tregarde three years ago, among others—had convinced him she would never willingly invite it into her life again.

In the end, she would give him what he wanted. They always did.

A plan. He had a plan. His throat relaxed, his muscles loosened with relief. A course of action. Finally.

At last, the sprawling stone walls of Maerleth Tainn came into view. He made for his usual point in the darkness of the mountains and Changed to man-beast to scale it. Once over, he Changed back to full wolf and ran around the outskirts of the city enceinte toward the massive castle. He entered through one of a network of subterranean passages, traveled between labyrinthine walls and dozens of windings.

Stale air gave way to the myriad scents of Tainn Castle, and soon he pushed a panel open into his quarters. Since his first Change, he had seen clearly in the darkness, something he'd had to hide from his family and everyone else for fear of death. He closed the panel and, in complete darkness, quickly donned a pair of black silk pants.

He headed to the washbasin and scoured the dirt off his skin. Unlike men and beasts, he didn't tire but for extreme exertions, but he could do nothing about the dust and grime of the forest floor, traitors eager to spill his secrets before all eyes. He scrubbed his feet and dried them. Such precautions were necessary if he wanted to avoid the fates of the suspected werewolves among his ancestors, necessary honor killings performed in secret. Stillbirths. Beheading. Quartering. Burning at the stake. Sometimes uncanny accidents.

He eyed his desk, where in a locked drawer, he kept what journals he'd found about the beasts of the Marcel bloodline, all firstborn sons of firstborn sons. His grandfather's older brother had been stillborn, and it had been decades since there had been a werewolf among the Marcels. *Until my first Change eleven years ago.*

But every day he remained a werewolf risked his life. *And that coldhearted bitch can't be bothered to care.*

He longed to return to Tregarde, to hear Liliane's counsel; although she never approved of his intrigues, she could always be counted on to assess them. She had been his bodyguard and his first, taught him the ways of the lover, the courtier, the plotter. At forty years of age, she was his oldest friend, if a Companion of the Camarilla could be called such. And yet, she knew nothing of his curse, his suffering. Even she might recoil from the monster. She had to be kept in the dark, like everyone else save for Rielle. He fought back a growl.

He threw the towel aside.

Distant, soft footsteps came from the hall—a woman's. He grabbed the washbasin, rushed to the garderobe, and poured out the dirty water.

As he finished, he caught the scent of jasmine and warmth. Mother. She knocked softly.

Silent as death, he crept into his bed and covered himself with a blanket. "Come in," he rasped.

She opened the door, letting in the illumination of a single candle. "Brennan? Are you abed?"

"Yes, Mother. Is everything all right?" He sat up, grabbed the flint and pyrite to light his bedside candle.

Clad in an elaborately embroidered dressing gown, her long brown waves unbound, she was the picture of elegance. She placed her candlestick on a table, and sat on the edge of his bed. "Your chamberlain said you weren't in your quarters earlier."

"I wasn't. Not in *my* quarters."

She eyed his bare chest and still-damp skin and raised an eyebrow. "Please, tell your mother no more." She patted his blanketed ankle. "The guard has warned your father—a large black wolf mysteriously appeared inside the city walls again tonight and has been seen prowling the grounds. I know you come and go as you please to Tregarde and elsewhere, so I wanted to make sure you were safe and that you take care."

If he didn't know better, he could almost believe she was warning him that the guards had seen him. He studied her even forest-green gaze, gentle and placid as ever.

No. She didn't know. She couldn't know.

She was genuinely concerned a wolf might hurt him. A novel thought. In addition to a dueling master, Father had paid his own weight in gold to buy his only son hand-to-hand combat training from a Faris grandmaster in Sonbahar, and he still employed a Faris master at Tainn Castle to train his knights.

He took her hand. "I can handle myself, Mother. I promise."

She studied him with searching eyes until she finally squeezed his hand and nodded. "I love having you here."

His smile faded, and he looked away. "But?"

She shook her head. "You're turning twenty-seven this autumn, and you're my only son. You should have your own children by now. Half a dozen, at least."

His back stiffened, and he fought back a smile. "Mother—"

"I don't blame you, but that girl has humiliated you long enough." Her face set, she could fit in among any army on a battlefield.

"It is I who have humiliated her, Mo—" He stopped short. He wasn't about to tell his own mother about the shameful deed he'd done.

"That was three years ago."

He swallowed. She'd heard of it? Mother, of all people, was privy to what he'd done to Rielle? "You know?"

She raised an eyebrow. "My son, there is nothing about you I don't know." She held his gaze a moment. "You're strong, intelligent, capable, rich, handsome. That girl is disgraced, only getting older, working for the

Divinity like some commoner, and has no other prospects. If she came to her senses, she would thank the Great Wolf for her good fortune and marry you."

If only it were so easy. "Yes, well—"

"And the only person more adamant than your father about adhering to the marriage contract is you." She took a deep breath and sighed. "Remind me again why it *must* be her."

Because she's the only one who can break my curse, but she hates me so much that she won't share my bed unless it's to do her marital duty and consummate as the scion of House Lothaire... Even the ridiculous answer would get him killed. "Because I love her. I've loved her ever since I was a boy. I made one stupid mistake, and I will spend the rest of my life trying to make up for it if I have to." The honeyed words were enough to make him retch, but there were few believable answers.

"Fortunately it's only eleven more months. You could learn to love another woman."

"Not like her." He clenched his teeth.

Mother let the silence settle for a moment. "When your father mentioned the black wolf, I told him it was none other than the Great Wolf himself come to protect His most faithful servants during this difficult time, now that the king is dead."

His breath caught. "The king is dead?"

Was this the bad feeling about the capital that Rielle had mentioned?

"Yes, my son. King Marcus, Prince James... the Faralle line. And many eyes turn to your father now." She rose with effort. "All the more reason you must take care. Although I believe the black wolf is He-Who-Carries-Away-All, our most holy god, my hedge witch has called it the Black Dog, *le Rongeur d'Os* of legend, omen and bringer of death. Watch your step, my son, and the eyes upon you." She kissed his forehead, reclaimed her candlestick, and left the room.

He blew out his own candle and stared into the darkness, willing the cold sweat from his body as smoke stung his nostrils.

Watch your step, my son, and the eyes upon you.

The breath abandoned his lungs. *She knows.*

Did she? Could she? He gasped. He could wait no longer. He needed the curse broken as soon as possible—by whatever means necessary.

10

The cell door slammed shut behind Archmage Olivia Sabeyon, and the lock clicked with a metallic hiss. A right turn, twenty-eight steps, a left turn, two flights of stairs, a right turn... Always the same. Every day, a Crag Company mercenary came to her cell, blindfolded her, and took her to the Hall of Mirrors. She could tell it instantly from the scent of iron and something like frankincense, light lemon notes and evergreens. Recondite. No other place in Trèstellan Palace smelled so heavily of recondite but the Hall of Mirrors.

And every day, some mercenary would tie her to a chair and simply stand over her but for the rare slapping, flogging, and cold blade pressed against her skin. Soon enough, the whole ordeal would end. She was always taken back to her cell to continue the next day. Like today. Like tomorrow.

She spun and threw herself against the door.

"Let me see James!" she shouted. Prince James Maximilien Breckenridge Faralle, Duke of Guillory, the king's brother and her lover, had been alive when last she'd seen him. *Please be alive, James.*

The Crag Company mercenary merely regarded her with a sneer and departed, along with the light.

"Who's on the other side of the mirror? Who?" she screamed down the darkening dungeon corridor. Her voice echoed in the blackness to no effect.

These dark walls had become her bower, silent but for the skittering of vermin and rush of faraway water, and cold as the grave. That day, that fateful day, the great hall in Trèstellan Palace had shone, golden, brilliantly bright, in only the light of the magnificent crystal chandeliers and sconces. Hosting a Sileni prince and his son, King Marcus had hoped to arrange a marriage for his youngest granddaughter. And no expense had been spared.

How deep had the treason gone? Filtered through the ranks of the guard, the army, the household?

A priest of the Order of Terra had arrived, bearing an urgent message for King Marcus from Paladin Grand Cordon Guérin, and as the king had beckoned him to his ear, the air had been hot, full, weighed far more heavily than its three hundred guests.

Five hundred breaths had stolen the air, from the corners, from the shadows, from the cover of magic, and as the strange priest leaned in, his dagger sharp into the king's flesh, two hundred blades pierced flesh from the corners, from the shadows, from the cover of magic. She had turned, caught an edge to the shoulder, immediately tried to cast a sleep spell but found her magic inert. Arcanir poison.

Her attacker's arm quickly dislocated from his shoulder, by none other than James.

Blood darkened the red brocade of James's doublet. A wound to the chest. But he lived. Without a word, he swept her away, the room a spinning top of spattering blood, a chaos of screams and wet gurgles, the marble damp with death and laden with bodies. Before they disappeared behind a curtain, she glimpsed King Marcus, lifeless on the table next to his sons, Crown Prince Robert and Prince Basile—and their wives and children. All dead.

A panel opened and shut, and she trembled in the darkness, borne away by James's arms alone.

"Are you loyal to the Divinity?"

Darkness amplified the screams, choked her.

"Olivia," he rumbled, shaking her as he dragged her along.

"I am loyal to King Marcus," she breathed.

Voices echoed from afar, and he slowed, his grip on her hand tightening, but he did not stop. "There is a wren in my quarters. In the bedchamber."

She'd seen the bird every night for the past two months. "I know it."

Screams sounded, muffled, from the other side of wall. Cut short. Men's furtive voices. Her mouth went dry.

"There's a black ribbon in the drawer next to the cage. Tie it to the bird's leg and set it free."

Distant doors slammed. More screaming.

"Olivia." James's firm voice. "The wren."

She swallowed. "Yes," she replied tremulously. "Black ribbon. Set it free."

"Good." He pulled her along faster, his palm dampening with cold sweat.

"James—"

"The recipient will know what it means. Do this, Olivia. The entire kingdom is at stake."

A rumble of shouts—nearer, and James paused, drawing her back to him, clamping a hand over her mouth. Footfalls thudded on the other side of the wall. Crashes. Shattering. A door slammed, then another, farther away.

James's hold loosened on her mouth.

"What about you?" she whispered.

He drew in a deep, shaky breath, then took her hand anew and led her down the black corridor. "The queen wasn't present tonight. I must find her."

She swallowed. Queen Alexandrie had been ill with heart problems for many months and resisted all healing. Her final months had taken a toll on an already weakened body. But given what had happened in the great hall, Queen Alexandrie's quarters had to be a killing floor. "James, if you go—"

"I know." He came to a stop and put his ear to the wall, then after a moment, pushed open a panel. "These are my quarters. Go, and then flee, *mon rêve*. Live." He kissed her—hard, deep, hungry for eternity, his arms so strong around her she believed he'd never let go—and then he did.

He pushed her through the open panel, and disappeared once more in the black corridor.

With panic quickening her heart, she took in the familiar bedchamber, where she had experienced such joy, but its warmth didn't fill her up as it always had. It was just a place. Just walls, furnishings, stone, wood, and fabric.

No time. She rushed to the birdcage and did as he had bidden—yanked open the drawer, grabbed the black ribbon, opened the cage, coaxed the wren with a trembling hand, and tied the ribbon around its leg. As she opened the window, a door outside the bedchamber creaked open.

Fly! She set the bird free and then tossed out the birdcage. Her gaze darted about the room. Unable to use magic, she would be helpless. She snatched a letter opener from the desk as the door to the bedchamber flew open. Before she could raise it, a masked stranger blew a dart from a Kezani blowpipe.

It hit her in the neck.

And it was all she remembered of that day before waking in her cold, dark grave of a cell. It had been the last time she'd seen James.

The Crag Company had taken her alive. Her—born of a commoner family, with no hope of ransom. A worthless prisoner. They'd bound her in arcanir cuffs before the arcanir poison could wear off. No hope of escape. Her only hope lay in a rescue, and only one person near and dear to her heart would even consider coming.

"You should come see the palace libraries," she had told Rielle the day of her planned departure from the Tower of Magic to the capital city of Courdeval.

Rielle pursed her lips knowingly. "The palace libraries, or you?"

Rielle could always be counted on for familiarity bordering on rudeness, and the palace would be a colder home for the lack of her.

Olivia embraced her. "It just won't be the same without you." Committing Rielle's wistful smile to memory, she pulled away slowly.

"You'll do fine. Have faith. You're Archmage now," Rielle added, her smile broadening. "The only woman among the king's advisers."

Something she'd worked very hard for—a commoner elevated to a respected position among the Grands, the king's High Council. She smiled. "Archmage..."

"And no matter how far you travel, how long, how high, our souls will always call to each other, Olivia." The bright blue of Rielle's eyes had shone.

Her words heartened.

Olivia nodded. "Don't make me cry, or I'll have to leave in tears." She grinned. "Besides, I'll see you at Midwinter. It'll be here before you know it."

And it had been the last time she'd seen Rielle.

She'll come for me. Olivia squeezed the bars of her cell. She had to believe Rielle would come.

There was no way the Divinity would sanction a rescue mission now that she had sworn her allegiance to the Emaurrian Crown. Rielle would face excommunication for undertaking such an unsanctioned mission.

I know Rielle. She'll come.

But she won't throw her life away without knowing I'm alive. She'll visit a spiritualist. Emaurria was home to a precious few spiritualists, but there were two at the Tower. Thank the Divine that Feliciano Donati was no longer there. He was the last person Rielle should ever meet again, or he'd break her precarious recovery. Olivia shook her head.

As long as she wasn't encased in arcanir, a spiritualist could find her anima. Spirit magic could find her—or anyone—anywhere. Not even the Crag Company's three heretic captains could stop it.

She shuddered. Phantom, Flame, and Shadow, as they were known, were General Evrard Gilles' illustrious mage captains, retained in exchange for certain promises after his embarrassing loss in Signy five years ago. Or so rumor said. The illusionist, Phantom, disguised their attacks; Flame, the elementalist, laid waste to all; and the elusive shadowmancer, Shadow, obfuscated their exit.

As formidable as they were, they could do nothing about a spiritualist's seeking.

Except kill me.

But it hadn't happened yet for a reason. A reason she hoped would persist until Rielle arrived.

11

*R*ielle slouched in the saddle. Jon's bitterness had been exhausting, but without conversation, the day dragged, and it was nearly dusk. The area around the Tainn Forest here was plagued by underground ruins and unsteady ground, so she needed to find a good, safe campsite. But as much as she disliked the endless ennui of the road, the prospect of settling into camp with a scowling Jon was less than appealing.

The night she'd asked him about forgiveness, he'd been friendly, caring even, until that caustic remark. *Your idle musings aren't my concern. Why don't you keep them to yourself next time so I can get some sleep?*

What had that been about? He usually acted so personably, but as soon as she'd begun to expect that, all hope had fizzled.

Although she set their pace, somehow he was always ready and waiting to leave in the mornings before she'd even properly opened her eyes. This morning, after training with his sword, he'd caught her watching him shave. Papa had always insisted on doing it himself, and seeing a man shave always took her back to sunlit mornings as a little girl, tugging on Papa's tunic, begging to go riding or swimming or sailing while Mama laughed heartily.

At her looking, Jon had almost smiled, as pleased as the wolf that caught the hart. Then he had turned bitter and muttered something about it being rude to stare.

Cursing under her breath, she clenched the reins. First hot, then cold. She could handle either, if he'd just make up his mind. But the constant fluctuations, the uneven ground, made her head spin, and her spinning head would twist clean off if the rest of the mission continued this way.

By nightfall, the horses were spent, and so was she. She spotted a potential campsite. On a slight rise, the small clearing was flat and well drained, in a grove of Emaurrian larches with a gap to the east that would let in the morning sun. If the ground supported the larches, it would support their camp. "How about—"

Jon urged his horse right past her and into the trees. She blew out an exasperated breath.

She followed him in, and they repeated their routine: she placed the ward, he built the fire, she tended to the horses, he pitched their tent. Tonight, they ate their supper of cheese and moistened double-baked bread by the fire and then enjoyed the warmth for a while. Perhaps the night would pass without incident.

Divine willing. She sighed and warmed her hands by the fire, letting its heat permeate her skin, her tired flesh and aching bones, to slowly devour the day's ravels like kindling. It was her constant companion, friend and enemy, the fire, with its versicolor hues as numerous as its powers. The power to warm, the power to kill, the power to light, the power to consume, to protect and to scare, to comfort and to hurt. It had borne witness to the brightest and darkest spots of her life. At times, she cursed its power, wished it doused, and always, always, she turned again to its familiarity, sought again its warm embrace.

Jon sharpened his sword, his constant companion, glancing her way from time to time. He'd been at it for hours—honing sections of the three-and-a-half-foot double-edged arcanir blade from guard to tip with one hundred strokes each on the rough-grain damp whetstone, polishing with a soft cloth, then the medium grain, polishing, the fine grain... Firelight seduced the mirror edge, a blurred dance claiming the blade to the measured hum of a nearby stream and the soft churring of a nightjar.

His eyes hard set, he worked with unflinching discipline, unwavering, patience and control in every identically repeated action. She watched him from beneath stray locks of hair, stealing glimpses of his stern face, the heat of the campfire warming her furthest reaches, and then those hard-set eyes fixed upon hers, turning the thousand suns of his concentration upon her while he continued honing the blade uninterrupted.

Her breath caught; a frisson of need shot through her, and she squeezed her knees together. The blade's tempered moan ended with a slow hiss, and his intense gaze locked with hers, he polished its length with a languorous stroke from base to tip.

The air spilled from her mouth, and she bit her lip. That look... He wasn't angry; he was...

She swallowed and turned away, a plant soaking too much sun, and her gaze settled on the tent. Tonight would be another night sleeping side by side in close quarters, and Divine be praised if she'd get a wink. At least they'd soon be in Bournand, in separate rooms, among other people.

The previous night, she'd hardly been able to sleep at all, for different reasons, frustrated by his confusing behavior and his damnably intoxicating scent of—she'd discerned after some rumination—linden wood and smoke. Papa had used a shaving balm that smelled just so, and it made her think of home and her childhood, safe and laughing in Papa's arms, sunny days, the salt on the air from the Shining Sea—

A feather fluttered along her ribs—an echo of magic reverberating through her. A breach of the ward. She jolted upright. Something large.

She surged to her feet, and so did Jon, the whetstone abandoned, eyes scanning the surroundings.

Someone had dared to cross the threshold. Brennan had met with her the previous night—and wouldn't return for a month.

An intruder.

"The ward's been breached." She looked beyond the campfire, peering into the woods. The elements were at her disposal, at least until her anima went dark, but there was no danger of that unless an entire army had breached the ward or serious healing was needed. "Stay here."

Already arming, he fixed her with a stubborn glare. "I'm coming with you."

No surprise.

"You'll only get in my way. You'll be safer here." Divine's flaming fire, the last thing she needed was for him to get hurt or killed fighting an intruder, or hitting a patch of unsteady ground. As she stowed their valuables in her recondite satchel, arcanir clinked and leather hissed.

Shaking her head, she stalked through the tall grass, wizened by the onset of autumn, in the direction of the intrusion.

His footsteps followed as he trod through the brush behind her. Arguing with him would probably require more effort than defending him in battle, so she didn't waste her breath.

Her inner barriers pulled to the southern edge of the perimeter, her body tensing and favoring that direction. The ward breach had occurred there, a short walk into the Tainn Forest. When she'd laid the protections, the twilight radiance had still granted her sight. In the darkness, however, a candlelight spell would give away their location. The forest's darkness protected them, and in lieu of the spell, she stopped, listened.

Jon's breath huffed on the nape of her neck—hot, close. Somewhere in the distance, a wolf howled.

She closed her eyes and signed the earthsight enchantment over them. And blinked.

The world was still dark, but faint white threads wove together before her in intricate patterns—in the shapes of grass, trees, and brush, with small, moving points of brilliance she knew to be rodents, owls, nighthawks. The glowing tree shapes shone ahead of her, their anima very much alive, the world woven and its life exposed.

If they were quiet and careful, they would see the intruders before being seen themselves.

Metal clinked softly behind her. Jon's fingertips brushed gently against the back of her coat.

"Stay close to me and be silent," she whispered. With earthsight, not only would she be able to spot the aura of a trespasser, but also the telltale loose threads in the ground, where the subterranean ruins might have crumbled and caused unsteadiness. Their campsite seemed well used and was safe enough, but here, there was no such confidence.

Taking a step forward, she peered past her own brightness at the anima of the grass beneath her boot glimmering faintly and, as she raised her foot, brightening once more. She led him toward the edge of the ward, weaving through the trees and the brush, and paused when a tiny ball of light darted across their intended path.

Jon stopped behind her, so still and so quiet she couldn't deny a begrudging respect for him.

"What is it?" he asked, barely audible, his mouth a hair's breadth from her ear, the tingle making her shiver.

All that newfound respect disappeared. "A rabbit," she grumbled in a hushed tone.

If he didn't keep his mouth shut, then all her effort at stealth would be for nothing.

He didn't reply, and she continued on, expecting to see anima the size and shape of at least one person ahead. However, as they neared the edge, nothing indicated a person. The ward had been breached—that much was certain—but they should have encountered the trespasser by now. *Someone* had been out here.

She looked left and right before turning around to look behind her—

An abundance of light.

Anima.

With a gasp, she receded and averted her gaze from the brightness. *Great Divine.*

"It's only me." Jon held out his hand in peace.

Unmoving, she blinked away the floating ghosts of light in her vision and allowed her gaze to settle upon him once more.

Silver brilliance shone from his face, uncovered by arcanir. Bright and shimmering, a marvel to behold, far brighter than only life.

Magic.

"You're a mage," she whispered. There was no time for this now; somewhere out there, a trespasser lurked. Could someone really have triggered the ward but not seen their camp, nor meant them any harm? She couldn't let her guard down.

Jon is a mage.

There was a tense silence.

Unable to see his facial expression for all the light, she couldn't fathom his reaction. Despite the disdain he'd shown for mages, he'd been one himself all along. Perhaps that was the reason—the guilty self-hatred of a *doué* paladin. A magically gifted paladin.

He muffled a sigh and raked his fingers through his hair? The brightness of his anima made the motion difficult to discern.

She scanned their surroundings. Clear.

He trudged through the trees, and she followed.

"I don't practice magic," he said, pacing a small clearing, his voice soft even in its insistence. He fidgeted with his wrists—loosening and removing his gauntlets.

"But you can learn to."

"I don't want to." He twirled that ring again.

"You're a mage—whether you want to be or not."

It did not matter whether he used his magic or not—he had been a mage long before now, before even his *éveil*, the awakening of his magic at puberty; he had been a mage since birth. "You've had an éveil."

He nodded. "While training with another page when I was twelve. He was bigger, stronger—pinned me. Wouldn't let me up, his knee pressing into my chest"—his palm settled over his sternum—"and I could hardly breathe. Everything was going white, and then... he was across the yard."

Force magic.

She could still hardly believe it. Rare and unexpected. In a kingdom of twenty million people, less than two thousand were known to be mages, many of them nobles. And here, one of the few mage-born, an enforcer, wasted away in the Order of Terra.

"Why are you a paladin?"

He stepped toward her.

The anima threads in the ground beneath him loosened. Divine, that meant the ground was—

A rumble. The anima threads broke apart.

He looked down. The ground collapsed.

He slid into the void below. She hurtled toward him, reaching out with both hands to catch his arm. The ground beneath her crumbled away.

They plunged into the darkness. She only tightened her grip on his arm.

The weightlessness of falling. The raw life of the hold between her and Jon. Her fingernails dug into flesh. A chunk of earth crashed through their joined hands. She didn't let go.

He pulled her into his arms. Her earthsight dispelled. She struggled to breathe in his hold as they plummeted together.

Geomancy—no, aeromancy—

The sting. Nothing. In the clutch of his arcanir. No magic at all.

Rushing air pulled at her coat.

The ground came too soon. The grotesque sounds of clashing armor, thudding bone, and crashing flesh.

Pain burst from every part of her, what felt like a kick in the chest expelling her breath, leaving her struggling for air. Everything went white. Agony crawled from her limbs inward, paralyzing. She tried to get up, but her body wouldn't cooperate. What had—?

Beneath her, Jon convulsed and wheezed.

The copper tang of blood filled her nostrils. She reached out for him, avoiding his arcanir, and muttered, *"With Your Light, Divine, grant my will, / Illume the flesh, reveal all ill,"* a healer's diagnostic spell. She inspected him through her hand, his every injury outlined with the Divine's light in her mind's eye.

Broken ribs, a dislocated shoulder, and after removing his helm, a cracked skull—she couldn't handle any more. Her hand was sticky with blood, his or hers or some mixture thereof—

Her rudimentary knowledge of healing magic would have to serve. Using non-innate magic required incantations. She'd never mastered dulling pain, but flesh and bone she could stitch together.

Not bright enough. Her anima wasn't bright enough.

She didn't have enough to heal them both entirely and retain something for potential threats. No, rather than repeating the incantation until his whole body healed, she would heal each injury individually to conserve anima, saving bruises and small cuts for later.

"This will hurt." She extended a trembling hand to unfasten his sword belt, and urged the leather between his teeth, then placed her hand on him to heal his skull fracture and whispered the incantation. A soft white glow from her hands permeated his body.

His reaction was instant and violent. He ground his teeth as bone shifted and fused together beneath his flesh, as she forced the swelling to subside. It was excruciating. She knew firsthand. Yet his reaction indicated he was still conscious. A good sign.

"You will live," she croaked, her own voice hoarse and weak. With a twinge of prickling sensation, she healed his ribs, his arms, his legs—and most of the broken rest of him, anima flowing from her to him.

She faltered and collapsed. Her body rebelled, and a wave of crippling pain flooded her.

Adrenaline had delayed the realization. *Broken bones.*

Head turned away from him, she vomited what little she'd eaten that day, reeling from the dizziness of movement. She took his sword belt and wedged it between her own teeth, then forced herself through the healing, starting with her head and working her way down until her legs were healed. The leather barely survived.

She reclined once more, her pain-addled mind vaguely recognizing rough stone tile beneath her. They were in a ruin; one of its crumbling support pillars must have collapsed and led to the ground giving way.

Next to her, Jon stirred, perhaps at last coming from the daze of crushing pain, and cautiously tried to sit up. *No, don't move yet.* He wasn't fully healed. She reached out, searching for his shoulder. He drew in a sharp breath, and she winced.

Found it. With a quick diagnostic spell, she saw all that still required healing and breathlessly muttered the incantation Olivia had taught her.

"*Sundered flesh and shattered bone, / By Your Divine Might, let it be sewn.*"

Anima left her weakened body and wove the magic, repairing his shoulder. He ground his teeth in a horrible creak.

His major injuries healed, she relaxed despite her remaining soreness. After the broken bones and the ordeal of healing without pain management, bruises and a few cuts were tolerable. The aching vacancy of her nearly dark anima, however, was harder to ignore.

There was a soft pressure on her shoulder, and she started. It was Jon's hand.

"You healed me." His voice was quiet but filled with awe.

Meaning to wave off his awe, she realized one of her hands still gripped his wrist and gasped.

She'd never let go.

"Are you all right?" he asked.

"Maybe step lightly next time," she grumbled, and he laughed softly.

He gave her shoulder a light squeeze, and then the darkness of the unknown pervaded. In the silence, she looked inward in meditation, and her dimmed anima ached for completion. The suffocating pressure of a thousand hands closed in on her presence, pushing, pressing, yearning.

Spiritseve was close. The anxiety of the earth mounted up to the night when the Veil was at its thinnest, less than two months away, and the dimmer her anima, the more she could feel it if she attempted meditation. After using so much magic unnatural to her, her anima was dim. She never allowed such a risky condition to persist and was disinclined to let it persist now.

Had it been the case before their fall, she would not have had the anima to heal them both. With a shudder, she retreated and shook off the feeling. She wouldn't willingly meditate again until Hallowday. "I need resonance."

And there was no one to offer it but Jon.

"I..." He hesitated. As a forsworn paladin nevertheless dedicated to the Code, he'd probably be unwilling.

"I'm not a healer," she bit out. "That was costly. My anima's dim, and who knows what we'll face in here?" She gestured around the dark ruins. "I need to be at my full power. I need resonance from another mage. And in here, you're all there is."

He slowly shook his head. "I'm a paladin. I have sworn—"

She heaved an exasperated sigh. "I'm not about to rip your clothes off and tackle you!" She snarled. "It's a touch. A simple touch, that's all. Would you have us die because you refuse to even touch me?"

With a sharp exhalation, he ran a hand through his hair. Unsettled. "Resonance, I... I don't know how."

Then he would have to learn. Teaching it to him and using it would cost them time, but the security of having her anima at full brightness was worth the risk. The protests of her aching body ignored, she rose to her feet. "Stand."

He didn't move right away but eventually stood. Despite her dim anima, she cast a candlelight spell so that they could see each other.

She jumped back with a horrified gasp. His face was streaked with dirt and blood, his hair matted with dark red, and his armor suggested he might have just crawled out of his own grave.

In a way, she supposed he had. "You look terrible."

"So do you." He closed the gap between them and ran concerned hands over her white mage coat, inspecting every tear, every injury. Paladins relied on mundane medicine for healing, and he clearly had some training. His inspection descended down her body. Her instinct was to pull away, but at the stern crease of his brow and the determined gaze beneath it, all she could do was swallow.

When he dropped to a knee, pulled aside a bloodied corner of her coat, and inspected a cut on her upper thigh, she froze and leaped away.

"I'm fine."

"That wound could become infected if we don't treat it soon."

Obviously. They didn't, however, possess any supplies to treat it, and she hesitated to dim her anima any more unless she was certain it could be brightened.

"After this, I'll make sure every cut is healed." She gestured to his armor. Arcanir interrupted a mage's spellcasting ability when in direct contact, and it deflected direct spells. If she came into contact with his arcanir, their resonance would be interrupted. "This won't work if you're in contact with arcanir. Take off your armor."

He cocked an eyebrow but begrudgingly did as she bade.

When he had stripped down to his clothes, she reached out, holding her hand over his. "May I?"

He grimaced. "If you must."

Off to a fantastic start already. Grimacing, she placed her hand on his. "Close your eyes, and try to look inward."

He closed his eyes, and so did she. He would need to reach his own anima first, in order for her to accompany him. Their contact would allow her eventual access to it.

"Envision a black sky, shimmering velvet with only the moon to light its darkness. Like the wind, you are floating through it, whisper soft and ethereal. You feel the cool air on your skin, and you smell water. Your gaze follows the moonbeams down beneath you, settling on the illuminated waves of a radiant sea," she said. "That sea is your pool of anima. Descend to it, into it. Do not be afraid. It is life to you, breath to you, and you are safe and most alive deep in it."

Soon, she saw him free-falling before a black canvas and felt the same falling sensation. She gasped when he hit the wet, silvery surface of his bright anima, feeling the cool, watery energy on her own skin.

"This is your anima." Reaching it sometimes took months for novices, and for Jon to find it instantly, he must have possessed unusually strong focus. "Now, for us to brighten each other's anima, I'll think of you and you think of me."

The resonance would both restore her and marginally deepen her anima—and his—permanently raising the potential of its brilliance.

As expected, she felt pulled, as if he'd taken her hand and fallen back. An invitation to connect. He was a quick study indeed.

She pulled back, and their psychic links slid languidly against each other until they caught. Forged a connection. She gasped.

The azure pool of her own magic rippled with a silver aura, its edges shimmering—Jon's doing. The ripple widened, a vibration spreading throughout her entire body, a steady drumming echoing off her inner barriers, intensifying, resonating until it hummed through her veins, radiating pleasure. Gradually, heat built inside to blazing, and her body heated up to match, relaxing, easing, slave to the resonance.

A sharp exhalation—his—made her shiver, the motion rousing the heat inside.

The vibrations were strongest at their point of contact—her hand on his—rapturous origin, but soon pleasure inhabited her entirely, from her head to her feet. Every hair follicle brimmed with electricity, a pleasant hum that made her mouth water.

Even the tips of her fingers and toes tingled with a pulse of power that shook her to her core.

She moaned. Overwhelmed with pleasure, her flesh contracted, the feeling so good it hurt, and she cried out. Strong arms held her in a tight embrace, close to his muscled chest, their bodies flush together at every possible point of contact. She breathed deep, blood, earth, wood, smoke, the very essence of him, her knees buckling but for his hold.

Holding her hand—the touch that had initiated this revelation in pleasure—he wrapped an arm around her waist, twisting hers with it. Closer. Deeper. More.

If he drew their joined hands farther up her back, it would hurt her arm, but she couldn't bring herself to care.

Upon her head, his every scintillating breath tickled a warmth from her crown to her spine. The resonance still tingling between them, she pushed her hips against him and relished the ecstasy of closer contact. His low groan gave her chills, his fingers shifting and kneading the flesh of her hip with unmistakable want. Somewhere inside him was a chained lover begging to be freed. She longed to engage him fully.

Power oscillated between them, overwhelming her with wave after wave of spiritual pleasure that only fed a different desire. A lusty exhalation escaped. He moved their joined hands to her face, slipped his hand free of hers, and lifted her chin. Just as his warm breath heated her mouth, so incredibly close to his, their resonance broke.

His hand parting from hers had broken their connection.

Like a hot coal, he released her, instantly breaking all contact. He held his arms clear of her and out to his sides, then took several decisive steps back. Wide eyed, he stared into the empty space between them. The color drained from his face.

She hunched over, unable to control her trembling body, trying to recover from the strongest desire she'd ever felt. Not even when she'd used *sen'a*, the pleasure-enhancing drug derived from the poppy, with Feliciano, had resonance felt so good. Her anima had nearly brightened to full radiance—a small measure permanently greater after the resonance—but it should have taken much longer.

It was the Magical Imperative—it had to be. The unseen force that brought mages together was taunting her with what she could never have.

Jon wanted to return to the Order.

Yet that reminder was but a ripple to the raging waves of his resonance.

Torture. The rest of the mission would be torture.

12

*J*on breathed raggedly, his mind racing with forbidden thoughts.
He blinked and shook his head, hoping to clear it. Before him,
Rielle doubled over and panted, her arched eyebrows raised and
her beautiful face flushed. The way her chest heaved, slow and deep—Terra
have mercy—was hypnotic, and even as he cursed himself, he struggled not
to look.

All these years, he had managed to repress the corruption of magic.
Always. Now he very keenly knew why. His blood raged through his veins
like pure fire. He forced his eyes to take in the dusty rock around him, the
crumbling walls, the rib-vaulted ceilings. Broken stone lying like shattered
vows. "What... was... that...?"

"The resonance—" she stammered, her voice tremulous.

Her lower lip, how it quivered as she breathed, full and soft and pink
under the glow of the candlelight spell. He could think of nothing else.

The floor. *Look at the floor.* He diverted his gaze, dropping it in a slow
path down her chest, her waist, her generous curves—how warm and
yielding they'd been. His fingers curled, and his hands tensed. Placing them
firmly on his hips, he gave them a distraction.

"Is it always so... intense?" He'd never felt anything like this in his life.
Ever.

She stiffened, still gasping for breath. "Intense, yes, but not like that."

She paused. Her gorgeous lips parted in what looked like epiphany.
"Sometimes two mages draw each other much more strongly than others.

Such pairs are called complements. I know of some complementary mages, but I've never found a complement myself." She shook her head. "Resonance is fuller, stronger. It can be... euphoric."

Euphoric. His blood sang at the mere memory. "Complement... Does it mean anything?"

She blanched. "It doesn't have to, no. Sometimes they become working pairs, and sometimes they end up..."

He held his breath. *They end up what?* She didn't finish her sentence, but the heat in his body, the hardness, and fire was answer enough. He wanted to drop and do push-ups until he regained control, but it would invite questions from her. Questions he didn't want to answer.

In just a few days' time, he was losing his restraint. Perhaps Derric's message discharging him from the Order had affected him more than he'd thought. When he'd received the letter at Villecourt, he'd hardly believed his eyes. Regardless of his current official standing, if he could just make it to Monas Amar with his honor still intact, then maybe the Paladin Grand Cordon could be persuaded to reverse the discharge; someone had lied to Derric, plain and simple, about whatever had gotten him discharged.

Jon steeled himself. He'd been raised in the monastery among celibate priests and paladins, and he'd been a paladin himself for nearly a decade. Paladins needed only their vocation for fulfillment. He was no different.

He donned his gear once more. The more arcanir between him and her, the better.

She unfastened her torn mage coat, swept it open, and examined the cut on her upper thigh through the tear in her trousers.

Shapely booted legs. Thighs and generous hips. An hourglass waist pulled in by a leather vest. A rounded bust beneath a white linen shirt. Flawless, porcelain skin exposed by her décolletage. Beneath that mage coat, she had been even more stunning than he'd remembered from the night at the Tower. He swallowed.

She whispered an incantation, and the cut closed, the flesh whole once more, a white scar merely sheened with remaining blood.

"Come." She bent, retrieved his gauntlets, and held them out to him. "We need to find a way out of here."

He put them on, picked up his helm, and checked that Faithkeeper was secure in its sheath, and for his dagger at his side.

Under the luminance of the candlelight spell, she walked down the corridor. Carved scrollwork adorned the ancient stone walls around them and the pillars bearing the ceiling's burden. Half-sunken beneath dirt and rubble, the shattered face of a statue sneered at him coldly from beneath a sculpted crown, a forgotten king curling his lip at their intrusion into his realm. Rielle's candlelight retreated, and darkness shrouded the broken visage once more.

As he caught up to her, his steps resounded. "Can't you just magic us out of here?"

She stopped, frowning. "There's no anima in this stone. It was made with arcanir. Trace amounts, I'm sure, but enough to make magic useless."

"Hands and a sword make most magic useless."

She grimaced. "You could always just pray for a way out."

Right. He grinned joylessly. "Do you know how to find an exit?"

"Yes," she snapped at him before taking off.

He passed on the guessing game and accompanied her down the corridor in silence. They came upon a crossroads, where she shined the candlelight spell a few feet into each of the four routes and then faced one of them. She held out her hand and slowly began to wave it. Curling and uncurling her fingers, she wove her wrist in a serpentine motion until a white glow engulfed her hand, its soft light cast against the gray. She turned her palm toward herself and beckoned.

The faintest swirl of white floated down the corridor to her.

It looked like an aeromancy spell, based on the illustrations he'd seen in books at the monastery. "Have your black arts solved the mystery?"

She raised an angry eyebrow but didn't reply. Instead, she repeated the action in every direction and then pointed to the western route. "There's some fresh air in this direction... eventually, which means—"

"An exit."

With a curt nod in reply, she shrugged and set off down the western corridor. The path branched, and she led them through an old library with countless shelves of ruined books. Here was a place he could spend hours, to see if it had been worth the fall.

The fall... When he'd plummeted, Rielle hadn't hesitated. She'd reached for him despite the danger to her own life and fallen with him. Why? Surely she'd known there was no way for her to keep a man of his size and weight from falling? Why did she risk herself even trying?

His gaze fixed on her backside, he almost didn't notice the large, dark figure ahead of them. His hand went to Faithkeeper's hilt.

A statue. One of the Immortals, sculptures littered across Emaurria and its neighboring lands. He'd encountered these wonders on his travels: a horned horse near a pond, a gigantic winged serpent carved into the side of a mountain, large and low lizards near caves, and most commonly of all, fey spirits in forests. Some nobles collected them, sending sturdy carts and groups of workers to secure the statues for extravagant stone menageries to impress their guests and rivals.

He paused before the figure, scrutinizing it in the glow of the candle-light spell. Sublime in its ugliness and majesty, the statue stood eight feet tall and had aged well, with no chips nor cracks, only an extensive layer of dust evincing its neglect. The creature's stone fur was meticulously detailed, and its huge torso appeared to heave in furor even in its stillness.

At first glance, he had taken it for a bear, but the ears and muzzle were all wrong. The eyes were perfectly carved, so lifelike, like the gorgons in the tales after seeing their own reflections. Thick, man-like arms tapered down to large, claw-like hands. Massive, powerful legs bore the heavy torso aloft, flanked by a long, lupine tail. It was one of the chilling creatures of legend, the Man-Beasts, Death-Bringers, Sharp-Claws—those man-eating, rage-fueled demons that village elders scared children with: the werewolves.

He thumbed a long, canine tooth, and in the silence, he became aware of Rielle's breathing and looked beyond the statue to find her glaring at him.

"Enjoying the sights?" Narrowed eyes speared him beneath her frown.

"Not nearly as much as the pleasant company," he said flatly.

"It'll only become more 'pleasant' if you don't start moving." She cocked her head toward the door.

As they left the old library, a distant light flickered at the end of the hallway.

He pulled her into a wall recess.

She extinguished the candlelight spell, and they pressed against the wall in the inky darkness. To avoid the sconce at eye level, he ducked his head, hunched over her like a gargoyle, his hand positioned over his dagger's hilt.

Pressed against him, she breathed gentle warmth against his neck. Thankfully, the dust overwhelmed the rose scent of her hair, which only made him long all the more to bury his face in it and inhale.

"The ward was breached underground," she whispered in his ear. "Our trespassers. Heretics."

Mages not of the Divinity.

He didn't know how far the ward's range had extended, but apparently, it had gone deep enough into the earth for the heretics here to breach it.

Tucked away, he and Rielle were deathly still, the occasional soft breath the only sign of life. Her shoulder moved faintly against him, her intoxi-cating scent just under his nose.

Their path lay through that hallway, but there was no telling what type or number of attackers they might face.

The distant light neared, its glow on the stone floor visible through the sliver of an angle available to him through the doorway.

She huddled closer, the silkiness of her hair brushing under his chin.

A pair of voices conversed casually as they neared. He held his breath.

The voices rose in volume, their plain chatter mere feet away.

"...plans to take down the Divinity but needs us to join as spies. A worthwhile meeting," a man said—by his voice's rough edge, middle-aged and a pipe smoker.

"As long as that hydromancer is dealt with before he reaches his destination," a woman replied gruffly. "If the siege lasts long enough, we won't have to do a thing more. It's been a blessing."

A siege? Where? He listened.

"Don't worry. The Grand Divinus will look like a fool."

The head of the Divinity of Magic? How did a siege make her look like a fool?

The voices faded as the speakers moved past, disappearing along with the light.

A siege...

War in Emaurria? After years of peace? If that were true, the paladins would most certainly be involved, protecting the populace, assisting in the defense. No one had mentioned a thing. Not Rielle, not the Proctor, Derric—

Had Derric sent a mage with him for protection because the paladins were otherwise engaged? Truly?

Rielle pulled on his hand. She wanted to move. Movement could betray their presence, but there was a chance the strangers could return. This could be their opportunity to reach the exit. He let her pull him through the doorway. They felt their way along the wall until they reached a corner.

The creak of a door came from the side. Rielle threw a ball of candlelight flame ahead, and her grip on his hand tightened.

She yanked him into a run. Already moving, he caught a glimpse of a figure silhouetted in the light streaming from the open door.

Shadows clung to the hall, illuminated by the faint candlelight spell, the glow from the open door, and a solitary torch. He and Rielle ran past the doorway, voices shouting in their wake.

Faster, Jon moved ahead and dragged her behind him, their footfalls echoing in rapid succession. He looked back.

A translucent blur of energy sped toward Rielle's back.

Turning on his heel, he threw his free arm around her and threw them to the ground. He landed on his back and choked out a breath.

She rolled out of his grasp, away from his arcanir, and onto her side, twirling her fingers before her.

He jerked out of the way and rose.

A whirlwind blew past and, with a wave of her hand, twinned with fire toward their attacker. Flame spun in ravenous embrace with a cyclone, razing all in its path to glowing embers and scattered dust.

A flash of violet. A red-haired woman in dark leathers charged out of the fire.

He drew Faithkeeper up and to the outside to block the strike of a conjured hand axe. The spelled weapon dissipated upon contact.

The woman's eyes brightened as she disengaged. "Paladin!" she called over her shoulder.

"Kill him!" a man ordered amid cracks, thuds, and crackling.

The char of burning fouled the air. Jon risked a glance at Rielle. She faced off against the man, an enforcer who threw large pieces of stone—bits of Immortals. She blocked.

Jon's attacker wielded a stone arm, her face contorted. She charged, swinging the full weight of the makeshift weapon.

He dodged and transitioned into a killing thrust aimed directly beneath her sternum. His blade plunged deep, through, and blood wreathed the arcanir.

Her eyebrows drew together in one last struggle before the stone fell from her grasp.

He pulled Faithkeeper free, unleashing a red spray.

A great flash blinded him. A massive ball of swirling flame saturated the hallway, barreling from Rielle's hands. An anguished scream choked —ended.

She rushed to him and grabbed his hand, cracks and rumbling sounding above them.

His pulse pounding in his ears, Jon dashed ahead of her, his grip on her hand unrelenting. Earthiness teased his nose—clean air, a forest—

The entire passage came crumbling down behind them.

13

Covered in dust, Jon panted in the cool forest air, the only other sound Rielle's fast, ragged breathing beneath him. He braced on his hands above her. At least he hadn't crushed her. They'd managed to get out alive. Barely.

He scanned the dark surrounding forest. No unusual sights or sounds. They were safe for the moment.

With a relieved sigh, he collapsed beside her, staring up at the waxing gibbous moon brightening the black sky. The sight had never been more welcome.

A green glow radiated next to him from Rielle's hands. Earthsight. Her irises became an arcane verdant green.

"We're safe." She dispelled the earthsight and inspected him under a candlelight spell. "Are you hurt?"

He moved his fingers and toes. "I'm fine." He rose on his elbow and studied her in the faint candlelight; gray all over, she was powdered with dust. "You?"

Her face tight, she nodded, but her pallor belied her answer. A sickly sheen broke through the gray veil over her wan complexion. When she held up her hand, two of her fingers bent at unnatural angles. Her eyes widened.

He shot upright in the grass and seized her wrist. "We'll need to immobilize them, wrap them with the adjacent unbroken fingers—"

A brief, faint smile, and she shook her head, grimacing. "Magic, remember?"

Magic. "Right." He released her wrist, but his gaze stayed on her fingers, on their distorted shape.

Looking at them even a moment longer—

He turned away. He'd held in a paladin's entrails to keep them from spilling out. He'd splinted broken bones. He'd disemboweled enemies. Such was the life of a paladin.

But the sight of her delicate fingers broken—he couldn't stomach it. He shook his head.

Mages were selfish hedonists; he'd heard it time and again among the priests and paladins.

And yet... A mage stranger had healed him once before, a few years ago. And in the ruin, Rielle had seen to him first, just as she did now. Even if her anima were dim, she would have healed him instead of herself.

He'd misjudged her. Perhaps he'd misjudged all mages.

"I've been through worse." She touched her fingers with a wince and whispered a healing incantation. Her teeth ground together as her bones righted themselves. She sat up, resting her elbows on her knees, and heaved breath after distraught breath.

He looked away while her breathing evened out, at the firm tall grass, the swaying larch canopy, the bed of soft wood ferns beneath, iridescent spikemoss in the moon's light.

It was already well past midnight, and they were some distance from camp. He rose, dusted himself off, and held out his hand. "Come."

As he pulled her to her feet, she braced a palm on his armored chest. That touch dispelled the candlelight. She stepped away.

A lesson to remember.

Faithkeeper lay nearby. He retrieved it, then pinched the blade between his thumb and forefinger and drew off the blood before sheathing. It had given him no pleasure to kill again, especially a woman, but she'd left him no choice. He bowed his head and said a prayer to send her soul along to the Lone.

Bathed in the moon's silvery light, Rielle covered her eyes. A soft, green glow flashed from her hands, and she uncovered her eyes. "This time stay behind me," she said, "unless you'd like to take another tumble."

With her spell, she'd see any unsteady earth. He had no desire to fall through the ground again. "Lead the way."

She took his hand, her skin clear of his arcanir knuckle-dusters. He hesitated at the contact but didn't pull away as they began the long walk back to camp. It would be easier to make their way through the dark holding hands. Nothing more.

But as she took him to the bed of ferns, he couldn't stop wondering if she'd ask him for resonance again.

She needed to be at her full power. He couldn't refuse her, temptation or no. He had the strength to resist breaking his vows, strength enough for them both.

Water splashed at his feet—a stream—and from farther away came the roar of a waterfall. They continued through the forest until a fire flickered in the distance. Their camp.

She stopped and checked the horses. "The ward was dispelled when you passed through it in your arcanir, but it seems no one's been here."

He pulled aside the flap to their tent and nodded, dust clouding from his head. He swept a hand back and forth through his hair, sighing at the never-ending puffs of gray.

"We can clean up in the stream." Her torn white mage coat was begrimed, too.

She rummaged through her packs and retrieved clothes and toiletries. He took a few items himself and stashed them in a knapsack. It was barely a quarter full, so he held it out to her and she stowed her things within— filling the bag to capacity.

He raised an eyebrow. "Do all women carry so much gear, or just you?"

She shot him a bitter smile and plodded into the forest. Somehow, her sour expression only made him grin. There was something about her that just made him want to tease her endlessly.

He followed her into the trees. Bathed in moonlight, the forest took on a surreal quality: leaves shining silver and lined with sable; trees a ghostly gray but backed with darkness, filtering the light effusing onto the leafy forest floor. Ahead, mist shimmered above a widening stream, where water fell over a ledge, joined by a brook farther along the rim of the basin. On most other nights, the drop would've been dangerous, but tonight, in the natural radiance, it was just visible.

She led the way down to the forest pool. At the bottom, she took off her mage coat, sat on the bank, and pulled off her boots. He offered her the knapsack, and she removed what seemed like a never-ending succession of items.

He left her to it and unfastened his armor, gazing out at the spray of the waterfall meeting the surface.

Dust wisped into the air. She'd unbound her hair from its braid and was shaking it out—a veritable halo of long, golden curls. He'd had no concept of its thickness until now, when it flared around her like an aura.

When she shed her leather vest and rose to unfasten her trousers, he straightened and turned away.

"You do realize I'm right here?" he grumbled.

"And?" A splash and a gasp indicated she'd entered the pool. "I knew you'd turn away."

"Did you?" Stiff, he tried not to dwell on the thought of what she might look like naked and instead focused on steadying his breathing while he stripped off the last of his armor.

"For all your superficial nastiness, you're actually rather courteous." Another splash of water.

He huffed. He hadn't been able to commit to being entirely rude, even for his own sake. "What, is courtesy so rare among practitioners of the black arts? How surprising."

A loud splash was her answer. Droplets spattered his back. He grinned.

"You can look now, by the way."

He turned around. In the reflection of the moon, she faced away from him, head and shoulders above the gleaming water, curls cascading down her back. For a moment, he was still, committing the sight to memory, and then she submerged and resurfaced, moved deeper in until the water reached her shoulders.

He shed his clothes, grabbed his soap, and waded in, dismissing his shudder against the cold. When he'd reached waist level, she turned to him, water lapping at her collarbone.

"Refreshing, isn't it?"

He crossed his arms. "How did you know I was in deep enough?"

With an impish smile, she shrugged. "Courtesy is rare among practitioners of the black arts, I've heard."

He smirked and moved farther away, then immersed his head in the water, the cold both shocking and revitalizing. Soap in hand, he popped back up and washed, the dust rippling away from him on the surface. "You think we'll see more of those heretics around here?"

"It doesn't matter," she said. "Out here, I'm in my element. Let them come."

What confidence. He raised his eyebrows. "I didn't catch all of what they said, but they mentioned something about spies, a meeting, a hydromancer..." He frowned. "A siege... and making a fool of the Grand Divinus?"

The splashing stopped. She paused. "I would've loved more answers, but I have my mission."

Right. Taking him for a walk to the monastery. He scrubbed the back of his neck.

"I'll need to send a dove to the Proctor when we reach Bournand. He'll want to send mages to investigate."

Of that he was certain. Had the same been said of the Order and the Paladin Grand Cordon, he would've sought to do as she did. It had to be uncomfortable that he'd been privy to Divinity matters, but it couldn't be helped.

A shrill squeal cut the air.

Adrenaline spiking, he whirled. She thrashed in shoulder-deep water, arms flailing.

"What is it?" He rushed to her.

"My foot!" Her face contorted. She reached into the water, drawing in breath after sharp breath.

With a gulp of air, he submerged into the dark water. His sight useless, he reached out for her leg. He found her thigh and then descended to her foot. Feeling to her toes, he encountered something smooth and hard.

A shell.

He could've laughed. A turtle had clasped on to her foot, nothing more. If he tried to pull it away, it would only latch on tighter, possibly causing injury. When he surfaced, she panicked.

He grabbed her shoulders. "Be still."

She gasped for breath but at last met his eyes.

"A turtle latched on to you—"

"I must've stepped on it." She breathed fast and deep, muttering in distressed tones to herself.

"He's just scared. If you stop thrashing about, he'll relax and let go." He rubbed her upper arms. "Be still."

Wearing a determined frown, she nodded but clenched her teeth. He watched the tension in her face, trying to soothe her as best as he could, until she finally gasped.

The turtle must've released her.

She ducked into the water and grabbed her foot.

"That snappy little bastard." She snarled and murmured a healing spell. "He bit right into me."

"You'll live." He could hardly contain his amusement. He'd seen the same fuss from children at the monastery, who ran up to priests and paladins with scratches and bites from the barn cats. " 'I'm in my element,' was it?"

She glared at him. "If you tell anyone about this—"

"About what? About a little animal making a mighty master of the black arts squeal in terror?" His lips twitched with the urge to laugh.

"I did *not* squeal—"

"You squealed." He crossed his arms.

She exhaled loudly. "Well, that turtle was savage—"

"Oh, vicious," he mocked, holding her gaze.

She bit her lip, but a smile fought its way free. A laugh followed. When her gleaming eyes met his, he couldn't help but laugh with her.

She squeezed her rosy soap. "Thank you, by the way. For helping."

Nothing could've stopped him. But he shrugged. "It's that damnable courtesy."

"So very damnable." An impish smile played on her lips.

"Two attacks in one night," he said with a mocking sigh. "You must have a target painted on you somewhere."

She chuckled. He met her eyes, cheerfully bright, but that brightness began to fade into something else. Something intense.

The stillness of the pool lingered, widened, until only the trilling of insects and croaking of frogs composed the sonata of the night.

She parted her lips, stilled as her breathing slowed. In the light of the moon, a wet sheen on her skin, she was stunning. Warmth simmered in him, and he became aware of his own nakedness in the dark water. And hers.

An owl hooted, breaking the silence.

He diverted his gaze and swallowed against the tension. "I should head back."

She was quiet a moment longer. "I think I'll stay just a few minutes more."

"Of course. Take your time." He backed away and waded through the resistant water, striving for some distance, then left the pool. The farther, the better. Water stirred behind him, but he didn't dare look back.

He threw on his clothes and, since they were away from camp, started a small fire, then began the lengthy task of cleaning and oiling his armor while he waited for her.

Had Terra joined their paths to test him? The more time he spent with Rielle, the more difficult it became to resist her. He could look at her for hours, poke her temper for fun, rise to meet her every challenge, but more than that, there was something that drew him in—that made him lie awake at night, flesh hot, heart pounding, grinning like an idiot. An attraction whose existence was becoming dangerous... and alluring.

He worked away the unwelcome thoughts of her, disciplining both mind and body.

When she finally emerged from the water, he stared pointedly at the Order's moon-shaped coat of arms on his cuirass while she dressed. His imagination chomped at the bit, but he nudged it aside.

She came to him wearing fresh clothes and holding a dusty bundle. "I'm about to wash my clothes. I'll wash yours, too, if you like. I was always much better at laundry duty than kitchen duty."

He swore he could hear the smile in her voice, and he wanted to look. Wanted to share in her amusement. To give in to her courtesy.

Better not.

He didn't look at her. "I can take care of it."

"It's no trouble. Besides, this means you're doing the cooking."

The longer she stood there, the harder it would be to avoid thinking about her.

He glanced toward the bundle next to his knapsack. "You have a deal. Thank you."

"You're welcome." She retrieved it and, along with her own, headed for the water.

While he finished with his armor, she did the wash, humming a familiar tune. He couldn't quite place it. Where he'd heard it was on the edge of his mind but remained stubbornly out of reach. It sounded nice enough, yet uneasiness spread through him. "What is that you're singing?"

She went quiet but continued washing their clothes. "I can stop, if it's bothering you."

"Please don't. I've heard it somewhere before and just don't remember the words."

She froze, staring out at the water, her brow furrowed. What about a song could cause such a reaction?

He drew in a breath. "Ah." He rose and hefted his armor. "Is it really such a bawdy tune?"

With a sharp snap of her head in his direction, her blush was scarlet even in the moonlight. She scowled at him.

Perfect. He leaned in. "Let's hear it, then," he challenged.

She turned back toward the water and continued with the wash. Trying to keep quiet, he wondered if she'd tell him the words or not.

"Winter wren, winter wren..." she sang, and the words blurred as the melody flowed into him, parting his thoughts to reach deeper. Spectral silver glimmered in her hair.

Beautiful—

The song. The song was beautiful. Captivated, he watched, listened, and yet something dark stirred in him, made his heart race, his breath catch. Screams. A settlement crowned with fire. Shining gold. Weakness. Blood. Shade... His eyelids heavy, he brushed his neck with haunted fingertips.

She sang on, and warmth rose inside him, yet the feeling of life seeping out of his desperate grasp ghosted through him, a specter that still haunted him some nights.

"I grew up with it," she added quickly. "In the North, it's a common song. I've heard it sung often enough, and the winter wrens nest in the spruce forests around Laurentine and Aestrie..."

She continued, but he could no longer discern her words; unintelligible memory spun his mind.

"Jon?"

He blinked, focusing on her kneeling figure, her shining hair. Reflecting silver, not gold.

"Hm?" He cracked his neck to break the malaise settling into his bones.

"You look like you've seen a ghost."

He knew a mage had saved his life five years ago in Signy—an apprentice healer, he'd been told. All he'd wanted was to thank her in person, but Tor had never told him her name, what she looked like, nothing. Instead, Tor had cautioned that paladins who chased after women often caught them. Yet, ever since that day, every young healer he met left him questioning.

Rielle's an elementalist. Could the healer also be from the North, where the song was common?

"I'm not much of a singer these days." Her shoulders slumped.

"It's not that." He could listen to her sing all day—but that song stirred such memories. "Maybe you'd care to sing another at camp?"

She laughed. "Only if you dance."

An attempt to cheer him up. Amused, he helped her to her feet. "Thinking I'll dance to your tune so easily, witch?"

Walking past him with a smug grin, she headed back. "You already are."

Speechless, he followed after her. Was he dancing to her tune? Was it mere teasing or something more?

I'm losing this battle. If he continued on the back foot for much longer, perhaps it would be time to beat a tactical retreat.

14

*R*ielle lay on her belly in the tent, writing by the light of the oil lamp to conserve anima. The Proctor would expect a full report. After the night they'd had, the last thing she wanted to do was stay awake longer to write a report, but it needed doing.

"Do you have any books in that bag of sorcery?"

She looked over her shoulder at Jon, who nodded toward her recondite satchel. "You read?"

"I do." A wry smile tugged at his mouth. "What a shame it would be for the world's greatest wit to waste away in a tent with an illiterate paladin."

She rolled her eyes. "No need to take offense. Obviously I meant recreationally."

"There *are* books at the monastery."

"What, like religious tomes? Histories?"

He nodded. "Not just that. We're more than just our vocation, you know. Think about it... Vows of sobriety and celibacy. What do you think we do in the evening?"

"Read?"

"Exactly."

"So what kind of books?" she asked, but before he could reply, she buried her hand in the recondite satchel and, with a smirk, thought of the perfect book for him. She retrieved it and handed it to him: the newest *Court Duelist* volume. Few had it so soon, but Gran knew the author and passed each one on early. The series followed a minor nobleman skilled in two things: romancing women and dueling, with the first skill getting him in constant trouble and the second getting him out of it.

She tried to contain her mischievous grin. What would he think of her favorite books?

His face lit up. "The sixth?" He swept a palm over the cover and opened the book. "How do you have the sixth volume so soon?"

She almost wanted to check to make sure her eyebrows hadn't shot through the tent and into the sky. *Court Duelist* was regular reading for him?

Forcing a shrug, she turned back to her report, but her mind wandered. Was he secretly a romantic? If he'd been raised at the monastery and into the Order, he had to be a virgin. Her cheeks heated. How much did forsworn paladin virgins know about romance?

A blot of ink had dripped onto her parchment. *Stay on task.* She had to stay on task. The uneventful journey, camp, the ward, the ward breach, the investigation into the forest, and—

After some more scrawling, she yawned.

"That exciting?" he asked from behind her.

She looked over her shoulder at him; he was already well into the book. "I'm merely ruminating on how to describe your unfortunate plunge into the ruins. Shall I go with *tumble, flop,* or *pratfall?*"

He glanced up from the book. "If you're going for the most effective anti-Order propaganda, the obvious choice is *pratfall,* for maximum comedic effect." He returned to his reading.

"Obvious—of course. How silly of me." She repressed a grin and turned back to the report.

Writing in the Divinity's code had become second nature after years of missions, both with Leigh and on her own, but it was still tedious. A touch of comedy made the task less so, even if it earned her the occasional finger-wagging from the Proctor.

Last mission, someone had stumbled upon the brilliant idea to pack only strawberry preserves for her food, highly unusual and suspect, considering her well-known and life-threatening strawberry allergy. Luckily, she and Rainier had managed to barter on the road for some standard travel fare—and some tobacco besides. With that, an otherwise dull heretic arrest in Caerlain Trel had become much more enjoyable. But she had let her displeasure about the food packing be known with a thorough log of all their meals, ingredient by painstaking ingredient, every detail of food preparation, in the coded mission report. She and Rainier had shared a laugh composing their reports.

The Proctor hadn't found it as funny.

But no strawberry preserves this time. She smiled. A small victory was still a victory.

She turned back to tonight's report. After mentioning the ward breach, the investigation, the revelation that Jon was a mage, and his... pratfall... into the ruins, she proceeded to include their injuries, her response, and their resonance.

In rather vague terms, of course.

The heat, the pleasure, the need were—she took a deep breath—*difficult* to put into words. The facts—dim anima, a mage at hand, resonance, bright anima—were all that needed to be said.

She cleared her throat. The Proctor didn't need to know any more about that.

Her face warmed, and she shifted on the bedroll. Resonance had always been pleasant, and although she'd heard of the better experience with complements, she'd never expected it to be... transcendental.

She bit her lip. The way he'd held her—tight, firm, close—had revealed a hidden boldness that begged encouragement. After that and his intensity in the forest pool, she knew he desired her.

And she desired him.

But he wished to return to being a paladin. It would be cruel to ruin that for lust—lust that she could slake elsewhere. And there certainly couldn't be anything more between them. If the disasters of her life had taught her anything, it was not to develop strong attachments. Or at least try not to.

Love led to madness. Madness led to fureur. Fureur led to death. Just like Laurentine.

It's in the past. Some things were better left buried. At least this report could help save people's lives from whatever the heretics were planning.

She shivered and continued writing the report, recording their search for an exit, the heretics and their conversation, the skirmish, and their escape.

Just what had the heretics been doing in an underground ruin, so close to the Tower?

Close to the Tower. She flittered her fingers. Perhaps preparing to attack there?

No, there hadn't seemed to be many of them. An attack on the Tower would have required many mages. Strong mages. War machines, for the arcanir-enhanced stone walls. The Towers had stood for centuries, perhaps longer—no one rightly knew who'd built them—and it would take a lot more than a few heretics to bring one down.

So close to the Tower... Were they meeting with an informant? A spy?

The heretics had mentioned a hydromancer. The only hydromancer in residence at the Tower was Kieran. Had he been sent on a mission, too? Were the heretics a danger to him?

Her disagreements with him aside, Kieran was still a mage, and no mage should have to suffer their interrogations. And suffer he would. The heretics were known for torturing mages into madness, branding their eyes to blindness, cutting out their tongues, maiming their hands, and leaving them to a twisted, morbid expiation of a life.

And the heretics had mentioned a siege. Where? There'd been no news at the Tower.

Great Divine. She straightened. No news. Leigh had said there'd been no news from the capital for days.

Berny had burst from the Proctor's quarters, teary eyed. *It's the cap—*

The daughter of a Courdevallan baker, scared, but unable to say more. *The capital.*

The black quill blurred before her. *Olivia.* She gasped.

"What is it?" Jon's voice broke into her thoughts.

Courdeval may be under siege. My best friend's life may be in danger. She mustered a thin smile. *It could be nothing. I need more answers.* "Just thinking about something the heretics mentioned, the siege."

"We could go back and find out more."

No, we can't. I have my mission. She lowered her head. "It's all right. I'll make some inquiries in Bournand."

It was probably nothing, but if a city in Emaurria was under siege, there'd be rumors in Bournand. She stowed away her writing supplies before settling into her bedroll.

Jon shut his book and then gestured to the oil lamp. When she nodded, he cupped the back of the chimney top and blew out the flame.

The canvas and wool rustled as he bedded down in the dark. "Do you suppose the Tower will send some mages to deal with the vicious turtle threat?"

Attempting to cheer her up? She grinned and shook her head. "Not unless you tell them about it."

"Your secret is safe with me," he replied, his amused voice an octave lower.

She burrowed deeper into her bedroll, snuggling against the cool night.

"Goodnight, Rielle."

She went still. He'd used her name. Perhaps they were becoming friends. "Goodnight, Jon."

Tomorrow, if they made good time, they would arrive in Bournand. If there was a siege somewhere, she would find out. *Olivia, please be all right.*

15

A torch shone at the end of the corridor, and Olivia shielded her eyes as it drew near. The constant darkness had become almost a comfort. Light now came as an unexpected and unwanted visitor.

There were two, a woman and a man. Dressed in darkest leathers, hooded, and masked, the woman's appearance was a mystery, other than her short stature and hourglass figure.

Ahead of her walked a tower of a man, over six feet of heavy plate bearing the sage tint of arcanir, flanked by a silver-trimmed black cloak of the finest wool. He had a full head of jet-black hair graying at his temples to match his ash-and-cinder stubble; the lines of his face placed him in his fifth decade. At his side he wore a sheathed blade a stunning five feet in length.

It could be none other than the infamous General of the Crag Company, Evrard Gilles. She had never seen him, but his infamy preceded him; Rielle had confirmed the details after one of her missions with Leigh crossed Gilles' path five years ago.

If Gilles is here, it's to kill me.

The blood-curdling screams of the king's guests in the great hall the night of the regicide echoed in her ears anew. She fought the panic rising in her chest and gathered her composure. If death awaited her today, she would go with dignity.

The woman paused before the cell door, her hand on the hilt of a sheathed dagger. "Attempt anything, mage, and I will take great pleasure in peeling the flesh from your face."

A shudder snaked down Olivia's spine, and she nodded.

The woman slipped the torch into a wall sconce, unlocked the cell, and entered, her presence invasive and menacing despite her diminutive height. She didn't move a hair from her ready stance while Gilles followed her in and locked the cell door. Then she moved aside.

Gilles peered down at Olivia and presented a small enameled box. It was not unlike some James had given her, containing expensive trinkets and jewelry, during halcyon days.

"Lady Sabeyon, how do you do?" he asked, in a surprisingly cordial tone.

She stiffened, then bent in the closest iteration of a proper bow she could muster. She tried to speak, but her voice failed her at first; rubbing her parched tongue on the roof of her mouth, she croaked, "The kitchen service could be better."

Gilles glanced at the woman, who wasted no time retrieving her own waterskin and handing it to Olivia.

Poisoned? But if they had decided to kill her, she would die. There was nothing to lose in drinking it. She brought it to her mouth and gulped down the contents.

Water. If it was poisoned, the poisoner was an artist, masterful in his craft.

She emptied the waterskin and shakily offered it to the woman.

"I come bearing a gift from your beloved prince," Gilles said sweetly.

James. How could he possibly get anything to her? "And what can I do for you, General?"

"Indulge me in conversation, my lady."

She risked a small smile. "Perhaps, General, we could converse somewhere more pleasant?"

An amused grin claimed his face, but he shook his head. "That's unfortunately out of the question, but your charm is considerable, Lady Sabeyon, and to your credit."

Many years ago, there had been some whispering about Evrard Gilles desiring to buy his way into the Houses, but when the king had made his disposition clear, Gilles had thrown away all hope and lain siege to Signy. Yet such pantomime of the noble mien spoke of renewed hope.

Gilles handed her the box.

She hesitated, but what choice was there? If violence could be avoided, she would try. She accepted the box, brushed her begrimed fingertips over the smoothness of the enamel. There were flecks of blue in it that reminded her of James' eyes—the breathtaking deep blue of the twilit Bay of Amar, luminous in the light of the fading sun. When he'd first turned them upon her, they'd frozen her in place; she'd lost herself looking into their horizon, contemplating where their brilliance ended. She still hadn't found the answer.

The box was cold in her hands, colder even than the frigid, humid air of the dungeon. Slowly, she opened the box and peered inside.

The deep blue of the twilit Bay of Amar, shrouded by a light-blue haze.

"Soon you may have a complete pair to gaze into," Gilles said, his voice eerily thoughtful. "How much can be cut away from a man before he can no longer call himself such?" he mused. "I have yet to learn the answer with His Highness."

With a quivering reverence, she gently shut the box, tears pushing against her restraint. *James...* She blinked and let them come.

At least he was alive. That was what mattered.

Her daily journey to the Hall of Mirrors came to mind then, and for whose benefit she'd been tortured in the chair. She couldn't bear to face Gilles. "It's him on the other side of the mirror every day, isn't it?"

The box's enameled surface was cool and smooth in her hands.

"The Faralles already had the system in place, did you know?" He sighed. "I learned of it on my last 'visit,' if it could be called such. Imagine, of all the recondite mirrors there linked to faraway, forgotten places, there are two linked within the palace. Sometimes His Highness needs motivation to talk, and while he seemed stubbornly resistant to torture, the sight and sound of torturing you is rather compelling."

That's why they were keeping her alive? A bargaining chip to keep James talking?

"What do you want to know?" she dared ask. Did it have anything to do with that wren James had made her promise to release?

"Don't worry your pretty head over it, my lady," Gilles answered. "He wouldn't have told you."

What wouldn't James have told her? They'd gotten very close; he'd even talked about his wife and children. "Then what do you want with me?"

"Why, to shower you with gifts," he answered, nodding toward the ring on her hand. The Ring of the Archmage, a ring of office, but he couldn't know that. "You're accustomed to it, aren't you, as a prince's mistress?"

Blood rushed to her face. *Mistress.* No one had called her that. Hardly anyone had known. Regardless, James and his wife were separated, estranged.

"I'll have another box for you next time, with gifts from your dearest friend," Gilles said, and his companion straightened next to him.

Dearest friend? She stiffened. Rielle. He meant Rielle.

"The Rose of Laurentine, isn't it?" Gilles continued. "A worthy prize, considering her dowry, but for her many thorns. Everyone knows about her little... *rebellion* against House Marcel. It won't matter." He huffed a laugh. "She won't be coming for you. You're not worth the risk."

Rielle would walk through fire for me. And I for her. She's coming.

"Do you see the unwavering faith in her face, Shadow?" he asked his companion. "You have nothing to fear. Keep your patience."

Shadow? Olivia regarded the woman with newfound respect. One of Gilles' notorious mage captains, the shadowmancer. Her prowess was legend.

"I have, sir, for nine years." Shadow turned her head to Olivia, her face shadowed where it wasn't masked. Her voice was a mix of harsh contrasting consonants, the accent of a Kezani islander. "Our ears report Lothaire took a Divinity mission after we took control here. She makes for Bournand with a charge, a paladin."

They wanted Rielle to come here? Olivia frowned. "What do you want with her?"

"You're worried?" Gilles asked Shadow. "Come, now. Have some faith in friendship, Shadow." He sneered, gesturing toward Olivia.

Shadow's voice rumbled in her throat. "The only faith I have is sheathed at my side, sir." She swallowed audibly, and Olivia leaned forward but couldn't see the woman's face for the shadows of her hood. "When I joined the Crag Company, sir, you promised me—"

Gilles' playfulness disappeared instantly. "Do not speak to me of promises, Shadow."

Shadow nodded and stood to attention.

"I dispatched Flame to handle it."

"But, sir... His madness... He'll kill her charge, but he might kill her, too, before I can—"

Gilles held up a hand. "Very well." He sighed heavily and thumbed a long scar above his jaw. "Make for Bournand, remove what troubles you, and return here."

Remove what troubles... Did Shadow intend to kill Rielle?

Shadow saluted. "Yes, sir."

"No!" Olivia shouted. "You have me. Why do you need Rielle? What do you want?"

Shadow strode to her and backhanded her across the face. "Justice."

Olivia covered the sting with her hand, pain simmering outward from the strike. "Justice? For what?"

Shadow moved to the cell door, and Gilles with her.

"For what?" Olivia shouted after them. "What do you want with her?"

"'Til next time, Lady Sabeyon." Gilles took a bow.

With a click of the lock, they left, taking the torch and its light with them.

Her heart swelled for James, a good man, strong and clever, made to suffer by the Crag like a mouse beneath a cat's paw until they were done with him. She clutched the box. Tears stung her eyes, but she didn't fight them. Would she ever count the stars with him again? Ever fall asleep in his arms again? Ever touch him again?

She dragged a dusty sleeve across her face. *He still lives.* She sobered. Her tears did nothing for him. Attempting to calm her erratic breathing, she turned her mind to other, more constructive thoughts. If she could get free, she could save him.

Why had they come?

She cycled their conversation through her mind. Revealing James' torture, they'd shaken her, perhaps enough to count on her face revealing the odds of Rielle coming to her rescue. Was this Shadow's axe to grind? Hurting Rielle?

Gilles had sent Flame and Shadow after Rielle. They had taken countless lives, those heretics well versed in death.

Flame was accustomed to being protected while he decimated large forces, Shadow to short and lethal skirmishes. If Rielle could survive the initial onslaught, her dueling abilities could tip the balance in her favor.

Against the most infamous mages in Emaurria. Olivia's spirits fell.

Have faith. There had to be a chance. And if Rielle could survive Flame and Shadow, she would come here. She would consult with a spiritualist. *Who'd locate me easily enough.*

And then Rielle would be walking right into Gilles' arms, into a trap of some kind.

A rescue mounted with the element of surprise had some chance of success, but this? Heading into the wolf's den with the wolf lying in wait? The last thing Olivia wanted, after all of this, was another loved one dead.

Stuck in a cell, there was no way to warn Rielle.

Spiritualists could find anyone, anywhere, using an object that person had handled. Their power was regarded as absolute—but for one exception: arcanir containment. If she could get herself into an arcanir cell, no spiritualist would find her. Rielle would think her dead and would have no reason to mount a rescue. And eventually someone would reclaim the capital, and Olivia could hold out until then.

She nodded grimly to herself. But how to get into one of the arcanir cells? She was already shackled in arcanir—

Shackles. Only shackles.

If she could get out of them, she could use magic. And if she could use magic, she could make a run for it. She'd either escape—she didn't hold much hope for that unlikely outcome—or they'd have to move her somewhere more secure... like an arcanir cell.

It was her only chance.

She needed to break her hands.

16

*J*on resisted waking, wrapped in heavy warmth. His thoughts had kept him awake last night, but afterward, he'd never slept so well in his life.

The songs of birds carried on the air, and the sunlight flirted across his eyelids. Resigned to waking, he blinked.

The weight on his chest... It was none other than Rielle, uncovered, sprawled across him and still slumbering in a white linen shirt, untucked from her trousers. Her face on his chest and her arm draped over him, she looked so comfortable and so serene he didn't want to disturb her.

The warmth—it was more than her flesh against his; it permeated him, deep, bearing fire to a hearth inside of him that had long lain cold. Rielle, although asleep, must have sought comfort from him in the night, and perhaps, in this small way, he'd provided it. The notion, for reasons he couldn't name, pleased him. He wanted to hold her closer, keep her warm, keep her safe.

Every day could start like this. The wayward thought infiltrated his mind, unbidden, but as he surveyed the fine golden lashes of her closed eyes, he allowed himself to entertain it. Were he a free man, never sworn to service, would the rising sun find him abed each day with her?

He'd claim her lips. Worship every inch of her body. Pin her beneath him. Make love to her, watch the pleasure upon her face, feel the grace of true union.

He thrilled at the mere thought.

Her thigh shifted across his hips, and his daydreaming turned painful. He peered down to see her leg draped across his lower body, warm and supple.

He gasped, and—Terra help him—she wriggled closer. His eyes rolled back. He wanted to stop fighting this, to simply pursue it, damn all the consequences.

But the idle fancy of mornings spent with her in his arms was just that —fancy. If he allowed anything to happen, he couldn't in good faith ask the Paladin Grand Cordon to reverse his discharge. He'd become an outcast from the Order, losing his adoptive father, his brothers, his friends, his mission in life, his profession, his home, and his life's work.

Without kin, aimless, defeated, homeless, and penniless, he'd not only have no prospects, but he'd be worthless, to himself and most definitely to any woman unfortunate enough to cast her lot in with his. Pursuing Rielle, inviting her into a life so devoid of value, would be irresponsible. Pitiful. Cruel.

Unthinkable. An orphan with nothing to his name couldn't support a wife and a family. As a paladin in the Order of Terra, he could change the world... but he couldn't change his own lot in life.

Terra has made me who I am.

But temptation had never figured so prominently. He'd almost lost himself last night in the pool with her. He'd wanted to, and some part of him still did, a foolish indulgence that would cost him everything.

He tried to think of something, anything, but her.

She leaned into him, a weight both heavy and tight, pressing against his hip—

Terra have mercy. He had to leave the tent.

Pulling away carefully, he replaced his chest beneath her cheek with his bunched-up bedroll. When she didn't even stir, he heaved a quiet sigh of relief.

His blood smoldered in his veins. He pulled off his shirt, strapped on his sword belt, and stepped out of the tent into the cool air. The morning breeze tempered him, and he closed his eyes to pray it would also quench his burning desire.

It didn't.

He said his morning prayers, then put all his bridled energy to good use —exercise, unarmed training, and sword drills until it left him in trails of sweat.

He washed and shaved, but his mind was only half-focused on the tasks at hand. In the past, he'd always managed to keep his distance from women who'd tempted him. Sharing a tent with Rielle, sleeping by her side, spending his days and nights with her—it frustrated temperance, and not only because he desired her. It was the combination of desire and something more that made continued proximity a risk. Pushing her away hadn't worked.

How he'd let that happen—he shook his head.

Although he didn't suspect her of pressing close to him deliberately, the result was the same. And moments like the resonance and the silent beat between them in the pool threatened to overpower his purpose entirely.

If he wanted to be a paladin again, he would have to eliminate the temptation. He didn't need a mage to escort him, protect him, watch him —he'd worked alone for years. If Derric wanted him to go to Monas Amar, he would go, but he didn't need a guardian. And he definitely didn't need fire in his veins every morning and a heart that threatened to burst from his chest.

And he couldn't lose his way of life, his family, his *home*.

He lifted the tent flap with care, but Rielle was gone—perhaps at the stream. She'd never agree to part ways. She'd made that clear enough. And he had to exercise his free will while he could. He grabbed his armor and rushed to the horses.

Thievery was repugnant, but he couldn't leave her any horses. He untethered them and clapped their hindquarters. They disappeared into the trees.

And so did he, arming himself as he went. Bournand was less than a day away. Once he arrived, he could stop at one of the Order's way-stations and continue to Monas Amar—without temptation.

He stayed under the trees' cover and, heading toward the road, listened for any sign of her. Nothing.

He tore through the dense forest, trying to put as much distance between them as possible.

Running steps.

He chanced a look behind him. Rielle chased him on foot, in her untucked linen shirt, trousers, and boots. Unbelievable. If he weren't so determined to break away, he might have stopped to laugh.

"Stop!" she shouted, panting.

He didn't. Even weighed down by his arcanir plate, there was no chance of her catching up to him.

"Turn back," he yelled, continuing on.

"Just stop!" Several winded breaths followed. "Or will I have to make you?"

With an amused snort, he kept moving, staying alert for any signs of magic. He knew her tricks now. He wouldn't hurt her, but he wouldn't fall for her indirect spells, either.

A tree groaned.

As it fell, he dodged.

Two ear-splitting cracks ahead—left and right.

He saw it now: she was creating a bottleneck to cut him off. He darted to the right, farther from the road, and sprinted. The forest floor shook. Birds lofted from the canopy.

Three cracks to the right, ahead, and to the left—

Damn her tactics. He backtracked as the aftershock rippled.

"I could do this all day!" she called out. "How many trees will it take?"

Fists clenched, he tried to navigate around the fallen trunks. If only he could bind her hands—

There was one way out—over the obstacles. But then she could create another pit and trap him again.

That left one other option. Pin her hands to prevent her casting.

When he turned and charged, her eyes went wide. Her hands glowed green with geomancy even as she retreated.

Closing, he reached for her. He tackled her, his arcanir against her skin.

Air puffed from her lungs. She wriggled under him, away from the arcanir. He was about to grab her—

The ground beneath them descended.

With it, they plunged into lengthening darkness from the halo of light at the top, some twenty feet on a smooth descent. When they finally stopped, the musk of deep earth burdened the air.

A slow smile formed on her lips.

Damn it all. Too late, he pinned her.

Again. She'd caught him *again*. Just like that night by the Tower.

He clenched his jaw and scowled down at her, but he got lost in the flecks of gold in her wild, sky-blue eyes and the indigo rim of her irises. "Let me go."

She laughed. "And fail my mission? Keep dreaming. You're stuck with me."

With a snarl, he tightened his grasp on her wrists. The mission? Was it only the damned mission? He wrestled with a yearning that threatened to undo him, and she was only concerned with the mission?

She raised her head and met his gaze squarely.

Vexed, he let her go and pulled away. Did she plan to wait him out, then force another bargain?

He could reason with her, threaten her, wait, or give in. "Can't you just stay in Bournand for a few weeks, and when I arrive in Monas Amar, tell your Proctor the mission is completed?"

It was reasonable enough.

She rose, dusting off her arms and her trousers. "And if you end up dead? I don't want—" She bit her lip. "I can't allow that to happen."

With an angry exhalation, he looked away.

The silence lingered, and she took a deep breath. "Do you hate me that much?"

Quite the opposite.

"If you're going to Monas Amar anyway, why separate? We're stronger together, and it satisfies both your High Priest's wishes and the Proctor's." She approached him carefully, ready tension in her fingers.

When she neared, he could see down her loose shirt. He raised his chin and averted his gaze.

"Tell me."

His back hit the side of the pit. There was nowhere else to go. He couldn't help but seethe.

She closed the distance between them and raised her hands to his helm. When he grabbed her wrist, her arm tensed. While she resisted his grip, he could either let her go or hurt her.

He let her go.

Her hands settled on his helm and removed it. Her bold eyes fixed on his. "You force my hand, Jon."

This was why he needed to leave. Every lingering moment risked his ability to return to the Order.

"Promise me you'll go with me." Her words commanded, but her voice was breathy, soft. She rested a hand on the cuirass covering his chest.

Focus on the goal. He grabbed her waist. The time for reasoning was over. "Take us up. Now."

"Or what?" She covered his hands with hers. "You won't hurt me."

He clenched his teeth. She was right. His fingers squeezed the supple flesh of her waist. His eyelids grew heavy at the pleasing give. The longer this went on—

"In case you haven't noticed, we're both trapped," he bit out, but his gloved fingers betrayed him as they caressed her. "You can't negotiate favorably this time."

"That's where you're wrong, Jon." She moved closer, close enough that he could smell the rose balm she used on her lips, and he closed his arms around her waist. "If you don't agree to work with me, I'll just follow you and guard you from afar. All you'll be doing is setting the pace." She leaned in.

Was she going to kiss him? He breathed raw, deep breaths as she invaded his space.

She turned her face aside. "So if you want to be rid of me," she whispered in his ear, "you'll have to kill me. Right now. Or you can promise to go with me. Your choice."

She could have kissed him. And he wouldn't have done a thing to stop it. He didn't want to stop it.

Desire blazed within him, made his chest pound, roused him to a painful state. Terra help him, he wanted to take her here, on the ground, please her in the dirt and mud until she cried his name. He wanted to be with her, be whatever she needed him to be, give her everything. The want of it all threatened to ruin life as he knew it.

With a coarse exhalation, he grabbed her shoulders and held her away. He wouldn't kill her, now nor any other time. And that meant she was right: his two choices were to go with her or be followed by her.

"Fine. I promise. Now take us up." He raked a hand through his hair.

"Your word."

He closed his eyes and took a deep breath. "You have my word. I promise to go with you."

The ground trembled beneath his feet as it began to rise. She grinned. "Wise choice."

He narrowed his eyes. "But—"

Her grin faded.

"You swear to never do this again." This saucy woman, this audacious mage, had not only stolen under his skin but into his heart. If she had but a sudden whim to cast, he would fall completely under her spell. Until they reached Monas Amar, he would have to be on his guard.

"Trap you?" A glimmer shone in her eyes.

"Twist what I feel into a weapon."

She gasped. "I—"

"Your word." He speared her with a stare. There was no denying she'd used his desire against him. So she would swear this. She would swear it, or there would be no peace between them.

She deflated. "I swear." Her eyes stole to his briefly. "I swear it, Jon. I'm sorry I—"

"Take us up." No, after what she'd done, she didn't get to alleviate her guilt. She didn't get to say the words and hold her head high a breath later. At the Tower, he'd decided to do as Derric had bidden, decided to go with

Rielle, but here, she'd taken his choices away, forced his hand, degraded him.

And if he heard the rest of that sentence, he would explode, mage or no, woman or no, promise or no.

Her eyes brightened feverishly and she rubbed her lips together, but she nodded and stepped back, gesturing a spell. Good. He'd have his space again.

If he held to his vows, he might be a paladin again. And if he didn't...

I will.

By tonight, they would be in Bournand. At least there he wouldn't have to share such close quarters with her. Even if his self-control waned, walls and doors would hold fast.

As long as he didn't allow himself to lose control and break them down.

17

*G*narled oaks lined the Kingsroad as far as Rielle could see. Their branches curved overhead like a lane of curious eavesdroppers awaiting some tidbit of conversation. She sighed. The wait would prove fruitless.

Jon had remained silent. Steadfastly silent. They'd found the horses without a single word from him, then had packed up and taken to the road.

She couldn't fault him. Although she'd never intended to use his feelings against him, it had certainly appeared that way. What would have been worse to claim—that she'd been manipulating him, or that she'd been pathetically attracted?

But he'd said *what I feel*... What he felt... for her.

Divine, it made her smile like a novice with a crush.

It had to be contained. If she opened that part of herself, everything would burst free, the pain, the anguish, the sorrow, the rage of nine years ago. The person she'd been that day. And that could not be allowed. Never be allowed. She winced.

For the rest of the mission, she'd respect his wishes and keep her distance, and in turn, perhaps she'd save herself... and him.

Storm clouds gathered on the horizon, and the hay-like scent of the forest's ferns intensified, mingling with the fresh, earthy smell of inevitable rain.

"We'll need to take shelter soon," she said over her shoulder. Not that he'd reply.

"Move!" Jon called hoarsely, reining his mount aside toward her, bumping her horse away. He dismounted, sent his horse running, and drew his blade.

A wave of fire rushed toward them.

Earth. Instinct took over. She raised a wall of earth before them, her hands aglow in the verdant green of geomancy. It spanned the road and beyond, thirty feet high and as thick as she could muster.

Jets of flame and searing heat shot past the wall's sides and top, trailing windswept dirt and dust. The dead smell of scorched earth stung her nostrils and irritated her eyes as it corrupted the air.

Bright orange flames licked the oaks. Sooty pillars of thick, gray smoke reached toward the sky.

Another elementalist. A heretic.

Rielle dismounted and swatted her mare, sending her galloping toward the trees. She scrambled for cover, and Jon ducked down next to her.

A wave of heat blurred the air. She craned her neck to see a tower of flames soaring up from the wall. It would build in heat and melt through.

Not much time.

Jon stole a glance at the trees, then fixed her with a resolute stare. "You keep him busy. I'll take to the trees and flank him. He won't see me coming."

A flurry of images rushed her mind, all in a split second. Flesh crisping. Faces melting. Screams burned to silence.

"Rielle," he grunted.

She blinked. Firelight glinting off unmoving armor. Glassy eyes fixed on the sky. Fair hair stroked by the chill wind.

"Now is *not* the time to vacillate!" He shook her shoulder. "I'll handle him." He rose and faced the heretic, sword drawn, as if no wall stood between them. Soon, no wall *would* stand between them.

He could die.

All those years ago, she couldn't save her family. She couldn't save Bastien. But she could save Jon.

She held out a green glowing palm toward him and curled her fingers inward. The earth beneath him rose at her command to form a circle.

It would build into a sphere an arm's length thick and large enough to encase him.

He peered down. The sphere formed to chest level. He turned to her, his face devoid of color. "Don't you—"

"I'm here to protect you," she said with a forced calm, wincing as the wall spell weakened. *I want you to live.* He'd be able to break his way out soon enough.

He swore, pressing against the spell-built earth. She'd conjured nothing, simply rearranged the earth into a new form with magic—built. It wouldn't dispel at contact with his arcanir.

"I don't need—"

She met his eyes, steely, burning with reflected spellfire.

He shouted her name, but the sphere closed around him, complete. She undulated her fingers, channeling the winds in white light. With a flick of her wrist, she sent the earthen sphere flying back down the road. He'd be furious, but he'd live.

The wall crumbled.

She rolled away, raising a fire shield at her arm. Her earthen wall disintegrated, its remnants hurtling toward her in a fiery blast. She held fast, the fire shield burning all to dust that swept over and around her.

Where was the heretic? She squinted.

On the road ahead, a man in a black leather coat stood cloaked in flame. Red-bearded, he had a shock of shoulder-length red hair to match.

Once the wall dissipated entirely, he ceased casting. Silence settled over the scorched road and burning autumn grass and trees. The choking smoke hung low.

She faced him resolutely and broke the silence. "Who are you?" she called out across the field of battle.

The man rumbled an amused laugh. "Flame," he said. "Perhaps you've heard of me?"

Flame. A shiver crept up her spine. There was one notorious mage by the name of Flame—but earning his attention took much more than traveling down a road. Since Signy, General Evrard Gilles of the Crag Company had corrected his company's deficit of mages. He'd recruited three of the most formidable and lethal heretics to ever prowl the kingdom. Flame had built his name burning the company's enemies—entire armies, villages, cities—to a cinder.

She stilled her racing breath. Now was not the time to lose her nerve. He meant to unsettle her.

Ego was a weakness. An exploitable weakness.

"Should I have?" she shouted back.

He gnashed his teeth. His face contorted into a grotesque snarl.

When his arm shot out, she was already moving, rolling, dodging. A surge of fire jetted from his joined hands, following her every movement.

She met it with her fire shield, one-handed, imbuing it with anima. A contest of focus.

"What impressive focus!" she shouted, hoping to goad him, and wincing from the exertion of maintaining the shield. "You must defeat novices with it fairly often!"

He snarled. The unending surge of fire intensified, and her shield with it. More anima, but it hid her better. The sky dimmed.

The storm. Behind her back, she wove an aeromancy spell, gathering a lightning storm to target him. The natural storm clouds would offer stealth to her magic, but the spell would take time.

She needed time.

"I can do this all day!" he shouted. "Can you, girl?" He laughed.

Shade descended over her eyes and line of vision as her spell wove seamlessly into the storm clouds, swirling above at her call, filling the air with the scent of damp earth and metal.

He would need to divert power from his fire surge if he was to defend against a lightning storm from above. Duels were won and lost with distraction.

She staggered. Plumes of flame wreathed her shield, ate away at it. No, it wouldn't hold much longer.

The clouds darkened to grim black. It was time. *Kill or be killed.*

Darkness shrouded the road. Heavy rain inundated the area, falling hard, pounding. Bolts of lightning sparked and converged around Flame.

One strike would end him. Adrenaline coursed through her veins.

Trapped in the lightning storm, he shielded with fire from above.

Now. She kept her fire shield with one hand and formed a circle with the other. The ground beneath Flame cracked and broke. He wove his fingers in a fire rune beneath him. The rune snaked a molten pattern and formed into a solid platform.

She abandoned the geomancy spell as he gestured—

A fireball.

His spell would burst on impact and burn from all sides. Her shield wouldn't protect her.

She dispelled it in favor of a flame cloak, clothing her entire body in thick threads of pyromancy. Whether it held depended on whose focus was greater—

He palmed the fireball as it grew in size to eclipse her.

She'd have to time it perfectly.

He raised his arms. She held her right hand above her and, with as much focus as she could muster, spelled three ice spikes shooting high into the sky. She didn't have long before they'd plummet back down.

Immediately, she raised three fingers on the same hand, her right, conjuring stone arrows behind Flame.

He threw the fireball her way. Whirring, it hurtled, a great consuming sun of flame.

She infused her flame cloak with anima as it hit, a raging inferno eagerly pushing against her power. Consuming. A relentless assault.

Her two stone arrows were ready, behind Flame, waiting.

The ice spikes plummeted from the sky.

No time.

With her right hand, she held the stone arrows behind Flame. Her left maintained the protection of the flame cloak. She needed another hand to direct the ice spikes.

She'd have to sacrifice her flame cloak. Dispel the only thing keeping her from the burning death of his fireball.

Trapped in the blaze, she beckoned with her right hand. Flame brought up a fire shield behind him, but she split her fingers, split the arrows—one to hit from behind and one from the side. He put up another shield at his side.

A split-second before they hit—the blaze around her persisted, but the ice spikes would hit the ground.

Flame cloak or ice spikes. She had to choose.

As the ice spikes nearly came down on her, she threw them with her left hand, her flame-cloaking hand, at his front and curled inward the fingers controlling the arrows.

Her flame cloak dispelled. Fire closed in on her.

With burning fingers, sweltering heat scorching her skin, she recast the flame cloak, hoping she wouldn't pass out. Throwing her arms up to cover her face, she fell to her knees.

"Sundered flesh and shattered bone," she croaked, *"by Your Divine Might, let it be sewn."*

Searing flames assaulted her from all sides. But her flame cloak held. The pain of healing strangled all inside her with a barbed grip, wrenched a scream from her throat. Fire roared in her ears.

She faltered onto her hands, remnants of her sleeves crisping away.

The fireball dissipated, and she chanced a hopeful look ahead, her vision blurry.

She ran her free hand over her body, finding her mage coat singed, tattered, but her flesh renewed. Her skin and hair had regrown. Recovered.

White light constricted her vision. Charred branches, doused with the rain, crumbled from the oaks and fell.

Flame lay on the black-scorched road.

Praise the Divine. Catching her breath, she collapsed into the mud.

Had Flame been working alone?

Her heart stopped. She tried to lift herself from the ground and faltered. Dizziness spun the rainy ground, and her weakened arms wouldn't cooperate. *Damn it, damn it, damn it.*

Jon. She scrambled to turn around. Dragged herself. Clawed into the ground until she could stagger on hands and knees.

Please be alive, Jon. Please. I can't—

What if someone had—

Past the blackened earth and charred trees of the dueling ground, the earthen sphere came into view in the pouring rain. An arcanir-clad arm protruded from a gap in the sphere, and the rhythmic thud of a pommel crushing against the dense earth came from within. Grunts of effort and exasperated curses accompanied the noise, her own name given pride of place among words she'd long considered unspeakable by paladins.

She sighed with relief, collapsed. The sky was a sea of white. Brilliant, spreading, blinding.

She dispelled the sphere. The loosened earth fell away, and then everything went white.

JON STRUCK the earthen cage again with the pommel of his dagger. It crumbled.

The pounding in his ears hadn't ceased. She'd stuck him in a cage. A *cage.* He cracked his neck from side to side. When he got his hands on her—

When he hit it again, it crumbled entirely. Seething, he stormed out. *"Rielle!"* he roared, booming. "Terra save you, mage, because I'm going to—"

The gathering storm had blackened, blotting out the sky. Smoke hovered in the distance, death lingering over charred skeletal oaks. Rain poured, pounding the ground into submission.

He lowered his gaze to the road. A dark heap lay there in the mud. In a puddle.

His cold fingers turned icy. He ran, his heart thudding in his chest.

She convulsed. Face down in a puddle, she shook violently. He raced to her, caught himself with a hand in the mud, slipped to the ground, and rolled her over.

Her face caked in mud, she went limp in his arms. He cleared off her nose and mouth, and shook her.

"Rielle," he said. He repeated her name, shook her harder. "Wake up."

No response.

He lowered his ear to her nose. No breath.

No.

He shook her again, clapped her back. She wasn't breathing. Wasn't—

Wake up. Terra have mercy, wake up. He lay her down, applied pressure to her abdomen. *Breathe.*

Nothing.

He raised her chin and respired into her mouth. Once. Twice. Again. Again. Again.

Come on. He fought the racing of his heart, on the verge of explosion.

Again. Nothing. Again.

She coughed, spluttered muddy water, and he rolled her to the side. He bowed his head, drawing a relieved breath through his nose. She was alive. Eyes closed, he let his head fall back. Another minute, and she would've—

He shook his head and peered at her. Coughing but breathing. Soot soaked her hair, like the rest of her, and all her clothes were blackened, crisped, singed, and now drenched in rain. Her sleeves were no more than tatters; her boots no more than scraps of leather barely held together. He opened his mouth, but no words emerged.

She'd nearly gotten herself killed, and him. What had she been thinking, caging him, sending him away? Dispatching a pyromancer would have been a trifle to him. He could have walked up to the heretic and run him through easily. Pyromancers posed no danger to paladins. None at all.

Instead, she'd caged him, taken on a dangerous enemy herself, and left him unable to defend himself or her. By the looks of it, she'd nearly burned to death and, by her own hand, left him trapped to await doom or destiny.

He drove a fist into the mud and clenched his teeth, grinding them until they creaked, radiating pain through his jaw.

She could have *died*.

He stared down at her, undecided whether he wanted to embrace her for surviving or shake her until some sense settled in.

Kneeling, he remained still until his breathing slowed and his muscles relaxed. He wouldn't touch her—not like this—not until he knew his own strength again. Calm seeped in as he watched her breathing steady, and he took in the frailty of her singed, curled form.

What had she been thinking? The finality on her face as she'd sealed him in the cage crept into his mind. The gravitas. Sacrifice. Trying to protect him?

She expected to do everything herself. Investigate the ward breach herself. Fight the pyromancer herself. Protect him herself.

He'd seen it before, people who acted alone, who preferred to fight alone. Survivors. People who'd lost someone and now thought themselves alone.

Mistakenly. People like her believed that if they just took on danger alone, no one else would die. People like her ignored their own weaknesses and others' strengths. People like her got others killed. And died.

Lying here like this, she appeared helpless, normal. No hint of her massive presence, her power. Her ferocity. All the things that drew him in and infuriated him. All the things that could make her stronger if she'd embrace them, if she'd open her eyes and cast away her willful blindness.

Rain soothed its way down his face and into his armor. She, too, lay soaked. He looked around—nothing and no one. He scooped her up and headed for the woods to find their horses. He needed to get her warm, comfortable. Somewhere safe, covered, when she awoke.

It was the least he could do; because when she finally came to, he'd give her hell. He'd give her hell, and she would never do this again.

*R*ielle shifted, soft fur smooth against her bare legs. Her blanket. She rubbed her cheek against the pillow, pressing her face into its pleasing give. The rousing scent of black tea and bergamot beckoned. Morning already? Too soon...

When had she gone to sleep? She frowned, trying to recall the previous day... On the road, traveling with Jon, and then—

Flame.

She stiffened.

Jon. She snapped her eyes open.

Soft lamplight illuminated the tent and Jon's stern face as he sat, watching her, his eyes half-lidded, his jaw set. He was here. Free. Unharmed. His dark hair was wet but clean, and he wore a fresh white linen shirt and fitted trousers tucked into his leather boots. He set down a steaming cup next to another.

He did not look happy.

She blinked under his scrutiny and struggled to sit up, her palms sticking to the bedroll's canvas. Sticking? The sheen of a poultice covered her angry red skin. She raised it to her nose. Yarrow and grease... goose fat. Her gaze meandered to her sleeve.

No, *the* sleeve. An oversized white shirt she practically swam in. Crisp white linen. One of Jon's. She glanced at him, but his quietly severe stare didn't waver. Although she pulled aside the covers, she didn't need to see her legs to know the shirt hit just above the knees and that her legs—and all beneath—was bare. Her cheeks heated.

She shot him an inquisitive look. He'd undressed her? Washed her?

His flinty eyes narrowed. Challenged.

That stare persisted, speared her. She looked away.

He was angry. Angrier than she'd ever seen him.

"Who was he?" His voice was cold, low. Unlike him.

"Flame," she replied, clearing her throat, "mage captain of the Crag Company."

He shifted, staring into space, an unfathomable world behind his eyes.

"Gilles." He froze and turned that storming world upon her, suffocating and blinding in its intensity. "General Evrard Gilles. Did the mage mention him?"

She managed to shake her head. Five years ago, in Signy, it had been none other than Evrard Gilles who had almost killed Jon. She kept her eyes from his neck.

"At the Tower, you asked how I got this." Jon raised his chin, and she allowed herself to look, the gruesome memory of that healing fresh in her mind. Blood. Wide eyes. Gurgling. A weakening grasp—"Courtesy of Evrard Gilles."

His unwavering glare pinned her.

"Do you think he's still after you?"

He looked away. "No," he replied. "While I have relived that duel in my mind almost every day since, to him I was—am—no one." He shook his head. "But to me, he's the man who killed my best friend."

Sir Bastien. In Signy, he'd kept her alive and helped save countless lives at mortal cost to himself. That's what happened when she didn't handle threats alone, when others helped. They died. Because she'd been too weak to handle the danger on her own, Jon's friend had died.

A shiver shook her spine, but she fought it. Controlled it. The wind thrashed the tent flap, a dreary late afternoon—not morning—haunting outside.

"I'm sorry for your loss." She reached for his hand, but when he clenched it into a fist, she stopped without touching him.

"It was five years ago, but I see it as vivid as yesterday," he said, his tone turning icy, "and I can't wake from that yesterday until I arrest Gilles, bring him to justice. For Bastien." He rose and reached for his armor. With his back to her, he re-armed.

"Where are you going?"

He didn't turn around but nodded at a spade in the corner. "The body."

She'd left Flame's body in the middle of the road.

Silence pervaded as Jon finished securing his weapons belt.

She couldn't leave things like this with him. Distant. Icy. Detached.

"You're angry with me." Her shoulders slumped.

His fingers flexed in their gloves, knuckle dusters catching the lamplight. He cracked his neck from side to side and took a deep, slow breath before glaring down at her over his shoulder. A muscle twitched in his clenched jaw. "That is the *last* time you will ever cage me."

The cold edge to his voice chilled her bones. She shuddered, curling her legs closer to her body. By order of the Divinity, he was in her charge. His survival was her responsibility. Her duty. "I did it to keep you safe."

He whirled to face her, fisting his hands. "I learned to walk with a practice sword in my hand. I've battled mages for half my life," he snarled. "I don't need *you* to keep me safe."

"I—"

"No." He shook his head. "Never again."

Never again...? She hadn't planned on the first time. Never in her wildest nightmares had she expected to duel one of the heretic captains of the Crag Company.

Flame had been alone... But what if he hadn't been? What if Shadow or Phantom—or both—had been there? She'd left Jon in the earthen sphere, knowing he'd soon free himself, but what if he hadn't in time? She looked away and plucked at her blanket.

Her impulsive decision to cage Jon could have gotten him killed. He would have died. *And it would have been my fault.*

And if Shadow and Phantom were coming—

He was right.

Her hands shook, and she folded them together. "Are you asking me to—"

He bared his teeth. "I'm not *asking.*"

She jerked her head back. *Oh?* She'd made a mistake, yes—a big mistake —but he now intended to dictate terms to *her?* In her years of service, she hadn't let a charge walk all over her, and she wasn't about to start now.

He'd wanted to fight Flame himself; is that what he had expected? To imperil himself when her duty was to keep him safe even at cost to herself? He wasn't the only person who'd sworn vows.

She wouldn't confine him again, but he had to accept that when there was a threat, it was hers to take on as his guardian and escort.

She rose. "I know I made a mistake—"

His eyes bulged. "A *mistake?*" He shook his head. "Don't try to minimize this." He swept a hand out angrily. "What you did was risk my life and your own. Foolishly."

"I wanted to save you!" she shouted back at him.

"Fantastic work," he shot back, wearing a tight smile that didn't reach his eyes. "Boxing your charge and wrapping a bow around him for your enemy—is that what the Divinity calls 'saving'?"

"You're alive, aren't you?"

A half-laugh escaped him. "By sheer dumb luck."

Dumb luck? Did he have any idea how long it had taken her to master those spells? How many lives she'd saved by what he reduced to "dumb luck"? She pressed her lips together bitterly, staring at the ground with all the ferocity she wanted to turn on him.

When Flame had attacked, she hadn't stopped to consider every option, every consequence. Only to make sure Jon would be safe and to keep Flame away from him.

But... Jon was right. She had endangered him. While he'd have been able to break the earthen sphere, if Flame had defeated her quickly, Jon would have been at his mercy.

But for her "luck," Jon might have been dead.

She scrubbed a hand over her face, wincing when the poultice stuck to her cheek. "I'm sorry."

He regarded her from a distance, warily, rubbing his sword's pommel.

"I only wanted to protect you... any way that I could," she said, her shoulders dropping. Her gaze fell to her toes pressing into the bedroll. "I didn't mean to put you at risk." She rubbed her lips together. "I won't do it again."

When she looked up, a line etched between his eyebrows.

Popping his jaw, he anchored his hands on his hips and looked away. "It's not just that you put *me* at risk," he said, his voice losing its edge. His eyes fluttered shut, and he frowned, taking a deep breath. "You could have died. Do you understand that?"

She took a deep breath, but before she could speak, he reached up and brushed aside a stray lock of her hair, then stroked her jaw, soulful intensity gleaming in his eyes.

His touch... She wanted to close her eyes and sigh, but she dared not move, dared not speak, dared not breathe until she heard his next words.

"You matter, Rielle." He thumbed her cheek. "And a guardian who doesn't value her own life is dangerous. She doesn't acknowledge her own weaknesses, or her charge's strengths. She makes poor decisions that could cost someone... far more than he is willing to pay."

She shook her head. "I'm not trying to throw anyone's life away. Yours, nor mine."

"And yet, you nearly did. On a whim." He squeezed her shoulders. "Did you stop to think what I could contribute?"

She blinked. No. Why would she have? Charges were a responsibility, not an asset. Countless typical missions had unfolded with her or her mage partner removing charges from danger, but she'd never worked without a mage partner. If she'd had one, he might have pulled back to guard Jon while she handled the threat herself.

"I'm a paladin, Rielle. A pyromancer, to me, is nothing. At least when I'm not stuck in a cage."

She frowned. A pyromancer... A paladin... Her mind flickered to the night at the Tower. The six mages afield, defeated.

Arcanir. Sigil tattoos. Shuttering her eyes, she heaved a sigh. This wasn't a typical mission. He wasn't a typical charge.

"I could have walked up to him, shrugging off all his spells, and defeated him. And I say 'defeated' because I wouldn't have killed him unless he refused to surrender. I would have arrested and questioned him."

Questioned... Why had Flame come after them? What did the Crag Company want? She eyed Jon, his thoughtful expression. Had she let him fight alongside her, they might have had answers.

But she hadn't thought about what he could do. Only what *she* could. "I just... prefer to handle threats by myself. It's safer for everyone that way."

He shook his head. "Is it? You don't think 'I'll handle this' are famous last words? People aren't solitary by nature; we were meant to be together." He straightened and cleared his throat. "To help each other." He exhaled a sharp breath. "You're accustomed to fighting alone. I understand," he said. "But I'm here. Trained, capable, and I've fought mages for half my life. Use me. Relying on your skills alone is willfully crippling yourself... and us."

She sucked in a breath. By trying to do it all herself, she'd exposed them both to greater risk. If she withheld her trust in Jon, she relied on her skills alone, and if she failed to protect him, he could be killed due to no decision of his own, but hers.

But if she trusted in him, she relied on both his skills and hers, and if one of them failed, the other might not; and if they died, they died by their own choices, fighting like hell.

He deserved a say in his own fate, the opportunity to defend himself should she fail, and her trust.

She nodded. "I understand."

"Good." He released her shoulders. "I'll handle the body."

With Flame dead, Shadow and Phantom wouldn't be far behind. She looked around the tent, wringing the hem of the shirt in her hand. "Are there any trousers? I'll come with you."

He shook his head, glanced at her legs, then averted his gaze. "I... couldn't find anything of yours, and the shirt was challenge enough with my eyes closed."

She grinned.

"You've been through a lot. Just stay here, find trousers"—he smiled— "and rest." He nodded toward the bedroll. "You don't have to do everything yourself. Let me take care of you for a change." He grabbed the spade.

She froze, but as he lifted the tent flap, he regarded her, a glimmer in his Shining Sea eyes. His lips twitched, but he made no further comment and left.

Staring after him, she waited for her pulse to slow. When it didn't, she collapsed into a heap on the bedroll.

She closed her eyes and exhaled slowly, picturing him trying to wash her and dress her without looking, and she covered an embarrassed smile with a poulticed hand. After her spectacular mistake, a lesser man would have left her stewing in mud and spell-scorched rags. Laughed under his breath. Enjoyed her pathetic state. Punished her foolishness with humiliation.

But Jon hadn't. He didn't wish her browbeaten, but taught. Wiser. Stronger.

She slipped a hand into the shirt—his shirt—and pressed a palm against her chest, feeling the thump of her beating heart. He was a rare man, Jonathan Ver. Rare, and all too captivating.

The poultice stuck against her skin. Healing. She needed a touch more. But air dense as oil surrounded her dim anima, the rising pressure of Spirit-seve, hungry outside forces pushing for a way in. It would not abate until Hallowday. The pressure pushed all the more against the dim; darkness didn't keep those forces away so well as the light.

She hadn't brightened her anima since the ruins. Fighting the heretics, healing, dueling Flame, healing again... It had strained.

Her options were few. Anima brightened slowly, over time; in a few days, it would glow again at least, but they'd likely reach Bournand tomorrow. There, she could find another—some other—mage at the Temple of the Divine.

Yet, if Shadow and Phantom hunted them, even a day was a danger-ously long time to wait.

Resonance.

Could she burden Jon with it again? She'd promised not to use his feel-ings against him, feelings he kept so well restrained. Resonance removed those restraints.

She chewed her lip. A distraction. She needed a distraction.

Barefoot, she crept to the tent flap and pulled it aside. A fire burned in a pit, and their tethered horses ate happily from their feedbags. Earthy petri-chor lingered in the air after the storm, soothing and electrifying all at once. She picked her way through the camp to their packs and retrieved some supplies from her recondite satchel. She'd have to teach Jon how to use it, for the next time—

The next time he undressed her, washed her, and clad her in fresh clothes? She pursed her lips. There would be no next time, would there? She'd never make the same mistake again, and he... he would never want to touch her again.

The rain had ceased, but gray clouds ominously hovered above. She spelled the campfire against the rain, blanketed the horses and stowed their empty feed bags, then tiptoed back to the tent to change. Undergarments, trousers, socks, fresh boots, and...

Her shirt waited, primly folded. She raised the cuff of Jon's shirt to her nose and inhaled. Fresh air, sunshine, and him. Like an idyllic summer day she could lounge in for the rest of her life.

Or at least a few hours more.

She left his shirt on and donned a fresh mage coat with trembling fingers. Anima withdrawal had already set in. She took a fortifying breath and stared at the steady flame in the fire pit.

Foliage crunched nearby. Out of the bracken, Jon returned, bearing the spade, a knapsack, and a belt pouch.

She inclined her head toward the bags. "Are those—?"

"Flame's." He dropped the knapsack and belt pouch near the fire pit and headed for their packs. He stowed the spade.

"I'm going to lay down the ward," she said, "and then we could go through his things together?"

He nodded and began unfastening his armor. "I'll see to supper." They were running low on provisions, but whatever was left would be sufficient for tonight. He looked her over, firelight glimmering in his eyes. "I see you found trousers."

She anchored a hand on her hip. "You know how to use a recondite satchel, right? You just think of what you need, and if it's inside, you'll get it."

He raised his eyebrows as he set aside his armor, then opened his mouth and closed it.

"Well?"

"I didn't want to risk accidentally thinking of shoes and triggering an avalanche."

"That's not how it—" When she caught his grin, she sighed.

Striding past her, he clapped her arm. "Thanks for the lesson, witch."

Shaking her head, she headed to the edge of the camp and circled it to lay the ward, the weave thick and large for trespass. Her hands flickered near the end, glowing so dimly she could barely discern the deep blue of her anima around them despite the dark.

Resonance. She'd have to ask Jon for resonance. He was finally in a good mood, and she'd have to ruin it.

Not yet. Throwing herself into practiced routine, her wretched heartbeat slowed, even if her face remained hot. The ward laid, she headed for the river to wash up, splash her face, and cool off before helping with supper. The water was clear all the way to the bottom.

She risked a glance Jon's way. He rolled up the sleeves of his shirt, approached the river bank, and started pulling off his boots and his socks.

"The river's shallow here, and there's just enough light to catch fish." He rolled up the legs of his trousers.

Indeed, the waxing gibbous moon was bright enough to illuminate the night, if not as well as a full moon.

She was about to ask him how he planned to fish without a rod when he stepped in without a sound, hardly disturbing the water, and moved toward the river's outside bend.

Spellbound, she observed, scrubbing her arms as he slowly dipped his hands into the water downstream from the fish and stood still, an exercise in control. Hours passed, or seconds... she couldn't discern. Barefoot and fishing with his hands, to her eyes, he was undeniably down to earth and masculine, in ways no mage at the Tower had ever been, and the sight was one she'd not soon tire of.

In his grip, a fish thrashed.

He tossed it past her onto the bank. His eyes met hers, and for a moment, he looked at her with the soft, silvery moonlight and the shadows of the forest canopy playing across his tattooed skin. As his gaze traced her entire form, the sound of the river's running water hummed between them. An owl called in the distance.

The cool night wind swept a chill caress around her shoulders. Watching him, she could almost feel his hands replace the wind's coolness on her body with his warmth, and the memory of his embrace in the ruins made it a challenge to breathe.

He took a deep, audible breath and looked away.

Swallowing a lump in her throat, she nodded abruptly in his direction and returned to the fire pit.

She busied herself with writing notes for her report until a frisson fluttered across her ribs—a ward breach. Jon. He returned with several dressed fish that he set to roast. River trout and graylings.

"I'm impressed."

He smiled and sat next to her. "It's a strange life that finds fishing impressive and casting spells commonplace."

She exhaled a half laugh. "Strange to you, maybe." If he was back to joking with her, then perhaps he wasn't angry anymore.

He nodded toward the knapsack and the belt pouch. "Shall we?"

Let's see what a mage captain of the Crag Company wanted with us. She grabbed the bags and upended the contents on the ground before her. Littered among various mundane things were some coded notes and a key bearing a hummingbird symbol with a *3* on the back. Jon picked out the key.

"I know that mark," she said. "It's a Bournand inn, nestled in the Weave. Cosette's. A by-the-hour place."

When he cocked an inquisitive brow, she shrugged. No, he didn't need to know how she knew.

"A favorite haunt of yours?"

She glared daggers at him. Had her reluctance to broach the subject been in any way unclear?

A sly corner of his mouth turned up. "Why the scowl, witch? I imagine you only enjoy the place for the fine... diversion." He'd chosen the word carefully and seemed pleased with his choice.

"Don't spend too much time imagining my enjoyment of fine *diversion*. You could go blind."

His eyes widened, but he quickly recovered. "We don't know how long he had been staying there"—Jon handed her the key—"so we'd best aim to go there soon after we arrive in Bournand."

"To investigate?"

"What else did you have in mind?" He grinned broadly, that dimple teasing.

She opened her mouth and closed it. *Bastard.*

"We need to get there as soon as possible," he said evenly, by all signs letting her off the hook.

We? Did he mean to invite himself on a Divinity of Magic investigation? "*We* aren't going there. This is an escort mission, remember? It's one thing fighting off threats together, but entirely another to willfully invite you to court new threats with me. I'm supposed to keep you safe."

"You can't guard me if you leave me behind." He thrust his chest out. When she shot him a chagrined look, his mouth twitched.

The *clever* bastard. "You don't even know he meant to attack *you*. He could very well have wanted to attack me."

Jon raised an eyebrow, his eyes lit with a mischievous twinkle. "And why would anyone ever want to do that?"

She folded her arms across her chest. No one but Leigh had ever teased her so mercilessly. Certainly never a charge. She wanted to tackle him for his insolence but was almost certain he'd have her on her back before she could touch him.

Her pulse quickened at the thought. *Stop it.*

He took two skewered fish off the fire and handed her one.

"Fine," she said, "we'll search Cosette's together."

With a smug grin, he dug into supper, and so did she, some moistened double-baked bread and nuts added to their meal. Jon studied her fingers, and when he raised his eyebrows, she followed his line of sight.

Damn. Her hands had started trembling again. *Not now. Not yet.*

She clasped them.

"What's wrong?" he asked.

She began to pull away, but he lunged and grabbed her wrist. He held out her hand and watched it quiver.

"Let go." She tried to yank her arm away.

His stare was unrelenting, his body rigid. "What are you using? Sen'a? Trux?"

Baffled by the accusation, she turned away. She'd been without for three years. But he didn't release her arm.

"Tell me."

Relentless paladin to the end.

"Anima withdrawal," she blurted.

He let her wrist go and frowned. "When were you going to tell me?"

"Tonight." She looked away. Resonance would shatter this peace between them. "My anima is dim, but as long as nothing major happens before we reach Bournand, I can find someone for resonance there."

" 'Someone'?" His face hardened.

Would he offer? She'd rather have resonance with him than a stranger, but she couldn't ask, not after giving her word.

If it was to happen, he would have to offer.

She paused. Waited. Her face heated, and her hands trembled so badly her arms quivered.

Nothing. She shook her head. It had been stupid to expect anything else. She knew what he wanted—or, more precisely, what he *didn't* want—and they'd agreed.

The silence lengthened, and he wouldn't meet her gaze.

Rejection.

"It's been a long day. Thanks for supper." Before he could answer, she rose, stalked toward the tent, and ducked inside. With a harsh breath, she plopped down onto her bedroll. What had all that talk of valuing her life meant when he refused to help her replenish her means of defense? Empty words.

But she would keep hers. Resonance stoked his desire, and she had promised not to use what he felt against him.

So be it. I'll spend the rest of tonight meditating and pray it's enough.

A rustle—he entered the tent and sat before her.

"I'll do it." Calmly, he shook his head. "We had no warning of Flame's attack. You may have enough power to fight again, but if one of us is injured, you may need more. I won't risk your life for the sake of my own... preference."

She crossed her arms. "I don't think you understand how an escort mission works. *You* are not responsible for *me.*"

"It's because of my pratfall into the ruins that you had to use healing magic at all, remember? Both inside and when you belly-flopped out and broke your fingers."

Just when she thought he'd managed to say it all with a straight face, the corners of his mouth turned up.

"Are you certain?" It couldn't be an easy choice. "I know that you—"

He rested his hand on hers. "Let me worry about that. Are you ready?"

She had barely nodded when the darkness enveloped her anima, and she descended inwardly through it to the azure pool, brilliantly aglow in the darkness. As soon as she thought of Jon, she felt pulled toward him, into him, and she pulled back, the connection made.

Goosebumps rose on her skin, its tiny hairs standing on end at the tingling of their union. He'd learned quickly, or perhaps it was being her complement that made it so. His presence began to enter her, a smooth flow of anima that sought hers and wrapped around it, just as hers did around his. He was warm—no, hot—and his heat flowed into her, through her, filling her furthest reaches until he brimmed inside her.

The watery surface of her anima began to vibrate with a rhythmic quake, its pulsing flood spreading through her body, her growing need making her shift. Her flesh quivered with the hot vibration, tremors contracting her muscles everywhere. Her entire body tightened, waited, yearned, and she writhed, unable to contain the keen wanting.

His silver built up the blue in her anima, then pressure—fast and overwhelming, filled her with one voluminous wave after another, pouring in, coalescing, surging into her until her anima overflowed, a waterfall of power rolling inside her. It pushed against her inner walls with the delirium of skin against silk, dizzying in its limitless caress. She shivered, trembling, overpowered; and the muscles of her belly drew taut, converging on the primal need springing there and saturating every inch of her until she hurt with desire.

His body collided with hers, sending her falling back onto the bedroll, and that ache exploded. Blossomed. A breath ravished from her chest, and beneath her, the fur blanket tickled in textured delight. *Yes.* Her head swam with ecstasy—his rough palm had broken her fall. Buttons came undone, her coat open and then cast away, the shirt raised, and his touch found her skin, cresting waves of pleasure. The heat of his breath on her neck made her shudder, frissons of anticipation tightening her skin, and Great Divine, she could hardly wait.

Please.

But he pulled back.

Braced above her, he breathed raggedly. Through the tent's opening, the wavering firelight cast a lick of illumination upon his face, light pushing against darkness and darkness against light. She froze beneath the hold of his pained, warring gaze, invisible armies battling for control, their carnage a clash of sea blue and shadow in his stormy eyes.

She reached up to stroke his face, and as soon as she did, the pleasant warmth of contact flooded her once more. Still connected, their anima flirted in a pleasurable undulation that swayed from his body to hers and back again.

He closed his eyes, and his breathing eased. Delicately, she ran her thumb over his mouth. He pressed his lips to it in a kiss before gazing down at her.

The tempest in his eyes had settled to still, calm waters, but the surface still rippled. She tensed beneath him, clumsy nervousness replacing the mindless desire of moments before.

He moved to sit and raised her hand to his cheek. His lust had been so keen moments before, but it wasn't lust animating him now. Not fire and need. It was something else entirely. Something gentle, thoughtful.

She slipped her hand free of his and let it descend along his body until her palm rested against his chest, absorbing the spirited beat of his heart.

He peered down at her. "Rielle, I..." He swallowed.

Her own heart pounded. They couldn't ignore the—whatever this was —much longer. The wind rustled the tent flap.

He placed his hands atop hers on his chest and threaded his fingers with hers. "I can't do this."

She looked from his face to their intertwined hands, perplexed by the contradiction between his words and the rest of him. *Can't. A loaded word.* "But you want to."

That's what his hands, his body, his heart said to her.

He brought her palm to his mouth and, closing his eyes, kissed it, holding the touch for a sensual moment. "Very much, I want to."

A rush of heat made her belly contract. She wanted him, and he wanted her. It could be that simple. "Then..."

Pressing his lips together, he gave a faint shake of his head. "To rejoin the Order—"

"Why do you need to rejoin the Order?" Why did he make his life so difficult? "Why deny yourself?"

It had been a long time since she'd risked rejection, but she wouldn't pretend she didn't want him any longer.

Gently, he extricated himself from her embrace, the resonance fading as his touch broke from hers. She cooled as he sat next to her and settled onto his bedroll. Her anima bright, swollen to abundance, she waited for his answer.

"I swore vows, Rielle." He pulled up his knees and rested his arms on them. "Eight years of devotion... I can't break my troth to Most Holy Terra on a mere whim." He lowered his chin onto his arm and studied the tent's opening as it wavered in the night breeze, shifting between darkness and firelight.

"A whim?" She clenched her teeth until they hurt. "Is that what I am to you?" Her voice broke.

His shoulders stiffened, and he looked at her wide eyed. She didn't turn away, but to wait for an answer was to stare at the sun. Pressure built in her face, and her cheeks burned.

At last, she could bear the heat no longer and shuffled into her own bedroll, turning away from him to the shadows.

He remained silent.

Fully awake, she stared at the side of the tent, trying to ignore the sickly pressure rising in her body.

19

*S*lowing his horse, Jon glanced at Rielle as she squinted into the darkness, her irises spelled arcane green with earthsight. Her eyes widened.

Perhaps Bournand at last? The question lingered on his lips, but he wouldn't be the one to break the silence. Last night would not be so easily smoothed over.

One last look around, and the magical color disappeared from her eyes. She lowered her gaze.

The Kingsroad had been clear and quiet all day, and so had she. But she'd faithfully done a check with earthsight every half hour and scanned the distance like a hawk, readiness tense in her shoulders. If Phantom and Shadow did lurk in the night, he and Rielle would not be caught unaware.

She did her best to protect him, even if he didn't need it. Perhaps he'd been too harsh with her. Despite everything, she'd acquitted herself admirably in the duel with Flame, if the body had been any indication. His mouth frozen in a silent scream, Flame had been impaled by two ice spikes in his chest and one in his gut. A decisive kill, and against a notoriously skilled mage, no less.

For a paladin, a pyromancer was an easy kill, but for a mage? Fighting Flame had to have been the equivalent of a paladin like himself fighting Gilles. Odds, experience, and status had all been stacked against her. But to win, she'd been willing to risk more than Flame had. To risk everything.

As Jon had trained this morning, Gilles had figured in his head as he did every morning, the blackguard who pushed his training to the limits. Gilles wouldn't deign to kill him, no more than a hurricane would deign to blow out a candle, and he certainly wouldn't risk his life to.

But I would risk mine to arrest him.

He eyed Rielle. In some ways, they were more alike than he cared to admit. He'd risk his life to defeat Bastien's murderer, and she had risked her life to defeat the man who'd threatened—

Me.

Misguided. Reckless. Foolish. But she'd been willing to die for his sake. For a charge she'd been ordered to protect. Was it only for duty? Or was there something more?

If it was duty, what had earned such loyalty? Divinity mages swore vows, too—obedience, allegiance, piety, and diligence—but had that been all? The Divinity's mission, something to die for?

She straightened, turned to him briefly and then away, passing the reins through her fingers.

A whim. He shut his eyes, reliving his ill-spoken words from the night before. He'd called her a mere whim. When she'd asked him if that was all she was to him—the look on her face as she'd waited for him to explain had been nigh unbearable. He'd wanted to kiss it away, tell her that nothing could be further from the truth.

The whim was not her. Not to him. The whim was making love.

Mages loved freely. He didn't know how many lovers had enjoyed her bed—and he didn't wish to know—but she'd kept none of them by her side. To indulge his desire without first winning her heart would have been indulgence in whim of the most dangerous kind. Sacrificing everything to offer himself as no more than a night's entertainment... when he would have wanted so much more.

In the tent last night, when he'd found his shirt beneath her mage coat, something of his embracing her, a woman whose heart could be his, that whim had nearly taken over. He had wanted to give himself to her, to keep or discard, to love or to break, to do with as she pleased... He'd wanted to sacrifice all that he'd been for all that she was, to whatever end.

The firelight had caught the arcanir center of his Sodalis ring, and he'd pulled back. Hard. To give himself to her would have been to lose himself, and no matter how much he craved the giving, the loss would leave him gutted.

He could never allow it. The Order meant so much to him, and he could offer so little to her.

His stallion's hooves crunched softly on the autumn leaves. After last night, she would have no more to do with him. There was nothing left but to let her escort him to Monas Amar. She'd never have to see him again.

The sky-glow over Bournand came into view at last, the city's torches shining brightly in the darkness. Past the north gate, lamps burned over the streets and in the windows of the few establishments still open to travelers on the main thoroughfare.

The Terran Vindemia festival, to honor the annual death of the Oak King, happened this time of year, but there was little indication of it. Black mourning flags waved in the wind before homes and businesses as they rode through, signs of a city's quiet bereavement.

A noble. Entire cities didn't hang mourning flags but for high-profile deaths. The count, perhaps? He turned to Rielle, but she wouldn't meet his gaze.

At the heart of Bournand's quiet was an enormous cylindrical building with a domed roof, a figure eight at its apex. The Temple of the Divine.

Rielle headed straight for the temple's stables, and he followed. There, an apprentice took their horses and a young black-haired mage with a two-bar chevron on his sleeves led them into one of the temple's towers, eyeing Jon and his armor the whole way. The temple wouldn't have welcomed paladins, but in Rielle's company, he had the rare privilege of entering.

Inside, their steps echoed off the sconce-lit hardwood hallways, quiet and dark. When they reached an office, the mage handed Rielle documents.

"We got a dove from the Tower a couple days ago. The Crowned Stag," he said. "Lucky for you. The refugees have been clogging up all the best inns."

"Refugees?" Jon looked up.

The mage hesitated. "You haven't heard?"

"Heard what?" Rielle glanced from the mage to him and back again. "I noticed the city was in mourning, but—"

The mage adopted a somber look. "About a week ago, King Marcus and Queen Alexandrie were assassinated, along with the entire line of succession."

The king dead? The queen? The entire line—?

"How?" Rielle squeaked. "How is that possible? The Royal Guard, the knights, the Emaurrian army, the city guard, every noble's force at court—"

"Who?" Jon closed on the mage. "When?"

"Olivia Sabeyon," Rielle croaked. "The Archmage. Is she alive? Do you know?"

The mage held up his hands, his eyebrows knitted together. "I haven't heard. I'm sorry." His eyes widened, and Jon followed his line of sight to Rielle.

She quivered, faltering on her feet. She took a step back and braced a hand on the stone wall, breathing harshly, her face pale, severe.

Jon steadied her with an arm around her waist. "Perhaps she escaped."

She eyed him and flashed a brief, watery smile. "She wouldn't have. Olivia's a healer... the Archmage. And a very caring person." Desperation beaded on her skin, and she winced, shaking.

In shock? He needed to get her to a chair, or—

She closed her eyes and breathed deep.

"Are you all right?" the mage asked.

She shook her head. "I'll be all right when I know Olivia's safe."

Her knees buckled, and she caught herself against the wall. Jon reached her, and under his palm, her tautness relaxed. At this rate, she'd collapse.

"Let's get you to the inn." He didn't wait for a reply before he scooped her up and bore her out. The mage's footsteps followed for a few beats, then ceased.

"Jon," she said half-heartedly, "I can—"

"Hush." As he carried her back to the temple's stables, her eyelashes fluttered. She frowned and opened her mouth, but whatever protest she'd intended died on her lips.

He'd seen it before, men after battle who'd lost their friends and brothers, who'd lost themselves, unable to speak, to think, to walk. Who'd needed calm and time. What she needed.

In the stable, he set her on a bale of hay, tethered her horse to his, then seated her securely on his black palfrey.

He swung into the saddle behind her, held her close. As they departed, she went limp against him.

Just hold out until the inn. He pressed his lips against the crown of her head. She'd be all right. If her friend needed saving, they'd save her. Whatever it took.

The Crowned Stag's wooden signboard came into view, bearing the image of a stag with a great rack of antlers etched in gold and a black flag next to it. He dismounted in the courtyard, holding Rielle tightly against his chest. He knocked with his boot's sabaton, more forcefully than he'd intended.

The innkeeper let them in, sending a boy out to attend their horses.

"What can I do for you, Sodalis?" the man asked sleepily, looking over Rielle with a rising eyebrow.

Jon nodded to her in his arms. "She's a Tower mage. Favrielle..." It occurred to him that he didn't know her surname. He waved the documents from the temple between his fingers.

The innkeeper grabbed them, donned his spectacles, and frowned. "This says two rooms, but there's already a Tower mage in one of them."

Jon went rigid. "Documented?"

"Yes. Official seal and everything. He was supposed to stay at another inn, but there was some issue with the refugees."

"One room will be fine."

The man's gaze meandered from him to Rielle and back again.

Jon narrowed his eyes. "With all haste, sir. She needs to rest."

The innkeeper jumped. "Of course. My apologies." He hurried to the staircase and led the way upstairs bearing a candelabrum. "Alfons will deliver your packs to you shortly."

"My thanks." He rearranged Rielle in his hold. Eyes closed, she hadn't moved since the temple.

The innkeeper unlocked the door, and Jon swept inside and accepted the key. The innkeeper lit a large beeswax candle on the nightstand, but as he pulled the door, Jon blocked it with his boot.

"I may need some supplies from the kitchen." He held the man's gaze.

The innkeeper nodded several times, eyes wide. "Yes, anything you need, please help yourself—"

"My thanks." He moved his boot, and with a bow, the innkeeper closed the door.

Jon laid her among the cool, stark-white cotton sheets and overstuffed pillows of the large four-poster bed. He pulled off her boots and covered her legs with a blanket, then watching her for any sign of change, removed his armor. Although her eyes remained shut, a line remained etched between her brows. Troubled.

A knock came at the door. He opened it and let in the boy, who brought in their packs, followed by maids who filled the washbasin and water carafe. Jon gave them a few copper cuivres, then turned back to Rielle. If she woke, needed anything—

He poured her a cup of water and set it on the nightstand, then pulled up the blanket to her waist and leaned in to smooth her hair from her face.

"I'll be right back," he whispered, the end of her braid sifting through his fingers.

When she didn't reply, he strapped on his sword, grabbed the nearby candlestick, lit it with the large beeswax candle, then headed downstairs, locking the door behind him. Quiet darkness claimed the hall and the stairs, and the kitchen was abandoned. He set a kettle of water to boil, milk to warm, and gathered some food and tea.

He shook his head as he stirred a bowl of porridge. When had the capital come under siege? Had Derric known when he'd sent the discharge? Had the Proctor known?

Even now, priests and paladins had to be mobilizing in Monas Amar. The Divinity, too, would have dispatched agents, perhaps even an army from Magehold. An army of mages would cause a stir in the Order, but per the Magehold Convention, the Divinity was bound to restore peace—and no more. At least the Order would watch their hands.

He took a heavily laden tray upstairs. The Crag, the Divinity, the Order... And Rielle's friend was caught in the middle. He couldn't allow Rielle to suffer the loss of a friend as he had.

He unlocked the door and shut it softly. Rielle didn't stir, so he laid the tray on the table and placed the warmed milk at her bedside.

When she woke, she'd be understandably distraught. Whenever he'd had nightmares as a child, Derric had always brought him a cup of warmed milk and stayed up reading epics until he fell asleep once more. Perhaps it would lend her comfort, too.

In the dim amber glow of the candle, he washed up and changed, keeping an eye on her all the while.

At last, she curled tighter in bed and her eyes fluttered open. He sat at her side, hoping to ease her waking before she seized upon the terrible news from the temple once more.

Her eyebrows drew together for a moment, then she blinked and sat up. He pressed the cup into her hands, his touch lingering on her wrist for a moment.

She took the cup, then sipped from it. "Thank you."

He offered a brief, sympathetic smile.

She looked around the room. "The Crowned Stag?" Her gaze wandered to the blanket and her boots in the corner. "If it weren't for you, I'd still be a heap at the temple."

"I know what it is to worry about a friend." He rubbed his chest. "You know I was raised at the monastery." With the surname *Ver,* his life was an open book.

She nodded.

"When I was seven, a boy named Bastien came to live there. His mother had died in childbirth, and his father, a sailor, couldn't afford to care for him any longer. From the day he arrived, mud on his face, he declared he would someday be a paladin. We became fast friends."

Leaning back, she gave an amused nod. "Two peas in a pod?"

"Oh, we got into so much trouble. We misbehaved so much, we spent more time punished with chores than the rest of the boys combined. One time, Derric fell asleep at his desk, and we filled his doorway with books stacked to full height, four rows deep." He huffed a nostalgic half laugh. "Five years ago, when the Crag Company took it upon themselves to clear Signy of bandits, they took over, hired themselves, and decided to charge for 'protection.' Bastien and I were among the many deployed to remove them. The Crag refused to vacate. There was a battle. Bastien and I were separated, and when I heard his position had been overrun, I—" He shook his head.

"He was like a brother to me," he said. A hard knot formed in his stomach, and his fingers went to his Sodalis ring. "Those moments when I didn't know whether he lived were some of the most difficult I've ever had to bear."

She covered his hand on the bed with hers. "I'm sorry."

"If I could spare you this, I would," he said gently, stroking her fingers. "At least there is hope your friend may yet live."

"She does." She intertwined her fingers with his. "I believe that."

He nodded. "No one else was downstairs, but we might learn more about the situation in Courdeval tomorrow."

His gaze lowered to their joined hands. He pulled away and leaned over to remove his boots.

Rielle cleared her throat softly, set down the cup, and left the bed. She padded about the room in her nightly routine, getting ready for bed.

Bed. He rose and stared at it. One.

He moved to the table and poured himself a cup of water. His grand plan after trying to escape from her a couple of days ago had involved separate rooms. Walls, doors, and space between them.

And here he was, enshrined with her in one room, with one bed, and no space between them to speak of.

From behind the privacy screen, she emerged in a full-length nightgown, white cotton and lace flowing about her soft curves, and brushed out her curls.

His fingers twitched. Wanting to comb through her hair. Traitors.

Her stomach growled, and she grinned at him sheepishly. "Sorry."

Fighting a smile, he nodded at the tray. "Too late for supper, unfortunately, but I scavenged what I could."

She sat with him and filled a plate with cured meat, cheese, and bread, and helped herself to a bowl of porridge. He ate his fill, too, then rolled up his sleeves. She followed the retreating fabric with her gaze, lingering over his arms, where the winding sangremancy sigils wove into aeromancy scrolls. Her sky-blue eyes dilated, tracing down to his hands, and her lips parted.

Did she like what she saw? He straightened in his chair.

Smoothing a hand over the skirt of her nightgown, she licked her lower lip. What would that lower lip feel like between his? Soft, warm—

She met his gaze and flushed. Terra have mercy, to be a stray thought in her head...

"I'll keep you company tonight," he said, keeping his voice even. There was only one room, so there wasn't much of a choice.

"Thank you."

She rose and laid the room's ward while he finished his water, then she withdrew to the bed.

Propped up on a pillow, she waited. For a moment, the silence between them was palpable. He approached the bed, grabbed a pillow, and tossed it onto the floor. From the armoire, he pulled out a blanket.

Even if he presumed to impose upon her and share the bed, it would have been beyond idiotic. His body had already abandoned any allegiance to him.

"Would you care to take the bed instead?" she offered.

As if he could ever abide sleeping on a soft bed while she suffered the floor. But she didn't offer to share.

Keeping her word?

He wasn't sure whether to be relieved or disappointed.

"Thank you, but I'm fine." He laid Faithkeeper next to the bed.

"Are you sure?" she asked, with a slight tremor to her voice.

"Completely." He spread the blanket on the floor. *Don't feel guilty.* Exhaling a quiet breath, he reclined, stretching out an arm and tucking it under his head.

She blew out the candle. Night blanketed the room, her breathing and his the only sounds.

"Thank you," she whispered, "for everything, Jon."

He nodded in the darkness. This day hadn't been easy for her, and the coming days would only become more difficult as worry for her friend would deepen. At least today, he'd managed to ease her suffering, in some small way. "Goodnight, Rielle."

Tomorrow, he would learn all he could about the regicide and the siege, but tonight, he would make certain the demons that had sapped her strength at the temple didn't return in the night.

20

The sun's morning rays alighted upon Jon, but even before he could open his eyes, he felt Rielle tucked cozily in his embrace. She'd cried quietly in the night, and he'd moved to comfort her, unable to stop himself from whispering away her fears. Eventually, she'd begun to drowse against him, and as he'd lain her down, he hadn't possessed the heart to disturb her when she'd finally fallen asleep, in his arms. He hadn't moved since.

None of this broke the Code, at least not in deed. But in spirit? Whatever this was, it drew him like a shrine drew the faithful. For all his self-control, tears from her and he could do nothing but keep her close. His face buried in her hair, he breathed her in.

She was still sleeping now, and deeply. Her night had been difficult, and she needed all the rest she could get.

Last night, the innkeeper had said a Tower mage, a man, had taken their second room. Shadow and Phantom were known to be women, so he hadn't troubled Rielle with the information. But he'd have to tell her today.

Careful not to wake her, he pulled his arm gently from under her neck. He sat up and, with one last look, said his prayers, did his morning exercises, practiced the sword, washed, shaved, and dressed.

As he laced a black leather doublet, a door slammed in the hallway. He flinched. It would wake her.

Rielle eased open her eyes.

Unlike him, she didn't spring awake with the rising of the sun. She greeted the world like the fields of immortelle around Monas Ver on warm summer mornings. As the sun had climbed the sky, the yellow blooms brightened slowly to radiant golden life, a flowery wildfire spreading toward the horizon, verdant hills dusted with gold in northeastern Emaurria.

She gave him a thorough look, her gaze trailing his fingers as he finished lacing the doublet. "It suits you."

The innkeeper's perplexed frown the previous night had been hint enough that a mage-and-paladin pair drew attention. The wrong kind of attention. The items the mages had packed for him had included some fine clothes—poorly chosen, as they'd make anyone stand out—but the well-made leather doublet was plain enough to suit his purposes.

"Perhaps we'll draw less attention." He took a seat.

Rielle gave him a once-over. "I doubt that."

A grin threatened to emerge, but he schooled his face.

Slender bare feet slipped from the bed as she sat up and stretched with a yawn, the hem of her nightgown rising from her ankles to reveal a glimpse of shapely legs. Long, flowing golden locks flared around her head and shoulders, down to her waist...

He tore himself away.

"Thank you," she said softly, "for last night."

His heart clenched at the memory. "You're welcome." He brushed it off. "We should head down to breakfast, see what we can learn."

"A few minutes." She hopped out of bed and crossed the room to the vanity.

He sat and waited until she emerged, clad in a fresh white mage's coat, her hair in a thick braid but for the stray ringlets framing her face.

He opened his mouth, then closed it. He'd seen many mages in his life —if from afar—but very few chose coats in white, as Rielle seemed to favor. Even her quarters in the Tower had been decorated with white everywhere —and he hadn't seen her wear any other color.

But it suited her.

"Let's go," she said.

Downstairs, the tavern was full, but instead of the merry faces and lively conversation, the somber-faced clientele huddled close and whispered amongst one another, snippets of anxiety over the Spiritseve rituals, Hallowday bells, and the capital. A fire crackled in the hearth, and a couple women served breakfast and hot beverages. There were three exits, one in the front, two in the back. At the far table, a man in his fifties sat wearing a merchant's garb, but his alert eyes were a warrior's. Retired mercenary?

"Good morning, *ma chère*," a lilting voice taunted from behind them.

Jon whirled. A man sat at the corner table, sipping tea. The same man who'd visited Rielle's room that night in the Tower. The libertine. He wore a black mage's coat with a four-bar gold chevron on each sleeve. Beneath the open coat, his garb was luxurious: a navy-colored velvet waistcoat, a cravat, and a crisp white shirt. His boots reflected an ostentatious shine.

His dark, Kamerish eyes gleamed with amusement. Looking no older than thirty-five, he nevertheless had pale white hair, eyebrows, and eyelashes. A wild mage.

The Tower mage who'd taken the second room.

"Leigh?" Stunned, Rielle approached the table. "What are you doing here?"

"Drinking tea," Leigh said with a crooked grin. He didn't bother to rise. "You never did catch on quickly." The mage's gaze turned to Jon, assessing his face and descending to his feet.

Jon drew himself up to his full height, but stopped himself from resting his hand on Faithkeeper's pommel. He disliked something about the man, and he'd been a paladin too long to dismiss his instincts.

"You're the hothead paladin from the Tower," the mage said, then turned to Rielle. "Escort mission?"

Despite the unexpected run-in, Rielle betrayed no signs of fluster—her face remained its natural alabaster tint, her breathing even, her shoulders loose, her mouth in its faint resting pout.

Leigh gestured to the seats across from him.

Exchanging pleasantries with a man who considered it acceptable to accost a woman at night, uninvited, in her bedchamber? Arrest was likelier. But clearly Rielle considered him a friend, so for her sake, he could keep his peace. He pulled out a chair for her and then seated himself.

The mage flashed him a thin smile. "So you shared the other room with my former apprentice?" He glanced at a scowling Rielle and back.

Unmoving, Jon held the mage's gaze.

"Why are you in Bournand?" Rielle asked.

"I had nothing better to do, so I came to Bournand for some... entertainment." Leigh took another sip of tea.

After a conspicuous look around the tavern, Rielle shrugged. "Well, you chose the wrong inn."

A serving woman brought eggs, bread, sausage, soup, and tea.

"My usual inn was booked up."

Rielle broke off a piece of bread and popped it into her mouth. "The Velvet Glove?"

The name of an upscale brothel. Jon raised a brow. A particularly brazen Velvet Glove courtesan had once accosted him and Valen. To no success. He helped himself to some eggs and sausage.

Leigh sighed. "Full. Most unfortunate."

"What can you tell me about Courdeval?" Rielle asked.

Setting down his tea, Leigh sobered. "Rumor has it, deep pockets hired Heartseekers to assassinate the king, queen, and their heirs. Barely a week ago. I suppose you were on the road and wouldn't have heard."

Deep pockets... Anyone hiring those assassins would have had to be flush with coin.

The king, queen, and their heirs... "What about Prince James?"

Prince James was a good man, a Terran; he'd visited Monas Ver from time to time as a friend of Derric's.

"We stopped by the temple on our way in last night but heard little," Rielle said.

Leigh shook his head. "I've heard nothing about the prince, but we can assume the worst. The Crag Company has laid siege to the capital."

The Crag Company. Jon straightened. Flames licking thatched roofs. Battle cries. Bastien unmoving on the temple's steps. The serpentine edge of a flambard, death wielded by a stern-faced mercenary—

Gilles.

It could be no coincidence that Flame had attacked them on the Kingsroad. The Crag Company had murdered the Faralles, controlled the capital, and perhaps anticipated some operations from the Divinity and the Order.

"The Crag employed heretics to destroy every dovecote and prevent doves from leaving the capital with the news," Leigh went on. "Everyone who could, or wanted to, has fled the capital, and only now is word spreading. The priests and paladins of the Order of Terra are assembling in Monas Amar to provide humanitarian aid and to negotiate the release of civilian hostages."

Of course they are. At such a time, they had to be. The situation was—if ever there were a need for the Order, it was now. And if the Paladin Grand Cordon would but have him, Jon would pledge his sword and his life to the cause. And not just to see Gilles arrested.

If. Jon quashed his sigh. The odds of successfully challenging a discharge were decidedly not in his favor. However, regardless of his official status, the Order was unlikely to turn away an experienced sword-arm during a crisis.

"The Divinity of Magic is mobilizing an army in Magehold, the Order is doing so in Monas Amar to 'eliminate the Crag' "—Leigh made air quotes—"each likely angling to influence who will ascend the throne, no doubt."

"Evrard Gilles." Jon glared at the mage. "Is he in the capital?"

Leigh shrugged. "Presumably. The Crag in Courdeval are three thousand strong at least. They've already repelled attempts by some of the Houses to retake the capital."

Gilles' Crag Company mercenaries included two thousand *doubles* in a total of sixteen thousand men. Doubles, named for the double pay they earned, filled out the front lines, trained in fearsome two-handed swordsmanship and the crossbow. Gilles was a formidable adversary, with a formidable army.

Rigid, Jon cast a speculative eye at the retired mercenary once again. A woman and two children had joined the man at the far table.

Jon folded his arms and leaned back. "The paladins, if they're gathering at Monas Amar, will number as many, if not more than three thousand, but the odds of victory are slim without some entry assistance, a diversion, some war machines."

"There's been no word in or out of Courdeval since the siege," Leigh said. "Nothing to suggest the survival or operation of a defending force within. No one can say who yet lives within or in what numbers, so I doubt the Order will be getting any assistance from inside. There may be some remaining forces from the defeated loyalist Houses that have stayed to assist, but without an heir to rally around, most are waiting for the Order and the Divinity to sort it out."

"Olivia," Rielle whispered, then turned her soulful eyes on Leigh. "Has there been any word of her? Anything?"

Leigh covered her hand with his.

Don't touch her. The thought sprang, unbidden; he glared at their joined hands. He'd have liked to rip the other man's hand off hers, push him away, but instead he unclenched his fists.

"Nothing." Leigh leaned back in a dejected slump. "If she'd made it out, we'd know by now. The Archmage is well known."

Taking deep breaths, Rielle rubbed an eyebrow, a forlorn look on her face. He wanted to do something, anything, to comfort her.

Her friend was the Archmage—adviser on magic and mages to the king. He remembered now. Over the summer, a young virtuoso mage from the Emaurrian Tower had been appointed to the king's High Council—a woman, and a commoner at that—to fill the vacancy left by the previous Archmage, an elderly illusionist who had died in office. The Houses had made their displeasure known, but the royal family had stood by the king's choice.

The Archmage's chief duty was to perform the annual Moonlit Rite on Spiritseve, when the Veil was at its thinnest. Predating both the Terran and Divinist faiths, the Moonlit Rite was said to protect the realm from an ancient evil. Emaurrians, both Terran and Divinist alike, believed in the rite's protection. Even among the paladins and priests, there were believers whose nerves didn't settle near Spiritseve until word came of Trèstellan Palace's bells ringing to announce the rite's performance. The Hallowday bells.

It was less than a month away.

Leigh's concerned gaze never left Rielle. "Will you be all right, *ma chère?*"

She shook her head.

Something about the way the man called her *ma chère* set Jon's teeth on edge.

"If I hear anything, I'll tell you," the mage said. Sympathy passed in the silence.

Jon could do better than listen for news. With the paladins, under the Paladin Grand Cordon's command, he could see Courdeval restored and, along with it, perhaps Rielle's friend. He could see justice done to Gilles for this, and for all his crimes.

"The Divinity will send someone," Rielle said softly. "There's the Moonlit Rite to consider."

Leigh huffed. "The Moonlit Rite... What a farce. No more than an attempt by the Divinity to endear itself to the Crown and the people."

Rielle's mouth twisted. "How can you say that? Don't you feel the pressure around Spiritseve, the push against your inner barriers?"

"That has nothing to do with the rite." Leigh crossed his arms. "If it did, you'd better believe the Divinity would shout it from the rooftops, so everyone would know just how indispensable we are."

She rubbed the table. "That's cynical of you."

Leigh shrugged.

The Crowned Stag's front door opened. Two cloaked figures entered.

By their carriage and gear, they were warriors—skilled hands—a man and a woman. They wore leather armor, well fitted and of high quality, with several throwing knives sheathed in bandolier vests and elsewhere. With a look, Jon guessed at the shoulder, the gauntlet, the belt. Both of them bore not swords but a pair of long stilettos in scabbards on their belts.

The man approached the innkeeper, gesturing lengthily with his hands

—about a sword?—speaking in hushed tones while the woman studied the diners.

A long sword.

Jon hitched Faithkeeper behind him.

They were looking for a paladin. But why?

Would the innkeeper give him up?

Jon barely had time to prepare himself when Rielle plopped into his lap and closed her arms around his neck.

Her hair brushed his cheek as she whispered, "Play along."

She pulled away, her nose almost touching his, and gave him a grave look, then caressed his jaw with the back of her fingers. A shiver rattled him.

Disguise. It was his only coherent thought. When he finally remembered to exhale, the sound emerged more like a groan than a breath.

She leaned in close to his ear, where she nipped him and exhaled, making him shiver. "Are they gone?"

Wrapping an uneasy arm around her hip, Jon looked over her shoulder. "Yes."

Leigh rested an elbow on the table and his chin in his hand, staring with mock interest. "Why don't you two take this upstairs?" he suggested with a patronizing wink.

"Come on." Rielle slid from his lap, took his hand, and urged him to rise. Uncomfortable in his fitted trousers, he followed her up to their room.

Inside, she turned around and pressed her fingers into his chest, pushing him against the door, and he allowed her to.

"Who were they? Why were they hunting you? What aren't you telling me?"

"They were clearly warriors, perhaps Crag. It's obvious they're looking for paladins."

"So they're hunting every paladin in Emaurria? If so, why would they look here?"

Just what was she implying? How was he to know? "I don't know."

Paladins were easily found at the way-station, and there'd be at least one performing services at the third night of the Vindemia festival tonight. Even if he'd seen coming here, he was just one paladin; why had they come to The Crowned Stag?

Was he mistaken after all? Perhaps they weren't looking for paladins?

"Do you know why your High Priest and the Proctor assigned me to you?" she asked in a low, seething voice. "If you do, tell me. I don't appreciate being kept in the dark." She pierced him with indignant eyes.

Her challenge made him want to throw her onto the bed, pin her, stare her down until she battled him for control, until she pulled him to her, twisting, tangling, intertwining—

He leaned in, invading her space. "I've told you all I know. Think what you like, mage," he replied, matching her low tone.

Her mouth dropped open. She raised a hand to grab his collar—

He seized her arm, fingers easily closing around her slender wrist, and spun to pin *her* against the door. She resisted, but the fight in her eyes faded. When she dropped her gaze, there lay only a finger's width between them. Only...

He released her arm. The whisper of an arpeggio plucked on a lute floated up from downstairs.

She lifted her chin. A blush reddened her cheeks, a touch of rose red across winter white. His fingers tensed, and before he could stop them, they stroked the softness of her cheek.

She quivered.

Despite all his efforts to push her away, longing persistently invaded his heart. Time and again. He cared, more and more each day. When they arrived at Monas Amar, would he be able to watch her fade into the distance and the past?

With a bang of splintered wood, the door flew open.

She tumbled into his arms.

Catching her, Jon kicked the door shut, but it caught. Held by some unseen force. Rielle whirled in his hold and faced the doorway.

He stared wide-eyed as Leigh sauntered in, holding up a hand with a blurry aura, then flicked his wrist and closed the door.

Rielle relaxed as her feet found the floor, her soft body serene against his. Warm. Close.

The mage had the worst timing. Or the best.

Leigh grinned. "One thing is clear. The Proctor assigned you an escort with good reason."

Satisfied that Rielle had regained her balance, Jon let her go.

Leigh eyed him. "You won't be able to carry your sword," he said, studying the arcanir armor across the room, "or wear your armor, despite its inherent advantages. In fact, you might want to consider getting it modified."

Jon scoffed. That armor had been made by the Sacred Blacksmith of Monas Ver. It was divine artistry rendered in arcanir. Modifying it in any way was blasphemy. "You must be joking."

"Those two sellswords came looking for a paladin," Leigh said. "You're one no longer, but arcanir does have its benefits. You can protect yourself by modifying the armor," he suggested, "or you can die."

"I can handle sellswords." Rielle pulled out a chair and sat. "He doesn't have to change anything he doesn't want to."

Leigh ignored her. "If you continue to look like a paladin, you endanger yourself. If you don't wear your armor until Monas Amar, you'll still be in danger, but Rielle will protect you." He pointed at her. "Either way, you endanger her, too. Needlessly."

Leigh was right. Jon grimaced.

"I can handle myself," she snarled at the mage, "and my charge. Stay out of it." She poured herself a goblet of wine from the decanter.

Leigh leaned on the table. "And the man can make his own decision. You may have charge of *him*, but not of his possessions. It's out of your hands."

She huffed and folded her arms across her chest.

As loath as Jon was to admit it, Leigh's reasoning was sound. He needed to be both disguised and armored, for his own protection and for Rielle's. Whether he preserved the state of his armor wouldn't matter if he died before reaching Monas Amar.

Finally, he nodded. "You're right."

"You're stating the obvious." Leigh waved a dismissive hand.

"But I don't have the coin to pay for such a thing." Jon received a small stipend every quarter, but not enough for extravagance.

"But I do," Leigh quickly offered. "And I'll help you, free of charge."

Jon furrowed his brow. The mage, of course, didn't care for him a whit —he offered for the sake of Rielle's safety, who scowled at her former master with bitter annoyance.

But in this, his interests and the mage's aligned.

"You don't want his money, Jon." Rielle upended her coin purse on the table. A pile of gold coronas, silver argents, and copper cuivres clattered onto the wood. "If you need anything, I've ample funds."

He could hardly take her hard-earned coin. If she needed to work for the Divinity, then she needed the money. "It's all right. I'll do as he says."

With a sigh, she rose. She swept the coins back into the purse. "If you're decided on this, we should see a blacksmith today. Such work will take time, and we have a schedule to keep. We're already taking longer than expected."

"I have just the blacksmith in mind." Leigh grinned. "I'll take your forsworn paladin there." When Rielle opened her mouth, he added, "Don't worry. I'll see to it that not a hair on his head is harmed."

Jon resisted the urge to remind them he was still in the room.

"Fine," she said. "I have to stop by the marketplace and the temple to send the Proctor my report. I... wasn't able to last night."

"The market's on the other side of the city," Leigh replied. "I'll be visiting the temple later. I can send your message."

Rielle removed a rolled piece of parchment from her belt pouch and handed it to Leigh. She trusted him so readily? If she did, perhaps the man was more than his demeanor suggested. *Just how close are they?*

Were they, he corrected. She'd told him at the Tower that she and Leigh weren't involved. They weren't lovers. At least not anymore.

Not that it mattered. It couldn't matter. Not to him.

Leigh tucked the parchment into his shirt and turned his attention to Jon. "How would you like to accompany me into the city center?"

Spending a day with the man wasn't his favorite idea, but he could handle it. He shrugged his assent.

"That thrilled, are you?" Leigh joked.

"As long as you don't kill each other." Rielle drank her wine.

"I'll leave my thirst for blood behind, then," Leigh declared.

"No chance your forked tongue will want to keep it company?" Jon asked with a grimace.

Wagging his finger at Jon, Leigh grinned. "Promising," the mage praised. "Very promising." Leigh passed in front of him and through the doorway. "Come. Let's take the horses." He didn't stop to wait.

Jon grabbed the pack containing his armor and shouldered it, and with a final glance at Rielle, he followed Leigh to blasphemy.

2 1

*O*livia remained calm as the Crag Company mercenary's steps faded down the dungeon corridor, along with the sole torch and its scant light. As darkness closed in, climbing the stone walls of her prison, she licked her bloodied lip.

At first, the darkness had been terrifying. Oppressive. She'd screamed, railed against it, pushed against it, and it... It had pushed back. Harder than she. Stronger than she. The yawning chasm of nothing, of emptiness, of oblivion. She'd wept, hot tears trailing down her face. Hot tears that reminded her she was alive.

Then, slowly, reality and the world around her had filtered in. Water dripping. Rats scurrying. Insects skittering. The ravings and screams of a distant prisoner. The faraway rush of a waterway. Even the odors—musty, dank, disgusting, putrid—were dust, mold, filth, death. All real, all present. Darkness was there, but darkness was not all there was.

Her trip to the Hall of Mirrors today had been long, and it had left her beaten, cut, and bruised. But unbroken. It had been the longest and most painful of her visits. She knew what that meant.

James is short of information for extraction... or unwilling to part with it. She swallowed. If the Crag torturers could elicit no more from him, he was not long for this world. *Nor I.*

She had to escape—to save herself and to find help for James and anyone else left here.

At best, she'd succeed. Escape the palace with her life and bring back a force strong enough to liberate James and destroy the Crag.

At worst, she'd be caught and Gilles would lock her in an arcanir cell, inadvertently cloaking her from any spirit-magic spells. Sparing Rielle from walking into a trap, if she hadn't asked a spiritualist to scry for her already.

All or nothing.

Tonight. She would implement her escape plan tonight. No one would return until supper, when they'd deliver her nightly crust of bread and water. Until then, she had a precious few hours to slip her shackles, burst from her iron cell, and escape Trèstellan Palace.

I have to try. At least they'd shackled her hands in front. Flexing her fingers, she grabbed her left thumb. A deep breath, and as she exhaled, she bent the joint inward and kept on pushing until it popped.

She gritted her teeth. Pain shot through her jaw, as excruciating as her hand. Tears burst from her eyes.

She shuddered, panting through the agony. Quickly, she pulled the arcanir cuff binding her hand—

And off.

One more, and she could use her magic. The second one would be worse than the first. This time, she'd know exactly how much it would hurt.

Now or never. She wrapped her left palm around her right thumb and, with another deep breath and exhalation, snapped it inward.

Her mouth opened wide in a silent scream, but she dared not make a sound. She pulled the arcanir cuff down her hand, gasping, tears pouring down her face—

It wouldn't come off.

The damned thing wouldn't come off!

No. She pulled harder.

No, no, no. It wouldn't move! She hadn't dislocated her thumbs for nothing. The Divine couldn't be so cruel.

Trembling, she raised her hand to her mouth and dragged her tongue across her salty skin.

Another yank at the cuff.

It went a little farther, but not enough to slip off. Sharp pain lanced through her wrist.

No use. It was no use. On shaking legs, she paced the blackness of the cell and then leaned against the bars.

The bars.

She rested the edge of the cuff against a bar and held it in place with her quivering left hand. It refused to cooperate.

Refusal was not on offer today. She forced it steady.

With all her might, she pulled the cuff against the bar—so hard her arm hurt as though it would pop from its socket.

Come on, come on, come on—

Her hand slipped free. She fell against the slimy stone floor of the cell and listened in horror as the arcanir shackles clattered on the other side of the bars.

No time to waste. She looked inward, found her shining white anima, willed it to her aid. It surged against her inner gates, rising, reaching for use. Unable to focus her healing magic with gestures, she wove it into her words, infusing a simple incantation with her will as she held her hands together. *"Sundered flesh and shattered bone, / By Your Divine Might, let it be sewn."*

Her thumbs moved into place and became once more as they had once been, and so did all else, every cut and bruise, with little dimming of her anima. A relieved gasp fled her parched lips.

She jumped to her feet and darted to the bars, then pressed herself to them as widely as she dared. To remove them, she'd need transmutation magic. Non-innate.

Another weaving, a thicker strand of pure anima made will. *"Earth to iron, iron to rust: / What is metal, turn to dust."*

The bars gave way to fine particles of rust falling like sand. She staggered forward but caught herself. Such a small charm, but non-innate transmutation magic had dimmed her anima much more than her healing spell.

She shuffled through the fine-grain piles. In the dark, outside her cell of her own volition, she had made more progress than she had in weeks.

A right turn, twenty-eight steps, a left turn, two flights of stairs, a right turn... Daily trips to the Hall of Mirrors had set an indelible route in her mind.

From her cell, she turned right and followed the path, creeping along quietly with as much haste as she could manage.

A stairwell came into view right where it should, torchlight curling around a corner, flickering on the stone floor. Shadows.

Guards. She could pass by them easily, but before they called for help? She clenched her teeth. Too big a risk.

They'd have to be swift deaths. No mercy.

With an emptiness in the pit of her stomach, she slunk toward the stairwell, each step slow and measured, and ascended along the wall toward the landing. When she heard breaths—two distinct sets—she gathered her courage, prepared her hands to cast, and wheeled around the corner.

Two of them.

She curled the glowing white fingers of both her hands downward.

The guards slumped against the wall, deep in slumber.

Counting her blessings that it had been only two, she continued, cautiously passing over the bodies to enter another stairwell.

At the top, she'd be on the palace's ground floor. She focused her anima on a winding gesture with her left hand. A protection spell. It would heal her next injury instantly, and she could sustain it for as long as she didn't cast another spell with her left hand—if she still had the anima.

Or just until I can get out of here.

Voices carried from the hall above, many more than two.

She pressed her back to the stairwell's wall, biting her lip to keep from making a sound. The conversation loudened, and her heart beat wildly. She could only put two targets to slumber immediately; a spell of calm could extend as far as twenty paces from her position, but there was no telling how far away the last of the voices were.

No choice. She would have to kill them all or turn tail back to the cell. Long ago, Rielle had taught her a deadly pyromancy spell, but it knew no bounds. It would consume everyone and everything without mercy.

Were they all Crag? What if some of them were innocent?

She focused on their discussion as long as she dared—for any sign there might be innocents among them.

They discussed shifts. She exhaled. Definitely Crag.

Knotting anima to lethal intention, she mouthed the incantation of the consume spell. *"Fire blazing, fire bright, / Spark to life, burn those in sight."*

She turned the corner. Her spelled gaze alighted on a dozen Crag Company mercenaries.

They ignited like kindling. Fast and violent. Flames consumed their bodies, their screams, their lives, and climbed to the ceiling.

Charred flesh and burnt grease assailed her nostrils. She pressed a grimy sleeve to her nose, looking past the flames to discern the hall. The tapestries caught fire and dropped from the walls in disintegrating heaps.

The Hall of Mirrors is not far. And just beyond would be the kitchens, where she could exit to the garden.

Forgive me, James. Not knowing where he was, she couldn't save him now, but she could escape. She could bring back help.

Smoke filled the hall, billowing in blackening clouds. Her nose covered, she sidled by, coughing.

"You're surprising." A woman's voice, honey-sweet, came from every-where at once.

Her stomach hardening, Olivia stiffened, gaze darting around the burning hall. No one was about—the consume spell would burn any who were.

Earthsight. Costly, but she could cast an earthsight incan—

"Not very clever, though." A giggle.

Too late. If she spoke the incantation, she'd only make a target of herself. Dismiss the consume spell. And likely die before she could finish.

"Show yourself," Olivia hissed. *So that you can burn.*

"You can't tell where I am?" the voice teased. "Perhaps here," it whispered, close enough that Olivia swatted at her own neck. "Or here?"

The other side, a brush of hair against her cheek. Olivia's legs weakened.

An illusionist. So frustrating in combat until they revealed themselves. There was no casting anything on this adversary until she could be seen—and focused upon.

There had to be some way to force her to reveal herself.

Olivia continued sidling toward the kitchens around a massive cloud of smoke.

The smoke.

She kicked the burning tapestry behind her until it puffed gray. The illusionist would have to walk through the smoke to follow her. *And then I'll see you.*

"What do you want?" Olivia whispered, trying to keep the illusionist talking, hoping to discern her location.

Voices called from the distance.

"What I want is irrelevant, Archmage Sabeyon." The voice came from all sides, a harmony—a spell.

Olivia studied the clouds of smoke, looking for a figure to break through somewhere as she continued creeping toward the kitchens, gulping down breaths to stay quiet.

Something came, something small—an arrow—

Gasping, she threw herself aside.

Not fast enough. It clipped her arm.

She grasped it, adrenaline spiking, gesturing a healing spell—

No.

Tingling, stinging. She could cast no magic.

Arcanir. It had to be. She rubbed the blood flowing from her upper arm, coating her fingers. The arrow. It must've been—

Arcanir poison.

Heart racing nearly to bursting, she turned toward the kitchens and ran.

Arms snaked around her, dragging her back, and she lost her footing.

Together with her captor, she tumbled to the ground, reaching in panic for anything she could grab—hair, flesh, eyes—

An arm closed around her neck. She thrashed, blindly grasping as black dots populated her vision. Dry curls slipped through her fingers, and she clutched them, pulled, but the blackness closed in, dark and unforgiving like a prison.

22

*J*on urged his horse through the crowd. After this blasphemy with his armor, the option of returning to the Order would likely disappear. But he wouldn't endanger an innocent life for the sake of his honor. Especially not hers. Never hers.

The city bustled. Here, uptown, there were all manner of fine things, from Kamerish silk to exotic pomanders to shimmering jewels and spices from Sonbahar. Leigh ignored them with all the nonchalance of a wealthy man, although he paused to resupply and didn't bother to haggle. He even paid to have his purchases delivered to the inn.

The vendors Jon had done business with as a paladin had traded for cuivres, not argents or coronas, and sold simple things like pork, potatoes, rye bread, rough-spun clothes, plain soap, and other necessities. This was another world.

They passed Vindemia baskets of apples and straw, which decorated the city despite the mourning colors displayed everywhere. Farther away, logs were being set in a large fire pit beside a barn while men carried in halved tree trunks to arrange as benches.

Tonight would mark the last night of Vindemia, the three-day celebration of balance and blessing around the autumn equinox.

Although most mages and nobles worshipped the Divine, the bulk of Emaurria's population—the commoners—still worshipped the Goddess. The villagers would offer thanks to Terra for a good harvest and make offerings to assuage her grief over the death of her consort.

A bonfire would be lit to consume offerings to Terra, cider would be drunk to protect the orchards' fertility, dances would be offered in gratitude, and wishes would be made. The streets would normally be lively with celebration, but given the grim events in Courdeval, the atmosphere would either be somber with mourning or riotous with escapism.

A blacksmith's shingle—Forgeron's—came into view. The Forgerons were well known as descendants of a regional Archon, a leader of witches from the Dark Age of Magic, long before the Divinity of Magic was founded. These days, the family was rumored to have ties to heretics, but Joel Forgeron, its current patriarch, was a respected community leader.

Inside, the smithy was small but sunny and clean, although no one was present to greet them. Jon set down his bundled armor on a counter. A short woman entered with a tired frown.

"What can I do for you?" She wiped sweat off her brow with a dirty hand and then gaped at Leigh. *"Galvan?"*

"Helene," Leigh acknowledged with a mirthful smile.

"I'd ask what you're doing in Bournand, but I'd rather not know." She cast him a suspicious glare. "My father warned me about your uncanny ability to find mischief anywhere."

If her father was Joel Forgeron, just how familiar was Leigh with him, and why? Archon families were no friends of the Divinity, and the Forgerons were one of the most well-respected Archon families Emaurria had ever known.

"That sounds like something he'd say about me," Leigh replied with a shrug. "This armor"—he inclined his head toward the bundle on the table —"we'd like it modified."

Jon flinched. Since taking his vows at eighteen, he had owned few significant things beyond the great honor and privilege of being a paladin: Faithkeeper, his arcanir dagger, a few necessities, his Sodalis ring, and this armor. And with this act, he would lose one of those few things and, possibly, another—his life as he'd known it.

If you continue to look like a paladin, you endanger yourself. If you don't wear your armor until Monas Amar, you'll still be in danger, but Rielle will protect you. Either way, you endanger her, too. Leigh's words echoed in his mind, seeping dread like an infected wound.

The blacksmith moved toward the bundle but didn't open it. Her narrowed eyes wandered from Leigh to him, dropping to his hands—the ring—and back. "It's paladin's armor."

"You'll keep that to yourself, won't you?" Leigh placed a corona on the counter.

Helene inspected all the pieces in the bundle. "What modifications did you have in mind?"

"Downplay the arcanir, but don't draw attention?" Leigh offered.

Helene looked to Jon for confirmation.

The moment to change his mind was slipping away. But he'd already decided. "I trust your best judgment in the matter."

"Very well. In the interest of getting Galvan out of the city as soon as possible, I can have it ready the day after tomorrow." Gathering up the bundle, she stared at Leigh. "Try not to break too many hearts in the meantime."

Leigh smiled facetiously. "No promises." With that, he led them out of the shop.

"Is there anyone you don't know?" Jon asked as they mounted their horses.

"You," Leigh replied. "But since you've taken to fooling around with my former apprentice, let's change that." He flashed a curious look as he urged his horse forward.

Fooling around? Frowning, Jon followed. The mage had proved himself rude, malicious, immoral, and glib, but Rielle seemed to trust him implicitly. If she trusted the man, there had to be some redeeming quality to him.

As he traversed the small city with the mage, Jon's shoulders slumped. Naked. He felt naked. There was no familiar weight of arcanir, no normal bulk. No arming jacket or cool metal. No shining surface catching the sunlight.

Just a weightlessness on his shoulders. How could weightlessness feel so heavy a burden? He exhaled lengthily, drawing his eyebrows.

He'd allowed himself an unforgivable blasphemy.

No, he'd dared. For the sake of a cheeky witch, he would have to beg the Paladin Grand Cordon's mercy and, even then, might face rejection.

How much more would he sacrifice for her sake?

When they passed a baker's cart, he recalled the last time he'd been to Bournand. He'd risked then, too. A couple years ago, he'd helped a young widow reap her wheat fields during harvest. Her husband, a mage, had overdosed on the resonance-enhancing drug sen'a, leaving behind a debt to a local sen'a baron, Feliciano Donati. Because of the debt, when her husband had died, no one in the city would help her with the crops for fear of retribution, even though she had three young children.

When the sen'a baron responsible sent ruffians to collect on the debt, Jon had dispatched them and headed to Donati's resonance den to negotiate. As soon as he'd entered, Donati had ordered his dozen mage minions restrain him, broken a bottle, and etched a cut into his eyebrow—*what came of looking into private matters.* And it had been a mere lesson, enough to mark him without inviting the Order's justice.

Outnumbered, blood seeping into his eye, he'd had no choice but to leave, and Bournand's paladin commander had refused to pursue the matter further, citing inadequate grounds.

Jon clenched the reins. Although King Marcus had threatened a ban on sen'a and trux nearly a decade ago, a dominant political faction of nobles, the Emaurrian Knot, had expressed their dissent. Against their massive influence, the king had backed down.

Sen'a and trux merchants, since they conducted lawful business, were immune to the justice of paladins, regardless of how many lives they ruined. The Code had always prevented him from stepping in, no matter how frustrating it was to turn a blind eye.

Leigh rode into the Chalice, Bournand's upscale entertainment district, and stopped before a large establishment with a rose-studded signboard— The Rose Garden. A boy took their horses.

Inside, laughter hung in the air, a collection of well-lubricated patrons spread out among low, round tables. Off to the side, a buxom redhead tended bar with several well-dressed gentlemen seeking her attention while flirtatious men and women wandered the room, chatting up customers and disappearing with them upstairs or to back rooms.

Jon froze in the doorway. Leigh shoved him in. Two bright-eyed women took their arms and led them inside.

Grimacing, Jon shook his head. "You've brought me to a—a—"

"And?" Leigh waved his hand dismissively. "The wine selection is fantastic. Just one glass, and we'll be on our way. Promise." He grinned roguishly and murmured into his female companion's ear.

"I don't drink wine," Jon growled. The woman escorting him squeezed his arm.

Kissing his escort's neck, Leigh studied him with one irked eye. He lifted his head. "So, how did you come to break your oath?"

Break my—

He scowled. The mage had skirted the word *forsworn,* but the intrusion was the same. The women led them to a table.

"We're not talking about that," Jon said finally. "And I'm leaving." He glanced at the door.

"How happy would that make our fiery mutual friend, hmm?" Leigh raised a pale eyebrow.

That smug look. Jon's fingers twitched, curling. He wanted to punch that smug look until it became something more like... humility.

He sighed. *More trouble than waiting for him to drink one glass of wine is worth.*

He settled in, and two other women joined them, one bearing a decanter of wine and two goblets, and the other running her fingers through his hair, making his entire body freeze at the unwanted contact. He scowled at Leigh, who appeared completely oblivious as a young lady fell into his lap.

"Why not discuss your oath-breaking?" Leigh asked, undeterred, as one of the women poured him some wine. "There are only a few ways you could've, really..." He ignored Jon's icy glare. "Purchase any lavish items? Drink any ale? Or was it the lure of the little death?"

The young woman in Leigh's lap giggled.

Jon looked away. He didn't need to give the mage further ammunition. There wasn't much to say, regardless, until he learned more at Monas Amar. An honorable discharge could be for any of a number of reasons—to reward service, to excuse physically or psychologically unfit paladins from further duty, to prevent the end of a line, to cull malcontents.

And, indeed, sometimes in lieu of dishonorable discharges for breaking one of the four Sacred Vows or the Code. It was one of the Order's worst-kept secrets.

But he didn't want to be discharged. He didn't want to give up his family, his vocation, everything—

Someone had borne false witness against him. That had to be it. Someone he'd judged, or fought, perhaps. Looking for revenge. Someone with clout, if it had happened so quickly.

At Monas Amar, he would demand the reason for his discharge and correct the record.

"Fine," Leigh said. "Keep your secrets. I suppose keeping your *oath* doesn't matter anymore, does it?" The mage's eyes gleamed as he sipped his wine.

"It does matter," Jon replied, "if I intend to get my discharge reversed at Monas Amar."

Leigh laughed into his cup. "You're not serious. They let you slip your leash, and you're staying in the kennel?"

"Finish your wine already, and let's go."

The woman who hung on Jon's arm tucked her hand into his shirt and rubbed his chest.

As she wandered lower, he grasped her wrist and cleared his throat. "I'm not looking for companionship."

"Oh, don't be such a spoilsport," Leigh chided, then spread his arms wide to the woman. "My friend here doesn't know what he's missing. Literally." He quirked an eyebrow.

Jon cracked his knuckles. Did all wild mages run their mouths without consequence, or just this one?

The redhead running her fingers through Jon's hair ceased and left to join Leigh, who drank deeply of his wine. With a woman on each knee, and two others giving him their attention, he appeared at ease, although he ogled an attractive man serving the next table.

"You must be a masochist, Jon." Leigh traced small circles on a woman's arm with his fingertips, making her shiver. Was this entire show—what, a taunt? Flaunting what paladins tried so hard to resist?

And what was the appeal of half a dozen women hanging off a man for coin? It didn't even compare to the love of one woman, the right one.

He shuttered his eyes bitterly. Indeed, circumstances had made a masochist of him. "I tried to leave a couple days ago, but she"—he lowered his voice—"captured me."

Leigh smirked. "That's my girl." He twirled a lock of a woman's red hair.

Shuddering, Jon let his gaze wander to nothing. Rielle's intensity in the pit still haunted him.

"You're past the point of leaving now, aren't you?" Leigh brought his cup to his lips.

Jon had promised not to, but the promise had proved more convenient now than simply binding. Even if he were free to leave, he couldn't say with certainty that he would. She'd made that difficult.

"You'll soon have a choice to make. Backward or forward. Known or unknown." Leigh sighed. "If you choose the unknown, make no mistake—"

"I would never hurt her," Jon interrupted, the words escaping his mouth without leave of his mind. But they were genuine. Not that he'd ever choose to break his vows, but just what was the mage insinuating?

"She'll eat you alive."

Jon grimaced. "What?"

Leigh leaned in, resting an elbow on the table. "She will reach into you" —he held out his hand—"grab your heart"—curled his fingers—"rip it out"—drew his hand toward his own chest—"and crush it." He clenched a fist and leaned back in his chair, eyebrow raised over an unflinching stare.

The whole show lit the mage from within, his dramatic pantomiming lending a gleam to his dark eyes. "The man who will ultimately stand at her side will be forged in fire. If you burn easily, don't even bother."

The mage speaks from experience.

Jon raised his eyebrows. "You love her."

Leigh scoffed and leaned back in his chair, letting the women resume their fawning. "You say 'love' as if there is just your kind—the aching, yearning, sweaty, romantic kind." He gave a careless shrug. "To her, I have been guardian, teacher, master, partner, lover, friend—spanning a decade. The kind of love she and I share is something you could never understand, will never understand. She and I are beyond romantic love." A wistful smile lit his face, then faded. "But she's lost everyone. And it would bring me comfort if she found joy." Leigh met his gaze soberly. "Do you believe you can deliver?"

His chest tight, Jon considered a reply when the doors opened.

The entire establishment hushed. A man entered, tall and handsome, with a devilish smirk and a confident swagger, his overcoat of the finest black velvet, a signet ring adorning his fifth finger. A noble, and a landowner at that.

Accompanied by two blond women, he claimed a large, plush curved divan in the corner with a view of the entire brothel, sprawling across it with unmistakable dominance. One leg hung over the divan's arm as he surveyed his domain with imperious eyes.

"Who is that?" Jon inquired quietly. He recognized the man's face but couldn't place it.

Leigh frowned in distaste. "Fortune shits on this day. That is none other than Marquis Tregarde, Brennan Karandis Marcel."

"Duke Faolan Auvray Marcel's son and heir?" Jon asked.

Tor, Jon's former paladin-master, was the duke's brother, making Brennan Tor's nephew. It had been years, but he hadn't forgotten the intense young man so unreasonably jealous of the attention his favorite uncle had paid his squire. Nor his beautiful sister, Nora, for that matter—who'd boldly declared her intention to pursue a paladin's squire. He grimaced. He'd spent the better part of a fortnight evading her.

"The one and only," Leigh said flatly. "He's considered one of the cleverest men in Emaurrian society, and one of the cruelest."

"Oh?" Although the marquis had seemed aloof in Maerleth Tainn, that had been the extent of his impression.

The women huddled closer, too.

"When he was nine, he was engaged to a girl five years his junior," Leigh began. "When she lost her family at thirteen, he went to where she was staying and begged her to return with him to Maerleth Tainn for her safety, that they'd marry within a couple of years, that he'd protect her. On his knees, before all the kitchen staff, he begged her." Leigh took a drink. "She refused him."

"Why?"

The levity in his face chased away, Leigh pulled free of the women. "She was scared. She felt safe where she was. I'm sure the marquis knew that, but refusal is difficult to accept for a duke's son." Leigh earned a few smirks from his entourage. "He left in a temper, and word of the refusal spread quickly among the Houses. He took lovers, one after another, and a few years later, she took one herself. Her relationship became public—humiliating the marquis to all society—but he was handsome, titled, and vastly rich. It should have been nothing to him. When her lover abandoned her, the marquis invited her to Tregarde."

"To put it all behind them?"

For a moment, the mage's gaze dropped to the table. "He lavished her with gifts, love letters, luxury... Heartbroken and lonely, she went, hoping to reconcile. Indeed, he held a fête, danced with her, romanced her. They stole away to the kitchen and, in a back room, did as young lovers are wont to do."

"Then he married her after all?"

Tregarde wore a relaxed smirk, an arm around each woman and his left booted ankle resting loosely on his right knee. Unlikely.

"During the fête, a few of his guests wandered in at an inopportune moment for her, but he called them in and said he'd be along presently, now that he'd had some relief. Shattered, his fiancée begged him before his guests not to forsake her. But viciously, he refused her—humiliating *her* to all society. She left in disgrace. Nobles have tangled with him rarely, and only to their detriment, since."

Looking away, Jon rubbed his eyebrow. If the story was true, then Tregarde was a malicious man. Without honor. "What happened to them?"

Leigh shrugged. "They're still engaged."

Jon frowned. "But how? They must hate each other."

"Nobles do not marry for love, but for power, position, and fortune. She brings an entire march as her dowry, being the last of her line. And he can make her a duchess. Nonetheless, she petitioned the king to release her from her marriage contract, but—no surprise—King Marcus denied it. Tregarde's father, the duke, has a lot of influence." Leigh's eyes went cold.

He slumped his shoulders and drained his wine. "The air in here has turned foul, ladies, so we take our leave."

In the face of several downturned mouths, Leigh furnished a handful of argents from his coin purse and extricated himself from the appreciative women. The mage was generous with his wealth.

"Now," Leigh said, "I promised Rielle I'd protect you—"

Jon bolted out of his chair. "I don't need your—"

"You and I both know Rielle's... concern for you goes far beyond this... venture." Leigh lowered his chin, his dark eyes frank. "If your presence—however bewilderingly—brings her joy, then I'm not letting you out of my sight until we're back at the inn."

Wide stance. Open demeanor. Relaxed posture. By all signs, this man spoke sincerely. Leigh drowned in licentiousness and inebriation yet seemed selflessly devoted to the happiness of a former lover. A friend. He defied quick judgment.

The suffocating protection grated, but Jon didn't want to delay their departure any longer. "Let's go."

As they made their way toward the exit, he glanced in Tregarde's direction. Tregarde turned his head then, looking directly at him, and gave him a knowing wink before returning his attention to the women with him.

Unnerved, Jon followed Leigh out.

23

A cold wind blew in from the open window. Rielle shivered and, rubbing her arms, moved to close it. Outside, people walked the streets in cloaks and warm clothes. The autumn had chilled, and soon it would be winter.

Winter. She and Olivia had made plans to spend Midwinter together in Courdeval, but Divine only knew whether the city would survive until the day. Courdeval was in turmoil, and Olivia might be there, trapped, hurt, or worse. And no one was coming for her.

Rielle buttoned her white shirt and tucked it into her trousers, chewing her lip. Interfering in Courdeval unsanctioned would deprive her of the Divinity's protection. No more contract to keep her safe. Brennan's father could enforce her arranged marriage.

None of it mattered. Not when Olivia's life was at stake.

But perhaps Olivia had somehow made it out. There had to be a chance.

She had to know whether Olivia was alive and in Courdeval before throwing her life away. She laced her leather vest.

In Bournand, there was one person who could tell her Olivia's current condition and location—the Sileni spiritualist, Feliciano Donati. Before he'd given in to his sen'a addiction, he had been a respected master doyen teaching at the Tower, his expertise the study of anima in resonance. A spiritualist, he was able to detect, enhance, disrupt, punish, and otherwise affect anima.

Feliciano was an epicure of anima, and quaternary elementalist anima was rare. Answers from him would come at a high cost, but she needed them. Badly.

She would pay whatever she had to.

But before she could justify it, she had to know that was her only option.

There was something Leigh wasn't telling her. She trusted him implicitly, but his booking an incognito Tower-reserved room at The Crowned Stag didn't make any sense. Even if The Velvet Glove was fully booked, there were a dozen other brothels he could have stayed at.

If he truly wanted to keep something from her, trying to drag it out of him would be an exercise in futility. She'd have to find out for herself. Maybe there was something there... anything... that could spare her Feliciano's price. If Leigh was hiding something, it would be something big; he didn't bother with anything but.

She winced. He had never given her reason to distrust him. It was weak, it was selfish, but she had to try. Anything that could spare her further wrath from Brennan.

She pulled on her boots, clasped her white cloak, locked the door, and headed for the stable.

Something Leigh wasn't telling her... She huffed. He wasn't the only one.

Those sellswords who'd come looking for Jon—*It's obvious they're looking for paladins*, he'd said. Just how stupid did he think her? Some adversary hunted every paladin in Emaurria?

She grumbled and saddled her mare. What kind of trouble was Jon in? Over the course of only one week, they'd crossed paths with two sellswords and Flame of the Crag Company. Either he withheld the details of his trouble, her own past had come back to haunt her, or coincidence laughed in her face.

If Jon could just be honest with her, she'd be better able to protect him.

Like this, however, he forced her to proceed blindly. Whatever it was, it couldn't be worse than endangering both their lives. But that's what came of trust. For most people, it was granted only to be broken. She had learned that well enough and often, and the lesson still smarted.

She hissed. *Leigh*. Was her trust still well placed with him?

Time to find out.

She pulled up the hood of her coat and took the long ride to the Beck, where The Velvet Glove and several middling establishments did business.

Despite the somber atmosphere, the city bustled with preparations for Vindemia. She pushed her way through.

After stabling her horse, she shouldered her way in, scanning the bar and tables for familiar faces. The Velvet Glove appeared unaffected by the national tragedy or, perhaps, even more populated than usual.

A well-dressed, pretty hostess bounced toward her in blush-pink skirts and a matching low-cut bodice. "Good morning, my lady. What's your pleasure this fine day?"

Inundated by a freesia-scented fog, Rielle shook her hand, sneaking a corona into the hostess's palm and eliciting an excited gasp. It was more than most made in a month.

She leaned in close to the young woman's ear. "Here to visit the guest in Leigh Galvan's room, if you'd be so kind."

The hostess beamed a high-noon smile. "Certainly."

She followed the hostess through the brothel's main room and into a hallway, where moans and laughter hung thick in the air. At the end of the hall, the hostess stopped and, with a courteous tilt of her head, gestured to a door. "Anything else, my lady?"

"That's all for now, thanks."

Grinning, the hostess disappeared down the hall.

Part of a broken pewter key protruded from the lock. Foul play. Steeling herself, she knocked. Twice.

No signs of life came from inside.

In the noisy hallway, she assessed the door, backed up, and took a preparatory breath, waiting to time the strike with the thumping a few doors down.

There. She side-kicked just below the doorknob—hard—with her heel. It budged but didn't open. The thud, thankfully, hadn't drawn attention. It blended in well enough.

Short of burning the door down or blowing it apart, she didn't have any other option but to continue. At least her sometimes-lover Launce had taught her a practical thing or two between bouts in bed. Broadsteel mercenaries possessed a different but useful skill set.

Timing it, she kicked the door in the same spot, and it bent inward a bit more. Again. Finally, she turned around and hit it with a back kick.

It flew open. Far from smooth, but acceptable. With a look down the hallway, she slipped into the room.

Empty.

With a sigh, she closed the door.

Nearly every surface was littered with clothes, papers, cups, glass shards, bread, apples, sausage, cheese, remnants of a broken chair. There'd been a struggle.

On the far wall, curtains billowed in the breeze of the open window. She crept near and peered out between laundry on clotheslines at the fast-moving stream below. Following its path, she spotted a long, cylindrical case caught among some reeds.

The Divinity used such cases for important documents transport. If the contents even resembled those she'd carried, it was valuable.

With a curl of her finger, she focused on the water, guiding a steady trickle up and apart from the stream to bear the case to the window. She pulled in more and more water, lengthening the spelled trickle, until at last the case was close enough to grasp. Checking for any witnesses, she reached out and took it, then dispelled the trickle of water. It splashed to the ground. She turned back to the room.

A man—

Instinct took over. She cast an ice shard at the large intruder. It thudded into the wall. Behind Brennan.

Where had he—

He seized her arm and twisted it behind her back, sending her face and chest crashing into the wall and the case rolling on the floor. Pain spiked in her cheekbone and clavicle.

He grabbed her other arm and leaned in.

"Calm down," he growled into her ear.

Her heart racing, she thrashed in his hold, but he only twisted her arm higher, until it hurt. "Let me go."

He pressed her harder against the wall. "Are you scared?" A taunting smile lurked in his voice.

Her chest crushed against the paneled wood. "Never."

"You should be." Something like a laugh rumbled in his throat. "I could do anything to you here, and no one would stop me. No one would even know."

She clenched her teeth. "Then stop talking about it and do it already. Give me a reason to destroy you."

He scoffed. "Your magic does nothing to me, and you know it."

Immune to all magic, Brennan had proved himself something of an anomaly, besides being a werewolf. Or perhaps all werewolves were immune to magic. She'd never met another to test her theory. But he healed quickly on his own and never fell ill, and had collected a series of sigils to justify his magic resistance to others. An empty way to spend thousands of coronas, but he'd kept his secret even from his family.

Brennan traced a finger down her cheek and then, with an effortless motion, unclasped her white cloak and continued tracing over her jaw, down her neck, and toward her shoulder. "You still think wearing white can ever make you clean?"

She recoiled. He certainly didn't lack for boldness when he didn't need the favor of her blood before the full moon. What did he want? What was this stupid game?

But he allowed her no reprieve. When he got to the collar of her white shirt, he yanked it down to her upper arm with a yielding rip.

She flinched, and as he brought his nose against her skin and inhaled, she froze. Too far. She threw her head back into his face.

He evaded, and she brought her heel down on his foot. He loosened his grip on her just enough for her to wrench free. Without a wasted second, he lunged, but she dragged a chair between them. Fire came to her palm—a shield between them like a scrolling, blazing rune.

He stopped short, pure amusement on his hateful face. An entertained laugh followed. "Who taught you that move? That brainless Broadsteel clod?"

"If you try to hurt me—"

"Hurt you?" His mouth cracked in a too-wide, unnerving grin. "I already have. Irreparably."

She didn't need the reminder. It had been years since she'd been able to show her face at home or at Gran's, thanks to him. No—thanks to her own naïveté. Never again.

Her eyes darted toward the cylindrical case. "What do you want?"

With a heavy, dramatic sigh, he looked off to the side, flexing his biceps in his black velvet overcoat.

He eyed her peripherally, flashing a crooked smile. "You know what I want."

Did he expect her to be afraid? She pursed her lips. No joy for him.

He rested his gaze just above her head. "I could feel you in the city. When you passed nearby, I was curious." He gestured around. "A middling brothel? Really?" He exaggerated a skeptical eyebrow raise. "We both know you prefer to fuck commoners. Try a place in Copper End."

Pain radiated from her jaw. How could he talk to her like that? But he was trying to get a reaction. She knew it.

She knew it, but she couldn't control the tremors that shook her body. All of her lovers had been commoners to a man, but not a common man among them. They knew how to respect a woman, to treat a lover properly, which was more than Brennan could claim.

"Jealous?" she cut.

A mocking puff. "Don't flatter yourself." He drew in a quick breath. "You don't yet reek of the new knave's sweat. Not common enough for you?"

Knave? She checked her urge to fight back. It would only whet his appetite for insults and draw more attention to Jon. And the last thing she wanted was for Brennan to take an interest in him.

Slowly, she raised her chin. "You seem very concerned with who shares my bed, for a man who's not interested."

" 'Concerned,' " he spat with derision, kicking aside the chair between them.

She held the fire shield before her despite its uselessness against him. At the very least, it made her feel stronger.

Brennan leaned in. "I'm only 'concerned' to the extent that it rattles you."

His vengeance would have no end. He would torment her to the end of her days, forever attempting to treat his old, festering wound with her misery.

She squared her shoulders.

"Nine years, and your ego is still bleeding." She braced herself for an attack, but Brennan only donned a joyless smile. He stared at her, his gaze unbroken, for an intense moment. Then he sighed and looked around the room.

"So what brings you here?" He paced the small room with a practiced nonchalance, opened a book on the table, and idly flipped a page. "Business? It's certainly not pleasure."

A shiver shook her spine. All his animosity had disappeared, as though it had never been.

What did he want?

She dispelled her fire shield but remained alert. How to answer him? *Investigating whether Leigh's story checked out?* No, she couldn't tell him that. "I wanted to know who was staying here."

"Have you tried asking?"

She rolled her eyes.

With a shrug, Brennan approached the bed and then crouched to pick up a shirt. He brought it to his nose and breathed deep. A frown creased his brow. "The mage who pushed you down the stairs in the Tower last year. What was his name?"

"Kieran," she answered.

But she had never mentioned the incident to him. On laundry duty, she'd been carrying a stack of folded sheets from the laundry to the fifth floor when Kieran had pushed her from the fifth-floor landing. She'd tumbled an entire flight of stairs and nearly cracked her skull open but for the sheets. She'd awoken in the infirmary. No one had come forward as a witness but for the apprentice who'd found her, bleeding and unconscious, and so before the Proctor, it had been her word against Kieran's. No reprimand.

Curiously, about a month later, Kieran had returned from the local tavern looking like one large bruise and had given her a wide berth thereafter.

"How do you know about that?"

Brennan crumpled the shirt in his grasp. "Rumor. People seem to think I'm interested in what befalls you." His hazel eyes brightened. "Your suffering amuses me."

Despite his words, she shook her head. Coincidence was no acquaintance of Brennan Karandis Marcel. "A month later, when he returned black and blue... that was you, wasn't it?" She frowned. "Some sort of possessive reaction?"

He rose and let the shirt fall to the floor. "If it had been me, only his shoulder would have been black and blue, from a congratulatory pat for a job well done."

She jerked her head back. Which was more shocking? Brennan making a trip to the Tower's village to interfere in a small spat? Or denying it with such effort?

A nervous laugh threatened to escape, but she contracted her belly, gulped a breath. He had always been intent on eliminating anything that threatened the source of his control over the curse. But she couldn't see why he'd step into such a trivial matter, nor why he'd lie about it.

It didn't matter. She had more pressing concerns. Brennan had made his point; maybe now he'd let her work.

"Kieran," she repeated. "Why would he be here?" She shuffled about the room, looking through various items, and then opened the cylindrical case. It contained maps of Courdeval, its wealthy Azalée District, the palace grounds, and Trèstellan Palace itself.

She rummaged through the drawers and every space she could think of for anything more. In a knapsack were mage's coats, some men's clothes, and toiletries, among other things. Her fingertips brushed the unmistakable texture of leather. A book. She pulled it out and opened it. *Revelations in Hydromancy.* Inside the book was a placeholder—orders from Magehold.

Hydromancy. She paused. The heretics in the ruins had mentioned something about a hydromancer. *As long as that hydromancer is dealt with before he reaches his destination.* Was this the work of the heretics?

Brennan walked to the edge of the bed and lifted the mattress, then pulled something from beneath it.

Glass.

He held up a vial on a chain, with a dark-red liquid inside. Blood.

She set aside the book and took the vial. "Why would he have this?" When no answer came, she glanced back at Brennan and then at the open window. "There's no sign of Kieran. You think he took a trip out the window?"

"Defenestration?" Brennan approached the area, bringing a breeze-borne curtain to his nose. "Could be. I'm guessing this mage didn't break off the key in his own door, either."

"Are there any other scents here?"

"Dozens," he answered. "But chief among them, I smell your master."

Leigh? He wouldn't harm another Tower mage... but she didn't rule it out. He'd been prone to indulging Tower whisperings of conspiracy and hidden factions and black operations—rumors he'd once dismissed with a wave of his hand, as she did.

Perhaps he'd investigated the room. But why hadn't he said anything? If he'd wanted it kept secret, why hadn't he destroyed the evidence? She clutched the orders. She'd learn her answer, one way or the other.

She unfolded them, her eyes widening as she read.

Orders to infiltrate the capital and the palace—along with instructions to perform the Moonlit Rite in the catacombs of Trèstellan Palace... All to prevent a catastrophe referred to only as the Rift. Bearing the sign and seal of the Grand Divinus herself.

Her breath caught. The Rift? The relief of pressure from the other side that came with Hallowday—was that because of the Moonlit Rite? What would happen if it wasn't performed?

It was less than a month away.

She'd just seen Kieran the night she'd captured Jon. He must've gotten the orders soon after and had made better time to Bournand somehow.

A sudden coldness struck her core. Berny bursting from the Proctor's quarters. *It's the cap—*

The capital. Had the Proctor known about the situation in the capital when he'd sent her as Jon's escort? Had he intended to keep her from Olivia?

No mention of Olivia in Kieran's orders. But if Magehold was sending someone to perform the Moonlit Rite in her stead, the implications weren't promising.

Teardrops fell to the parchment, and she sniffed, folding it up to stuff into her shirt. She wiped her face with her sleeve; she didn't need Brennan's ridicule.

At a distance, he eyed her, eyebrows drawn, fingers twitching. If he'd wanted to see her upset, then he'd gotten what he'd come for. It was far from her first—or worst—humiliation in his presence.

She clasped the chain bearing the vial around her neck and tucked it into her shirt. Keeping an eye on Brennan, she fastened her cloak, pulled up her hood, and exited the room.

Olivia hadn't escaped. And if the Divinity had sent Kieran to perform the Archmage's duty—

No choice. She pressed her lips together. She would see Feliciano and certainly relapse under his ruinous demands, but no matter the price, she had to know Olivia's fate. *If she's alive, excommunication or not, even if I have to bind myself to Brennan for the rest of my life, I'm going into Courdeval.*

24

*S*oreness climbed up Olivia's arms. An attempt to flex her fingers yielded nothing but pain. Voices diverted her attention, but she kept her eyes closed, feigning unconsciousness. The dark—whether of closed eyes or dungeon—was no stranger to her and honed her hearing.

"Coordinate with the Heartseekers in Melain and take one with you to handle the problem, should they make it past Bournand. Make certain her charge is dead." Gilles.

"All this for Shadow, sir?" The saccharine soprano of the illusionist.

"All this because I wish it, Phantom, and you'd do well to remember I keep you well supplied." He forced out a breath. "And never forget who keeps your son alive. Displease me in any way, and I promise you, he will know it. Keenly."

Phantom. Another of Gilles's mage captains?

"Sir."

"And to the other matter, make them understand—I don't care how many paladins they have to kill. Tell them to keep at it."

"Yes, sir." A rustle of clothes, and footsteps retreated.

Olivia's heart shrank. That she was privy to an exchange between Gilles and one of his mage captains could mean only one thing. Utter failure.

Defeated, she dragged her eyes open, squinting against the abundant torchlight in the familiar macabre comfort of her dungeon cell. The iron bars repaired, it looked the same.

She hadn't escaped. She hadn't even been moved to an arcanir cell.

When she attempted to raise a hand to her forehead, pain lanced her arm. With a grimace, she peered at her hands. No, the misshapen oddities that may have once been hands, now ugly, grotesque. She could do naught with them but make them hurt more.

"Ah, Phantom took some... liberties during her custody of you, Lady Sabeyon." Gilles maintained a pleasant mask on his stubbled face.

Olivia's stomach rolled, and she grimaced, repressing the whimper that threatened to emerge. Her attempted escape had failed spectacularly.

But all was not lost. She had planned with dual purpose, after all.

Gilles held up the arcanir shackles, so small in his large palm. "Still locked." He peered at them, dark eyes gleaming. "I'm impressed, Lady Sabeyon. It must have been quite painful to slip these."

She pasted on a smile and forced herself to meet his gaze squarely. "It was easy."

As she raised her chin, something moved around her neck. And stung. Instinctively, she raised her hands to it, but agony tore through her arms. She winced and suppressed a vocalization, glancing down at the item awkwardly. She could just make out a padlock. An arcanir collar?

"Ah, yes. Phantom's idea. Not so... 'easy' to slip." He smiled pleasantly.

A sour taste formed in Olivia's mouth. "But I'm poisoned. You shouldn't need anything but that."

A knowing grin. "Always seeking information, aren't you, Lady Sabeyon? The arcanir poison will have already worn off. Phantom used a diluted formula on you. We're saving the concentrated poison for something... special."

Her chest tightened, and she fought to slow her accelerated breathing. Now was not the time to show fear. If she wanted to get into an arcanir cell, she'd have to bait him.

"You think I will allow you to use me against James indefinitely? These bars are nothing to me," she said, purposely adopting a languid pose. "I escaped once, and I will escape again, or your men will kill me. Either way, you will have nothing left to use against James."

"You are a clever woman, Lady Sabeyon," Gilles said, pacing the cell. He toed an intricately carved box on the floor, and Olivia's blood ran cold. "And because you are so clever, if you truly hoped to escape on your own power, you would not posture so recklessly."

Perceptive. She had to hedge. "I am confident."

"Confidence, when on the back foot, is for fools and schemers." He speared her with a piercing stare. "And we are not fools, are we, Lady Sabeyon?"

She swallowed and fought back a shudder. Yet everything inside her trembled.

"Am I to believe, then, that you are so eager for death?" He rested his hand on the pommel of a massive five-foot blade he wore. "The new Archmage, a fresh twenty-six years of age?"

She looked away.

"Wrong answer, Lady Sabeyon." He crouched until his face was level with hers. "You want to be locked in an arcanir cell."

She drew in a deep breath. "Why would I want that, General? Escape, then, would be truly hopeless."

"So would spirit magic."

She fought to keep the disappointment from her face.

"I want the marquise to find you, Lady Sabeyon. I want her to come." At that, he rose.

Had it all been so artless? "Why? Why do you want her to come? What do you gain by all this?"

He leaned against the bars. "I gave my word to Shadow once that I now intend to fulfill. Keeping my word is its own reward."

How forthcoming. He was helping Shadow with some personal vendetta?

Olivia narrowed her eyes. "So was the invasion of the capital and the murder of King Marcus 'keeping your word' as well?"

"Invasion?" He crossed his arms over his massive chest. "I am keeping the peace after the horrific regicide of our most beloved monarchs."

She had heard tales of such "peace keepers" before, even of Gilles himself, who had "kept the peace" in Signy after clearing the area of bandits, seeking a "reasonable fee" for his unsolicited services. Leigh and Rielle had been tasked with ousting him.

"And is the next king inclined to be grateful?" she ventured.

Gilles sniffed. "It depends on how thoroughly I keep the peace." He smiled at her, torchlight softening the austere black of his hair. "It's a pity you can't be allowed to survive after your friend's capture. I enjoy your intellect."

A murderer enjoying her intellect. She sucked her lower lip, guarding reckless words.

"We climb from low and humble origins as commoners, Lady Sabeyon," he said softly, "but we have risen to great heights, high enough to gnaw at the scraps cast aside by the gods among men."

She wanted to scoff, but she couldn't. How far had she come from a thatched hovel, where she and her entire family had slept in one room? She could have lived comfortably at the Tower as a healer, a researcher, or a doyen, or perhaps posted in some village as a healer and one of the nouveau riche, but indeed, the air higher up seemed clearer, crisper, sweeter. And she had found herself advising the king of one of the region's strongest nations, and loved by one of its princes.

What she wouldn't do to feel James's hand in hers again, to lay her head on his chest, content and carefree.

And now I find myself in a dungeon, awaiting my death. "A great rise, General, may beget a great fall. Take care where you step."

He squinted, his eyes lit with an inner glow. "I will remember your cautionary tale, Lady Sabeyon." He pushed off the bars and left the cell, locking the door with a click, and nodded toward the box on the floor of her cell. "Some consolation for you."

With those final words, he strode down the corridor, leaving the torch behind.

Consolation?

Her gaze settled on the box, blurring as the minutes passed. One part of her wanted to open it; another didn't. Perhaps it would keep her company here, mysteriously, until the drawn thread of her fate was finally cut.

How long had she been locked up? Days? Weeks?

She would die here, the first utter failure of an Archmage, a girl born into a family of fishmongers in Caerlain Trel's Copper Bottom, who had risen to Emaurria's most decorated mage office only to end in the grime of a dungeon? She moved to wipe away her tears but yelped at the touch of her broken hands. There was nothing she could do.

Yet hope still glimmered in her heart. If Rielle came, there might be life after all of this, perhaps even saving the kingdom from the Rift, the tearing of the Veil, the return of every Immortal monster to have ever walked the earth. The end of mankind.

But unless Rielle came with an army to take back the palace for good, she would have to sneak in and out on Spiritseve, close enough to midnight to perform the rite.

But there was no way she could know it needed to be performed... *And that it won't be.*

Even if it had become no more than a simple tradition to some, even if no one outside the royal family and Olivia herself knew the full extent of the Rift, everyone in Emaurria assigned significance to the Moonlit Rite. There was a chance.

You will feel it in your blood, Rielle. And you'll know I wasn't here for nothing.

She'd left one note, a shorthand for herself, in her room under runic protection. Even if Rielle didn't come, the Divinity would send someone to perform the rite. It had to. If somehow the Moonlit Rite were performed, she could—

No. She shook her head. James. She could never go to her grave quietly while James suffered, and she remained the instrument of it all.

The box Gilles had brought sat, waiting in the torchlight, inviting her fingers to its lid. *Consolation*, Gilles had called it. Did James yet live?

To Gilles, which was the consolation? After such torture, was it life? Or death?

Her chest grew heavier with every shaky breath, and she crawled toward the box. Her broken fingers reached the intricate carvings on its surface before she could stop them. Pain wriggled up her arm.

James...

She had to know.

Breathing fast and deep, she raised the lid slowly, every muscle in her body resisting the pain with rigidity. With a cry, she threw it open.

James had touched her with hands roughened by battle yet soft in their caress, his fingers long and elegant but capable of strength, his palms broad but gentle.

The same hand that had stroked her so lovingly lay nestled on a bed of sea-blue silk.

25

*R*ielle squinted at the shops in the distance. Only the familiar grayed scrap of fabric hanging over the entrance marked the building as Donati's.

As she entered, a haze of smoke clouded her vision, and it took a moment for her eyes to adjust to the dim lighting. Several intimate alcoves accommodated six to eight people each, seated on sumptuous cushions and secluded by diaphanous veils in shades of aubergine, sapphire, and emerald.

Massive tapestries bathed the walls, depicting revelry, feasting, drinking, smoking, and swiving to excess, ripples of roisterous debauchery. Excess she'd already spent too much of her life drowning in. Such places had once held an irresistible allure, a promise of escape from painful reality to exquisite numbness.

False numbness.

Within the alcoves, patrons lay sprawled in disarrayed heaps, high on sen'a and the pleasure of resonance, revelers summoned from the tapestries behind them.

On the low tables tucked into each alcove lay trance pipes and pouches of dark powder: a higher state of being, reduced to fine grains to be smoked or consumed. Sen'a.

Her mouth watering, she took a deep breath and approached the counter. *Here to talk, not to use.* She placed her gloved hands on the uneven polished surface, scanning the room for Feliciano. Her gaze fixed on a half-full paper pouch nearby, and she drummed her fingers.

"Trance?" a breathy man's voice offered.

A frail young man with dull eyes stood behind the counter. The clerk partook of the goods himself. Unsurprising.

"I'm here to see Feliciano."

Feliciano famously had a lavish house in the city, but he'd always been hands on, especially when it came to sen'a. He would have spent most of his time here, in the thick of things.

"May I ask who wants to see him?" the clerk slurred.

"No." She didn't need rumor peddling her name linked to a resonance den.

The clerk lowered his head and peeked under her hood.

His eyes flashed an intense red. She tried to jerk away—too late. She'd seen such eyes before. Damned augurs, always prying where they weren't invited.

A chill shook her body like wind across naked skin. She shuddered, shrugged deeper into her coat. It was still on, Divine be praised.

"Burning sands at your feet. A walk through desolation. A paradise of torment. Red water," he announced, rocking. His eyes widened, vivid, blazing fiery rings. "Red water."

The augur shrugged back into his lazy stance.

Red water. She exhaled sharply. Augurs looked into the future and the past and spoke in fragments, riddles, and metaphors. Hopefully, whatever he'd seen was tucked firmly in the past. Divine knew she'd certainly spilled enough *red water* on missions.

"I'll tell him," he said. "Have a seat."

A shiver rattled her spine as he turned and trudged to the back room. Better those eyes meet someone else's.

The sound of melodic thumps drew her attention to her fingers.

They'd been tapping of their own accord. *Damned sen'a.*

She lowered her hand to her side, looking out into the den for diversion until her gaze settled on an empty alcove.

The turquoise and magenta pillows there looked soft and comfortable, inviting, the sheen of their velveteen texture illuminated by a paper lantern above the alcove's low table. *Come, stay a spell,* they said. The paper lantern bathed its immediate vicinity in faint yellow light but did little to brighten anything beyond the tray with two trance pipes, flint and pyrite, and other sen'a consumption accoutrements. Mere things. Not dangerous.

There's no harm in sitting. She took a deep breath and made her way there.

Not a single person paid her any mind as she passed. Thank the Divine for small favors. The last thing she needed was to be seen associating with Feliciano again. Word of this visit would make a rousing farewell kiss to her dreams of the magister's mantle.

At the empty alcove, she paused. It was only taking a seat. Nothing more. The cushions were softer than they looked. Comfortable. She rested her elbows on her knees, staring from beneath her hood at the trance pipe. It was long and elegant, despite its mean purpose.

The bodies writhing in adjacent alcoves appeared little more than shadows in a dream, their moans and languid, euphoric laughter ghostly amid the smoky fumes. And they *were* ghosts—ones who had long since forgotten the purpose of resonance was to prepare anima for greater endurance in service. Something she remembered. Remembered well.

Did they use magic at all anymore, or did they resonate only for the sheer pleasure of the preparation? Magic was anima structured, trans-formed, while resonance was primal—raw union. Was that how they lived, reduced to that primordial essence?

And none took greater pleasure in resonance than a spiritualist, whose magic ruled all anima. Feliciano had once told her resonance to a spiritualist was more immediate than reality—sight, taste, sensation, smell, sound— with each mage creating a different reality, depending on their magic and the shape of their lives. An experience other mages couldn't even imagine. And enhanced with sen'a, that reality lasted months, even years, in the span of hours.

Some spiritualists spent their lives resisting the lure of the resonance dimension. And others embraced it, becoming anima gourmands, wasting away their years in euphoric inertia.

Feliciano Donati wasn't a mere gourmand; he was a connoisseur.

Slowly, a slight figure approached from the periphery. Rielle reclined, her eyes fixed on Feliciano's chiseled face, his lips curved up in the most placid of smiles, framed by his jaw-length black curls.

He sauntered toward the lounge and descended to the cushioned seat, splaying out lazily like a lounging desert king, dressed in a long black brocade caftan tied with a gray silk sash, loose pants, and flat leather slip-pers. He faced her with that placid smile.

"We meet again, *Favriella*," he drawled pleasantly, with the alveolar trill typical of Sileni speakers.

She flinched, looking around to make sure no one had heard her name.

He glanced at the tray. "Will it be *como di comsueto,* the usual, my dear *fiamma?*"

The usual. She grimaced. Three years ago, when she and Leigh had been forced to part, she'd found solace in Feliciano's Tower rooms, in the bowl of a trance pipe. Minutes, hours, and days had passed in resonance with Feliciano and his trancers, her only cognitive moments the hazy awakenings in Feliciano's bed, when her fingers reached for the trance pipe of their own volition. There, in that dark, smoky room, she had tried to use sen'a, trance, resonance, and Feliciano to patch the wounds Leigh and her vengeful fiancé had left seeping.

It was a different time. A horrible, numb, lulling, comforting, rapturous time.

Even as she shook her head, she fixed her attention upon the trance pipe. "I need answers."

Looking away with a pout, Feliciano shrugged casually. "For that, *fiamma*, I'll require payment." He rolled up his sleeve and held out a wan hand adorned with gold, on nearly every finger and his wrists. The jewelry overflowed from his limbs to his neck, one of his ears, a nostril.

She peered down at the solitary black tablet in his palm. Concentrated sen'a. "I have money." *Take that instead. Please.*

"As do I."

She knew what he wanted. Tranced resonance, as always.

"Perhaps without the sen'a?" Her stomach churned, and Feliciano smiled. She held her breath, muscles taut, the fine hairs on the back of her neck raised.

"In another life, another time, *fiamma*. Do you wish for your answers?"

Inside her, a shrill voice cried a warning. Olivia had been there for her last time, helped her through the withdrawal—and she would never approve of this. She had elicited a promise never to use sen'a again. *Promise me, Rielle*, she had said. *Promise me. Never again. Never again, or so help me—*

But I need answers. Spiritualists were scarce, and Feliciano was the only one in Bournand, if not Emaurria. *I need to know Olivia's alive before I throw away the rest of my life.*

Forgive me, Olivia...

Rielle swallowed. The black tablet waited in his hand. "You don't even know what I plan to ask."

"I know that I will have an answer."

Feliciano did not move, nor did his repose falter.

"Isn't there anything else—"

"What can you offer a spiritualist who has everything?" Feliciano gestured lazily about the room, the sharp angles of his body obvious beneath the brocade—he'd been remiss in eating again. Too long in the resonance dimension. "Spirit."

She stared at the tablet. Such a small thing. It would be nothing, less than nothing, to accept it and render payment to him. Just once.

The judgment on Jon's face when he'd accused her of using sen'a or trux flickered in her mind. Paladins did not pollute their bodies with the likes of sen'a. Would he turn away from her in disgust if he knew? Would he hate her for what she was about to do?

I can't break my troth to Most Holy Terra on a mere whim, he'd said.

Even if she disgusted him, if he hated her, if he kept his distance, she had to do this. For Olivia's sake. And for her own.

After a long, slow drag of her glove, she reached for Feliciano's offering. The sen'a tablet was small and hard, but soon, it would bloom like a floret of ecstasy uncurling into a thousand blossoming bouquets, soft petals that would eventually harden to thorns beneath her skin. She shivered.

With a trembling hand, she raised it to her lips and held it there for a time, taking a deep, venerating breath before she accepted it into her mouth and swallowed. As it descended down her throat, she closed her eyes.

When she looked back at Feliciano, he was holding a goblet of wine out to her.

Time folding. She must have welcomed it, because its warmth still burned inside her as she peered into the mostly empty goblet in her grasp. She threw her head back into the pillows and rubbed her face against velvet while her hand dropped into his. The goblet clinked to the floor and rolled with a metallic whirl that faded... faded... faded...

The draw dragged at power in her veins, anima to anima. Feliciano's pulled hers, seeking connection through their fingertips. She waded through the phantoms clustering at the Veil, shouldering through, and attracted his in return until they made contact. Inside, the luminance of her azure anima took on a violet aura—Feliciano's—and shimmered. Finally, a ripple of pulsating energy erupted, bringing with it the promise of pleasure.

That pleasure spread languidly like an overflowing cup, saturating every corner of her until she trembled on the cushions, her skin sensitive to the faintest breeze. Far away, someone opened a door, and as the fresh air kissed her skin, she quivered. Feliciano exhaled deeply, and the chill of his breath reached her—a puff of air from the flap of a moth's wing, her head swimming with bliss as she writhed.

She forced her eyes open, and her vision blurred. A strand of hair before her, her own, came into and out of focus.

Her eyelids fluttering, she shook with sensation, and beyond that strand, she saw her hand on a turquoise pillow, relaxing and contracting. She rolled her eyes in Feliciano's direction. He sat with his head thrown back, and his closed eyes tightened in pleasure. Her view of him multiplied as he became two, four, six Felicianos, and she shut her eyes, frowning to contain a moan from the shiver that ran through her, flowing along her spine like the Divine's own caress.

Chasing the sensation, she focused on her shimmering anima and the pleasure that radiated from it, reveling in its throbbing for a time that stretched minutes, hours, days...

When she opened her eyes, her field of vision was narrow, no more than a dim slit of gossamer, tapestries, and a lit lantern. She reached up to touch her face, her hands deviating from their intended path until they dumbly felt her tense cheeks at last, bringing her to the slow conclusion that she was beaming from ear to ear.

She shook her head and laughed, intending only a chuckle, but somehow, it amplified and lasted for what felt like an hour, lasting until long after her teeth had grown cold from the exposure to the cool air.

"Fe... li... ciano." She rolled her head to face him.

He peered at her, a smoking trance pipe hanging from his lips. "What I wouldn't give for your now low tolerance, *fiamma*," he said between puffs. "Ask me your questions."

Questions...

She rolled her head back and blinked, trying to remember them. Her eyes jarred open, and she was cold, so cold, and alone. Feliciano was gone, and a heavy woolen blanket covered her. She tried to sit up, but her body refused to cooperate, and she collapsed into a fleshy heap.

Hands caressed her face—she looked up at the person they belonged to.

"I'd forgotten the rush of resonance with you—a quaternary elementalist." Feliciano peered down at her, seated upon the lounge, casually sipping some wine. "The ends, heights, and depths of the universe, *fiamma*."

"Olivia Sabeyon." She swallowed. "Does she live?"

He shut his eyes and, for a moment, glowed violet. When he looked at her again, his irises were purple. "She lives," he said, his voice an eerie harmony, "but her anima is bound." He blinked, and the glow disappeared.

"Bound?" she asked. "What does that mean? Where?"

"Arcanir bonds, usually," he replied with a shrug, then drew his brows together. "I felt her to the south, at the capital. Below ground." Clasping his hands, Feliciano leaned in closer to her face. "You are meddling in things much meaner than anima." His smiling mask flickered for a moment.

She tried to blink away the blur. Olivia was imprisoned—but alive. Bound in arcanir, underground... In the palace dungeon?

And no one was coming to help her. By the time the Grand Divinus's army arrived to break the siege in Courdeval, Olivia could be dead. There was only one thing to be done.

Rielle took a deep breath. If the Proctor found out, if the Magisterium found out, if the Grand Divinus found out—and they most certainly would—she would be excommunicated from the Divinity and forced to wed the man who had taken her broken heart, given her hope, then shattered it anew and humiliated her to all society. Who continually devised new ways to torment her.

But Olivia faced death.

It was no choice at all.

Olivia. I let you down today, but I won't let you die.

Come what may, Olivia would be free, alive, and well.

"How—" Rielle stammered. Her lucidity trailed in. The trance was wearing off. She eyed the doorway. "What time is it?"

The trance had felt like days, but it could have been minutes. The windowless building offered no clues.

"It is nearly dusk," Feliciano said.

She'd spent the entire day tranced out. Had Jon and Leigh finished their tasks? Her heart beat faster. And worse, would they come looking for her?

They couldn't find her here. Not Leigh. Not Jon. Especially not Jon.

She tried to rise from the lounge but faltered. Dazed, she slowly surrendered, sliding back down.

"Careful, *fiamma*," Feliciano cautioned. "Where are you rushing off to, anyway? *Puosso aiutarti a calmarti.*"

Calm down? Only if she could gather her wits about her and leave. "Then help me up."

Feliciano nodded, beckoning with two fingers for the clerk to come over. Shortly, the young augur arrived with a steaming mug of dark liquid and offered it to her.

"A favor for a good friend." Feliciano clasped his hands together and bowed his head.

Tendrils of steam rose from the black surface.

"Trux tea. If you must go, it will give you the ability."

Tiny white five-pointed stars, the flowers of the truxillensis plant, glimmered small smiles in stretches of endless desert flats, meek in their modest beauty. Heartwarming. Yet trux, made from its silky leaves, was known for its stimulant effects and, in high doses, could stop a heart dead.

It was not her first taste, and he was well aware. She had descended to such lows today, what was another few feet? Tipping the mug, she drank it down.

Feliciano rose and leaned over, eclipsing the paper lantern lighting the alcove. He tucked a small envelope into her décolletage.

She rolled her eyes up to meet his, beneath the mop of sable curls falling over his brow. He had such long eyelashes.

"In the event you require... *sollievo* later."

More sen'a—in case she desired to ease the withdrawal pains, if they came. The first time, about three years ago, after heavy use, had been excruciating, but she wouldn't make that same mistake again.

She nodded her understanding, and he pulled away enough for her to rise.

Her body cooperated. Good. Feliciano held his arms open, and she leaned in, allowing him to embrace her.

"Return to me should you require more. You know where to find me." When he released her, she nodded. "Any time, *fiamma*."

She staggered toward the door, acutely aware of the paper envelope against her skin, and its contents.

But there were far more important things than the weight she carried.

Olivia.

Looking inside herself, Rielle found her azure pool of anima, bright and glowing, and singled out the thread tied to Brennan—their bond. She tugged on that thread; he would come to her. Although she knew Olivia was alive, she would need his help to invade a heavily fortified city besieged by thousands of professional mercenaries.

But would he give it?

Brennan...

She shivered. At the end of this, when the Divinity dismissed her, she faced a lifetime of his punishment. The humiliation of three years ago, stretched over the waning years of her life...

26

Three Years Ago
The Emaurrian Tower of Magic

*C*urled up in her bed on a chilly afternoon, Rielle reread the last lines of Brennan's letter: *I humbly request the pleasure of your company this Midwinter at Tregarde. Forgive a foolish boy his ego, and do the wiser man the great privilege of a second chance.*

She had accepted his invitation, but what to make of this sudden change of heart? Last she'd heard, he'd taken up with Chantal Barthélémy Armel, the seventeen-year-old daughter of Marquis Jean Vignon Armel of Quatrebeaux and jewel of the Emaurrian court. Had that changed?

It must have.

Rielle folded the letter. Did he now understand she'd had to make a difficult choice six years ago, not to spite him, but to save those around him and herself? Her magic was less volatile now. Thanks to the Divinity, the Tower, the doyens, Leigh...

Leigh. More heartbreak there. After the outing of their affair and Leigh's demotion, he'd rebuffed her attempts to reconcile, flaunting one new lover after the next and breaking her heart anew. In truth, the thought of staying at the Tower for Midwinter, witness to Leigh's never-ending string of lovers, was intolerable.

And Brennan's letter... Could they put this old feud to bed, live as their parents had intended? His words gave her hope that she had scarcely dared to dream. And she did have much to tell him—not that he'd been in a mood to listen before. Leigh's position as a magister had granted her, as his apprentice, access to the forbidden section of the Tower of Magic's library, and she'd researched answers. There, she'd translated ancient tomes until she'd found one about sangremancy curses.

The Old Emaurrian text called the result of a sangremancy curse a *blood bond*, formed between the bloodline of a curse's caster and that of his or her target. Master and thrall. Long ago, a sangremancer of her bloodline must have cursed Brennan's to an eternity of beastliness, every firstborn son of every firstborn son—a spell paid for with the entirety of one's anima.

A mage in her family had died to curse his.

But a blood curse could be ended by uniting their bloodlines. By conceiving a *child*.

She'd kept the knowledge to herself, weighing the decision of whether to tell him or not. The curse made both her and Brennan its pawns; by conceiving a child, they could both be free, and yet, by doing so, they'd be more bound to each other than ever. She sighed. There were no easy answers.

In the weeks since she'd accepted his invitation, he'd surprised her with a lavish correspondence that included gowns, jewels, and trinkets, and love letters the likes of which she never could have anticipated.

If he meant these last lines...

Could the man she'd been engaged to since age five have forgiven her, welcomed her back into his heart? Was it as simple as that? She wanted to believe it.

If he had changed, if he wanted to marry her and she him, then perhaps it was time to discuss it.

Her heart swelled. If Brennan had become a man who could forgive, who could love her even at her worst, then she could allow herself to love him, too. She could marry him. She could do all that her parents had wanted for her and see them honored.

She rose from her bed, flattened the wrinkles in her new gown, and donned her new red cloak. Although she usually wore white, this was a gift. A gift from him.

She headed downstairs, where two novices had already taken her luggage to the elaborately decorated golden carriage, a coach-and-four, harnessed to four beautiful black horses. Painted panels and carved trim dazzled, with interior drapes in noble blue. The center panel showed a nobleman upon his knee before a lady. Extravagant, with a clear message as to his disposition.

The craftsmen would have earned a lifetime of gold with this alone.

The coachman greeted her with a bow and assisted her into the carriage. She took her place on the right-hand side of the rear seat, and when she was settled, they embarked.

Days passed outside the coach windows, with stops at village carriage houses. How had six years passed in hostility to precede this diplomatic overture? Every day gone by the carriage windows eased her mind a little more.

When she finally arrived at Tregarde, she looked out at Castle Delalune, where the marquis himself—Brennan—emerged to welcome her.

Twenty-four years of age, he'd let his dark hair grow out, a boyish contrast to his sculpted build. Voluminous on top, styled away from the perfection of his face. Effortless in appearance and begging to be touched. Her fingers twitched, eager to rake through his hair, to tug at it playfully. Turned out in a black brocade doublet, fitted trousers, and high-gloss boots, he cut a handsome figure.

"You've arrived, fiancée mine." His voice was rich, deep, and smooth like *hors d'âge* brandy, flowing into every corner of her being with languid sensuality.

Despite their silent monthly offerings, how long had it been since she'd heard him speak? Years, at least.

With a warm smile, he offered his hand to help her from the carriage. "How was your trip?"

Unable to tear her gaze from him, she accepted his hand and began to exit the carriage, but ended up stumbling over the first step and straight into his arms. *Idiot.*

But he caught her adeptly, closing around her in more than mere support. Divine, she'd forgotten how good he smelled, cinnamon spice and cypress. Luxurious imports thanks to his father's trade connections in Sonbahar. A sudden chill pricked at the crown of her head—Brennan breathing her in.

"Sorry, I—" she stammered.

"You never need an excuse to get close to me, fiancée mine. I am for you and only you." His rumbling whisper left a shiver in its wake.

Her cheeks flamed. A discussion. Of course. They had planned to discuss their future.

Had he asked her something? His amused eyes offered nothing.

"Your trip?" A grin played at his lips. Gentlemanly of him to repeat it.

"Wonderful! Thank you. It was wonderful. Everything was... wonderful." Her mouth had run away, leaving her sense behind. She winced. *Wonderful.*

But no sharp retort came. He held his arm out to her, and warily, she accepted it. While servants flurried around them with her belongings, Brennan led her into the castle, covering her hand with his.

Her heart lodged in her throat. "You really didn't have to do all this."

He stopped just inside the foyer. "Yes, I did."

With a finger, he raised her chin and met her gaze.

His eyes were the color of wet bark on the oaks, rimmed with moss green. At times, the edge seduced the iris, moss growing over rich wood. When he smiled, the warmth of the deep brown danced with the seductive green in dazzling intimacy.

So close, so warm, so gorgeous—she could hardly stand it. She tore herself away, but her gaze wandered back to his in helpless attraction.

"It's been some time since I've had the pleasure of seeing your face in the sunlight. You've grown into a stunning woman." He wound a loose straw-blond curl around his finger and pulled it only to watch it bounce back again. "You must have suitors begging for your favor."

After news of her affair with Leigh had spread throughout the Tower, hardly anyone looked her way without scorn. But Brennan didn't need to know that. She shrugged it off and gathered a few of her escaped wits.

"Does this flattery usually work?" she teased, feeling more like herself.

He chuckled. "Stunning *and* modest. Perhaps I should keep you hidden from the other guests."

"Desperate to get me all to yourself?"

"Desperation speaks poorly of a man." A slow smile tugged at his lips as he leaned in by her ear. "And yet..."

Her breaths heavy and ragged, she bit back a gasp. Had any other man spoken such things to her, she would have laughed him off, but when Brennan Karandis Marcel murmured these sweet nothings, Divine help her, she wanted to believe him. No matter how many locks she closed around her composure, he had all the keys.

As he pulled away, the foyer waited in silence, empty, and it wouldn't object to a moment stolen from passing, would it? She rose on her toes, wrapped an arm around his neck, and kissed him.

He swept her into a dark corner with him, exploring her mouth with a skillfulness worth the six years since their last kiss.

She raked her fingers through his hair, relishing the soft thickness of it, pulling on it enough to make him groan. Beneath her cloak, he swept a palm up her back, separated from her skin by too many layers of cloth. He drew her against him and held her tight enough that she didn't melt to the floor at the thought of what he'd do next.

He broke away then, and her question barely formed when a group of nobles walked past.

Werewolf senses—he never got caught doing anything unless he wanted to.

A true gentleman of the Houses would never allow others to see his lady in a state of indecency. And he wanted to protect her reputation. Or what was left of it. Her cheeks hot, she lowered her gaze and smiled.

He exchanged pleasantries with them before turning back to her. "Why don't I take you to your room?"

"Please take me," she replied, breathless. "To my room," she corrected. *Stupid, stupid, stupid.*

With a pleased arch of his eyebrow, he offered his arm and led her upstairs. "I had the lady's quarters redecorated in anticipation of your arrival."

The lady's quarters? The rooms for the lady of the castle? Blinking, she struggled to breathe and reined in her eager mouth for a full three seconds. "How thoughtful."

He straightened next to her, raising his head a little higher, and stole glances at her as he made polite conversation about the weather, visiting artists and bards, and the guests in attendance, until they at last arrived at the lady's quarters.

White walls decorated with floral carvings and paintings contrasted with ornate blackwood furniture. A white Sonbaharan rug with a golden, scrolling floral pattern lay beneath a four-poster bed draped in white velvet. Above, intricate stuccowork of white hinds framed an intimate, detailed fresco of an elven maiden caught bathing in a forest pool.

Crystal vases brimming with red roses lent their bright crimson to the room, a sweep of petals across the bed in invitation.

A shelf of books on magic, botany, and theology waited nearby, with two volumes of *Court Duelist*, her guilty pleasure, stacked on a nightstand with a brown-ribbon-wrapped box. She grinned. Sugared almonds, her favorite.

It was the most beautiful room she'd ever seen.

Brennan smiled. "Do you like it?"

There were no words. How did he know her so well? All that he'd done for her—the invitation, the letters, the careful choices of gowns and gifts, the elegant coach, his thoughtful decoration of this place, this room that was somehow a reflection of her own heart and mind—

Her knees threatening to buckle, she tightened her grip on his arm and faced him, met his eyes unabashed, and unclasped her cloak. With a whisper, it fell to the floor, and with its descent, he lowered his gaze to her chest. It lingered.

A step closer. She traced a line up his coarse jaw, slow as the breaths passed between them, and he exhaled measuredly. He met her eyes, brushed a curl from her face; his finger stroked a heavenly path over her cheek, and her eyes fluttered shut as she raised her mouth to his.

A chaste kiss led to another, and another, and another, until she teased his lip between her own, drew at it, challenging his tongue to seek out hers, and he did, sweeping her into his arms, leaning against the closed doors, coaxing her mouth to voracity.

Divine, she wanted to kiss him forever, to love him forever, to marry him and bear his children and break the curse and live her life by his side forever.

She pressed into him, provoking him, daring him.

But he cupped her face, held it, her lips a breath away from his. "Marry me, Rielle... Let me love you for the rest of my days."

She shivered. Since her early childhood, she'd always imagined her fiancé as her knight in shining armor, and she his lady, and after that dream had fractured six years ago, she'd kept the pieces together with nothing but hope. But now—now—with a single word, the fracture could disappear. And her weakened heart desired it, longed for it.

"Yes," she breathed, and he gave her quivering lips another soft kiss.

"Before the party tonight," he said, inhaling a sharp breath as she leaned into him, "I have some arrangements to see to. At the end of the night, we'll make the announcement. A summer wedding."

Goosebumps pebbled her skin. A summer wedding. A bride. A wife. A mother. A duchess. The life her parents had always wanted for her. She inclined her head in agreement.

Brennan knotted his hand in her hair and pulled it back, urging her to look into his dark eyes, bringing his mouth achingly close to hers. He held her there, leaving her wanting, needing, on the cusp of begging, the air frozen in time while her heart pounded away.

The moment she thought he would kiss her again almost came. Almost came. And almost came. His heat warmed her face, made her lips long for his to sear her like a brand for a lifetime.

"'Til tonight," he whispered.

"Tonight."

He lowered his gaze to her mouth, exhaled a ragged breath, and his touch slipped away, leaving behind the promise of the evening.

She could hardly wait for her new life to begin.

A FEW HOURS LATER, the herald announced her, and Rielle entered Castle Delalune's great hall, which was hung with banners in Tregarde's red and gold overlooking a room rippling with activity. On one end, a meticulously staged scene featured players as the triune god's second facet, the Oak King, arriving to defeat and slay his third facet, the Holly King, so that he would reign in the Waxing Year.

Many tables filled the hall, covered in embroidered white tablecloths and dishes heaped with tarts of mushroom, spinach, beef, and pork; pear custard; peacock with ginger; stuffed capons stewed in wine; herb-roasted quail; a small tower of profiteroles wrapped in caramel threads; and roasted venison in red wine. The spiced creamy scent of her favorite custard tarts teased, although she couldn't spot them among the abundance spanning the tables.

Nobles swarmed the tables like butterflies, adorned in colorful silks, jewels, gold, and ornaments. A band played a duple-meter movement of moderate tempo on the harpsichord, the harp, violins, and horns.

Swaths of sapphire, crimson, emerald, violet, turquoise, and white swirled in breezy grace on the dance floor in a quessanade—all spins with joined hands, hops, rotations, and lively kicks. The first movement of the suite, then. The quessanade would be followed by a sprightly courante, then the passionate and scandalous sarabande, and finally, the gigue.

A soft bubbling splashed nearby amid the activity. Deep-red wine cascaded from fountains—no doubt built for the occasion. A dazzling woman in her early thirties impressed a group of guests nearby with a lively tale, her radiant face framed by golden locks. She wore a peony-pink gown decorated with pearls, soft and lovely, luxurious and elegant.

Brennan's long-time Companion, Liliane, who'd turned a boy into an impressive courtier and had been the object of Rielle's jealousy for many years.

Like all Companions, she was a person of beauty and talent, educated in the fine arts, etiquette, politics, and combat. They often served as bodyguards, entertainers, and sometimes paramours. Although loyal to the Camarilla, Companions were renowned for their discretion and confidence to their patrons. Most nobles retained one or, if their finances allowed, sometimes several Companions—Brennan's father, Duke Faolan, had four.

It was a well-known fact that Liliane was Brennan's closest friend. And she would never betray him—assured by the Camarilla's three vows: *I serve at the pleasure of my patron. I offer all that I am, apart from my love. I keep the confidence of my patron, but give my loyalty only to the Camarilla.*

Liliane sent a wistful smile her way, and her ocean-blue eyes dulled, taking on a somber grayness; she inclined her head and returned to regaling the guests surrounding her with some tale.

Rielle inched away toward the beverages and the men liveried in red and gold, serving port.

Port. She peered down at her white silk gown, embroidered with rosebuds, a gift from her fiancé. Probably not the best idea to sip a burgundy-colored drink while wearing it.

Best to drink it quickly. She drained the glass. "Another."

"It will take more than a few glasses of port to forget *your* troubles, scarecrow."

Scarecrow? *One* windy day during a hunt, and—

Only one lady had ever dared call her that. Rielle spun and met the sculpted-pleasant smile of Chantal Barthélémy Armel. Chocolate-brown curls pinned in an elaborate array framed a fine-boned porcelain face, bright sage eyes overwhelming a small nose but balancing full lips. Even from a young age, she had been expected to be a true court beauty, worthy of not mere nobles but princes and kings. Her parents had their pick of marriage contracts for her.

What was she doing here? There had been rumors of a dalliance between Chantal and Brennan, but he must've ended it.

Don't let her know I care.

"Chantal," Rielle acknowledged with a nonchalant sigh. "To what do I owe the torture?" She brought the glass to her lips and sipped, scanning the great hall for the only person who mattered.

Chantal's face sagged in splendid annoyance. "Is that any way to greet your cousin?"

Rielle fought back a snort. "You're no cousin of mine."

"We're of the Houses, scarecrow. We're all family."

Admittedly true. "What do you want?"

Chantal gazed out at the dance floor, and Rielle followed her line of sight to spot perfectly coiffed dark hair and bronze skin—Brennan—presented to best advantage in deep crimson brocade and black. He swept his beautiful younger sister Nora, recently married to the Count of Vauquelin, about in a courante, a sweet, hopeful piece. Sharing her brother's attractive features but for her long, bouncing dark tresses, they were a matched pair.

Across the hall, Brennan's eyes found hers, a slight raise of his eyebrows his silent greeting as he danced in ideal form, not a finger deviating from the full choreography. He held her gaze a moment longer, until the heat began to swell inside her, and then turned back to his sister.

In her periphery, Chantal's face blurred through a range of emotions.

"...when I am speaking to you." Chantal glared at her. "Bedding your master at the Tower while engaged to the marquis? A common-born mage, no less? How can you even show your face? I'm genuinely curious."

Rielle smiled. "That common-born mage is the most powerful man in Emaurria."

Chantal scoffed. "With a stroke of the pen, my father can make anyone's life very difficult—"

"And with a stroke of his hand, my former master can make anyone's life end." Rielle set down her half-full glass, gestured an ice spell over it, and savored Chantal's flustered expression as the remaining port froze solid and fractals of frost spread outward. "And so can I." She raised her chin as Chantal's mouth dropped. "Scared?"

Chantal's mouth clicked shut.

"Just doing what scarecrows do. You understand." The courante finished, and Rielle met Brennan's eyes as he strode toward her.

Half the faces in the hall turned to her. Brennan approached, and when Rielle offered him her hand, he kissed it with a lingering look over her dress. "Beautiful."

"It was a lovely gift." Her cheeks warmed.

A slow smile seduced his face. "I wasn't referring to the dress."

He held out his arm, and she curled her own around it.

Chantal cleared her throat. "You've outdone yourself, Tregarde."

Brennan looked over his shoulder. "The night is yet young, Chantal. Observe and enjoy. I expect news of tonight to spread far and wide."

News of our forthcoming wedding. Rielle tried to ignore the fluttering in her belly as he led her to the dance floor.

"Would you care to dance the sarabande, fiancée mine?"

A scandalous dance, few nobles dared participate lest committed to their partners. The harpsichordist and flautist began a slow, stately movement in triple meter accompanied by castanets. Some of the dancers fled the floor.

With the discretion he'd shown in the foyer, dancing the sarabande with her only meant one thing. Commitment.

Holding Brennan's gaze, she nodded. Eyes never leaving his, she followed him to the center and, once in position, started with the dance's coupé, changing her feet one in front of the other, and into the chasse, a slide.

To coy notes, they circled each other, undulations of the body and massive hip movements an extended flirtation; he closed in on her, and his hands nearly brushed hers, then swept away, a game of tease and denial, a sensual pantomime of seduction, conjuring dizzying images of lips on lips, skin on skin, moments behind closed doors. Relentlessly, his eyes sought hers out, dark pools inviting her to the depths where pleasure and little death awaited in breathtaking excess.

Heat spread through her, an inner fire that burned for him, and would burn until he sated it. She swallowed, trying to ignore the pulse of her body, but it had already invaded her every movement.

A smug smile curled a corner of his mouth, but his motion didn't deviate from perfection: controlled, slow, sensual. Tease and denial, tease and denial...

Great Divine, she couldn't bear it another second. She forced her body through the steps, glancing about the exits. After this, she would have to run outside and throw herself into a snowbank to cool off.

And just like that, the music ended, and Brennan offered his arm, leaning in.

"Respite?" A soft, brief whisper; barely audible.

Please. She inclined her head as subtly as she could manage, chest heaving and pulse refusing to slow.

Before three hundred watching faces, she followed his lead to the beverage table, where he handed her a goblet of wine that she drained instantly. Although his mouth remained immobile, his eyes gleamed. He leaned over to pour another goblet full.

"Exit to the right and follow the hall," he said quietly. "I will find you shortly." He stood tall, eyeing her over the rim of his goblet as he sipped.

Find me. Her body throbbed painfully, urgently. Invitation.

When he lowered his goblet, he inhaled lengthily, and a predatory grin stalked his mouth.

Great Divine, he knew. He *knew.*

She bobbed a hasty curtsy. "If you'll excuse me, I must rest," she said, loud enough to be heard. She tried to look weary, but a fire threatened to burn its way out through her skin. And she couldn't wait to tell him about the curse breaking; he would be so relieved.

Brennan bowed, every muscle in perfect place, begging to be touched, kissed, teased. "My household will see to your needs," he replied in kind, as a proper host should.

Mouth watering, she tore herself away and glided to the door on the right as the musicians began the gigue. She breathed deep, inhaling the space and respite, wishing she could claim its peace for her disquieted body. The hum and music of the great hall faded in the corridor, sparsely lit with sconces.

She fanned herself with her hand. Divine, Brennan could have had her right there, on the dance floor, and she wouldn't have remembered the other guests at all. She swallowed and focused on a well-lit room at the end of the hallway. Perhaps there she could compose herself.

A shadow swept from an open doorway, pillaging the breath from her lungs and stealing her away into darkness. Cinnamon spice and cypress. His hot mouth covered hers, his body eager against hers, and he pushed her back against a wall, imprisoning her in his tight embrace. The scents of freshly baked bread, garlic, and herbs mingled with his—a kitchen.

"I have been waiting for this all night, all my life," he whispered between kisses. "Tonight, I'll proclaim to the world my intention to marry you, my intention to make you mine, my wife, my duchess, mother to my children—"

She shivered, desire burning to unbearable heat within her, and invaded his mouth with her tongue as her anxious fingers unfastened his doublet. His grip slid from her hip to her backside, and he palmed her flesh, squeezed, pressed, harsh rhythmic breaths escaping his mouth. She spread his shirt open and admired the vast expanse of his hard chest with awed hands as she devoured his mouth, lingering before she reached for his trousers.

He spun her, turning her back to him, and pulled up the skirt of her gown. The mere thought made her gasp—but no, she pushed him against the wall and turned to face him once more.

Nothing held him there but for her wishes—if he wanted to, he could have her any way he liked—but she had other designs, and he allowed them. Stroking him, she dropped kisses from his chin, down his neck, over his chest and abs and lower.

Fingers gently raking her hair, he gasped, his breath catching as she took him, and she relished his enjoyment as her own, savoring every breath, shudder, and oath, keeping him paralyzed by sheer force of will, slave to her pleasuring, captive to her passion, until she drew him over the brink, lovingly and fully, until he unraveled over the edge, over and over and over, released all hold on the other side, and transcended into pure rapture.

His spent breaths, his satisfaction, his fingers stroking through her hair made her mad with desire. She loved him.

"Rielle..." He knotted her hair and pulled her away, cold eyes peering at hers. "You didn't think I meant all that, did you?"

She drew her eyebrows together. *What—?*

Gasps and laughter fogged in from the room's edges, and when she looked up at him—painfully as he tightened his grip on her hair—he smirked, eyes dark and shimmering.

But the smirk wasn't for her.

"Will your scarecrow be joining us for the rest of the party?" Chantal's voice lilted from across the kitchen, accompanied by the chuckles of several others.

Heart gripped in a panic, Rielle gazed up at Brennan, tried to rise, but he trapped her hair so securely—

This can't be—there has to be—he's about to make it right—

"You made this so much better than I had planned." He looked down at her, eyes narrowed to slits, then turned to the others. "I'm done with the little tart. She can find her way back to the Tower."

The blood drained from her face. It couldn't be. Couldn't. A tremor rattled her, and tears rose in her eyes; she could barely see, but she looked at him, willed her eyes open, because it couldn't be, all of everything couldn't have been for nothing—their betrothal; their years, almost decades, together; the heartbreak at the Tower; the years of silent offerings; the invitation; the gifts; the love letters; the carriage; the lady's quarters; the party; all his time with her—

All of this for *revenge?*

Her chest hurt, a claw the size of Brennan's wrath wedged in her heart, and he just peered at her, face set in a grimace.

Soft steps drew near, and Chantal kissed him. "Happy Midwinter, my love. Did you enjoy your gift?"

Brennan yanked his hand free of Rielle's hair and left her to fall to the floor, peered at her, then grabbed Chantal and kissed her passionately. "You've outdone yourself, sweet." He righted his clothes. "Let's return to the party."

And just like that, he and his tittering guests swept out of the spare kitchen.

It was a dream. It had to be.

No, a nightmare. Surreal.

But her hand found a stone wall for support, and she pressed into it, scratched her skin against it until it bled hot, red reality. The crack in her heart fractured, crumbled into pieces, and it was all she could do to curl up on the floor.

She recalled Liliane's somber glance. Piteous, she now realized, but bound by her vows as a Companion to keep her patron's confidence.

How could she have been so stupid? To think that Brennan Karandis Marcel would ever forgive her for slighting him? She wrapped herself tight on the kitchen floor.

Kitchen. She covered her mouth. Just like at the Tower.

He'd planned it all to perfection. And dancing the sarabande? He'd all but announced his intentions to the entire room.

What had he said? *The night is yet young, Chantal. Observe and enjoy. I expect news of tonight to spread far and wide.*

A public rejection.

She staggered to her feet and scrabbled against the wall, searching for an exit through blurry eyes. He'd been with Chantal all along, who'd been, what, his accomplice? Helping him plan this elaborate scheme?

Her throat tight, Rielle slapped the wall. He never could have accomplished it without her own gullibility.

She paused against the wall. The pain robbed her body of its strength, but she had to move, had to leave this place tonight and forever, to get away from it and them and him.

But she'd see him again. He'd find her every month, get to her, no matter what.

A sob escaped. They would never be free of each other. She would see him again before the full moon, before every full moon, for the rest of her life... unless she broke the curse.

No. Unthinkable.

She swung her head from side to side. She would never let him in again. Ever. Not after this.

Not after this.

At last, she found a door to the outside, and ignoring the guards, she threw it open, threw herself from the hateful castle into the white purifying cold of the snow. She wandered the grounds, found the stables, and trudged through the knee-deep snow to them.

Her teeth chattered, so she cloaked herself in flame, an aura of fire that brimmed around her body and protected it. Warmth seeped into her weary bones, but not any deeper.

She'd loved Brennan before, and he'd made her choose between controlling her magic and marrying him, then abandoned her.

She'd loved Leigh, who now showed off a new lover every week with no regard for her feelings.

And she'd been stupid enough to fall for Brennan again.

Would it ever be worth letting another man into the mess of shards that was her heart?

Better to play at love than to love. Better to pantomime it than to live it. At least the hurt, when it came, would be false, too.

It would serve her, and it would serve everyone around her. No one to hurt her and no one to hurt meant no one to lose. No one to cause fureur. She dabbed at her eyes. It would all be for the best. Yes, for the best.

She stumbled into the stable, dispelled her flame cloak, and began to saddle a bay horse.

"Theft is a crime."

A violent shudder tore through her, and her head ticked in the direction of the hateful voice. Brennan leaned against a pillar, arms crossed, grotesquely handsome and emanating satisfaction.

Burn. She wanted to burn the stable, the grounds, the entire place, but she'd only succeed in killing everything but the one man she wished to reduce to ashes—and likely getting herself excommunicated from the Divinity.

She scrambled for some measure of composure and continued saddling the horse. "What, did you come here expecting applause for your performance?"

A slow clap beat the air. "I definitely applaud *yours*. Skill born of much practice, no doubt."

She strode to him, scowling. "What did I do to deserve this? Did I say a single word when you seduced your way through the Houses? Did I?"

He grabbed her shoulders and shook her, eyes wild, blazing amber, face livid. "We are *not* the same." He held her mere inches from himself, from a hate-filled gaze. "You *know* we're not the same. A betrothed nobleman can have his conquests, but a betrothed noblewoman—"

"Can what? Waste away in loneliness until her thin-skinned, weak boy of a fiancé decides she's suffered enough?" She spat in his face.

He threw her aside, and she tripped over a hay bale and landed on the ground. He dragged a sleeve across his face.

"In the war of love, who flies conquers. And I have conquered you. I have won." He chuckled, a sharp white smile eerily joining primal eyes. "Don't be a sore loser. Or do. I don't care. I'm going to find a way to marry Chantal."

Marry Chantal? Was that the point of all this? Good riddance. They deserved each other.

He clenched his teeth. "I don't need you anymore."

Sad laughter ripped out of her, strong and throaty, deepening until she laughed herself to tears. "But you do. Every month. We both know that."

She would elicit one small victory out of this nightmare. "And you should know, *fiancé mine*"—she savored his favorite term of endearment, spitting it back at him with venomous satisfaction—"that, in the Tower library's forbidden section, I learned how to break the curse. I was going to tell you tonight." Laughter bubbled within her anew.

The color drained from his face. He fixed his eyes on her.

Now she had his attention. All of it.

She savored the moment. "To break a blood curse, one bloodline cursing another, you must unite the bloodlines."

Realization dawned on his face, and she let herself laugh into a stupor.

He sobered. "Rielle—"

She only laughed harder. Divine, the comedy of this moment, how he'd thrown away freedom from the curse for petty revenge, without even knowing it! The grim amusement masked, if only for a time, the deep wound he'd clawed into her.

He looked at her, eyebrows drawn, pleading. "Rielle, not an hour ago, you were happy at the prospect of bearing my children. Give me another chance and free us both."

Never. She beamed a smile so wide her face hurt, and shook her head. "You'll come crawling to me again before the moon is full."

She led the horse out, willing her composure to last just long enough to leave.

"You're lying." His voice, now thin, carried from behind her.

She scoffed and mounted. "You can tell I'm not. We both know that."

He followed her outside. "You're not going to get very far with one horse and no money."

She held up her signet ring. "I'm the Marquise of Laurentine. I'll make do."

His upper lip curled. "I hate you."

She flinched but straightened quickly. "The feeling's mutual, *fiancé mine*," she mocked. "See you before the full moon."

A gossamer net held back the flow of tears and sobs as she rode away, but it held long enough to see her far from Castle Delalune toward the city.

Another chance. She'd given him a second chance willingly.

But not a third. Never a third.

27

*R*ielle shuddered, picking her way through the crowds. The grim memory of that night three years ago was never far. She'd closed off parts of her life—the Houses' society and love—but now that grimness stretched before her feet, a black road she would follow into the horizon, if it meant Olivia's rescue.

Night had fallen when she finally found her way back to The Crowned Stag, the vial of blood on its chain around her neck and the cylindrical case in tow. The smell of cider was thick in the night air, and a bonfire rose in the distance. She stabled and tended her horse, trying to quiet her doubts. She couldn't worry about what came after. She had to focus on now.

When Brennan arrived, she would ask him to contact the Black Rose, an assassin's guild in Courdeval whose illustrious leader owed her a favor. If the woman was still there, Rielle would have it repaid.

But there remained the matter of convincing Brennan to help. He was her only chance at getting a message into the capital fast enough and over its walls unnoticed, but at what cost? She would never admit to him that the Divinity would excommunicate her, and when it happened, she would fight to her last breath to resist marriage to him. The only thing he truly wanted, a child, she would never give him, and little threatened him personally.

If anything, she was the weak point in his armor—if something were to happen to her, he'd have no means of control over his curse.

Finished caring for the horse, she headed for the front entrance, trying her best to clear her mind. Tonight, she had the unenviable task of confronting Leigh about Kieran, and she needed to keep her composure.

In the tavern, amid nearly a full house, Jon sat at a table, all broad shoulders and tense muscle, nursing a cup of tea, his leather doublet unlaced at the neck. A trying day, then. Chatter filled the air, punctuated by the occasional thunk of dinnerware and cutlery on tables and the crackling of the fire.

When she approached his table, he looked up and rose. With a deep breath, she laid the cylindrical case down on a chair, and they sat.

"What's that?" He tipped his head toward the case.

"Maps."

He frowned.

She glanced about the room, full of unwanted ears. "I'll tell you all about it later. Where's Leigh?"

"He had some business at the temple." Jon sipped his tea.

He'd abandoned Jon here? She fought back a grimace. But perhaps Leigh was sending her report to the Proctor. Good. He would know about the heretics in the ruins sooner rather than later. "How did your errand go?"

"Your former master knows Helene Forgeron fairly well, it turns out," he said. "She accepted the job and said it would be ready the day after tomorrow. Then Leigh took us to a brothel."

Unsurprising.

"And you?" he asked.

"I went to a brothel, too." She tried to hold back an impish grin.

Jon crossed his arms and leaned back in his chair, gaze smoldering.

"Was your coin well spent?" he asked, a slight growl in his throat.

"Oh yes," she answered, enjoying rattling him far more than she should. "I found the staff there most accommodating."

The leather of his doublet crackled.

Rattled indeed. Perhaps she'd tell him a little. She sighed and patted the cylindrical case. "A whole corona to bribe my way into a vacant room, but I found these."

Relaxing, Jon nodded toward the case. "Maps, you said? Whose, and of where?"

After a look around—no one sat nearby—she leaned in and beckoned Jon to do the same. "Turns out, a mage booked Leigh's usual room at the usual place. A mage on a mission to perform a certain rite. The maps are of the venue."

He thumbed his ear and raised an eyebrow. "A certain rite and a venue... down south?"

She nodded.

"And he just let you walk off with them?"

She shrugged. "He was nowhere to be found."

Jon hesitated and then lowered his voice even more. "You think Leigh had something to do with it?"

"When he returns, I intend to ask him." The thought was troubling, but it only grazed the surface of her concerns.

"Hopefully, it can wait until after the Vindemia festivities tonight. I've never missed the offering or the group prayer, and I don't intend to tonight. It is only by expression of our gratitude to Most Holy Terra that the harvest is abundant each year." With a heavy sigh, he leaned back in his chair, his gaze wandering the inn with detached interest.

"Oh?" But those mercenaries had come to the inn looking for a paladin. And Shadow and Phantom were still out there. A shadowmancer and an illusionist... She and Jon would never even see them coming. There was no certainty the threat had ended with Flame. "Attending the festival is inviting risk."

Jon eyed her resentfully as he folded his arms across his chest. "Trying to cage me again?" he hissed, the raging sea of his eyes crashing into hers. "After last time, we agreed: never again."

This was different. Flame was a risk they'd had no choice in facing. If another unavoidable risk turned up, she wouldn't send him away again. But she could hardly expose him to needless danger for the sake of—what, fun?

She shook her head. "The answer's no."

After clenching his fists and flexing his fingers, he laid his palms on the table and rose, leaning over it to scowl at her. "I didn't ask."

Livid, she stared him down. Did he plan to renege on his oath to her? He'd vowed not to sabotage her mission. But if they went to this festival, out in the open, surrounded by people and chaos, and he got himself killed, he'd be doing just that.

And it wasn't just about the mission anymore. She rose and rounded the table to face him. "You promised—"

He straightened and took a step toward her, invading her space. "I know what I promised, witch." He closed in. "I did *not* promise to ask your permission to practice my faith."

"Good," she snarled. "It spares you the disappointment, then, since it would be denied."

Scowling, he opened his mouth, but then he closed it. He glared at her, holding the silence like a blade to her flesh.

Let him fume. If she had to cast every spell in her repertoire to keep him from doing something stupid and getting himself killed, then that's what she would do. He might have been keen on endangering himself, but luckily for him, he didn't make the decisions on this mission.

A smile soon replaced his scowl, and his eyes gleamed. "Never mind."

What? What did that mean? And why was he giving up so easily?

Jon picked up his tea and drained it as he strolled around her.

Dumbstruck, she looked around the room. Everyone was watching. Had they taken in the spat? Simpering, she took off after him while he deposited the teacup on a serving woman's tray and headed for the stairs.

What had convinced him? Had it really been so simple? Perhaps he'd realized all the threats still out there—especially Shadow and Phantom.

No, it was a ploy. Or a ruse to soothe the spectacle. Had to be. What game was he playing now?

She caught him on the stairs and gripped the railing. "What did you mean by 'never mind'?"

"I meant never mind arguing downstairs."

"What?" Her face burned.

"We can discuss this upstairs." He continued up the stairs.

She followed him. "You want to go to Vindemia so badly?"

He turned and raised an eyebrow. "Badly? Tell me, why would I want to go to a celebration germane to my religion that I have attended every year without fail? Speak sense, witch."

She slipped past him into their room. As she took off her coat, she lost her balance. *Damned sen'a.*

Jon moved to stand before her. Close. He grabbed her coat. "What would it take to convince you?"

"It's dangerous."

"I won't let anything happen to you," he said, hanging her coat, "or to me. I'll be on my guard. And there will be other paladins there. It'll be safe, trust me. I wouldn't recklessly endanger you."

"But Shadow and—"

"They'll never attack us in a crowd like this." He tipped his head toward the window, where throngs of people clogged the streets. "Not tonight. Not here. It would be suicide. The streets are full of paladins. We will never be safer than in that crowd."

She searched his eyes. Of course, anyone bold enough to attempt a murder in such a crowd would find escape nigh impossible, and the increased paladin presence meant a quick arrest.

And perhaps she was being closed minded. Divinists didn't attach as much meaning to ritual as Terrans did. His faith was important to him.

She could check the vicinity with earthsight every so often... and stay close enough to him to be mistaken for a part of his body. At least if Shadow or Phantom appeared, she'd have some warning with the earthsight and would be close enough to shield Jon.

And... they were at an inn. Where she couldn't capture him with geomancy. If he truly wanted to go without her permission, she could do little to stop him. Even on the city streets. He'd respected her enough to discuss it. She could compromise, too. "Fine. Let's go to the festival."

Jon leaned against the door, arms crossed, looking like the cat that ate the canary.

She retreated behind the privacy screen to change into her white batiste chemise, her corset, and her cotton bodice and skirts—as "festive" as she'd get—careful to keep Feliciano's envelope in her décolletage. "But only for an hour, and if you die, I'll"—*Kill you?*—"be displeased."

"I'll do my best to keep you pleased," he replied.

Frozen, she bunched the fabric of her skirts in her hands, holding her breath with a growing smile. *Is that so?*

"By staying alive," he corrected, clearing his throat.

She remembered to breathe. "Of course."

What am I doing? She scolded herself. Was she really allowing this man, who had already rejected her, to get to her now?

Olivia flashed through her mind, suffering and hurt, imprisoned. Tears waited impatiently to make their entrance.

Vindemia. She sighed. With the capital, the rite, and Olivia on her mind, how could she attend a festival? When Olivia could be in chains? Arcanir chains. Surrounded by a hostile army.

She pinned her arms against her stomach, fighting its upset. With Olivia in danger, the last thing she wanted was to go to a festival.

But she emerged from behind the screen. Jon twirled his ring around his finger; his eyes downcast, he could have been miles away or years.

He glanced up, looked her over, and his face went slack. His gaze lingered, seeking across the distance between them. "Are you all right?"

Was her worry that obvious? Pressing her lips together, she looked away and raised her shoulders in a halfhearted shrug. She fought the tears that threatened to invade.

Not now.

Divinity mages did not weep before their charges. *She* did not weep before her charges. Or anyone, if she could avoid it.

But Jon followed her, didn't let her turn away, bent to glimpse her face. He approached her with all caution, his careful observation equal parts soothing and disconcerting. Why did he care? Hadn't he turned away from her before? Hadn't he made his decision?

Yet when he touched her upper arm, let his fingers glide down to her elbow, every trace of her nervousness disappeared, replaced by familiar, warm comfort.

"We don't have to go to Vindemia." He rubbed her arm gently through the cotton fabric. "We can stay here, do whatever you want. I'm sorry."

Settled in here for the night, she'd think only of Olivia and wait for the sen'a withdrawal to come. Perhaps there was a way to keep moving, keep her mind off everything, and keep Jon from recognizing the withdrawal when it came.

"You can talk to me, Rielle."

Her older brother, Liam, used to say that to her. Then Olivia had become the only one to truly listen, the only one she could bare her heart to, without fear or reservation.

Her hands shook. Useless. Alone, she could do no more than throw herself at the Courdevallan gates, a raging wave breaking against the immovable cliffs, but break she would, if it would see Olivia free. If only.

Stupid tears—there was no stopping them now—but Jon was there, and she pressed herself against him, buried her face in his doublet, his shirt, his chest. He welcomed her, invited her in. Cautious arms closed around her, tightening against a fleeting hesitation, and he rested a cool hand on the back of her head, his fingers soothing into her hair.

She angled her body away from him, her ribs squeezing, her body collapsing in on itself... But when he offered a tranquil whisper to her ear, the brush of the gentle summer breeze that eased into Laurentine from the Shining Sea, she closed her eyes and let herself lean into him.

She would give her all to save Olivia. But until that time came, she would borrow strength from Jon, if he'd lend it to her.

His fingertips coaxed the distress from her with subtle strokes, sweeping it away to distant air. A moment in his embrace gave her much-needed relief, but before she could daydream about another night in it, a moon, a lifetime, she drifted away. A storm darkened his eyes, and she attempted to ease the worry there with a small smile.

"We should go," she said. "You're Terran. You belong there. And I..."

Well, I'll keep you safe. And getting out of here for a while might do me good."

A dense pause followed, but the tempest cleared from his gaze, and he let his hold slip from her arms, down to her hands, and apart.

"As you wish." His soft tone belied the words' meaning, yet he moved to open the door. "After you."

With a look over her shoulder, she mustered a smile, then headed downstairs and outside, with Jon close behind. It was time to steal some joy before the torture that would become her life after Courdeval.

28

*W*hen Jon stepped out of The Crowned Stag with Rielle, lamps and torches lit the dark streets with dancing flame, casting everything in a warm glow. City folk reenacted scenes, dressed as the mournful Maiden and the dying Oak King.

Thanking Terra for another good harvest and asking her blessing for the coming year was an ancient tradition, and he hadn't missed the daytime festivities for as long as he could remember, so today was a first. But ever since Tor had taught him to dance, he hadn't missed the evening celebration, either.

Rielle spelled her eyes, and her irises turned that arcane green of earthsight. Squinting, she looked around.

If an assassin wished to strike from stealth, this crowd would be cloak enough. But since he'd taken his vows, risk had been his faithful shadow. Paladins wore wealth that attracted greedy hunters, and for that greed, he'd dealt death before and would deal it again. A man who feared his own shadow was no man.

Although armed only with his dagger, he could ably defend her and himself, and she was a capable mage besides. Convincing her to attend had seemed reasonable, and yet, at the sight of her aggrieved face in the inn, he had regretted it all.

Olivia. He'd busied his mind with Gilles and the Crag Company, the capital, his armor, even Leigh Galvan and his tales, and had forgotten that

Rielle didn't know whether her best friend was dead or alive. And he'd pushed her into attending a celebration? He winced.

If she wanted to take her mind off the unanswerable question, then tonight he'd do his all to lift her spirits.

As they made their way through the crowds to the bonfire in the distance, her gaze darted from costume to costume. The city's women would have worked on them for weeks; their discipline and devotion showed in their well-crafted patterns, myriad colors and designs, and painstaking stitches.

A small group of revelers broke through them to pass by, and when he and Rielle reunited, she locked her arm with his.

He stood taller and fought the urge to grin like an idiot. She wanted to be near him. Close. And it felt good.

It had no right to feel good. He eyed her warily.

"Don't flatter yourself," she grumbled. "I just don't want to lose you in this crowd."

When he scoffed, she elbowed him playfully.

I don't want to lose you either.

A shadow passed over her expression. She spared him a quick grin before turning back to the spectacle. "I don't think I've ever been to a Vindemia bonfire."

"I've never missed one." He flashed her a half-smile, and she waved him off.

"Well, it's hard to miss one when you're a paladin."

Yet this year, but for her last-minute acquiescence, he would have. He would have stayed in that room with his arms around her for as long as she needed. A part of him wanted to go back to that moment and never leave. "I'm glad we came."

A group of jovial celebrants danced past them and tossed vine necklaces over his head and Rielle's. She lifted hers, examining the weave with a curious eye.

Ahead of them, several pots steamed with spiced cider.

Rielle squeezed his arm. "Do you mind if I...?"

"Not at all."

They made their way through the crowd. He'd always wondered how the beverage tasted, but had never broken the second Sacred Vow.

Before they could reach the cider, a group of men clad in vines handed them each a large cup of wine. Thankfully, Rielle accepted them both with thanks and drank deeply, laughing as the other people in the crowd drank and cheered.

He couldn't help but smile.

In the orchard, the circles gathered for the offering, and he led her there among them.

"Is it all right that I'm not—"

He nodded. "Terra welcomes all."

She opened her mouth, then closed it and smiled, joining him in the outer circles. A priest stood before the altar with five black candles—one for each of the quarters and one to unite the circle—and lit incense of frankincense, myrrh, sage, and cinnamon. The circles filled and tightened, the thankful closing in and in and in, and then the priest called the four quarters, masked representatives.

The Stag of the North brought an offering of apples to the altar; the Fox of the South an offering of wheat; the Hawk of the East brought an offering of onions; and the Trout of the West an offering of wine.

The priest recited the introduction and lit the first candle; the Stag the second; the Fox the third; the Hawk the fourth; and the Trout the fifth.

The chant began at the altar. Jon closed his eyes along with the crowd.

The chant spread. "Great Goddess, give; Great Goddess, keep; Great Goddess, sow; Great Goddess, reap." And repeated.

I am done with indecision. From tonight, I'll walk my destiny with purpose. He laced the words with hope and intention and prayed Terra would give him strength and take away his weakness.

The chant finished, and he opened his eyes. Rielle looked around, her eyebrows raised. She was interested, then; and it pleased him.

The priest reminded them of the four quarters' work, their energy placed upon the altar as tokens of repayment to the Goddess, and that they would receive the gift of another—balance celebrated. He stepped away from the altar, and the four quarters rotated, each taking a gift they had not provided.

"We thank you, Great Goddess!" the priest called.

"Praise Terra," Jon replied, one of the countless voices in the crowd. Rielle's brows knitted together, and he gave her hand a squeeze. She smiled.

The inner circle turned sunwise; the next widdershins. And each of the circles alternated until theirs turned sunwise, and as the outermost circle spun, the group prayer rose up on countless lips. "Lady of the Harvest, Mother of the Earth, / Most Holy Terra, Goddess of death and rebirth: / The grain has been threshed; the grapes have been pressed. / Hear our thanks; we have been blessed!" And twice. And thrice.

And the prayer was done.

Rielle looked up at him with wide, curious eyes.

Hear my thanks. I have been blessed.

Off to the side, a band played a quick and lively dancing tune. A bourrée, but in triple time with the crowd clapping the beat.

"And now?" she whispered.

The crowd headed for the dance floor and moved to the rhythm with an energy only a Terran festival could spark. Even Rielle tapped her foot to the beat.

"And now we show our thanks." He inclined his head toward the band. "You dance, witch?"

"I haven't—"

"You're about to."

When the dancers drew into a tight circle, he led her to join them. The city folk accommodated them happily. He joined his right hand to the others at the center of the circle, and so did Rielle. They went sunwise, stepped, widdershins, stepped, and broke to spread out on the dance floor, stepped, and wove through one another to mirror it all.

Rielle tracked the dancers with bewildered eyes, her steps quickly falling into line as dancers braided through one another only to pair once more in a tease of spaced, mirrored movement and a clap to the beat. When she spun, he orbited her, feet practiced, heart amateur; the immaculate white of her bodice and skirts brought out the gold of her hair, her cheeks rosy pink as she danced with abandon, and he couldn't look away. The world around him colored with warmth—amber light, golden hair, the honey-colored hay bales.

They circled each other, a dance of intricate steps and layered gazes, her cheer igniting to fire, to an intensity he couldn't look away from. He swept an arm around her, took her hand in his, joined the many pairs twirling; her eyes held his captive, her frame so right in his arms that when it came time to break, he could hardly will his limbs to cooperate. They circled each other once more; she spun away; and they wove through the other couples, Rielle slipping from his grasp.

Right hands returned to the center of the circle—her soft hand beneath his—and they went widdershins, stepped, sunwise, stepped, and spread into a wide ring, holding hands.

As the last sounds of the hurried tune faded, the ring of dancers freed one another's hands, but he drew her in, indulging in the pleasing encore of holding her close.

Terra have mercy, nothing had ever felt so good, so right, so whole. Panting as he did, she smiled up at him and moved even closer, sparkling as she glanced at her hand in his. Her sky-blue eyes widened. Her gaze flickered, and she drew in a soft, giddy gasp.

I love her.

A chaotic line of dancers moved past, and raising her eyebrows in invitation, she grabbed his arm.

"Jon?" A man's voice.

Jon whirled, sweeping Rielle behind him.

Sir Valen Boucher, a paladin and one of his closest friends—a thirty-one-year-old bear of a man with rough features and cheery eyes, clad in full arcanir plate, a longsword on his belt and his shield on his back.

"Valen," he greeted in surprise, clasping Valen's arm and leaning in to embrace him. "Terra's blessings upon you, my brother."

"And upon you." Grinning, Valen gave him a once-over. He turned to Rielle, and his mouth dropped as he squinted. "Terra's troth, you found her."

"Found?" Jon repeated, raising an eyebrow. He looked at Rielle, whose gaze darted away.

"The healer." Valen's cheery face went slack. "From Signy?"

Jon's breath hitched.

Rielle's mouth fell open, her head shaking in quick little swipes. Fiery and fair as ever. Her notes of "Winter Wren" from the forest pool threaded deeper, a faded fiber of something older, worn, a threadbare tapestry of rooftops aflame, fire reflected in golden hair.

The familiar song in his heart.

Merciful Terra, the healer-apprentice who'd saved his life? It couldn't be. "You're an elementalist. How can—"

She cleared her throat and released his arm. "Why don't I give you two a chance to catch up?" Her eyes were wide, too wide, and then she blinked rapidly, shifting her weight. Her gaze darted away. "I'll be at the bonfire."

No attempt to even deny it. "Will—"

She bowed and rushed away. How could—

He planted his hands on his hips, stared at the blades of grass at his feet until he couldn't see them anymore.

"Jon?"

He shook his head. "Are you sure that's her?" But he already knew the answer. Valen had been at Signy, too.

Valen made the sign of the Goddess. "I was there, Jon—fighting beside Tor while you were dying. She saved you. By my life, that's her."

You could have a healer fade that for you, she'd said to him on the night they'd met at the Tower.

Terra have mercy. All this time. She'd known. He backed up until he hit a hay bale.

"What's wrong?" Valen touched his shoulder.

It was her. It had been her that day, that fateful day. Rielle had returned him to this side of the blade. Not a healer. An elementalist who'd healed him. *An elementalist.* Had the other paladins not known the difference?

It didn't matter. A face like hers—he would have remembered. He should have. Except that he'd been dying.

So little had stayed with him from that time beyond the crippling loss of Bastien, the battle, and his own imminent death.

And at the Tower, it had been her, one and the same, savior and captor. All this time, she'd tolerated his ingratitude, his rudeness, and hadn't voiced the one thing that would have humbled him completely.

Rielle. His chest ached.

Valen frowned. "Where's your arcanir?"

Jon folded his arms across his chest. "I've been discharged from the Order."

"What? *You?*" Valen leaned against the hay bales with him. "Honorably?"

"Yes."

"Any idea why?"

"No." Jon stared at the ground, at feet shuffling by toward the bonfire. Toward Rielle. "I got word from Derric about ten days ago. Then I met her." He caught Valen's easy grin in his periphery. "I'll petition Paladin Grand Cordon Guérin for reenlistment."

Valen pushed off from the hay bales. "What?" He swept his hand toward the bonfire. "A blind man could see the affection you bear that woman."

Druthers had always been murmured in monasteries, but the rarity of oath-breaking spoke to paladins' dedication. And he'd pledged his. "I know my place." He took a deep breath. "I swore vows, Valen."

"Yes, you did. We all did." Valen grabbed his shoulder. "But you've been honorably discharged. You are beholden to those vows no longer."

"Is that what it means to swear a vow? To intend it at the time and then seize the first available opportunity to abandon it?" He clenched his teeth.

"It is Terra's will. She set you on your path for reasons you may never understand. Or is it so common to you that you should cross paths, unbeknownst to you, with the woman who saved your life?" Valen gave him a light shove. "Are you of so little faith? What is it that you fear?"

Fear? Was that it?

"Do you have any idea how many of us would rejoice at the chance to have our service ended with honor, to have fulfilled the mission, and to be released to please the Goddess with a fruitful life?"

A fruitful life...

Rielle perched on a log bench near the bonfire, her head tilted, her back to him, rigid. She'd already found her way into his heart. There was no denying it.

Even released from his vows, what could he offer her? All he had to give her was himself, a man who only knew how to be one thing, that which he could be no longer.

It wouldn't be enough. It would never be enough.

A woman like her deserved more than he could give her, more than he could ever be. More than a destitute man who could scarcely secure a roof over her head. No matter what he felt about her, inviting her to join him in such misery wasn't in him.

"If I'm not a paladin, what is there for me?" he thought aloud. "I have nothing. For men like us, service is life."

"You can still serve." Valen stepped back. "You're going to Monas Amar to turn in your arcanir, right?"

"Yes." Jon eyed him warily. A paladin would never suggest joining up with irregulars. Pledging a sword-arm once sworn to Most Holy Terra to take life indiscriminately for coin was no option.

"Horrible tragedy—Courdeval," Valen murmured solemnly.

So much loss of life. Unnecessary. Unspeakable. The Crag Company had gone too far. Yet again. "When Parliament elects the new king, perhaps Gilles will finally face justice."

"That, and... when the new king is crowned, go to Courdeval and swear your fealty to him. He'll need knights. With an honorable discharge, you'll get a recommendation from the Order. Maybe you'll be chosen for the Royal Guard."

Service—a different kind of service. A knighthood.

At the bonfire, Rielle turned, her arcane-green eyes searching the area with earthsight, then she dispelled it. She pulled in a knee to her chest and rested her chin upon it, staring into the fire.

A knighthood. Money. A home. Perhaps even—

Fiery hues shimmered in her hair.

"If ever there was a sign..." Valen's voice drifted off. The faint trace of envy and awe in his tone lingered in Jon's ear. "An honorable discharge and crossing paths with the woman who saved your life are it. Ask for your lady's hand, start a family—"

Jon winced.

"—and let me visit your bounteous clan on furlough." Valen elbowed him in the ribs and grinned.

He shoved Valen back light-heartedly. It was easy for someone who was one of seven siblings to talk like that. If only things were as simple as Valen's far-reaching ideas.

And yet, his words made sense. Jon rubbed his chin and—that idiot grin had returned to reclaim his face.

"She's a mage, you know," Jon said as Rielle played with a flame in her palm. "And works for the Divinity."

"And you have an awful temper. We all have our faults."

A smile tugged at the corner of Jon's mouth. For a paladin, he had never been known for his restraint. Cooling his hot head was a lifelong challenge.

"Don't keep her waiting. We can catch up at Monas Amar," Valen said.

"You'll be there?"

Valen nodded. "Orders. Heading out tomorrow with some of our brothers."

The sellswords at The Crowned Stag. It could be nothing, but... "There's something else. Earlier today, two sellswords came to the inn where we're staying, looking for a paladin. You need to watch yourself and pass the word along to our brothers."

With a grave frown, Valen nodded. "I saw a couple of those types hanging around near the way-station, but they made no move. Still, we're all on notice." A warm smile. "Watching my back as always, eh, Jon?" Valen clapped him on the back and drew him into an embrace. "Goddess keep you, my brother."

"And you."

Valen let him go, but then he lingered a moment; he opened his mouth, but no words came. He smiled, and they parted ways.

The bonfire rose higher. But he hung back. Rielle traced her finger over the flame in her palm.

He headed toward the bonfire, stopping only for a cup of mulled wine.

No. He hesitated. Tonight, he would take the first step toward his destiny. That first step was breaking one of the Sacred Vows.

The entire journey, he'd made it clear to her that he'd planned to keep them. Made her promise not to interfere. And now he wanted her to do the opposite.

It wasn't her burden to bear; it was his. Unless he made his intentions clear and secured his own freedom, he could not in good conscience court her.

A second cup of wine. He poured another.

Walk my destiny with purpose... He strode toward her.

Her eyebrows drawn, she turned toward the direction he'd come from, then back to him. "Are you all right?"

He handed her one of the two cups, then sat next to her and took a deep breath. "Why didn't you tell me?"

Her shoulders slumped as she studied the bonfire, pensive in her hesitation. "When I was an apprentice, Leigh and I were sent to Signy to rescue the viscount, but when the paladins needed help with a burning temple and the people trapped inside, I volunteered." She gave a little shrug, her gaze dulling. "Sir Bastien covered me while I got them out—"

Bastien? She had known Bastien?

By name?

"But there was a girl, unconscious... she needed to be carried out. He..." She shook her head, staring into the cup.

"He died a paladin, honorably, fighting for what he believed in." Jon thumbed the rim of his cup. "I saw Gilles kill him."

The image of Gilles running Bastien through had been seared into his mind, and even now, when he closed his eyes, not a detail of the gruesome scene had faded despite the worn fibers of all else.

His scar burned, a hot brand on his neck. Leather creaked. He'd gripped his dagger's hilt to numbness. He inched the blade from its sheath, just a bit; the fire played on its reflective surface, reminiscent of the light cast by Signy's burning buildings.

"I charged in, thirsting for vengeance, and I fought him," Jon said, the memory vivid, "but in my hatred, I lost my focus. Gilles outmaneuvered me, tripped me over two of my dead brothers, and impaled me through the neck." He raised his chin at the mention, the gurgle of blood rumbling in his throat anew; he had stared at what he'd believed to be his last sight: up the blade of a flambard to the grinning face of his best friend's murderer.

He'd fought that duel a thousand times in his mind since.

"I... left him behind, and he died for it," she said, her voice tremulous, her eyes haunted.

"But you came back for him."

"Too late."

"You found me instead." He traced the entry wound on the right side of his neck and the exit wound by his ear. Rage gripping him, he'd refused to die until Gilles faced justice for Bastien's death—not that it would have mattered.

Left there, he would have lost his life. "I should have died, but thanks to you, I didn't."

She took his hand in hers. "I'm glad for it."

It had been difficult to be happy about surviving when his best friend had died. It had taken a long time for him to wade through the guilt, to remember Bastien as he'd been instead of how Gilles had left him.

He put his arm around Rielle and poured some wine out for Bastien.

Then he drank some himself. He would bear the burden of oath breaking and free himself. To love her, if she would have him.

She gasped, staring at the cup. "Jon... your vow—"

Broken. A shudder rode his spine, exhilaration and finality mingled.

"Tonight, I'm swearing a new vow," he said, peering at the wine, "to live a new life."

"You are?" She swallowed. Reflections of the flames danced on her trembling lower lip. "But are you—"

"I'm certain."

Silence had its say as her eyes searched his, a slow but warm smile claiming her lips. Fortunate, enviable smile, master of such coveted territory.

She raised her cup. "To new beginnings."

"To new beginnings." He struck his cup to hers, then drank.

Most Holy Terra, he'd actually done it.

The night wind whispered past, and she shivered beside him. He set down his cup and removed his doublet, then laid it gently around her shoulders.

"Thank you," she whispered, placing one hand upon his. It was freezing.

He took hold of her hand and raised it to his mouth, cupping it and blowing his warm breath onto her skin.

Her eyes widened, and her cheeks bloomed. But she didn't pull away. She touched his lower lip and, painstakingly slow, smoothed her fingertip across, her gaze locked with his.

With no more than a touch, she teased something awake in him, something wild and untamed that now hungered. Something he'd always caged.

He pressed his lips to her fingers in a reverent kiss.

Whatever lay between them slipped sight, but it lived, breathed, filled him with a tangible fullness that would not be denied. His gaze fell to her neck, where her pulse beat visibly. The same, steady throb inhabited his own body, heat flowing through him, awakening his senses.

A group of carousers catcalled them, elbowing one another and raising their glasses in toast. Blushing, Rielle responded in kind with her cup, and he followed suit.

But a certain selfishness wished to lay claim, surround her and banish all else, save for her breaths and his, her hands and his, her mouth and his—

"Perhaps it's time we head back."

She drained her cup. "You read my mind."

When he rose and offered her his arm, she took it and huddled close. Even through his shirt, the cold of her skin and her trembling fingers were undeniable.

As they made for the inn, an autumn storm rolled in. The first drops of rain fell.

Holding her hand, he rushed with her, careful to stay at a pace she could manage. The rain fell faster, heavier, lightning flashing in the distance moments before thunder rumbled. Everywhere, celebrants ducked under eaves, into buildings, torches hissing as they doused.

By the time they made it to the inn, they were both soaked. His shirt clung to his chest, a sopping mess.

They shuffled past the innkeeper and the tavern to the stairs, Rielle peeling back the wet locks of hair plastered to her rain-streaked face.

Their room was dark but for the lambent glow from the window. Once he closed the door, her breaths, soft and quiet, became the only sound.

She took a step, two, and reached for his shirt collar. Gentle fingers descended to the buttons and unfastened them slowly, purposefully. Droplets of water fell between them from her hair, and he smoothed the wet tresses away from her face, tucking them behind her ear.

Lightning flashed, brightening the darkness in the room. Breathless, he lifted her chin, and she gazed up at him, chest heaving.

Beautiful. The woman he loved was beautiful, glistening with rainwater.

She shivered. His leather doublet rested on her shoulders, soaked like the rest of her. And he wanted to warm her, hold her until every hint of vulnerability disappeared from her eyes.

He slipped the doublet off her shoulders. With a glance for permission, he reached for the laces of her bodice and, when she nodded, pulled the fine cords undone.

A rustle. Paper? Something floated to the floor.

29

*R*ielle caught Jon's gaze and held it. Feliciano's envelope lay on the floor. *Don't look down, don't look down, don't look down.*

He looked.

She lunged for the envelope, but he barred her with one arm and snatched the envelope up with the other. Before she could reach for it again, he checked inside.

Her world froze. His face went slack, then he pressed his lips into a thin line.

No, no, no... As he rose, his fingers closed around the envelope into a tight fist, and he turned his back to her. Her heart pounded.

"Where did you get this?" he asked, his voice low, hoarse, pained. "Sen'a?"

She clutched her bodice to herself and then grabbed a pillow.

"Rielle." Even hoarse, his tone demanded an answer.

She wavered. "I... needed to know what happened to Olivia," she said, "so I went to a spiritualist for answers. She's bound in Courdeval, but alive." When he only exhaled, she continued. "He required... payment for his knowledge."

"Payment," he repeated, wooden.

A pressure formed behind her eyes. "Resonance."

Silence lingered in the air for too long. He was rigid, full of a tension that displaced all else.

She swallowed. The pressure behind her eyes turned into a blurry haze over her vision. "With sen'a."

Fastening his shirt and his weapons belt bearing his dagger, he withdrew.

"I was addicted once," she said, the words spilling out of her mouth, "but that was three years ago, and I've been without until today."

Years ago, when the embarrassment of bedding her master and Brennan's humiliation of her had spread far and wide, the immense pleasure and resulting numbness of sen'a had presented a favorable option. It had been a clear victor compared to facing the scorn of the Tower, the guilt of Leigh's demotion, his never-ending string of bedmates, the ridicule of society, and the painful prospect of being an outcast.

A sharp oath later, and Jon rubbed his forehead. His shoulders were stone, his hands clenched into fists. "You used sen'a?"

"It was his price for answers."

"Who?" He crushed the envelope in his fist. When she didn't answer, he took a deep breath, but it did nothing to relax the hard lines of his face. "This spiritualist. Was it Feliciano Donati?"

There was an intensity in him she had never before seen.

"You know him?"

Jon whirled to face her, coiled aggression in his taut body. The tension in his face threatened to crest into rage. Before she could ask another question, he grabbed his doublet and marched to the door and out, slamming it shut behind him. The quick drum of heavy footsteps faded down the stairs.

Where—

She stumbled to the window.

He trod in the direction of the Shade.

Great Divine, he was going after Feliciano Donati.

She scrambled to the coat rack, grabbed her cloak, and raced outside, her fingers busy relacing her bodice. She pulled her hood over her head and ran through the rain toward Donati's. Years ago at the Tower, mages had dueled Feliciano to their detriment. Although addicted to sen'a, Feliciano was still a powerful mage with an immense anima.

But Jon's a paladin. Sigiled against all magic but healing. He could resist every one of Feliciano's spells and overpower him physically with relative ease.

But there were other mages at the resonance den.

How many had it—

Hadn't Jon taken on six fully capable mages on the Tower's property?

A group of tranced mages would be unlikely to subdue him, but he'd be fighting many. Too many. Without arcanir armor.

He still had his sigil tattoos. They'd keep him safe... wouldn't they?

Please be all right.

She quickened her pace, ignoring the looks she got from passersby still about in the night.

Finally, the gray banner came into view. Two tranced mages spilled out, clutching their limbs. She darted between them and through the doorway.

A mage slumped in one corner. Two mages leaned against a wall, hissing and guarding dislocated shoulders.

"By the Divine." Breathless, she pushed in. A tranced mage—the augur —was out cold, sprawled on top of rubbish that had once been a table.

I needn't have worried.

"—make quite an entrance, *bello.*" Feliciano's voice, muffled from the back room.

"Your sycophants accosted me." Jon, venom poisoning his tenor to a bitter hiss. "I disarmed them."

"It seems you have learned nothing since you last meddled here. I believe I etched my displeasure into your flesh quite clearly, *bello.* Would you like your other eyebrow to match?"

Other eyebrow?

When she'd stared at the scar slashed across Jon's eyebrow, he'd said, *Broken bottle. Apparently the usual greeting when faced with meddling paladins.*

Had Feliciano been the one...?

"You're short of men to hold me down, mage," Jon snarled. "But I'd love for you to try. Give me one more reason."

Feet frozen in place, she waited, prayed Jon would abandon this course. Feliciano had penetrated local government long ago, and Jon was a paladin no longer. If he hurt Feliciano now, the connétable would see him punished, if not killed. At the very best, he would become a fugitive.

"By your own Code, you can't touch me," Feliciano replied with his typical charm.

"I am bound by the Code no longer."

A moment of quiet.

She didn't dare shift. Not even a mouse would dare breathe until Feliciano answered.

"Why are you here? Who has you tied in such knots, *bello*?" Feliciano asked, his voice equal parts surprised and intrigued.

The rustle of paper.

"Not Favriella?"

Metal scraped against wood in an abrupt sweep. A chaos of objects crashed against the floor.

The hairs on the back of her neck stood.

"The eager *fiamma* came here with a question, and she purchased her answer."

She bit her lip. Her heart pounded so loudly they might hear it through the door.

"She wanted it," Feliciano spat. "You know nothing of the depths of her wanting. She desires it. She salivates for it. It stalks her every day, haunts her troubled mind, chases her. And, more than anything, she wants it to catch her. All I've done is help her attain her deepest desire."

Another cacophony beyond the door.

No.

She burst into Feliciano's quarters. Before the bed, Jon held a wincing Feliciano's arm twisted behind him, and a dagger to the back of his neck. He pressed the point into yielding flesh, a bead of blood swelling until its weight rolled down.

"Stop!"

If Jon killed Feliciano without lawful cause, without the protection of the Order—if, because of her—

She couldn't breathe.

Jon turned to her, his snarling face full of wrath.

"Please." She waited, her skin tingling.

Divine, he would do it. He would kill Feliciano.

She couldn't watch Jon follow wrath to certain destruction, but she couldn't turn away.

There is only one thing I can say to stop him. "I wanted it."

Jon's agonized gaze fell from her face to her hand.

It's over. He's disgusted by me. He hates me.

He loosened his grip on Feliciano's arm.

"Leave us," Rielle said to Feliciano.

He raised a rebellious eyebrow, but he would find no room for argument.

The air between them became dense, charged.

Then, with most of his usual Sileni repose, Feliciano lowered his eyebrow and took a deep breath.

Jon threw him free and then sheathed his dagger with an angry flourish. Fixated, she chewed her lip, heat surging under her skin. *Unsettling.*

Feliciano gave Jon an irritated glare as he rose to his feet and dusted himself off. He approached her, followed by Jon's watchful eyes, and gave her a pitying once-over before leaving and shutting the door behind him.

Pity.

Yes. She had yet to love a man and not have it go down in flames. Every man she allowed into her heart only broke what remained of it into smaller pieces. Jon was just the next in a long line of disasters.

But he wouldn't want her now, and it was better that way. *I won't be able to hurt him, and he won't be able to hurt me.*

"You wanted it?" He wouldn't meet her eyes.

She wouldn't have to let him in, share all her secrets, bare herself to him in all her fragile vulnerability and hope he didn't shatter her. Better they keep their armor—she her secrecy and he his distance.

"To learn whether Olivia lived, yes."

He raised his gaze to hers. "That's not the same."

The sea-blue of his eyes stormed, wild, untamed. He had come here to thrash a sen'a baron, and whatever had possessed him to abandon the Code was an indelible part of him now. *Fire.*

That much had changed... But had anything else? He disapproved of her way of life, her magic, her. He was disgusted by sen'a. By trancers. By her. "Does it matter?"

He took a step toward her, the turbulence in his gaze unrelenting. "Rielle, I—"

Didn't he know that he could have been killed? And for what? To punish someone else for her choices? And she could have come here to find him—to find him—

She stalked to him, brimming with fury. "What were you thinking, throwing your life away? A resonance den full of mages? You could have died!"

She curled her fingers into her palm, but he took her wrist.

His eyes met hers, intense, unblinking. "I'm in love with you."

Her mouth fell open.

"I broke my vows. I chose a new life. I chose you."

His vows were broken. He'd drunk wine tonight. He didn't just desire her; he *loved* her.

Fureur, pain, loss—"Jon, I bring hurt to all who love me."

He closed the distance between them and drew her against him. "Then give me memories to live in when the hurt comes."

Her knees weakened. A trembling fear wove through her, fear of hurting him and of being hurt by him, fear she'd long carried about love. But faced with the warm, firm reality of his embrace and the passion in his eyes, it faltered. He still burned, battle ready and raging beneath her touch, his chest hot despite the layers of rain-soaked leather and cotton. But he burned with different purpose now. His embrace awakened every part of her. *Yes.*

He lowered his mouth to hers. A fiery bloom of sensation consumed her fear and doubt until it burned away, met her hunger with his ferocity. Every rebellious thought standing in opposition to him wavered, swayed, knelt. His lips pressed against her own before teasing her lower lip between his, sending a shiver down her spine. Shaking the last discordant notes from her body, letting her be no more than who she was here, in his arms. A true self, a bare self... a scared self. He buried his fingers in her hair and knotted it, held her gently and coaxed her walls to fall open to him.

And her mouth, and every part of her, did open to him.

When he slipped his tongue into her mouth, her heart threatened to burst. Inhaling the heady scent of him—leather, rain, woodsmoke—she wrapped her arms around his back, willing him closer, deeper. And he explored her with slow, reverent hands, with a madding patience that only stoked the fire raging beneath her skin. He traced a line down her back—it came alive at his touch—and to the curve of her backside, palming her flesh.

She rotated her hips against his, could have cried at the ache of waiting.

A groan into her mouth, and he lifted her; she wrapped her legs around him and closed her arms around his neck. It was all happening in an instant, but she didn't care. She cared for nothing but the feel of him against her. Him. Her. Here. Now. Step by painstaking step, she edged him to the bed.

He braced an arm and a knee upon it and lowered her to the softness, his breaths heavy, long, deep.

Her mouth never leaving his, she unfastened her cloak and slipped out of her damp bodice. Beneath it, she wore a corset, and he followed the line of its busk with spellbound fingers.

"You know I've never—" The rawness of his rasp on her hot skin made her shiver.

"You're about to," she said, returning the words he'd given her at the festival.

His eyes widened, but his gaze turned dark with desire before he brought his mouth down to hers once more. She wrapped her wanting arms around his neck, squeezed his hips between her thighs. She wanted him. Now.

His firm hands planed down her back to her waist and over her backside, fingertips testing the firmness of her flesh as he gripped her, at last lowering a palm that encouraged her hips.

She set about unfastening his shirt with trembling fingers. He hissed in a breath above her; she would elicit many more before the night was through.

She kissed his neck, reveling in the salt of his skin, its firmness against her lips. At last, she threw open his shirt, baring the divine artistry of his body. A winding maze of sigil tattoos, firm corded muscle rippling beneath her touch, pure strength begging to be worshipped.

And worship it she would.

He threw off his shirt and doublet, then enclosed her between his arms, and she pulled him down to her. Her body pulsed in need; a loud exhalation, and she knew he'd felt it, too.

Dizzy and squirming, she craved his mouth, craved him, and what only he could give her. The press of his lips against her chest, and the tension in her body had reached its limit.

She reached for his waistband; he took in a sharp breath, then began unfastening the laces.

Great Divine, yes. Heart hammering with anticipation, she threw her head back.

Voices came from outside the quarters, from the resonance den.

She held her breath. *Not now, not now, not now.* But Jon paused above her, too.

Heaving breaths, she looked up at him, acceptance slowly sinking in. *Divine's flaming fire.* "Our time's up, isn't it?"

A grin broke through the determined frown on Jon's face, and he laughed.

More noise came from the other side of the doorway, and she turned an angry eye on the lock. She glanced around the room until she spotted a full bath. Gesturing a spell, she pulled the water to ice the lock—and the door, and the frame, and the wall.

Perhaps her body, too. And the rest of her. For several hours.

"It'll hold for a little while, at least," she said, "but not nearly long enough to... finish what we started."

With a sobering breath, he rose from the bed only to descend to the floor, his hands palm-down under his shoulders. His back straight, he lowered himself nearly to the floor and pushed back up again, then repeated the exercise. And again. And again. And again.

"Is now really the time?" She righted her clothes and grabbed for her cloak.

He didn't stop. "Give me a minute."

"For what? Must you do this *now?*" She gestured toward the door, where more voices now murmured on the other side. "They could be—"

"Yes, I must," he bit out between repetitions.

She left the bed and watched him with a raised eyebrow. He did a dozen more before the doorknob rattled. As the blood rushed to his face, her own cheeks heated.

He jumped to his feet, threw on his shirt and doublet, then grabbed his weapons belt. He secured it and took her hand, remarkably composed. "Let's go."

He led her out the back of the resonance den.

A quick survey of the alley—no one was about—and they slipped out into the night. He looked back with a roguish grin and gave her hand a squeeze.

He'd said he was in love with her. Warmth rose to her face, and she fought back a smile of her own.

"Back to the inn?" he offered readily.

This time she freed her smile. Every part of her yearned to return to The Crowned Stag as soon as possible, to finish what they'd started.

"With all haste," she said, earning a puckish grin from him in return. "This way."

30

*R*ielle looked over her shoulder. No one followed them. Good.

With a spell of earthsight, she scanned their surroundings. A healer here, another there; a few city folk with magic. No sign of a shadowmancer or an illusionist.

She held Jon's hand, and in the street's faint light, they made their way back to the inn. A group of laughing people crowded the street.

Sensations from the resonance den flooded her mind. Raw breaths. A hungry mouth. A firm hold. An intense gaze. *I'm in love with you.*

Her heart raced, a runaway horse galloping far from restraint, logic, reason. Divine, he'd said the words. And they'd felt like a soft caress that stroked beyond her longing flesh, deeper, found a flower in the shade and coaxed it toward the sun.

Fureur. Heartbreak. These shades lingered in the darkness of her, haunted. Letting Jon in had opened a doorway that risked both fureur and heartbreak. She could close it.

Jon's grip on her hand tightened. A paladin patrol passed by.

But his face lit with a warm smile, summoning that dimple that made her melt. Not worry. Happiness. She mirrored his expression.

She could close that doorway. But she didn't want to. Not now, not tonight, perhaps not ever. Not to him.

Fureur, heartbreak—she had fought powerful mages, assassins, armies... She would fight these shades, too.

The night streets of Bournand's thriving textile district did not ordinarily teem with folk as they did during the day, here in the center of the Weave, but tonight unfastened the ordinary and embraced the extraordinary. Even in the dimness of lanterns and candlelit windows, boots clicked on the cobblestones as people wove into taverns, out of inns, and between shops. Smiling. Happy. Together.

As she and Jon avoided a small crowd leaving a smoke shop, laughter burst nearby.

A group of carousers exited a tavern. Above them, a signboard hung, bearing the weather-worn script: *Cosette's Inn and Tavern*.

"Cosette's," she whispered. Where Flame had been staying. But they'd left the room key at The Crowned Stag.

Next to her, Jon paused, his smile fading to the grim line of duty.

Her runaway heart slowed a little. Flame had come after them. Shadow and Phantom were still out there.

He creased his brow. "There could be some trace of Gilles's whereabouts among the mage's things." He hesitated. "Shouldn't we...?"

Although he studied the signboard, his thumb softly stroked her hand in his. She gave his hand a squeeze, and he looked her over, sucking in a breath as his gaze lingered over certain of her curves.

The feeling was mutual.

"The Crowned Stag," he murmured. "Definitely The Crowned Stag." He fixed his eyes on hers and held them.

Desire pulsed like a drum.

Great Divine, *yes*—they could lock themselves in their room for the next two nights to learn the meaning of exhaustion...

But Flame's room could be cleared by then. If it hadn't been already. And they'd be as blind going forward as they'd been so far.

With a heavy sigh, she tore herself away and looked out at the tavern. "As eager as I am—and believe me, I'm eager—we need to know why Flame attacked us. Since we're already here, we should investigate his room."

A pull at her hand, and she tumbled into his arms. He raised her mouth to his, claiming her lips with a hungry kiss.

"I'd love to disagree," he whispered, his voice deep and sultry, "but you're right." He brushed his lips against hers and exhaled a shaky breath.

Hunger. Him.

He pulled away.

She nearly stumbled—

Legs. Feet. Street.

But he offered her his arm. She grasped for some sobriety. A blur of people moved past them as he walked her to Cosette's.

Protecting Jon came first. Had to. If Flame left behind any information, it could help keep Jon alive.

The thoughts straightened her spine, and she took strength from them, raising her chin as they approached. *Focus.*

Below the signboard, an image of a hummingbird sipping from a tankard made plain the nature of the establishment.

She leaned in close to his ear. "Pretend we're very anxious. Rent us a room for an hour."

Jon stiffened, then raised a teasing eyebrow. "Pretend?"

His eagerness coaxed a small smile from her.

The inn's door swung open, and revelry spilled out, along with a dance of lamplight and shadows. As Jon caught the door, she tucked herself under his arm and sauntered in with him.

The tavern swelled with wenches, merrymakers, carousers, and drunkards at tables abundant with food and drink. Laughter, song, and conversation dominated the atmosphere. This was a crowd trying to ignore the plight of the kingdom. Trying very hard.

A large fireplace graced the center of the room, its flames playing around the reddened embers and roasting chickens.

At the counter, a flush-faced woman with flyaway curls greeted them. She glanced expectantly from Rielle to Jon and back again while a loud guffaw echoed from the tavern.

"A room, please," Jon said.

Here to work. Intent on that reminder, Rielle nuzzled Jon's arm. A cheerful drinking song started nearby.

"And how long will you be staying?" The woman dipped a quill in an inkwell and opened a book.

"An hour," Jon replied.

The woman winked and grabbed a set of keys from a hook. "That'll be five cuivres." She placed the keys on the table. Tankards clinked behind them.

Jon slid over five copper coins and picked up the keys. "Our thanks."

Lips twitching in an almost-giggle, the woman gave them a gladdened nod and gestured toward the stairs. "If you'd like some ale, just let one of my girls know!"

The innkeeper tipped her head toward a serving woman, and Jon nodded.

He swept Rielle off her feet and carried her to the stairs in what had to be an inspired bit of acting, earning whistles and cheers from the tavern-goers. As he carried her upstairs to the accompaniment of the crowd's lively encouragement, her blush required no pretending at all.

The noise returned to drinking songs and laughter, and Jon set her down on the second floor.

"I didn't think you had it in you to be that shy," he teased in her ear. His low, husky voice made her wish they'd actually be using the room. "It was entirely unnatural."

"Underestimate me at your peril, Jonathan Ver." Flashing him a playful grin, she breezed past him.

"Wouldn't dream of it." He unlocked the door.

With a gesture, she lit a nearby candle. The room was tiny but cheery, its drabness warmed with a vase of wildflowers on the nightstand and a bright needlepoint of a sunflower hanging on the wall. A colorful, home-spun patchwork quilt perked up the small bed. The personal touches made her sorry they actually weren't staying.

Jon's breath warmed her ear; his gaze locked on the quilt, too.

"Well," she said with a cleansing breath, "we have some business to attend to."

"Business. Of course." His whisper teased her ear like a wisp of smoke. She longed to breathe it in, deep, slow...

Business.

Smiling to herself, she opened the door and checked the hall; it was empty. As she exited, Jon was right behind her and shut the door softly.

At one end of the corridor was a small stockroom, and at the other end, a door and an alcove for linens off to the side. Although she had left the key at The Crowned Stag, the fob had said *3* on the back; she matched it to the corner door.

They were almost at the door when footsteps sounded from the stair-well. She grabbed Jon and pulled him into the linen alcove, pressing her back against its wall. The footsteps neared, a door opened, and there was a short lull before the door closed, and the footsteps departed.

For a moment, there was only breath, warmth, and close proximity.

"The room," Jon whispered, taking a step back.

With a check of the hallway, she moved toward the door and reached for the doorknob. The chances of it being unlocked were slim, but she had to try.

No good.

"It's locked," she said softly.

He nodded for her to stand aside, and she took a couple steps away. He faced the door squarely, his knees slightly bent. When a wave of merry-making sounded from downstairs, he snap-kicked the lock with the flat of his booted foot.

The door swung open.

He moved to catch it when she looked at the floor just inside the room.

She pounced on him before he could enter, tackling him to the floor in the hallway. The noise from the tavern below drowned out the sound.

Shocked, he fixed her with a wide-eyed stare. "What—?"

"My knowledge of healing magic doesn't extend to reattaching limbs." She cocked her head toward the doorway. Just inside the room, an ornate fire rune was inscribed on the floor. Upon contact with anyone but the caster, it would explode. "And I happen to like your limbs. Very much."

He flashed a brief smile. "I'm sigiled, Rielle. All paladins are. Direct spells, even runic spells, can't hurt me."

Of course. She shrugged. *Smart. Really smart.*

She held her hand over the fire rune and dispelled it. Standing, she scanned the floor for more runes. When she found none, she was about to enter when Jon preempted her. Per usual.

Inside, she spelled the candle aflame and took inventory. On the desk, papers of all kinds lay scattered and weighed down with a variety of items—focus crystals, inkwells, coin purses, candles. A thick book lay on the night-stand, a partially written letter upon it. Perhaps Flame had been composing one the night before he'd left to attack them on the road.

Jon approached the desk and picked up a paper, frowning. He held it out to her, a full page of unintelligible script.

"It's written in code." She took it from him, folded it, and tucked it into her shirt. Leaning over the desk, she pulled out papers, searching for anything useful while Jon riffled through the book from the nightstand.

"Ancient blood rites," he said, presumably reading the title.

She paused—the Moonlit Rite and the Rift. Perhaps the book contained answers. "Take it with us."

A stack of letters on the desk were written in plain Emaurrian, a personal correspondence with no names or locations. Some details on recruiting efforts and replies to Flame's status reports.

There was a crackle of folding paper.

Jon held up the partially written letter from the nightstand. He read, " 'I'm heading out onto the Kingsroad to handle the problem.' A message left for someone?"

"One of the other captains?" *I hope not.* "Any clue on who it was meant for?"

Jon fanned out the papers before him and shook his head.

She gathered the letters and stuffed them into her clothes. Jon paused, a frustrated crease etched on his brow.

"Anything about Gilles?"

"No."

A creak came from the window.

Behind the glass, a shadow darkened the view of the Weave's streets, hanging from the window frame. A hooded figure.

The spy dropped from view.

Jon bolted from the room, book in hand.

"Wait—" Rielle spared a fleeting glance around the room—out of time —and ran to the hallway. By the time she reached the lower level, Jon was already out the door.

Ignoring the dumbfounded innkeeper, she burst out into the crowded street.

Jon broke a path through the people. She chased after him, shouldering through the drunkards and carousers.

Ahead, a blade glinted in the light of a shop's lantern.

She began to close the gap, focused on Jon's back, but then a hand grabbed Jon's arm, twisting it behind his back.

31

*P*ain seized Jon's shoulder. "I don't want to hurt you," he said, earning a low laugh in reply. His captor drew Jon's arcanir dagger and flung it into a wall twenty feet away.

A burst of fire flared around him—it had to be Rielle, although he couldn't see her. But it didn't slow his attacker.

He wrenched his arm loose and turned, meeting the thrust of a dagger with the book he held. The blade would have slid between his ribs and pierced his heart.

A woman.

With the dagger stuck, Jon dropped the book and grabbed her gloved hand, twisting it into a wrist-lock. He kicked at a knee.

Dodging, she swept back and around him. He released her, evading a kick to the head. Fast. Too fast. She struck at his face with a palm. He pulled back.

A punch to the gut followed—he couldn't dodge, but he braced. Unyielding, she doled out strike after strike with nary a breath in between, met with blocks.

Sparks of fire blazed nearby, but she was too agile. Passersby darted away, screaming. Magic in the streets of Bournand—

He blocked and evaded her attacks, but it couldn't last. He would have to go on the offensive or lead her somewhere emptier, away from bystanders.

He dodged a short side kick to the head, seizing the opportunity for a hook kick to her jaw.

Evaded.

Dropping to the ground, he swept his leg in a low roundhouse kick.

It didn't connect. She evaded him in a puff of shadowy smoke that obfuscated his immediate surroundings—magic.

A shadowmancer.

Shadow.

Alert, Jon listened for anything that would give away Shadow's location.

Nothing.

A hand to the front of his chest, and a pair of thighs closed around his neck. Within seconds, Shadow threw him onto his back. His breath burst from his lungs. He wedged a hand into the lock to create space and struck her in the kidneys.

Her thighs released him, but hands closed around his neck. He reached out and grabbed a smooth neck in turn, his other hand seizing her wrist in a crushing grip that made her arm tremble.

His reach and strength were far greater. Her neck in his grip, he managed to push her away, forcing her to choose between continuing to choke him or having her own neck snapped.

Shadow threw the weight of her body to the side, her thigh perpendicular to his arm. He had to let her go lest his elbow break.

Still unable to see anything in the shadows, he sprang to his feet.

Noise—panicked sounds of the escaping crowd—he tried to filter it out.

Thunder rolled. Magic. A crack of lightning rent the air. A gust of wind blew past, and the shadows receded. She fled.

As the smoke cleared, Rielle raced past him, bringing her hands up in a green glow.

Roots erupted through the cobbles after Shadow, green sprouts surging from the tree-flesh in winding vines amid clouds of dust. At the head of the chaos, Rielle ran, Shadow just ahead of her.

He chased after them, leaping over the arcs and spikes of wood erupting from the cobblestones. He evaded the smaller hooks and notches, then jumped over a large loop. Shadow rounded a corner and disappeared in a wisp of darkness.

Rielle palmed a growing flame. With an angry roar, she threw it in the direction of the woman.

The fireball flared past the corner.

It dissipated without hitting the target. Rielle chased after it, then snarled and stopped at the corner, staring down the small corridor at the darkness between the dwellings. Her hands on her knees, she breathed hard, winded.

"Divine's flaming fire!" She frowned, fixated on the empty corridor. "Was that—?"

"Shadow." He looked down the alley with her.

"Divine, what's next? Are the twelve magisters coming for you?" She brought a shaky hand to her forehead and then let out a huge breath. "I think we've seen the last of her, for some time at least." She eyed the mass of roots dominating the street and, with a descending palm and green glow, returned them to the ground. "Is everyone all right?"

"I think so." No one seemed harmed—the streets had cleared. He spotted his arcanir dagger in the nearby wall and pulled it free, then sheathed it and traced back to where he'd been attacked. On the cobblestones lay the book, an obsidian dagger buried in it.

He dropped to a knee, placed his booted foot on the cover, and yanked the blade free. He turned it, and the dim light of a nearby shop's lantern reflected off its beautiful black surface. It was long and serpentine, as sharp as a dragon's tooth.

But for the book, it would have killed him. Was it because he'd given chase? Shadow had seemed content enough to spy on them before he'd pursued her...

He tucked the dagger into his belt and then picked up the book. Were the Crag hunting paladins, or just people interfering with Crag affairs? If Derric had known the Crag Company had been hired to kill paladins, perhaps that explained his request of the Tower's Proctor. And Rielle.

When he rose, he found Rielle standing there, her intense eyes fixed on the dagger's hilt, her stare blazing. Lethal. She stood frozen, mesmerized, a madness tainting the single-minded violence in her eyes.

Slowly, he approached her and reached for her limp hand.

Her eyes still fixed, she inhaled sharply and swallowed. After a moment, she met his eyes. Her nostrils flaring, she heaved labored breaths. "I need to see Leigh. Now."

Why? The madness in her gaze belied the asking.

Paying no heed to the looks they received from the few agog bystanders, he put his arm around her and headed back to the inn.

32

*R*ielle knocked on Leigh's door. No answer. She knocked harder. Not a sound on the other side.

That dagger—she'd seen its like before but couldn't place it. When battle fury took hold, there was the fire, as always, the fire, and the memory felt so real. The flames had singed the hair on her skin all over again.

Murderer. Demon.

And all she wanted to do was kill. She hated it, couldn't stand it. But when battle fury took over, it repressed her will, imposed its own. To end life.

While she fought battle fury for control, she could direct it, if not reliably stop it, but without a kill, it intensified, unsatisfied, clamoring for full fureur. And if she had something, someone, to lose, the fight for control became more difficult to win.

No kill had satisfied battle fury tonight, but she had managed to bring it under her control, reciting her oath to the Divinity as she always did. *I, Favrielle Amadour Lothaire, pledge myself, from now for eternity, to the holy Divinity of Magic.*

I declare to take freely and solemnly this oath of obedience, allegiance, piety, and diligence...

With this oath, I state my strong and irrevocable intent.

It was as far as she'd gotten. As far as she'd needed to get for her mind to retake control.

With a heavy sigh, she laid a palm flat against the door and shook her head.

"Perhaps we should talk to him tomorrow," Jon said.

He had come to danger because of her once again. When she had seen that dagger, its aim between his ribs—the thought of it finding its mark had ignited battle fury, the gateway to fureur. It was only his survival that had stopped her from flaring into fureur in the midst of a crowd, in a densely populated city.

She closed her eyes. The carnage would have been unspeakable. Unforgivable.

If she'd fallen into fureur tonight, all of Bournand could have gone up in flames, Jon included. If he had been killed—she didn't want to consider that possibility.

Her feelings for Jon were dangerous. Not just to her. Not just to him. To anyone in their path, should his life be in danger.

She needed to talk to Leigh.

"Tonight." She grabbed the knob and turned.

It was unlocked.

Before her, on the large bed, Leigh lay sprawled, shirtless, with a decanter of wine on a wet nightstand. The cups were across the room, on the table.

She cleared her throat.

No response.

A little louder.

This time, Leigh cracked an eye open and perked his head up. Slowly, a smile brightened his face.

"*Ma chère,*" he greeted. "Please, have a drink." He waved a shaky finger toward the decanter. "You too, Jon." He chuckled to himself.

"We're fine," she replied while Jon studied the decanter with a frown.

"Pity. It's port, your favorite, fourteen hours decanted." Leigh made no move to rise, so she reached for the serpentine dagger at Jon's belt.

She held it up. "Ever seen one of these?"

Without a word, he extricated himself from the disheveled bed and rose, wearing nothing but fitted black trousers, an unfastened belt, and boots. He poured the rest of the bottle of port into the decanter and drank straight out of it in loud gulps, burgundy rivulets trickling down his neck and bare chest as he headed for the nearby table.

Jon sighed, crossing his arms and bowing his head to pinch the bridge of his nose.

"How long have you been drinking tonight?" she asked.

One cold eye transfixed her, a fearsome stillness possessing Leigh's body.

All the air drained out of the room. She swallowed. Leigh's warning look had always petrified her. No matter that she was no longer his apprentice.

Jon cleared his throat. "Up for a discussion?"

Leigh dragged a chair out from the table and planted himself in it. He gestured to the two other places available.

They sat, and she placed the twisted obsidian blade on the sticky table. "We were attacked by a woman wielding this. Do you know anything about it?"

Leigh grabbed the blade and scrutinized it. His eyes widened. "Did you defeat her?"

"I couldn't. No more than I could defeat shadow and celerity. We suspect it was Shadow of the Crag Company."

"Shadow?" Leigh cocked his head. "What would Shadow want with either of you?"

"I don't know. What does the Crag Company want with the paladins? But we were attacked on the way to Bournand by a man claiming to be Flame."

Leigh bared his teeth. "And you've waited until *now* to tell me this? *Ma chère*, you try my gentility."

"He's dead," Jon interrupted.

Leigh regarded him with a glassy stare. "And you think you've done well, do you?" He turned back to her. "If the Crag Company is after either of you, they will not stop, all the more if you've killed Flame. The general will not let that stand."

"I have my mission." But it was strange that, although she'd tried to kill Shadow, the woman had not tried to engage her. *Almost as though she tried not to kill me.*

"Flame would have been the easiest of them for you, knowing his tricks as you do, but Shadow and Phantom will test even your considerable dueling abilities."

"Shadow ran."

"You cannot be so naive as to think that's the whole of it. Shadow-mancers always want to fight on their terms, and they will disappear like the receding tide only to return in full force once more. She will wait until you are distracted, vulnerable, and then she will strike again."

"And I'll be there," Jon replied, his voice hard, his neck stiff and corded.

"Until the end of the mission, perhaps," Leigh shot back. "And as likely to distract as to defend."

Jon bristled.

"And Phantom—you won't even see her coming before it's too late. *Ma chère*—" Leigh shook his head.

"I can handle them." When Phantom would come for her, when Shadow would return, she'd be ready.

"At least while you're here, near me, neither of them would dare engage you." Leigh ran his finger across the flat of the dagger's blade. A line of runes glowed in reply. He grimaced. "Did you study this at all?"

Between the search, the chase, the fight, battle fury—she shrugged.

"Naturally," Leigh said flatly. "This is a soulblade."

She coughed—she had forgotten to breathe. Soulblades were made of a rare volcanic glass infused with sangremancy—to avenge. Embedded into the target of the sangremancy curse, it could kill instantly.

"Soulblade?" She gaped. Damn it all, an infamous heretic shadow-mancer had nearly killed Jon with a soulblade, and they weren't even halfway to Monas Amar.

"What's a soulblade?" Jon asked.

"A rare and priceless weapon designed for vengeance. The runes are chiseled with recondite. Not even a paladin would be immune to its magic." Leigh sighed, brandishing the dagger. "She'll be back for it, I'm sure."

"If she does, I'll give it to her." Sharply. Deeply. Painfully.

"That's my girl." With a heartening grin, Leigh reached for a cup and poured himself some more port.

At least he was using a cup. Progress.

She slid the blade into her boot and laid the cylindrical case on the table. "In any case, it also turns out that Kieran was sent to Courdeval." She opened the case. "Maps of the capital—Azalée and Trèstellan Palace, specifically."

Leigh peered down his nose at the maps. "Is that so?"

Was he really going to play dumb? "There were signs of a struggle in his room."

"Did you find a body?"

"No," she replied. "The room overlooked a waterway. Where a body might easily have been disposed." When he didn't meet her eyes, she added, "It was at The Velvet Glove. Your usual room."

His gaze locked with hers.

No more games. "Did you kill Kieran?"

"Yes."

Next to her, Jon shifted in his chair.

"Why?" she asked Leigh.

He spread his arms wide. "The man provided plenty of reasons," he replied bitterly. "But if you knew the things he threatened to do to you—"

She balled her hands into fists. "You killed him because he threatened to do something to me?"

Hardly believable, but not impossible. Kieran had always hated her for winning the apprenticeship to Leigh—and his hatred had only escalated to open war between them.

Leigh inhaled an incensed breath. "He rented a room personally instead of taking the Tower's reservations. If he knew you were coming through Bournand and wanted to enact his plan—"

"Or he just wanted to stay there."

Leigh rose. "He told me that one day he'd kill you." His eyes were narrowed, dangerous, a clear warning she knew well: to proceed with caution. "I did what needed doing."

She stood. "If he threatened me, why didn't you tell me?"

He paced toward the window. "You would have felt responsible if I did."

He was right. And she did feel responsible. She *was* responsible.

A threat wasn't reason enough to kill someone, but she'd told Leigh that Kieran had reported their affair to Magehold and had pushed her down the stairs last year. Brutal, decisive action was Leigh's way.

"That hydromancer wanted to kill you, *ma chère*. I say good riddance." Leigh settled back into his chair. "Wouldn't you agree, Jon?"

Jon crossed his arms and frowned contemplatively. Then he looked up at her. "Hydromancer."

Hydromancer. That heretic in the ruins had said, *As long as that hydromancer is dealt with before he reaches his destination.*

Jon's eyes flickered from hers to Leigh and back again.

Pensive, she blew out a soft breath. *And so the hydromancer has been dealt with.*

There was no way Leigh would be working with heretics. To what end could he possibly? Leigh had been working for the Divinity since before she'd had her éveil, and they'd been so close—as close as two people could become—for years. If he worked against the Divinity, he would have told her.

She shook her head at Jon. There was no way.

"Kieran was on a mission from Magehold to Courdeval," she said to

Leigh, "to perform the Moonlit Rite. Someone else will need to do it." She grabbed Kieran's orders and handed them to Jon.

When he finished reading them, he passed them to Leigh.

Eyes narrowed, Leigh slipped on his spectacles and read, crumpling the orders in his hand when he finished. He sighed. "Don't tell me you intend to do this? Sneak into the capital, do the rite, see if Olivia's alive?" He didn't wait for her to answer. "And why are you revealing orders to an outsider?" He glared at Jon.

Sitting up straighter, Jon scowled back at him.

The last thing she needed was another brawl between them. "The mission was high priority. The way I see it, I have two options. The first is to return to the Proctor with all of this. The second is to finish my mission and then Kieran's."

She sat, folded her hands together, and looked from Jon to Leigh.

"You have your orders," Leigh said in the authoritative tone she knew all too well. "Magehold will have a contingency plan. Unsanctioned missions lead to excommunication and punishment. You know that, and you can't risk it." His gaze flickered to Jon.

She shivered. There was the very small matter of her unwanted betrothal to Brennan. She'd wait him out under the Divinity's contract until his father gave up on her and arranged a new marriage. That, of course, would be difficult if she were excommunicated.

And however irrelevant her betrothal, Jon deserved to know. She needed to tell him. But not tonight. She bit her lip.

With a nod, Leigh took the cue well and quickly. "If you want to become a magister, you need to complete your mission, no more and no less, and get your next commendation. Focus on that."

Avoid Courdeval? "What about Olivia? I can't just leave her there and this... Rift, whatever it is, to happen."

Leigh sighed. "I don't want to abandon Olivia either, but I'm not in favor of sacrificing one former apprentice to save another. My trip to Bournand is just a pleasure trip. I can take Kieran's things back to the Tower and talk to Pons. He'll send someone."

Jon took her hand. "You should do both missions, Rielle." He fixed her with a ruminative stare that made her hold her breath. "I'll help you."

Leigh scoffed, earning a warning look from Jon.

"But... I'm supposed to take you to Monas Amar."

"You will," Jon replied, "but if I choose to go to the capital afterward, then I don't see how you can stop me." He smiled warmly. "There's a lot at stake, if these orders are to be believed. The Rift sounds disastrous for not only the city but the kingdom. And no one can begrudge you wanting to save a friend," he said, his eyelids falling heavily for a moment.

He had to be remembering the friend he'd lost. Sir Bastien.

"And I won't turn down an opportunity to destroy the Crag Company." Jon's expression turned hard as he stared at the maps.

She met Leigh's scowl directly. "After Monas Amar, we're going to Courdeval. It's the right thing to do."

He rolled his eyes. "You don't even have this vial mentioned in the ord—"

She pulled out the vial on the chain around her neck and held it up defiantly.

"Oh fine," Leigh grumbled. "Shadow and Phantom, along with the rest of the damned Crag Company, hunt you, *ma chère*, and you want to infiltrate a heavily guarded city. You know I'm not about to let you run off to your death with only a forsworn paladin for support."

Jon began to rise next to her, but she covered his hand with hers. He glared at her but kept his peace. Her former master had never been a mild man, but his heart was in the right place.

"Now get out. I need to sleep off all the insanity you've just spewed at me." Glowering, Leigh tipped his head toward the door.

Her stomach rolling, she gathered everything from the table and handed it to Jon. "I'll catch up in a minute."

Jon hesitated, looking from her to Leigh and back, but finally nodded. "I'll see if the kitchen can send up supper." With a glance at Leigh, Jon left the room and closed the door.

"He's jealous." Leigh raised a knowing eyebrow. "At least you finally have someone cleaning out the cobwebs."

If only. She bit her lip. Was that why he'd riled Jon so much? Testing him for reaction? Hoping jealousy would give away the truth of the matters between them?

"You wanted to speak to me in private. Something you didn't want to discuss with your new lover present."

Lover. She dropped back into the chair, her heart pounding.

"You love him."

She buried her face in her hands. For three years, she'd managed casual dalliances, kept her heart safe, herself free from risk and others safe from the ever-looming possibility of her fureur.

Enter Jon. She sighed. Her desire for him had come quick, strong, so heady she hadn't thought past it. She'd only fallen for him harder, deeper, since. And now, she risked him, herself, and everyone around her if anything ever happened to him.

"Fureur," she croaked.

He raked his fingers through his long white hair. "How close were you?"

"A dagger strike away." She rubbed her forehead and pulled at her bodice. The blasted thing had become terribly uncomfortable, made all the more so by the aches inhabiting every inch of her body and the crawling sensation beneath her skin.

He closed his eyes, massaging his temple with a finger. "Three years ago, the Grand Divinus's hensarin cuffed me with arcanir. They knew there was a good chance I loved you and that we would be parted. A wild mage in fureur—it's unthinkable—but in arcanir, I was harmless. I don't know what would have happened without it when the Magisterium advocated for moving you to Magehold, but I'd like to think I would have withstood battle fury and not gone into fureur. I don't know."

She gasped. "Then it's true. You sacrificed the magister's mantle to keep them from transferring me." After the demotion, he'd shut down, distanced himself from her, and had never opened up about the proceedings despite all her questioning.

"I should have never allowed what happened between us to happen. I failed as a master, and as a man."

"I pursued you." Even as an apprentice, she'd been bold.

"It doesn't matter. What happened was my fault, and I wouldn't let you suffer for it."

She met his earnest eyes and nodded her thanks. "What you did, I'm grateful—"

He shook his head. "I'm not telling you this for your gratitude. I don't need that. I never did. I'm telling you this to remind you that unless you make peace with yourself, there are only two ways fureur ends—death or arcanir."

Death or arcanir.

He pulled a small satchel from his belt and emptied it into his palm, then presented the contents to her.

A small, sage-tinted ring.

"It's—" She'd never forget it. "Nine years ago, when you found me in Laurentine, you put that on me. An arcanir ring."

He closed his fingers around it. "When I was accepted as a novice at the Kamerish Tower, the Proctor gave me this... because I'm a wild mage. My fureur could destroy the world."

The destruction of the world. It should have been a ridiculous proposition, but she believed him. With a link to the earth's anima, a wild mage's fureur could truly end everything.

"I was taught not to love, not to develop attachments, not to cling to other people as we are born to do, all in order to prevent fureur." He drained his cup and tipped it on its side.

She already loved Jon. Could she... stop loving him?

"Were you able to?" In her heart, she knew the answer.

"No. You know that." He avoided her gaze. "But that is the advice given to us by the Divinity."

She frowned. "And you... don't trust that?"

He righted the cup. "What is magic, *ma chère?*"

"Anima."

"And anima?"

She shrugged. "Everything. It's in everything."

"Nature," he said. "Anima is nature. Magic is nature. And love? Is it natural?"

She raised one shoulder.

"Do you suppose magic would require the inhibition of something so natural as love? What does it serve? Whom does it serve?"

Whom did it serve... If the Divinity was teaching mages prone to battle fury to inhibit love, it meant fewer attachments. Powerful mages with fewer priorities. Available to pursue the Divinity's priorities. "That's ridiculous."

"Is it?" He brought the decanter closer, swirled its contents. "Do you know what battle fury is?" When she shook her head, he dragged her chair close to his. "It's disharmony... between this"—he touched her forehead—"and this." He touched her chest, just over her heart. "Your mind comprehends someone you love in danger, part of a truth your heart knows in full. A truth it must accept."

She waited, but he didn't continue. "And that is...?"

"We—battle mages—are governed by the heart. Our passions are strong, our hearts violent. We don't know how to love with restraint. But if we try to impose those restraints, if there is disharmony within ourselves, we can't control our magic. Something else takes control." He poured a full cup.

"Fureur."

He nodded.

Although she understood his words, if there was an answer in there about preventing fureur, it was in code.

"Making peace with yourself is the answer to fureur, *ma chère.*"

"How do I make peace with myself?"

He drank. Slowly. Very Slowly. "What keeps you from giving your heart free rein?"

She frowned and shook her head. Fear? Pain? Danger? "I don't know."

"Well, you need to find out, and make peace."

Make peace? How did one make peace with fear? With pain? With danger? She wrinkled her brow. "And if I can't?"

"You need a safeguard." He put the arcanir ring back in its satchel, then stashed the satchel back in his belt pouch.

On the black market, it was worth a thousand times its weight in coronas. Paladins were sometimes hunted and killed for it.

Swallowing, she rose. Her stomach churned, and she rubbed it. Sen'a withdrawal was setting upon her; she could feel it. "Thank you... for everything." She headed for the door. "Goodnight."

He smiled. "Go back to your lover and make it so."

She left the room, then paused in the hall to gather her composure.

Loving someone, loving Jon, meant not only putting herself at risk but him, too.

I can't lose him.

And if, Divine forbid, she *did* lose Jon, she'd go into fureur and kill everything and everyone near.

Unless she made peace with herself. Whatever that meant.

33

*J*on set down the glass of wine, staring at its unsettled dark red until it stilled. The maid had brought up supper—fine baked veal pâté with figs, cornichons, warm partial-rye bread, and a hearty pea soup—luxuriously far from the country pâté of chicken liver and pork that was his favorite. And here it sat, this expensive meal, nearly gone cold.

Rielle still hadn't returned from Leigh's room.

Probably some internal Divinity matters. Nothing more.

He spread out the papers they'd taken from Flame's room and lifted a sheaf to read. Coded. It would take some time before they'd learn the contents.

And just why had she trusted the mage so easily? He'd killed a man, lied to her, and she just took his word?

Jon set down the paper and crossed his arms, leaning back in his chair.

With a sigh, he threw his head back. Candlelight swayed with shadow on the ceiling.

Was Leigh trustworthy? He'd shown up in Rielle's bedchamber that night in the Tower, clearly wanting something she hadn't planned on giving, and now he'd just coincidentally shown up in Bournand? In the same inn? Lying about a murder?

Something didn't fit. His easy demeanor suggested no jealousy—so he didn't seem to be after Rielle. So why the late-night visit at the Tower? Why the appearance here?

And this Kieran—the victim—had been a hydromancer. Like the heretics had mentioned.

The candle's glow flickered, shadow claiming the ceiling for a moment. He'd seen countless liars over the years, questioned them, unraveled them, sentenced them. And Leigh Galvan was a liar.

Leigh and Rielle were close. That much was certain. The mage had made it clear they'd meant a lot to each other in various ways for a decade.

And I've known her for a week. He sighed. Rielle trusted the mage. Without question.

I don't. She gave the mage the benefit of every doubt, but that didn't mean he had to.

I'll watch him.

The door creaked open. He straightened.

Rielle poked her head in and smiled, wavering but warm. With a swish of her white cotton dress, she entered, then cast a ward before the door.

He grinned. "Finished plotting the conquest of the universe?"

She chuckled softly, tongue in cheek, then shut the door. "Ah, yes. I updated my black-arts overlord on my symbolic victory over the paladins." She removed her boots and set them next to his by the door. Together.

"You mean on your acceptance of a willing surrender."

She cast another ward at the window, then strode by, touching his hand and stroking her way up his arm to his shoulder, and leaned in close. Close enough for him to inhale rose balm and rainwater and *her.*

"Are you ready to continue negotiating the terms?" she whispered into his ear, raising a pleasant shiver.

Elementalists were fearsome indeed, if they could reduce a man to cinders without casting a single spell. Perhaps it was just *his* elementalist.

He turned his head to hers, her lips a soft breath away from his. "You have but to ask, witch."

A mischievous smile curled her mouth, and the sky blue of her eyes shimmered. She licked her lip—enviable, enviable tongue—humming a quiet moan that teased more than it answered.

She slipped away and disappeared behind the privacy screen. And he could breathe again.

Water splashed.

His chest pounded. Terra have mercy, what was he doing?

His tongue had taken leave of his senses and boasted without a shred of experience to call upon for reinforcement.

He shuffled the pile of papers. There had been stories of famous rakes and their exploits. How they pleasured women. He had read those.

Books on anatomy. He'd read those, too.

Casual talk. He'd heard his fair share in towns and villages, men boasting of their conquests. Among the abundance of tall tales, there could have been some small whit of practical advice.

As a squire, he and his friends had carefully studied erotic illustrations they weren't supposed to have. Ah, contraband. It had been endlessly fascinating. Although... the Sonbaharans had drawn feats of human flexibility that gave the imagination a week's worth of long-sword drills. Per page.

Those among them who'd come to the monastery later, who'd had some experience with girls, had been asked to recount their tales a thousand times over. In detail. All variations of fumbling in the dark, earth-shattering ecstasy, comparisons of breasts, and everything being over far too soon.

These were the things he knew about lovemaking.

He scrubbed a hand over his face, dropped his head in his hands. Merciful Terra. What was wrong with him? He could train all day and every day, resolve disputes ranging from petty squabbles to the most violent of crimes, kill men in battle, hold to strict vows for years on end—but this... *this* was... beyond—

The papers crunched beneath his elbows. Crumpled. He flattened them and then undid the first few buttons of his shirt, his gaze settling on the bed.

The bed.

He'd slept on the floor last night. But tonight, after what had happened at Donati's, would she—?

Light footsteps. Rielle padded across the room barefoot, small perfect toes peeking out from under her full-length white nightgown, lacy, feminine, soft. She'd unbound her hair, long golden cascades shimmering in the candlelight. They swelled around her in wild disarray, untamed and shining and ferocious. Just like her.

She strode to the table and poured herself some wine, then took her glass to the vanity, where she rifled through her packs until she pulled out a jar. A pinch of its contents went into the wine.

A powder. She wasn't ill—that he knew of. There was a common preventive women used, also a powder—was that it? A preventive taken daily, for...

He raised his glass to his mouth and drank down its bittersweet contents all at once. Wine was relaxing, fortifying. Or was supposed to be. Any second now.

Flushed, she came and sat next to him. He looked back at her with what he hoped was a completely normal facial expression. Then her gaze dropped. To his lap.

She reached out and rested a hand on his bouncing knee.

Terra's troth. *Idiot.* He stilled. "It's, um—must be the—"

She rose and sat in his lap, wrapping an arm around his neck. Her eyes met his, their clear skies sparkling.

She found this all amusing, didn't she? Smug little witch. He wanted to laugh, but held back. In the resonance den, he'd been a man possessed, his mind silent, but now?

Mind. That was it. Too much time to think.

For a long moment, he held her gaze, losing himself in her intensity, and then he wrapped his arm around her waist, drew her in, and brushed her lips with his. Natural. Warm. Soft. She met his kiss slowly, the smoothness of her lips caressing his, teasing his nose with hers.

Playful. He huffed an amused breath, but before he could say anything, she covered his mouth with hers, kissed him hungrily, explored him with her eager tongue. Wanted. She tightened her hold around his neck, shifted in his lap against his hardness. Goddess, he wanted her. To make her moan, make her cry out in pleasure, make her his. He held her in place, a hand on her thigh, his fingers pressing her yielding flesh through the nightgown's cotton.

Beneath, bare skin. Immaculate thighs, begging to be touched, caressed, parted. He exhaled sharply against her mouth.

"Take me to bed, Jon," she whispered to his lips. Tenderly, she kissed his jaw and moved down his neck.

He went rigid, a fullness swelling inside, bigger than his body, brimming, burning through his skin. Eyes locked on hers, he gathered her into his arms and carried her to bed. He descended to her, claimed her mouth, let his unlearned hands explore the curves of her waist, her hips, warm and supple, and he gathered the fabric of her nightgown.

She grazed the coarseness along his jaw and slipped her fingers over his neck and into his hair, grabbed, pulled, hard enough to hurt. Hurt with the utmost pleasure.

Mouth never leaving hers, he shifted to lie next to her, and finally his palm found the warm, smooth bare skin of her thigh. And he touched. Caressed. Parted.

She hurried through unfastening his shirt, at last stealing in, her palms planing over his chest, his abdomen, and he gripped her backside, stroked the curve as she unlaced his trousers and braies and at last freed him.

A soft murmur in her kiss, and she smoothed a palm over his abdomen and lower, lower, lower until she stroked him slowly, firmly. His eyes squeezed shut. *Terra have mercy.* Her touch, it was—*Goddess*—he'd thought about this a million times, and it was—finally, it felt—

So good. His fingers met silk—lingerie—and traced the waistband, tugged a delicate ribbon, slipped between it and soft skin. Found heat, blessed wet heat, and she raised her hips to meet his touch, moaned.

He exhaled sharply between kisses.

This was Rielle. He was with her. He loved her, and she—

She—

Did she? She did, didn't she?

Her strokes firmed. Deliciously. He tensed.

She hadn't said, had she?

Blessed Terra, it's—

How many men had she given her heart to?

—a world away from—

How many had she taken to bed, men she didn't love, and promptly discarded?

Until the end of the mission, perhaps, Leigh's voice rang out in his head. Terra have mercy, of all things—and now—

No.

He groaned and broke away, ravenous and frustrated and ravenous. And ravenous.

Wild eyes met his for a moment; breathing hard, he glanced away and moved to sit next to her on the bed, anchoring his elbows on his knees and his head in his hands. Not how he'd envisioned the night going.

"Jon?"

She sat up with him, still and quiet. "Talk to me," she whispered, resting a hand gently on his arm.

Talk to her? Tell her what? That he had no idea what he was doing? That he blindly followed his body's demands, letting it lead him into a murky darkness he didn't understand? That he needed to understand.

What was this to her? Sex? Love? He knew his own heart, but hers? How did a man tell whether a woman's heart was in it? Every part of him wanted to be one with her, to bring her pleasure, to let her pleasure him. But that was the squire in him, flipping through erotic illustrations and wondering what it would be like to feel a woman beneath him. And answering that wonder wasn't enough. Wasn't anywhere near enough.

She was sophisticated, experienced, knew her way around a man, a heart, and these matters. If he told her any of it, wouldn't she laugh?

He could wait. See. Learn. He could accept that.

But her laughing at him? Not that. Never that.

"Tell me what's on your mind," she said, and he couldn't remain silent.

"I've been a paladin for so long, Rielle, but always a man first." He took a deep breath but couldn't look at her. "I've thought about this moment so much, tortured myself with it."

She rubbed his arm softly. And Terra help him, it only made the ache in his body hurt all the more. "It's all right if you don't want to."

He took her hand in his, intertwining their fingers. "No, I want to." He almost laughed. "Believe me, I want to so badly it hurts."

She hesitated. "Your decision, then... It hasn't changed?"

Never. He met her eyes, unblinking. "I love you. I want to be with you, in every meaning of the word."

Her eyes widened, and a soft smile claimed her swollen lips. "I love you, too."

He brought their entwined hands to his mouth and kissed her fingers. The tension imprisoning his body began to recede, his disquiet slowly soothed.

Her eyes were earnest, her lovely face calm, her body relaxed. She meant it.

Even so, all of this was fast, flashing like lightning into the celibacy of his life, a sky-splitting bolt from the heavens to the earth, full and instantaneous. Kissing her had been a revelation, a pleasure, one so soon blinded by the next and the next.

He sank back onto the bed, and so did she. He moved closer, then brushed her cheek with his hand. Was it selfishness to want to savor a lover, to learn every nuance of her kiss, the exact shape of her hand, the feel of her and only her beneath his touch, and yes, at long last, every breath, every whimper, moan, and movement of hers in the throes of pleasure? A great part of him desired this, more than the quick conquest of a mystery too long left raveled.

Soft warmth from the candle flame set her eyes aglow as he drew a path to her neck, over her shoulder, and down her arm to her waist. He let his fingers settle there, stroking over the curve of her hip, and she leaned into his touch.

"As much as I've thought about this, for so long, I don't want to just rush through it. And all of this is so new, tense, fast. And right now, I'm too"—he drew his eyebrows together—"in my head, the virgin paladin lying awake imagining what sex might be like. This, between you and me, I want it to be... right." Not just getting it over with.

She blushed pink—

Rosy—

Red—

She hid her face.

He straightened. "Terra have mercy, Rielle, if you laugh at me right now—"

She kissed him... to silence her laugh or to silence him? As her lips played against his, whatever care he might have mustered unceremoniously surrendered.

"Why don't we just enjoy each other? And whether it's minutes from now, hours, days, or weeks, when you're ready," she whispered, slowly wrapping a leg around him, "I'll be waiting."

He hissed in a breath, raised her chin, and took her mouth with a ravening ardor, threading his fingers into her hair.

Selfishness? Perhaps...

But one he would allow.

RIELLE'S EYES FLEW OPEN. She wriggled, damp with sweat, her knees aching with the need to move.

The light of the waxing gibbous moon cast its eidolic glow through the window's lace curtains, silvery apparitions indolent upon the white bedspread. Beside her, Jon slept soundly, his chest rising and falling steadily.

She lingered, wishing to memorize the way the moonlight cast shadows across the planes of his face, his high cheekbones, the sweep of dark lashes almost too genteel a companion to his chiseled jaw, dark and coarse. Her fingers twitched as if to touch him, although she moved no closer. Just below, on his neck, was that scar—that blessed and terrible scar—the bitter-sweet beginning of all this and, she hoped, so much more.

He breathed softly, his lips slightly parted—lips that sparked her heart to flame.

A smile claimed her mouth. They'd spent hours kissing, tangled in each other, breathing the same air and chasing the dawn. Every part of her had ached for him, but she had resisted pushing for more, and he hadn't pushed either. Every kiss, every touch, every breath, every whisper—had meant all the more.

A perfect night.

No man had ever stopped to question when she'd offered herself. Pleasure was pleasure, greedily consumed whenever on offer—whether the time was right or not.

But not last night. Not with Jon. Her face had warmed to such heat, she'd nearly burst into flames.

Until she learned how to make peace with herself, her love was a liability, frightening, but as she closed her eyes and gave in to the swell of warmth inside her, what she felt for Jon—it was irresistible.

Beneath her skin, movement—restless, crawling, unyielding.

The sen'a.

Shifting, she raised the sleeves of her nightgown with clammy hands to give them something to do. No matter how she shifted, her legs hurt; she just had to move.

All her muscles rebelled, as if awakened from a thousand-year slumber and relearning the meaning of use. It was happening. The withdrawal. Moving her toes back and forth, she lay her hand next to her face on the bed and focused on it, trying to quiet her anxious mind.

For a moment, her hand stayed miraculously still.

Her finger jerked.

Exasperated, she eased off the covers and sat up, staring out the window while she swung her legs over the edge of the bed. Not a soul moved outside. It was at least two hours before dawn. Unable to sleep or stop moving, she surrendered and rose, padding across the room to the water carafe to pour herself a cup. She brought the cool water to her lips and sipped.

Jon stirred, his eyes still shut. "Rielle?" He yawned. "Is everything all right...?"

"Privy," she whispered. There was a chamber pot in the room, and although they'd dispensed with a lot of privacy, she certainly wasn't prepared to dispense with that bit of privacy.

He nodded and shifted his head on the pillow.

As she set down her cup with a shaking hand, tension claimed her body. Abrupt. Quick. Complete. The distinct pull of the bond from Brennan. He'd answered her call. She hated having to ask him for anything, but she needed his help if she had any hope of getting into Courdeval.

Another pull of the bond. Brennan was near. Very near.

She headed for the door, and with a final reassuring look at Jon, she laid a ward and left.

Barefoot, she went down the hall and, finding no one downstairs, headed out the back toward the stable. The ground prickled, chilled, and hurt her feet, but anything was better than their damned restlessness. In these predawn hours, Bournand was finally quiet.

She entered the stable. Sweet-smelling hay crisped underfoot, dewy. It was far warmer in here than outside, but it was too quiet. Something was amiss.

Her back thudded against the wall, the breath beaten from her lungs.

She couldn't move.

Horses snorted their protests from their stalls.

An arm pinned her, pressed across her chest. Nothing disturbed the darkness until the faint glow of amber eyes.

"Let me go, Brennan," she spat, and he released her. She rotated one of her shoulders, frowning at the ache. "You didn't have to do that."

"And you didn't have to pull on the bond earlier tonight." Even as a man, his voice rumbled like a growl. "Do you have any idea how long I had to wait before everyone was asleep... just so I could wait around some more in a stable?"

"Quit being so dramatic." She dusted off her nightgown, but due to her sweat, all the dust was now caked on. Wonderful. She took a step away when he trapped her between his arms, his palms meeting the stable's wall on either side of her head.

"What do you want?" His exhalations steamed her face in short, irritated puffs.

"Besides a little space?" she shot back, but he didn't move. She wouldn't be intimidated. "I found out Olivia is alive but bound in Courdeval."

The sound of his usual scoff was more pronounced in the dark. "And now you're finding out I don't care."

"I need you to scout the road to Melain for Crag Company outposts, then the road to Courdeval, and do some reconnaissance there."

"Is that all? Shall I single-handedly oust all the Crag? Perhaps resurrect the entire Faralle line?"

Sarcasm was a paper wolf. He could have his small victories—they didn't hurt until they came to tears, blood, and bruises.

"There's a Black Rose assassin named Nicolette stationed at Del's. She owes me a favor, and if she's there, I'm calling it in. On Spiritseve, I need a diversion to keep the Crag off my back, as far away from Trèstellan Palace in the city as possible, ideally a couple hours before midnight and lasting as long as she can manage."

He stayed silent, the only sounds in the stable his breathing and her restless toes tapping against the ground. He swallowed. "You're going to Courdeval to save this Olivia?"

Why did he pretend not to be familiar with Olivia? Rielle nodded. "Yes, I—"

His fist pounded the wall. "Are you insane? The place is crawling with mercenaries. You don't need reconnaissance to know that. It's suicide."

She didn't answer. Maybe it was, and even if it wasn't, this seething wolf would be her jailer for the rest of her life. But Olivia needed her, and someone had to prevent the Rift. The Grand Divinus's army wouldn't cross the Shining Sea any sooner than Spiritseve, and she couldn't count on the Order to retake the capital. There was no one else. "You're right. Maybe it is suicide. But we all have people we'd die for, and I'm going there whether you help me or not."

Unless he wanted to live with the risk of losing control of the Wolf, he would do all in his power to keep her alive. She knew it. He knew it.

The distinct heaviness of menace hung in the air. She wanted to move, to leave, but every instinct kept her frozen in place.

Her heartbeat quickened, but she refused to gratify him with the unnerved response he no doubt desired.

"You smell of wine... sen'a... and *him.*" As he lowered his head, his stubble brushed against her forehead, and then his mouth was a whisper away from hers. "I could steal you away right now, and there wouldn't be a thing you could do."

And yet his voice was low and sonorous. Not threatening.

She scrambled for answers—with magic useless against him and his preternatural abilities, what could she do to him? A shudder rippled through her. "I could shout your secret to the four winds," she hissed, "and let the good people of Emaurria deal with you."

An amused laugh puffed onto her chin, and even in the darkness his smile was white.

"Could you"—a finger grazed from her ear, down her jaw, and he clamped his hand over her mouth—"with my hand just here?"

Why did he—

Her lips pressed against her teeth, painfully. She grabbed his arm and pulled. No use. The pressure intensified.

The coppery tang of blood pricked her tongue.

"Could you, in fact, utter anything?" The smile persisted in his voice.

She struggled against him, snatching for his face, but he drew away. When she spiked her knee toward his groin, he caught her strike with a palm and laughed quietly.

"Could you do anything? Anything at all?"

She trembled—from fingertips to feet, quaked, filled to bursting with anger—sparked to blazing. She dug her nails into his shoulder and raked them down his arm. He sucked in a shaky breath.

In pleasure?

He released her mouth only to take her shoulder, burying his face in her hair. She wanted to slap him, curse him, banish him from her sight, but she needed his help if she was to increase her odds of surviving Courdeval. *And he knows it.*

It was then that a knee parted her thighs and traveled upward.

Her breath caught in her throat. Too far. He was toying with her. Mocking her. "It's times like this I wonder why I don't whip you for your insolence."

"Perhaps because I'd like it?"

He actually would. She pressed herself as close to the wall as she could, shuddering as the heat of his knee reached her flesh. "Brennan..."

"You've dreamed of being under a lover who doesn't tire"—he pulled down the shoulder of her nightgown—"who is more wild beast than man" —he brought his nose to her skin and breathed deep—"who can satisfy your every desire and keep pushing you past heights you've never envisioned." He raked his teeth against her skin, making her hiss with revulsion. "You could have an intoxicating dream tonight, every night, every day if you wish it, for the rest of your life."

A stare was all she gave him. He didn't really think she'd just acquiesce and fall at his feet, did he? That he'd see the curse broken so easily?

No. He wanted her to scream, wanted to unsettle her. But that was his condition for victory, not hers. She needed his agreement to help her in Courdeval. He'd soon tire of this game anyway and leave her be.

"You lack the most important quality of a lover," she whispered in his ear. "Love."

"A mere word forgotten in blinding pleasure." He pressed searing hot lips to her shoulder.

Once, they would have melted her to an aching, pining, pathetic puddle on the floor. Once.

She swallowed, looking away. "I'm in love, Brennan."

He scoffed. "You're what?" He straightened, all artifice abandoned, and loosened his hold. Wide eyed, he looked her over from head to foot and back again.

Did he think she meant with him? "I'm in love with Jon."

He paused, inhumanly still, listening? To her heart, perhaps. He could hear a lie, but in this, he would hear none.

"A commoner? Unworthy."

She shook her head.

He narrowed his eyes, their amber glow a mere slit from darkness. "He'll end up no more than a dalliance like all the others."

She stiffened. The conversation lurched toward an ugly destination. *Time to return to the matter at hand.* "Will you help me with my 'suicide mission' or not?"

He snarled. "Fine."

A lantern filled the stable with soft, yellow light.

Who— She turned her head to its source.

The stable boy's eyes were wide as saucers.

Indeed, they must have made a bewildering picture: a barefoot woman in a sweat-soaked nightgown pinned against the stable wall by a... a... *naked* man. *Divine's flaming fire—*

"You saw nothing," Brennan said, with the unmistakable imperious tone of a noble. He speared the boy with a glare.

The boy gulped and nodded, then retreated into the night. Before the light disappeared entirely, she faced Brennan, catching a glimpse of his smoldering hazel eyes, human eyes, before blackness dominated the stable once more. She opened her mouth to say something, then closed it.

He was already gone.

34

*R*ielle woke to a gentle caress gliding along her cheek, then her neck. As it trailed over her shoulder and down her arm, whisper-soft, she smiled and opened her eyes. Jon rested on his elbow next to her. With a playful grin, he stroked an iris flower toward her inner wrist. Amused, she brought the bright amethyst petals to her nose, breathing in the powdery, earthy scent.

His grin soothed away all trace of indignation from meeting with Brennan. When she'd returned, she'd washed, changed, and gone back to bed. Jon had pulled her close.

"As captivating as it is to watch you sleep, I couldn't resist waking you." His finger traced the iris's path from her hand to her cheek. He slipped his hand to the nape of her neck, and kissed her, his mouth deliciously sweet and a touch tart, like...

Rosehips and hibiscus.

"Jon," she whispered, sweeping her hands down his body, "you taste like... tea." Over his shoulder, two cups steamed on the nightstand—he'd already completed his morning routine. "Can nothing keep you from rising with the sun?"

He gathered her into an embrace, chuckling softly in her ear, and she melted into the bed's warmth and his.

"I would have entertained arguments, but you weren't awake to make them." He dropped a kiss on her shoulder.

"I was in no state to resist sleep," she replied, stroking his arm.

A devilish laugh. "Is that a concession, witch?"

"Concede?" She raised an eyebrow. "Never."

Then her stomach had the audacity to growl.

Jon huffed an amused breath in her ear. "A truce, then, while you quiet the dissension among your ranks." He tightened his hold briefly, then pulled away. "Come, let's eat."

Eat? On the table sat a large breakfast. Her stomach rebelled. The sight of food made her gag, but she sat up and reached for one of the two cups on the nightstand. With an expectant look, Jon took a seat at the table.

The last thing she wanted was to burden him with the effects of her sen'a withdrawal.

"You go on," she said, with a dismissive wave. "I only want some tea just now." When he raised an inquisitive brow, she added, "Really. I'm not particularly hungry, contrary to"—she glanced down at her belly—"rumor."

While he ate, she eased out of bed. It was past time to glean what knowledge she could from Flame's letters and to learn what she needed to know about the Moonlit Rite. She washed again and dressed, but her body, needy for sen'a, still refused to cooperate. She cringed at the inevitability of the throbbing pain that would soon invade her senses, worse than the night before. At least some research would distract her.

Nearly all of the letters bore the same thin, sloped script. All from the same sender. They were vague in their contents—preparation, setting an event in motion, discussing a target. Probably elaborated upon in the coded letters.

But the code symbols offered no easy answers. Without a cipher, comprehension would be impossible. She picked up her quill and began making notes of repeated words and their positions in sentence structure. Surely they'd be common enough? If she could guess at one or two, derive a test cipher, and see if it worked...

Nearly an hour later, Jon poured her some water from the carafe. He rested a hand on her shoulder and looked down at the line of letters. She, too, stared at the letters until the symbols blurred into one another. Why didn't the Tower teach code breaking? She sighed.

"This is hopeless." She leaned back in the chair.

Jon rubbed her shoulders. "Let me try."

She rose, and Jon took the seat. He laid the coded letters side by side and looked across them. She left him to it and sat at the table.

Codebreaking wasn't one of her few skills, but she could still read a book. Perhaps she'd find some answers about the mysterious Moonlit Rite. With a slow stroke, she brushed the knife hole in the cover of *Ancient Blood Rites,* Flame's book. It had saved Jon's life, and was all the more precious now.

She pulled out Kieran's orders, which contained instructions to the rite, and read: *During the midnight moon between Spiritseve and Hallow-day, find the Lunar Chamber in the catacombs of Trèstellan Palace...* A reference to a map. *Trace a sacred circle and a pentagram with rowan ash, and spill the vial of king's blood in the center while the full moon is at its zenith. There will be no second chances.* Diagrams and page numbers. They matched pages in *Ancient Blood Rites.*

A pentagram etched in the Lunar Chamber matched the layout of anima threads around Veins—where the Veil was thin, where wild magic bubbled close to the surface, close enough to touch, close enough to die to, or to become a wild mage.

Was there a Vein in the Lunar Chamber? What did Veins have to do with Spiritseve? She frowned. Pondering the questions repeatedly yielded a headache, but no answers.

She slammed the book shut. Sacred circles and pentagrams. Not exactly her forte. She rubbed her forehead, then paged through the book.

An illustration took up an entire page, a copy of an engraving. A naked man holding the hand of a naked woman in a clearing, under the stars. Behind them was a handful of people, one of them holding the halter of a doe. Beneath was a caption: *The Earthbinding, a mythical rite performed for the favor of the Dead Gods, binding a king to his land.*

She raised an eyebrow and read the facing page, which presented theories as to the nature of the mythical rite. At a Vein, the king was to couple with a virgin representing the land; as they became one, so did the king and his land. Earth brought from all corners of the realm gave him sense of all corners; and a representation of enemy intentions, taken far away, became a prayer to keep the land—and so himself and his bloodline—safe.

The Earthbinding allowed a king to influence his land's health, prosperity, and strength. She read on. The last Earthbound king was rumored to have been the first of the Faralles, a warrior king, the Blade. Tristan Armand Marcel Faralle.

The Lothaires'—her family's—only claim to royalty came from the Blade, who'd married Rosalie Vignon Lothaire, a wayward lady and pirate queen who'd brought a fleet under the Emaurrian banner as her dowry. Together, they'd ruled the land and the sea for half a century.

She thumbed the vial of king's blood she'd gotten from Kieran's things. Which king's? King Marcus's? King Marcus—and the current generation of Faralles—were all descended from the Blade, who, if this book was to be believed, had been the last Earthbound king. That vial was all the more precious now, with all the Faralles dead.

The Blade's blood flowed through the Faralles. Was in this vial. If that blood had to do with the Earthbinding, it could mean protecting the land from something. Something that had to do with Veins and the thinning Veil.

The maid came and went with trays, food, and water. Jon worked at the letters, and she turned over the same few questions in her tired mind.

She squeezed her eyes shut and looked inward, plummeted to her own anima. The heaviness of a massive presence crowded around her, dozens of phantom hands pushing against her inner barriers. More and more appeared, pushing harder and harder, crowding closer, closer—

She opened her eyes with a start.

This pressure would become suffocating unless relieved the night of Spiritseve, as it was every year.

Spiritseve... when the Moonlit Rite was to be performed.

If it wasn't—

Perhaps this pressure would continue. A natural culmination. And then an overflow.

She imagined her inner barriers—what made her anima hers and not just of the earth—gone, and shuddered. Every mage's barriers. The earth's barriers. If they were gone, what would come over?

She frowned.

Spiritseve... When the Veil is at its thinnest.

The Veil. Barriers. She drew in a shallow breath. Everyone knew that on the other side of the Veil was the Lone, the after realm, a matter both Divinists and Terrans agreed on. What if the Veil tore open?

Whose phantom hands pushed for entry?

Was that the Rift?

Nausea beset her with a sickly warmth. She could hardly think without craving sen'a.

"I'm on to something." Jon's excited voice.

Weary, she pushed her chair back and stood to look at the spread of letters arranged in a perfect line from left to right on the desk. Jon ran his index and middle fingers across the first line of every letter.

"The first word is always different," he said, "but the second word... In all the letters, only two different options appear in that second space." He rearranged the letters, placing on the left side those with one word and on the right those with the other. "A few of them use the first word, while the vast majority use the second."

That relationship could only mean one thing.

"The month," she said over his shoulder, impressed with his work.

"Yes." He looked up at her. "Flame wouldn't have been stationed in Bournand very long. He was probably supposed to have burned them to prevent just this. The first word in every letter, although different, is likely a coded, written-out number for the date. The two options for the second word in each letter end in the same exact construction, so they're likely the month—Chaudoir or Aimadoir."

It made sense. If they could decode two words, a full cipher would eventually follow. Her heart leapt.

She shuffled to her pack to retrieve her extra quill, inkwell, and some parchment and handed the supplies to Jon. Right away, he began scripting a cipher. As he steadily linked symbol to letter, one after another, with a determined crease on his brow, she could not help but grin.

Jonathan Ver was a capable man.

But just how did a former paladin, trained daily in combat, develop a scribe's abilities? She smiled to herself.

"What?" he asked with a lilt of casual amusement as he worked.

Her lip twitched as she tried to hold in a laugh. "I don't know, just trying to imagine you, all brawny and broad shouldered, as a bookworm hidden in some candlelit corner, reading long into the night—"

"Find it funny, do you, witch?" An amused gleam in his eye.

"Only a little."

"It's not far from the truth. I received quite the education at the monastery. Some of it even had the tenacity to remain, even after all the blows I've taken to the head."

She snorted. But she couldn't help a brief inspection of his head anyway.

When both words were translated on the parchment, Jon set down his quill. "There. I can decode most—if not all—of the rest, given time."

She curled her arms around him, and he swept her onto his lap. When she kissed him, he exhaled lengthily.

"Anything else the Divinity needs a forsworn paladin to do?" he joked.

She leaned in close. "I can think of a few things."

She kissed him again. A very masculine sound passed from his mouth to hers.

"And you?" he whispered against her lips between kisses. "What did you find in that ruined book of yours?"

"It may be ruined, but I've got a soft spot for it now."

"Oh?" Jon glanced at the cover, a corner of his mouth turning up fondly. He traced her lower lip with a reverent thumb. "Why would that be?"

He wanted her to say it? Aloud? "It—"

Her stomach growled.

Jon fixed her with a stern glare. "It's nearly dusk. You haven't eaten anything since yesterday."

She left his lap and poured herself a glass of water. The mirror caught her reflection. Her horrid reflection. The sen'a hadn't been content with the aches inhabiting every inch of her body and the crawling sensation beneath her skin; it had also darkened the skin beneath her eyes and made her wan. She looked like a resurrected corpse. Or a ghost.

"Rielle." A scrape followed—the chair.

Forcing a smile, she shrugged. "I'm not hungry." It was true enough, although it was her churning stomach's answer and not hers.

"Is it the sen'a?" He directed a nod at her tapping foot.

Immediately, she stayed it, although her restless legs rebelled. The hurt, the pity in his face was too difficult, and she looked away, but she wouldn't lie to him. "Yes."

His gaze was upon her, she could feel it, and Divine, she didn't want to look—she couldn't.

They had only begun to explore love; she hardly expected any man to suffer through something like this with her after only so little time together.

"Jon," she began, trying to keep her voice even, "you don't owe me anything. I understand if you—"

When he swept her into his embrace, the pressure inside her finally broke.

"I'm here for you." The strength in his arms matched that in his voice.

"You won't want to be," she croaked. The restlessness, the crawling, the pain—it was unbearable. She hurt everywhere, her entire body a throbbing bruise, and it would only worsen. If the past was any indication, she'd say terrible things, hateful things, be some monstrous shade of her true self. Olivia had put up with it, but she'd known Olivia for years, had been best friends for years. But Jon—

He rubbed her back softly, his breath warm on the crown of her head. "I'll help you through this."

She didn't deserve it. There were many dark things in her past, not to mention her engagement to Brennan. She longed to tell Jon—even now, just so he'd know the true nature of the woman he had begun to love. And she would tell him all of it, so help her, before she took him to Monas Amar.

He gestured at the table full of food. "You need to eat something."

He arranged some bread, fruit, and chicken on a plate and placed it on the table in front of an empty chair. She looked away, swallowing thickly. He approached her and, cupping her cheek, tilted her face up to his. "Come. Eat."

"I'm not hungry." But she hadn't intended the agitated tone with which she'd spoken. She sighed. The last thing she wanted was for him to see and hear her vomiting all night. "I'm fine."

"You're not." He fixed her with a serious look. "You need to keep your strength up. At least eat a little. Even if you only keep some of it down, it's better than nothing at all."

He was right. Staring down at the fresh food with all the enthusiasm of a convict facing the gallows, she rose and seated herself at the table. He brushed his palm along her back as he came around to sit next to her.

It was far too difficult to turn him down. It was a wonder she hadn't simply let him walk away from the skirmish at the Tower.

She speared a forkful of chicken and shoved it into her mouth. Perhaps if she didn't think about it, she could chew and swallow it without retching.

Chew, chew, chew. Swallow.

Second forkful. Chew, chew, chew. Swallow.

It wasn't pleasant, but she could manage.

Warmth simmered in her belly and spread, but it settled in her body like malaise, radiating nausea. She paused at the third forkful, the smell of roasted chicken polluting her nostrils while her stomach rolled.

The chair raked the floor and fell over when she ran for the chamber pot and, grabbing its rim with both hands, vomited. The sting of acid in her nose burned so keenly that she could hardly spare a thought for her bulging eyes.

And then she realized Jon had been there all the while, keeping her hair away from her face, an arm around her waist to hold her steady. He'd witnessed the entire disgusting thing.

"Don't... look... at me," she managed to say, wiping her mouth, but he didn't move. She shoved him away, but he didn't budge and instead handed her a towel.

With a grunt, she accepted it and dabbed at her face, hoping to stave off the dry heaves. Restlessness dominated her limbs, and as she looked at the mess before her, she fidgeted with the towel. The aches filled her up, and she slung her arms around herself, trying to rub them away.

She reached for the water carafe. "I need to clean—"

Before she could grasp it, Jon lifted her and took her to the bed. The objection died in her sore throat before she could make it. He laid her down softly, a font of calm, then handed her a nightgown.

"Try to get some sleep," he whispered. "I'll be right here next to you soon." He planted a kiss on her cheek, then returned to the mess.

Changing into her nightgown, she tried to ignore the protests of her body. Under the covers, she curled into a tight ball.

True to his word, he came to bed and, much to her shame, placed an empty chamber pot on the floor near her. He doused the candle with his fingertips, settled between the sheets, and drew close, reaching out to stroke her hair softly while she writhed in pain.

He embraced her with one secure arm. "Tomorrow will be better."

She didn't deserve this kindness, not from Jon, not from anyone, not after all she'd done. Still, even in the depths of her humiliation, his embrace was a comfort. But if he knew about Brennan, if he saw the shadows haunting her, would he still be here?

I'm a murderer.

Her body convulsed with a violent shudder.

Tomorrow, they'd be back on the Kingsroad, in constant danger. Hopefully she'd make it through tonight with some strength left to protect the man she loved, whose caring arms she'd neither expected nor deserved, but now couldn't imagine living without.

35

*D*uring the midnight change of the Crag Company guard, Brennan scaled the wall in man-beast form and descended into the darkness of Courdeval's Chardon District.

He kept to the shadows of the wooden buildings. The streets here were empty, although his werewolf ears pricked at voices in the distance, muffled from underground. He Changed to full wolf and padded toward the sound, sniffing his surroundings cautiously.

The Crag Company skimmed every corner of the city that mattered, cheap leather boots pressing old Courdevallan blood into the cobblestone and dust roads. Few Courdevallans remained in the city—alive—but those who did kept to the destitute districts like this one, where the penniless and the lawless burrowed underground, in ratholes ignored and forgotten.

He'd overheard the guards talking about a resistance. Would the Black Rose assassin Rielle had mentioned know anything about it? Rielle might have been content to throw her life away on a suicide mission, but he needed her alive to continue their monthly meetings, to be free of the moon's control. If a resistance could help her odds of survival, then he would seek it out, as well as this Nicolette—he tongued his teeth in distaste —even if it meant openly acquiescing to Rielle's wishes.

She certainly wouldn't approve of his little bloodbath on the Kingsroad, but she didn't have to approve. She just had to survive long enough to free him of the curse.

So he'd killed all the Crag there. Better dead than alive. Only once had he bitten someone and let him live. He'd ended up having to behead the man—no, the werewolf. Never again. There was nothing to gain by leaving behind living, breathing evidence to come seeking hush money. Or worse, to spread word of a certain nobleman who turned into a monster at will.

He growled.

At The Rose Garden, the wild mage had said Rielle's concern for the commoner extended far beyond her mission. That his presence pleased her.

She'd had brief dalliances before. Brief. But perhaps this commoner was different. Maybe he was more to her than a warm, willing body.

A tool to father a bastard, the next Marquis of Laurentine? Was that how she planned to circumvent the betrothal, by bearing a bastard?

No comparison to a Marcel, of course—she'd be foolish to pursue that course. But it couldn't hurt to bring his fiancée to heel. He'd already tried shaming her for carrying on with a commoner. To no effect. He'd tried seducing her in the barn—to some success, if his nose hadn't betrayed him —but not enough. It was time to consider other cards.

A reasonable offer, and if that failed, a change of targets. If she proved immovable, the commoner could be handled. No commoner could withstand the full force of a determined Marcel.

The voices grew loud enough for his wolf ears to discern. He slowed his steps. Stopping at the door, he read the shingle above it: Del's.

"...they have nightly meetings there, and we'll just have to hit them hard, when they least expect it," a woman said firmly.

There were murmurs of halfhearted support amid the din. "Nicolette, the Divinity is no doubt already sending an army—"

Nicolette. She was the one.

"So what? We should just wait? Keep starving? Keep suffering, only to be bargained off as hostages later?" Nicolette shot back.

"This is not what we do," a man argued in a smooth, calm voice. "We're the Black Rose, not the damned militia."

"We are residents of this city, Ben, and if there is no one left to stand for it and for us, then even we assassins must stand." She paused for a moment. "We need to free our brethren."

Brennan pulled back. If Rielle meant to infiltrate the city on Spiritseve, then this could be the well-timed diversion needed to reduce the risk involved considerably.

He'd approach this Nicolette, but there were questions to consider of how he'd entered the city, and how he'd be leaving. Even if he name-dropped Rielle.

Stalking into an empty hovel, he shifted to his human form and searched for clothes. His spoils were sneer worthy—an over-sized woolen tunic, a rawhide belt, patched and too-large woolen pants, and old rawhide shoes for his feet, at least two sizes too small, and all stinking of sweaty *commoner*. He groaned, but this was a part of being a werewolf attempting to blend into human society—*common* human society.

Once dressed, he slipped out of the hovel, slinking along walls and in shadows until he reached Del's Tavern once again. He closed his eyes and exhaled, letting a mask of calm settle over him, then opened the door.

Only a couple patrons sat within, nursing ale steins nearing empty, muttering about ghosts, phantoms, and the Lone—the other side of the Veil.

An elderly barman drying an ale stein with a dishcloth eyed him warily. "We're closed."

The presence of the two patrons spoke to the contrary, but the barman glowered at him.

"I'm here to see Nicolette."

The barman set down the stein and placed his hands on the table. "She's not here."

The oldster had some fight in him. Good. That would keep things interesting.

"She'll want to see me," he said. "Tell her Favrielle is calling in a favor." The name-drop would smooth things over. He stood still, fixing the barman with an unrelenting stare.

The barman frowned but finally gave in and left the bar, presumably for the cellar. Brennan released the tension he'd been holding in his shoulder blades and waited, listening to the voices and footsteps.

The two patrons rose and, eyeing him warily, left the tavern. *Wise choice.*

Within moments, a small brunette emerged, her eyes wide and curious despite the taut anticipation of her body. She stopped in the doorway, her hand resting on its frame. She wore her hair high, secured tightly, and a fitted coat, trousers, and boots of the darkest black.

"Nicolette, I presume?"

"Who's asking?"

"A friend of Favrielle's."

She tilted her head in skepticism. "What do you want?"

Brennan drew in her scent, the fragrance of almond oil, ale, and woman. "She's calling in a favor."

A vein flared in her neck, pounding with the blood from her heart. She stepped closer.

"And what does she want?" She planted a fist on her hip.

"She intends to retake the palace. She can get in without trouble, but the whole of the Crag Company cannot be waiting for her there."

Nicolette brought her head down in an epiphanous nod. "She needs a diversion."

"Yes," he answered, restraining the wide grin begging to be released. "On Spiritseve, beginning a few hours before midnight and lasting as long as you can manage."

"Will she free the prisoners?"

"Yes."

If the assassin believed it, then she'd be motivated enough to do her part.

Crossing her arms, she stopped, eyebrows drawn. Typical. Soon, she would ask him whether he was trustworthy, how she could be certain that he would deliver.

"How do I know I can trust you?"

"You don't," he said, "but if I were a Crag spy, I wouldn't come here alone to trick you. I'd come here in force to kill you and anyone else trying to mount a resistance."

Nicolette's wary eyes appraised him for a moment. "Those clothes are not yours."

He laughed. "Of course not." He received a crooked grin in reply. Her scent hit him again, strong and tantalizing. "So, can I tell Favrielle you'll deliver that favor, or will she be on her own?"

She put her thumb and index finger to her lower lip, then nodded reluctantly. "I'll need to talk to my people, but... even if they don't help, I will. I owe her."

The little assassin had as much spunk as he'd initially thought.

"A signal," Nicolette said. "The northeastern gate tower. Extinguish the light the night of Spiritseve, and that's when you'll have your diversion."

Rielle could extinguish a fire easily enough.

"Good." As his mouth watered, he backed up toward the door. He would hunt a fine young doe tonight and feast on warm flesh to sate this hunger. Clicking his teeth shut, he felt for the door behind him.

Nicolette followed after him, her feet closing the very necessary gap between them, practically jumping into the wolf's mouth.

"Wait! Who are you?" she hissed after him.

He gave her a toothy grin. "Brennan."

He slammed the door shut. It was time to face his snarling little she-wolf and see if a reasonable offer would prevail where a hand of courtship, scorn, humiliation, and seduction had not.

36

*R*ielle curled tight, tossing, turning, twisting. The tide of pain in her veins swelled, clotted out even the soft lambency of the night, leaving only the blackness and punctures of bone-needling agony.

But Jon held her all through the black, and whenever pain shot through her, when she crumpled and winced, his hold tightened until the bout passed.

The cramps woke her from the fitful storm. Then the shivers, and the goosebumps, descended. Uncomfortable, but nothing compared to the horror of the previous night. She cringed. As much as she'd tried to keep her sen'a withdrawal secret, it had poured out.

Near dawn, Jon arrived with food. He'd been the one ray of light in the thorough dark of the past night, and she could hardly bear to face him. But he sat in bed with her while she ate some of the toasted bread, broth, and plain rice, and sipped the mint tea, as much as she dared—which amounted to little.

Stomach full or rotting, she had to go. They had to go. Staying in one place too long was too risky.

He set down his mint tea and took her hand, held her gaze with that patient stillness of his. "You need to recover. Give yourself time."

"I'll be fine." She stroked his knuckles softly. "Thanks to you." Her belly contracted, a cramp clenching tight. She winced.

"Are you all right? Perhaps you should rest a while longer."

Forcing a smile, she shook her head and rose. "We have a schedule to keep."

He narrowed his eyes but nodded.

Quickly, they gathered their things, settled their bill, and found Leigh before making through the morning crowds for Forgeron's.

The blacksmith presented a modified suit of armor, dark and unrecognizable, but a shining and elegant deep gray. Jon stiffened, then reached for the arcanir, hesitating before he rested a palm on the new cuirass. He gave a somber nod to the blacksmith, then she came around the counter and helped him arm.

Perfectly tailored. It suited him. Over his shoulder, his once-white cloak was now a deep, cobalt blue. His lips curved beneath somber eyes. "Thank you."

The blacksmith inclined her head. "Wear it well." She slitted her eyes at Leigh. "Now get out of my shop."

Leigh held up his hands and smirked. "Give my best to your lovely papa."

As they left, Rielle took Jon's hand. "Your armor"—she looked him over—"do you regret it?"

"No." Grinning, he helped her into the saddle. "But if you want to cheer me up later, I still welcome all efforts."

He mounted and, with a lingering look, rode past.

Leigh followed, rolling his eyes. "Really," he muttered, just barely audible.

With all the talk of refugees, the Kingsroad to Melain should have been bustling, but it was clear, with nothing but greenery and wildlife to distract them. Even so, she checked for Shadow and Phantom constantly with her earthsight.

No sign of either. Perhaps having Leigh along was all the deterrence needed.

With the road safe and clear, the journey would take only two days, but it would be a taxing two days. Although her sen'a withdrawal tapered, her moonbleed had her wincing through the ride.

The first night, they camped at dusk and rested fully in the safety of her wards. The next day, their route took them along the Kingsroad through the Forest of the Hart, a dense wood said to be protected by Solis—Sun God, Oak King, and Holly King—the triune god of the Terran pantheon, taking the form of a great stag.

The sky still bore the intense pinks of dawn when they set out—*much* too early—but Leigh set their schedule. Ahead of them, he led their small cavalcade, bespectacled and withdrawn, reading a tome on legendary immortal creatures.

Farther from Bournand, the forest had thrived and become overgrown, its tangled woods ablaze with reds and golds pressing tight against the road. Serenaded by the clopping of her mare's hooves, Rielle gazed at the canopy, catching only occasional glimpses of the sky between the densely leafed branches rippling in the wind. The autumn chill made her shiver, but when she closed her eyes, she could feel the heat of Jon next to her beneath the thick coverlet at The Crowned Stag, holding her close, taking care of her.

Jon had sacrificed, greatly, only to be tangled into the mess that was her life. There was still so much she needed to tell him, chief among all subjects her engagement to Brennan.

Her breathing turned shaky, and her mare stiffened. Rielle whispered words of comfort and patted her softly.

She and Jon did not need the added pressure of this discussion now. And there were still two mage captains of the Crag Company out there. If she told him everything and he decided to end things, would he still accept her protection? Or would he try to leave on his own?

And how would I protect him then?

If he took off as he had after Feliciano, he'd be all alone. He could handle himself, but against Shadow and Phantom? It was too risky. He could get hurt or killed.

She tightened her white scarf around her neck.

It would have to wait until they were close to Monas Amar.

Once they arrived in Melain, she'd ask Gran's support in breaking her betrothal. At least that much. If anyone had the political clout and broad influence, it was Gran, but the Auvrays had long nurtured close ties to the Marcels. It had seemed hopeless for years and seemed hopeless now, but she had to try.

Something lurked in the distance. She squinted.

A massive sculpture of a beast the size of a caravel, with a huge spiked maw and long sharp claws, seethed its rage among the bright-yellow growth of autumn hawkbit.

The Serpent of Mel. One of the Immortals, it was made in the shape of a great winged dragon, a legendary creature that had rained terror from the skies on villages, farms, and castles.

Still hours away from Melain, Leigh brought his horse to a halt, and she and Jon followed suit. Her sore backside would be grateful for a reprieve from the torture device—saddle. And she'd make some tea to soothe the residual queasiness from the withdrawal.

She dismounted and secured her horse, then moved to the Serpent's head and reached out to rub a long tooth, easily the length of her arm.

Jon approached with his horse in tow, then tied it off to a nearby tree next to hers. He leaned in and kissed her softly. "What's on your mind?"

Too much. She shook her head. "Just thinking about the weeks ahead."

He raised an eyebrow. "With such a frown? Should I be worried?"

She hugged him, resting her cheek against the arcanir of his chest. It stung, but she didn't care. His arms closed around her.

"I'm very selfish, Jon," she whispered.

He snorted a soft breath. "I think you're mistaken. You've risked your life to save mine, more than once, and you're on a mission to rescue your best friend. Few would call that 'selfish.'"

His words elicited a small smile. There was little she wouldn't do for those she loved.

"If you are pursuing your own happiness," he said softly, "then in that, our goals are aligned." A smile lilted in his voice. "So don't waste another minute frowning." His hold tightened.

If he knew the truth of the matters worrying her, would he say the same?

Leigh rode by, beckoning her to follow with a jerk of his head.

"I'd like to make some tea." She rested a hand on her unsettled belly.

"We'll catch up," Jon added, leaning against the serpent of Mel with his arms crossed.

Leigh cocked an eyebrow. "Ten minutes. I'll scout ahead." He rode ahead.

She pulled away from Jon and offered him a thankful smile. There was time for some peppermint tea, which would hopefully make the rest of today's riding a little less *entirely uncomfortable.*

"I'll gather some firewood," Jon said.

"Together." She smiled, and when he offered his gauntleted hand, she took it.

They entered among the trees, picking their way through the dense foliage as they gathered sticks and twigs. She'd only need a little bit to get a fire to blazing and a kettle of water boiling.

A fallen bough lay nearby, full of sprigs she could break off. Her foot caught, and she tripped with a yelp.

He darted to catch her but lost his balance, too. She landed atop him, hard, her breath knocked out of her lungs. Stunned, she took a moment to collect herself before lifting her head. *Graceful. Very graceful.*

When her eyes finally met his, Jon was grinning.

A putrid odor invaded her nostrils. Not the crisp freshness of a forest.

"What is it?"

She sniffed. "Don't you smell that?"

He paused and smelled the air, then nodded. She searched the ground. Her gaze wandered a little farther.

A severed hand.

Her breath caught. It was small for an adult. Probably a woman's hand. The point of separation was far from clean—a mess of torn flesh, tubes, and bone at the gruesome end of a blood trail on the forest floor.

Before she could venture beyond the scene to follow it, Jon grabbed her arm. She rounded on him with a scowl.

"I'll take a look." His grip slid down to her hand, and he squeezed it in reassurance.

She wanted to stop him and say she'd be the one to go, but he wasn't just her charge anymore. Things were different now. Barking orders at him was no longer an option; she couldn't even bring herself to. They'd just have to work together.

"Not without me, you won't." She conjured a flame in her hand while he drew his sword and moved alongside her.

They crept through the brush, following the blackened blood trail to an arm, thin and grayed by death. Farther still, a headless torso clad in bloodied leather armor lay among the filth and leaves, a short sword not far from its grasp.

She knelt beside the body. Amid the shredded flesh were puncture wounds and claw marks.

Brennan.

She held her wrist to her nose. Jon crouched near the body of—a boy, probably no older than sixteen, a new recruit perhaps. But he stared elsewhere. She followed his line of sight.

Detached limbs reached out, mouths on decapitated heads hung open in silent screams, bodies lay torn asunder, and drowning it all, a dried pool of bloody terror soaked into the leaf-strewn ground. The disarray of pieces amounted to at least a dozen bodies.

Swords, knives, axes, and bows littered the area. Some torsos still bore bloodied red tabards—a black mountain flanked by the sun.

"Crag Company." Jon scanned the scene and examined the spread of the bodies. "They tried to retreat."

"Wolf attack," she murmured. If he needed an answer, that was the only one she could give.

Jon closed the young man's eyes. Slowly, he rose and shook his head. "The bodies are ripped apart, but not much is missing. No predation."

She couldn't tell him that no, it hadn't been a pack of wolves—nor even one.

Jon sighed. "Enemies or not, we can't leave them like this. It's not right."

"We can tell the guards at Melain," she offered, her throat tight. She watched him awhile, standing with his hands up in offering, praying to his Goddess.

A rustle came from the forest. Clear in the silence. She nodded to Jon, who acknowledged.

The thrash of a run through dense vegetation—

Casting earthsight, she tracked the sound. The bright figure was clear as day—a person, and a mage at that.

"Stop!" she shouted.

She and Jon wended through shrubs, bushes, and brambles as quickly as they could. The bright aura grew smaller, gaining distance. They closed in, when—

A snap. Blinding pain. A crunch. A scream. Her own.

Pain shot up her leg from her ankle, so excruciating she couldn't think. She collapsed.

Jon was at her side, his back to where they'd come from. A roar in her ears, images came to her in disarray. He took her in his arms, shouting words she couldn't hear, his alert eyes flitting to the surroundings and back to her. Pain immobilized her, breaking her focus.

Her earthsight dispelled, she lost track of their quarry. On the ground, her booted ankle bent oddly, caught between two metal jaws. A wolf trap.

Jon wedged his arcanir dagger between the jaws, his voice reassuring but unintelligible. Her ankle throbbed in agony during his ministrations. Pain seared. Dizzy, she squeezed her eyes shut as he pulled her free.

"You'll be all right," he said firmly. But his eyebrows were drawn together, and he breathed quick, shallow breaths. He held the leather sheath of his dagger in front of her mouth. "Bite down."

The taste of leather and oil frayed at the ends of sharp, shooting pain— he removed her boot—and she clenched down. Her palm shot to slam the ground, an instinct, but Jon grabbed her hand midair.

"Don't." He tipped his head toward the ground.

Leaves littered the forest floor, glimpses of metal peeking out here and there.

Traps.

Tenderness—Jon's feather-light touch—at her ankle made her squirm. She peered at the jagged shape.

"I'll need to splint this. We need to get out of here." He surveyed the area.

Attempting to heal it, she spat out the sheath and murmured an incantation but couldn't focus her magic. Arcanir.

"Jon," she said, her voice strained, and he turned to her. "I can heal it, but you have to let me go." She nodded at his armor against her bare leg.

After a moment's hesitation, he let her go. She whispered the incantation and suffered through the healing. When it was finished, Jon looked from her ankle to her face, murmuring soft thanks to his Goddess.

Metal screeched. Armor. Jon jerked forward. A gasping cry forced from his mouth as his hand flew to his chest.

He slumped onto her.

The shaft of a crossbow bolt protruded from his back.

Cold fractured her inside.

She shook it off, tried to assess his state with healing magic—no good. Contact with his armor prevented casting. He breathed raggedly as he unfastened his left pauldron.

A second shot whizzed by her ear. The angle—from above—meant a crossbowman in the trees. A warm, wet substance coated her hands.

Blood.

Jon's blood.

With his arcanir against her skin, there would be no earthsight. No elemental magic. No healing.

She needed to move him.

Wary of the traps, she readjusted her hold on him and, with his help, dragged him behind the trunk of a cedar. The crossbowman would need time to get another angle on them.

Granted a moment's safety, she frantically unfastened his cuirass and inspected the wound. Deep.

Bright-red blood seeped. Arterial blood.

"You have to run," he bit out, his face paling. "Arcanir poison. I feel its sting. If it hits you—"

Quickly, she untied her scarf and pressed it into the wound to slow the bleeding.

His hands clenched. He exhaled heavy breaths through his nose. The white lambswool knit against his wound reddened. The pressure and the scarf wouldn't stem the bleeding.

He would bleed out.

"Rielle."

She broke all contact with his arcanir, then whispered an incantation over the injury.

Resistance. A wall stopped her magic.

The bolt had been coated in arcanir poison.

"No," she said, her voice breaking. Her heart raced as precious seconds ticked by. Blood pooled on the forest floor, soaked up by decaying leaves. He didn't have much time.

A shudder ran down her spine.

Not him, she prayed. *Not him.*

She stole a glance at his face and nodded with a confidence she didn't feel, even as her heart threatened to burst from her chest.

He needed to get to Melain. She had to try bandaging him and make for the castle.

She wiped the wetness from her face, then her unsteady hands began their work. After removing her scarf from the wound, she felt around the bolt tip. She reached for his sword belt and pulled the sword free, then held the belt before his mouth. He clenched it between his teeth.

"Steel yourself."

He nodded. She grabbed the bolt shaft and broke it.

His eyes shut tight. He bit into the belt. Hard.

She dropped the fletched end, then removed any splinters she could. Trying not to push the bolt tip in deeper, she tied the scarf around the wound as tightly as she dared. His jaw twitched as he clenched the belt between his teeth.

His eyes fluttered open, and he spit out the belt. His elbow on a bent knee, he rested the uninjured half of his back against the tree. Pale and drenched in blood, with a red-stained scarf binding his wounds, he was a chilling sight.

"You'll be fine," she affirmed, taking his hand, surprised by the sticky contact. Her hands were covered in blood up to her elbows. The metallic smell inundated her nose as her adrenaline faded.

So much blood.

Somewhere out there was the person who had almost killed Jon. She flexed her hand, smeared with blood, dark and sticky. Before the day was done, she knew it would be soaked in more.

"Wait here," she said.

He nodded.

Casting her earthsight, she scanned her surroundings. Back the way they'd come, up in the trees, a dull aura descended. A non-mage. Chasing the first figure, she and Jon had run right past a crossbowman.

Carefully weaving between traps, she caught the angles to ignite every tree surrounding her target, the canopy, and the forest floor. She kept the blaze carefully controlled, preternaturally hot.

"Nowhere to run," she called to her target, watching for any sign of him through earthsight.

When he held out an arm, a bolt tip plainly visible, she expanded her fire spell to where she presumed the heavy crossbow to be. The aura's limbs spread wide. He dropped the crossbow.

He was trapped. She spelled aside all vegetation in her way and approached the target. Her soon-to-be prisoner.

He dropped into the fire.

Agonized screams tore from the flames.

She dispelled the pyromancy on the forest floor. Too late.

At the site, only a charred body remained, next to it three unburned arrowheads. They had to be coated in arcanir poison. She snatched them up and, confirming with her earthsight that the second target wasn't in the area, hurried back to Jon.

His face was pale as a shroud—

Her outstretched hand trembled its way toward him to disprove her eyes. She brushed his skin with her fingertips, smearing blood.

"Jon?" She shook him gently.

His head lolled to the side.

Tears stung her eyes as she shook him harder. "Jon," she called, taking in a deep breath through her mouth.

His face, but for its ghostly color, looked as it always had.

No magic. No medicine.

She shook.

"Help!" she cried, her hand sliding down the length of his arms to his wrist. Her limbs refused to cooperate, buckling and faltering when she needed them to stay still, so that she could focus on some sign of life she could measure—any sign. "Help! Leigh!"

Nothing. But he couldn't be far.

Raising her arm with an aeromancy gesture, she shot sparks of lightning high above the canopy to burst in the sky. A signal. Leigh would see it. He had to.

She swallowed. With the arcanir poison in Jon's body, her fingers could feel nothing but her own fear. Seconds passed like years in her trembling, the rising hysteria inside threatening to burst.

"Jon!" she yelled into his ear, as loud as she could, spasms wracking her body. "Wake up." That familiar red feeling began to spark and burn in her chest. *Murderer. Demon.* "Wake up!"

No reply.

No, no, no, not me, I'm not—

She collapsed against his uninjured side, the tears trailing down her neck, feeding the pressure building in her chest. The blood coating her hand had saturated the grain of her skin, a branching chaos, a shattered pane of red glass made liquid.

The blood of the man she loved.

Her fingers curled into fists, coiled so tight that her fingernails broke the skin. The pain—it burgeoned, bloomed into a gateway, magic drumming a battle march in her veins. It was dreadful delirium, a vision of fire and ash before her wide, unblinking eyes. Her hands grew hot, unbearably hot, invisible fire climbing up her arms, awakening every part of her body, armoring it, a flame cloak for magic personified.

She could smell it—the ash, keen and bracing, a rallying cry. The world would reek of it.

Then—noise—a voice—movement—

Darkness.

37

Olivia rubbed the back of her head against the rough stone wall, hoping to relieve the persistent itch in her greasy hair. She stared into the darkness across the cell, where the two boxes lay. Where James's eye and hand lay.

It would be so easy to wish it all away, pretend it hadn't happened, invent a happier dream-world and wrap herself up in it. But that path was dangerous. That path could kill. She'd been taught at the Divinity about imprisonment survival strategies, and disengagement led to complacent prisoners, ones incapable of fighting.

Instead she tortured herself, staring at the boxes. Imagining their contents. And how they'd been acquired. Staying in pain. Staying alive. James's love was real. His life was real. His suffering. She refused to close her mind, and her heart, to him—no matter how much it hurt not to.

Hope. She needed hope. But here it seemed in short supply.

A smooth tail slipped along her ankle. A rat. She kicked out. "I'm not dead yet."

The croak sounded unfamiliar to her. Her own voice. She hadn't spoken in two days. No one had come. No one bearing food or water, no one to drag her to the Hall of Mirrors. She swallowed and shook her head, shaking that thought free. She didn't want to think about what that meant.

"Hmm?" A voice swept in from down the corridor. An unfamiliar voice.

She shuddered. When her spine finished trembling its shock, she jolted upright and held her breath. Had her starved mind conjured it?

Footsteps echoed. Not measured and self-assured as her former guard's had been. Softer, unsure. Someone new.

Someone new.

Hope.

She seized it, wriggling closer to the bars. "Yes?"

A light shone in the distance, and she squinted her eyes against it.

"I'm here." She forced an eye open, flinching against the pain, trying to discern something, anything, from the blur of flame-gold light and shadowed black before her.

A figure neared. Tall. Broad shouldered. Slender. A man. He had a crown of hair the color of the Aes River sandbar north of Caerlain Trel, a sandbar with a stand of cottonwood trees, black poplars. If she closed her eyes, she could see the leafy branches softly swaying in the wind.

No. It was not yet time for them. After all of this, she would go there. She would go there with James.

At last, he came into full view, willowy and young, his torch shining overbright, but she could just make out his features. His face bore fading scars—a slash across the cheek, one along the nose, and another across the chin that disappeared into short, well-groomed facial hair. It was a face that had seen too much and wished to see no more.

He bore a—not a box, Divine be praised. A tray. He dropped to a crouch before the bars and laid his burden beside him. A full cup and bread. Her mouth watered.

Black bread. The Crag must have exhausted the palace's supply of wheat and turned to rye. Loyalists had to be raiding supply lines. The siege couldn't last much longer.

"Gods above," the young man swore, and turned away. "To a woman..."

Did she look so horrific? With her wrist, she swept tendrils of greasy hair away from her oily face. How long had it been since she'd bathed? The sting in her eyes had burned badly at first, and now that she recalled it, the stinging resumed. She'd gotten used to it.

The smell. She bit her lip. Had it been two weeks since she'd been able to wash? There'd be no mercy coaxed through flirtatious wiles. Not here, not even from this man, with his warm, oak-brown eyes and hair like the sand.

"I'm Olivia," she whispered. *A name for the wretch before him.* Perhaps he'd treat her kindly if she had a name.

Warily, he turned to her and clenched his teeth. "Anton. Your... new guard."

Guard. Her spirits fell. Someone new all right. But no hope.

Anton. Her previous guard hadn't given her a name. Hadn't introduced himself at all. Was this one new to the Crag Company? A pliant recruit, perhaps?

"What happened to my old one?" she asked.

Anton drew in a slow breath. "You... killed him."

"I did?" When was that?

He stared at the torch pointedly.

She gasped. "Ah, I did?" She'd burned him during her escape. Had to be. "I mean... I wasn't aware that I did," she quickly corrected. "It's—"

He waved a hand dismissively. "How about this: I will make sure you have food and water, and I don't end up crispy like my unlucky predecessor?"

She almost smiled, and then she allowed it. Hope. "Deal."

He removed a cup of water from the tray and, through the bars, placed it before her. Kneeling, she wedged it between her palms and brought it to her mouth.

She drank it, sweet, soothing, as if she'd never drunk water before. "More?"

"I'll return with more later tonight." Anton accepted the empty cup from her.

Was that allowed? Her previous guard had brought her bread and water once a day, if that. But she wasn't about to question him.

He passed the chunk of black bread onto her side of the bars. It took all of her self-control not to pounce on it immediately. Making a pig of herself would surely detract from what minimal charm she had left.

He stayed in a crouch, frozen. When she moved to grasp the bread with her broken hands, he lifted his gaze to hers.

"Is there anything I can get you for"—he nodded to her hands— "that?"

Why was he acting so kind? That had to be a facade. He wanted something. Had to. But she couldn't expose him, alienate him. Better he thought her naive, liked her, even... and kept bringing her food and water.

She raised her head to better expose the arcanir collar. "The key to this would be nice."

An amused laugh faded into hollowness, and he stroked his blond beard. "Somehow I don't think General Gilles would approve."

No, he wouldn't.

"Then we won't tell him." She mustered her most charming smile.

With a long sigh, he lowered himself to the floor and sat cross-legged. "I don't even have the key."

No chance, then. "And to the cell?"

He shook his head. "Not trusted enough for that, either. 'Glorified but powerless kitchen boy' is the sum of my accomplishments."

No key to the arcanir collar. No key to the cell. His openness gave her pause—a ploy to get her talking? She wouldn't tell him anything worth knowing.

"You seem a decent sort," she whispered cautiously. "What are you doing with the Crag?"

He averted his gaze. "Robbed travelers for a living with the Black Mountain Brigands, ever since I was old enough to hold a blade." He glanced back at her and drew in a breath. "No killing, mind. Just robbing."

She nodded encouragingly. Hopefully he'd keep talking. Maybe he'd tell her something she could use.

"Then Serge took over. He did things... differently. I wanted no part in it, thought, 'Join up with one of the Free Companies. Help some people for coin.' Signed the papers a month ago, enlisted for a year. You can see how that turned out." He hung his head.

"They forced you to do this?" she asked cautiously.

He huffed. "No, my company—and several of the others—were brought in to quell a coup d'état. A faction arisen among King Marcus's men—insurrectionists. They'd killed the king, his heirs, all the Faralles here. The loyalists were said to have abandoned the capital. We were brought in to eliminate remaining traitors—the Emaurrian Army, the Guard, anyone who put up a fight. We were to take control and hold the capital until Parliament could convene and settle succession." He drew in a deep breath and released it. "Only, when we arrived at the palace, General Gilles was already there. Along with Phantom, Shadow, and Flame. And hundreds of men. Where had they come from? When had they arrived? 'Forlorn hope,' they said. 'Vanguard.' Right."

If this fellow could be believed, most of the Crag Company had been deceived into treason.

She remembered to breathe. "You were lied to."

"So I've gathered." A lengthy exhalation. "There were a few outbursts of doubt, protest. Quieted. 'Paranoia,' the officers say. And we don't dare object. No longer."

A reckless wish sprang in her breast, to convince this man to abandon his Free Company and incite rebellion among the Crag, but there was no sense in it. Against the organized Crag officers and men who had knowingly committed treason, a few low-level dissenters had no hope of victory. And they well knew it.

Moreover, convincing men who had drowned their swords with the blood of the Emaurrian Army, the Guard, and innocent countrymen attempting to defend their realm that they would not be tried as traitors was a losing battle.

But Anton had no love for Gilles or the Crag Company. No dedication to their cause. If he could be believed.

"James. Can you get to Prince James?"

Anton shook his head. "Heavily guarded by Gilles's most trusted doubles."

Her heart swelled. "He's alive?"

Eyes shadowed, Anton nodded. "If it can be called that."

Gilles's words needled her mind. *How much can be cut away from a man before he can no longer call himself such? I have yet to learn the answer with His Highness.*

No matter what Gilles did to him, James was James. She closed her eyes and could see him raising her hand to his lips, eyeing her with sea-blue magnetism, requesting a dance with her at the Ignis ball last spring. His muscled build had belied his grace, and he'd moved with the fluidity of a consummate dancer. In his skilled arms, faced with his refined handsomeness, she'd melted into him. That evening, when the ladies had run into the King's Wood for the maying, she'd wished for him to find her. And he had. That night, under the stars, in a bed of soft grass, they'd made love for the first time. She smiled at the memory.

As long as he lived, he was the man she loved. No matter what.

But there was nothing Anton could do for him.

"Do any of the Faralles yet live?" she asked. James had gone to find Queen Alexandrie after all.

Anton shook his head.

None? Not even any of the little princes and princesses? Not even—

She stifled a sob. No, she couldn't think about that now. She frowned, considering further options. "Can you get a message out—"

"Not allowed any messages out."

She sighed. No keys, no access to James, no messages, no rebellion? What *could* he do?

What if he's lying?

She bit her lip. If he was lying, he might pass on everything she said to Gilles. Would the general have her killed?

Killed... No. Then he could no longer use her against James.

And if Rielle hadn't yet used spirit magic to find her, he could no longer use her to lure Rielle here either.

No, she was too useful to Gilles alive.

But if Anton truly did bear the Crag and Gilles ill will, if he truly did wish to help...

"The Moonlit Rite."

His eyes widened. "What about it?"

If there was one thing, above all others, that could be done to help the realm, the Moonlit Rite was it. And Anton was the last remaining hope to see it done.

She would test him. And if he passed, she would tell him everything.

38

a soft hand squeezed hers, and Rielle opened her eyes.

Red. The chamber was appointed in all things red, from its priceless Sileni drapes to its Sonbaharan cotton bedding. It had once been her favorite, before she'd had more than her fair share of red in her life.

She inhaled. Lily of the valley and amber, a scent from her childhood.

Next to the bed sat Gran, regally attired in a long-sleeved violet dress of the finest velvet, her silvered hair spun into an elaborate style that empha-sized her sky-blue eyes. A fine crease had settled between her eyebrows.

"Gran." Rielle shifted toward her.

"Are you all right, child?"

Gran. Melain. Rielle clutched the red coverlet. Red. Red. She jerked upright. "Jon—"

"He's alive." Gran stood and took her shoulders. "My House Physician, Cyril Féron, is operating." Her palms rubbed comfort through unfamiliar fabric.

Rielle looked down. A simple white chemise and side-laced bodice. Hands clean of blood. And on the bed lay a bolt tip, coated in a waxy substance.

"That man said you should keep it close, that it would be of help if you needed to calm yourself."

That man. Only one man had the dubious honor of being called such by Gran. *Leigh.*

Rielle rubbed the bolt tip. Arcanir poison. It was designed to both prevent its target from receiving magic and to prevent casting. Before all had gone dark, she'd felt battle fury nearly break her.

No, not mere battle fury, not stoppable, reversible battle fury.

Outright fureur—

Gran's fingers slipped down to hers. "Tell me who did this, my child."

Rielle thumbed the bolt tip's greasy coating. "A team of two. A crossbowman and... a mage." Her vision blurred. "One burned to the death. The mage escaped." Memories of the mangled bodies of the Crag camp invaded her mind. "We stumbled upon a camp of dead Crag Company mercenaries. The attackers... they could have been Crag as well."

"Gautier," Gran called. Her armor of calm and propriety remained in place.

The door creaked open, and within moments, her impeccable Companion was at her side, one of two she patronized from the Camarilla —one as a bodyguard and the other as a bard.

Gran's constant sentinel and Companion for as long as Rielle could remember, Gautier had changed little over the years. Tall, broad-shouldered, with not a single gray hair out of place. During her childhood visits to Melain, he'd been a perfect gentleman to her and Lady Rosette, her doll, during tea parties.

As always, his face was a calm and pleasant mask. His flawless manner and carriage evoked competence, capability, and somehow, despite his advanced age, a deadly air.

"Please make inquiries with the connétable," Gran said.

Gautier inclined his head and, after a punctilious bow, left their presence. If Gran was sending Gautier, then she was keeping the matter limited to those she could trust.

Jon. Was he all right? Gran had said he was alive. But how badly was he hurt? "I need to see him."

"Of course." Gran rose. "Cyril is still with him, but we can wait outside the chamber."

As soon as the physician finished, she would be waiting. The first to see Jon. She sat up, donned the slippers set by the bed, and followed Gran into the hall. Farther down, in front of the White Room, some household knights and Prevost Castle's Master Healer, Narcisse Blanc, awaited.

Bows rippled as she and Gran approached.

Outside the White Room's door, two guards stood watch. Behind that door was Jon.

How hurt was he? Would he live? She reached for the knob.

Gran cleared her throat and gestured to a set of fine upholstered chairs placed against the wall.

Rielle smiled thinly, folded her hands, and sat while Jon fought for his life on the other side of this wall.

He'd tried to tell her about the arcanir poison. She'd felt it for herself.

Arcanir.

There was nothing she could do. His life was in the hands of Gran's physician.

Please live. I need you.

It wasn't so long ago that his life had been in *her* hands, his wide eyes fixed on what lay beyond while he slipped away. Divine be praised, he hadn't. Five years ago, she never would have guessed that the young paladin she healed would now mean so much to her.

Her hands, clasped together, hadn't so long been parted from his. Strong, big, rough, and yet so gentle. Loving. Warm. As they'd dashed from Donati's to Cosette's, he'd held her hand, squeezed it, grinned at her. She smiled, and her palm tingled at the memory.

The red of Jon's blood filled in its lines.

Heart racing, she blinked it away.

Gran placed her hand on Rielle's. "Cyril is highly skilled."

She swallowed. Of course. Of course he was. Jon would be fine. He had to be.

"I know. Thank you, Gran." She closed her eyes and leaned her head against the wall. The wolf trap snapped in her head, her jagged ankle, Jon's wild eyes, the way he'd searched the trees for a moment before tending to her—

A man arrived, lithe, in his late thirties with thick black locks. He had a kind face to match his gentle mien; it was Benoist, Gran's Companion for nearly a dozen years, renowned for his musical talent.

He inclined his head with a sad smile and a slow blink of his long lashes, offering his sympathies most gracefully before taking his place at Gran's side.

Rielle dropped her gaze to her own lap. White knuckles. Fisted fabric.

"It's been a long time since you've visited, my child." A slow smile brightened Gran's face.

Trying to make conversation. To keep her mind off Jon. Rielle's muscles relaxed. She nodded.

It had been over three years since she'd last visited. Since Midwinter in Tregarde. Since word had spread among all the Houses, Gran's included. When all eyes saw her through the veil of that night, even mustering presence among the Houses was an ordeal. "I wish I could have come sooner, and under different circumstances."

Gran's eyes shone. "Don't trouble yourself, child. You're here now. I am hosting a small number of displaced nobles from the capital... and Marquis Tregarde."

Stiffening, Rielle pressed her lips into a thin line. Brennan had already returned from the capital, then. At least he'd behave in Gran's domain. Probably.

"Not your favorite person, I know," Gran remarked, "but he *is* still your future husband."

Rielle shook her head and exhaled sharply. "Tregarde's cruelty is inhuman, Gran."

"And yet obligations remain." She heaved a sigh and lowered her gaze as she clasped her hands and rested them on her knees. She had lived those words, in one way or another, like countless other noblewomen. "Your parents carefully planned your union. Their reasons are still valid."

As much as political marriage repelled her, the day would come when she'd have to pay the price for being the daughter of Corbin Fernand Lothaire and Sylviane Amadour Lothaire, née Sylviane Auvray Amadour, Gran's granddaughter.

While nobles enjoyed great freedom, she would not be able to elude the duties of governance, propagation, and honor forever.

Just not with that sadist.

The door to the White Room opened. The physician emerged, and she stood from her seat, wringing her hands. He turned to Gran, who nodded toward Rielle and took Benoist's arm to rise.

"The patient should make a full recovery," the physician said, eyeing Rielle. "The bolt just barely nicked his subclavian artery. Leaving the bolt tip saved his life."

She shuddered and lowered her gaze.

"He will need his dressings changed twice daily and this salve applied." He handed her a medium-sized jar. "There are no signs of infection, but this should prevent it and decrease inflammation." He thrust a tall canister into her hands. "Serve it brewed as a tea thrice daily until it is gone."

She opened it and sniffed. Yarrow, among other herbs.

"There is no antidote for arcanir poisoning, but his body should filter it out in about two to three weeks. He can then be fully healed by magic. Otherwise, he's in good health and will recover with rest and plenty of fluids."

Good health. Recovery. "Thank you," she breathed.

He inclined his head. "He's awake. You may see him now, if you wish."

Gran smiled her encouragement. "Go."

Heart pounding, Rielle entered the room and closed the door behind her. What could she say to him? He'd come to harm in her care. She'd failed him. If not for Leigh, he might have...

A fire blazed in the hearth, and a large bowl of reddened water sat on the table. Next to it rested the broken bolt—Leigh must have brought it—and the rhombic tip, upon a piece of canvas. Gently, she set the medicine down next to it.

A few steps through the antechamber and around the corner, and the bed came into view.

Jon sat against the pillows, his chest and back bandaged. He greeted her with sleepy eyes, a corner of his mouth raised, at ease as though this were any other day.

Her heart leapt. Although he was still pale, some color had returned to his skin. Alive. Awake.

She ran to the bed, where she fell to her knees and buried her face in the bedding. He could have died due to her carelessness, but he hadn't.

His fingers roved through her hair as he consoled her with a quiet, soothing sound. Reality slowly sank in, a warmth seeping back into her bones. She knelt there in silence awhile, his comforting hand on her head, until the tears stopped flowing.

Although he'd been the one shot, here he was, comforting *her*.

"What happened?" he asked. "I don't remember much after getting shot... I know we were ambushed by at least two enemies. One lured us into the other's sights."

She swallowed. Fureur. The rise of truth would at last meet the surface. "I tried to trap the crossbowman, but he killed himself rather than face capture."

"Odd." Jon shifted. "Such loyalty is rare, especially among mercenaries. Perhaps a Heartseeker? They're more of a religious order devoted to Nox than assassins."

It could be. There'd been no magic used—at least none that she'd seen —but the runner had possessed a bright anima. Perhaps a mage. One of the Crag's mage captains? But if it were Shadow or Phantom, why not finish the job? Had Leigh been so close by?

She shook her head. "If we are dealing with Heartseekers, then we won't find his partner until he wants to be found."

He ran his fingers through her hair, slow, soft, coaxing. "After you defeated him, what happened?"

Her worst nightmare. She chewed her lip. "I came back, and you were... unresponsive. I shouted for help, but no one came, and I..." She took a deep breath. "There's something you need to know."

He drew his eyebrows together, watching, waiting.

She took his hand. "Some mages are predisposed to a condition called battle fury." Mages who'd experienced traumatic events and never could move past them. There was a fear left behind. She licked her lip. "Do you know what that is?"

He nodded. "All paladins do. Spells are anima constructed into magic. That construction is mindful, complex, meticulous, and as a result, delayed. Battle fury is an involuntary response to fear of a threat. It lowers the inner barriers between a mage and her anima, enabling faster, more natural spell-casting at a cost of..." He pressed his lips together and lowered his gaze.

"Mind," she supplied softly. "It's all right. In battle fury, our minds are affected by that fear. But fear can keep you alive." Battle fury was a short-cut. It skipped questions, theories, excuses, and cut straight to sorting threat and non-threat. Straight to survival. "We're controlled by instinct, bloodlust, violence, until the threat is destroyed."

"We?"

She nodded, and his hold on her hand tightened. "If that fear turns to madness, those lowered inner barriers can disappear completely. And so can the mind."

"Fureur," he rasped, wincing as he sat up. "You went into fureur?"

Eyes watering, she looked up at him, her chin quivering, and nodded. "When I thought I'd lost you, I—"

"Lost yourself." His voice dropped. "You could have—"

"I know."

A deep line settled between his eyebrows. "Like a berserker..."

She nodded.

"Except at the end of it, you'd—" He swallowed, shook his head, and pulled his hand away. "I can handle a lot, Rielle. But no matter what happens to me, your"—he closed his eyes and took a deep breath—"death isn't one of them."

But he hadn't felt the loss when she had. Entire. All consuming. Hadn't felt the fureur settle in, taking on the pressure, setting her mind free as it took over.

The sea of his gaze turned cold. "Fureur is caused by fear," he murmured, "when a mage or loved ones are threatened."

No, no, no. If he decided he would try to prevent her fureur, this would go somewhere horrible.

She shifted. "I had no choice."

"In fureur taking over?"

"In loving you."

The line between his eyebrows faded.

"Believe me, I *wanted* to want no more than a cheap thrill. That's all I've allowed myself for years. Those first few days on the road with you, before the promise I made you about not using your feelings against you, if you'd pinned me in the dark, I would have gladly enjoyed some pleasure and no more—"

His eyebrows shot up.

"—and I would have been fooling myself. Because by the end of this mission, I would have completely and utterly fallen for you. No matter what." His mouth fell open, but she pressed on. "And even if you tell me now that, for my own good, this is over between us—"

He took her hand again. "Rielle—"

"Even if you tell me that," she continued, her eyes locked on his, "that won't change how I feel about you at all."

He looked away, but his mouth twitched. When he looked back to her, he was grinning, that dimple playing below one of his twinkling eyes. "If I'd pinned you in the dark?"

She frowned. "Jon, I'm serious—"

"How often, exactly, did you think about that possibility?"

With pursed lips, she eyed him.

"Because judging by how readily you said that, it seems like you've given it a lot of thought." He raised an eyebrow. "*A lot.*"

She exhaled sharply. "Jon—"

"I know," he said, sobering. "Fureur. We'll face it together."

"It's not that simple—"

He held her gaze. "When problems come up, we face them together. It is that simple. Done."

Done? Just like that? She drew in her chin. He was lying here because she'd gotten caught in a trap, because she'd made a mistake, and now she'd told him about fureur, the risk to him, herself, and everyone around them, and he was... taking it in stride?

He cleared his throat. "How is your ankle?"

She scoffed. Her ankle didn't matter. With a sniff, she murmured into the sheets, "Don't ever do that again. Promise me."

"Don't get shot? Got it." His soft chuckle broke into a cough.

"Jon," she chided, "you could have died."

"I would have," he said, taking her hand, "but for you." With some effort, he urged her onto the edge of the bed.

"But for Leigh, you mean." Frowning, she pulled her hand free and turned away from him. If she'd been more vigilant, he wouldn't have been hurt. He was trying to comfort her, still. She slumped. "If I hadn't gotten caught in the trap—"

"Let's lay the blame where it belongs... with the one who shot me."

"He's not here to punish, is he?" She sighed.

Jon held her against his uninjured side. "Stay with me."

As if she'd leave. As if she'd want to. "Someone has to make sure you don't die abed... at least not from battle wounds."

The sound of his soft laughter gave way to a pained grimace. With Jon afflicted with arcanir poison, it would be some time before he'd be fit for travel—and for battle—again. He would be well protected here, and they had no choice but to wait the two to three weeks. A wait would mean not only Jon's recovery but also a delay in approaching the capital until Spirit-seve and the rite.

A serious delay. She'd have to send the Proctor an update—

Or he might think it's a stalling tactic. A lie so that I can step into Kier-an's shoes and go to Courdeval on Spiritseve.

And what would the Proctor do then? Send explicit orders not to go? Send someone to stop her?

No. There could be no more reports, not until this was over. Not until Olivia was safe—even if it meant incinerating every mercenary in the way.

She was through hiding from the Crag, defending against them. Jon lay, barely alive, bleeding and bandaged in a bed. This was what came of hiding and defending.

Until Jon fully recovered, battle was too risky for him. But not for her. It was time to find their enemies and kill them first. Kill Phantom and Shadow so they couldn't strike from stealth.

She would just have to track them down somehow. But all she had was her memory and the broken bolt.

The broken bolt...

Brennan might get a scent off it. Perhaps he would have some insights that could lead her to the mage captains... and their final resting place.

She wrapped a cautious arm around Jon, looking about the White Room.

The White Room. In Prevost Castle, Gran's home. She stiffened. She needed to tell Jon who she was—among other things. She shook her head. One step at a time.

"Jon," she began.

"Hmm?" He caressed her arm.

"We're in Prevost Castle in Melain, home of Duchess Madeleine Duclos Auvray."

"I know that."

"My great-grandmother."

He frowned.

"I am Favrielle Amadour Lothaire, Marquise of Laurentine."

He went rigid, opened his mouth. Closed it. A line formed between his eyebrows. "You did not introduce yourself as such."

She hadn't thought it would matter when she'd captured him. Hadn't foreseen that the stubborn paladin stuck in her spell would become so much more. "At the Tower, my title has no bearing. I'm just a master mage, no more, no less."

His gaze downcast, Jon stole a glance at the fifth finger of her left hand, where she should have worn her Laurentine signet ring. It was a badge of difference, isolation, identity, and a constant reminder that her future was not entirely her own. She kept it in her recondite satchel.

"I have lived away from the Houses and their politics for a long time... I've lived as no more than a mage for almost a decade." She paused. "I love you, but there are some things you must know about me before you can truly feel the same. My past. My duties—"

"I know what I feel." He caressed her cheek, shaking his head slowly. "We can figure the rest out later." He tipped her chin up to his mouth and kissed her.

39

*T*ension seized Rielle's body. Suddenly. Quickly. Entirely. Brennan pulling on the bond, the sensation powerful. Close.

She opened her eyes. It was still dark, and Jon still slept beside her, his arms encircling her, his chest rising and falling steadily. His skin was cool to the touch.

She tugged the covers a little higher. Better he be warm, comfortable, anything to bring him back to health, especially with Shadow and Phantom still out there, and who knew what else hunting them.

Dragging a shaky hand through her hair, she rose from the bed. Jon lived. But how long until the haunting fear of his brush with death dissipated? Maybe never.

Being with him was so new, and yet somehow, it felt like she'd always known him. In so short a time, he'd managed to carve a place in her life all his own, one she couldn't fill with anything or anyone but him. It scared her—the chance of losing someone always did—but it pleased her, too, to have this man, this person, who belonged only to her.

Slipping free of his embrace, she pulled aside the covers and wrapped herself in a silk robe. In case he woke soon, she topped off his water, then poured herself a goblet of wine. She padded to the vanity table and mixed in a dose of queen's lace powder, smiling. Although she hadn't needed it yet, it was always better to be prepared.

Next to it lay the canvas-wrapped bundle containing the remnants of the bolt. She grabbed it and slipped through the glass-paned doors that led out onto the balcony.

They'd moved to the Red Room, and its best asset was its full view of the Lady's Garden, a vibrant and internationally renowned collection of exotic flora tended into the shape of a labyrinthine blooming rose.

The night-blooming flowers welcomed her, and she closed her eyes to inhale their alluring scent. She brought the goblet to her lips. Alone, in the quiet of the night, she could gather her thoughts until Brennan arrived.

On the stone balustrade, she unwrapped the bundle, revealing the broken bolt. Cedar shaft. Goose-feather fletching. Standard. The bolt tip was rhombic—crafted to penetrate plate armor—and although the crossbow didn't require special skill, it was a very expensive weapon. Prohibitively expensive, because it had the power to kill a noble in the costliest of plate. Which meant that the crossbowman's employer had possessed ample coin. She frowned.

She and Jon had stumbled into a massacred outpost of Crag mercenaries, courtesy of Brennan. The attackers could have been survivors, but Brennan wouldn't have left any. Investigators, maybe?

Too soon for them, too. Perhaps scouts checking in?

She sipped her wine. A crossbow countered armor. The target had been Jon.

Arcanir poison, however, could dispatch a mage easily or prevent a target from being healed. Useful for handling either her *or* Jon.

But they couldn't have known she loved him. That hurting him could trigger fureur... Which would have happened. At least if Leigh hadn't come along to hit her with arcanir.

Thanks were in order. She would visit him soon. Gran, of course, didn't want "that man" staying at Prevost, regardless of his good deeds. She grimaced.

But the attack... The Proctor and the High Priest hadn't been wrong in assigning Jon an escort. The question was why. Were all paladins in danger now, or only he? Was the target actually his adoptive father, the High Priest? Did someone hope to prove a point to him?

She turned away.

There, to the left and just below the ledge, was a living fixture embedded in the castle wall. Brennan.

"Do you come here often, or is tonight an oddity?" she asked softly.

With a snarling smile, Brennan rent a set of claws free only to dig them into the stone just above him, scaling the last few feet with ease to perch upon the balustrade like a wolfish gargoyle, somewhere between man and beast.

"If you're asking whether I visit the Lady's Garden often, the answer is yes," he hissed, with a grin too wide to be human. "If you're asking whether I cling to the castle wall below this balcony every night, then no." He casually polished his claws, the black fur of his man-beast form shining under the starlight.

She pursed her lips, fending off a smile. Sometimes he could actually be tolerable. She sipped her wine and looked out at the garden.

His nostrils flared as he sniffed the air.

"How convenient to lace the wine with preventives," he remarked, his voice low and rumbling. "Makes it easier to swive with abandon." He observed her darkly through slits.

Smug bastard. "You'd know all about that." She leaned her back against the balustrade.

"Judging by your scent, you're out of practice." He huffed a soft bark. "Do you need a review?"

Sucking her tongue, she regarded him disdainfully. "I'm still smarting from your last lesson."

His back stiffened, and his upper lip curled. "To business, then," he said, his monstrous voice gravelly. He stalked to her on the balustrade, more wolf than man, and sat within her reach.

Good. She needed a favor.

"You killed those Crag scouts." She ran her fingers through his long, thick fur, and he closed his eyes and groaned.

"They were there to kill you." He sighed. "They needed to die."

When her fingers stopped moving, he opened an eye, looked at her, and then turned his wolfish head. He reached out with a clawed hand to grab her wrist, and she met his endless, dark depths.

His black fur disappeared as wolf ceded to human, replaced by bronze skin and a man's powerful physique. "I will always do all that I can to protect you. As a man, as a beast—it makes no difference."

"To preserve your means of control."

"Not only." His human, hazel eyes were earnest and yielding. "I want to marry you." He grinned, exuding both confidence and calm, as though the outcome of their extended game was both certain and in his favor.

Grapes would ripen on the willows. She scoffed.

He leaned in. "Long before I knew about how to break the curse, I agreed to marry you. That day I came to you at the Tower, I knew only that your family was gone, that you were alone. I offered you everything, and you threw it back in my face."

"I was thirteen," she shot back. "Did you really want a child bride?"

"Of course not," he hissed, his face contorting into a grimace. "But marriage was the only way to get guardianship of you. We would have been wed in name only until you were old enough and felt ready to make it a reality. You know that, but the Divinity filled your head with poison."

She shook her head. "I was scared and had just lost my whole family, then you showed up talking about marriage while I worried about not killing you and your family by accident. So of course I couldn't go with you. And you exacted more than your fair share of vengeance six years later."

He blew out a breath. "You refused me like some knave. Is it any wonder?"

Her refusal. It always came back to that. No matter how many times she explained to him her fear, what her needs had been, her intentions—he always blamed her for his resulting humiliation among the Houses. If he'd actually cared about her needs, he would have left her in the care of those who could actually help her.

But he'd pushed for the marriage. Hard. A terrifying prospect for an orphaned thirteen-year-old girl.

She swallowed. "Tell me, if you'd known how to break the curse before Midwinter at Tregarde that year, would you have done anything differently?"

He clenched his teeth. "Maybe. Would you have deserved it?"

The air escaped her lungs, and she turned away. His old wound still bled. They could argue about this for hours.

He winced. His gaze bored into the stone beneath him.

Either she had hit the truth, or he still played his game. Either way, she wouldn't indulge him.

It didn't matter anymore. She didn't care. She would never marry the man who'd treated her so cruelly.

The intensity ebbed from his gaze. "I made contact with Nicolette."

A change of subject. Divine be praised. "Anxiously awaited news. Did she agree?"

"Yes." He heaved a breath.

"Thank you."

He tipped his head toward the bolt pieces lying on the canvas. "That almost broke your commoner plaything."

"He has a name."

Brennan curled his upper lip. " 'Commoner' will do."

She rolled her eyes. "We were attacked by a team near the Crag outpost. A mage and a crossbowman. I killed the crossbowman. The mage disappeared." Her blood simmered at the thought.

"You're losing your touch."

She sighed; he didn't even know the half of it. "I went into fureur."

That couldn't happen again; she'd have to make peace with herself, as Leigh had advised.

She traced the bolt tip's edge with her fingertips. "Leigh stopped me with the arcanir coating on this bolt tip."

Quiet for a moment, Brennan's face went slack. "That team almost killed you, then."

"Almost."

He approached the bundle and brought the pieces close to his nose. "All I am getting is the overwhelming smell of your commoner's blood, kestair oil, and arcanir." He examined the tip of one piece, followed by the fletching of the other.

"Then I'll have to find the mage myself."

"Leave that to me." Brennan wrapped the bundle. In his savage eyes was the unadulterated fixation seen only in lethal predators.

"As if you care."

He clenched his jaw, baring his teeth wolfishly. "You could have been killed. I would have spent the rest of my life an uncontrollable beast, howling at the moon—if I should have been so lucky as to live. I would have nothing."

No matter his faults, Brennan could always be trusted to protect his own interests. She nodded.

"I'll investigate the scene and see what I can find." Black fur spiked out of his skin until it became a full coat covering a muscled, tailed, clawed, snouted beast resembling a wolf but possessing the figure of a man. His beastly amber eyes held hers for a moment.

He bounded to the corner of the balcony and leaped off.

With a gasp, she threw herself against the balustrade, looking down—

He lifted his head from the garden a final time before he stalked off into the night. She exhaled and backed up to lean against the castle wall, shaking her head.

Did he have to be so dramatic? Did it please him to know she cared whether he lived or died?

Fire ran through her veins. She managed to settle her gaze on the goblet she'd left on the balustrade.

The doors creaked open behind her.

Jon. His eyes brightened.

Bandages interrupted the tattoos of his bare chest, the break a visible reminder of his brush with death.

She wouldn't let it happen again.

"Here you are," he whispered, walking carefully toward her.

She rushed to brace him. "Did I wake you?"

His hands settled on the stone, then he wrapped an arm around her to embrace her from behind. He kissed her head. "No," he answered quietly in her ear, "I just awoke to find you gone."

She closed her eyes, savoring the feel of him against her back and gently stroking his arm.

"What are you doing out here?" he asked.

She turned in his embrace to face him, but his gaze had wandered to her goblet.

"Black arts stuff." She smiled. "Communing with ghosts and monsters, drinking witchy concoctions, casting my love spell on you—"

He kissed her, swaying with her in his grasp. "A love spell?" He laughed under his breath. "That explains everything."

She scoffed. "Bastard."

"Witch."

Her lips twitched. He seemed to enjoy teasing her almost as much as she enjoyed chiding him.

She rose on her toes as if to kiss him, but when he descended to meet her lips, she stopped just short. "You're lucky you're injured, or I'd show you what happens when you mouth off."

He gave her a squeeze. "Don't you mean 'unlucky'?" His voice dropped an octave lower.

Unlucky indeed. Held together by catgut sutures and bandages, he was in no shape for a proper reprimand.

"Take it up with the physician." Before he could reply, she took his hand in hers, wrapped his arm around her shoulders, and helped him back into the bedchamber.

Somewhere far beyond the balcony and the garden, in the outlying wilds, a wolf howled.

40

The afternoon sunlight peeked through the dense canopy, illuminating patches of ground with a golden glow as Brennan made his way through the Forest of the Hart. The magic-tinged smell of ash still disturbed the air. But the earthy fragrance of oak, beech, little-leaf linden, and silver birch dominated these woods, the common dogwood on the outskirts—he inhaled—no, winter-flame. The moon would be full tonight, and the Wolf clawed close to the surface, heightening his senses even more than usual.

Separating its scent from the moss, the rot, the trees, and the other shrubs, he breathed it in. Its leaves would have turned orange-yellow by now and fallen to reveal the beauty of its red-tipped, amber winter stems.

The winter-flame gave way to pungent hoarwithy, with its vermilion leaves and toxic gray bark. Crisp foliage crunched underfoot to the unmusical, noisy song of a common starling and the chattering of far-off finches above. Elsewhere, magpies, wrens, and a golden oriole staked their claims.

His sharp nose picked up the markings and filth of a bear, deer, foxes, and the myriad forest rodents. From a distance came the scents of a pack of wolves—they'd give him a wide berth, as always. The Wolf liked its space.

The bodies of the Crag scouts had been removed, but the slightly sweet, acrid smell of old blood and decomposition still clung to the earth. Mingled with the stagnant scents, fresh ones—men from the Connétablie of Melain, knights, and men-at-arms.

And *her* scent.

It lingered, along with the commoner's. Brennan gnashed his teeth but followed. The ash grew stronger—scorched trees, scorched earth, scorched human—

The char of burnt wood overwhelmed his nostrils.

A crater. Massive, black, everything incinerated for thirty feet in every direction. The wind riffled the ash, sweeping it by. On the fringe, trees lingered with amputated limbs and disfigured trunks, blackened at the points of separation, still shaping what looked like a perfect sphere. Unnatural.

He shuddered.

Fureur. This was what it looked like.

All those years ago, he'd raced to Laurentine. Right after. Stone walls had remained like a cage with nothing inside. Instead of floors, furnishings, animals, people—nothing but a fine powder. Ash riffled by the wind. He'd knelt in it, brought it to his nose, reached across the bond to no avail. She was in that ash, gone, dead, and the Wolf had crept just beneath his skin and clawed its way out—

Until he'd felt her presence flood him once more, a rush of warmth and joy. An illusion. Just confirmation of the bond. Not real.

And the absence, the death that he'd felt, had been false, too. Arcanir. The same absence he'd felt two days ago.

The Wolf had fought for freedom and had it in the wilds—days of mad ranging—until that warmth and joy rushed in once more.

Arcanir... If that was how it felt for her to be in contact with arcanir, he didn't want to entertain the idea of her death.

With a deep breath, he rounded the crater, tried to leave the dominion of its overpowering odor. So much had burned, but traces remained.

Blood—the commoner's. Brennan leaned toward a tree, brought his nose flush against it. The bleeding commoner had braced against it. Arcanir and kestair oil.

A collection of disarmed traps sat in a pile nearby, one tampered with, marked with the scent of Laurentinian leather. He recalled his balcony meeting with *her* and couldn't remember any marks from such a trap on her body.

Rielle.

He snarled. He'd never met such an arrogant, infuriating woman. He offered her the sun, moon, and stars, but she rejected him because she liked the dirt. Wealth, power, strength, intelligence, good looks—every other woman he'd pursued had fallen for these, and easily. But not her.

Snarling little she-wolf. She'd refused him. Him, heir to Emaurria's most prestigious dukedom. Brennan Karandis Marcel. Refused by a naive thirteen-year-old orphan.

As if that wasn't humiliation enough, she'd debased herself a few years later by having an affair with her master, a Kamerish commoner.

His fiancée had cuckolded him with a peasant-born foreigner.

He punched the rough trunk of an oak, sending splinters flying, the Wolf clawing inside for a way out. Mutilated flesh and fractured bone radiated pain up his arm.

Thanks to her indiscretion, the scandal had spread far and wide, animating every Emaurrian noble's tongue to wagging. Whispers of his degradation had infected every noble function, and they had not been kind.

When her common-born lover had abandoned her, a little vengeance had been in order. Brennan had wooed her, captivated her, seduced her—pledged her his love, his loyalty, his protection, his hand in marriage, everything her broken heart had longed for. And when he'd finally gotten her to her knees, revenge had never felt so good.

But his guests walking in on it had made it all the better. He'd rejected her. Viscerally.

You didn't think I meant all that, did you? A stroke of pure genius. How she'd paled! *I'm done with the little tart. She can find her way back to the Tower.*

Public humiliation. As she'd done to him years earlier. It should have felt good, equalizing, but even as he'd laughed at her with his guests, a knot had formed in the pit of his stomach. Her feverish, over-bright eyes pleaded with him, haunted him, even now.

Begged for a different reality.

Lamented.

But if he had defended her then and there, she never would have known the keen suffering she'd inflicted on him nine years ago. She'd never have understood it if he'd taken her in his arms, enshrined her in a bedchamber, comforted her the rest of the night and the rest of his life. Married her. Conceived their heirs.

But after that night, she'd understood.

And was that—

That *was* more important.

He swallowed and shook off the thoughts, then rubbed his bloody knuckles raw and watched them begin to heal. So she'd had her heart shattered. So some nobles had gossiped about her, made her an outcast to society. It was three years ago and trivial compared to his curse.

It was time to move on to his next strategy to bring her to heel. Her new commoner plaything was only a distraction, but she had risked her life to save him. The commoner's survival was something she wanted.

Brennan smiled. He wanted something from her, too. Perhaps the commoner could be useful to him. A bargaining chip.

With a sigh, he returned to the task at hand. The last thing he needed was an assassin robbing him of his betrothed—his redemption. He inhaled the scents, setting aside the stronger, more recent ones in favor of the fading. Besides the Connétablie's men, the knights, the men-at-arms, the Kamerish foreigner, Rielle herself, the commoner, and the scorched man—he breathed in, his left nostril picking up another.

He followed it to the faint scent of a footprint, then another—stronger. And another. And another. In five steps, despite the changing wind, the changing humidity, nearby deer feces and rabbit urine, he tracked the footsteps with his superior nose through the oaks, birches, and ferns in the direction of Melain.

A clear print in the dirt.

Brennan crouched. It was small—a woman's. He followed her path, but the footprints ended. The stench of magic lingered.

Illusion magic.

But the silver birch nearby—it bore the scent of leather.

No—Sileni leather, from a Barda cow. The distinct, brisk smell of trux. And a woman's scent. Danewort root, olive oil...

A recipe for curling hair. He knew that scent, had smelled this woman before.

Grimacing, he invited the Change, let the Wolf out, and began the journey back to Melain.

41

*J*on escorted Rielle downstairs to the duchess's great hall for dinner, passing the watchful eyes of Prevost's household knights and men-at-arms. Good. They were alert, then, as well as they should be after Courdeval.

Although he'd served in Melain before, he hadn't been inside the castle. Lengthy, tight corridors, its wide spaces insulated deep within. As defensible inside as it was outside. His first time in the city, Tor had taken the opportunity to pair his lessons on city defense with a view of the towering machicolated walls and the northern gate. Its heavy, latticed iron portcullis and three-foot-thick Kamerish teak and iron doors had kept out Northerners, bandits, and in ancient days, entire armies.

The Auvrays had held Melain unbroken since the second Farallan king had taken the throne, and Her Grace, Duchess Madeleine Duclos Auvray, held it now. Under her control, the guards kept the city locked up tighter than an arcanir mine.

And the duchess's great-granddaughter walked by his side. The Marquise of Laurentine. His love.

With a deep breath, he straightened, raised his chin.

He checked a button on his cuff. Fastened.

After two weeks recovering in a soft bed, it was past time to properly thank the duchess for her hospitality. It would go well. Perfectly. It had to. A lot hadn't... but this would.

After that golden night by the Vindemia bonfire, when he'd imagined spending two weeks in bed with Rielle, he hadn't envisioned being critically wounded, weak, and hardly able to move. He'd held such strict dominion over his body for so long; although he'd suffered injuries before, this one had been a lesson in humility. Even reluctantly allowing the household's valets to help him bathe and walk to the garderobe—Terra have mercy, he could hardly stand needing assistance for those tasks—had led to flares of neck and back muscle spasms, pain that radiated from his back to his legs, tingling, numbness, tremors, palpitations.

Rielle had spent night and day by his side, tending to him, reading to him, telling him about Olivia, magic, experiences in the faraway lands of Pryndon, Kamerai, and Silen. Her nearness was bittersweet agony, spellbinding, tempting, and deadly all at once. Even soft kisses, warm like the hearth, escalated to blazing, spiking his circulation, kicking his pulse into a frenzy.

Don't you dare die, she'd said to him, her delicate palm pressed against his chest, against the thing that hammered erratically within, too strange to call a heart.

He'd had to drop that pursuit, to retreat, suffer the wait, the experience made all the more excruciating by the delicious temptation of her so close.

But for the past few days, his strength had been returning. He'd begun to walk on his own again, tend himself again without the valets' assistance. It was no longer inability but pain that crippled him.

Pain he could fight.

Progress.

He'd even taken Faithkeeper in hand again and returned to training before the sun—and Rielle—had risen.

She'd kill me if she knew. His beautiful witch had strictly forbidden anything strenuous, but his choices in this weren't hers to forbid. No matter how far she believed her imagined dominion to extend. He fought back a smile and glanced at her.

Her full-skirted brocade gown matched his own cream-colored attire, trimmed in golden-yellow lacing and embroidery. Much to his chagrin, a valet had insisted on helping him dress for tonight's occasion—in better clothes than he'd ever seen, much less worn.

Her hair ornately secured atop her head in cascading curls, Rielle gave him a reassuring smile.

Not an hour ago, she'd pinned him and demanded he drink the medicinal concoction the physician had ordered. He had been feeling much better, and the brew was entirely unnecessary, and... tasted like having his face shoved in the Monas Ver garden.

But his sadistic, beautiful witch had cast a spell, one that had rendered him powerless: *Please... I know you think you don't need it, but I worry about you all the time, and this little draught makes me feel like maybe I can worry less, that you'll be all right.*

He'd gulped it down, the entire herbal torture, without complaint.

"You look confident," she whispered.

Then Tor's lessons in masking his emotions had proved fruitful. He covered her hand on his arm with his palm, caressing her soft skin. "After drinking that terrible brew, little can unsettle me."

But the Duchess of Melain was now arguably the most powerful woman in Emaurria, moving mountains with a flick of her wrist. And he was a forsworn paladin bastard in love with her noble great-granddaughter.

She laughed, and there—he could see it clearly—that tiny spark gleamed in her eye. Sadism? "You needn't worry, Jon. Gran is lovely."

He nodded. Here, in her home, he'd been at the duchess's mercy and had survived. That counted as a good sign. "Will Leigh be joining us at last?"

She winced and looked away. "I told you—Leigh decided to stay in town."

It was hard to imagine Leigh turning down castle food, drink, and accommodations. "Why?"

Taking a deep breath, she looked around the opulent hallway. He'd only seen such opulence matched at Maerleth Tainn, the home of Tor's duke brother.

"Rielle?"

She sighed. "Gran wasn't pleased with the way things ended, with the disciplinary action at Magehold. She may have... insinuated that if he ever showed his face here again, he'd be parted with his... most cherished jewels."

His most... cherished...

He chuckled softly.

But if the duchess had made such threats to Leigh, a powerful wild mage, over the end of his relationship with Rielle, what would she say to a common-born forsworn paladin who dared love her?

He quickly quieted and then cleared his throat.

They proceeded down the palatial hallway and its endless portraits. Noble after noble after noble. Who else could afford to be painted, even once in his life? He exhaled lengthily. The odds of being well received looked grimmer and grimmer and grimmer, and then one of the portraits—

He stood, gaping.

A young woman in a dazzling white gown embroidered with golden peonies, neckline plunging provocatively, her waist accentuated by a full skirt—extravagantly full. With a dense crown of golden hair atop her head, a few curls daring to break free, she regarded him with a gleam of challenge in her bright sky-blue eyes, a coy smile gracing her beautiful oval face. A golden signet ring adorned the fifth finger of her delicate left hand.

He reached out to touch her but stopped himself before his fingertips could make contact with the canvas. Rielle. Regathering his composure, he turned to her. "This is...?"

Blushing, she looked away. "Gran had me sit for one every year since... Since I could be made to sit long enough for the painter to work."

"When was this one?" It could have been yesterday.

"That's the last one I sat for..." She shrugged. "It's from three years ago."

"None since?"

"No." She took a deep breath and exhaled it heavily. "Gran sent the painter every year, but I..." She stiffened, looked at him, and flashed a fleeting, nervous smile.

Just what made her so nervous? She could tell him anything. And why she hadn't sat for a painting in three years couldn't have been such a grave secret.

He eyed the portrait again, at her coy smile and challenging stare. She exuded spirit, fearlessness, boldness, like she played through life with a winning hand. And she did, didn't she? A powerful mage, a rich noble, a woman of character, skill, and beauty. Her world appeared so perfect.

But when he looked away from the portrait to her, she didn't exude spirit, fearlessness, and boldness. They were part of her—and he well knew that part—but those qualities were caged, on occasion flashing bared teeth through the bars, but for most of the time bound. What were those bars made of? Fear? Obligation? Weariness?

What had changed in three years?

"So when this was painted," he began, "you were..."

"At the Tower." She shot a wistful look down the corridor toward the great hall.

Three years ago... "Back then, you were... involved with Leigh?"

Her cheeks reddened. "No, this painting was after. Not long after, however."

The portrait didn't depict the face of a heartbroken woman; the affectedly demure mouth, the provocative eyes, the confidently raised chin—it was the face of a woman in love.

He frowned. If not Leigh, the man she had devoted years to, whom did this young woman in the portrait love?

"This isn't an interrogation, is it, Sir Jon?" She gave his arm a squeeze and winked.

He huffed a laugh. "That depends. Are you hiding anything?"

"Everyone has their demons." She smiled. "Shall we?"

She had yet to share those demons. Someday, when she was ready, he would get their full measure.

But not here, in this hallway, while the Duchess of Melain awaited them both.

"Yes," he answered. "Let's not keep the duchess waiting."

Her features relaxed into a relieved grin. She felt like Rielle again, the one he'd known on the road, rather than the landed and titled noble. They continued down the hallway.

Two footmen—liveried in the household violet and white colors—opened the doors to the great hall.

"The Marquise of Laurentine, Her Ladyship Favrielle Amadour Lothaire, and her companion, Monsieur Jonathan Ver," the herald announced.

Within, the duchess, dressed in an indigo gown, sat at the head of a table flanked by a host of servants. Soft music welcomed them—a harpist off to the side. Innumerable candlelit sconces glowed against the tall latticed windows, revealing the dark star-studded backdrop of night outside the castle walls. Only one of the enormous room's dining tables was set, with but three place settings.

"Welcome." The duchess examined him with a probing gaze as they approached.

"Terra's blessings upon you, Your Grace." He bowed from the waist.

"And upon you, Monsieur Ver."

"I am humbled by your generosity and hospitality, Your Grace." He inclined his head. "I am in your debt."

"It is in my domain that you came to harm. It is the least I could do. Please." With a wave of her hand, she directed them to the two open seats on each side of hers. "I am pleased you're able to join us. I expect the empty hall comes as a surprise, but as it has been some years since I've seen my great-granddaughter, I wished for us to speak freely. Rest assured, Benoist is entertaining my other guests expertly."

"Thank you, Gran." Rielle grinned warmly.

They sat, and the duchess laid her napkin upon her lap as servants emerged with the apéritif, an anise-scented liqueur.

She shared a smile with Rielle, then took a drink. "Forgive me, Monsieur Ver. Normally, we take the apéritif in the salon, but I thought it best we avoid too much movement."

"My thanks, Your Grace," he answered, "but my strength returns quickly." The last thing he wanted was to appear needy and impose on the duchess any more than he already had.

The servants brought in trays of colorful hors d'oeuvres. Rielle selected a gougère. "I haven't left his side for more than a minute. He still needs rest and time to recover."

In truth, when she'd pledged to nurse him back to health, he'd wanted to test the limits of her fussing. The high, high limits. Watching her fret over his every movement, he'd decided a prank was in order.

She raised an eyebrow, then the other, too. "What, was all that just for *fun?*"

With an inward grin, he lowered his chin. Ah, it was her nature to overreact. To brim with ferocity.

"My child," the duchess said, eyes sparkling, "your complaint rings hollow." She offered Jon a charming smile, and he was only too pleased to turn to Rielle with her own great-grandmother's validation.

Rielle's fierce eyes narrowed, gleaming with the promise of sweet revenge later.

And he wanted it, all of it, and to provoke her all the more—to elicit her overreaction, her passion, her amusement, her joy, her pleasure. To meet like flint and steel.

"I'm glad you two still have joy, in the midst of... all this," the duchess said, her voice pleasant despite its somber undertone.

Rielle sobered. "Have you heard any news, Gran?"

The servants brought in the appetizers—smoked fish, pâté, sausages, quiche, and some foods he'd never seen—and the first bottle of wine.

"Yes, my child," the duchess replied, "and none of it good. The Crag Company's control of the Kingsroad is extending ever closer to Melain. Unfortunately for General Gilles, my city is well guarded. His control will extend no farther, lest he risk relaxing his hold on the capital merely to monitor a roadway."

Gilles.

Jon clenched his jaw. How he longed to put that blackguard behind bars, let the Order and the Crown bring him to justice for all his dark deeds. But Gilles's mercenary company was formidable. The dead squad of Crag mercenaries he and Rielle had encountered on the road had been scouts—what awaited them in Courdeval was far worse.

"Monitoring?" Rielle asked. "For what?"

The duchess drew her eyebrows together. "There are whisperings about the Moonlit Rite going unperformed. And the Crag Company, some of its men with black-market arcanir, has made it unsafe for any mage to travel toward the capital. My child, it is good that you are here. Protected."

"There are people who need help. A mage's help. For them, I do not fear combat, Gran."

"You should," the duchess scolded, and Rielle's fingers curled. "Do not fool yourself, child. You have gone on your missions, yes, but this is war. War is ugly. I know you are strong, but it takes little more than a single well-placed bolt to warrant a dirge."

At that, Rielle's fists loosened. Her face went slack.

Beneath the table, he brushed her foot with his and, when she perked up, gave her a reassuring look.

They were both alive. That bolt needn't trouble her any longer.

"If you are taken alive," the duchess continued, "war makes beasts of men. It is no place for a woman, let alone a lady. The best you can hope for is to be kept prisoner and ransomed, if you are lucky."

Rielle's slender wrist disappeared under the table. He'd seen firsthand the victims left behind by an army like the Crag Company—treated them, comforted them, counseled them, buried them. Some had even been sold into slavery, to lands beyond Emaurria's free shores, by greedy mercenaries.

Rielle planned to infiltrate the capital, which teemed with such men. Only her magical ability and competence stayed him from dissuading her.

"Don't trouble yourself, my child. We will retake Courdeval before the first snow. The Order is mobilizing. No doubt the Grand Divinus will send a force. I've reached out to Faolan and the other nobles. Once we hear back from them, Courdeval will be cleared of that rabble without you having to lift a finger."

"Gran," Rielle said quietly, "I know you mean well, but I am no gentle lady." She raised her head and met the duchess's eyes squarely. "And there are those trapped within Courdeval's walls who won't survive until the first snow."

An icy grip seized his heart. Some primal part of him wished to secure her in a sanctuary, somewhere safe from everyone and everything, with all she needed and could ever want.

But the woman he loved could never sit idly while the world burned; Rielle would always see herself as a mage first.

The duchess regarded her great-granddaughter with a resigned sigh.

"Very well, child. Then just promise me you'll be cautious. The instability in the capital is quickly spreading."

"Of course," Rielle answered, perhaps a little too quickly.

As the servants brought in the main course, the duchess shot Jon a meaningful look and glanced toward Rielle and back.

He would keep an eye on her great-granddaughter; that went without saying. He gave her a grave nod.

The main dish was served—a veal tenderloin stuffed with a fragrant mushroom mixture, accompanied by roasted vegetables and potatoes, with a medium-bodied red wine alongside.

"Is there any news from the capital?" Rielle's foot, apparently freed from its shoe, stroked his leg gently, entirely removed from the serious tone of her voice and topic of discussion.

This was it, then. Sweet revenge. Did she want to make him squirm?

En garde, my love.

"No news from Courdeval, I'm afraid." The duchess paused between bites. "There is some talk of the late king's niece once removed laying claim to the throne, but married to a Sonbaharan prince, her claim is weak. Emaurrians would never accept an El-Amin dynasty of kings."

It would be a sunny day in the Lone before Emaurrians would accept a foreigner as king above any man of their own.

"Even if the Crag can be ousted, then, our land would still be in turmoil." Rielle's foot ascended his leg, but she evaded his hand.

A bold advance.

"There are those among the Houses who would support the return of an older dynasty," the duchess said carefully.

Rielle's foot reached his thigh. *Lunge.*

He took it gently in hand. *Parry.*

He brushed a finger across her sole—her foot jerked, her knee bumping the underside of the table with a soft thud. *Riposte.*

He quickly brought his goblet to his lips to keep from laughing at her pointed scowl.

Even the duchess hid a smile.

Rielle cleared her throat. "Not the Duke of Maerleth Tainn?"

The duke? Jon straightened. He'd visited Maerleth Tainn with Tor. "Duke Faolan Auvray Marcel?" Marcel was a master negotiator, businessman, and strategist.

"You know the duke?" The duchess turned to him, and Rielle stiffened.

"I squired for his brother, Your Grace."

"You squired for Torrance?" Warmth colored the duchess's expression.

"Yes, Your Grace."

She smiled. "I knew him when he was just a boy. He was a fine young man, and his success among the paladins is well earned."

Success. The duchess referred, of course, to the likelihood Tor would succeed Paladin Grand Cordon Guérin, who'd hand-picked Tor as his squire decades before. Guérin had been a favorite of King Marcus's father, and Tor was the younger brother of the most powerful man among the Emaurrian Houses. Bloodlines figured even among a non-governmental entity like the Order of Terra.

"If I may ask, Your Grace," Jon said, "is there any news of the paladins?"

The duchess leaned back in her chair. "There is little. Nearly every paladin in the land has been summoned to Monas Amar. Although I do not know their plans with certainty, I can guess. The Order has never been able to look away from injustice, and what has happened in Courdeval—and continues to happen—is injustice given form."

He couldn't agree more.

"It seems, however, that just as it is unsafe for mages to travel toward the capital, so too is it for paladins. Two groups from Monas Tainn were attacked by rogues, one paladin among each killed before the assailants were defeated."

Killed?

The thought became solid, a lump in his throat. Not Valen—he'd just seen him in Bournand. It couldn't be him. Florian, who played the lute and had been transferred last spring? His former squire, Stefan, who'd gone on mission? Not Tor—he'd be in Monas Amar, wouldn't he?

Rielle's foot rested against his under the table, and when he glanced at her, her gaze shone, soft. Solidarity.

Finding his voice at last, Jon asked, "Do you know their names, Your Grace?"

"Forgive me. I confess I do not. They were both young. That's all I know," the duchess answered quietly. "You have my sympathies. I know paladins to be good, honorable men."

Countless names flew through Jon's head as he considered who the victims may have been.

"Heartseekers attempting to cut off reinforcements to Monas Amar?" Rielle cut in.

The Heartseekers were naught but blades, wielded by a swordsman of wealth. The same one who had hired Gilles and his mercenary army. Had

Derric known of this? Was this the reason why he'd requested a mage escort?

Was it that Derric considered him a son? Clearly the other paladins hadn't been afforded extra guard, nor perhaps even warning.

He glanced around the table, at the duchess's signet ring and Rielle's. Was it possible...?

Was it possible he was some noble's bastard, like many other paladins? One of the "Order of Third Sons," as the Order of Terra was sometimes called?

He'd squired for a former noble, been trained in strategy, manners, educated beyond most paladins. Many in the court had lost their lives, and if some nobleman's heir and spare had died, a bastard paladin son could well be the last of his line.

Or maybe Derric just loved him that much. The years they'd spent together, father and son in all but name, spoke convincingly.

The doors to the great hall opened then, footmen staggering after a man walking through, but the duchess waved them off with a sigh. The same man he and Leigh had seen at The Rose Garden. Tregarde, heir to the dukedom of Maerleth Tainn, Duke Faolan Auvray Marcel's eldest son.

"His Lordship," the herald announced hesitantly, "Brennan Karandis Marcel, Marquis of Maerleth Tainn, the Marquis of Tregarde, the Baron of Calterre."

The tall, handsome, well-muscled man with dark hair, bronze skin like his own, and hazel eyes strode through the doorway, garbed in high fashion —a black doublet and black trousers trimmed in gold. On his left hand, a golden signet ring engraved with a fierce wolf's head adorned the fifth finger.

The marquis had an air of distinction, his keen eyes fixed on the table through dense, dark lashes. As he neared, the man revealed his sharp, white teeth in a fleeting, imperious grin.

Jon's shoulders grew tight.

"Good evening, Your Grace," Tregarde said to the duchess, his voice equal parts convivial and masculine.

The duchess's eyes widened—stunned but not unwelcoming. "Brennan," she greeted, "what a pleasant surprise."

Tregarde approached the duchess and took her hand. "I could not countenance missing the pleasure of your company, Your Grace." His eyes dancing, he raised her hand to his lips while she waved off his flirtation.

"You cruelly flatter an old woman," she replied while Tregarde rounded the table. He approached Rielle, who sat stiff as stone, her face drained of all color, as if death itself were taking her hand in his and greeting it with a kiss.

"Favrielle," Tregarde said, his voice smooth and languorous while he flowed around her chair to the next, close. Too close. He took the seat next to her, and at once, servants flitted around him, bearing plates, utensils, food, laying a napkin on his lap—while, blasé about all the commotion around him, Tregarde stared across the table at Jon.

"I don't believe we've met." Tregarde hooded his amused eyes and offered a matching smile, holding out a goblet that a servant quickly filled.

Before Jon could answer, Tregarde cocked his head and narrowed his eyes.

"No, I stand corrected." He sat up. "Tor's loyal shadow, aren't you? Years ago, you bewitched my sister Nora with your pleasing visage, you know. Made her impossible to live with for days. She still asks Uncle Tor what's become of you, commoner though you are."

"Brennan, you will address my guests respectfully."

"My apologies, Your Grace. A slip of the tongue." Tregarde never looked away.

Neither did Jon. Tension coiled in his body, the way it always did when combat was imminent. He allowed the coldness he felt to chill his voice. "And now you know what's become of me."

Smirking, Tregarde looked over at Rielle, whose pallor—impossibly— had increased.

"Yes, it seems I do." Tregarde stared at Rielle dreamily. "I suppose it falls to me to tell Nora a different lure was needed to catch her prize."

Every muscle in Jon's body went rigid. Pain blossomed on his chest and back, but all that mattered sat across from him, unsettled by the man leering at her. Her lips a thin line of distress, Rielle moved not an inch, but as Tregarde's vulgar stare persisted, at last she flinched.

Polite company or not, he wouldn't allow this violation a moment longer. He pushed his chair back, but Rielle's abrupt turn toward Tregarde stayed his rising.

"What do you want?" she demanded, terrified, pleading, enraged—he couldn't discern.

The duchess glared at Tregarde. A clear warning.

With every passing second, Jon's fists clenched tighter beneath the table. Whatever this man had done to cause her such anguish, Jon wanted to bring him to his knees for it.

Tregarde smiled, blinking away the intensity of his gaze. "Nothing more than to look upon my betrothed. Is that so wrong?" He turned to Jon with an arched brow.

Betrothed.

Rielle's eyes widened, her lips parting.

As the word sank in, his chest ached with pressure. Fit to burst. He turned his head to Rielle, willing her to say something, anything to dismiss Tregarde's claim. Her chest heaving, she eyed the table.

His heart raced. Had he abandoned the chance to rejoin the Order for a woman promised to someone else?

It wasn't true. It couldn't be.

Slowly, she raised her face to meet his. She said nothing, but her haunted eyes said it all.

Terra have mercy, it was true.

All this time, she'd pursued him, tempted him, kissed him, loved him, and she'd had a fiancé all the while?

"The shadow bleeds," Tregarde's wry voice cut. Tregarde—the man who had a legitimate claim to the woman Jon loved.

"Brennan," the duchess warned.

He's considered by many one of the cleverest men in Emaurrian society, and one of the cruelest. Leigh's words echoed in Jon's mind. His nails bit into his palms.

Shattered, his fiancée begged him before his guests not to forsake her. But viciously, he refused her—humiliating her to all society.

His heart stopped. Terra have mercy, she was the one?

Rielle was Tregarde's fiancée.

And Tregarde the man who had hurt her.

When Jon turned his attention to him, all he heard was the pounding of his own heart in his ears, all he felt the heat of his own blazing blood, all he saw—

His hands wound into fists so tight his knuckles cracked. His hostile body rose from the chair of its own volition. Kill him. He would kill him.

"Your stitches." A voice. The duchess's. She nodded toward the left side of his chest, where all eyes aimed.

Even he, teeming with rage, glanced down. Sure enough, just above his heart bloomed the stain of blood. As he watched its languid spread, he cooled just enough to regain control of his body, if nothing else.

Keep it together. He had to keep it together. He held on to that control with every last shred of his strength.

"Forgive me, Your Grace." His entire body throbbing, he bent to the duchess. "I must take my leave and see to this at once." Attempting even another minute of control courted disaster.

"Of course," the duchess replied.

Without sparing a glance in Rielle's direction, he headed for the doors. He had to leave, lest his boiling blood overpower his sanity.

"Jon," Rielle called after him hoarsely.

His hands numb with tension, he had already crossed half the great hall and didn't stop.

42

*R*ielle gaped at Brennan, curling her fingers against the violence coursing in her veins.

"Did he not know?" Brennan's casual expression did little to hide the venom in his mocking tone. He raised his eyebrows in feigned innocence before taking a long drink from his goblet.

She wanted to throttle him, but finding Jon and explaining was more important. He'd been livid, even angrier than when he'd hunted down Feliciano. Although his smoldering gaze had fixed on Brennan, she hadn't been exempt from it either.

Hiding her betrothal from Jon... The choice between truth and secrecy had seemed impossible: telling him would have pushed him away, and yet, so had not telling him.

Her hands shook with the need to do something, anything to salvage what they shared. "Gran, I—"

Gran nodded toward the doors. "Go."

Rielle spun to leave, but Brennan caught her arm. "No kiss goodbye?"

She slapped him.

He opened his mouth and popped his jaw. Gran stood.

"Monster," Rielle snarled at him, wrenching her arm from his grip to hurry for the doors.

"Marquis Tregarde!" Gran bellowed. "Stay where you are."

"I only wish to speak to her, Your Grace." The sharpness of his tone belied the politeness of his words.

Rielle hadn't even crossed the threshold when his determined footsteps clicked behind her. She walked faster.

"If you harm even a hair on her head—" Gran threatened.

"Wouldn't dream of it, Your Grace," he hissed.

Perhaps the one woman who could truly jeopardize the Marcels' position economically and politically, Gran was never to be taken lightly. Still, Rielle quickened her pace and didn't look back.

Behind her, the echoes of his pursuit drew ever closer, and although she ran, she couldn't outrun him. *Stupid shoes. Stupid dress. Stupid corset.*

Just as she reached the staircase, Brennan grabbed both her wrists and twisted her arms behind her back. He drove her into the stairwell and pressed her to the wall.

"Let me go," she bit out, her cheek flattened against the stone, "or—" It hadn't occurred to her what yet; he was immune to magic.

"Or what?" he taunted. "You'll use magic? You know you can't hurt me." His breath came hot against her ear, his body hard and flush against her back, his cinnamon-and-cypress scent invading her nostrils.

What was this? Why antagonize Jon? Her? "What do you want?"

"You know what I want," he rasped harshly. "I do your bidding, protect you, and what do you do? Refuse me and parade around your lover." He breathed her in despite the hoarseness in his voice. "I tire of waiting, Rielle. I need to know I'll be free of this curse. Accept my offer."

He'd never stop hurting her.

"Never."

"Damn you!" he growled back at her, pushing her into the wall with renewed force. Scraping pain bloomed in her cheek, a blunt ache in her ribcage. He held his cheek to her head, his lips almost touching her ear. "Any other man would just take what he wanted."

And whatever the cost, she would see him dead if he tried. Still, the thought did little to calm the terror creeping over her skin, seizing her paralyzed muscles already at his mercy.

"Have at it, then, if you're so sure of yourself—reveal what kind of man you are," she spat. Insult, her final maneuver before she'd bring the stairwell down around them. "A jilted, spoiled libertine who can't come to terms with rejection."

He exhaled sharply into her ear.

"An artless boor who, to get the woman he needs, must *force* apart her thighs." Even as she uttered the bold words, she trembled against him.

At any moment, he could overpower her, and she knew it. Perhaps she'd always known it.

"I—" He hesitated.

His painful grip on her wrists loosened as he backed away. She whirled to face him.

Wide eyed, he looked upon her. Did the remnants of her fear show in her face?

She narrowed her eyes. Good. If he could see her fear, he knew she took him seriously. Serious as death.

He sobered, the tautness of his bearing slowly fading.

"Rielle," he began, "I don't pretend to be a gentle man, but you know I would never—I've never—"

"Damn you." No explaining this. No smoothing this over. If their war of barbs had changed from words to weapons, then it was time to shed the shadows and face each other openly.

He snapped his mouth shut, and a muscle worked in his jaw.

Enough. She headed for the stairs, but he blocked her path with his arm, his palm flat and firm against the wall at her side.

"Wait."

She flinched, then hardened from foot to head. "Let me pass." One sudden move, and she'd level this place around her and scream for Gran's guards. Let him fight them all. Let him *try*.

"I just—" He sighed. "I don't want to be a monster, beholden to you or anyone else. Can't you understand that?"

Her blood burned beneath her skin, scorched by the memory of weeping in a kitchen, the stone floor rough beneath her as he laughed with his guests. It wasn't the Wolf that made him a monster.

"You've forced me to this, Rielle. You keep from me the one thing I need. I've tried everything. I tried befriending you, courting you, pursuing you, ignoring you, hating you—" He paused, directing an anguished stare at the floor. "Like it or not, you are my only chance at redemption."

Her jaw tightened, cracking her clenched teeth. "You squandered that chance three years ago."

"Tell me what I must do. I'll do anything, give anything. Just grant me this one boon. You needn't even marry me if you find me so repugnant. Just. Break. This. Curse."

She closed her eyes. He wanted his suffering to end—that was understandable—but she owed him nothing; she wouldn't force herself to endure the humiliation of his bed in order to redeem him.

And even if she did, she wouldn't leave any child of hers in the care of such a cruel man.

She opened her eyes. "There is nothing you could ever do, *ever,* that would convince me to lie with you."

His fist struck the wall. She raised her hands, rooting her magic in the stairwell's stone.

"You dare to judge me?" he snarled, fixing her with a maddened glare. "Mark my words, Rielle, one day you will *beg* to share my bed."

"Never."

He opened his mouth, but she didn't give him the chance to speak; instead, she ducked under his arm and rushed up the stairs.

"Your parents weep in the Lone at how you sully their good name with that commoner."

The words stopped her in her tracks. How dare he drag her parents into this?

Her eyes stung, but she refused to blink.

All he understood was power and powerlessness, the hunt and the kill, pleasure and pain; he did not understand what it meant to love someone with all his heart, to put someone else before himself. And she wouldn't waste her breath explaining it to him.

"I'll see you soon," he called out to her.

He was inescapable; she needed no reminder. With a shake of her head, she dispelled her geomancy and continued up the steps.

"Marquis Tregarde." Gran's grave-cold voice. She stood in the stairwell's entryway, flanked by guards, and nodded to Rielle.

Air hissed out of Brennan.

Good. Then he wouldn't follow.

She hurried up to the Red Room.

43

*I*n the Red Room, by the light of a candelabrum, Jon pulled off the ruined doublet and threw it on the bed. Beneath it, the immaculate white of his shirt was also stained red. Wincing through the pain, he picked up some spare gauze on the nightstand and tucked it into his shirt, pressing it against his reopened wound while he gathered all of his things.

All of his things.

With a bitter laugh, he glanced at the lot of them: Faithkeeper, the sword of an oath breaker; a set of desecrated arcanir armor; and a coin purse half-full of argents and cuivres. It was as much as he deserved for being such an idiot.

And for all his desire to place some distance between himself and the man he ached to kill, he couldn't even find his own clothes. Simple and rough spun, they had disappeared, probably taken away and discarded to be replaced with frippery.

Replaced with something superior in every way.

The barest of necessities—he would take the barest of necessities from the wardrobe. When he opened it, a length of white silk caressed his skin. Rielle's nightgown.

He pinched the bridge of his nose.

The man who will ultimately stand at her side will be forged in fire. If you burn easily, don't even bother. Terra have mercy, Leigh had known it all and warned him.

Jon exhaled lengthily. He'd loved her even then. Blinded by it, he'd been a fool.

A noblewoman like her would be betrothed. She'd kept it from him and that stung, but he'd been stupid not to think of it.

And while paramours weren't uncommon, it just wasn't in him to accept her someday sharing that man's bed. No, the very contemplation of it imbued his shoulders with tension so keen it ached.

But he loved her. Fire or not, there was no turning back... And yet, in his position, he had nothing to offer.

He had to get to Monas Amar and see what awaited him, the reason for his honorable discharge. There, he would set everything right and focus on Gilles and knighthood. At least then, he'd be more than nothing. Never Rielle's equal, like Tregarde, but more than he was now. More that he could offer her.

As he buckled his sword belt, the door creaked open behind him, and quiet footsteps stopped just past the doorway.

He didn't turn to face her. He wouldn't. Not now.

"Jon," she said. Soft. Apologetic.

He didn't reply, selecting some of the simpler clothes from among the luxurious collection.

"I was going to tell you."

With a heavy sigh, he paused and anchored a hand on his hip, crushing a shirt in the other. He was angry with Tregarde, but the woman he loved had lied to him, deceived him. Deliberately. "How stupid you must find me."

"Don't say that." She took a quiet step nearer.

He stuffed some clothes into the knapsack. "I threw away all I ever knew to be with you, Rielle. You could have mentioned you were betrothed."

"I was waiting for the right time to tell you."

"The right time? You've had weeks."

"Was I to open with it, then? 'Nice to meet you, I'm betrothed'?" Her tremulous voice rose in volume. "There was no reason to tell you at first, and later, it's not as though we had a discussion before we kissed. Bringing up potential impediments to marriage so soon is more than a little presumptuous, isn't it?"

He took a deep, calming breath; she was being facetious, and all the more frustrating. "Spare me. A betrothal to another man is important enough to merit a single conversation."

She hesitated. "I'm sorry." Her voice broke, the words sounding heart-felt, if abrupt. "I love you."

Terra have mercy, how good it felt to hear those audacious words, even now. He finished packing and fastened the knapsack.

He had no right as a forsworn paladin and commoner to request that she reject Tregarde—none at all—and yet it lingered on the tip of his tongue. He needed to get to Monas Amar as soon as possible. Perhaps then, he could resolve everything, one way or the other.

His head hurt.

"You're not leaving, are you?"

He had to, lest he meet Tregarde again, murder him, and end up in the hangman's noose.

"Neither the House Physician nor Gran will let you leave until you're healed. It would be irresponsible. You have a few days until the arcanir poison leaves your system. And then, I will still—whether you like it or not—escort you to Monas Amar. It is my mission, after all, but you'll only have to... to... endure my presence a few days more."

He would gladly endure it for the rest of his life.

A shuffling came from behind him. He turned to see her gathering her belongings in the shadows. "What are you doing?"

She threw her hairbrush into a bag. "You stay here in the Red Room." She continued to pack. "All your medicine, your things are here. I'll go."

As she bent to retrieve her toiletry bag, the candlelight illuminated her face—her scratched, bleeding face.

A trick of the light. A mistake. It had to be.

He grabbed the candelabrum and approached, holding it up to get a better look.

No.

The front of her gown was snagged and dirty. Her hair disheveled. Her chest and face scratched, like she'd taken a nasty spill onto a stone floor. And her wrists... Hand-shaped red marks ringed them.

His chest grew so tight he could barely breathe.

She turned her marred, tear-streaked face to him, but upon meeting his gaze, peered down at herself.

Paling, she raised her hand to her scratched cheek.

He already wanted to kill Tregarde, but—"Did he do this?"

"Well—yes, but it's—"

He slammed the candelabrum onto the vanity table, checked for Faith-keeper at his side, and then stormed out of the room.

His hands quaking with pressure, he forced them into fists. He would have no relief until Brennan Karandis Marcel answered for pain with pain.

A chambermaid passed in the hallway.

He grabbed her arm, and she yelped. "Marquis Tregarde. Where is he?" She cowered.

He gave her a shake, and she gasped.

"The Black Room, directly downstairs... on the Sonbaharan garden."

With a curt nod, he let her go and made for the stairs, Rielle's echoing steps chasing after him.

"Jon, don't do this!" She seized his arm and yanked; he dragged her futile weight behind him. "Nothing happened!"

Nothing? She called *that* nothing? Why did she defend that monster? What about his cruelty years ago?

No matter. Nothing would stay his hand now.

At the stairs, she released him but bounded down after him.

He reached the ground floor and stalked down the hall, fixated on the door to the room below his own. The Black Room.

"Listen to me, please!" she called behind him. "He's dangerous! *He'll kill you!*"

The door opened to Tregarde's surprised face. Jon smashed his first and second knuckles into his nose. Cartilage crunched.

A large man, Tregarde staggered to the floor, dazed. He brought his hands to his bleeding nose. In the glow of the sconces, his stunned gaze finally found Jon. His countenance darkened, contorted.

"Rielle, get him out of here," Tregarde snarled, his voice low and rumbling as he rose. She rushed through the doorway and threw herself between them.

"Stop! Please, just—" she cried out to Jon.

He nudged her aside as he approached Tregarde. "You dare raise a hand to her? Rise. You will answer for that now." He headed to the garden doors and kicked them open, shattering a glass panel. "Outside. Now."

He stepped out into the garden, and Tregarde followed, Rielle scrambling behind them.

Tregarde's eyes turned a glassy amber in the darkness, the bones of his face appearing to shift beneath his flesh—

Not possible.

Rielle slammed her palms on Tregarde's bare chest. "Control yourself!"

Tregarde's hands still covered his nose and most of his face, but—

No, it couldn't be—his fingernails elongated to claws.

"No," Tregarde said from beneath his hands, pure menace in his voice as he eyed Rielle contemptuously. *"Let us see your lover's answer."* His voice, an eerie harmony—

She pounded on Tregarde's chest. "Damn you! Stop this right now!"

The muscles of Tregarde's arms and shoulders bulged, twisted, rearranged. Tregarde moved his arms to his sides, revealing his face— monstrous and disfigured, long and sharp teeth protruding from his mouth.

Magic? Dark arts of some kind?

Black fur burst from his skin to cover his enlarged body.

What? Jon reached for Faithkeeper. He surveyed the garden—dark but spacious. Enough room to maneuver.

"Rielle." He needed to get her away—now.

Tregarde's arm swiped, and fabric tore; she rose, clutching the front of her dress, and rushed to Jon. He swept her behind him.

She grabbed his left arm. "Jon, you have to get out of here. Please."

"Go." He took a step back, pushing her toward the open doors.

Hunched, Tregarde rumbled an animal snarl, his muscles aligned to aggression.

Instinct took over. Left foot leading, Jon drew Faithkeeper.

Sparks shot from Tregarde's claw strike as Jon parried. He pulled back and raised Faithkeeper, tip pointed at Tregarde's throat.

The beast's throat.

With the length of the blade between them, the claws and teeth the beast relied on for close-range attack would be useless unless the gap was bridged. The beast's movement arced and angled. But Jon followed with perfect footwork and distance.

There was no telling whether he faced a man or a beast. But whatever the Marquis of Tregarde was now, he was prepared to fight him to the death.

44

rozen, Rielle stood several paces behind Jon, giving him the space he needed to maneuver in the garden. Divine, this was all wrong. Although over the years Brennan had become increasingly malicious, she'd never expected anything like *this*. And Jon, afflicted with arcanir poisoning, risked death if he was gravely injured here.

She needed to do something, a spell—

And yet, tipping the balance now had risks. Unforeseeable risks. Changing the field of battle could end up hurting Jon. But she had to stop them somehow... without getting him killed.

She bit down on the inside of her cheek.

Right shoulder forward, Jon faced Brennan in profile. At the point of his sword, Brennan menaced in man-beast form in the dark, circling, Jon matching step for step. The sheen of moonlight fled along the blade.

Brennan moved to the right—No, lunged.

A slash—evaded—and Brennan closed swiftly, his jaws wide. The sword was between them again as Jon stepped back and off line, covering, the five-foot span dividing them.

The men traded strikes, Jon working to stay covered, sword ready, avoiding the close range of those jaws, those fangs.

Brennan means to bite him.

A werewolf's bite transmitted a fatal sickness that claimed its victims, if the violence of facing a werewolf didn't. However, when coupled with the blood of the Wolf, the bite could transmit the sangremancy curse, leaving the bitten victim to the same terrible fate. Or the victim could take fever and die.

Great Divine, Brennan must have believed her, that she'd never give him what he wanted. When he'd believed he could win her over, he'd been more reasonable.

But now, he would force her hand by afflicting Jon. If Brennan succeeded in transmitting the curse to him, the only cure would be a breaking of the blood bond between her and Brennan.

Leverage.

But if he bit him and failed to afflict him, Jon would be dead.

Her fingers quaked with the need to be useful, but what use was she here but to potentially worsen the risks?

Brennan lunged for Jon's head—

A parry with the middle of the blade, his claws beaten wide to Jon's left as he passed to the right. Jon cut him from jaw to knee, blood, a thrust to the chest—

Bleeding, Brennan receded, dark eyes narrowing, and dropped to all fours, met with a low guard. When he lunged again, Jon struck—the sword caught mid-strike.

He broke away—but not fast enough. Brennan raked his claws across Jon's chest, deep enough to bleed.

Her breath caught in her throat, every inch of tension in her body drawn together to a fine point.

Jon pulled back, the blade spattering blood.

Divine, she needed something, *anything*—flowers, curtains, goblet... On the flagstones, there, lay glass. The remnants of a shattered panel from the door.

She scrambled for the largest shard, tore a strip of fabric from the skirt of her dress, and wrapped one end to hold. What to do, what to do? She followed their every move, every strike, every evasion. Everything she knew about blood bonds was useless here. Blood bonds, blood bonds, blood bonds—

Blood.

Brennan needed her blood. Brennan needed *her.*

Leverage.

A feint and an upward thrust of the sword, between Brennan's ribs. A killing blow—

For any mortal man.

Brennan's eyes widened, met Jon's, but his claws clasped Jon's sword hand. By the Divine—

Jon twisted the blade. Jaws snapped shut where his shoulder should have been.

"Brennan!" She clenched her teeth and plunged the glass shard into her belly.

A cry tore from her lips. Ripping, jagged agony doubled her over.

Jon yanked his sword free. Blood spurted from Brennan's ribs and hands. Jon ran to her side, dropped the sword to the flagstones.

As her balance failed, he caught her, carefully bringing her head against his bleeding chest.

Brennan crumpled, a violent roar tearing from beastly lungs. He turned his wolf-head to her, his amber eyes wide, wild.

The front of her dress was wet, stained. Blood seeped from her wound. *Divine...*

She held his gaze. *Keep redemption alive or lose it right now.*

It had come to this—to protect what she loved, forcing Brennan to choose. She had a short window of time to heal in which she needed him to agree to her terms.

As she gripped the shard, Jon's hand hovered just above hers.

"Rielle—what have you done?" he asked, his voice raw.

Pain twisted in her gut, sharp, burning.

Behind Jon, Brennan knelt, fell to his hands, writhing. He curled his hulking shoulders inward, his face frozen, wide eyed, gaping. "Heal yourself. Now."

Even as she trembled, she shook her head. *"Divine take me,"* she said through gritted teeth.

Brennan scoffed. "You don't have it in you to—"

With an anguished cry, she shoved the shard in deeper. It hurt, it hurt, it hurt—

His mouth fell open.

"*Rielle.*" Jon shuddered, his face drained of color, brows drawn tight. "Stop this. Stop..." He rocked her on his knees.

Too many people had already died on her account. Papa, Mama, Liam, Dorian, Viviane, Dominique, the Laurentine household. Sir Bastien.

Not. One. More.

She wouldn't lose anyone else. Ever again. Not if she could help it.

Still, as the weakness spread, she began to question the merit of this particular course. But she'd gone too far to turn back without a vow.

Beastliness melting away to humanity, Brennan crawled toward her, covered in cuts, bleeding, his gaze roving over her bloodied dress.

A chill settled over the garden, or over her.

Jon grabbed his sword but didn't let her go. "Touch her, monster, and Terra help me, I will see you dead."

Eerily still, Brennan stared at the blade. A night wind bent all in the garden to its will but for his immovable amber stare. "If she dies, then just do it, commoner, or a mob will beat you to it. Without her control, how long before the locals come bearing torches and pitchforks to kill the monster?"

That stare turned to her. Glassy, ghostly. Faded to hazel. Softened. "You would die just to spite me?"

So tired. She was so tired.

Brennan fixated on the wound with feverish eyes. "Tell me what you want."

White shapes floated across her vision, twirling, transforming, dancing. Beautiful. Surreal. Jon's face brightened until she almost couldn't see the hollow darkness in his eyes.

"Promise you'll never hurt the people I love," she said to Brennan, "or me... or anyone, in order to influence me."

A cold frown. "I promise," Brennan hissed.

"Release me from the marriage contract."

A rustle. He moved closer. "I can't. You and I are only terms in an agreement between our parents," he said, swallowing, "but, for my part, I will never force you."

Her grip weakened. She yanked out the glass with an anguished cry and tossed it. Cold. She shivered—or thought she did.

"Rielle—" Brennan began.

Jon forced her face to meet his scowling, over-bright eyes. "Enough of this."

Cruel. She was so cruel. Forcing Jon to watch her do this. Depriving Brennan of his redemption. But no reasonable option had presented itself.

She inched her hand toward her wound, dipping her fingertips in blood. It should have felt warm, but it didn't. Life seeped from her body. She had gone too far to...

"I won't lie to promise something that I can't deliver." Lips pressed in a paling line, Brennan watched her.

No, he could not, in honesty, promise her what was beyond his control. And she couldn't die for it.

She wouldn't.

Although... she had the agreement she needed: his word that he wouldn't hurt Jon or anyone she loved.

"Sundered flesh... and shattered... bone, / By Your Divine Might... let it be sewn."

Pain choked out of her in the healing, cry after cry, more excruciating than the glass had been; her teeth screeched against one another, so hard her head hurt, but she persevered until it was done. Jon held her hand, even as she clenched it tight.

She sucked in a breath. Light. So light she could almost float. She moved her fingers and toes, testing her ability.

Gasping, Jon pulled her close, held her. "You will be the death of me," he whispered in her ear. He kissed her head.

Reaching to touch his face, she found a wet streak.

Booted footsteps thudded near—knights, men-at-arms, servants. Soon, a halo of people gathered, voices bleeding into a cloud. Jon helped her to her feet, but light-headed, she clung to him.

Brennan had disappeared.

"An accident," she assured everyone. "I was injured, but I've healed my wound."

"Your Ladyship—" a Prevost knight began, his brow furrowed.

"I thank you for your concern, but I am well. Monsieur Ver will see me to my quarters." She nodded at Jon, pleading with her eyes that he agree.

His face hard, he stared out into the night. He glanced in her direction, then turned to the knights with a thin smile. "It is as Her Ladyship says. I will see her safely to her quarters."

The knight vacillated, then barked orders, dispersing the group. Jon met her eyes and glanced in the direction of his sword.

Damn. His bloodied sword. Lest everyone assume he tried to murder her, she had to help him retrieve it somehow before they noticed.

Behind her back, she gestured a wind spell to blow out the Black Room's candles. A commotion spread through the dwindling number of Prevost staff.

Without missing a beat, Jon bent to retrieve his sword, shook it off, a whisper of metal against cloth, and then he sheathed it. Cold and quick, no doubt something he'd done countless times.

"Allow me," she declared. With an elaborate gesture, she lit the Black Room sconces.

The few remaining knights, servants, and men-at-arms gaped, but before they could speak, Jon scooped her up.

She struggled to keep her torn bodice closed as he carried her from the garden into the Black Room and to the hallway, square shouldered and stiff. His jaw hard set, he faced forward and wouldn't meet her gaze.

"Jon?"

He peered down at her coldly for a moment, then looked away again. "Do you have any idea what you just forced me to endure?" His voice rumbled, raked raw. A shudder shook through him, solitary and unsettling. "Making me watch you almost..."

Her breath quickened, pulling the risk of tears along. No. Not now. She wouldn't cry. She wouldn't. The oath, calming and safe, came to her. *I, Favrielle Amadour Lothaire, pledge myself, from now for eternity, to the holy Divinity of Magic...*

One calm breath, then another.

She'd done something horrible.

But she'd stopped Brennan... and exacted a promise that he wouldn't hurt anyone she loved. If it had cost her—if it had cost her Jon's love, she wouldn't pay it happily or easily, but to save his life, she would pay it. "I thought if I could just—"

Jon drew in a sharp breath but didn't look at her, his cold, narrowed eyes staring down the path before him. His chest expanded, tense, under strain.

"I'm sorry."

He shook his head. "I watched you nearly die. I dueled a monster to whom you're betrothed. He's abused you both emotionally and physically. And has gotten away with it." He exhaled roughly.

The tightness in his face, his clenched jaw, his corded neck—every part of him aligned to violent intention.

Any attempt on Brennan would only end in tragedy. And he didn't know Brennan the way she did. He knew a few terrible things, but not their context or history. As contemptible as Brennan could be, contempt was not his sum.

Yet the prospect of defending Brennan to Jon in any way knotted her stomach.

As Jon ascended the stairs, he rearranged her in his arms. Not all too gently.

"Jon," she began, "I know you feel that way now, but isn't it a bit extreme—"

When he glared down at her, wild eyed, she shivered.

"You're defending him?" he snarled, nostrils flaring. "Him?" His hold on her tightened to discomfort.

A tremor rattled her bones.

His eyes widening, he relaxed and swallowed. "I'm sorry."

"No matter what he's done, he's still the heir to Maerleth Tainn. Killing him would cost you your life."

"I know."

When he cooled, she allowed herself to rest her cheek against his chest.

At the wetness of his blood, she gently pulled aside his shirt to inspect his wounds. Indeed, he had pulled some of his stitches, but he wasn't bleeding profusely. She would need to treat the claw wounds, too. "How you fought like this, I don't know."

"Slower," he replied, "but if I let pain stop me, I wouldn't be much of a paladin. Or alive."

Still, he would need care. "I have my travel treatment kit in our room. Let me take care of you."

Jon hesitated, then nodded.

There was no doubt she'd hurt him with her stunt. And as upset as he was about her keeping the betrothal from him, the revelation of Brennan's werewolf nature had revealed even more duplicity. Where did they stand?

She'd tell him everything, come what may. At least then, if he turned away from her, she will have tried all she could to convince him of her trustworthiness. "About Brennan—"

"He was the one who killed the scouts."

So he was putting things together. "Yes."

"And you met him in the forest that night you asked me about forgiveness."

"Yes."

He lowered his contemplative gaze, opened his mouth to speak, then closed it again. Eyes shadowed, he looked anywhere but at her face. "And how many times, exactly, did you lie to me to keep his secret?"

She froze, holding her breath as he carried her. She had no love for Brennan, but as the only werewolf she knew of, hiding his true nature just so he could stay alive, she hadn't been able to bring herself to tell anyone his secret. Not Leigh. Not Olivia. Not even Jon.

Time and again, she'd made the conscious choice to lie, to omit, and it wasn't right, wasn't fair, but revealing Brennan's secret and possibly putting his life at stake wasn't right either. No matter her decision, telling or lying, it would've always been the wrong one. "I did my best not to lie to you, Jon. Not directly, anyway."

He exhaled a sharp breath. "Let's not pretend keeping it from me wasn't lying."

"It was. I know it was." She dropped her voice to a crestfallen croak. "I wish I could say I was sorry, that given the opportunity to make that choice again, I'd choose differently. But that wouldn't be genuine of me. Lying to you wasn't fair, but revealing someone else's mortal secret"—she winced as Jon clenched his teeth—"even *his,* wouldn't have been fair either. I wish I would've never been in that position, forced to do one wrong thing or the other, making a choice that disrespected you, but I can't change that."

He still wouldn't meet her eyes.

"But I'm in that position no longer." At least one good thing had come of this entire mess—the truth was out. "You can ask me anything. I promise I'll answer truthfully. Anything you ask." No more lies.

He hesitated but finally glanced at her. "How are you two bound?"

"An ancestor of mine cursed his bloodline—every firstborn son of a firstborn son to become a werewolf." She paused when he tensed, but he didn't interrupt. "When I was a child, I accidentally formed a blood bond with him. I provide him with control over his beastly nature, and he provides me with service... when it suits him. We are drawn to each other monthly before the full moon."

Jon raised an eyebrow. "To do what?"

"I... give him my blood." When his eyes narrowed, she added, "Just a drop. Really."

"He's a monster," he hissed.

Brennan was a werewolf, but calling him a monster painted him with too broad a brush. Much more had spanned the long years of her betrothal to him than she could relate. Despite his brashness and temper, he'd helped her when it suited him.

She took a deep breath. "The only way to break the curse is for our bloodlines to become one."

"To have a child," he said, his voice barely audible.

"Yes," she confessed, "but I have no intention of doing that." Grapes would ripen on the willows before it came to that.

Cold eyes paralyzed her. "Then your choice is either to conceive a child and never be free of him... or not to, and never be free of him."

Her chin dropped to her chest. Jon was right. She would never be free of Brennan.

45

*I*n the Red Room, Rielle spelled the candle in the nearest sconce alight, and Jon set her down. Clutching her torn bodice, she pulled a chair out for him from her vanity table. No more bleeding allowed —these wounds of his needed treatment. "Sit."

He unclipped his sword belt, placed it on the vanity, and dropped into the chair, his face frozen in an empty stare as he spun his silver Sodalis ring. She gave him a towel and bade him hold it to his reopened wound.

She headed to the armoire and, in the dimness, shed the bloody, ripped remains of her dress. Blood coated her skin from her belly down—she washed hastily and threw on her white silk robe.

Jon was quiet. Too quiet. What was he thinking now, his face so expressionless? That he was angry with her? Disappointed? Or perhaps he was beyond caring anymore.

If she asked him, he might tell her to leave him alone altogether. She pressed her lips together and, with a pull of the robe's sash at her waist, hurried back.

"Sorry," she whispered for the delay, but he shook his head and perhaps —if her eyes didn't deceive her—smiled a little. She retrieved her treatment kit, poured a cup of brandy, then laid out the tools and tinctures she needed. She moved aside the towel he still held, and grabbed his shirt to pull it over his head.

So much red. A quick candlelight spell illuminated the blood caking his wounds. Although it looked serious, as she began to clean it away, his injuries weren't so severe.

Plunging the wet cloth into water, she nodded toward the cup of brandy. "It'll help with the pain when I redo the stitches."

He glanced at it and then at his sword. "I'll be fine."

Why wouldn't he choose to dull the pain? But the words died in her mouth. After so much fighting tonight, she couldn't handle any more. She only hoped her ministrations wouldn't hurt so much.

The coppery smell of his blood thick in the air, she went back to cleaning his wounds, then treated the claw marks and re-stitched the surgery incisions. A slight tensing of his body revealed pain. A clenched jaw that only betrayed the slightest twitch. Hard eyes. And not a word.

So distant. So closed. She couldn't stand it.

The length of his reticence stretched on until she reached the next stitch and blurted out, "Do you still love me?" Divine, *stupid*, so *stupid*, but—

His chin jerked, and his gaze shot to hers. "Of course I still love you." That same fiery anger rolled in his voice, but then he glared down at his empty hands and exhaled lengthily. "You didn't trust me. You could have told me at any time that you were engaged to a vile man who turns into a monster, and I would have fallen in love with you anyway." He pinned her with a long, pained look, then broke eye contact. "But you chose to manipulate me."

She continued stitching, but her eyes watered. She should've told him sooner. At least he knew now.

"I was wrong. I should've told you about the betrothal." She finished the stitching.

"The worst of it is that I can't do anything to free you from him." He clenched his empty hands into fists. "That monster has humiliated you, disgraced you, abused you—and he's gotten away with it. He's lost nothing and learned nothing, while you are bound to him, betrothed to him. Stuck with him."

Through blurred vision, she stared at her feet.

He reached out to rest a hand on her waist, imparting the warmth of his reassurance through the robe's thin silk. "It's destroying me," he said, raw. "Hangman or not, I want to kill him." His fisted knuckles cracked.

"And I love you for it, but you can't." Heart swelling, she leaned over and applied a tincture to the re-stitched injury to prevent infection. The strong scent of myrrh and cloves became overpowering.

Brennan had been born into privilege, the kind not afforded the man she loved; if Jon pursued this, he wouldn't be insulated from justice like a noble would. Like a Marcel would. She could handle Brennan's moods, but not losing Jon.

"You need to let this go." Finished, she cleaned her hands and inspected her work, then offered him a small smile, hoping to assuage his quiet intensity. "Especially after I've worked so hard to keep you alive." She was about to walk away when his strong, firm hands settled on her hips.

"Rielle," he said, his voice smooth and deep, "I am past letting go." His hold lowered. "Far past."

They weren't talking about Brennan anymore.

Silence beat between them.

"Then don't." Swallowing, she covered his hand with hers, her heartbeat quickening.

He reached for her silken sash, grabbed it, and pulled. The knot slowly came undone. When her robe parted, his gaze traveled the length of her body, and his palms found her skin. Leaning forward in the chair, he encircled her waist, closing his hold until he drew near enough to lavish her bare skin with kisses.

She embraced him, raking her fingers through his hair. She closed her eyes, relishing the feel of his hands, his lips on her skin, the rising heat in her own body, the tension coiling in him beneath her touch. He held her tighter, rising—

Not with those injuries. She pulled away, took his hand, and led him to the bed.

She broke away and slipped the robe off her shoulders and to the rug while he pulled off his boots, trousers, and braies, his gaze consuming.

His bare form could have been sculpted by the Divine's own hand. Perfect. Ready. Wrapped in his order's exotic tattoos from neck to foot. Divine, he was art. She longed to memorize every line, scroll, and symbol, to learn each one with her eyes, her hands, her mouth.

She closed and urged him onto the bed; his gaze never leaving hers, he stood firm a moment too long, only the slight narrowing of his eyes and twitch of his lips betraying his curiosity before he acquiesced and then leaned his back against the pillows and the headboard. She wouldn't have him pull those newly sewn stitches, even at the height of desire.

No, she had *much* different plans for him.

She sat at his side, facing him, his wide eyes. Burying his fingers in her hair, he drew her in and kissed her, but she traveled downward, kissing his neck, his chest, worshipping her way down his hard body slowly, methodically, eliciting a growl. Audible anticipation. Smiling, she dropped another kiss on his abdomen. When she at last reached his lap, she took him in her mouth—and was rewarded with a drawn-out moan as his head hit the headboard.

He hissed an oath—words that only emboldened her.

The nervous tension that had coiled in his body ebbed away as she pleasured him, replaced by something else. Mounting urgency. His hands smoothed over her back, caressing, kneading their way up to her neck to tangle in her hair. His touch was a loving gentleness, familiar as if he'd always been part of her, and she of him, always intended, to be close, to be one, his whispered breaths reaching beyond sound to stroke something deeper, something that reveled and craved. He tensed and urged her upward, and she did as he wished, let him pull her in to kiss her between panted exhales.

He rested his forehead against hers, smoothed her hair, and blew out a raw breath. "That was—"

A shiver shook through him. He kissed her again, brief but anxious, hungry, with lips that had been abandoned too long and craved union. He gently raised her chin, and she looked at him, her lover, how he brimmed with passion and a beating intensity, a tender depth.

He stroked her cheek. "I wanted to see your eyes. I want to see your eyes."

Her face heated beneath his gaze, and smiling, she leaned in to kiss him once more. She brought her knees down around his hips, and he seized her, drawing her close, capturing her mouth with his. His breaths quickened, deepened until she had him in hand between her thighs; he shuddered an exhalation, and with the sound, her need built up to a level not unlike pain.

When she began to descend onto him—slowly, carefully—his entire body went taut beneath her until at last, she was gloriously filled.

He swore, holding her close.

Stunned at the incredible sensation of fullness, she rocked her hips against his, each rough movement sheer bliss, yet intolerable, bittersweet torment. His mouth trailed from her lips to her neck, awakening her sensitive spots, kissing, nipping, sucking. Unbearable anticipation. His hold on her hips was so firm it hurt, but she didn't care, moving with his urging, savoring every motion.

He drew against the skin at the curve of her neck and broke away to exhale a cool breath, making her shiver. He grazed her shoulder with his teeth, and she writhed in pleasure, riding him hard. Rough. Merciless. She wanted him to never stop touching her, kissing her, making her whole. But her peak was so near, irresistibly near.

His strong hands braced her, aiding her movements, and she broke away from his mouth only to focus on the mounting urgency at the heart of their colliding hips.

Release—her body begged for release, the tension of her core heightening and heightening.

She gasped—almost within reach, she could feel it, she could almost touch it, in desperate need of relief, moaning with every thrust, again and again, and then, it was there, right there, within reach, and she took it, a high note of ecstasy escaping her lips as she peaked.

Everything went white, intense pressure in her skull ripping out of her throat in screams, powerful, unstoppable, impossible to contain, all to the throbbing primal beat in her blood, and she tightened her arms around him, riding out her climax. Her body contracted in waves that whispered a tide of pleasure to every corner of her being, flowing and flowing until her blood hummed. Squeezing her eyes shut, she threw her head back, secure in his hold, and let her body arch as it pleased, limbering as she kept moving against him. Divine, it felt good, so good, the pleasure of him.

In a dreamlike blur, she caught his intense eyes fixed upon hers. The rhythm of his breathing changed—he was close. She sucked in a breath, and summoning renewed vigor, she took him.

Each breath louder, stronger, deeper, he slowed his movement, his firm hold on her hips matching her pace to his own, until finally he found his own release, forcing out breath after breath with each thrust, his body rippling. Wringing out the last of his pleasure, she watched his awestruck face in gaping fascination until he was utterly spent, the sight caressing something wild deep within.

That look—that spent, lazy, blissful look—she wanted to see it again. And again. And again. To elicit it over and over. And over. And over.

His eyebrows drawn, he could have been contemplating the great mysteries of their time so intensely, or the sublime marvel of two halves finding completion.

The tension that had hardened his entire gleaming body took its leave, relaxation left in its wake. Their fire banked, his eyes went dark, locked with hers in a moment of shared revelation.

A hint of a grin teased his mouth. Pleased with himself. Pleased with her. She couldn't help but kiss him. His embrace tight, he reclined onto the bed, taking her with him.

After checking his stitches, she collapsed onto his uninjured side.

Tracing figures on his skin with her finger, she let her mind empty, dominated into numbness by sensation while he stroked her hair gently.

"Perhaps I should pull my stitches more often." The rumble of his voice reverberated in his chest beneath her.

Grinning, she rubbed her cheek against him, toeing the red sheets in idle play. "Pleased?"

He blew out a breath. "In ways words cannot express."

She chuckled softly. If she could spend the rest of her life like this with him, she would ask nothing more. Delightfully sated, she closed her eyes. She would regain control over her lower half eventually, but for now, she couldn't bring herself to care about anything but the bliss whispering under her skin.

"Was that..." he began, then pressed his lips together. "I mean, are you..."

She beamed a wide grin. "Oh, yes. Very."

For a moment, he shared her grin, then glanced away. Shy?

"Are you sure you haven't done this before?" she teased.

He rumbled a low laugh and shook his head. "I think I would have remembered."

With a toothy smile, she traced a spirit-magic sigil on his abdomen. "So what you're saying is that it was *memorable*."

That laugh again. "I'm not altogether certain I'll remember anything else ever again, witch."

"If you do, we still have plenty of time to make an amnesiac of you yet."

The bed shifted as he shook his head, toying with a lock of her hair. They lay there in a comfortable silence, breaths slowing, pleasure fading to a contented lull.

He took a deep breath. "Rielle," he began, "there's something I'd like to discuss with you."

Enjoying his fingers combing through her hair, she hesitated to open her eyes. "Hm?"

His arm tensed. "You know I was discharged from the Order."

Her eyes fluttered open. Long had she wondered about the circumstances. Staring into the darkness, she waited. He continued to stroke her.

"It was an honorable discharge, or so I was told." His fingertips trailed through her hair, languid and pleasurable. His touch felt so good, a distraction when she now wanted her wits about her.

Frowning, she took his hand and brought it to her chest, holding it close. "Why wouldn't you mention that?"

He shrugged beneath her. "Because I didn't know what it meant. The message didn't say why, just that I was honorably discharged and to report to Monas Amar. I was on my way to Monas Ver to confront Derric the night I broke through the Tower checkpoint."

"Isn't an honorable discharge a good thing?" She lowered her chin, and he traced his thumb along her lower lip.

He squeezed her hand and held her closer. "Now it is, yes. I get to be with you." He kissed her head. "But at the time, it gutted me. I had taken my vows in contemplation of serving for life, and the concept of no longer being a paladin was unthinkable."

"It's a reward, though, isn't it? An honorable discharge?"

"Sometimes," he said. "But paladins far more decorated than I hadn't been given such a reward. It's also granted to paladins rendered physically or psychologically unable to continue service, but clearly, that's not it either. Rumor says it's also done to quiet dissent that can't be dealt with otherwise."

"Is that what happened to you?"

"No. I've never made waves in the Order, just did my duty and kept my mouth shut. If someone didn't like me, well, an honorable discharge is like blowing out a candle with a hurricane."

She snorted softly. "What's your theory, then?"

He pulled himself up a bit, and she did, too. "Well, I'm not decorated enough to be honorably discharged for excellent service. I'm not physically or psychologically unfit. I'm not important enough to be discharged for political reasons." He sighed. "The Order is sometimes snidely referred to as the Order of Third Sons or the Order of Bastards. Since priests and paladins can't inherit, noblemen often enlist their third sons, after the heir and the spare reach manhood, or their bastards, to keep inheritance from getting bloody. Still, the unpredictable can happen. It's why the Order has the Last of the Line clause."

Her mouth fell open. The last of a line? She craned her neck to gape at him. "Your father's a noble?"

He raised his eyebrows, staring into space for the span of a few breaths. "I don't know, but I have no other plausible explanation. And it would explain why I seem to be the only paladin assigned a mage protector." He offered a smile that soon faded. "My whole life, it never mattered to me who my parents were. Derric, Tor, and the other priests and paladins who raised me, cared about me—they were my family. My bloodline never mattered to me. Until now." He reached for her hand, cradled it in his own, caressed her knuckles with his thumb. "But if I'm not a nobleman's son, if no inheritance awaits me, I plan to pledge my sword to the new king."

She drew in a long, slow breath. At dinner, when Gran had mentioned Duke Faolan being a likely candidate for king, a part of her had recoiled at the possibility of Brennan rising to princedom. But the duke was ignorant of Brennan's condition, and to consolidate his power, he would surely see his only son wed to no less than royalty to legitimize his reign, breaking the betrothal.

A disgraced Emaurrian marquise would never be accepted as a future queen by Parliament or any king in his right mind.

Although she shuddered to think what kind of prince—what kind of *king* someday—Brennan would make.

But she could be free. Free to be with Jon. He'd either be a knight, titled, albeit lowly, or a lord if his suspicion proved true. It was a long shot, but even so, her chances of freeing herself from the betrothal were now better than ever. "If it's Duke Faolan—"

He raised her hand to his lips, kissing her fingers. "I know, my love." He lowered her hand and peered at it pensively. "If Duke Faolan becomes king and the Paladin Grand Cordon tells me I've inherited a title, some lands—"

Freedom from the marriage contract. Jon with a knighthood, perhaps more, no longer a commoner... And she, free to marry him...

He retrieved his belt pouch from the nightstand and removed a small, round glass bottle stopped with a cork. Inside, dried flowers retained a sunny yellow in a cluster of blooms. "It's home. Immortelle. I cut this cluster about four months ago outside the monastery. Traveling north, when the fields are golden with its bloom, home is not far."

The dream in his eyes was home, a happy longing, and when he placed the tiny bottle in her hand, she blinked. "You're giving it to me?"

With a slow, playful smile, he skimmed her cheek with his fingertips.

Her heart skipped a beat, and she clutched the bottle close. Time and again, her hopes for happiness had been dashed, but maybe this time, it would be different. Maybe fate, despite all she'd done, would let her be with Jon and be happy while she worked her way to magister, helped where she could, made herself useful to the world. Plenty of mages lived outside the Towers, taking missions as they received orders.

"It's the foolish dream of a forsworn paladin," Jon said, with a self-deprecating laugh, "and I hardly dare give it thought, let alone voice—"

Breathless, she leaned in and kissed him, then broke away, just barely. "If you're trying to seduce me again, Jonathan Ver, it is working."

A hint of a puckish smile appeared. "Saw right through my plan, did you, witch?"

Grinning, she nipped his lower lip. "And I have it on good authority that it's an opportune time to set it in motion."

"Is that so?" He took her face in his hands and captured her mouth with a kiss that soon escalated to more.

It was all she could do to nod. Lips locked, she let Jon ease her back onto the bed and pin her beneath him.

46

*A*t the edge of the Lady's Garden, Brennan kneaded his eyes with the heels of his palms. Foolish woman. The faraway look in her eyes—to exact that promise, she had been willing to bleed to death. What was he to do with her?

Tonight the nightblooms here blossomed just for him, the air thick with their spicy scents. Somehow in darkness, they flourished. He closed his eyes and leaned in to sample the jasmine's fragrance. The plan had been flawless. The castle guards were far, the garden had been dark, and the commoner would have been bitten—the perfect incentive for Rielle to break the curse for them both.

Flawless. Until she'd threatened herself. The beat of her heart had been honest. Determined. Irrefutable.

He'd overplayed his hand, pushed her too far. Cursing her lover would have forced her to break it, but now—

That was hopeless now.

He closed his eyes, let the defeat sink in. She'd never willingly give herself to him the way things were now, and he'd promised not to force her. Whatever he was, he would keep his word.

And *she*—she was...

The strength of her convictions, the ferocity in her eyes—she could stare down death without flinching. Even the Great Wolf would admit a fondness.

Steps neared, light but not cautious. Confident. A woman with an agenda.

He caught her scent on the wind. Lily of the valley and resinous amber. The duchess entered the garden. No guards.

She'd confined him to his quarters earlier, and although he was defying her now, that defiance no doubt paled in significance to the rest of the night's events.

He didn't move, tried not to give away any sign that he knew she'd arrived.

"Out for an evening stroll, Marquis Tregarde?" The cold edge to her voice belied her casual question.

He kept his tone even. "A beautiful evening for it. Wouldn't you agree, Your Grace?"

She remained silent too long. "You think I don't know what's happened between you and my great-granddaughter?"

He exhaled softly. So much had happened between him and Rielle over the course of their stormy engagement. "What in particular, Your Grace?"

"Everything. Her refusal to leave with you at the Tower nine years ago after the pirates killed her family. Your mistreatment of her three years ago. Your repentance. Her continued rebellion. The duel between you and her lover tonight. As I said, everything." Her steps neared.

Everything.

Almost. No one knew about his werewolf nature, the blood curse, and the bond except for Rielle, and now—he curled his upper lip—her *commoner* lover. Perhaps Mother knew, but if she did, the duchess wouldn't be her confidante.

No, the duchess didn't know; if she did, her treatment of him was curious. "And you let me live? Why?"

"Because I know your heart." She rested a hand on his shoulder. "You don't hate my great-granddaughter. You love her."

He snorted an amused breath. "And here I thought with age comes wisdom."

The duchess sat on the garden's ledge in a luxurious violet dressing gown, eyes warm. "You've convinced yourself that you hate her because that is the only way you can stomach her rejection. It's easier to hate someone who doesn't want you than to love her, Brennan. Unattainable grapes are always bitter."

Bitter grapes? "You don't know what you're talking about."

"Mind yourself, boy, when your betters are speaking." She straightened, but then heaved a slow sigh. "I don't say this to shame you, but to help you.

You and I want the same thing—a stable, profitable marriage between our two lines, with plenty of legitimate heirs."

Heirs? Is that what this was about? Then the duchess wanted to strengthen and consolidate her political and economic powers—a marriage tie and a blood tie to the Marcels. Shrewd old she-wolf.

"But my great-granddaughter follows her heart, as you well know."

The foreigner. The commoner. This stupid mission saving her friend. The girl was willing to drug herself, stab herself, die for those she loved. It was exhausting just trying to keep her alive.

"And you will never win her heart with malice."

He looked away. "What, a few kind words will erase the past few years?"

There was no turning back now. *What's done is done.*

She moved into his line of sight. "No. Love her. Love those she loves. Convince her you want to make amends, and convince yourself. Then make them. Rielle resists opening her heart to others, but it is not impenetrable. And I'll make sure the new king doesn't grant her any unnecessary favors."

Like breaking our marriage contract. Rielle's petitions had fallen on deaf ears for a long time, thanks to Father's influence with the Faralles—

Or... was the duchess the one who'd kept King Marcus from granting Rielle a breaking of the marriage contract?

"I want what's best for my great-granddaughter and her House, even if she disagrees with what that is. And it can happen, if you resolve to be honest with yourself. You love her. Let yourself feel it. And see our lines united."

She glided away, quiet steps disappearing behind the thud of a door.

Her suggested strategy... not courtship, but an extended game to win favor.

He inhaled the soothing jasmine and gazed up at the night sky. He wouldn't overtly pursue Rielle but entice her to pursue him. Let her think it was her decision.

The idea had merit. If he succeeded, she'd never realize the game was being played until it was over and he had won.

Let myself feel my love for her.

Love. Did he love her? He needed her, but did he love her as a man loved a woman? The ties between them knotted like honeysuckle and hazel, and he couldn't tell which was which anymore.

He couldn't tell, and he didn't want to, need to. It didn't matter. He required one thing from her, and it wasn't love.

The old woman was wrong. Yes, on that, she was mistaken. Had to be. But she was right about one thing.

Currying favor.

He sighed.

An overture... He needed a diplomatic overture, something she wanted but didn't expect from him.

A gift. He'd make her a gift of Phantom.

47

*S*hivering, Olivia sat against the iron bars in the torch's fading light. The rats here were braver than most and the torchlight didn't bother them, but at least she could see them. Gilles hadn't returned, and neither had any of his mage captains.

Her gaze flickered to the two boxes in her cell. Was James still alive? At first, she had asked Anton each day, but the longer she went without a trip to the Hall of Mirrors, the more fear gathered in her heart that Anton would avert his eyes and shake his head.

She hadn't been to the Hall of Mirrors in a month's time. Gilles must have at last gotten James to talk.

What had it been? What secret had James held so close that not even *she* had been privy to?

Whatever it was, he would never give Gilles anything important. James was intelligent. Brilliant. He well knew that when prisoners finally elected to speak, the issue wasn't eliciting information but eliciting true and useful information.

Endure, my love. She didn't know when, or how, but they would survive this. They had to.

Thanks to Anton, she still clung to life. True to his word, he had returned every day—sometimes twice a day—with bread, water, and a willingness to help. Divine be praised, he'd even occasionally sneaked in basic human necessities. Not enough to garner notice, but enough to deserve her eternal gratitude. She'd never been so grateful for a bar of soap, tooth powder, and some water carafes.

But could he be trusted? Was this kindness truly to rebel against Gilles and do right, or was it simply a deception to coax some true and useful information from her?

Her words had to be carefully measured with him... except about the rite.

The rite... She drummed a finger against the muggy stone floor—or tried to. She winced. Too stiff.

It didn't matter if Gilles knew about the Moonlit Rite. In fact, better if he did—perhaps he'd see the wisdom in performing it. Few knew how humanity had come to sit upon the throne of the world; contrary to some legends, it hadn't been through glorious battle. No, the ancient Emaurrian texts had revealed the truth of the matter: it had been through the secretive spellweaving of witches.

When the first men had finally achieved a decisive victory against the elves and conquered Emaurria, they hadn't held it with military power. They'd held it with magic. Mankind's kings used magic to bind themselves to the land—to strengthen it and to draw strength from it. The Earthbinding.

And beneath Trèstellan Palace lay the Lunar Chamber, housing a Vein, a connection to the earth's anima. Originally, the elves had used it to sever the souls of evil that couldn't be killed, leaving behind great petrified monsters. On Spiritseve, the night when the Veil between the living world and the Lone thinned most, they could send a soul to the Lone without a dark god's guidance.

Humans had corrupted its use. The Keepers, human hunters of immortal beasts and beings, had collected the blood of each immortal race and brought those ingredients to the Lunar Chamber on Spiritseve. There, upon the Lunar Chamber's Vein, an Earthbound king had severed the soul of every Immortal in Emaurria—and beyond. How far, the texts had never specified.

The first Moonlit Rite had secured mankind's conquest, but the Immortals ever pushed against the Veil, longing to return to their petrified bodies, their pressure rising in strength until each performance of the rite, which maintained the Veil.

The Moonlit Rite prevented their Immortal souls from returning. Every performance kept the door closed. If it opened—

If it opened, hell would reign on earth.

When she'd told Anton about the Moonlit Rite, he'd left the dungeon and had returned the next day looking five years older. But he'd greeted her with the all-important words: *Tell me what must be done.*

Rowan ash. The blood of a Faralle. A mage skilled in ritual magic.

She patted her chest. There lay a pouch of rowan ash Anton had sneaked from her quarters and a vial of James's blood, secured from the torturer's boy for a bribe. At least the blood meant James was alive.

A month's maneuvering had taken them only so far. She still had no way out, and they had no other mage to perform the rite either.

She peered at her ring, the Ring of the Archmage, an enchanted emerald set in recondite. Worth many times more than the golden Emaurrian crown, it had been borne by each Archmage for a secret, singular purpose: to open the doors of the Lunar Chamber.

Without the ring, the rite could never be performed. And in the wrong hands, it could enable the severing of any soul, any time.

To trust Anton with it or not? She had wrestled with the decision for a month, and every day he left the dungeon without the ring, the chance of opening the Lunar Chamber doors for a mage to perform the rite dwindled.

And yet... If Anton served Gilles, if the general had the blood of someone important, someone he couldn't capture to kill through conventional means, the Ring of the Archmage and the texts in her quarters could grant him the power to eliminate anyone.

The footsteps came at last. Soft, uncertain. She pressed her cheek to the bars to try to see down the corridor.

He shed the shadows—Anton, bearing water and more black bread. With a half-smile in greeting, he approached the cell.

She smiled back.

She flinched. Smiled back? When was it that her face had taken such liberties with Anton before her mind calculated them?

Trust... She trusted him.

Intuition, let me down and I'll never believe you again.

When he knelt at the bars, the torchlight illumed the bruise on his cheek. He was hurt? How? Why?

He passed her the bread and cup of water.

She accepted the offering with a frown. "What happened?"

He sat and stroked his sandy-colored beard. "Well, that conjurer I mentioned... Asked her if she'd be interested in some side action outside the company."

She eyed him. " 'Side action'?"

Anton waggled his eyebrows, a sportive gleam in his oaky eyes, and slicked his white-blond hair back. Indeed, he had a sly handsomeness to him. "I don't kiss and tell, Liv."

She rolled her eyes.

"I asked her if she'd be willing to take on a side job. A spell for a nice sum of ten coronas, which our beloved general might not quite sanction." He rested his elbows on his knees.

"And what did she say?"

He turned his face, giving her full view of the bruise. "She let her five fingers do the talking."

She sighed and hunched over, deflated. This conjurer was the second mage to turn them down. And their second liability, who could report Anton's doings to Gilles.

He leaned in. "Reserve your worrying. I got a lead on a healer in the Coquelicot District."

If Anton really wasn't a Crag spy, this was risky for him. With every task he performed on her behalf, he risked exposure and punishment.

She leaned against the bars. "And this is worth it to you? What stops you from just waiting the siege out, taking your pay, and parting ways?"

He pursed his lips. "You know... you're right. Maybe that *is* the smarter choice."

She froze—her body refused to move until he cracked a smile. She grimaced.

"In the summer, the mosquitoes here are bad enough. When I imagine having to swat little naked pixie men away, I don't need any more persuasion to see this thing through." He winked.

She gave him an encouraging smile. "So you're an altruist, then? Just doing it to stop the Immortals from coming through?"

"In part, perhaps." His smile faded. "Signed on with the Free Companies to do some good. Gods know the army wouldn't have me. But this...?" He shook his head. "Can't bring back the dead. Can't save His Highness, Prince James. Can't free you. Can't defeat Gilles. The fact is, Liv, I can't do much." He heaved a deep breath. "But I won't let Gilles tell me who I am. With this, every man who willingly follows him endorses his actions— killing the king, the queen, the rest of the royals, nobles, women, children, old folk; conquering the capital; mounting insurrection; imprisoning young, beautiful women, abusing them, and torturing those they love," he whispered, grabbing one of the bars. "Won't endorse that. Won't become a murderer, conqueror, insurrectionist, abuser. I refuse. That much I can do."

She rested a hand on his. "Anton..."

He lifted his gaze to her hand and frowned. "Gods, Liv, how could they have done that to you?"

With a shrug, she pulled her mangled hand away. "If you're willing to do wrong when you tell yourself your cause is just, there's little you won't do."

She stared down at her hand, at the Ring of the Archmage. If she hesitated in order to save the life of some heretofore unknown person, the Veil could come down. Immortals could walk the earth once more, claiming countless lives.

That couldn't be allowed to happen.

She raised her ring finger to her mouth and moistened it. The ring had always been loose, but her fingers had been broken; it was snug now. Praying the band would come off, she put her finger in her mouth and, using her teeth, pulled at it.

Anton grabbed the bars. "What are you doing?"

The thing was stuck, but she didn't relent. Little by little, she dragged it, and at her proximal joint, her pulling sparked agony. Would the damned thing come away only *with* her finger?

But at last it gave. She spat it into her palm. "You'll need this."

"What?" He stared into her palm, his face lined with deep furrows.

"The doors to the Lunar Chamber are secured with a recondite lock that only this ring opens. You insert the stone into the lock. It closes quickly, so when it opens, wedge something there, if you can. Otherwise, no mage will be able to enter on Spiritseve." She held out her palm to him.

He swallowed. "This must be worth—"

"One of Emaurria's most priceless treasures."

"And you trust a former bandit with it?" He raised his gaze to hers.

She shook her head. "No. I trust *you* with it."

He drew in a shaky breath and accepted the ring. "I'll bring back the ring. Promise."

She smiled her encouragement. "I know you will."

Regardless of what happened, she'd have certainty. Certainty that she'd done all she could do to see the rite performed. Certainty that, if Anton returned with the ring, she could trust him enough to tell him about Rielle coming.

And, if he didn't return with the ring, the certainty that she'd given Gilles everything he would ever need to control the kingdom of Emaurria.

48

*B*reathless, Rielle gazed down at Jon. Divine, he was persistent. Against a sea of red bedding, the morning sunlight swelled behind him through the sheer panels. Bliss. He lay with his head against her inner thigh, his loving mouth intimating daydreams of afterlife—ascension —a world bathed in warm. Unrelenting. Pleasure.

Her breath quickening, she closed her eyes, writhed against the pillows, overwhelmed with sensation—cool, smooth cotton and the soft give of down, hot sweat spirited away by the chill air, a firm hand anchoring her bucking hip, unyielding warmth and pressure. A wave of white blinded her, and she squeezed her eyelids tighter.

Her heart raced, bliss throbbing through her entire being, pounding in her blood, in her ears, pulsing bright against the canvas of her vision. Cries —hers—chased away the quiet, and Divine, she could take no more, but he pushed her past her limits, pleasured her past her concept of pleasure, persisted until nothing else remained to animate her spent body, no more sound to escape her gaping mouth.

White. Pure, radiant white.

As the throb ebbed, he kissed her inner thigh before resting his head upon it once more with a smug sigh. They had spent most of the night and the morning in each other's arms, exhausting each other—in the bed, on the desk, in the bath—

And when he'd insisted on exploring her, there had been little she could say to dissuade him. Curious, captivated, determined, he'd tested her response to every touch, kiss, and more, then put it together to leave her a consumed heap.

"You're not as dead as you look, I hope."

She chuckled weakly. "If I am, you killed me. Too much of the little death."

A playful fingertip grazed her tender flesh, and she shivered.

"The witch yet lives."

She opened an eye.

His wry grin faded into softness. "You're beautiful."

She suppressed a smile. His light touch trailed across her sensitive skin, swept across her thigh, coaxing gooseflesh and shivers.

A knock sounded at the door.

The light in the room dimmed—a cloud shuttering the sun. She sighed. It had been too much to hope for a lazy day abed with Jon.

Go away. "Just a minute," she called.

Jon left the bed with a wince, rotated his left shoulder stiffly, and she followed, assessing the strain on his stitches with cautious fingertips.

Grasping her hand, he smiled. "I'm fine. Truly."

She shook her head. Arcanir poison still flowed in his blood, and until it was gone, she'd worry.

"I know that look," he said, a twinkle of amusement in his squint. "Stop worrying. Really. I'm all right."

But he wasn't. Not until the arcanir poison was out of his system. She would simply have to be stubborner than he.

"You'll mind those stitches, Jon, or else." She put on her robe and pulled the sash tight.

"Don't provoke me, witch," he said, his voice an octave lower. "Or I may have to 'kill' you again."

She swallowed. The promise of pleasure glimmered in his eyes, and she raked her gaze over his strong, bare form. Provocation had never been so tempting.

Another knock.

Of course. Breathing hard, she walked backward to the door, leaving Jon as he dressed and shot her a challenging look. Her breath caught.

Walk away, walk away—

With a last check of her robe, she answered the door.

Muscle rippling in black leather, Brennan filled the doorway, fixing her with a knowing look, the hint of a sly smile slinking around his mouth. He gave her a slow once-over and flinched. "How long does it take to answer a door?"

She was of half a mind to slam it in his face. "Have you gone soft in the head?" she hissed, trying to push him out into the hallway, but he wouldn't move. "Showing up here, after last night—"

"What happened last night?" He only moved into the hallway when she stopped pushing. "Your lover survived. You relished bringing a beast to heel. If anyone should have cause for umbrage, it's me."

"The victim of your own tale, are you?"

He shrugged. "What's a little blood shed between intimates like us? We have weathered worse, you and I. The bond continues unbroken. Let us not pretend, fiancée mine, to now have delicate sensibilities. You will continue to give me relief. I will continue to protect you."

Albeit unpleasant, it was the truth. But she shook her head. "I don't need your protection."

Coolly, he lowered his chin. "Do you have preternatural reflexes?"

She scoffed. His talents weren't the only way.

"Then you need my protection," he said with a victorious grin. "Especially considering I have a lead on your missing assassin. We'll be going into town."

He'd found the assassin?

Well, he did have skills she needed. Loath as she was to admit it, she required his help. When his attention shifted to something behind her, she stiffened.

"You," Jon snarled.

Brennan smirked. "Me."

Jon stalked past her toward Brennan and leaned in. "Give me one reason why I shouldn't gut you."

Unmoved, Brennan shrugged with his usual nonchalance. "For one, I promised Rielle I wouldn't hurt you, and it wouldn't be very sporting of you to attack a man who won't fight back," he said, with all the condescension of a parent explaining something to a small child. "And for another, while you're held together by some catgut and stubbornness, you're still *far* too weak."

Jon clenched his teeth. "Try me."

She rolled her eyes. "Both of you," she interrupted, "stop."

Drawing a deep breath, Brennan held Jon's gaze and smiled icily, his eyes brimming with either amusement or hatred—she couldn't guess—but he kept his peace.

What had changed between last night and today?

But with the way Jon glared at him, how long would that peace hold?

She cleared her throat and darted between them to face Jon, whose glare remained fixed on Brennan. "He said he has a lead on the other assassin."

"On friendly terms with the enemy, no doubt," Jon bit out, his neck corded.

"No," Brennan replied. "If the assassin had *succeeded,* on the other hand—"

When Jon anchored a palm on her shoulder, she interrupted before he could nudge her aside. "I'm going into town with Brennan to deal with—"

Jon turned the full force of his glare upon her. "I'm coming with you."

She shivered. Not a question. A declaration.

With his injury and the arcanir poisoning, he couldn't—and he had to know that. Looking away, she gently urged him back toward their quarters.

Brennan leaned against the doorjamb and crossed his ankles. "If you don't want your plaything broken, leave it in your room, fiancée mine."

When Jon tensed, she preempted him and turned to Brennan. "Silence." Her pulse sped.

Brennan held up his hands, then crossed his arms. But he'd already drawn blood.

She turned back to Jon, who bristled, staring down Brennan.

"I'm coming with you," Jon repeated. Not a question.

"Jon," she pleaded, her voice barely above a whisper. What she had to say to him would hurt, but she hoped her care would lessen the blow. She led him into the room, away from Brennan, and gently shut the door. "You know you can't."

He shook his head vehemently. "I won't allow him to—"

"Even if you were recovered from your wounds, which you're not, you're still afflicted with arcanir poisoning. If anything were to happen to you, I'd be unable to heal you. You could die." She stroked his shoulder.

He pulled back. "I can handle myself, mage."

Mage. She winced. The last time he'd called her that, she'd been as a stranger to him. She lowered her gaze to his clenched fists. When she reached out to take his hand, he drew away.

Even if he did feel affronted, she couldn't let him take such a risk to protect her, neither as her lover nor as her charge. He had to see reason.

"Brennan won't hurt me."

He rolled his eyes.

"In fact, he has good reason to protect me, and you know it. I'm safe with him."

"I can protect you."

She shook her head. "No, you misunderstand me. I don't need his protection. I'm just telling you he has no reason to allow harm to come to me." If he wouldn't see reason to stay behind for his own survival, she had to try to convince him another way. "And, as much as I'm touched by your care, I don't need your protection either. What I need from you is to stay here, so that my focus isn't split."

He recoiled.

But she'd told him the truth. "This is mission related, so I say this to you as your guardian and escort. My mission is to protect you. Your arcanir poisoning has complicated matters. I know I can trust you to fight well, but if something happens, I can no longer rely on healing you—and I am no physician. Knowing that one rare blow can, without healing magic, kill you —I don't want that to happen to you. Ever."

She couldn't bear it if anything happened to him. If he wanted to protect her, the best way to do that was by keeping himself safe here, behind a ward and the castle walls, under Gran's guard. "Preventing that requires a level of attention that could compromise my own safety. And I would—if we *needed* to take the risk, but we don't. Do you wish me to risk my life to suit your preferences?"

While he stood speechless, she moved to the wardrobe to leave the vial of king's blood and her signet ring in her recondite satchel and to dress in her shirt and trousers. "That is why we're still in Melain. Because it's riskier for you to be out there now, even with two mages to protect you."

He stormed after her. "I never asked for—"

"No," she interrupted, tucking her shirt into her trousers, "you didn't. The High Priest did. The Proctor did." She put on her leather vest, then began taming her hair into a braid. "And you may have never asked for me to be assigned as your guardian, but I am, and one way or another, I won't let anything hurt you. Whether that means you staying behind here or me splitting my focus to protect you out there is in your hands."

He forced out an angry breath. "If there were nothing between us, you wouldn't—"

"If there were nothing between us, we wouldn't be having this conversation. You'd be confined here while I handled the threat to your safety." She buckled her belt. "But because I love you, I want you to understand why this is the only reasonable course of action. And I want you to agree. I want there to be no resentment between us."

He crossed his arms and looked away. "You want me to cower in the bedchamber while you go into battle?"

She put a finger to his lips. "I want you to live." She paused, and his eyes softened. "I need you to."

A shadow passed over his face as he took her finger and peered at the hand he held with a contemplative frown. He then removed the singular ring he wore, the silver one he was so enamored of twirling pensively. Forged with ivy vines engraved on the band and the Terran moon at its center, it bore the Sodalis crest. A symbol of his oath, a paladin would part with it about as willingly as he would with his arcanir.

He took her hand and placed the ring in her palm, then closed her fingers around it.

"Jon—"

"The center stone is arcanir."

Indeed, at the center was not silver but arcanir, its sage tint faint but present. If she felt battle fury, she would have but to touch it for safety. His eyes locked with hers.

"I know you don't need my protection," he said, his eyes flaring and his voice rising at the words, "but take this ring at my insistence. It will make all this more—tolerable."

"I can't accept this. It's too much." As helpful as it could be to her, he had few things to call his own, and parting with even one could not be easy.

"Accept it, with my love."

She uncurled her fist to reveal the ring in her palm. A way for Jon to be with her, to help her from afar. "I'll treasure it." She slid the ring onto her thumb, the only finger it wouldn't slip from easily.

He swept her up, held her close, then tipped her chin up to his mouth. Her lips parted to him, and her eyes fluttered shut. Being with him felt natural, like coming home, a wave inside her flowing in to shore. He stroked her hair, keeping her close, inundating every bit of her doubt with love. Breaking away with one last light kiss, he cupped her face, and they breathed the same air.

This wasn't goodbye; he would be safe here, and she would return with the assassin in custody.

He released her and stroked her cheek. "I can't believe I'm agreeing to this madness." He sighed heavily, his body held still by a thousand unspoken arguments. "Go, before I change my mind."

She gave him a faint smile. "I'll see you soon."

He grinned, but it didn't reach his eyes. He couldn't be pleased with the circumstances, and so his acquiescence meant all the more.

When she pulled away, a line etched between his eyebrows, but he stood unmoving, his every muscle taut. She warded the quarters against intruders and headed for the door.

It was time to hunt the assassin.

49

*O*utside the castle, Brennan could finally breathe.

It was too much. Too damn much. She reeked of her lover's scent, and that commoner bastard had been bathed in hers, drowned in hers. It was enough to make the Wolf raise its hackles and claw to come out. He hadn't missed the Sodalis ring, either. The paladin was actually trying to claim her. *My betrothed.*

He gulped the city air, grateful for the odors of the unwashed masses, the rotting garbage, the dust, the cats, rodents, and stray dogs, the Melainese dumplings cooking, even the damned tannery so far away but close enough to add to the millions of scents diluting hers. Lifeblood. Surfacing from the crushing depths of her and *him*, he inhaled.

"Are you all right?"

"You *reek.*" Countless women nearby smelled like sex, but this one was his betrothed. *His.*

"I—" Her face contorted. "No, you know what? I'm *so sorry* you can't tolerate me having a partner, despite the countless women you bed. I'm *so sorry* about your fragile little ego cracking. *So very sorry.*"

He forced a breath from his nose, listened to her racing pulse, smelled her anger. And she was right. He did bed whomever he pleased. But reminding him of that didn't assuage his indignation. Some passersby glared their disapproval at what must've looked like a lovers' quarrel.

An angry response would just vindicate her, bolster her fury. No. Let her stew in guilt later—that was the better choice.

He mustered his most indifferent sneer. "Apology accepted."

While she fumed, he merely headed for Nilda's. Rielle would follow. She had no choice. And indeed, she fell into a heavy, stomping stride behind him.

"What are you smiling about?" she asked bitterly.

"Your folly." He paid her a lazy glance.

"*My* folly?" She spat. "What about you, threatening Jon? Did you think that would work?"

"It almost did, until you poured your guts out."

She glared at him and then jerked her face away, wisps of golden hair misbehaving in the dirty city breeze. Conversation was out, then.

He led her on a meandering route through the city, down shadowy alleys and into fetid gangways, through the more presentable districts toward the Mélange, where poverty, opportunity, and debauchery met at an ever-bustling crossroads. A street performer's lute, myriad disjointed voices, and the stench of piss and garbage shrugged a welcome to the crush of bodies moving in seedy self-interest. Full of thieves, whores, sen'a and trux peddlers, smugglers, counterfeiters, and the honest poor who could afford no better home, the Mélange also housed Melain's largest immigrant population.

Past the whisperings about the dead Faralles and the Moonlit Rite, under a brown canvas awning, a woman sat splayed in a chair, her bony knees pitching a billowing black batiste skirt, its hem dusted with the road's filth. The bodice, once presentable perhaps, had laces worn with use, fastened and unfastened by countless eager, uncaring fingers. Her head thrown back, her glassy eyes consumed the nothing above; her olive face dulled in a frame of fraying sable tresses, curled with weather, age, neglect, and Nilda's pomade.

Rielle halted and stared. "You've brought me to a—a—"

"Resonance den," he supplied. He pulled his black hood up. "We're going in."

Her chin trembled, but she set her jaw. With a curt nod, she pulled up the hood of her cloak and followed him.

Her weakness for sen'a had long been known to him, written to him three years ago by his Tower spies, and a mere moon ago, she had been trancing again. In Bournand.

But he wouldn't coddle her. She needed to master looking into the abyss without falling in. The next Duchess of Maerleth Tainn, Marquise of Laurentine and Tregarde, Baroness of Calterre, could not afford such vulnerability.

Nilda's was a poorly lit nest of alcoves, begrimed with writhing trancers and furious truxheads, all in varying stages of pleasure and decay, lolling and fucking, and somewhere in the back, fighting—no, the whisper of a death rattle—dying. All beneath a shroud of smoke.

No sign of the assassin.

Sen'a, trux, filth, sex, body odor, and curling pomade dominated the air, but somewhere farther in, there was a stale smell. Old earth. Dust. A cellar.

No one had stopped to question them. A clerk lay sprawled over a desk, trancing. Brennan smirked. *Some guard.* He nodded to Rielle, but she stood, frozen, her gaze fixed on a trance pipe. She exhaled a quivering breath. Weakness.

Resist.

He grabbed her hand and led her through the resonance den, following his nose to the cellar door. A soiled curtain swayed ahead of them, and he threw it aside. A private room. She yanked her hand free and looked around.

Cushions covered the seats in a lounging booth, but his sense of smell had taken them to the right place. He tossed aside two worn cushions to reveal a door and a ladder descending into the darkness. Behind him, Rielle gasped, but he merely opened it and gestured to her.

Her face tightened, but she drew in a preparatory breath and descended. He replaced a cushion atop the open door to camouflage their entry as well as he could, then followed her into the dark.

Down here, the scents of a number of people lingered—truxheads, leather-clad thieves, sea-washed smugglers, mages. Sen'a and trux scented the air heavily. A hub.

Sileni leather. Danewort. Olive oil.

The assassin woman. She'd been here, perhaps still was. He'd know her scent anywhere. Four years ago, when he'd gone with Father to Mor on business, this woman, cloaked and hooded, had been in the villa's study with him. Upon Brennan's entrance, their meeting had hastily concluded.

If Father had anything to do with her—with any of this—all the more reason to kill her. No loose ends. Protect the family.

The only light was a distant torch until Rielle's hands glowed a mossy green. She raised them to her eyes. "Divine. The place is teeming with people. I can see them through the walls, winding and myriad like veins."

In this network of tunnels, she could see people through the walls, but he didn't need magic to know how many humans littered the place. Scents inundated his nostrils, dozens, along with traces of recondite.

He swept his fingers over the walls, their telltale grooves. "Ancient recondite mine."

"The assassin's down here?" A rustle and a whisper of air—she removed her hood.

He shrugged. "If she isn't, she was."

"She?"

"Yes. An illusionist with curly hair, wearing Sileni leather. A truxhead." Even if he relayed everything of significance to her here, she could hardly dismiss him now.

"Could be Phantom." A soft scuff—she angled her body toward him. "You've seen her?"

"No." Not recently.

A pause. "You got all that from a scent?"

All that and more. His lungs expanded to their fullest. With a hint of a grin, he stalked toward the torch, trying to pick up the assassin's scent amid the many. The clean smell of ice mingled with the stormy musk of elemental magic—Rielle had conjured an ice shard behind him. As they proceeded, the human scents intensified.

Changing, even partially for the claws, would make for easier battle, but not a single person could see his Change and live to tell the tale. But down here, he couldn't ensure death for all witnesses. Too many twists, turns, and rat holes.

Black powder. The odor hit him, heavy and near, and he grabbed Rielle before she could take another step.

"Tripwire," he whispered.

A flash, and she conjured candlelight in her palm and crouched, illuminating the trap and the small kegs rigged to it. Candlelight in one hand and ice shard in the other, she puffed an exhalation.

An explosion would exceed her infamously meager healing abilities.

Unease settled in the pit of his stomach. He could kill mages and warriors threatening her, but against severed limbs and hemorrhage, there was little he could do. And it grated.

He breathed deep, tensed his muscles. "Tread lightly, and let's go." He cocked his head toward their destination.

Rielle lit their way, the ice shard still glinting in her other hand. The candlelight would give away their advance. He didn't need it—the narrow mining tunnel, although dark, was clear to his eyes—but against loss of limb for her, it was a necessary risk.

They crept toward the torchlight and a door of some kind in the tunnels. As they neared it, he motioned for her to take up a position to the left while he took the right, where it opened. Immune to magic and with preternatural healing, he took point.

Mouthing a countdown to Rielle, he reached for the doorknob.

Footsteps. Damn.

The door opened. Two men walked out.

He seized a throat and ripped it out. Blood spattered, a gurgle marking the end.

The other turned to him, eyes wide, trembling hand reaching for a dagger.

A shard of ice burst from his chest, drenched in red. The man's shout emerged as a whimper, screaming death hushed to a pathetic end. He thumped to the ground. No others nearby.

"Let's find your assassin."

She nodded and conjured another ice shard. "Lead the way."

He passed through the doorway. The perfume of sen'a—sickly sweet, floral, rounded with a certain thick richness—prevailed. Sparse torches lit the chamber, crates stacked to the ceiling to form a maze to the other side. He moved through, Rielle tiptoeing behind him.

"Eastern distribution," she said, her voice matter of fact. "This place probably supplies all of eastern Emaurria." She was silent awhile. Stable. "What do sen'a suppliers have to do with assassins?"

King Marcus had threatened a ban on both sen'a and trux over a decade ago. If the assassins were Heartseekers, perhaps King Marcus had reconsidered the ban—and the smugglers had planned for both eventualities, hiring assassins to kill him but expanding the underground tunnels in case they failed.

Heartseekers with access to this hub would use it as a base for nearby operations. Perhaps the Heartseekers had contracts for Rielle and paladin reinforcements arriving in Monas Amar. More blood would flow.

"Let's find out." He took her through the narrow winding path between the crates until they reached another door. He sidled up to the right side, she to the left. No one nearby, although his ears picked up distant steps, faraway voices. A dozen, perhaps.

He inched the door open and peeked through a crack. A long, dark corridor ended at another door, lit by two torches. A dozen smugglers loitered in front, half playing cards at a primitive table, the others sparring, drinking—the one mage among them, an enforcer, napping.

Enforcers always smelled the strangest, like a winter's night in the Tainn Mountains. Icy, crisp, slightly sweet—tingly. And although they were dangerous to him as mages went, this one was sleeping. Brennan shut the door softly.

"Your turn," he said softly to Rielle. "Twelve targets, distracted. One mage, enforcer, asleep."

A determined nod. She dispelled the ice shard and conjured fire in her palms. It blazed high, bright, arcing between her hands with an excited roar. There was the slightest curl to the corner of her mouth.

Mistress of flame—warmth and destruction. Death incarnate. Blessed of Nox. Some part of her had to love it. The power to comfort. The power to kill. Power of any kind.

She assumed a ready stance just out of the door's path and inclined her head to him.

He mouthed a countdown, then threw open the door.

Rielle gestured and unleashed a torrent of flame. Scorching down the corridor, it charred the walls, consumed all in its path with fiery hunger as it surged toward the doorway.

Explosions boomed—small barrels of black powder combusting.

Close behind the spell, he charged. Screams barely emerged before the deafening roar of the pyromancy burned them.

The stench of charred flesh conquered the air, even as the fire left nothing but ashes and a bewildered enforcer behind a repulsion shield.

Brennan tackled him, grinning as the enforcer's desperate spell failed, and snapped his neck.

The door and its wall burned, flames licking the sides of the tunnel. Rielle made her way to him.

Behind the door, rustling, stepping, creaking. Entirely resistant to the pyromancy, Brennan kicked it open.

An arrow hit his shoulder.

He rushed the archer, ripping out the arrow midway, and tackled her. She fell to the ground, and he crushed her skull.

The room was clear, but on the other side, the door was open, still moving. The scent of Sileni leather, danewort, and olive oil lingered. He listened for footsteps—and there they were, a door opening and closing, the turning of a lock, and then, silence.

He smiled. Nowhere to run.

Rielle entered. Her gaze darted to a map on the wall, and when she approached it, so did he. Several duchies, marches, counties, viscounties, and baronies were marked, linked with black thread, all over Emaurria. Even Maerleth Tainn.

"A distribution map." Rielle moved to a nearby table and pushed it toward the wall. Slowly. Pathetically.

With a sigh, he grabbed her hips and lifted her.

"What are—"

He carried her to the wall. She grimaced but began taking down the map, squirming against him as she worked.

Great Wolf, she felt good in his hands—satisfying, soft, substantial. Those trousers of hers did little to camouflage that generous curve of her hips, her ass, luscious thighs, soft and...

What would she be like in bed, that softness wrapped around him, at his fingertips...?

His mouth watered, and the Change brushed up against his control, tufts of fur spiking through his skin, sharp teeth protruding in his mouth. Even the Wolf hungered for her. *Patience, Wolf. Patience.* Fur and teeth pulled in, the Change subdued.

She wouldn't have him. Not before. Not now. Maybe never, if he failed to convince her of his repentance. What would it take?

"Got it." She folded the map.

He let her slide along his body to the floor, suppressing his need. She gave him a once-over and raised an eyebrow at him.

He sighed. Some things couldn't be *suppressed*. "Beyond my control," he snarled. "Don't flatter yourself."

"For that, I'd have to care." With a dismissive shrug, she wandered to the various surfaces in the room, leafing through papers, opening containers.

He let her enjoy her little victory, the knowledge that he lusted after her. It didn't mean much—he lusted after many a woman.

When she struggled with a chest, he swept her aside, broke the lock, and threw it open. Letters piled within. She shuffled through them and carefully pulled one out.

" 'Advance payment to silence dissent until we can nominate and confirm a candidate of our choosing,' " she read aloud. Her eyes widened. "A 'candidate'? A king?"

" 'We,' " Brennan repeated. "There's only one 'we' that can nominate and confirm a king."

She sucked in a breath. "Parliament."

He shrugged. "Some members, if not all. Whether one or more, they must be influential, if they claim to have such control."

"Treason." She stared at the wall and shivered. "King Marcus's own nobles had him and his family killed."

The map—

Maerleth Tainn had been among its points.

But Father would *never* risk treason. He was far too smart for it.

Or, if he did, he certainly wouldn't get caught.

Other nobles, however...

"Ambition knows no satiety," he said while she gathered up every document she could find.

"We'll take the letter and present it to—" she paused. "The Paladin Grand Cordon. The Order of Terra would be obligated to investigate such a thing, especially in the absence of a Lord Chancellor or Constable of Emaurria."

Two of the Grand Officers of the Crown, the Lord Chancellor and the Constable of Emaurria, would have to be appointed by a new king, one who could be complicit in the treasonous plot. Unworkable.

Indeed, the Order of Terra would be as impartial a judicial body as could be found.

A new king... Rumor said the king's niece once removed was laying claim to the throne with her husband, but married to an El-Amin prince, she would be as welcome in Emaurria as a plague. No, the Houses wouldn't support her, not when there was another, older, line of kings headed by a powerful, intelligent, rich man.

Father. Brennan peered at the small chest of letters.

However, without the actual payment and clarification of "candidate," there would be little to prove the guilt of any member of Parliament.

A new king.

Father could be king.

And I could be—

No. Too remote. "I scented the assassin earlier. She was here." He cocked his head toward the open door. "But she ran out before I entered."

Rielle straightened. "Then let's catch her."

She stuffed letters into her shirt, and together, they headed for the door.

50

*R*ielle entered the dark corridor with Brennan. *That letter...* King Marcus's own nobles had plotted his death and that of his heirs. They'd been so threatened by the Farallan agenda that they'd hired the Heartseekers and the Crag Company. So much tragedy over...

What? Politics? Money? Ambition?

No matter. They now had solid proof and could, with time, identify the nobles involved.

Brennan guided her over another tripwire and toward a door. The assassin would be there; she had to be. Capture her, question her, and they'd be back at the castle. Jon wasn't here and Brennan was immune to magic, so there was no danger from battle fury nor fureur.

She'd had to kill, but it was kill or be killed.

Brennan held her back. "There's a lot of movement." He stared at the door, his eyebrows drawn.

"Let me handle this."

He cocked an eyebrow but moved aside. With a quick bit of pyromancy, she set the door on fire. While the flames consumed the wood, she cast a wind spell, blasting the door open.

Fire blazed through and inside.

Ear-splitting screeching—

She cloaked herself in flame and followed its wake. Inside, several figures burned—all women with long, black curls, wearing leather armor, daggers strapped to their belts.

No, the same woman. Doppelgangers.

They all smoldered until they vanished, wisps of smoky red.

"You're brazen." A woman's mellifluous voice came from everywhere at once. "I'll give you that."

A laugh came from behind. Rielle turned.

A giggle from the side. She spun.

"Not very smart, though."

An illusionist. It had to be...

Flame, Shadow—and this must be—

Phantom.

I need a shield spell. The flame cloak would work. Impervious to blades and dulling to blows. As long as her focus didn't break.

Brennan paced the room, his shoulders tense, a crease between his eyebrows. Tracking the assassin's scent, no doubt. An illusionist could hide from the ungifted, even from mages, by disguising herself and her anima as anything else. Earthsight would be useless.

But even Phantom could hardly hide from a werewolf.

"Quite the bloodhound you have there," Phantom's voice echoed from every corner. "How does a mere man develop such a skill?"

Brennan hissed. "A lapdog could smell that shit in your hair from a town away."

Silence.

A dozen curly-haired doppelgangers emerged from a corner, each wielding two sharp daggers.

Rielle called flame to her palm, burned anything that closed in while maintaining her flame cloak.

Brennan dispelled one—two—five doppelgangers.

"Here I am," Phantom's voice teased from the left.

A slash—barely evaded.

It wouldn't have cut through her flame cloak, but it would've connected.

"No, here." A laugh.

Pain radiated from her cheekbone. Rielle caught an arm and incinerated the snarling doppelganger to a cinder. Games. This was all fun and games to Phantom. Behind her, Brennan fought the last few.

"He should have died in the woods, that paladin." Sharp, clipped. "But now, he's going to die in the Red Room of Prevost Castle."

The flame cloak blazed white. Larger. The Red Room? Was someone—

How did—

A face flashed before hers. No, shimmered. A distraction spell. The woman aimed to flank her. Revealing her position, if only briefly.

Rielle conjured a stone arrow across the room behind the woman. Shot it.

A body thudded against hers. Together, they fell, the flame cloak between them. Screams and the stench of singed hair rose like a bonfire.

Tangled in burning curls, Rielle rolled her over, spelled the woman's wrists and hands to the floor with earthen shackles, and then her ankles. Dispelled the flame cloak.

The woman thrashed. Rielle pinned her, seized her throat. Felt the blood pulsing in her neck. Saw the whites of her eyes. Heard the labored breathing, thumping, pounding, drumming—

Blood hummed in her ears, the pounding, the drumming—

That face paled. Blued.

A deep breath. Smoke. Ash.

No. *No. She could be lying... He might not be...*

She pressed the arcanir of the Sodalis ring to Phantom's flesh. Eyebrows rose. The remaining doppelganger disappeared in Brennan's grip.

"How do you know about the Red Room? What are you planning?" With a glare, she conjured fire in her palm and held it over Phantom's arm. Incentive.

Phantom stared up at her, eyes wide. Grinning. Grinning. "If you hurry, his body might still be lukewarm."

Bright red draped her vision. Blood. Jon's blood. "Answer."

A twitch of her mouth. A smirk. A laugh.

Rielle tightened her grip around the woman as the fire in her burned hotter. Flesh went stiff below her.

The fire... Brighter. Hotter. Scorching.

"Rielle—" Brennan's voice.

Burn. Fingers twitched. *Burn.*

No, no, no.

I, Favrielle Amadour Lothaire, pledge myself, from now for eternity...

The fire inside banked a measure. "Answer."

Phantom stared up at her. Gaze unbroken.

Burn. Burn.

Not yet. Was Jon in danger? She'd warded the room, but—

Divine, he could be—

And she was *here*, and not—

Burn and burn and burn. Her breath short and furious, she leaned in, brought the white-hot fire of her palm to the woman's arm.

Shrieks rose with the heat as the fire ate away leather, cloth, skin, and flesh. Bulging eyes fixed upon hers, capillaries bursting, a mouth open so wide it tore and bled at the corners.

"Rielle!"

Need to go back.

Not yet.

Burn.

I declare to take freely and solemnly this oath of obedience, allegiance, piety, and diligence...

She pulled her hand away, the flame dancing along her undulating fingers. The odor of scorched flesh filled the room. Residue coated her palm. The fire had eaten the arm away to the bone.

She slowed her breathing. Divine, now was not the time to be losing ground to battle fury. "Did you send someone to the castle? Or are you just toying with me?"

Phantom raised her trembling head from the floor and spat.

Rielle slowly drew a sleeve across her face and wiped the spittle from her skin. Her flame grew, large and lively, blazing with the desire to destroy. *Destroy.* "Tell. Me."

"You will all—die—"

A hand dropped onto her shoulder.

"Rielle," Brennan said softly. "Heartseekers don't talk. You know that. Let me deal with her."

"She's not a Heartseeker." She peered at the woman beneath her, whose eyes widened for a fraction of a second. Just enough. "This is Phantom, one of the Crag Company's mage captains."

The woman flashed a thin rictus grin. Still posturing.

Or pleased... That someone was finishing the job at the castle.

Her chest tightened. *Never.*

Brennan folded his arms. Good. He knew better than to interfere.

Heat simmered inside, prickling her skin.

"I'll talk," the woman sputtered. "A Heartseeker has already killed him. Another body for the fire." Laughter bubbled in her throat and boiled. "If you let me go, your mage friend in Courdeval might be spared... more or less."

Killed... Jon... Olivia.

Grabbing the woman by the shoulders, she stared into her eyes, their veiled fear, their spite, their trux-induced mania. *Demon* mouthed on the woman's chapped lips.

Murderer. Demon...

The fire just beneath Rielle's skin licked at the surface, making her fingers glow a volcanic red. She closed her eyes and plummeted deep, down into the heat of liquid flame below the land. A drum beat in her heart, in her blood, in her head, welcoming the smoldering heat of the earth's core. Mage no more, self no more, one with the fire. Fire.

She opened her eyes. The glow of her fingers intensified to a blazing vermilion, grew brighter against those shoulders, to a voice that screamed uselessly, painfully, loudly, each note kindling for the flames, another drum to the line. The bright heat permeated every ounce of the body below until it shone like a lantern, roared like a bonfire.

More. Consume. More. A primal voice inside.

And hands—the hands that burned and burned and burned—those fading hands did not hold shoulders anymore but an ash hulk. Entirely grayed.

Her fingers spasmed.

The hulk disintegrated into dust. Specks of gray settling onto the floor, coating its stone.

Her eyes watered. She dusted off her hands, the debris puffing away. When she looked down at her palms, ash filled in and darkened the lines.

Ash.

She blinked. Ash coating little fingers and palms, lines filled in with death. With loved ones. Mama, Papa, Liam, Dominique, Viviane, Dorian...

Her hands shook.

She rubbed them, rubbed the lines, attempting to push the ash out and off, but the stain only smeared deeper into her skin. Death. The hot tremor spread up her arms, through her, into her, until she rattled like a disturbed bone chime, and the fire spread within, wild, unfettered.

She broke the threads of anima. Tried to. Again. Again.

No.

Didn't break. They didn't break.

She shivered, rubbing her blazing arms—trying to—her hands, they wouldn't move. *The ring.* Jon's ring. Jon. She twisted a finger toward the arcanir center—

To no avail. It wouldn't—

Jon.

She shook. A sickly feeling pervaded, squeezing tighter and tighter, and heaving breaths, she closed her eyes.

It couldn't happen now. It just couldn't. In the city. In the middle of the city—

Please. Someone... Anyone...

Leigh. Make peace with herself, she hadn't even—

"You must—" *Stop me.* She turned to look at Brennan, at his lined face, but it was not his face she saw anymore.

Mama, Papa...

I, Favrielle Amadour Lothaire, pledge myself, from now for eternity, to the holy Divinity of Magic.

Huddled in the corner, she shook like a leaf in the wind, watching their terrified faces. Next to her, Dominique, Viviane, and little Dorian cried.

I declare to take freely and solemnly this oath of obedience, allegiance, piety, and diligence...

Sunlight reflected off the sharp, black edge held to her brother Liam's throat, its sinister shape a stark contrast to its bright sheen.

With this oath, I state my strong and irrevocable intent.

They took him into Mama's room and slammed the door.

To pledge my magic, my life, and everything that I am to the cause, defense, honor, and further knowledge of the Divinist religion, the Divinity of Magic, and of my mages in camaraderie, to the lands under the Almighty Divine's protection...

She tried to make herself as small as possible, holding her knees in to her chest, squeezing her eyes shut and thinking of the dagger, praying the man would stop hurting Liam, that the men would let him and Mama and Papa go, and Dominique and Viviane and Dorian.

To submit to the Rule of our Holy Grand Divinus Eleftheria II, to the Conventions, Laws, and other Decrees and all statements issued in conformity with the Code of the Divinity; to the Hensarin, the Proctors, the magisters, and all high officers of the Divinity, singularly and collectively...

Liam never cried, but he cried then, and it hurt, it hurt, it hurt. A... warmth coated her skin, a fever.

To love my brothers and sisters the mages and to help them, their children, and their partners with my magic, my advice, my means and wealth, my credit, and everything in my power, and to favor them, without exception, over those who are not members of the Divinity...

Rocking back and forth, she tried to choke back a sob, but it escaped. The man said to be quiet or else. He pointed a dagger at Dominique and smiled.

"Your mother's next." He smiled, his teeth catching the light of the winter sun, sharp and shining, and how, how could he be smiling, while the other men were hurting Liam, and Mama begged, she begged, and then it felt so hot inside, the fever spreading everywhere, pushing with the pressure of a headache, and why, why had they come, why were they hurting Liam, why?

To fight the heretics and the non-believers with my example, faith, charity, and convincing arguments; and with lethality to fight the heretics and non-believers who attack the Divinity with their own...

"Rielle," said a man's voice—No, it had been Mama's.

They burned—her hands—they burned, no, no, no, and everything burned, and she couldn't stop—it wouldn't stop. Everything burned, fire hiding away everything that hurt, and Mama, she cried but she said, "I love you."

It wouldn't stop, why wouldn't it stop, why? The crying, the fire, the screaming, she couldn't look, couldn't bear to see—

To live in happiness as One with the Divine and to defend to the death others' right to live in happiness as One with the Divine...

Tears streaming down her cheeks, and the flames licking at her heels. The stench of burning flesh. The ghostly echo of death throes. The hot stone against her hands. The smoldering hallways. A nightmarish hellscape that had been home.

A girl, a murderer, a demon. Full of love, full of rage. So many loved ones in her heart, so many loved ones dead around her. Murderer. Demon. Lock her away. Leave her behind. All that she was, all that she'd been, all her love, all her rage. Leave it all. Reforged in the flames of death.

Blazing steps seared the soles of her feet, unable to carry her fast enough down the stairwell, and her eyes oozed sweltering tears caked with ash. The smoking air scorched her nostrils as her lungs inhaled breath after desperate breath, until finally, the castle spewed her out like soot onto the cold ground.

Inside, nothing remained but the trembling need to find something to hold on to. Anything.

No looking inside.

Look outside.

Help. Someone.

This oath I pronounce loudly before the mages present at this Tower. I sign it and confirm it by my blood, as I am registered to this Tower and witnessed by the mages...

A sting. Chilling. Strong arms.

Glory to the Divine.

Everything went black.

JON PACED the length of the Red Room's bedchamber. What was she thinking, venturing out alone with that monster? Brennan Karandis Marcel had no honor. There was no telling what he might do.

And I... gave her a ring and let her go. He winced, snarled, and scrubbed a hand over his face.

Her reasons had been convincing. Yes, he was poisoned with arcanir. Yes, that was a risk. Yes, she could take care of herself. And yes, the monster needed her alive.

Alive. But safe? Free? Neither was a certainty.

He glanced at the door, his hand hovering over Faithkeeper's hilt.

No. He'd given his word. She could take care of herself, and she trusted the monster.

Sighing, he raked his fingers through his hair. Something to do. He needed something to do. Anything but fuming and contemplating.

A stack of letters sat piled atop the desk. The coded letters from Flame's room at Cosette's Inn and Tavern.

After the shooting, the surgery, the duel with the monster, and—he sucked in a sharp breath—getting closer to Rielle... Terra have mercy, but last night had been—and this morning—

His lips twitched. He suppressed a grin. Decoding the letters had lost its urgency.

But there was no better time than the present. With a sigh, he pulled out the chair, dropped into it, and worked, finishing the cipher.

Then, letter by letter, line by line, he decoded them all, transcribing them onto clean pages.

...three thousand strong... led by General Gilles... Courdeval...

He set down the quill and leaned back in the chair. So Leigh had been right. Three thousand Crag Company mercenaries in the capital.

And Gilles himself.

Jon rested his palm on Faithkeeper's pommel. He'd arrest Gilles. At the earliest opportunity.

Vengeance was against the Code, and as much as he'd called it *justice*, it was merely a white scabbard for a black blade. But he wouldn't lower himself to Gilles's level by killing him. No, the Order would deal with him.

He heaved a sigh. When Rielle had killed Flame, he'd scolded her for not conducting an interrogation first. Interrogating Gilles was risky. If he somehow escaped—

He won't.

He drew in a deep breath, picked up the quill, and continued.

Heartseekers... Black Mountain Brigands... cut off movement to and from Monas Amar...

He frowned. The Black Mountain Brigands? They were bandits, highwaymen, but in recent years, they'd become better organized than most such groups. Gilles used them? Or whoever had hired Gilles had also hired the Heartseekers and the Black Mountain Brigands.

A massive effort.

A costly effort.

And if there were Heartseekers and Black Mountain Brigands surrounding Monas Amar, then he, Rielle, and Leigh would have their work cut out for them. But at least they could prepare.

He blew on the page's fresh ink and set it aside with the others. Outside the balcony window, the sky was already aflame with the intense orange-red of the setting sun.

The whole day had gone by, and Rielle still hadn't returned.

He rose, strode through the balcony doors, and looked out toward the city. The red burned hottest there, molten, bright.

Burned.

He squinted, staring far into the distance at the brightest spot. A trick of the light. Had to be.

I gave my word.

Everything was fine, or he would have heard otherwise.

A creak. The hallway door.

He turned.

A young woman flush against an invisible barrier.

He dove.

A fast blade. Two. Three.

Thud. Shatter. *Thud.* Two blades embedded in the window pane, one through the glass.

Crouched behind the bed, he peeked out to the doorway, quickly pulled back. A throwing knife flew past the bed post and thunked into the upholstered wall.

A grunt from the doorway.

The woman was wearing the duchess's violet and white. A member of the household. Could she get through the ward?

He unclipped Faithkeeper from his belt. In this room, it would be useless. Across the bed, on the nightstand, was his dagger.

If he peeked out from cover one more time, she'd throw, and he'd have a window of a few seconds to roll to the other side of the bed, grab the dagger, and take cover behind the—

Footsteps. Two light ones. On the balcony.

Warded... Was the balcony warded? Clenching a fist, he angled toward the balcony doors, shrouded in whispering white sheer panels. Whoever came in would regret it.

Platinum-white hair swept up by the wind. A blurred radius—a repulsion shield. Leigh.

He walked in through the balcony doors, knives glancing off his shield spell, then raised his arm.

A broken shriek.

Jon glanced out from cover toward the doorway, where the woman hovered in the air, whimpering, her body smaller and smaller, blood trailing from her nostrils, her mouth, her ears, her eyes—

He looked away. A crunch and a squelch ended the whimpers. A heavy thud hit hard marble.

Leigh dispelled his shield, straightened his waistcoat and overcoat, then approached. He cleared his throat and smiled. "Feeling better?"

"Much." Being alive helped. He stood, keeping a watchful eye on the doorway. "All this time, and you didn't visit until now. Should I be offended?"

Leigh shrugged. "I would have loved to see my surly former apprentice hand-feeding you and tending you like a puppy. Alas, I've grown quite fond of my jewels, and the duchess once promised to relieve me of them if I ever showed my handsome face at Prevost Castle again."

"Handsome?" Jon raised an eyebrow. "Did she really say that?"

"I do have very prominent cheekbones," Leigh drawled, raising his chin and angling his face this way and that. "She might be jealous."

"So what are you doing here?"

Leigh bowed his head, and when he looked up once more, all levity was gone. "It's Rielle. She went into fureur."

51

*S*hivering, Rielle opened her aching eyes. Her forehead pulsed with a staggering headache, but she was alive and—she shifted, sinking into a mattress—in a bed. Ghostly fingers grasped toward her anima through a gossamer net, pushing, prodding, reaching, and she shook them off.

Spiritseve draws ever near.

Anima withdrawal. She raised a trembling hand to her forehead. Her hand was bare but for Jon's Sodalis ring.

So was her arm.

And the rest of her.

She squirmed, raised the coverlet. Naked.

Warm, diffused twilight glowed through the single window, shimmering on the plain furnishings clinging to wooden walls. Nearly dark. On a small, crude table, an old bottle housed a few spikes of hooded amethyst blooms. Monkshood.

Tensing, she checked herself for injuries. What had happened? Where were her clothes?

The door opened. Brennan, bare to the waist, held a dirty curtain wrapped around his hips. His face lit up.

"You're awake." He shut the door and sat on the edge of the bed. It creaked beneath his weight.

She sat up, carefully covering herself. "Where are your clothes?" She bit her lip. "And mine, for that matter?"

With a sigh, he eyed her, and a corner of his mouth rose in a lopsided grin. "You burned them, along with everything else not immune to magic in the tunnels below Nilda's."

Of course. She'd executed Phantom, burnt the woman to ash. Her stomach rolled, bleeding a queasy malaise throughout her body.

There had been no humanity to it. No mercy.

And Jon—

Brennan glanced at the Sodalis ring. "When I grabbed you, the stone of that ring touched you—the arcanir, I assume, stopped you."

Battle fury—battle fury had taken over. No, fureur had taken over. She swallowed. *If not for the ring*—"Brennan, what have I done?"

He shrugged. "The Mélange was on fire—"

"The Mélange?" Her breath caught in her throat. An entire district? "Is everyone..."

"—but they found some hedge-witch pyromancer to put it out... who is now conveniently also a suspect." He shrugged again. "Some smugglers, Heartseekers, and that Crag Company mage captain dead. Sen'a peddlers. Maybe a few trancers... whoever was around the resonance den. But don't worry—the fire didn't even come close to the castle."

She blinked. "What?"

"Only commoners."

She clutched the covers, bunching them up at her chest. Divine, she'd gone into fureur and... killed. Perhaps even innocent people. She raked fingers into her hair, held her head.

"Look at me." Brennan rested a hand on her knee, and she raised her heavy head. "I haven't heard anything about deaths other than those in the resonance den. Those below deserved it, and those above... The fire wasn't instantaneous. They escaped."

Escaped. Yes. Maybe they escaped. She scraped fingernails through her hair. No reason to believe innocents had died. Reports would come in if they had, wouldn't they?

That was wishful thinking. No, she'd confess to Gran. Take responsibility. It was the right thing to do. The only thing.

She took a deep breath and looked around the room. "Where are we?"

"Bonny's," he replied. "It's a brothel, but it was the closest place to Nilda's I could take you, wrapped only in this curtain as you were." He nodded to the fabric around his waist.

"If I was wrapped in that curtain, what were you—"

He cracked a smug smile. "No one complained."

She shook her head, suppressing a laugh. No, they wouldn't have. She pulled the coverlet even higher, to just under her neck. "Is that everything that happened?"

He stared at the fabric over her chest. Through it. His delinquent gaze met hers. "You have nothing left to hide from me," he said with a heavy-lidded once-over, "but it's not as though I had the leisure to really *peruse*. I was preoccupied with getting us out of there before the sen'a and trux barons discovered their inventory had been destroyed. I brought us here, rented the room on my good name, and washed the... ash off both of us."

Warmth rose in her face.

Thumping from the other side of the wall interrupted the silence. *Could—*

"And no, obviously I didn't violate you."

Of course not. After all they'd just been through, it was ridiculous to even consider. She couldn't help but laugh. Nervously. "I know."

With a grin teasing his lips, he planted his hands on the bed, trapping her hips, and leaned in, less than a whisper away, his breath warm on her skin. "And when I do finally fuck you, I'll expect a lot more than you lying there like a dead fish." That grin turned wicked.

Sucking in a breath, she shoved him away. "Idiot." She held the coverlet closer, her fingers bunched up so tight in the rough cotton that they ached.

He laughed and rose, then strode to the window, where his mirth faded as he looked out. "He's here—"

"Who?" They had no clothes, no coin, and now a visitor was coming?

"—and he brought a friend."

"Who did?"

He scowled over his shoulder. "Phantom mentioned the Red Room and your commoner, so I sent a message to your former master. Better he check and make certain the bitch was lying."

She flinched. He'd written Leigh about checking Jon? Her every muscle tensed. *Breathe.* "Is he all right? Tell me. Is he?"

He lit an oil lamp on the table with a match. "Calm down, woman. He's here, isn't he?"

"Don't tell me to—" Here? Jon was here?

Footsteps thundered down the hallway's creaky floorboards, and she smoothed her hair and wiped her face but sighed at the futility. There was no way to preserve her dignity here. Jon and her former master would walk through that door, find her compromised under a blanket, hiding naked-ness and weakness beneath. Knowing she'd started a fire in the Mélange. And she couldn't do a thing to stop it.

A pronounced knock on the door, and Brennan opened it.

Jon pushed past, his cobalt-blue cloak trailing, and stormed to her side. Wild eyed, he took a knee and glided assessing hands over her covered limbs, cupped her face. "Are you hurt?"

She shook her head, clutching the coverlet tight. "Are you?"

"I'm fine." His gaze dropped to her fisted hands.

Boots clicked from the hallway. Leigh strode in, bearing a leather satchel and a bitter smile. An unfastened black master's coat hung from his shoulders over a golden-yellow brocade waistcoat, white shirt, trousers, and polished black boots. He looked every bit the magister he'd once been, power donned like perfectly tailored finery.

His dark eyes found hers, cold as shadow, making her shiver. He pressed the satchel to Brennan's chest and entered, then stopped before the bed and clasped his hands behind his back, lips pressed tight as he peered down at her through dark slits.

She winced. He didn't need to say a word. Disappointment radiated from him. She met his eyes. "Leigh—"

He squeezed his eyes shut and hissed in a breath.

The words died in her throat.

"I told you," Leigh growled, "in Bournand, that you needed to make peace with yourself." He opened his eyes. "Did you hear a word of it?"

She wanted nothing more than to leave, but with no clothes, her gaze fell to the bed, to the wild roses embroidered on the coverlet. She had heard every word. Had committed it to memory.

But making peace with herself... After her family suffering, their deaths, her culpability, how was there any way to make peace? What could possibly relieve the sins of that day?

She shuddered, shutting her eyes to the room, to their reactions. Divine, even now, she could see their faces all anew, ablaze, in pain.

"Rielle!" Leigh shouted, rumbling fury, commanding her attention. "Do you think yourself above the realities we live by? Do you think yourself exempt? Do you?"

The bed shook as he slammed his hands atop it. She started, her eyes flying open. He braced himself on the bed, his eyes wide, livid, and his face hard.

Jon put himself between her and Leigh, facing him, and they rose together, gazes locked. At his full height, his formidable presence dominated the room. "Back off, mage," he said icily.

The air between them froze, radiating a cold that made her shiver.

Fiery red played beneath Leigh's skin, flaring—but at last giving way to a banked warmth. "This can't wait any longer," he said to Jon. "Even you must see that."

"It will wait until she's dressed." Low. Firm. Jon stood, unmoving, shoulders hard, holding his gaze.

Leigh exhaled sharply, rolling his eyes, and left the room. Jon turned to Brennan, who smiled smugly, shrugged, and followed.

The tension left Jon's bearing, and he looked over his shoulder. A pile of folded clothes dropped in her lap.

"Thank—"

"We'll be out in the hall," he said, the ice still in his voice. "When you're dressed, we'll talk." He strode out of the room and shut the door.

Quiet settled in, and the pile of clothes in her lap felt weightier.

He hadn't been willing to leave her trapped, forced to take Leigh's scolding, but that gesture didn't mean he approved. It didn't mean he wasn't angry.

And why shouldn't he be? She'd nearly burned down the whole city, but for his Sodalis ring. Hearing him out—and Leigh—would be the least of her penance.

She dressed in the delicate undergarments, crisp shirt, trousers, white wool riding coat, and buttery soft boots. Every last button was fastened, and she ran her hands over the coat, smoothing out every last wrinkle.

A glass of water sat at the bedside, and she drained it. A deep breath.

Raised voices came from the hall, and a thud against the wall. A fight?

RIELLE RUSHED OUT THE DOOR.

Brennan's back was flush against the wall, Jon's arm pressed against his neck, the point of a dagger at Brennan's flesh.

He held Jon's narrowed gaze, a faint grin lingering about his mouth.

Leigh cleared his throat from behind them. "Could we please save the brawl for another time?" Behind him, a small group of women eyed the scene caused by... What, exactly?

"If this commoner can manage to control his temper." Brennan remained still, calm, smug.

Jon clenched his teeth, glaring, then with a grunt, broke away and sheathed his dagger. He stalked into the room.

"Give them a minute," Leigh said to Brennan.

Thumping came from across the hall. Again.

Brennan breathed deeply, adventurously. "I'll give them thirty. Tell me you brought coin."

Leigh tossed him a small coin purse. Of course. Brennan raised an eyebrow at her, and she nodded. He headed downstairs.

"We're not done," Leigh said to her.

"I know," she whispered.

He followed Brennan.

Eyes shut, she took a deep breath. *Make peace with myself.* She exhaled lengthily, returned to the room, and shut the door.

Jon stood at the window, his back to her. The cobalt-blue cloak hung from his shoulders over a brown leather brigandine coat. He rested his hand on his sword's pommel. There was an alertness, a rigidity to him, like a guard on watch.

She swallowed. "I'm sorry you had to come all the way here just to bring me some clothes."

He turned his head and glared at her coldly, eyes narrowed.

Not the right thing to say. Not right at all.

He drew in a long, deep breath. Some of that rigidity faded, his bearing eased, and he scrubbed a hand over his face. "When the sun had nearly set and you hadn't returned, I thought—" He looked her over with pained eyes. "You're all right?"

She nodded.

He moved in, held out his hand, and she took it. He ran a finger over the Sodalis ring. "Tell me what happened."

"First, what about you? Was there something at the castle?"

He smoothed some hair from her face. "There was an attacker camouflaged among the duchess's household, but the ward kept her out, and Leigh dealt with her."

She'd left Jon alone to be attacked. "I should have been there."

"Yes, you should have." He glared at her, but then his expression softened. "I'm sorry." He sighed. "Being poisoned... I don't like being weak. Watching you go into battle while I stayed behind. And I just... When I saw that fire..." His eyebrows drew together.

"I'm sorry," she whispered. There had been many bad choices to make, but no right one. "It shouldn't have happened."

"What did happen?"

The resonance den, the loss of the evidence, the fureur, and... It was time to tell him about Laurentine. For whatever existed between them to survive, he had to know whom he loved.

"We found the assassin," she said. "Well, Brennan did."

He narrowed his eyes again.

She cleared her throat. "It was Phantom, the third of Gilles's mage captains. I... defeated her." When he didn't reply, she said, "She didn't tell us anything, but we found a map in the sen'a hub—"

"Sen'a hub?" His hold on her hand tightened briefly.

Watching him carefully, she said, "Phantom was holed up in an old recondite mine beneath a resonance den."

"Need I ask?" His voice dropped.

"No," she replied with a faint but earnest smile. Her knees faltered under her, and when he led her to the bed, she followed and sat. He leaned against the wall, arms crossed.

"They used the old mine as a base of operations for smuggling and, well, for plotting treason. I saw a map there of sen'a distribution and a chest of letters."

"Letters?"

She smoothed a hand over the coverlet's embroidered thorns. "One mentioned advance payment—to silence dissent until they could nominate and confirm a candidate of their choosing. I think the 'candidate' is none other than the next king of Emaurria."

" 'They'? Do you have the letter?"

Eyes fixed on the nearest thorn, she shook her head. "It burned... along with everything beneath the resonance den."

He clenched a fist, knuckles whitening, the color draining from his face. If he was frustrated by the loss, she couldn't blame him. Evidence like that might have kept corruption from the throne. At least the worst of it. But now...

His gaze dropped to the ring on her thumb, and she brushed it with a fingertip.

"I succumbed to fureur," she admitted, her voice just above a whisper. "It's thanks to your ring that I didn't destroy the city." With every word, her muscles constricted.

She looked down at her hands as they shook.

He cast off from the wall and anchored himself on the bed next to her, pulled her into his embrace. In his strong arms, with her cheek pressed against his chest, she felt warm, loved, safe.

But it wasn't only her own safety she risked.

She closed her eyes. "Do you know what happened in Laurentine nine years ago?"

"Pirates... attacked the port."

If only that had been the full extent of it. She drew in a long breath and swallowed. "It was in the heart of winter, one of the coldest days of the year. The watch, huddled in the guard towers, didn't see them coming in time to keep them out.

"I was told later that a heretic aeromancer had dispersed sleeping powder over the city. I don't know." She paused. "My whole family was bound in one room, and they were about to bind me. One of the pirates was... hurting my brother, taunting my mother, and I—It triggered my éveil," she croaked.

He'd told her about his own, so he knew how they tended to be. Usually, an éveil would happen during a mildly emotional moment, just a spark and quickly noticed, controlled, celebrated. Not hers.

He'd gone still against her.

She pulled away far enough to see his face, his hold loosening around her. "It was during the trauma of the attack that I had mine. I hadn't been bound in arcanir like the known mages in my family."

The horror flooded her mind anew, but she tried to blink it away. "Magic burst from my body, setting everything—everyone—on fire. My family was bound in arcanir, and although that stopped them from using magic, it did not stop them from being..."

Burned to death by it. She hadn't the heart to finish the sentence. "I-I was trapped in my body, a prisoner, watching it all happen. The pirates, the servants, my mama, my papa, Liam, Dominique, Viviane, and Dorian—all of them, I... Everything burned."

The inhuman rage of fureur had taken over, insatiable, unstoppable, indiscriminate. Her entire family—reduced to ash. "I killed them all."

The emptiness inside widened until she could hardly breathe.

When Jon didn't immediately reply, she said, "I should have died. I managed to get out, and by some miracle, Leigh found me there, stopped me with arcanir." She wiped away the moisture on her face. "N-no one but Leigh and Brennan know, and Leigh thought it best that I keep it..."

Jon stared at her, his face void of expression and color, but he drew her in close, pressing her against him.

Her voice died in her throat. With all the blood on her hands, could he see her the same? A liar? A murderer? A demon?

52

*R*ielle knotted Jon's cloak in her hands but pushed for no answer.

At last, he drew in and released a deep breath, rubbing the back of her neck. "It wasn't your fault."

She froze. "But if I had just been stronger, if I could have controlled—"

"There was nothing you could have done. You were only a child confronted with her éveil."

"There was," she bit out, tears flowing. "It was the weakness in me that killed them. I had to be stronger, find the strength to control my own power. I couldn't be that girl, that murderer, that demon. When I am a magister, only then will I rest."

It was why she'd chosen the Tower, why she clung to it so fiercely. Years of diligence had hardened the pain into ambition to master her magic. And she would not rest until it was mastered. And safe. Used to do some small amount of good in this world through the Divinity to atone for so much bad.

"Sometimes, something triggers the memory, and... I don't know what happens exactly, but Leigh has told me that I shut down until it's over. I've learned to control it with a mantra, but... it seems that has now failed me." If the mantra no longer worked, there only remained making peace. And where to begin with that? "I can't always predict when it'll happen."

"So you push people away." He stared at the door. "Some part of you dislikes others getting close, tries to maintain a distance."

It had been her way to protect her loved ones—and herself. As long as they were safe, she was safe, and so was everyone else. "The farther those I love are from me, the safer they are." She couldn't kill them if they weren't around. "The farther you'd be, the safer—"

"How can you even say that to me?" His voice descended to deep, cold depths.

"I killed my family, our household, probably anyone who died in Laurentine that day. Capable mages. Knights. Warriors. Even the pirates." Her shoulders tensed.

"I am a paladin. You couldn't kill me with magic if you tried."

"Would that matter if an entire castle came down on you? If the ground gave way beneath your feet? For all your sigils and arcanir, would you be any less dead?"

He reached for her and turned her chin until she looked at him. "I love you. If I risk death at your side, then so be it. It is my choice."

She shook her head free and rose from the bed. His choice? He would *choose* to risk death?

No. Why would anyone choose that? Could he really—did he accept her, the deadly, dangerous, ugly true self she had so long hidden? Telling her it wasn't her fault... did he... forgive her?

She shook her head and swallowed. No. It had been nearly a decade, nine years of hiding the horror of that night, bottling it, locking it away, wearing an innocent face, a false face, one that neither asked for nor received absolution, one that hid evil. True, disgusting, unclean evil, rotting and malignant, burrowing deeper and deeper, never to see the light. Never to be cleansed. Absolved.

Had all that—all the hiding, the lies, the suppression—been for nothing? All this time?

She walked to the mirror, ignoring her throbbing head, and once there, the white wool coat faced her in the reflection.

White. Since that day, she had endeavored to only ever wear white. Clean. Pure. Innocent. Good. A reminder of who she wanted to be.

A guise hiding what she truly was. A part of her.

Her fingers assailed the buttons, trembling to undo them, and beneath —a white shirt, even whiter than the coat.

Running her hand over her face, she felt its texture and had never longed for a bath more than now, to wash away the day, the years, the rot of her life, to start anew. Her hand fell to her side.

Jon stood silent, eyebrows drawn. She had said too much.

"The fureur tonight," he whispered. "How did it happen?"

She sniffled, forcing Phantom's face before her eyes. Her spiteful words. Her threat to Jon. "She... said you were dead."

He took hold of her shoulders and peered into her eyes in the mirror, jaw clenched. He lowered his gaze, and his hands descended to hers. "I need you to understand something."

She waited.

"What is the greatest pain you can imagine?"

Imagine... She didn't have to imagine. She'd survived the greatest pain —losing her family. "Losing someone you love."

He searched her eyes, twined his fingers with hers. Slowly, he raised her fingers to his lips, pressed a kiss to her skin. A deep breath. "Do you know what would cause me the greatest pain?"

She blinked. "I—but I'm all right."

He lowered their joined hands, wrapped them around her. "Yes, you are. But this is the third time that you've nearly died when faced with the prospect of my death. Even if I *did* die, the last thing in the world I would want is for you to meet the same fate."

"I know that, but..."

"Loving someone is loving yourself as they do. Loving yourself enough to go on, if not for yourself, then for them."

She opened her mouth, then closed it.

Mama wouldn't have wanted her to succumb to fureur. To die. Neither would Papa. Nor any of her brothers or sisters.

Nor Jon.

When their loss crept in, when the fear ensnared her, it became absolute and turned to rage. A great black sky, stretching as far as the eye could see. And the sun would never rise again, shine again.

But it did rise again. It did shine again. And they wanted her to see it.

"If I were the... if you... if because of me, you—"

He squeezed her fingers gently. "I'd forgive you."

Pressure pushed against her eyes, and she drew in a deep breath. "Do you think they... do you think they would..."

"Yes. They already have, Rielle."

She closed her eyes in a futile attempt to keep the tears in.

"You hold your loved ones at a distance, but with that mantra, that distraction you use, you distance yourself from who you were, too." He kissed the side of her head. "That little girl from nine years ago, so loved by her family, didn't mean for any of that to happen. She needs to be forgiven. She needs to be held. Loved."

She turned in his embrace, wrapped her arms around him, and he held her, stroking her hair.

"Do you understand, Rielle?" Jon squeezed her, a comfort, his hold warm and familiar.

Making peace with herself. "But how do I do that? I don't... I don't know where to even begin." She covered his hand with hers, rubbing it for the feel of his skin, relishing its familiarity. Whatever lay ahead, she resolved not to let it go.

"For that, you need to look inside yourself, my love." He held her close, held her safe, and kissed her shoulder. "Forgiving yourself is never easy, but I'll be here to help you through it."

The inner glow of his eyes embraced her in its softness, surrounded her. She was his, and he was hers.

For nearly a decade, the notion of home had unsettled her, scared her, evaded her. She'd reduced Laurentine to ashes once. She didn't belong there with the ghosts of her family. She didn't belong at Tregarde or Maerleth Tainn with Brennan. She didn't belong at the Tower with the mages who hated her.

Jon's eyes reflected her, and in them, she saw where she belonged. Saw herself as he did. If she could hold on to that, perhaps battle fury couldn't rip her away into fureur. Perhaps, with his eyes, she could see the little girl she'd been. An innocent. One who needed forgiving.

And if that was so, then the answer to her fears had been the one she'd spent the last nine years pushing away.

She rested a palm on his chest, just beside his stitches. Had he recovered? She removed his cloak, then reached for the fastenings of his brigantine and undid them. With his help, she removed the armor, then unfastened his shirt enough to slip her hands toward the stitched wound. When she glanced at him for permission, he nodded.

Whispering an incantation, she healed the wound beneath her touch. She moved on to the claw marks Brennan had raked across his chest, and those healed, too. Her anima was dim, but she'd ask him for resonance later.

"All better." She smiled up at him, and he reflected the expression. Wistfully, she traced the scar on his chest with a finger. She hadn't the talent to remove it, just like the one on his neck. "You'll need a healer to remove this."

He took her hands in his, interlacing his fingers with hers. "I think I'll keep it."

He reached out to her in resonance, pulling her in, and she pulled back. A brief frisson of ecstasy, and the intense connection oscillated between them until she was filled to abundance, brightening and brilliant as the rising sun.

He wanted it, he wanted her, he wanted all of it. He knew her—every last dark corner—and loved her. If it was a dream, she would keep dreaming it as long as she could.

When she looked up at him, brimming with power and desire, it was all she could do to take his mouth with her own. His strong hands claimed her body, spun her, pinned her against the wall. Something fell to the floor with a clack—a sketch, a painting—

His mouth wanted, demanded, and she leaned into him, smoothed needy palms over his hard body.

A knock rapped at the door.

She exhaled sharply, deepened her kiss.

He broke away, heavy-lidded eyes dark. "Tonight," he whispered, and she sighed her regret.

"Tonight."

Holding her gaze, he raised her chin and brushed her lips with his, then turned away to the window. She righted her clothes as her breath slowed, then answered the door.

Leigh came in scowling, rubbing his temples. He'd worn that look before, usually when she'd acted spontaneously on missions and succeeded. Like today. An exasperated anger bubbling beneath a precarious lid.

She was in for it.

"Do you realize what could have happened? What you could have done?" The disapproving look he gave her almost made her bite her tongue.

But she nodded.

Unspeakable things could have happened today. She brought her thumb to her palm, pressed the firmness of the Sodalis ring against it.

Arms crossed, he watched her, his fingers in restless movement, drumming on his arm.

Worry. He'd always been harsh with her... Because he cared. Whether that worry surfaced as anger or whether he masked it so, she never did find out.

"I want you to live, *ma chère*," he said. "Divine knows I've tried to teach you, but maybe..." He shook his head. "Maybe I'm not—"

Brennan walked in, holding the curtain about his waist, and picked through the satchel Leigh had brought. He held up a commoner's rough-spun tunic and pants.

"Peasant's clothes?" He scowled at Leigh.

Leigh shrugged. "I never did like you."

Brennan dressed, yanking on braies, the pants, the tunic, and a pair of rawhide shoes. "Why does it always have to be—" he muttered, then sighed.

She allowed herself a small smile until she sensed Jon's intense presence behind her. A look over her shoulder, and—

Jon scowled.

A shiver rattled her spine. She should've looked away. Definitely should have looked away.

Her lips pressed together, she sobered as she turned back to Leigh. "I know it's late in coming, but I think I know how to make peace with myself."

Leigh's skeptical gaze flickered to Jon and back to her once more. "You do?"

She nodded. Soon she'd test her theory and pray it would work.

His lips curved slightly. "Good."

Brennan raised an eyebrow. "What?"

"The answer to fureur," she replied.

He shrugged.

"Tell me what happened," Leigh said, pulling a chair close and planting himself in it.

She relayed Brennan's leads—the essentials—the old recondite mine, the sen'a crates, the smugglers, the map, the letter, Phantom, the Heartseekers, and the fureur... as much as she could remember. And that Brennan was sigiled against elemental magic—which he was, for the sake of appearances—to explain how he'd survived. Jon stiffened next to her but didn't object.

"One group of nobles hired the Crag Company," Leigh said, "which in turn hired the smugglers and the Heartseekers. That group calls itself the Emaurrian Knot. Some of them are involved, if not all of them. Nearly a decade ago, when King Marcus had threatened a ban on the sen'a and trux trade, they blocked it with countermeasures. There had been whispers of another such attempt of this ban not five months ago."

"All this—over a possible law?" She shook her head. Most nobles didn't care about the law until it meant sacrifice. Usually monetary.

"How much did they stand to lose?" Jon asked.

"Millions of coronas." Leigh paused. "We'll have to rely on the Order's support to hold the capital until a new king can be crowned."

A new king. She leaned against Jon.

He tipped his head toward Leigh. "You, advocating for Order support?"

"I want the capital saved as much as you do," Leigh replied. "For good.

The two of us have better odds of actually saving someone in a siege with ground forces. Now, if we were tasked with leveling the city—"

"Three of us," Jon said.

Leigh glared at him.

"You said two."

Brennan cleared his throat. All eyes turned to him. "Two, three, whatever. Enjoy your little squabble." He tipped his head to Rielle, a mischievous smile lurking about his mouth. "I'll see you soon."

That was always the case.

He took his leave with his chin raised high, peasant clothes and all. Visible or not, the cloak of nobility always hung from a Marcel's shoulders. She sighed.

Jon's narrowed eyes traced his exit. "When do we leave?"

"Tomorrow." She just had to say goodbye to Gran first. Take responsibility for the fire.

And ask her help to break the betrothal.

53

*O*livia curled up in the corner of her cell, cloaked in darkness. The chill had taken on a biting edge, and the humidity made it almost icy. She rubbed her bare ring finger with a stiff hand.

It had been at least two days since she'd seen Anton. He had the Ring of the Archmage. And he hadn't returned, not even to bring her food, water, or a new torch to chase away the darkness. She hadn't rationed her bread or water; she'd trusted him. The dizziness and weakness had set in.

She'd trusted him, and he hadn't returned. Hadn't brought back the ring. Hadn't kept his promise.

Gilles could end whomever he wanted now. Thanks to her.

She'd failed. Failed in every sense. To stop the regicide. To perform the rite. To guard the ring. And, soon, to stay alive. The realities were too much. She closed her mind, and her heart, to them and their hurt.

Curling up tighter, she nuzzled the stone tile with her cheek. Sometimes, if she pretended, it almost felt like the walls in the palace stairwell leading to her quarters.

There, James had surprised her once during the summer and pressed her to its rough stone, his hands firm upon her. "Come with me to Vercourt, *mon rêve*," he'd whispered between kisses.

"What's in Vercourt?"

"I have some business nearby. Come with me."

A trip? They'd been inseparable for some weeks but hadn't spoken much about what lay ahead. He was married, albeit estranged from his wife, with several adult children. A prince.

Yet she—she was... What was she? "James, what am I to you?"

Eyelids drawn, he regarded her intensely, the air between them dense as he leaned in and kissed her cheek. "Friend."

Was that all? She squirmed, but he gently lay a finger to her lips, his smile broadening until she quieted.

He kissed her. "Lover."

The sea of his eyes glittered, and she fought to hold back a grin.

He lowered his mouth to her chest and, eyes closed, pressed his lips there, in the very center, his breath warm and awakening. "Dream."

Head leaned against the wall, she inhaled deeply, her hips swaying toward his of their own volition. "Dream..."

"Of the life I always see, have always seen, when I close my eyes."

A dream. Not fleeting, but deep seated, an aspiration. And yet... One couldn't marry a dream. Have children with a dream. "And what can you promise a dream?"

It was a naive question. She'd known his bonds. Royal. Matrimonial. Paternal. All unbreakable. She'd always known. But the days with James that had turned into weeks had given way to thoughts of months and years. Someday, she'd need to be more than friend, lover, dream.

He cupped her cheek and stroked her skin softly. "To respect you. To love you. To give you all that I can. To never promise anything I cannot provide."

The words were soft, warm, sincere. She covered his hand with hers. "Will that be enough?"

"That is for you to decide, *mon rêve*," he said softly. "It is not for a man to tell a dream when it is satisfied."

She'd melted into him then.

Now, in the dungeon, the cold stone floor wasn't as loving, as yielding, as warm as he, but if she pretended deeply enough, it was almost like the walls of that stairwell, and her imagination could wrap James's arms around her, whisper his words in her ear, press his lips to hers.

A sound filtered in—not the usual rush of water, drip of leaks, or skittering of rats—a light but labored rhythm. A struggling gait.

She laid her palms to the stone floor, raised herself, crawled to the bars. She pressed her cheek against the iron and squinted down the corridor. A faint light glimmered far down, blurry. A visitor.

She had heard Anton walk this corridor for a month. His steps were always soft, a little uncertain, but regular. She'd know his gait anywhere, and this wasn't it. Hardening herself against a shudder, she rose, dusted off her dirty frock, and raised her head high. If the executioner had come for her at last, she'd not give him the satisfaction of cowering fearfully, no matter what trembled within her.

The irregular steps neared, and she swallowed, trying to slow her racing heart to no success. A tired grunt accompanied the unusual gait. She tilted her head. Strange. Had the executioner been so overworked? She took a hesitant step toward the bars.

"Liv?" Deep, rasping, but it was Anton's voice. It was him. He'd returned.

Her breaths came harsh, hard. She wanted to run to the bars, throw herself against them, but she couldn't will her feet to move.

Yellow torchlight suffused the entire corridor, and despite the ache, she forced her eyes open, strained to look.

When he came into view—

Anton kept his weight off one leg and, despite bearing a tray of black bread and a waterskin, held an elbow close to his ribs. His face... One eye swollen shut. An array of sickly ochre, titian, and puce. And a faint smile with a split lip.

She gasped, ran to the bars, gripped them painfully. "You—" What had happened to him? "I—" She'd spent so much time wondering whether he'd betrayed her, and he'd been—

The faint smile broadened. He passed her the bread and water, then tipped the tray toward his face. "What, this?" He shrugged and quickly winced. "It's nothing."

"Nothing?" She huffed. Why was he minimizing this? She bit the waterskin's valve, yanked it open, and took a deep gulp. Water... She'd never take it for granted again. "I've seen rainbows with fewer colors than your face is wearing now."

He chuckled, torchlight silhouetting his form. "Clever."

"What happened?"

He bent to place the tray on the floor, his movement stiff and slow. "Would have come sooner, but couldn't move until today. Told another merc to bring you food and water, but"—he looked her over with his one available eye—"clearly she didn't."

Clearly. "Never mind that. What happened?"

He heaved a sigh. "Followed our plan. Got caught after trying to open the Lunar Chamber. I was trying to sneak past the guard after, but he woke." He rubbed his neck. " 'You picking my pocket?' he asked me. He assumed. Didn't correct him. And this"—he glanced down—"is justice."

Trying to do her bidding, he'd gotten himself hurt. Could have been killed. She took a deep breath and exhaled slowly. No, he had wanted to do this, too. She alone couldn't bear the burden of guilt. "Did you do it?"

"Pick his pocket?" Anton smiled and crossed his arms. "Nah. Is that what you think of me, Liv? A mere pickpocket, after all we've shared?" He winked.

The bastard was teasing her. She waved him off. "No, you ninny. The Lunar Chamber."

" 'Ninny'? 'Ninny'!" He scoffed. "After all I've done—"

"Anton—"

He leaned in to the bars, his sandy-colored hair catching the light of the torch. "Yes," he whispered, gripping them, his battered face close enough to hers for his answer to breeze onto her skin. "Did everything you asked. Wedged a whetstone there, between the doors. Should hold."

He took her hand in his, urged it between the bars. His skin was warm. Callused. She shivered, struggling to remember the last time anyone had touched her but to hurt her.

James.

Anton pressed something into her palm, gingerly handling her broken fingers to curl closed. "Did you miss me?"

Against her own reluctance, she smiled anyway. "I missed sustenance."

"One and the same by now?" Grinning, he covered her hand, enshrined it between his warm, callused palms, and gently guided it back to her.

She swallowed. He'd become her only friend here, the one person who came without demands or harm. She peered at her palm.

The Ring of the Archmage. Returned. She'd been right to trust him.

Eyes shadowed, he gripped the bars, clenching them tightly. "It's not going well with His Highness."

What? "It's not... How do you know?"

Anton shook his head slowly. "It's better if you don't know, but just... prepare yourself. He doesn't have much time left."

"Then... Then let's find a mage to perform the rite, and—" Pointless.

Even if they found a mage to perform the rite, there was no way for her to escape her cell and save James. In her heart, she'd always known it, hadn't she? Hope had been a distant dream, but she'd dreamed it, despite all she'd known, all that the world around her had been shouting in her reluctant ear.

James had never promised her forever. But what had he said? That it was not for a man to tell a dream when it was satisfied?

But Gilles would. He'd decide when her dream with James would come to an end. And here, behind these bars, she couldn't fight to keep it alive. To keep him alive.

"I'm sorry." Anton bowed his head, his light locks shrouding his eye. "Told you I had a lead on a healer who might do us that favor. Well, now I have a reason to visit her." He gestured to his array of bruises and flashed a brief smile. "Think it'll all go well." The words were bright, but he still clenched the bars.

Hoping to distract her, to cheer her up?

She forced a smile. "Yes, it will. I'm sure it will." It had to.

He pulled away, then bent stiffly to retrieve the tray. "Hopefully, I'll be able to return tomorrow with some answers."

Would those answers come as expensively as opening the doors to the Lunar Chamber? She held the ring tightly, ignoring the ache of her hand. "Try not to get yourself killed."

He flashed her a quick smile. "I won't, Liv. Promise."

She watched him leave until his form passed away into the darkness, and the unnaturally quiet isolation returned, her constant companion.

This was the last risk he had to take. If they managed to convince a mage to perform the rite, at least Emaurria's people would be safe. And, after that, so would he.

And if they failed—if they failed...

She shook her head.

It would go well.

It had to.

54

*R*ielle shifted on the sofa, its seat hard and uncomfortable. She'd never been skilled at drawing, but as she glanced over Gran's work, it was obvious that the deficiency hadn't descended from the Auvray branch of the family: the wolf catching the doe depicted in Gran's drawing was vivid.

"Brennan was right to do as he did." Gran leaned back and studied her work.

Rielle shook her head and leaned forward. "Surely you don't mean that. I put the entire city at risk. I need to be held accountable. And the hedge-witch pyromancer who extinguished the fire needs to be cleared of suspicion and rewarded." If innocent people had been hurt, their recovery was her responsibility. If they'd lost their homes or belongings. Their fears. Their panic. If there were consequences from the Connétablie or the Divinity, she would face them. As she should. No more secrets. No more lies. No more regrets.

"Everything has been taken care of, child. Master Blanc has tended the injured personally. I have financed the rebuilding of homes and replacement of possessions. All will be as it was."

Warmth washed through her. Gran had money enough to cover the victims' losses... but no money would ever make them whole. To replace their keepsakes and mementos, their bottles of immortelle and Sodalis rings. "But it can't be. *I* won't be the—"

Gran took a lengthy breath. "There is no need to disgrace yourself. You are already punishing yourself quite ably."

"Disgrace myself?" She straightened. "I don't care about—"

"But I do." Gran resumed her work, shading in shadows. "Is my duchy better served when I am strong and trusted, or when I and my relations are dangerous and doubted?"

Rielle opened her mouth, but no words emerged. Dangerous and doubted. She was a liability, best kept quiet and managed. Her actions could reflect poorly on Gran, in her duties as duchess...

In her political relations.

In her business negotiations.

In all matters.

Could. No, they probably already had. She winced. "Gran, I'm sorry. I know I haven't had an ideal, illustrious few years..." She pressed her hand to her cheek. "*Decade.* And what I've done can't have—"

Gran turned away from her drawing, set down her burnt-umber chalk, and sat next to Rielle on the sofa. "Is that what you think? This is all about my reputation?"

"No, but—"

Gran took her hand. "What good will shouting the truth from the rooftops do?"

Her chest ached, a knot pulling tighter.

"You believe it will ease your burden. That their judgment and ire will allow you to punish yourself less for your flaws," Gran said softly.

Wouldn't it?

"But there is only one way to ease a burden. Set it down."

Rielle's hand instinctively went to her chest, where the solitary vial of king's blood she needed for the Moonlit Rite lay just beneath the velvet of her gown on a silver chain, along with her signet ring. "Walk away?"

Gran nodded. "You have no sensible reason to continue tempting fate by doing fieldwork for the Divinity. Retire to a quiet life. A safe life. For yourself, and others."

Rielle stood from the sofa, rubbed her forehead. Retiring, locking herself away, wasn't the best she could offer the world.

She paced to the windows. So many had been consumed by her power. Innocents, criminals, loved ones, strangers.

But destruction wasn't the whole of her gift. Outside, the smoke had cleared, and somewhere to the south was Olivia. She palmed the cool glass. Today it was Olivia, but there was always a use for her magic. A good use, a worthy end, helping someone in ways others couldn't. The way Leigh had helped her after the burning of Laurentine.

"I still have work to do," she whispered.

"Sometimes, the best thing you can do is nothing at all." A soft voice. A loving voice.

She squeezed her eyes shut. "Is that why I have magic? Why I was born to this world? For nothing at all?"

"Child—"

Rielle straightened, every bone and muscle in perfect posture, and raised her chin. There were more choices in this world than destruction and nothing. There had to be. Difficult, uncomfortable choices. Challenging ones. Paths full of stones and brambles, breaks and scars, that led somewhere worth going. She turned back to Gran, whose watery gaze closed around her. "There's something more for me, Gran. There has to be."

"Will you marry Brennan?"

Her palm found the wall. Then her back did. "Do you wish me to, Gran?"

Gran gestured to the space next to her on the sofa, and Rielle sat. "Someday, and it may not be today or tomorrow, you might change your mind. You might wish for something this life you lead can't give you. Stability, children, legacy. If you do not start planning it now, you will regret its lack someday. Take it from an old woman—nothing brings me more happiness now than my children, grandchildren, and great-grandchildren." She reached out to brush the back of her fingers lightly against Rielle's cheek. "And Brennan, despite his faults, can offer you not only a family but the kind of stability a life at the Divinity cannot."

A life at the Divinity, with a commoner as her lover. "I don't love Brennan the way—"

"The way that a woman loves a man?" Gran offered airily. "Love is what lovers are for. Even Queen Alexandrie was rumored to have lovers. Love is transient—it waxes and wanes. A marriage must be made to endure. The secret to a good marriage for us nobles is not love, but a combination of respect, trust, and communication."

She and Brennan lacked those things. Severely. But there was no explaining that to Gran, not without mention of what had happened at Tregarde. *I'd rather pull my own teeth.*

And how could one separate love and marriage—? "Gran, it's not only a lack of love on my part, but outright animosity on his. You witnessed how Brennan treated me at dinner. Sometimes it is worse."

Gran folded her hands together. "You see animosity, child, but for a man to be so hostile to a woman requires animus. Intense passion that would not exist but for frustrated love."

Love? She choked back a gasp.

Brennan needed her and rued that need, but Gran couldn't know about the bond. Perhaps, to her, it looked like frustrated love.

Yet... Long before she'd told Brennan how to break the curse, he'd borne that animosity toward her. When she'd rejected him at the Tower, he'd been so cold, so hostile, and hurtful beyond her wildest nightmares. Could that have been, as Gran said, frustrated love?

And if it was so then, was it possible that now—

She shook her head. "If this is how he shows his 'love' now, Gran, then if we're married, I fear I won't survive any escalation." When Gran didn't immediately reply, she added, "He may love me, he may not—but I deserve better than to be mistreated, manipulated, hated, no matter what he's feeling. I will never accept becoming a sacrifice to him, to endure his frustrations, to tolerate suffering as though his emotional wellbeing were my responsibility."

The doe in Gran's drawing seemed to come alive, her gleaming eyes fixed upon the wolf with its teeth buried in her hind leg. Gran lowered her gaze.

"I can't live agonizing over my every step, walking the edge of a cliff. But that is my life, Gran. And it is terrifying." After rescuing Olivia, she'd be at the Divinity's mercy. And likely end up at the bottom of that fall.

Gran looked from the drawing to her, shook her head, and pulled her into an embrace. Rielle laid her head in Gran's lap and closed her eyes as Gran stroked her hair softly. It was fifteen years ago, and she was a little girl in this very room, napping in Gran's lap while Mama and Grand-Mère Geneviève laughed and sketched.

"I won't condemn you to that fate, child, but neither will I act hastily. There are few unbetrothed suitors of worth for a noblewoman of your wealth and title, and it will be difficult to make a proper match. Men at Brennan's age can be capricious, but perhaps he may yet surprise you." A pensive silence lingered while Gran smoothed her curls. "A compromise, then. If, by the end of the summer, you remain unconvinced about Brennan, I will do all in my power to dissolve the betrothal."

Rielle opened her eyes. "You would do that?"

"Child, there is nothing I would not do for your sake."

And that was the world. "I love you, Gran."

"I love you, too." Gran gave her shoulder a squeeze.

She wouldn't proclaim her guilt about the fire in the Mélange, but

Gran was right. The way to relieve her burden was to set it down. And she could do that by ensuring she never succumbed to fureur again.

It was time to test whether she could truly resolve it once and for all. Jon had promised to help rescue Olivia, and that would mean he'd be by her side in Courdeval—over six feet of arcanir and the man who loved her to stop her fureur if necessary. The perfect chance.

Just a few days. A few days more.

AFTER THEIR GOODBYES, Rielle and Jon made their way across the city to The Copper Flagon. They needed to collect Leigh and finalize their plan for breaching Courdeval. It was finally time. *We're coming, Olivia. Just hold on a little longer.*

After the hostler took their horses, Jon opened the door.

Leigh's wide eyes greeted them from the dining area. "Well, well, such distinguished personages! To what do I owe the honor?" He threw back an ale stein and drained it. Dressed in an open, black master-mage coat over a quilted green cotton doublet and trousers, he looked comfortable, if not assimilated with the clientele.

She headed straight for the table, shedding her white cloak, and pulled out a chair. "Nice to see you, too, Leigh."

He eyed her. "Learned your lesson?"

"Working on it." She pressed her lips together.

Jon joined them, his armor clattering as he settled into the chair. Given the letters, it was best to take no chances on the road.

"All healed?" Leigh asked.

"Better than ever." Jon helped himself to some rye bread laid out on a tray between them and buttered it.

She nodded to the staircase. "Shall we?"

Leigh rose while Jon stuffed the bread in his mouth, and then he led them up a flight of creaky stairs, to the end of the hall, and into a room. The packs were piled near the door, and on the solitary table in the room, a map lay sprawled, a large candle anchoring its upper right-hand corner.

Jon moved to the table's edge. He traced a winding path on the parchment with a finger. "This route takes us directly through bandit territory." He looked over his shoulder at them. "The Black Mountain Brigands run the area east of the Kingsroad there, and they're on the Crag's payroll—we have the letters to prove it. Just a few miles west, and we should avoid them."

She pulled the stack of letters from her satchel and handed them to Leigh.

He riffled through them and sniffed. "Why waste the time?"

Jon turned to him with a hand on his sword's pommel. "The risk of battle and the time it would take to regroup. I've planned on quick battle before and found myself"—he eyed Rielle—"thwarted."

The Tower. She suppressed a laugh.

Nevertheless. "We can't risk late arrival at the capital," she replied. "We will have to assume the risk and rely on healing for recovery, arcanir poison notwithstanding."

Jon crossed his arms and eyed the map with a sigh. "Very well."

"It is quite likely that you won't need to draw your sword at all. Two mages can wipe out an army. What hope do a few bandits have?" Leigh shrugged. "Do we have a way in?"

"Yes," she said. "I have made contact with the resistance in Courdeval, mainly the Black Rose. They will provide a diversion for a few hours on the south side of the city."

"Can they be trusted?" Leigh set down the letters.

"They want the Crag out as much as we do." Mentioning Nicolette's involvement—and thus explaining how someone, namely Brennan, had made it over the city walls—was out of the question. She moved to the map and pointed to Courdeval's northeastern gate, where they would enter. "We'll come in here. We'll have to extinguish the light at the gate tower to signal the Black Rose." Moving her finger to the southeastern gate, she said, "Here, in the Coquelicot District, the Black Rose will stage a diversion, which will help us cross the Violette District, Alcea, Orchidée, then breach the citadel's northern gate to enter Azalée and fight our way to the palace."

"We'll just 'breach the citadel's northern gate'?" Jon raised an eyebrow.

She and Leigh exchanged a smile.

Jon drew in a long breath. "Terra have mercy. Tell me how."

"The black arts are mighty." With a grin, she pointed to the palace's southeastern service entrance. "That's our way into Trèstellan Palace." She thumbed through the maps until she found the palace's fourth-floor plan. Tapping the Archmage's study, she glanced from Jon to Leigh. "Here are Olivia's quarters... We can check there for anything related to the rite."

"And the Lunar Chamber?" Leigh's eyes searched the map.

She found the maps of the palace's lower levels and traced the edges of a large room, separated from the dungeon by a sealed space. "Here. I'll perform the rite, then we'll break through these sealed chambers"—she indicated them on the map—"and make our way to the dungeon. Once we find Olivia and release the Black Rose prisoners, we have a few exits." She pointed to two staircases, an entrance to the catacombs, and three sewer grates.

"Sewers?" Leigh shuddered. "It won't come to that."

"It might," she replied.

"It shouldn't," Jon said. "Once I reach Monas Amar, I'll convince the Paladin Grand Cordon to seize the opportunity provided by the Black Rose's diversion. It's the kind they will have been waiting for."

"It's as good a plan as we'll get." She anchored her hands on her hips, staring at the dungeon on the map. *Olivia, please be all right.*

Leigh pushed away from the door. He went to the table and rolled up the map with the letters. "Let's go."

Downstairs, Leigh paid the innkeeper, picked up one of the packs, and left. She and Jon grabbed the remaining bags and headed for the stable.

Brennan lounged on a bale of hay in full black leathers, his eyes flitting up to hers and hooding as he grinned. She threw down her bags and glared at him.

Jon took her arm and leaned in close to her ear. "What is he doing here?"

"We're about to find out." She pulled away and approached Brennan. "You could have found us inside."

Brennan huffed a half-laugh and spread out his arms. "I'm quite comfortable here with the rest of the beasts."

Leigh pushed his way past Jon. "What are *you* doing here?"

Brennan dismounted the hay bale in a fluid movement. "I'll be joining you," he answered, his voice matter of fact.

"No," Leigh said.

She glared at him. That was her *no* to say.

"Marquise Laurentine is my fiancée," Brennan said firmly. "If I allowed her to enter a besieged city without my support, my father would raise an uproar the likes of which the realm has never heard... the brunt of which *I* would be bearing"—he looked Leigh up and down—"and sharing with Her Excellency, the Grand Divinus."

"Fuck the Grand Divinus," Leigh hissed.

Brennan's eyes narrowed even as he smiled, but she shook her head at him. If he so much as touched Leigh, all bets were off.

Brennan's smile widened as he clasped his hands behind his back and straightened his posture, drawing himself up to his full height. "I'm a skilled fighter."

Leigh crossed his arms. "You're no mage, you have no weapons—"

"I *am* the weapon." Brennan locked eyes with him. "I have trained with a Faris grandmaster of hand-to-hand combat since early childhood."

House Marcel bred expert fencers, including Brennan, but the duke had employed a hand-to-hand combat master from Sonbahar for well over a decade.

Leigh turned to her. "And you're all right with this? After all he's done to you?"

There it was. Out in the open.

Brennan, to his credit, pursed his lips in what seemed a valiant attempt to beat back a proud grin.

Something had changed in Brennan after his duel with Jon, after she'd... stopped him. Had he accepted that he could force nothing from her? Had he finally resolved to befriend her?

She glanced at Jon.

He held her gaze for a blazing moment, then at last grunted his displeasure and looked away.

"Yes." The period of utter stillness after her answer may have lasted a decade in the span of a minute. A horse snorted a few feet away in one of the stalls.

Leigh rolled his eyes but shrugged. "Very well."

She caught sight of her horse in the farthest stall, cleared her throat, and strode to it. She opened the half-door, reached for a dandy brush and, wishing to vanish, did her best to make it come true as she brushed her mare. More for herself than the horse, but she received no complaints.

"If he so much as looks at her wrong, I will gut him." Barely audible, Jon spoke several feet away.

She froze, her hold on the brush loosening.

"Personally, I'd prefer a force-magic spell crushing him to a fine paste," Leigh retorted. "But your way's good, too."

Jon exhaled a deep, calm breath. The unmistakable heavy footfalls of his booted heels followed. She raised her head just high enough to spy him fuming. He hadn't tried to impose his will on her, but he needed to cool off.

"Folly, isn't it?"

She swung her head toward the sound.

Brennan crouched in the corner of the stall. His ability to move about in stealth never failed to amaze.

"Nothing to do with you, of course," she hissed, returning to her task.

He examined his nails. "I wanted to tell them that they're so obsessed with the fifteen minutes of pleasure you gave me three years ago when what they really should be doing is trading stories with each other. Now *that* would be cause for obsession."

The brush slipped from her hand. She tried to catch it only to bounce it farther away. Clenching her teeth, she glared at him before fetching it. She'd rather fight a hundred duels than listen to even one second of the nightmarish discussion he described.

"What?" he asked quietly, loosening his shoulders. "I knew you wouldn't go for it, so clearly, I abstained."

She seized the brush and picked the straw out of its bristles. The insuperable barrier between Jon and Leigh about their romantic experiences with her was a gift from the Divine. "Why are you here, Brennan?"

He scoffed. "You know why."

She tossed aside the last of the straw, and he grasped her hand. Held it until the searing heat of his contact forced her eyes to his. "I'm here for *you*, Rielle," he said, his voice so quiet she wasn't sure she'd heard correctly.

She pulled her hand away and returned the brush to its place. "What new trick is this?"

"No trick. I want to ensure you make it to the other side of this, and not just because I want this curse broken. I want to make amends."

"You don't mean that," she whispered.

"I do. I want to earn your forgiveness, if I can."

Forgiveness? She shook her head. Brennan thrived on bitterness. Could any man who'd enjoyed hurting someone for so long have a change of heart like this? She was a fool for even wondering. Playing right into his hands. Paws.

"You're lying." She rose and coaxed her mare out of the stall.

He sidled up next to her.

"Would I lie to you?" he asked, his voice a lingering caress as he moved past.

" 'You didn't think I meant all that, did you?' " She snarled his own words from Tregarde back at him.

His upper lip stiffened. "One time. Am I never to get another chance?"

"Another chance at what?" Her hands shook; she fisted them. *At marriage? At love? Never.* She'd already given him two, and he'd squandered both.

"At peace between us," he hissed, invading her space. "I know I hurt you. I'm sorry. Let me try to make it up to you." He brimmed with tension, coiled tightly beneath his skin.

Make it up... If he wanted peace—whether real or false—it was better than cruelty. She wouldn't turn him away. But she wouldn't trust him entirely either. "Fine."

The tension dissipated from him in waves as he relaxed. "Good. Let's be friends, Rielle."

Kind words from him had turned bitter far too often. But maybe his intentions were sincere this time. Maybe...

Leigh walked his horse out of the stable.

With a final glance toward her so-called friend, she followed and paused near Jon. His eyes caught hers just as he managed to get his horse out.

"Are you all right?" he asked, his voice low, still rumbling.

She slumped her shoulders. "Are you?"

He inhaled deeply, as if the intake of air were panacea to violence. Perhaps it was.

"I can handle myself." She could feel his eyes on her, but she didn't have the heart to meet them.

He stroked her cheek softly. "You don't have to, not alone. Not anymore."

Together. They would face the world together. She looked up at him, and slowly, he leaned in and kissed her, his lips playing softly against hers. His gloved fingers moved from her cheek to cradle her head, inviting her closer.

She surrendered to him, let him pull her in as his back met the stall's wall. Deep breath after deep breath, never enough. The warmth, the dizziness of him, the sting of arcanir—His hand wandered lower, pressing into the small of her back, pulling her close. How she wished to feel his body against hers again, lamenting all between them.

His eyes narrowed at something over her shoulder.

"This is really titillating, but I need to get by." Brennan's voice.

She broke away. Brennan stood behind her white mare and held the reins of a dappled gray destrier. The massive horse bobbed its head and tapped the ground with an anxious foreleg.

She could do nothing but nod and lead her mare out of the way, but Jon stepped in front of Brennan and eyed him coolly.

"Commoner," Brennan said dismissively.

"Monster." Jon alighted upon the word with a grim twist of his lips that could no longer be called a grin. He took a bold step forward and leaned in. "If you so much as *look* at her wrong, I will have your head."

Brennan remained rigid. Controlled. "It won't come to that. My betrothed and I have an understanding."

She fought back a shiver.

Jon blew out an amused breath, but in an instant, his face turned hard, unforgiving. He held Brennan's impassive gaze for a moment longer, then turned his horse aside.

Wordlessly, Brennan led his destrier past and only gave her a passing glance, calm and unaffected. Who was this Brennan who held his tongue? Well, mostly?

Jon approached her, and together they exited the stable. Brennan had tried to kill him only a few days ago. If Jon needed time and some coarse words, then she wouldn't complain. And Brennan had earned a lot worse.

They mounted their horses and set a course for Melain's southern gate and their perfectly planned route.

55

*J*on scanned the horizon as he headed into the woods. Empty. Quiet. The day's ride along the outskirts of the Forest of the Hart had been long and uneventful, made bitter by the late-autumn chill. And the monster that stalked Rielle.

Brennan pitched the tents. Completely unobjectionable. She watched, too, casting a wary eye from time to time while she laid the camp wards. If she didn't trust him, good. She shouldn't.

Even now, Faithkeeper ached to be drawn. His hand hovered over the hilt, but he curled his fingers.

A low babbling hum came from nearby. The quiet flow of the stream. He took a deep breath. And then another. And then another. And headed deeper into the woods. No campfire yet. No firewood. Something to do.

He wove through the tangled shrubs and thorny bushes of the dense mixed-oak forest, searching the ground for hardwood, so their fire would burn long tonight to combat the ever more biting cold.

He passed Rielle, who dispelled her earthsight and gave him a soft smile. A thin smile. He knew that look—a brave veil over doubts. All day, she'd been unusually quiet and positioned herself carefully between him and Brennan; she didn't trust him to control his temper.

Then again, after Melain, he'd given her little reason to.

He nodded to her but didn't disturb her as she warded. Later, in the relative privacy of their tent, they'd talk.

A sizable oak branch, thicker than his arm, lay split not far from the stream, where Leigh had brought the horses. Leigh glanced over his shoulder. "You've been quiet."

Not for lack of words. Jon crouched and splashed his face. Terra have mercy, it was bone cold. He shook off the chill. "In Bournand, when you told me about Tregarde... You could have mentioned his fiancée was Rielle."

Leigh rubbed his horse's back pensively. "Did it matter?"

Had he known...

Had he known, he would have still fallen for her. Perhaps there were men who believed they could decide whether or not to love a woman. Foolish men. "No, I suppose it didn't."

Leigh crouched, cupped his hands, and brought some water to his mouth. He shook out his hands and stood. "I'm glad you two worked it out."

"Glad?" Jon arched a brow. "Then what was all that 'she'll rip your heart out' business?"

Leigh patted him on the back. "Oh, she *will* rip your heart out. Only it's not yours I care about; it's hers."

"Touching," he replied. "For you, anyway." With a nod to a grinning Leigh, he crossed the stream toward the split oak branch. He grabbed both pieces and dragged them back while the setting sun shined its farewell rays. The sky darkened.

His and Rielle's plans relied on many variables, too many to rest comfortably. What if the worst happened? He gritted his teeth. What if the Divinity excommunicated her, he couldn't get a knighthood, and the new king didn't break her engagement? Where would that leave them?

Stolen moments in dark corners. If she had to marry another man, if she had to marry *that* man, it was stolen moments in dark corners or nothing. Dishonor or despair.

He left the firewood and headed back into the woods for more. In his lifetime, he'd been struck by despair over and over, but he'd defended. Despair could only land a fatal blow if allowed. His parents had abandoned him. His best friend had been murdered. He'd been discharged from the only family he'd ever known. All defended. He was still standing.

But now the only woman he'd ever loved could be wed to another man.

If Most Holy Terra wouldn't spare him this strike, his perpetual duel with despair would continue. But it was no longer only himself he defended. Rielle marrying *that* man wouldn't only destroy him; it would destroy her, too. Never seeing her smile again, leaving her to the whims of that monster...

He shook his head and broke off another oak branch. If his continued love of her, in secret and in dark, in adultery and in dishonor, brought her some measure of joy... could he withstand the pain and dishonor? If that were the only way? A shadow lover...

Foliage crunched softly behind him. He turned, his arms full of small beech and oak branches.

Rielle bent and retrieved one herself, a candlelight spell hovering above her, setting her braided golden hair aglow. As she straightened, she smiled and tipped her chin toward his bundle. "You put me to shame."

He bridged the space between them and kissed her softly, the contact of his armor against her hand dispelling the candlelight spell. "It's been a long day of riding. Why don't you rest at camp and let me finish up here?"

"Rest?" She pursed her lips, then looked away. "You know, don't you?"

After she'd grimaced her way through the entire ride today and hurriedly brewed raspberry-leaf tea whenever they'd stopped, even a paladin would know it was her moonbleed.

For the past four days and nights, they'd chased pleasure at every available opportunity. Making it through the day without falling asleep and out of the saddle was a wonder, having slept so little. And still, he desired her, to see her face tighten, to hear her primal cries, to feel her fingers press into his flesh, her sated body curl into his. He would always desire her.

She softly stroked an oak branch in the bundle he held. "Not the greatest timing."

"We may not survive," he teased.

"Dreadful, isn't it?" she asked, a soft lilt in her voice. A smile. "Disappointed?"

Desire wasn't everything. He tossed aside the bundle of wood and drew her in, kissing her full on the mouth once more, savoring her softness, her nearness, *her*. "Like blessed water to sun-parched lips."

"What?"

From the Code of the Paladin. A verse about Terra's grace. "You are to me as blessed water to sun-parched lips. You could never disappoint."

Rising on her toes, she kissed him once more, a soft hand tracing along his jaw. "Neither could you."

Give me a lifetime, and I'll prove it.

She pulled away and retrieved some of the firewood he'd dropped. He joined her. Together, they made their way back to camp and built the fire.

Leigh read a book while Brennan, if the lamplight in his tent was any indication, had elected to isolate himself. He'd pitched his tent and theirs on opposite ends of the camp.

A courtesy? Jon mulled it over as he boiled, then fried, some of the salt pork they'd packed in Melain. Brennan had minded his tongue and kept his peace since the duel. But whatever he was doing, it couldn't be as genuine as he pretended.

Still, if he could fall in line to keep Rielle safe, then a truce was tolerable... for her sake. If not complete trust.

He fixed a plate for himself and Rielle and joined her in the tent, where she lay on her belly, frowning over a tome. "That good?"

She looked up, and her face brightened. "My Old Emaurrian is rusty, that's all." She held out her hands, and he turned over the plates.

He began unfastening his gauntlets. "What's it about?"

"A history of Trèstellan. I asked Leigh for help, but he can't be bothered. I wish Olivia were here." She sighed, her breath abandoning her and leaving her slumped. "Well, for many reasons more important than this."

"We'll find Olivia. Have faith." He removed the rest of his armor and joined her.

She offered him that thin smile again, then nodded and brightened. "I know that. I do. But it's good to hear you say it. More real somehow."

They ate their fill, then lay back, watching the firelight skirmish with the shadows on the tent's canvas. He curled an arm around her and held her close. She wriggled closer and nuzzled his bicep.

With her in his arms, the bleak possibilities that might await them seemed more distant than ever. But if the unthinkable happened, forcing her to marry *that* man...

He had sacrificed everything to be with her. If he had to sacrifice more to stay by her side, he would. No matter how much it hurt. Those stolen moments would still be blessed, perhaps all the more so in their scarcity. And the rest... his pain, dishonor, anguish, loneliness... The rest wouldn't matter.

But surely it would never come to that.

Would it?

AT THE SOUND OF FOOTSTEPS, Olivia smiled and sat up. Anton had arranged to meet with that healer the night before. Maybe they'd finally found their ritual mage for the Moonlit Rite. She crawled over to the bars and peeked out for the familiar glow of torchlight.

And it was there, down at the far end of the corridor.

Good news. It was going to be good news.

Leaning against the bars, she waited, listening to the set of steps echoing.

No—*two* sets of steps. Had Anton brought the healer? Risky of him. She stilled and focused on the sounds. Soft, light but sure steps. And the other—a regular beat. Wide, large steps. Purposeful. Confident. Arrogant.

Not Anton.

Gilles.

A shiver spiked up her spine, and she scrambled to her feet, backing up to the walls. Divine, if Gilles was here—

Her breaths turned ragged, her mind reeled with thoughts of plans revealed, the Moonlit Rite thwarted, punishments to follow—and Divine help her, she'd endangered not just herself, but Anton, too.

She pressed a palm to the wall, rubbing the stone grain into her skin. Calm down—she had to calm down. Perhaps Gilles didn't know anything. He might have come to gloat again... Or to coax free some answers, as he had before, about Rielle.

Soon, the lighter set of steps faded—stopped. Only the arrogant set remained.

She stared at the bars and braced herself.

Gilles strode into her field of vision, six feet of muscle clad in black-market arcanir plate, his silver-trimmed black cloak flaring behind, and he set a torch nearby. He bore his five-foot flambard sheathed at his side and...

A box.

She cringed and swallowed the lump in her throat.

Another box.

Expressionless, he proceeded to unlock the cell door, set down the box, then strolled back through and locked it once more. He set off back toward the end of the corridor.

Just like that, he was going to leave? No word, no answers, no taunting? Where was Anton? Had Gilles done something to him? And the general was going to just stroll away?

She stumbled forward. "Where's my guard?" she blurted out.

Gilles slowed to a stop, let his head fall back, eyes closed. A corner of his mouth curled upward. "That lanky fellow?" He tilted his head and looked at her, his eyes cold and empty but for his usual amused glimmer. "I needed a liaison to accompany my sigilist, and he intimately knew the group with which I needed him to liaise."

Gilles had a sigilist? Recondite was tightly controlled by the Order and the Divinity, as were the tools and knowledge of sigilists. How had he found a rare defector?

And group? What group?

All he'd told her over the past month... The only group she could think of—

The Black Mountain Brigands. Anton had said he'd been a member before joining up with the Free Companies, a robber until the group had changed... And that he'd hated it.

Had Gilles sent him there to prevent anyone from performing the Moonlit Rite? Or as a punishment? She stopped herself from biting her lip. She'd die before letting Gilles know she feared for Anton's safety. If Gilles detected anything more than a guard–prisoner relationship, Anton—and their whole plan—would be in danger.

Gilles smirked. "Why? Have you taken a liking to him?" He turned toward the bars and grabbed them, leaned in. "After His Highness, a lowlife such as he would be beneath you." He sneered, and although he sobered, an ill glint shone in his narrowed eye.

"Because I've appreciated the food and water."

Gilles looked her over with a calculating eye. "I see you've been well fed."

Considering the guard before Anton, that likelihood must have been rare. Although she kept her face a stone mask, she scrambled for explanation. "Yes, well, he exacted his price."

Gilles peered down at her through the bars, his stare appraising. "Between the bars? Truly?" He leaned away. "Few can claim to have enjoyed such favors from a prince's mistress."

Prince's mistress. Of course. Even after all she'd accomplished, history would see her as a prince's mistress and no more.

But the general seemed to have accepted her explanation. At least Anton wouldn't suffer for the kindness he'd shown her.

She mustered her most nonchalant shrug. "Even a prince's mistress will do what she must to survive."

Gilles crossed his arms. "People like us, Lady Sabeyon, no matter how high we ascend to equal those gods among men, we never quite leave behind the streets, do we? We do what we must. And we survive."

She forced a grin—a predatory grin. "Is that a promise?"

He laughed. "I wish it were so, but you had the grave misfortune of finding yourself in my path, Lady Sabeyon, and of the two of us, I am the better survivor."

She smirked. "They must have been quite persuasive, then."

He stiffened and canted his head. "What?"

"The favors you have provided between the bars to those 'gods among men.'" She grinned, fixing him with a piercing glare.

Gilles flinched.

She'd unsettled him. Good. She'd grown tired of his smirking arrogance.

His flinch proved a fleeting waver; he donned his smirk once more. "Such a mouth, Lady Sabeyon. If not for your necessary and inevitable end, I would have kept you as a concubine and enjoyed it."

Disgusting. And a lie. The way he looked at her—detached and calculating—he'd never looked at her lustfully. His tongue, speaking those words, attempted to wield power, not desire.

And she saw through it. It was her turn to smirk. "But I'll never see the day. What a pity."

He clenched the bars. "You think yourself so clever, don't you?" The leather of his gloves crackled as he tightened his grip even more. "You suppose I don't know exactly how much bread makes its way down here? When and how much hot water comes down in which tub and for how long? Nothing happens in my company without my knowledge."

Her breath stopped.

Divine, had she misread the situation so egregiously?

She looked away from him, her gaze settling on the box. "Why have you brought this?"

But she knew the answer. She'd known it from the moment she'd seen the thing. To punish her. And yet the question spilled from her mouth, a prayer hoping against hope.

The general tore himself away from the bars. "How should your attempts at manipulation be rewarded? I don't care if my men find a little comfort with a prisoner, but when one steals from me—"

By the Lone. *Rewarded.* Someone had suffered for her actions. Anton? James?

She suppressed the tears. Trembling took over her body, its conquest spreading unhindered until the whole of her quaked.

"What have you done?" she asked, despite her quivering jaw.

Gilles took a deep, calm breath and clasped his arms behind his back. "When someone steals from me, a lesson must be taught. My men, and the world, must know what happens when some conniving little schemer like you tries to take advantage."

She stared at the box.

James.

The pressure behind her eyes broke, and tears burst free. Gilles had cut the punishment not from her body, but his.

"Enjoy your evening, Lady Sabeyon." Gilles smiled, bowed his head cordially, and strolled away. The steps departed, serene but wide—a pleased man, an arrogant man.

Her gaze settled once more on the box, and tears flooded her determination to pool at the corners of her eyes. Cold whispered against her skin, quiet words that shivered through her being, so chilling even the tears rolled away.

Her chest tight to bursting, she scrambled toward the box on her knees and elbows, rasping desperate breaths.

She could feel it in her heart. Feel the missing part of her, right there in that box.

"James—" *Divine, please spare him, let him live—Terra, Nox, you gods of the old world, all of you, any of you—*

She grasped the box with broken hands, biting her tongue against the pain. Blood pooled in her mouth as she opened the wooden lid.

James.

James was dead for her scheming. His head lay there, the suffering of the past weeks permanently etched into his flesh.

His voice. She would never hear his voice again. Feel his touch again. See him stride confidently through life with unbreakable composure. He'd been broken here, forever, and the man she loved was gone—disrespected, dishonored, defiled.

And his murderer had strolled away. Smiling.

56

*R*ielle shivered. She shrugged deeper into her cloak as the wind beat against her back. Although the days had grown colder and the riding made her sore, at least her moonbleed had passed.

The country landscape was stark; the once golden-crowned canopy of the early autumn trees had given way to bare dark limbs, the land slumbering beneath a heavy shroud of foliage.

Ahead, Jon's shoulders moved with his horse's gait as he kept an unflinching watch at the front of their group. He knew this land better than any of them, and his unease was unnerving. If he was on edge, they'd be fools to relax.

They kept to little-traveled roads, paths the map had laid out in bandit territory, avoiding the exposed Kingsroad where the Crag would be watching. Brennan brought up the rear, his face set into a stony mask. As mischievous as he could be at social functions, he was devoid of that mischief now.

He tossed something to her.

She raised her hand and somehow managed to catch it. A...?

An apple, its color a dewy red and its flesh firm. She wanted to thank him, but he'd already turned away, his focus back on their surroundings.

With a shrug, she faced forward again and bit into the fruit. Juicy. Sweet.

"The Heartseekers," Leigh said from next to her. He shut the book he'd been reading and cocked his head toward Jon. "Is that what's got him in knots?"

She chewed slowly and studied Jon, then took another bite. "Why don't you ask him?"

"I did."

"What did he say?"

Leigh sighed through his nose. "He told me that I waved my tongue like a palm frond, with just as much significance."

Laughter and bits of apple exploded from her mouth. Brennan smiled wryly and shook his head. Jon looked over his shoulder at her, eyebrow raised.

"Even if navel-gazing is his life's calling, there may be hope for him yet," Leigh said to her.

So they were getting along. Somewhat.

A shadow passed above. A raven flew ahead of them and disappeared into the distance. At least something else was alive out here.

"You once burned with purpose, *ma chère*."

"What do you mean, 'once'?" She frowned.

Deep lines tightened his face, but he blinked and they disappeared. "What if I told you that the Divinity wasn't as... well intentioned... as you think it is?" he asked in a hushed tone.

She drew in her chin. The Divinity had saved her, taken her in, given her structure and purpose. She'd devoted her life to it and its goals. Not well intentioned? He'd been drinking again probably.

"What if I told you a lot of the Divinity's 'services' to governments are actually manipulation and deception? Ways to pursue its own ends? That it isn't as righteous as we're all led to believe?"

She pursed her lips, but a half-laugh escaped anyway. "That's ridiculous. All the missions that I've ever—"

"There are other missions, Rielle," Leigh said, his voice lower than before. Conspiratorially low.

Covert missions. Black operations. Dark dealings behind closed doors. Actions shrouded in mystery! She rolled her eyes. Rumors abounded wherever the Divinity's name fell from flapping lips. Tales of attacks and extortion, assassinations and schemes. And yet, every mission she had carried out or heard of had the clear purpose of advancing righteous causes. But of course, rumor didn't like reality.

Fearmongering. That's all it was. "What proof do you have?"

Leigh wrinkled his brow. "There are mages, people who say that—"

She shook her head. No solid evidence. It was no different than gossiping about whether some noble lady polished her guard's sword.

"Gossip is hardly proof of anything, except that some people have time to waste."

He frowned. "You won't even listen."

"I *have* listened to this all my time at the Tower. And will never get those minutes back."

He scowled at her.

"These are the same rumors that have always haunted the Divinity. They haven't proved true in all this time, and you with your swaths of no evidence aren't pulling back the curtain either."

Several factions segmented the Divinity's membership, all with different ideas about what the Divinity should and shouldn't do. Factions full of people with time to waste: the Pillars, the Protestants, the Integrationists, and the Anarchists. As these time-wasters ascended to the Magisterium, the Hensar, and Proctorship, each faction vied for influence, wielded rumors like blades to cripple the others.

All of it was a feckless debate that stole attention from practical reforms championed by people who weren't conspiracy theorists. Who lived in reality. She clenched the reins tight. Rather than squabbling about *how* mages were organized, why not focus on *what* they could do today? Tomorrow? Help people who needed it. Actually *do* something instead of arguing *how* to do something.

"All I've heard is self-indulgent ranting," she said.

He rolled his eyes.

"It's easy to say that something is imperfect, but it's a much more difficult task to actually perfect it. Everyone has an opinion on the future of the Divinity, but the people seeking to break it up aren't thinking beyond themselves. The Divinity has been keeping peace since the Magehold Convention. Tell me, what happens to the world when the bonds holding it together are dissolved?"

"If they're holding the world together with unthinkable acts and unconscionable methods, then we owe it to everyone to find out."

"If." She locked eyes with him. "You're willing to burn it all down based on *if.*" She exhaled lengthily while he shook his head. "Until there is something to prove any of this, it would be reckless to destroy the only protection keeping the world from destroying itself."

"*We* keep the world from destroying itself, Rielle. We mages. Don't ever forget that it is *we,* and not some *institution,* who guard the gates of chaos."

Of course mages kept the peace. But without the Divinity, they'd squabble over *whether* and *how* to keep that peace than actually keeping it. Decentralize power, and suddenly every idea was the best idea. Until it wasn't. And there was no sheepdog to herd the straying flock of wool-brained morons. It had happened in Parliament—King Marcus had been a weak king, and the nobles had been strengthened. And he was dead now. Along with his entire line. And Courdeval was in shambles. "Look how much good we've—"

Hooves thundered.

Brennan pulled up on his destrier. "Horses," he announced grimly. "At least forty head."

So much for a quiet trip. Rielle gave Brennan a grim nod. He dug his heels into his horse's flanks and cantered up to Jon.

"He can't possibly know that." Leigh hunched forward and stared into the distance.

She cast earthsight over her eyes. An incoming fleck of light appeared in the distance. Riders. It would be battle.

She dispelled the earthsight and assessed their surroundings. The path ahead, the woods, the plains, a cliff—

"Let them come," Leigh bit out.

She tightened her grip on the reins. "We don't know what we're facing."

Jon and Brennan pulled back their horses. "The woods," Jon said, jerking his head toward the trees.

Split their attackers' greater numbers, use the terrain—

"We don't need the woods," Leigh grumbled.

"Unless anyone has a better idea in the next second, we have run out of time." Brennan urged his horse toward the trees, with a wordless glance behind him. They hurried to follow.

In the tree cover, they slowed toward a small clearing on an incline and dismounted. She clapped her mare's hindquarters and sent her deeper into the forest along with the other horses.

"Cover me," she said to Jon over her shoulder. He drew his sword.

She gestured a cross, and her finger glowed azure. She backtracked and hastily inscribed runes on the forest floor—round ancient symbols, just like the ones at Cosette's. Pyromancy runes to immolate them, geomancy runes to drop them into pits, aeromancy runes to blow them back, throw them off their mounts—

A low hum rose from nearby. She stole a glance through the trees, off to the side, as she worked.

"The Mor Bluffs," Jon said softly, his back against an oak next to her. "It's a long way down."

"It will be. For them." She inscribed the runes in an arc, as far around them as she could manage, two rows deep.

Jon hissed and tipped his head behind her. Brennan.

She nodded, and they receded toward Leigh, who leaned against an oak, polishing his nails. Jon eyed her from the cover of the trunk next to hers. He donned his helm, visor still open.

They'd survive this. They had to.

"Your efforts are unnecessary, *ma chère*." Leigh always did prefer impulse.

She shrugged. "Well, if all else fails—"

"Pray and flambé?" he offered, with a smug smile.

A long silence claimed the woods, stilling all but the hum of the Mor River and their soft breaths. Hooves clopped in the distance.

Calls, scattered and clipped, echoed through the trees.

A series of thumping footfalls nearing.

Branches breaking. Foliage crunching.

The hiss of blades drawn.

A silent moment stretched for ages.

"Why don't we just—" a voice yelled.

"Shut it, Anton," another cut in. "Nobody asked you."

"Now!" A battle cry.

Boots pounded the ground. An arrow flew past and hit the trunk of a tree with a whine and a thwack.

A massive repulsion shield sprang before them—Leigh's. He held it with his fisted hand. An arrow, two—a dozen glanced off, diverted.

A great boom shook through the ground. Screams. Another. A series of deafening booms and shrieks. The hiss of fire and crackling. The yawning groan and creaking of a tree falling, and one more—

Rattled their footing.

The runes.

She peeked around the trunk through the blurry distortion of Leigh's repulsion shield. Fire gorged on the forest in an arc that spread over pits, fallen trees, and crumpled bodies.

Horses screamed as they jumped through the flames. A second wave of about fifteen men charged straight for them, with more behind.

Leigh unfurled his clenched fist. The repulsion shield rippled out toward the riders. Horses and men were thrown back toward the flames, cries tearing through the air.

Half a dozen riders still charged. Arcanir, sigils—?

She grasped the anima threaded in the trees mere feet away. Yanked them down.

One by one, massive trunks collapsed to the ground, braiding in falling quakes, and with her other hand, she turned their anima. Tumbled them down the incline toward the riders. Destroying all ahead in an enormous, thudding clamor—

It stopped.

"Geomancer!" Brennan called from ahead, where he leaped over two fallen trunks.

Distant stone spikes erupted from the ground and sped toward them in a twenty-foot swath. Leigh pushed blurry force magic directly down and levitated.

She shielded herself in an aqueous bubble, overfeeding it with anima until its waters grew and grew and destabilized. It wouldn't hold much—

She directed its overfed force into a tidal wave toward the geomancer.

Wood splintered, obliterated to dust as a compressed century of tides hit stone.

The waters split, dispelled. A man advanced through, followed by two others. Had to be—

Trees collapsed toward them. Hit Leigh's repulsion shield. They fanned out and thudded to the ground, falling in a ring. She spelled her flame cloak in place.

A man fled the scene on branches as if they were a bridge that bent and molded to command. Leigh shot force-magic projectiles at him.

One hit a trunk and shattered it.

One hit the ground—exploded.

Still the geomancer evaded. He had to be stopped. He was hers.

She immolated the trees ahead of him. Flaming branches curved under his feet, and yelping, he jumped to another bough she burned.

An axe-wielder charged past Jon toward her amid a chaos of weapons, blood, and magic. Jon spun behind him, sweeping his sword through the man's neck. A head toppled to the ground.

A second and third man advanced; he faced them, his helm spattered red. An arrow glanced off his pauldron.

The geomancer tumbled to the forest floor in a wreath of flame. She enclosed him in a circle of fire as bushes and shrubs sprang into a cage around her. Enemy magic. Denser and denser and tightening.

She fed her flame cloak anima until it burst, blasting open the cage in flying splinters, then spelled a wind wall into place to repel incoming spells.

The geomancer raised a dais out of the circle of flame. Jumped off onto a glowing bridge of braided vines that formed out of nothing.

This slippery bastard wasn't getting away—

Rain.

Holding the wind wall in place, she gathered the groundwater, days of rain and remnants of her tidal wave, widening control of her anima as far as it would go, spreading in a massive circle that stretched past him in every direction.

She pulled it all together.

Torrents of surging water converged in one location. Unrelenting pressure. To keep stable, it required anima, more and more and more.

She gave and gave and gave. Kept the geomancer within. Stone cut from the inside, but she fed the indomitable water the anima to obliterate it.

If he had the brighter anima, he'd win this test of endurance. Arrows hit her wind wall. No matter. She'd hold out for the geomancer, then deal with them.

Blood hit her shield. The carnage in her periphery swung his sword, slicing through flesh with deceptive ease. Jon.

An attacker closed in on him from behind, short sword raised—

The geomancer still—the arrows—

"Jon!" Her heart thundered. Divine.

He spun and parried with his dagger and punched the attacker in the face with his knuckle-dusters. Bloodied teeth flew.

The fight in the convergence of water died. The geomancer.

She dispelled it. Only red water remained.

Her shield broke.

A shadow passed over her.

She fell back. A heavy club thudded into the ground where she'd stood. A flame cloak sprang into place around her, and fire scattered from her fingers.

Upon contact with her attacker, it sputtered and died.

Sigiled—a lieutenant, perhaps. "Time to die, bitch."

Not today. She pulled the ground under him, but he jumped toward her with an agility that belied his size.

Shooting pain in her arm. Not cooperating.

In spasms of movement, she dragged herself a few feet back under a massive oak bough. No time.

Another strike. She dove aside.

Attack—she had to attack—but her throbbing arm wouldn't cooperate and she didn't dare stop moving.

She dug into the hard earth with her other hand and scrambled away from another hit. He raised the club again—

Evade or cast.

She brought down the bough above them.

An eerie wail escaped him. Cut off. Brennan tossed the head aside as blood sprayed from a severed neck. A blade buried in Brennan's shoulder—he tumbled.

The club plummeted onto her ribs—

Breathe. She couldn't—

Her vision flashed white.

Excruciating pain pulsed from her side. She curled up on the ground. Gnawing waves wracked her body, but she couldn't give in—wouldn't.

Heal. She had to heal. But she couldn't afford to focus inward during a battle.

Someone screamed her name.

She swallowed hard, pain forcing tears from her eyes as she crawled behind two dead bodies amid the shouts and roars. Mumbled the incantation.

Pain spiked, ripping a scream from her throat.

Too painful to heal. Through the dizzying fog, she saw Jon, his sword and helm gone. Men with targes and bucklers surrounded him.

His eyes met hers, wide and savage like those of a maddened animal. For a second. Less than.

Hand to hand, he fought the bandits crowding him, thrashing violently among them, elbows and fists flying while they attacked him in numbers.

Her head swam. She needed to—to get to—

Brennan fought his way to Jon, throwing men aside. He broke through, bringing his back against Jon's. Flowing like a Faris master, he dispatched the flankers, his grappling more of an art than combat. She squinted sluggishly. Beautiful, really. Bright... White, almost...

A giant of an attacker pinned Jon. Grunting with effort, he pushed an axe haft away, keeping the sharp edge looming just inches from its mark, the effort of his hands the only obstacle preventing its descent into his neck.

Blinding light flooded the corners of her vision. Fought for dominance. Pulsed. Pounded and spread. Power sang in her blood. She closed her eyes for a sliver of a moment, indulging the sound, swallowing as her mouth watered.

No. He wouldn't want this. She didn't want this. *Never again.*

She blinked. Her fingers hovered over the Sodalis ring. He would...

In the distance of space and memory, a teary-eyed blond girl trudged out of a burning castle, wearing flames like great regalia. Each footstep steamed, melting knee-deep snow, as she faltered away from the wall. Murderer. Demon.

Such a small thing. A child. She hadn't meant for this to happen, couldn't control power inherited from ancient magical lines, profound beyond her comprehension, stronger than her young grasp could hold.

Rielle watched from afar, wrapped her mantle tighter—a magister's mantle. Leigh's. Her feet—his—hurried toward the girl as whips of flame shot forth.

Batted aside with a repulsion shield.

Another lash, and another, and another, and the girl's horrified eyes, the shaking of her head, the futile tears as her magic acted in its chaotic nature, its shadow nature, divorced from her self. Pushed away from her self. Distanced. For the sake of her sanity.

Two feet away, he sent a wave of force knocking her back into the castle wall, stunning her, and pulled the metal from his pouch as he rushed her. Pressed its sting into her blazing-hot hand.

Heat hissed as it dissipated, as magic retreated, as the girl became only the girl once more. Her eyes met his, blinking weakly, and he held her hand. *It's all right. You're safe now. It wasn't your fault.*

It wasn't your fault.

Rielle blinked. Suddenly Leigh's hand holding the girl's was her hand holding the girl's. *It wasn't your fault*, she said.

The girl squeezed her fingers weakly. *I kept the fault for you. All these years. I kept Mama, Papa... everyone. Their pain and their love. Pain and love.*

Rielle's chest tightened. *I didn't know how to feel it. How to bear it.*

The girl smiled sadly. *Bear their pain with their love. Bear pain with love.*

Rielle shook her head, shrugging deeper into the magister's mantle. She hadn't been able to bear love, true and deep, without fear of that pain, memory of that pain. But like a set of scales, where love sat, pain sat opposite. Where pain sat, love sat opposite.

For years, she'd locked away that part of herself, the part that could feel either. When pain or love became too intense, intense as fureur, she locked it away in this girl she'd left behind nearly a decade ago. Her way to move on, forward.

The emptiness of those missing parts as she locked them away filled with something else. Someone else. Power. Pure, raw power, with a will of its own.

No more.

It'll burn you, and it'll warm you, the girl said.

Rielle nodded. *But it'll be me feeling it. Either way. I'll be there.*

The girl raised her hands and intertwined fingers with Rielle.

The girl, the snow, the castle wall faded away, far back into time and memory, vanishing from sight but not existence, leaving her feeling greater than her whole, somehow. Fuller. Stronger. Herself, who she hadn't been in ages.

Her heart pounded as she took in the tall trees, the deadfall, the pain—her arm, her side—

Steeped in red, Jon rolled from the shadow of the body before it collapsed, his dagger buried deep between the ribs. He grabbed his sword and cut a bloody path through the foes surrounding Brennan. He grabbed the blade by its leather-wrapped ricasso, below the hilt, and faced the remaining men closing in.

His eyes darted to hers. Speared her.

She was useless like this.

A blur came between them. A repulsion shield. Leigh.

Good. She collapsed behind the two dead men. Reached for her belt with her only cooperating hand, then stuck it in her mouth. Pressing her palm to her side, she winced but began the healing incantation.

The shattered bones had splintered into her flesh in agonizing chaos. There would be no time to finish healing entirely, but even a start would help.

Mouthing the words through the belt, she rushed her work. She closed the internal wounds, working through the shooting pain to make herself whole. Her teeth ached, radiating waves into her jaw as she bit into the leather. But pieces of bone and tissue came together, returned to their place. She bound them, grinding the belt down.

Shouts rang out. Two men across the clearing pointing to her.

She raised her arm, signing a storm.

Above her, a small darkness gathered and grew, swirling in a storm-gray whirlwind. The two men turned their heads in her direction.

The short channeling period would have to do.

She brought her hands down and rolled away, her arm and partially healed side throbbing.

Leigh faced them, a hand of force magic for each.

Her flashes of lightning descended, willed to each target. Clouds of black smoke dotted the surroundings, the smell of ozone thick in the air.

Leigh glared at her. Displeased at being preempted.

Blood and the tinge of burnt flesh saturated the battleground. And silence. Dead silence.

Jon's eyes met hers as he pushed his dagger between the breastplate and pauldron of a fallen foe.

He was all right. She was all right.

Leigh dusted off his coat. Brennan slit a throat with a stolen blade.

Over. It was over.

Divine, if the Black Mountain Brigands had been so prepared—with sigils and arcanir—then what in the Lone awaited them at Courdeval?

Shuddering, she dispelled the fire and the storm clouds, the ground around them brightening with a tentative gray light as scorched trees sizzled. Jon, Brennan, and Leigh stood surrounded by bodies and weapons in every direction. Leigh was already tending his wounds.

She throbbed with the need to finish healing.

A twig snapped behind her.

57

*W*ith a flame ready in hand, Rielle spun.

A young blond man stood with his hands raised in surrender. One of the bandits.

"Stop! Don't"—he glanced down at the fire—"burn me."

Shade blackened next to her. Brennan at her side, cold menace shadowing his face, his body drenched in dark blood.

"Allow me." Snarling, Brennan cracked his knuckles.

She blocked him with her arm, her hand pressing against his chest.

Judging by the man's unblemished clothes and skin, he had abstained from the fight. A coward or a spy. The Divinity had a draconian No Quarter policy on missions—the worth of certainty far outweighed that of mercy, apparently. But perhaps he had information. "Speak."

His tense muscles relaxed even as his eyes shifted. "Used to run with the Brigands for nearly a decade. Until Serge"—he tipped his chin toward the large man whose head Brennan had taken—"took over. 'Need to make a name for ourselves,' he said. 'Need the threat to mean something, so the marks turn their purses readily.' No thanks. Not for me. Won't lie—I'm no hero—but I draw the line at raping and massacring cooperating patrons."

" 'Patrons'?" She arched an eyebrow. Brennan smirked next to her.

The man smiled and shrugged. "Simple, really. For a small fee, we provided safety to those who crossed these lands."

"From yourselves, you mean." She pursed her lips. Their business model was not uncommon. They'd take over territory that the kingdom couldn't afford to guard in force, and they stopped unsuspecting travelers, intimidating them into paying for protection. An exciting career in wealth redistribution and personal security.

"I vote we kill him," Leigh's voice lilted from several feet away while Jon dragged bodies into a pile. The terrible stench of the battlefield flooded her nostrils, of blood, viscera, and singed flesh.

Jon came up next to her, wiping sweat off his brow and leaving a bloody smear. "We can't release him."

"My vote's for living," the man offered with a hopeful smile. "If you're tallying."

Killing him—as the Divinity expected—would ensure he wouldn't bring the Crag information and that he wouldn't return to kill them in the night. However, letting him live could mean, at the very least, a safe way through the wilds. If he misled them, he could just as easily be killed later. Of course, disobeying the Divinity would mean a demerit... or worse.

She shrugged. If she was being excommunicated anyway after Courdeval, what did the Divinity's expectations matter anymore?

She turned to Brennan. "Bind him."

He nodded, then approached the nearest bodies and pulled off sword belts.

"That's my girl," Leigh remarked.

"We're not killing him," she said. "We'll use him to get through these lands unhindered."

Brennan bound the man, who offered no resistance, and tied him to a singed oak. One of the few left standing. She'd have to restore this forest. Well, perhaps after washing off all the blood and guts.

Leigh grimaced. "You're no fun anymore."

"What, was all that not enough fun for you?" she joked.

"*Ma chère*, you really should know better after all these years."

She snorted. But even Leigh would have to admit they'd bitten off more than they could chew. The Black Mountain Brigands with sigils, arcanir, and a heretic geomancer? Horses, good equipment, and information? None of that boded well for Courdeval.

The man wriggled against the oak, testing the bindings; Brennan had secured him tightly.

"Let's see what he knows." Jon stared him down, his face stained blood red but for the whites of his eyes and teeth, despite his attempts at wiping it away.

She probably looked no better. The bottom of her braid was spattered with red. "At least he'll know that if his information is useless, we could always wear his insides like a face mask."

Brennan shot a grin her way and then a surly look at their captive.

"Who wants to search the dead?" she asked.

"Searching messy corpses?" Leigh furrowed his brow. "I nominate Marquis Happy-Face over there." He nodded to Brennan, whose mouth was still a grim line as he stared down the tied-up man.

"You're too good to get your hands dirty?" Brennan crossed his arms.

Leigh side-eyed him. "Indeed. Well said." He patted Brennan's shoulder with lips pursed in distaste. "Perhaps you're not a *complete* asshole. Some part of you may just be buttock."

Brennan exhaled lengthily and headed for the bodies. "Come on, foreigner. Don't make me drag you along."

Sighing, Leigh followed.

She and Jon approached the prisoner. Despite his slender build, he had a large frame. Lanky. He had hair the color of straw, the kind children usually grew out of in their teens to become brunettes. The texture of his skin—and his knowing dark eyes—he had to be in his late twenties or early thirties, but that hair lent him a juvenile air despite his many bruises.

Jon stalked to the oak and thudded his knuckle-dusters into the bark beside the man's head. "Where's Gilles?"

The man flinched, widening his eyes, then inched his pleading gaze over Jon's shoulder at her.

No, no help here. "Don't look at me. Answer the question."

He swallowed. "In the capital?" he offered, looking back to Jon. "Haven't seen him in a few days. Look, I'll tell you all I know. I'm a sure thing."

Jon lowered his fist and took a step back, resting his hand on his sword's pommel. Unmoving, he locked eyes with the man, who looked away quickly.

She rested her hand on Jon's gauntlet, but he didn't waver. She tipped her head toward the prisoner. "What's your name?"

"Anton." He met her eyes. "You?"

She grinned. "Stick to answering."

"That's a mouthful. Got a nickname?"

Jon went rigid, but she shook her head at him.

"Anton," she said, testing the name. "The Brigands knew about us?"

"Gilles sent me to them with information."

Jon leaned in. "Gilles? What does he know?"

Anton raised his eyebrows. "I'm just a grunt. All I know is what was in the message... To expect two Divinity mages and a paladin, and believe me, the Brigands had the influx of coin to keep watch. Delivered it myself."

Then Gilles knew they were coming. Knew about her. About Jon. Even Leigh... but not Brennan. "You're very forthcoming with this information."

"I like to live." Plain. Serious. Matter of fact. "The Brigands were once respectable robbers, taking a cut from traveling merchants and sending them on their way. But their new way wasn't the life I signed up for, and I don't want to die for it—or for the bloody Crag Company. 'Is this really the hill I want to die on?' I ask myself. No. Might have something to live for after all this."

"What do you think we are to Gilles?" Jon asked, eyes narrowed.

"I don't know—Sent to stop all this, to—"

Jon winced, gritted his teeth. He coughed into his hand. Blood.

She grabbed Jon's wrist, looked him over. Behind the arm he held in front of his torso was a huge set of dents in his cuirass. "What is this?" she demanded, staring into his blank eyes.

He shrugged. "I'm fine. We need to know—"

"What. Is. This."

He drew in a slow breath but coughed before his lungs filled.

"Off with the armor. Now."

He held her gaze, face an unflinching mask.

Oh, he could resist. He sure could. He could resist if he wanted her to climb him like a sycamore and undo all the straps herself.

Footsteps crunched from behind. "He took a flanged mace to the ribs." Brennan's voice. Jon glared at him, but Brennan shrugged. "And apparently wants to drown in his own blood. Maybe we should let him."

Jon scowled. Blood trickled from his hairline down his face—from where, she couldn't tell. She'd need some water.

The Propré River was nearby, branching from the Mor. The falls. "Anton's not going anywhere," she said to Jon, then turned to Anton. "Are you?"

Anton shook his head. "Couldn't even if I wanted to."

"See?" She raised her eyebrows at Jon. "So you're coming with me, and I'm going to clean these wounds and heal you. Then we can talk to him as long as we want later. Got it?"

Jon hissed. "Mage—"

"I'll even keep an eye on him," Brennan interrupted. "So go on."

Shaking his head, Jon took off toward the river. She nodded her thanks to Brennan and got a quick smile in reply as she trailed Jon.

Leigh tethered the horses to a nearby tree. Good—he'd found them.

"Anything on the bodies?" she called as she walked by.

He smirked. "Weeks of unwashed stench. Want to check?"

"Better you than me." As she passed the pile of bodies, she ignited them. The hotter-than-hot fire would reduce them to ash.

Ahead of her, Jon shed his armor piece by piece, then his arming jacket and his shirt, too.

Even from behind, his side looked bad—heavy bruising on his ribs. How he still had the wherewithal to trudge—

"Would you just stop?" she called after him. "Why are you so angry?"

He turned, walking backward, and narrowed his smoldering eyes at her as he clipped his weapons belt back over his trousers. He turned his back again. She ambled to catch up to him.

"Jon."

"Why am I angry?" he asked the canopy above. "Why could I possibly be angry?" He shot a piercing glance at her and looked away, his mouth a thin line. "Could it be because you told me you hated your fiancé, were never going to marry him, couldn't *stand* him, and now he's your—and everybody's—best friend?"

"That doesn't mean—"

"Or could it be that I warned you all that *this*"—he jerked an arm toward the field of battle—"exactly *this* would happen if we took this route?"

"We couldn't—"

"Or *maybe* it's that Gilles knows we're coming, is prepared, and we're walking right into his trap?"

"Can I just—"

He grabbed her shoulder, yanking her to a stop, and whirled her to face him. Fresh blood streaked through his hair down his face. "Or could it be that I just had to watch you nearly die over and over. And over. And over—"

Her chest tightened. "Jon..."

"No." His grip on her shoulders clamped harder, the storm in his eyes wilder. "This was just a preview of what awaits in Courdeval. And have your plans changed?"

"No, we—"

"So what could I possibly be angry about? Other than, of course, us nearly getting killed, this reckless plan, your new best friend, and you foolishly walking straight to your death?"

She ripped away from his grip. "Don't you dare." Pressure formed behind her eyes. "I am *not* some doll for you to lock away. Look at yourself"

—she raked eyes over his array of lacerations and bruises—"and then try to tell me *I* shouldn't go into danger."

He spread his arms. "I'm not saying that, am I?" He turned on his heel and stalked toward the river.

"Then what *are* you saying?" she shouted after him. "Tell me what you want from me!"

"Nothing," he barked back over his shoulder, then stopped. "Everything."

"What do you expect me to do?"

He just stood there, taut as a bowstring, ready to snap, and... He didn't. Didn't move. Didn't speak. Didn't... anything.

The rush of water figured in the silence. Ahead of them, boulders and large rocks littered a river bank. The ruins of an old stone bridge over the Propré River, branched from the Mor. Here, the Propré was about forty feet across, with banks that eased into the water. The sizable remnants of the bridge broke up the Propré's shallow autumn flow. Interrupted it.

"There's nothing to do about any of it. That's what's so infuriating about it," he said quietly, but his voice vibrated like a fist clenched too long.

He strode to the river bank, knelt, and splashed his face. Water ran down his face and chin, and he kept his eyes closed, taking a moment. He just breathed.

"You look like you needed that."

He washed his head. "Things have just been... tense lately."

"Tense?"

Water fell through his hands and dripped into the river. "I've always been of single mind before battle," he said, pressing his lips tight for a moment, "but having your fiancé along, and the threat of battle, and this— it's all made me very... aware of how much I have to lose when I finally speak to the Paladin Grand Cordon."

She moved next to him and reached for the contusion to his ribs, to start the healing process. He caught her fingers in a light grip, her injured arm, and when she flinched, he released her.

His gaze dropped to her injured side. "I saw you take that blow from the falling club. Your ribs are broken, and so is your arm."

"Nearly healed."

But he was right. She hurt all over.

"Take care of yourself first." The look in his determined eyes left her no room to argue.

Her anima had dimmed by more than half—ghostly pressure pushed against her inner barriers—but she'd have enough to heal them both. Biting down on a twig, she touched her broken arm—shattered in several places. Whispering the incantation, she began, using magic to pick the bone shards free of the flesh and return them to their proper place, knitting together muscle, closing open blood vessels, struggling with the pain of it all.

She resolved to give healing magic another good-faith effort the next time she returned to the Tower. *If I am ever again welcome at the Tower.*

When she finished healing, she opened her eyes to Jon's creased brow. "I'm fine. Promise."

His mouth twisted.

"Whatever happens, we'll find a way."

"I know. I've just been preparing myself for the... worst case."

She swallowed. "Worst case?"

He looked away. Bloody water dripped from his chin. "If nothing awaits me at Monas Amar, if the new king won't hear your petition, isn't Faolan Auvray Marcel—"

She held her breath, not wanting to hear the words, not wanting to hear that if she had to marry another man for the sake of her line, this would end between them. But she knew it. "There's no need to—"

"I still want to be there." Dauntless, he held her gaze, strong and vulnerable and brave and afraid. He'd sacrificed all he'd ever known for her. And he offered to sacrifice even more.

She stroked the contusion to his ribs.

He gasped, and she held a stick before his mouth. He bit it.

"Sundered flesh and shattered bone, / By your Divine might, let it be sewn," she whispered, threading her anima to reshape his bones, seal his internal wounds, make him whole.

The river babbled quietly, the current breaking against the stone ruins that had stood steadfast in its path for centuries, if not millennia, and withstood the constant force with unwavering strength.

If the tables were turned, being a mere mistress to the man she loved would be... Watching him with a wife who bore his name and his children, who was his partner before all the world, who had everything she could only ever want. And then being the black mark that tarnished something beautiful, a leech to what a real family offered, stealing away just enough love for her heart to subsist on. Ruining his chance at pure joy, and ruining her life by being in his, yet unable to imagine life without him. The pain, the torture, would be crippling. "Why? Why would you?"

He submerged his fingers in the river and let the water flow between them. "These past few days, I have asked my own heart what, for your sake, I would not do." Slowly, a resolute smile spread across his face. "The answer is nothing." Unabashed, he met her eyes. "For your sake, there is nothing I would not do, nothing I would not suffer. You have become... everything to me."

Everything... everything that could make him happy, or that could destroy him. "Jon—"

"My mind is made up."

Beneath his unwavering stare, she averted her gaze. "That worst case will never happen."

He splashed some water in her direction, and she yelped at the cold water that sprinkled her skin. "Even if everything goes wrong, we'll fight. We'll fight with everything we've got. When the enemy takes your sword, you must draw your dagger."

Nodding, she shook off those distant thoughts. They were together now, and they had hope; it was more than she'd had in a long time, and she wouldn't waste this day pondering clouds that only might portend future storms.

While he scrubbed in the river, she sat on one of the rocky ruins and unbuttoned her stinking coat. The sooner she washed her clothes off, the better. When she leaned over to take off her boots, Jon came up and held out his hands until she surrendered her foot to him.

He removed one boot and then the other. "You know, I have given *much* more thought to our other, more optimistic fates."

"Have you?" She grinned and gathered up her coat.

He nodded. "They all begin with taking you out into the country for the winter. A cottage." His intent eyes met hers as he paused and tenderly drew her trousers down and off, revealing a cut on her thigh. "Somewhere only for you and me."

She liked the sound of that fate already.

"And then?" She inspected the wound, removing a few blades of grass.

He knelt and flushed it with water. "I'll hunt and fish and cook, and you—you'll do whatever chores it is you know how to do—"

She gave him a playful shove. "Hey! I know how to—um..."

"Right." He grinned smugly, that sinful dimple of his appearing. "We'll enjoy each other. We'll read books by the fire. We'll take walks—"

She smiled dreamily, her wound forgotten beneath the cool water and Jon's touch.

"I'll teach you how to use a blade—"

"And I'll teach you how to use magic."

He leaned in and winked. "Let's not plan anything too drastic."

She pursed her lips and watched as he returned to his ministrations.

"And of course, I plan to make love to you until we forget our names."

She raised an eyebrow. "Until we forget our names? Don't let that stop you."

The soft rumble of a chuckle was his reply. "Done."

She liked that plan. She liked it very much. But she had plans of her own, which included, at the very least, making up for a solid decade of his celibacy. Indeed, he might forget his own name, but he'd remember hers— the one he'd be calling between gasps of ecstasy. She allowed herself a mischievous smile.

The wind stinging against the wound on her thigh interrupted her planning. Placing her hand over it, she murmured the incantation until it finally knitted shut.

Definitely giving healing-magic lessons another shot.

"We should head back, retire," she said. "Early start to get to Monas Amar tomorrow." Where they'd part ways, for who knew how long... unless he convinced the Paladin Grand Cordon to join the invasion of Courdeval tomorrow.

He stared at her closed wound. Still fascinated by magic? She seized the moment and examined the seeping cut in his hair. Caked with blood, it bled anew. Without stitching—with threads of catgut or magic—it would continue bleeding.

She combed her fingers through his soaked, matted hair and healed the cut. He held her gaze through the incantation, through the healing, by all signs unaffected by the pain.

When she finished, he kissed her bare inner thigh, the soft contact sending a shiver through her body.

Memories of Melain sparked in her mind, of squeezing her eyes shut in unbearable pleasure.

He leaned in to kiss her thigh again, a little higher up, fixing his provocative eyes upon hers as he pressed his lips to her skin once more.

Her heart beat faster as she watched him, dirty and blood soaked, passionate and tender, his penetrating gaze a question she answered with a bewildered nod.

58

*B*rennan hissed and threw the brush aside. His leathers shone like a wolf's eye in the moonlight.

He had run out of menial tasks.

The curse had never been content to simply force him into a beast's form from time to time. It was intent on drawing blood. He could hear breaths—quick, shallow, deep, belabored, relaxed—and heartbeats—normal, fast, irregular—and know what those closest to him felt. He could smell them nearby or their scents on one another. He could tell when a woman he pursued took a paramour, or when Father was cheating on Mother again.

Sometimes, he thought that this was the true curse, coexisting with humans so used to artifice, yet he with the ability to see through it as beasts did.

With Rielle close, the Wolf in him was sated, but the man in him rattled in his cage. The scents, the sounds from the forest would not vacate his mind, repeating the torture over and over and over. Her gasps, moans, and cries of pleasure, another man eliciting them. Someone making her happy. Someone else.

Playing nice was flaying him alive.

Busy. He had to stay busy.

Long after the sun set, his hands stayed moving—building, fixing, sharpening—the only peace they could muster.

She returned with the commoner, both of them smiling, glowing, laughing, a pair of foxes thinking themselves so stealthy. They made eyes at each other through their camp chores—insufferable—and then retired to their den of a tent, whispering.

Great Wolf spare him the annoyance, but he could hear the whole thing. His ear hadn't yet learned its place, always seeking her damn voice. He didn't want to hear the loving words, the soft kisses, the delicate pleas. None of it.

Before Melain, before the duel, the sen'a hub, before all of that, it had been simpler to ignore her. But now, after the duchess's allegation that he loved her, it was nigh impossible.

Eyes front, he focused on the crackling of the fire, trying to overpower her noise. He added a log, his gaze lingering on the hole in his leather overcoat's sleeve. He'd taken a dagger through the shoulder—a dagger he now called his own—but the wound had already healed.

It was, at least, something he could do.

He dug out Rielle's sewing kit, and thumbing the box in his hand, he returned to the campfire, removed his overcoat, and sat. He opened the kit and gathered the supplies he'd need.

"A paladin and a mage?" Anton asked, tied up, sitting on the ground, leaning his back against a tree. His tunic, an unusual marshy shade of green, made him almost blend in. Almost. "If that celibacy bit's been relaxed, maybe I should join. The new armor is stylish." He grinned. "Think a fine palace lady would be impressed? I think she would, don't you?"

Brennan scowled at him. "Why don't you return to just thinking about it and shut up?"

"You don't want to interrogate me?"

"Do you know anything?"

Anton frowned. "Plenty."

At least it was better than listening to Rielle's noise. "Such as...?"

"You're headed for the capital."

That much was obvious. "You'll say anything to keep breathing."

Anton raised his lamb-white eyebrows. "Yes. I will. It's the right thing to do."

"How fortunate that you found your conscience when you noticed which way the wind was blowing." Conscience was convenient when the other option was death.

Anton gaped. "Serge was threatening to disobey Gilles' orders. The Brigands weren't to kill the woman, not even hurt her, just disarm her and bind her with arcanir, then take her to Courdeval for safekeeping."

The man's heart beat true. He wasn't lying.

Someone had wanted Rielle unhurt. Someone high up. Someone at Gilles' level... or above. Perhaps even the one who had hired him.

Someone who needed Rielle alive.

He rose and stood above the man, who shrugged and looked away with a smug grin.

"Got your attention now?"

Brennan peered at the still-gaping hole in his overcoat. If the Crag Company wanted Rielle alive, it had to be because their client did. Their wealthy client. And there was only one wealthy man he could think of who might insist on Favrielle Amadour Lothaire's survival.

Father.

Word of this could not survive.

Brennan moved closer to the man. "Have you told my friends yet? They'll be eager to learn this information." *Friends.*

"Not yet."

Rielle and Jon were in their tent, Leigh in his.

The man frowned contemplatively. "Don't suppose any of you know Archm—"

"I'm about to turn in for the night. Did you need to...?" He cocked his head toward the forest.

Anton raised his eyebrows. "For hours. Thought you lot were going to leave me here high and dry. Or... wet."

Brennan set down his overcoat—no need to mend the hole anymore. He untied Anton from the tree but kept his hands bound as he marched him into the forest. No sounds but crunching leaves, water, and the creatures of the night.

"Got a woman?" Anton asked.

Brennan laughed under his breath. "Any time I want."

Anton shook his head and kicked up a pile of leaves. "No, no. Someone special."

Someone special. Rielle counted. She was *especially* infuriating. "She's... beyond reach. At least for now. You?"

A wistful breath. "Oh, I wish. If yours is beyond reach, mine is the moon."

"Maybe you should look a little lower." Brennan walked him right up to the bluff overlooking the Mor.

A half-laugh. "Or learn to fly." Tied hands fumbled with the marsh-green tunic and roughspun trousers.

The waxing gibbous moon was massive in the sky tonight, a tease playing almost within reach. Her silvery kiss was mesmerizing but ghostly, will-o'-the-wisp and not lover. Never for these arms to hold. Always beyond reach.

He took a step back, Changed his fingers to claws, watched the man's shoulders a moment, silhouetted against the moon. Just a moment.

He clawed off a piece of the tunic and pushed him over the edge.

The man turned his head, a last wide-eyed look of recognition.

Then a gasp and no more. No scream going down. Just the gasp.

He drew the dagger and contorted to stab himself in the back with it. Exactly where he'd been stabbed the first time.

He headed back to camp. His overcoat lay by the tree where he'd left it. He put it on and fastened it, reached across his shoulders to check that the new wound and the overcoat's old hole aligned. They did. He stowed away Rielle's sewing kit, just as he'd found it.

In the morning, he'd say the man had pulled a dagger and stabbed him, then fell in the altercation. He'd tried to save the man—he crumpled the shred of marsh-green fabric in his hand—but hadn't been able to.

No one else would know about Father's involvement with the Crag. No one would ever have the evidence to put the Marcels on the chopping block. He raised his chin and flexed his neck.

The man hadn't deserved to die. But against the lives of Mother, Nora, Caitlin, and Una, his life was a paltry sum. Yet Father had gambled with them all.

Never again. He was done cleaning up Father's messes. It was time to put an end to the scheming for the crown, once and for all. After they retook Courdeval, he'd talk some sense into the old man.

He closed his eyes, letting the song of the night in once more. The renewed silence drew his hearing back to Rielle's tent, but he resisted, listening to the other sounds of the autumn night—the soft breath of the horses, an owl hooting, the wind rustling through dried foliage, the river splashing in the distance.

Blood oozing from his wound, he bedded down in his tent. He shut his eyes and imagined the Change. At least tonight, he'd lose himself in the forest of dreams, forget about the bandit, Father, the commoner, Rielle. Everything.

59

*J*on clenched his fists and invaded Brennan's space. "He tried to kill you? You expect us to believe that?"

Rielle stepped in his path, planted her hands on his chest, and pushed him back. "Jon, please—"

Brennan shook his head and sighed. "Believe me or don't. I wouldn't go out of my way to kill him any more than I would an insect."

"Right. Because that's all commoners are to you. Insects."

Brennan shrugged.

"No one believes you." He reached for Faithkeeper. The narcissistic, conceited—

"*I* believe him!" Rielle shouted.

She—

"He was no threat to us. There was no reason for him to kill the man. We didn't check him for weapons—"

He narrowed his eyes at her. "What, so you take his side?"

She beat a palm against his chest. "He's not the one shouting in a —rage."

A rage.

A *jealous* rage. He took a step back, and her pushing hands sent her tumbling right into him. "Why don't you just say it, Rielle?"

She straightened and crossed her arms. "I don't want to fight."

"Then you shouldn't have started one."

Her mouth dropped open.

They'd spoken last night about many things, but none of the ones they'd needed to resolve. Certainly not about Brennan.

"It's not even dawn yet. Do you really want to spend this morning fighting?" She drew her eyebrows together, summoning that little crease that was designed to make him answer with whatever she wanted to hear.

She'd used it last night, too. And—he had to admit—they'd spent the night doing far more enjoyable things than fighting.

A tent flap flew open, and Leigh stormed out, half-dressed, his long white hair unbound and disheveled. "*Why* is there shouting before the sun is up?"

Jon jabbed a thumb in Brennan's direction. "Because *he* murdered the prisoner."

Leigh threw his hair back from his face and nodded at Brennan. "Well done. I like to travel light."

Rielle shook her head, and Brennan bowed his—at least he offered the pretense of remorse.

With a long inhalation, Jon turned and headed for the horses. They'd lost their only source of information on Gilles, the Crag, and the siege, and no one else seemed to care. Rielle was too busy defending Brennan to concern herself with the advantage they'd lost.

Were they insane, or was he?

He did his share packing up the camp. Rielle avoided him, only meeting his gaze quickly when she tucked Shadow's soulblade in her boot. And looked away just as quickly.

He sighed. Maybe the death of one bandit could be set aside, at least today.

Today he would finally arrive at Monas Amar. Finally turn in his arcanir. Finally look the Paladin Grand Cordon in the eye, formally end his service to the Order, and ask every single question that had been haunting him.

And then do his all to persuade the Paladin Grand Cordon to join the fight against Gilles. Finally get justice for Bastien.

The death of one bandit could be set aside. At least today.

He said a prayer for the man before they departed. Terra willing, he'd fare better in the Lone than he had here.

They chanced a route with Brennan at the lead, and hours passed without incident. After a long day's ride, the stone battlements of Monas Amar came into view at last, a square-toothed edge against a pink twilit sky. A Terran fort, the largest in Emaurria, it protected the monastery within, currently home to hundreds of priests and thousands of paladins, his brothers. Tents spilled over into a faubourg outside the stone walls to surround the fort.

Rielle stared toward it, that persuasive crease summoned once more. Perhaps *she* should convince the Paladin Grand Cordon to join the battle.

He rode close. "We didn't fight today, did we?"

She eyed him peripherally, then a little smile emerged. "No... We cuddled all morning, laughed and grinned, and weren't angry or upset about a single thing. At all."

He chuckled under his breath. "We have the same memory, then, so it must be true."

That little smile of hers brightened, but as she stared into the distance, it faded.

"I'll find you in Courdeval. I promise."

She looked away and nodded. "I know."

Her voice was too high. Thin. She wasn't really assured.

It didn't matter. She wouldn't be able to dispute reality when he showed up in Courdeval later.

They neared the path into Monas Amar, and they all dismounted. Leigh gave him a respectful nod—a gesture he returned.

"You were as annoying as any paladin the night we met," Leigh said, clapping him on the shoulder over his pauldron, "but in time, you became slightly less annoying."

Jon raised an eyebrow. "Take care, Leigh."

From beside his destrier, Brennan observed the leave-taking with an apathetic eye. Good riddance. With any luck, they'd never meet again.

Jon turned to Rielle and took her hand in his, raised it to his lips in a whisper of contact, a soft kiss, and shot her a playful grin. "This isn't good-bye." He gave her hand a gentle squeeze. "The paladins will join the battle, and I'll find you in it."

She intertwined her fingers with his, smiled, but it didn't reach her eyes. Forced smile.

She raised her hands to her neck and unfastened a silver chain, at the end of it—a signet ring. Her Laurentine signet ring. She held it out to him.

"I can't accept this." He shook his head.

"Just keep it until we meet again."

This was her assurance, then. What she needed in order to believe what he'd already told her.

He accepted it and fastened it around his neck, cupped the side of her face. "You'll have it back tonight." He leaned in, tracing her mouth with his thumb.

Her breath slowed, wavered, then he tipped her chin up and kissed her, the softness of her lips, the taste of her mouth awakening memories of the night before, and every other time he'd held her in his arms. And that night in the forest pool when he should have but hadn't.

She melted into him, and he caught her, held her tight, pressed a kiss to her forehead and inhaled her hair, faraway roses and her own intoxicating scent.

Someone cleared his throat—Brennan—and she pulled away. Jon stroked her cheek softly, and they shared one last smile before he accepted the horses' reins; he'd stable them at the monastery.

"One last thing," he said with a wry dimpled grin, "watch your step, witch. You never know what you might find underfoot."

The unspoken word gleamed in her sparkling eyes. *Turtle.*

Her pinched lips did nothing to keep the smile from her eyes.

After a final nod, he led the horses toward the monastery.

AMONG THE SEA of white tents, his blasphemous deep-gray armor and blue cloak earned him bizarre looks from paladins and priests. The camp itself teemed with activity, paladins sharpening swords, training, and transporting supplies while the priests tended refugees, offered blessings, led prayers.

Ready to retake the capital from the Crag Company. From Gilles. Once the general's wrists were in shackles, a new life awaited.

His shoulders hardened as he walked toward the command tent.

A paladin commander halted him, a stout hulk of a man. Commander Noren. "Report."

Jon stood to attention, brought his right hand to his heart in salute, and bowed. "Sir Jonathan Ver, eighth rank, Monas Ver First Company, sent by High Priest Derric Lazare of Monas Ver to see the Paladin Grand Cordon regarding my discharge."

Noren's eyes widened, looking him over, his armor, Faithkeeper, his face. He gestured to two paladins behind him, who approached and accepted the horses. "Jonathan Ver?"

"Yes, sir."

Noren heaved a deep, dissatisfied breath. "The Paladin Grand Cordon expected you a week ago." He beckoned to four paladins. "Take him to the Paladin Grand Cordon at once," he said to his men.

They surrounded him and led him through the camp like a prisoner. He straightened, tensed, but there was no use. If the Paladin Grand Cordon wanted to throw him in a cell, then that's exactly what would happen.

On the way, perfect order functioned around him. He'd always loved the structure of the Order, the clarity that came with knowing exactly what to do, when to do it, and how.

But he didn't miss it anymore. His future would be gloriously chaotic, and its existence depended entirely on what the Paladin Grand Cordon had to say.

Sweat coated his palms and his limbs tingled, but he tried to ignore both. Soon he'd have an answer, whether for good or ill.

His paladin escort took him to the great hall, which had been repurposed as a war room. Among a small cadre of paladin grand officers and high priests stood Paladin Grand Cordon Raphaël Guérin, a broad-shouldered and sable-haired man in his late forties, in his highly polished, intricately detailed arcanir. Holding a black ribbon, he moved markers on a map, assessing it with intelligent eyes.

The paladin escort saluted, and so did Jon. "Sir Jonathan Ver, eighth rank, Monas Ver First Company, sent by High Priest Derric Lazare of Monas Ver regarding my discharge."

Paladin Grand Cordon Guérin set down the ribbon and approached with slow, heavy steps.

Then he bowed his head, saluted, and dropped to a knee.

Every priest and paladin in the room followed suit.

"Your Majesty, you have arrived."

Jon whirled around to look at the new king, but behind him, the paladin escort detail had bent the knee, too.

His mouth fell open. Terra have mercy, they couldn't possibly—

The head of the Order was on a knee before him. Blessed Terra. "Paladin Grand Cordon, sir, please rise. I'm not—"

"You are King Jonathan Dominic Armel Faralle," said a voice from the side of the room. Derric.

How? It couldn't possibly be—but he was—

There was no way. No possible way. "What?"

With his shaved head and kind eyes, standing there in his white robes, it was unmistakably the man who had raised him. He'd straighten this out, tell everyone the truth, fix this.

"Derric." He went to embrace him before he remembered himself.

"It's true, son." Derric's expression was grave, even if a smile shone in his honey-brown eyes. "You are the son of Queen Alexandrie and the king's younger brother, Prince James, Duke of Guillory."

His commoner mother had abandoned him at the monastery; that was what he'd known all his life. A bastard, but never—

"King Marcus discovered their affair," Derric said, "but allowed her to bear the child in secret at Monas Ver, as long as she relinquished him to the custody of the priests, keeping him out of the line of succession and the public's eye. That child is you. I was present at your birth." Derric held up some parchment. "Queen Alexandrie and Prince James defied the king and signed a legitimization in secret, witnessed by me, placing you seventh in the line of succession."

Derric approached and handed him the parchment. "It's why you were discharged right after the coup. But telling you the reason would have endangered you."

His head swam. He stared down at its aged seals and signatures. Slants and curls and lines. *My parents' seals and signatures. My parents.*

Derric picked up the black ribbon. "A wren bearing this ribbon came from Trèstellan Palace. At your birth, your parents warned me that, if you were ever in danger, I would receive this. Unless any higher-ranking heir remains alive within the palace, you are king." Derric gave it to him.

His parents had kept this. For his sake.

His heart pounded a battle march. This was madness. A royal love affair and lines of succession and kingship? It was incredibly convenient for the Order of Terra if one of its own were king.

He'd be no one's pawn. "That's a fine tale, but it doesn't prove this king is me."

Not a single kneeling man in the room moved.

Derric's calm didn't waver. "I raised you from infancy, taught you all the subjects a prince should learn, saw you squired to a noble who could teach you what I couldn't. I know who you are. But if you doubt my word, read near the bottom."

Shaking his head, he peered at the document once more. "Straight hairline, attached earlobes, cleft chin"—he read the description, pressure building in his chest—"no facial markings. Birthmarks on the left hand above the fifth knuckle, on the right outer elbow, on the right inner ankle —" He didn't need to read a single word more.

This was why he'd been left in Rielle's charge. "This is—"

"You." Derric fixed him with a confident stare, then he, too, dropped to a knee. "Your Majesty."

Your Majesty.

The son of Queen Alexandrie and Prince James.

Prince James. Prince James had stayed at Vercourt from time to time and would come to Monas Ver and tour the grounds, talk with the priests and paladins—

Talk with *him.*

One summer day, sparring with Stefan, his first squire, Jon—all of twenty years old—had hit him with the flat of his blade, and while Stefan had followed the sword with his eyes, Jon had swept a leg low to knock him to the ground.

"Eyes on the man, not the weapon," he'd said, "and don't let your opponent put you on the defensive if you can avoid it." While Stefan rose, rubbing his backside, Jon had moved back into ready stance. "Again." Jon batted aside a lunge from Stefan.

"Perhaps you are the weapon, Sir Paladin," a stranger's voice had interrupted from behind.

The fourteen-year-old's mouth fell open, and he dropped his sword. Irked, Jon tapped Stefan with the flat of his blade. When the boy didn't move, Jon sighed and turned, finding himself face to face with a tall, fit man in his late thirties, clad in finery befitting a king. The man had a neatly trimmed dark-brown beard, shoulder-length hair, sea-blue eyes, and a tall and well-muscled, but not bulky, physique—a duelist's body. Prince James.

Jon planted his sword in the ground and dropped to a knee. "Forgive me, Your Highness. I didn't see you."

The prince had visited the monastery before and spoken with priests and other paladins; although His Highness had watched him before, Jon had never heard him speak. Hadn't recognized his voice.

Prince James rested a hand on Jon's shoulder. "You'd make a poor master if you didn't keep eyes on your student, now wouldn't you? Rise, son."

Swallowing, he rose. When the prince watched him expectantly, he turned to Stefan and motioned for him to take his sword. Stefan hurried to do so, bowing profusely as he made his exit.

Prince James gestured to the practice yard, and Jon joined him, walking the outskirts and watching paladins, squires, and pages spar.

"How long have you been a paladin, son?"

He exhaled slowly. "Two years, Your Highness."

"Do you enjoy it?"

"Yes, Your Highness." When the prince gave him an exasperated look, Jon scrambled for words. "It's all I've ever known. I was raised at the monastery, among the priests and paladins. They helped people, enjoyed their lives and their calling, and I... I felt called to do the same."

"To help people?"

"Yes, Your Highness."

Prince James stopped and leaned against a wooden-post fence, watching two pages spar clumsily. "But does it make you happy?"

He took a deep breath. "I have the privilege of serving Most Holy Terra, dispensing justice, and helping Her faithful, Your Highness"—when the prince pursed his lips, Jon grinned—"but I also get to travel the country, meet new people, listen to their stories, advise them... And when I return here, I trade tales with Derric and my brothers. Train with them. Celebrate with them. I learn. I read. I've taken a squire under my wing, and teach him the sword, the Code, and how to be a man. Watching him learn has been a great amusement and joy."

Prince James, looking out at the practice yard, slowly smiled. "You mentioned Derric?"

It was Jon's turn to smile. "He raised me, Your Highness." Was the amusement and joy he felt teaching Stefan anything like what Derric had felt raising him? Considering the sheer volume of pranks Jon had played on him, probably not. "Derric's the closest thing I have to a father."

Prince James scanned the horizon then, but his eyes could have been a world away. "So you're an orphan?"

He nodded. "Yes, Your Highness."

Prince James turned to him then and extended his arm. Jon accepted it, and the prince shook his hand.

"You do this land a great service. Seeing the man you are now, your parents would have been very proud of you. I know it." Prince James gave him an encouraging nod and released his hand. "Thank you for taking the time to talk to me."

"It has been my pleasure, Your Highness." It had been the first time he'd ever spoken to Prince James—or any member of the royal family.

The prince had returned from time to time while traveling on business, and although he spent most of his time in Derric's company, sometimes he spoke with the priests and paladins, Jon among them.

But Prince James hadn't just come to see Derric and enjoy the serenity of Monas Ver.

He'd come to see his son.

My father. Jon looked around the room, at all his brothers, Derric, and the Paladin Grand Cordon himself bending the knee.

60

*N*ight had fallen by the time Brennan reached the edge of the oak trees outside the city walls with Rielle and Leigh, but the darkness suited his needs. He crept among the dark-green cork and kermes oaks to the hobbled downy oaks, nestled among their fall russet-brown leaves as he scanned the wall. To open the northeastern gate, he would scale the wall in man-beast form, dispatch several guards in silence, and single-handedly lower the drawbridge over the city ditch, then draw up the outer and inner portcullis.

Just a few yards from open land, Rielle and Leigh stood in obscurity while he attempted to string together a believable lie as to how he would realistically accomplish all that. It was all too much for a mere man, but perhaps the wild mage accompanying her would overlook mystery in favor of advantage.

"No light," Brennan murmured. "We don't want to alert the guards."

Leigh nodded, despite the dark. "How will we know when to approach?"

"Watch the gate tower. When it's clear, I'll extinguish its torches and open the gate." The gate tower going dark would be the signal for the Black Rose to initiate the diversion at the southeastern gate.

"And why must you go alone?" Leigh inquired, eyeing him peripherally.

Rielle stiffened.

So much for overlooking mystery. "I'll have help—a turncoat I've paid off—and if he sees anyone but me, he might panic. You'll just have to trust me."

Maybe the ex-magister knew better than to question a gift: the city walls were coated in a priceless arcanir solution, and the ground beneath them soaked in it. Nothing short of war machines and flashy, indirect magic would penetrate the capital's defenses if stealth failed.

Brennan took a deep breath. "Stay here and wait for my signal."

Rielle grabbed his arm. "Try not to die."

He smiled, a pointless act in the dark. "You'd miss me too much." He pulled away and stalked to the trees.

At the edge, he undressed and, neither hearing nor scenting anyone nearby, shifted to full wolf and dropped to all fours. He gathered his leather overcoat, trousers, and boots between his teeth in an unwieldy bundle and skittered across the open plain, swift and low.

The city ditch quickly approaching, he vaulted over it with all the force he could muster, shifting mid-air to man-beast and digging his claws into the wall.

Above him on the ramparts, a lone guard stirred, his footfalls nearing the battlements.

Brennan kept still, clinging close to the stone.

Whether the guard looked through the machicolation or over the parapet would determine the success of this stealth plan. Midway between a bastion and the gate tower, both heavily guarded, he had planned to escape notice.

Up between the two nearest corbels, the guard's breath puffed softly over the parapet above, between the battlement's merlons.

Then disappeared.

Departing footsteps.

If not for the mouthful of leather, he could have grinned. The laziness of not wanting to look through the machicolation had just cost that guard his life and the lives of his comrades.

He pulled his claws free, only to dig them in a little higher. He scaled the wall up to the supporting corbels of the battlement and then around.

No more claws. The sound of them cleaving into the masonry would give him away. Still in man-beast form, he eyed his hand, willing his claws to retract. He'd use his fingers for a hold on the crenel above without a sound.

Placing his hand on it, he listened for a change in the guard's heart rate. None.

He retracted the claws on his other hand to follow suit. Jaw clenched, he dragged himself up and onto the crenel, crouching low, hidden between the merlons. A guard looked out over the plain just a few feet away. A few feet away from his end.

Brennan took the clothes out of his mouth and noiselessly placed them on the crenel next to him, extending his razor-sharp claws anew. An easy kill.

He listened for any nearby guards. None on the wall. Only far-off voices in the gate tower and in the bastion on the opposite end.

A quick loosening of his shoulder muscles, and he leaped. The whites of the guard's eyes flashed. Brennan swept his claws across the man's throat, silencing a scream into a quiet gurgle.

The smell of blood thick in the air, he dragged the body against the battlement and threw it over the parapet, far enough to avoid the city ditch and its telling splash. He sidled against the edge, darting toward the cover of the gate tower.

He eased open the door. Two hearts beat within.

Quick work. He exhaled a preparatory breath and dove for the nearest guard, ripping his throat out in a flourish of claws. He flickered to the man on the opposite side, closing his gaping maw over the guard's face. The cover drowned a shriek as he shredded flesh and crushed bone between his teeth.

A flurry of steps and racing hearts—

Four guards upstairs stirred in varying stages of alertness. There would be little time before they rang the alarm. Spinning, he launched himself onto the stairs, gouging the stone steps as he scrambled up.

A guard on the nearest landing.

Before he could draw his sword, Brennan lunged for him. He plunged his claws through the man's leather armor to seize his spine and crunch it in an instant.

Another guard charged down the stairs, short sword drawn. A slash— evaded—and Brennan surged upward, snapping the man's neck between his jaws.

A flash in his periphery—the glint of the alarm bell. He turned on the guard about to sound it and threw himself at him, scratching, ripping, shredding, leaving no larynx with which to scream—

Sharp, shooting pain bloomed in his side—a blade between the ribs— and his breath shallowed.

He tore out the heart of the man beneath him with a wet tatter, then angled his massive wolf head around at the man holding the sword.

He kicked out with his clawed back leg, sending the man flying against the wall with his sword yanked free—dazed.

Laboring through the burn of the sword wound, he turned and sprang onto the dazed man before he could react. Slower, but fast enough. Buried his claws in the man's mouth, pierced through his tongue and into the back of his throat. He seized an arm between his jaws and thrashed his head until it rent free.

Hope you miss it in the Lone, bastard.

The last tower guard dead, Brennan breathed heavily, clutching the wound at his side even as it began to heal. It was bad, enough to kill a mortal man, and although he would soon heal, his injury slowed his pace. He crept down the tower's steps, bracing himself against the wall, extinguishing all the torches, and then he staggered onto the battlements to fetch his clothes. The tower going dark would not only signal Rielle and Leigh to approach the gate but also Nicolette and her diversionary force.

The battle had officially begun.

He re-entered the gate tower, shifted back to his human form, and descended the flight of stairs to the lower level, pausing only to throw on his trousers, overcoat, and boots. The leather stung against his open wound, but he steeled himself.

He made his way to the winches for the drawbridge, outer and inner portcullises, seized the hand crank of the first winch, unwound it until the bridge lowered. Then he drew up the outer and the inner portcullises.

Finally. He exited the gate tower on the ground floor and peered around the corner. Two figures traversed the plain in the consuming darkness. He waited until he could discern Rielle's face before leaning against the tower.

He applied pressure to his wound. It would take much more than that to kill him, but this night would no doubt test those boundaries.

61

*R*ielle cast a stoneskin spell on herself. A dull gray layer of geomancy hardened over every inch of her skin. Sustained spells were costly, but being killed by an unnoticed arrow before completing the mission was costlier. And stoneskin, at least, wasn't as visible as her instinctive flame cloak—nothing said *look over here* like a walking human torch. She would still have enough power left to penetrate the citadel, cross the Azalée District, and fight through Trèstellan Palace—hopefully.

Leigh followed suit with a repulsion shield.

Ahead of them, the drawbridge had been lowered over the city ditch. Brennan had succeeded. They crossed the drawbridge and darted past the two portcullis gates, the threat of the meurtrière overhead dormant but not forgotten, the hole in the gatehouse passageway ceiling opportune for spilling tar or boiling oil. A fond farewell to avoid on their exit.

Flames licked the night sky in the distance: the darkened gate tower had either gone unnoticed or the guards were more concerned with the growing fire beyond the rooftops on the south side of the city.

She had just about run past the gate tower when she caught movement in her periphery.

She stopped, raising her hand to cast.

Brennan slumped against the tower, clutching a hand to his side.

Was he hurt?

She bit her lip. He was fine. Of course he was fine. Wasn't he?

But once she approached him, her hands checked from his head to his neck, his shoulders, through his parted leather overcoat over his chest and his back, until her fingertips found the wetness of blood in his side, seeping through his fingers. "You're hurt."

He chuckled softly and grazed his fingers against hers. "Maybe you should keep checking."

"You can't keep—"

"Stop." He pushed her away. "It looks a lot worse than it is, and you'll need your strength. Believe me, I'm already feeling better."

His werewolf healing had already kicked in, then.

She frowned. "All right, but stay out of trouble."

He shook his head, smiling crookedly. "If I'm following you, then I'm already way past staying out of trouble." His gaze shifted toward Leigh, who stood alert, watching for enemies at the nearest crossroad. His brows drew together, and his mouth thinned to a fine line. "You need to go."

She slid her hands out of his overcoat, away from his touch. "I know," she said, "and what about you?"

"I'll rendezvous with Nicolette and her group in the Coquelicot District by the southeastern gate." He hesitated. "I'll be fine."

She lowered her gaze to his ribs, visualizing the hemorrhage there.

"I didn't know you cared," he whispered, a sharp edge riding his voice.

Of course she did. As deeply as he'd hurt her, she still cared. The boy she'd met as a child had been kind, and she still remembered him, even if Brennan didn't. Her gaze wandered back up to his. Narrowed and gleaming. Cynical.

"We need to go," Leigh warned.

"I'll find you in the palace." Brennan pulled her in and kissed her cheek. She jolted.

He chuckled and, before she could smack him, departed.

She turned to the peaks of Trèstellan Palace. *I'm coming, Olivia.*

She strode past Leigh down the city street, keeping her eyes on the citadel beyond the canal enveloping the Azalée District and the palace. Those walls were meant to keep armies out, their arcanir-soaked earth and coated stone a barrier to most mages.

Most mages.

Their main obstacle would be General Evrard Gilles. The city outskirts, the citadel, and especially the palace teemed with Crag Company mercenaries.

"It's a good thing war waits for heartfelt goodbyes," Leigh grumbled from her right side.

She rolled her eyes.

The shouts in the distance grew nearer. No time to lose.

Maintaining their shield spells, they traversed the rich Alcea District and entered the Orchidée District—housing nobles not rich enough to purchase property in Azalée within the walls of the citadel. The voices drew closer, and she led Leigh from the cobblestone boulevard into a small thoroughfare between villas. They ducked shoulder to shoulder behind a row of hedges.

She raised her head. The citadel's regal northern gate into Azalée was right there.

"Planning to visit your home away from home?" Leigh asked her in a hushed tone.

Couronne, her family's long-unused villa in Azalée, was close by. "Why, Leigh, do you need a break for dinner?"

He cracked a grin. "A nap would be nice, too. And tea."

"Why don't you earn it first?"

A platoon of about forty mercenaries shuffled down the cobbles. The voices they'd been hearing.

Many. Too many. Were they sigiled? How many of them?

She stayed hidden as they passed, then slunk along the hedges to the edge of the thoroughfare and peered around the corner.

The platoon marched toward the citadel. To reinforce it, no doubt, which would make their plan even more difficult.

Not a chance. She channeled wind in one hand and fire in the other, dismissing her stoneskin spell, and stepped out of cover.

Setting the wind spinning upon the ground, she imbued it with fire. In a matter of seconds, it grew into a fiery whirlwind before her, four bodies wide and two tall.

Voices ahead—time to let it go. She sent it toward them, a cyclone consuming the avenue in a conflagration of screeching wails, dragging men into its spinning inferno.

It left only char in its wake.

She rubbed her hands together. The spell's intensity raged in a blazing moment before she swept her hands apart to dissipate it.

The fire cooled. The wind died. The smoke cleared.

Embers glowed upon the blackened cobblestones. The mercenaries. They hadn't been sigiled.

Wind drove down the avenue from behind, hurtling past her to gather up the ash and surge toward the towering gates of the citadel. A rustle made her snap toward the sound—Leigh emerging from the thoroughfare, his repulsion shield dismissed.

Eyebrows raised, he nodded his approval, lowered his gaze to the ash, and winced. "Bad way to go."

"I was fresh out of old age."

"Always out of stock." Grinning, he studied the arcanir-coated gates ahead. "We'll knock. Very hard."

She and Leigh—an elementalist and a wild-mage enforcer—could penetrate any wall. She stared into the murky waters of the Arsen Canal. "The canal. Cover me."

They crept from cover to cover toward the walls of the citadel. Archers lined the citadel's battlements, but she and Leigh kept out of sight. Time dragged as they advanced toward the canal, the city's skyline silhouetted against the growing fire to the south. The Black Rose distraction—good. Occasional shouts rose from amid the din. The sounds of revolt.

Cover became scarce as they neared the canal.

A call. The archers unleashed a wave of arrows.

Leigh's repulsion shield was up, deflecting them all. Using his free hand, he magically pulled individual targets from the battlements to their deaths.

"Take your time," he grunted.

The canal flowed several feet away from them, just close enough. She focused on it, channeling current control to magical excess, both sculpting a new path for the canal with her hands and willing its waters up and away toward the battlements.

Several archers gaped at the canal as it flowed up through the air to the wall, the rampart its new channel. A shadow, enormous and dark, cast wide below the tons of water. Men fled, screamed.

She flooded the top of the wall in a torrent, the blasting water sending screaming mercenaries flying from the battlements with incredible force to the ground below. It burst through the door of the gate tower and exploded from windows and doors, continuing on its path of destruction around the entire wall of the citadel.

She fed it, willing more and more of the canal's water to the wall until it seeped from every crevice and poured through the battlements' crenels. Stones and beams burst; water pounded to the ground and back into the canal.

She ceased channeling the spell. Her surroundings spun for a brief moment, and then—

Ah, I feel light as a feather.

Serenity brimmed beneath her skin—no, quivered. She sighed heavily, opening her eyes to see Leigh's blurry, panicked face while he lightly patted her cheek. She winced as the blur cleared, and clenched her jaw at being slapped repeatedly.

"I'm fine!" she shouted at him, and he pursed his grinning lips. "You can stop hitting me!" She looked inward. Her anima reserve was dim. With about a tenth reserved for Brennan, she'd also expended about half of the rest. Controlling the canal had cost her much.

Holding her a foot off the ground, Leigh seized her hand, and she felt the familiar pull of resonance, unsolicited but sorely needed.

Her anima begged for completion, and instinct made her pull him, too. Her blue pool of anima shone with a blinding endless white light, Leigh's magic, a force that shook her anima, making it ripple as it pulsed, radiating outward through her entire body, its familiarity both comforting and invigorating. Every part of her vibrated with power, a hot energy that filled her up and compressed into a pressure that begged for release. Her skin tingled until the hand holding his sizzled.

Her eyes fluttered open, every part of her awakened and alive. Her gaze locked with his, star-white eyebrows drawn, dark eyes intense—pinned against the door to his office, bunching fingers in his heavy winter magister robes, *You will be my undoing* a soft caress against her ear, a shiver, opening her mouth to his, stifling a soft moan—

She pulled her hand away. Memories from years long past.

"What are you doing?" he groused, rolling his eyes. He let her go, and she fell the short distance to the ground with a gasp. "You needed resonance."

Her face burned. Resonance, once so casual and utilitarian, had become a thing of beauty with Jon. Intimate.

Nevertheless, Leigh was right. She had regained nearly half of the anima that she had lost, and every bit would matter until the rite was done and Olivia was free. They were both mature enough to separate a biological response from intention.

"Thank you," she conceded, despite the certain bruise forming on her bottom.

He replied with an irritated nod and watched the citadel while she rose to her feet.

Before she could address how they would pass the gates, he turned to the cobblestone avenue, his hands glowing with bright power. She knew that look, and prepared to observe art. Leigh Galvan never disappointed in that regard.

The stones ripped from the pavement, forming a magical arrangement of steps ascending from the bank of the canal to the battlements, only Leigh's force magic control holding them in place.

Once the last stone was placed, Rielle headed toward Leigh's creation, offering him a small appreciative smile before ascending the steps. He sighed, the annoyance between them dispelled, and followed her.

As soon as they set foot on the damp stone battlements, the cobblestones collapsed behind them in a clamoring heap, a chaotic monument splayed across the canal and onto the bank.

She glared at Leigh, and he shrugged.

"I'll restore it all later." He peered over the other side of the wall. "Let's head into Azalée."

"One stop." She spun toward the gate tower. Opening the citadel gates could mean that the Black Rose and the paladins, if they came, could enter Azalée to support them.

"Why bother?" Leigh trailed after her while she approached the doorway into the gate tower, its door hanging off a single strained hinge.

"Why not?" She hurried down the nearby staircase to the level above the meurtrière between the inner and outer portcullis gates. It was soaked, with a body face down in the corner. The torrent of water had trapped the Crag mercenary on this level, even with water draining through the meurtrière.

She found the winches that controlled the drawbridge, outer portcullis, and inner portcullis, and proceeded to open them all.

"Come," she said to Leigh. "We don't have much time."

Their entry into Azalée had been less than stealthy. It wouldn't be long before Gilles brought the full force of the Crag upon them.

She exited with Leigh, the long road through Azalée and the causeway to Trèstellan Palace ahead of them.

62

*T*hick smoke filled the air, stinging Brennan's nostrils—the blaze had nearly spread through the entire district. The oil the Black Rose had procured had not only ensured that the fire would burn long but also incredibly hot.

By the time he'd made it here, his wound had nearly healed. The impoverished residential area lay in molten ruins, with the uproar of battle raging near the gates. He quickened his pace, running toward the center.

"Kill them!" a man yelled above the pandemonium.

"Let's put the hurt to these bastards!" Nicolette shouted wildly.

The clangor of parried blades rang nearby, mixed with cries of the dying and roars of the victors, myriad hearts beating in racing, raucous cacophony. Tuning them out, he cleared an alley to see the chaos of fighting between the Crag and the assorted band of assassins, thieves, swashbucklers, blacksmiths, merchants, and other citizens armed with everything from pitchforks to meat cleavers to wooden beams with nails.

The Crag here amounted to a company of men. Although the resistance was about even at near a hundred fighters, Crag reinforcements closed in from the adjacent Chardon District. It was only a matter of time before more forces would arrive from farther districts.

The resistance would be crushed. And then the diversion would be over. The Crag would turn their eyes to the palace.

He rushed in and drove a flying kick into a Crag tabard, dodging a sword slash as he landed.

A mercenary threw a roundhouse kick. Brennan dropped and spun a low sweep kick, taking his opponent and two others to the ground. Barely a breath later, he grabbed two necks and crushed them before rolling to avoid an axe strike. He wove through a bedlam of warring bodies, knocking out knees, breaking arms, snapping necks. At least the curse had its uses.

Nicolette fought at the back of the militia. "Get that gate open, men!"

Several rebels exited the gate tower, coughing. The tower itself was on fire, the smoke no doubt too thick for them to open the drawbridge and the portcullises. Beyond the wall, thousands of voices roared in rally.

Paladins.

Someone had to let them in.

Someone like him.

He made for the smoke-filled gate tower. The howl of air cut by a blade had him moving, but not fast enough—

Searing pain sliced into his shoulder.

Grinding his teeth, he seized the back of the short sword and yanked it free from its flesh-and-bone anchor. He pulled it forward, bringing its bearer's face directly into his punch. With a gratified hiss, he relished the crunch of bone and cartilage against his knuckles.

His teeth elongated.

Not now. Not fucking now.

He drew his lip over them, struggling to keep them hidden. The lengthening points of his nails dug into his flesh as he tried to keep pressure on his cleaved shoulder. His Wolf skulked at the edge of control.

Making his way to the gate tower, he focused on the bond. The precarious hold meant Rielle was weakening. Passed out, or—

The thundering steps of approaching reinforcements meant he needed to get that gate open.

He evaded his way through the battle to Nicolette.

"Brennan." Her eyebrows rose as she dispatched a mercenary with ease while the rest of her assassins made quick work of others. Outside their usual stealthy element, they still seemed capable enough. But the Crag's numbers countenanced the losses easily.

He nodded as he moved past to the gate tower, where two more men exited, one dragging the other.

"What are you doing?" She blocked a slash with her sword and sliced a throat with her dagger. The spray of blood laid a fresh coat on her already bloodied leather armor.

He surveyed the inside, waiting for one last man to emerge. "I'm opening that gate."

She laughed, and her sword and dagger found flesh once more. "Nox give you strength!"

With a grin, he was inside the tower, heat and smoke stinging his eyes and nostrils. Through the gray haze, he searched for the stairs.

There. At the back.

He raced toward them, one boot sloshing. Blood had run all the way down from his shoulder to pool at his sole. The burn of healing heated the flesh, but not as hot or as fast as usual. He applied pressure with his palm while hustling to the staircase, and took the stairs two at a time.

Smoke filled his lungs before he spotted the winches and rushed to them. While his head swam, he seized the first crank, finding it already partially drawn. The humans had made some progress.

Once the drawbridge was down, he moved to the outer portcullis winch, then the inner, his breath shallow and painful as the smoky gate tower spun around him.

But the gate was open.

He fell to his knees, then to his face. Fresh air and the clamor of charging paladins filtered in through the meurtrière. His strength flagged, draining from his body along with his blood.

RIELLE PEEKED around a rose bush at the southeastern service entrance.

No one manned it. Good. She nodded to Leigh.

With many of Gilles's sigiled men on the wall to repel the invasion of the city, she and Leigh managed to cross Azalée and enter the palace grounds quietly enough. They'd encountered and fought small pockets—with a swiftness that only unsigiled opponents could offer.

She ran to the door. No keys. Her hand against the metal, she heated it to molten while Leigh kept watch.

When it dripped down the door, she finally allowed herself to exhale.

Leigh took position at the side of the door as she wrapped herself in a flame cloak and gusted the door open. The bond faltered, and she stiffened.

Two arrows grazed her arm and shoulder but didn't cut through the cloak. Leigh threw his repulsion shield before her, deflecting two more arrows.

Was Brennan all right?

A couple of Crag guards stood within the first-floor service hallway.

He had to be all right. He had to.

Calling the wind, she flourished her free hand and spun a cyclone down the hallway, swirling it larger and gathering both of the guards. She pulled her hand back and stepped out of the way.

The two went flying toward her and burst through the open door, screaming as they soared through the air and over the causeway, then plummeted into the Azalée District, their screams fading until they died.

"Aren't we dramatic?" Leigh mumbled, entering the hallway. Clapping, he inspected the first-floor service corridor of the east wing.

She frowned and searched for the stairwell. At the end of an adjoining hallway was a tower with a narrow spiral staircase.

They'd have to clear the damn stairwell first. If alive, the palace's original inhabitants were locked in the dungeon, so she summoned a sphere of searing heat.

The bond tightened like a tendril of a braid pulled taut; she clenched her teeth. Brennan had to be seeking greater control—which meant things were going poorly in Coquelicot. At least he was alive.

Divide and conquer. Perhaps he and Nicolette needed the diversion now.

Swirling the sphere of fire into an ascending spiral in her hand, she cast its route and, with a push, released it up the stairs. Flames licked the walls as it traveled, and she ran outside until she could see the top of the stairwell's tower. Leigh chased her out as the flames burst through the windows on the top floor.

He scowled at her. "If the Crag didn't know we were here, they do now."

Fresh air blew in through the meurtrière's holes, and Brennan sucked it in voraciously, the second wind he needed. He crawled to the staircase and tumbled down the steps, then landed on his back, the wind knocked out of him.

Dazed for a moment, he gathered only enough of his will to drag himself to the exit's open door.

His eyes stinging, he blinked several times at the picture outside—a deluge of armored paladins pouring through the southeastern gate, coursing through the Crag fighting the militia, and crashing against the reinforcements with brutal force. A large Order of Terra platoon broke off to reinforce the wall. They could hold Coquelicot with their numbers.

He looked up at one of them standing over him. Tor smiled down at him, his hazel eyes dancing and his dark hair covered in ash.

"Does Faolan know you're here?" He surveyed Brennan with a raised brow and a narrowed eye.

"Uncle Tor." It was always good to see him. But on the other matter—he sighed. The less Father knew of his dealings, the better.

Of his uncles, Tor and Desmond had always been the friendliest, not to mention vastly better men than Father. The youngest of four brothers, Tor had shunned courting marriageable heiresses, and had inexplicably chosen service as a paladin. He had been the best warrior among them, something Brennan had admired and respected since childhood.

Tor extended an arm, and Brennan took it and struggled to his feet, receiving a pat on the back that made him wince.

"I won't tell him if you won't." Brennan added an audacious wink with a stinging eye.

Tor examined the wound on his shoulder, but it had already nearly healed, leaving naught but a shallow cut. "You should get this treated." Tor eyed the blood drenching the entire right side of Brennan's body. "The priests have set up a medical tent just outside the wall."

Brennan shrugged, his usual excuse ready. "It looks much worse than it is."

The smoke inhalation had been the greater annoyance.

"Tor," a familiar voice bellowed—the commoner?—and he turned around. "You have command. Subdue the Crag on the wall and the district's outskirts, rally the militia, then wait for Captain Perrault's orders."

Covering his heart with his right hand, Tor bent at the waist.

What was this? Since when did forsworn paladins issue orders to their elders? Behind Tor stood none other than Jonathan Ver. Did he now outrank Tor somehow? Or was he relaying the captain's orders?

If Jon was surprised to see him, he didn't show it when their eyes met. Blood spatter adorning his face and armor, he'd clearly seen some battle. Gray ash covered his pauldrons and the helm that he held under one arm; the paladins must have been in position outside the gate during the fire.

"Tregarde." Jon inclined his head. The battle continued raging far behind him.

"Ver," Brennan replied.

"Have you two become friends?" Tor asked, looking from Jon to Brennan.

Friends... with *him?* Brennan snorted. "I wouldn't go that far. I only saved him from decapitation a couple times."

He savored Jon's scowl with no small amount of satisfaction. A few days ago, the commoner's neck would have been a deliciously indulgent crunch between his jaws, but killing him would mean losing Rielle's good graces forever. Better this dalliance run its course.

The sound of upheaval carried from the distance near the citadel. It likely meant one thing: Rielle had invaded the Azalée District.

Jon glanced toward the citadel, where black smoke curled from a palace tower, and pointed to it. "That's where I'm headed."

"So am I." Before heading out, he turned to Tor. "Good luck, Uncle."

Tor nodded, but his gaze shifted toward Jon and he took a preparatory breath. "Perhaps you should—"

A look from Jon, and Tor stayed his tongue and stood to attention.

"Terra's blessings upon you." Tor gestured the blessed circle with his open palm toward them.

"And upon you," Jon replied while Brennan nodded his thanks.

They turned to the north and began the long advance toward the citadel through groups of wounded soldiers, prisoners of war, and heaps of corpses. The city remained dark but for the burning buildings, and quiet but for distant cries and fighting.

The exchange between Tor and Jon had been strange. The bow meant it hadn't just been a relay of orders. Jon outranked Tor, but how could that be? Had the Order taken him back among its ranks? Perhaps his assistance with entry into Courdeval had even gotten him promoted?

If so, the Sacred Vows would govern him once more. His tie to Rielle would be severed. She'd be free.

Brennan fought the broad grin threatening to emerge. One fewer obstacle. Perhaps he'd break the curse yet.

Only a couple of hours remained before the Moonlit Rite would have to be completed. Hopefully Rielle would survive the damned night—she had a habit of nearly getting herself killed. The last thing he needed was her dying. Especially now.

"Your injuries look severe," Jon murmured as they crossed from the Coquelicot District ringing the city into the Dandelion District, known for its sprawling bazaar.

"I've had worse." Bleeding wasn't entirely unpleasant. Perhaps his rapid healing had colored his impression of pain. "I'll be fine." His werewolf healing would restore him soon.

" 'I'll be fine,' " Jon imitated, with that insistent down-note on the end that was so familiar. "You sound like Rielle." He looked ahead solemnly as they moved through the marketplace's wrecked stalls.

True enough. By now, they sounded like old soldiers reminiscing about battle wounds. But there was something different about the man; his heart beat faster. Perhaps stressed by his return to the Order? Or was it just the uncertainty of battle?

He scented the faint smell of Jon's blood on the wind. A diagonal cut along the cheekbone. "What about you? Are you redecorating your face?"

A stern glare. "I've been dodging arrows all night."

"Looks like you've gotten better at it since Melain." He could hardly hold back his grin, and even Jon's glare cracked.

A strange, faraway sound. Brennan tilted his head. A creaking, kind of like—

Jon opened his mouth when Brennan lunged to tackle him.

They tumbled behind a fruit stand in a loud clatter, sending fruit rolling away. A barrage of arrows impaled the spoiling apples, pomegranates, and pears next to them.

63

Smoke rose from the stairwell, and Rielle drew in a deep breath. Yes, doubtless the Crag now knew they were here, but it would take the pressure off Brennan, Nicolette, and the Black Rose at the southeastern gate.

Their time would soon run out. They needed to complete the rite, find Olivia, and get out. She raced past Leigh and entered the smoking tower.

Leigh held the black wool of his sleeve to his nose as he followed her in. She spelled a gust that blew the smoke away.

"Now that the Crag know we're here," Leigh said, "there could be hundreds of mercenaries coming our way. We may have to choose between Olivia and the Moonlit Rite."

Gilles would send his best men to the palace. Sigiled men. Those who could stand up to magic. And the Crag had shown its access to black-market arcanir. Spell shields were useless against arcanir weapons and arrows... magekillers. And in cramped quarters—buildings—indirect magic would be risky.

But she'd come here for Olivia. Although the Moonlit Rite couldn't be ignored, he had to know she'd choose Olivia.

She looked back at him. "I'm doing both, with or without you. So make up your mind."

He bridged the few steps between them and grabbed her upper arms. "Don't you understand yet?" he asked in a hushed voice. "These traditional rites are so old, no one knows why we even need them anymore or *if* we need them. As long as people believe that the Divinity protects them, it retains its power—control—over all of us, over every aspect of our lives."

She pulled away, clutching at the vial of king's blood hanging from her neck. "It may very well be a manipulation. Who knows? But we can't take the risk."

"Oh? What are we risking, then?"

Shaking her head, she shrugged. "Fine. I don't have all the answers. But Olivia does. And she chose to perform the rite. I trust her judgment."

He turned away and sighed. "Then let's go get her."

Great Divine, if only it were so simple. "I found out in Bournand that she's bound in Courdeval. Who's to say they're not keeping her locked in her quarters, chained up with arcanir?"

"If I took control of a palace, I know where I'd put my prisoners."

"The most secure part of the palace? Before we put *ourselves* in there, we should be sure our risk is warranted, shouldn't we? It could be a trap."

Leigh scoffed, but didn't reply.

A loud boom roared from the south. She darted to a nearby window and looked out at the darkness of the city, lit only by the moon and the scattered fires beneath it. In the distance, a massive fiery glow rose over the city. A battle. Jon.

"The Order is doing its job," Leigh said. "It's time to do ours."

"I—"

"I'll go in first."

Chewing her lower lip, she followed up to the fourth floor. So she'd managed to convince him to check Olivia's quarters first, then. At least for now.

Leigh cast his repulsion shield while she assumed a position to the side of the doorway.

He entered the hall and cast a flurry of force-magic spells. Anguished cries and the crunch of bone—

She stepped out of the doorway. Two guards lay on the floor, bent at odd angles.

A third collided with the floor, the ceiling, and then the floor again.

With earthsight, she scanned both hallways stemming from the tower stairwell. No more movement.

Leigh stood ready, still as stone, his brow creased.

She moved past him down the hallway toward Olivia's quarters—no brightness there either. Empty.

She dispelled the earthsight and, with a wave of her hand, lit the hallway's many sconces. Tapestries saturated the walls, priceless antiques filled in alcoves, and the vaulted ceiling figured high above them in majestic, lofty arches. Most of the stained-glass windows were still intact, representing generations of monarchs in their immortalized glory.

The Crag hadn't ransacked the place. Their employer—the anonymous lords of Parliament calling themselves the Emaurrian Knot—had prioritized keeping the palace in good condition.

Gilles would say he'd defended the capital and defeated the assassins and traitors who'd killed the Faralles. And who would remain to refute him?

She wasn't the only one who needed to find Olivia alive. All of Emaurria needed her alive.

The Archmage's quarters were unlocked, and they entered a parlor. Off the parlor were several doors—the first of which had a large blackwood desk covered in papers, artifacts, and supplies. The drawers and their contents lay scattered on the floor.

The magic laboratory and the storeroom appeared much the same while the small library remained orderly. The Crag didn't seem to think books were worth cracking.

The last of the doors opened to private chambers. The dresser's drawers were open haphazardly, the armoire emptied, the bed overturned, and the storage chest's lid hung off its hinges against the foot of the bed. Next to her, a solemn Leigh browsed through the contents of a bookshelf.

Olivia had lived in this room for the past few months: a vanity with toiletries, two night stands piled high with books and papers, a dresser in utter disarray, and a small table with writing implements and an incomplete drawing of a cat on some official document. Olivia's quarters at the Tower had been full of sketches; her mind tended to wander when she mulled over a problem.

Like the rite.

On top was a requisition order for alchemy supplies. She flipped it over. Nothing. And beneath it, a letter: *You say you can't, but you want to. Meet me in the stables after the banquet. A moonlit ride. Just you and me.*

She ran her thumb over the ink. The words of a lover. Had the attack happened later, would Olivia have been safe, outside the palace, in the arms of her man? Someone honorable and steadfast like Jon, or mysterious and volatile like Brennan, cold and wry like Leigh. Did she love him? Would she see him again?

A lump formed in the back of her throat, and she tried to swallow, but couldn't.

Leigh came up to her and put an arm around her shoulders. "We'll find her."

They would. They had to. She nodded. "Let's go. There's nothing here."

He squeezed her shoulder gently, lowering his gaze to the drawing. "She always did have a cat thing."

He was stalling.

"Leigh—"

"Fine. Let's go. The dungeon it is."

It was unlike him to be so indecisive. He'd always been a man who shrugged off opposition and smiled at challenge. Who boasted that, no matter what, he'd accomplish his goal.

Who was he tonight? Eyeing his back warily, she headed for the door.

BRENNAN POPPED his head up just long enough to spot the archers readying another volley from behind a cloak stall.

Jon dropped to a crouch and took cover as they let their arrows fly. A pear flew off the top of the fruit stand and rolled across the ground, an arrow embedded in its flesh.

"Is there an archer in this kingdom who doesn't want to shoot you?" Brennan bit out.

Jon peered around the stall's edge. "I'll let you know when I meet one."

Brennan followed his gaze. The archers were splitting their formation, some drawing swords.

"They're going to flank us," Jon murmured.

Brennan gathered a couple apples. "I'll draw their fire, and when the opportunity arises to attack, you take it."

"Are you insane?" Jon's gaze snapped to his. "Out of cover in nothing but leathers? You'll be—"

Brennan got in position to run. "I'll be fine." He flashed his teeth. "You're the one they like to shoot so much, remember?"

He bolted. Arrows dotting his wake, he ran in an arc away from the fruit stand. The arrows followed.

Jon dashed to another stall and another and another until he crouched behind a spice display, just behind the archers.

Arrows whizzing close by, Brennan dove toward a clothes rack. In midair, he hurled two apples—each hitting an archer in the forehead—and rolled to a landing through a shelf of boots. He darted toward the cloak stall and took cover on the opposite side.

Only two remained, their hearts hurried and erratic. The rest approached the fruit stand with swords drawn.

Brennan rounded the cloak stall and grabbed the two archers' jerkins, knocked their heads together.

He kicked aside their bodies and stayed in cover, just in case the swordsmen switched back to their bows.

Metal cut the air. His ears perked.

The crunch of a blade connecting with body after body. The coppery scent of fresh blood competed with a cacophony of screams.

He peeked around the cloak stall.

Jon stood, blood-drenched, an arrow lodged in his armpit through a weak point in his armor. A scattered array of body parts, bows, armor, and fruit formed a grotesque circle around him.

"Not bad," Brennan murmured under his breath. The arm of an archer jerked next to him. He twisted the man's neck.

Jon removed his blood-spattered helm. Its visor hadn't protected his face from the crimson spray. He offered a grim nod to Brennan, then looked beyond the citadel toward the palace. "We're close." He shook off his sword, wiped it, and sheathed it.

Brennan grabbed two black cloaks from the stand.

Jon jerked his head toward the palace. "You can shop later. Let's go."

Brennan tossed him a cloak, and Jon caught it, wincing. "It's free now. You might not be able to afford it later, on a paladin's wages." He smirked. "Besides, we look like someone killed us, dug us up, and killed us again."

Jon strode toward him and past, grabbing hold of the arrow protruding from between his cuirass and pauldron—it had just barely split and penetrated his chain mail—and pulled it free with a grimace. He threw the black cloak about his shoulders.

Donning his own, Brennan walked up to him. "Looks like your dodging still needs work."

"So did theirs." Jon put on his helm once more as they headed toward Trèstellan.

RIELLE HAD SEEN this tapestry already—a man slaying a dragon. They had the same eyes. She turned the map of Trèstellan's ground level. The door was supposed to be here somewhere. "Are you sure we haven't been here already? I think we're lost."

Leigh shrugged. "Whenever I came here, I didn't exactly spend time wandering the halls. If we were trying to find our way around a bedchamber, however—"

She sighed, the map crumpling in her hand. It had revealed only one way into the ritual chamber in the catacombs—steps beneath the ancient temple at the heart of the palace. They'd rounded the temple at least once.

It was through the ritual chamber that they'd get to the dungeon, too. Unless they wanted to traverse the entire palace to enter through the barracks. But Gilles' best sigiled troops incoming made that no option at all.

There was no one to ask either. Not that the Crag would tell them, but she and Leigh had dispatched the few guards they'd encountered. The temple should have been heavily guarded, but it appeared deserted. Perhaps the Crag Company had sent out too many troops to reinforce the Chardon District. The Crag's long trek back to the palace was supposed to be a blessing, if she and Leigh could find the damn stairs.

"Divine's flaming fire," she blurted, and kicked the tapestry. She kicked too far, and her boot thunked against wood.

Wood? She glanced at Leigh, who shook his head and pulled the tapestry aside. A heavy door wrapped in iron.

"Welcome to your stairs," he murmured.

"Why behind a tapestry?"

"Would *you* want the door leading into an ancient ritual chamber out in the open?"

Probably not. Her cheeks heated. The thought should've crossed her mind, but she'd been too busy looking over her shoulders for Crag, staying alert—

He held up a hand, distorting the air, and curled his fingers.

When he pulled his arm back, the door ripped free, flew across the hall, and thudded into the other side.

Shouts echoed from the distance. Had the Crag already arrived? Time was dwindling.

They entered, carefully replacing the tapestry over the entrance. Her candlelight spell guided their way down as they carefully avoided broken stairs; stray cobwebs caught fire above them and smoked away like ephemera.

As they neared the bottom, a faint glow emanated from the corridor outside the ritual chamber. It should have been abandoned. Perhaps it was.

Perhaps a mere torch shone at the bottom, left behind by some singular visitor.

But she spelled a wind wall before her. Leigh followed suit with a repulsion shield.

Their defensive spells intact, she enchanted her eyes with earthsight.

No fewer than two hundred men awaited them.

64

*R*ielle froze. An army stood in their way.

"Well, now we know where all the guards went," Leigh murmured.

Turning back wasn't an option. Somewhere past them was Olivia, and the Lunar Chamber.

"Welcome, Marquise Laurentine," a man's gravelly deep voice bellowed, his arrogance rumbling down the corridor. "Come join us. We won't hurt you. Yet."

Leigh extended his repulsion shield before her. But if the Crag had arcanir weapons and arrows, neither Leigh's repulsion shield nor her wind wall would mean anything. With a swallow, she descended step after painstaking step, the heels of her boots clicking like isolated, discordant notes.

At the bottom of the stairs, she looked through an archway.

A mountain of a man stood at the front of the large company of men, holding his five-foot flambard across his shoulder. He wore a plumed helmet and a massive suit of armor with a black, silver-trimmed cloak. The General of the Crag Company, Evrard Gilles.

He wasn't the leader of the most sought-after mercenary organization for nothing; his men maintained perfect formation behind him. At least two platoons of doubles stood with him, bearing their iconic two-handed swords.

"I hope you've enjoyed your stay," he drawled. "It's about to come to an end."

"The reception could have been warmer," she replied, with forced bravado.

Gilles laughed. "Yes, I've heard you like playing with fire," he replied, chuckles rippling through the company of men. "Don't look so upset," he teased. "I'm not entirely heartless. You can still turn around and leave." More laughter accompanied his words.

An offer to leave.

He'd just given her something useful.

"If you intend to break the peace here, it would save me the trouble of having to clean my blade of your blood," he quickly added. Perhaps he'd seen the epiphany on her face.

No matter. He'd already given away that this show of force was born of necessity. A soldier of fortune, he wouldn't offer her a way out unless he knew the battle would cost him.

So he'd gathered troops here, but were there enough sigiled men among them, enough arcanir to give him the favorable odds he needed? Maybe most, if not all, of his sigiled men had gone to the Black Rose's diversion at the southeastern gate. Maybe they had fewer arcanir weapons and projectiles than he required. Maybe he'd never expected her to get this far.

Or... Maybe that's what he wanted her to think. Maybe he was toying with her. All these men could be sigiled. Like paladins.

With the Lunar Chamber here, she couldn't risk indirect magic that might collapse the walls or the ceiling.

The walls or the ceiling...

She examined the stone floor tiles between them. An inward grin. "I'm not entirely heartless either," she called out, pushing that forced bravado as far as it would take her. She couldn't lose her nerve now. "You and your men can still leave. It would save me the trouble of having to wade through your corpses." She made a show of narrowing her eyes. "But if you don't, no quarter."

Leigh relaxed next to her. Perhaps he'd realized it, too. He dipped his chin ever so slightly in her periphery. A simple yes.

Even if the company was sigiled, they still had options in the environment to use. There was a chance.

Across the corridor, Gilles stood in silence.

But no answer came. No, the Crag Company couldn't afford to retreat, to gain a reputation for failure. Not Gilles. And if his men didn't know her reputation or Leigh's, they wouldn't know what awaited them. If they did, they'd flee... unless they all bore sigils and wore arcanir. Gilles relied on their ignorance to bluff now and try to retain his reputation.

She and Leigh blocked the exit, and the mercenaries wouldn't trust two strange mages to let them pass by peacefully.

It would be battle. And a prayer to the Divine that they survived any arcanir arrows.

Gilles lifted an arm and signaled toward them. The doubles with crossbows readied shots in their direction. How many were arcanir?

Leigh's repulsion shield remained in place. He'd hold it.

She raised a brow at Gilles, smiled coyly, and gestured. A quick spell extinguished the candles. Every last flame hissed out of existence in a blink. The chamber echoed with silence as if every last member of the Crag held his breath. *Let them feel fear. Let them know doubt.*

In the pitch black, she and Leigh darted apart and crouched. Quickly, she visualized the anima threads glowing in the stone tile underfoot, grasped them and brought them together, amassing the stone between them and the repulsion shield. She wove the threads into a large orb, nearly the size of the corridor. The stone tiles clenched together like an enormous fist.

The bolts hit. Most glanced off the repulsion shield. A few made it through—dispelled the shield that Leigh continually recast—and hit the stone orb as it grew in size. The darkness's gift.

Shouts rang out from the company.

While Leigh protected her and himself, she bathed the stone orb in fire and sent it rolling toward the mass of men, a fiery, stony inevitability that filled the corridor.

Flame and stone lumbered toward the mercenaries, larger than life, eclipsing the other side. Smoking, crackling, bright. Firelight shone on their contorted faces. If they wouldn't surrender, they had to die. Olivia would wait no longer.

"Mercy!" A shrill voice cried from the other end.

She cringed. That time had passed.

A great rumble filled the corridor, the very floor trembling with the massive moving weight. Orders echoed.

The screams.

The orb wheeled over the Crag forces.

The squelch of mangled flesh joined the crunch of pulverized armor. As her creation meted out crushing violent death, flames crackled and licked steel, searing flesh and singeing skin. The stench of gore and burning hair thickened. So much loss of life. Senseless loss of life. Gilles could have surrendered. Should have.

Dust and fragments crumbled from the ceiling. She cast a wind wall above them, and it repelled the debris in all directions.

The flame-stone orb struck the end of the corridor with a reverberating thud that rattled the walls. She channeled fire in her free hand and immolated target after target with unyielding torrents. Firelight fought a pitched battle with the dark, granting enough sight to hit a target and then snatching it away.

Gilles and some of his men had squeezed between the orb and the walls, their number reduced to little more than seventy bodies. Roaring, they charged through the bloody, fiery mass that had been their comrades, their faces grotesque in desperate determination.

Leigh held the shield with one hand. With his other, he spelled tiles from the floor and hurled them at their enemies.

Some dodged, but not all. The stone squares plunged through the attacking force. Men were sent flying through the ranks. Crossbow bolts glanced off the repulsion shield.

Some made it through—arcanir tipped.

A bolt flew past her neck. A sharp sting—

She recast the wind wall. No arcanir poison—just a mere cut to her neck.

Their spells flew and struck, but the mercenary army forged onward, now numbering about fifty.

No good. The mercenaries would reach them before she could call the flame-stone orb back to crush them.

Still, she tried, willing it forward again, but her anima was dimming. The massive weight and fire claimed some of the back line, but not enough.

Gilles and just over two dozen men closed in on them, some with sage-tinted weapons and armor.

A few ran past to the exit. Cowards. Survivors.

Swaths of black flew in from behind her and Leigh, dark wool gliding on air. Two men charged past, blood drenched and fierce.

Jon and Brennan.

With them came a breath of relief. Jon was alive. Alive, and he'd kept his word.

Her heart swelled at their arrival, but there was no time. They took on the arcanir-clad Crag at the front with deadly determination. The rest of the company closed in on them in force.

Leigh threw spell after spell at any available target.

"Rielle!" Jon screamed a warning at her, his wild eyes darting ahead. His blade bound with a Crag mercenary's, he was stuck.

Half a dozen more closed in around him.

Gilles charged her, a massive two-handed sword drawn.

Just as he brought it down mere feet from her, she pulled up a stone wall from the floor to block him, and rolled away.

He rounded the wall, and she shot a torrent of flame at his face.

Unburnt—sigiled, probably. But the enormous blade's waved edge glowed orange. The flambard. She hadn't forgotten it from five years ago.

It lacked the sage tint of arcanir and had no sigils inscribed on it. Opportunity.

He brought his sword back up. She directed fire at the blade, heating it to a molten red from tip to guard.

It tumbled from his gloved hands like a hot coal. "Couldn't leave well enough alone, could you?"

"I could say the same to you!"

He bridged the distance and caught the side of her face with a backhand.

Sent flying, she felt like her eye would burst from its socket. Agony bolted through her face, rippling and blinding and dazing while she clutched her cheek. It throbbed beneath her hand.

"Sundered flesh and shattered bone," she whispered, but the words were slurred. Her jaw, it—*"By Your divine might, let it be sewn."*

Over and over, she tried to heal it as she crawled away. The words were wrong, and she couldn't—

"You don't know what it is to have your life, your destiny controlled by lesser men with greater titles," he said. A step thudded closer. Then another. "No more. My family will want for nothing."

His family?

No, she couldn't think about that now. She had precious little time to kill him before he killed her.

Blood ran down her broken face, and she spat a mouthful of red onto the floor. Men with sage-tinted weapons cornered Leigh. Jon and Brennan disappeared behind a wave of blades.

She rolled onto her back, the blinding white light clearing. Cast a wind wall.

The trembling—No, not now, her anima—

He walked through it. Dispelled it. "That's right. You've lost. Surrender."

He picked up a dead double's two-hander.

Never.

She clawed for a dead mercenary's short sword. She would not die on her back. Not here. Not like this. To her last breath, she would fight. Her hands closed on the hilt. Gilles's sword came down toward her arm.

Sword clashed against sword. Jon stood between her and Gilles, unyielding, pushing back against the general.

"Go," he bellowed at her. "This is my fight!"

Gilles broke away, but Jon followed. The two men measured each other.

He'd anticipated this moment for five years. Justice for Sir Bastien.

The Moonlit Rite and Olivia awaited. Clutching her throbbing jaw, she clad herself in a flame cloak. Fire had always been second nature.

She scrambled to her feet, feeling for the pouch of rowan ash secured to her belt and the vial of king's blood around her neck. Amid the chaos, the doors to the Lunar Chamber were on the far wall.

Her anima was dim—only a couple spells left.

She ran, all the while scanning the battle for Leigh. A crossbowman loosed a bolt. She threw herself to the ground to avoid it. Leigh caught her gaze as he threw a spell at the attacker.

Her heart pounding, she struggled to her feet and charged the entrance to the ritual chamber, finding the double doors closed.

65

*J*on stared down Gilles, holding Faithkeeper in low guard as they circled each other, shouts and the hissing of blades and spells surrounding them. Broad-shouldered with massive arms, the General of the Crag Company stood level with him, over six feet in imposing heavy plate.

Gilles was infamous—a mercenary for three decades, he had taken hundreds, if not thousands, of lives. Both his blade and his pockets ever thirsted for more.

Gilles wielded a two-handed sword five feet in length—as long as the glowing flambard on the ground. He assumed high outside guard, and Jon matched. With the length of the blade, Gilles's reach exceeded his own, but with a few feints, he'd test the man's measure.

Since Signy five years ago, he'd fought Gilles in his mind a thousand times. He'd been learning the sword his entire life and training all the more rigorously for the past five years. Faithkeeper, in his grip, had become an extension of his own body. He hadn't been ready five years ago.

But he was ready now.

Gilles wore a firm but focused expression. The battle blazed around them—Leigh and Brennan cut a bloody path of carnage through what remained of the company.

"Arcanir sword but not the Order's armor," Gilles observed, eyes slitted. "James's bastard, is it? Amazing what torture can elicit. You know, my men found him after he'd killed your mother. To silence her about you, no doubt. He was about to off himself, too, when we caught him."

Gilles wouldn't distract him. Couldn't.

"Surrender. You've lost." Jon studied the man's movement. It hadn't changed much since Signy.

Gilles smirked. "Not to you." Battle ready, he nonetheless cocked his head toward the Lunar Chamber, where Rielle had gone. "Not to her." He laughed. "Broke her face, in fact."

Jon set his jaw. The general tried to rile him, nothing more. But if he only spoke of Rielle and not Bastien, then clearly Gilles didn't remember him.

"Does that make you angry?" Gilles spat. "I watched your pathetic father die, too. There's not enough left of him to bury." He sneered.

His heart thundered in his ears, but Jon fought it. Rage would make him careless, a liability he couldn't allow.

When a force-magic spell darted past, Gilles struck high. Jon blocked. Their swords crossed, Gilles pressed his advantage and advanced, but Jon matched him step for step with retreating footwork.

They disengaged.

Angling, Gilles transitioned to middle guard and immediately struck again, fast. Jon met his strike and closed the distance between them to strike under Gilles's arm. Weak point. His opponent fought back with ruthless efficiency.

Jon turned and parried Gilles's follow-up attack, and coupled it with a riposte. Gilles counter-parried flawlessly.

Impervious. Jon growled. They broke away, circling each other once again.

Gilles laughed. "I'll kill you easily."

"Try hitting me first."

Gilles roared through clenched teeth. He lunged, looking to Jon's left. Signaling. But his shoulders betrayed the feint. Jon bound Gilles's sword aimed for his chest.

I'll defeat you even if it kills me.

Metal chimed in strike after strike, Gilles meeting his every effort. Jon raced through his options. He parried a thrust. Immediately, he reverse-gripped Faithkeeper and closed the distance between them to deliver a heavy pommel strike to Gilles's helm.

A clang resounded. No time to hesitate. Moving Faithkeeper over his shoulder, he struck.

Gilles recovered. The pommel strike should have dazed him, but Gilles worked through it.

The general's experience would prompt him to conclude the fight as soon as possible. More time meant more time for mistakes. Jon's gaze darted to the fallen men surrounding them. Vengeance.

Gilles lowered the point of his sword, taking advantage of his sword's greater range. Jon couldn't match it and win.

Risking all, he brought Faithkeeper down in a crown strike to the top of Gilles's head. The general would be forced to block instead of striking. Or he'd risk taking the blow.

Gilles blocked, crossed swords with him. Directed the point toward his shoulder. Right into the wound left by the arrow in the market.

Through the shoulder—

Wincing, Jon angled, their swords bound, maneuvering Gilles in front of two bodies—dead doubles. Gilles' blade plunged deeper.

Caught.

Roaring through the pain, Jon grabbed the sword and advanced as Gilles took the expected retreating steps.

And tripped over the bodies.

It was over.

Jon pinned the general's right wrist with an armored foot, crushing it until Gilles released his sword, and pressed Faithkeeper's tip to the weak point in Gilles's armor at his neck.

He yanked Gilles' blade free of his own shoulder and glared at the vile man beneath him.

The general didn't remember him, but it didn't matter. He'd longed for —envisioned—this moment countless times, imagining what the swell of justice would feel like when Gilles was finally behind bars for killing Bastien.

"I surrender." Gilles pushed away his sword with sluggish fingers.

Jon glared at him. "Soldier of fortune," he said coldly, "waging war and taking life for coin..."

He could finally arrest Gilles...

Bastien's life. His brothers' lives. His family's lives. His people's lives.

He stared into the general's visor until he saw the whites of the man's eyes. The Code demanded he accept an enemy's surrender.

He was bound by the Code no longer. "I don't accept your surrender."

The general's eyes widened.

Jon thrust his sword through Gilles's neck.

66

*W*ith a frustrated roar, Rielle tried to pull open both of the doors without success, her face pulsating with pain.

No choice.

Focused on one door, she stepped aside and cast a gust spell behind it.

Both doors flew open, wind tearing through them to sweep the mercenaries in its path against the back wall. Something—a whetstone—flew past her.

The doors were open.

Time to perform the rite.

She cast a candlelight spell above her and entered, trying to whisper the healing incantation. Sharp agony shot through her face as it healed, blinding white.

And that was it. There would be no more magic beyond a single spell until she had resonance.

At least the rite was powered by blood.

When her vision cleared, she looked about the chamber. Massive, its large stone construction predated anything she'd seen on the palace's upper levels. Darkness cloaked most of the area, but moonlight poured in from high above, illuminating a dais of wood, about fifty feet wide...

With roots buried in the stone?

A tree stump?

She climbed onto the stump and moved until she stood at the center of the light, then looked up to see an open circle at the top of a tower, the moon nearly filling it. It had to be two hundred feet tall, easily going through the temple above.

"The Lunar Chamber," she whispered.

Around her, a pentagram lay carved into the wood, circled by an ouroboros. Carvings, deep, ancient, and dark; mages had performed this rite for centuries, and witches had for ages before that, and perhaps before them, practitioners with no name, only magic seeping from their fingertips, anima shining within their inner barriers, and a soul that reached deep into the earth when they closed their eyes.

At her feet, a star-shaped crack in the wood, blackness at its center, reached into those depths. This was it. She followed the edge of the circle with her eyes up to the head of the serpent. Rushing toward it, she reached for the pouch of ash on her belt to trace the lines.

It wasn't there.

She looked down, feeling all around her belt for the pouch. It was gone.

"Looking for this?"

She whirled to see Leigh in the doorway. He entered and shut the massive doors.

Dust grayed his face. A smattering of blood darkened him. He held up the pouch of rowan ash.

Thank the Divine. She hurried toward him.

"I found it on the ground outside the chamber." He held it at his side, and when she approached him, he offered it to her, placing one hand on her shoulder. "Are you sure you want to do this?"

"Of course." She met his narrowed eyes.

A pull at her neck and a snap.

He threw the vial of king's blood upon the ground, shattering it.

Its precious contents soaked into the dust.

"You gave me no choice," Leigh said flatly. He stepped away from her.

How...?

She clutched the pouch of ash close and fell to her knees. The canvas grated her fingertips. Her palm pushed dust, blood, and shards of glass. Uselessly. Hopelessly. Her heart clenched in an unforgiving vise.

How could he?

"It had to be done," he said, his voice wavering despite his words, his dark eyes haunted.

Her mind was numb.

"The Divinity has long acted without conscience. It secures peace by removing all opposition."

No words would come.

"Monarchs seek the Divinity's approval to enact laws. Grand Divini determine the legitimacy of governments. And no country may deny the Tower without consequence."

Her eyes narrowed, lessening him.

"The Divinity is setting itself up to become the world's government unless we, the mages, rebel. Starting with you and me."

Her hands clenched. Dust. Blood. Glass. A throb began in her fists.

"To the Divinity, you are an expendable soldier, but to every mage out there torn from her home, forced under the Divinity's rules, regulated to the point of every personal decision, you'll be a role model and a rallying cry. Join me. Let's return to the old ways of Covens and Archons—mage communities that served all mages. No more of this... tyranny. You have to understand, Rielle, I would never hurt you. This is best for everyone."

Useless words. His paranoid vendetta, the imagined slights, and the unfounded accusations made her stomach roll.

The kingdom had been expecting, anticipating, praying for the Moonlit Rite, and it was the Divinity's responsibility. Olivia's responsibility. Kieran's responsibility. Hers.

And he'd pretended she'd had a meaningful choice, when he'd been prepared to do this if she disagreed with him.

She stiffened. In the ruins, the heretics she and Jon had overheard spoke of joining someone planning to take down the Divinity, of stopping a mage from reaching his destination, of making the Grand Divinus look like a fool.

"It wasn't a coincidence, you being in Bournand," she said.

Leigh lowered his gaze. "No."

He'd been working with the heretics.

He'd betrayed the Divinity.

But worse than anything, he'd betrayed *her*. When they'd always, *always* trusted and protected each other. "And all this time, you pretending to be there to help me... it was all in anticipation of this moment," she said, sharp pain blooming in her palms, "when you would betray someone who has always loved you?"

The throb spread up her arms, her hot arms, to her shoulders, scorching shoulders, and up, through, out—

He shook his head. "It had to be done, *ma chère.*"

"Don't you dare!" Pain burned in her palms, her hands, and coursed through her; pure flame marching through her veins. "In Bournand, did you even send my report to the Tower?"

He didn't answer.

Deep, calming breaths. The Proctor wouldn't know about the heretics in the underground ruins. About what they'd said. No clue leading to the heresy happening now. And she was implicated.

The only Divinity mage who could tell him.

And Leigh—

He stood there, still, full of conviction, over-bright eyes boring into hers. She was a loose end now. He'd already betrayed her. Did he also plan to—?

"And now..." Her searing skin tightened, begging for transformation, to be part of flame made flesh. "You just destroyed our only hope of completing the rite. And I'm the only one left to tell the Proctor."

He said nothing. Stood. Watched. Unmoving.

A familiar power surged beneath her skin, longing to burst free, set her alight.

She stared at her fiery fists, feeling the pressure build to capacity inside her. To burn, and burn, and burn until only embers and ash remained. Bright as the sun, far as its light, until eternal night.

But it didn't fight for control; it came to her call. *It'll burn you, and it'll warm you,* the girl had said. *She* had said, to herself.

"Wait," a voice called out, reaching through the fire. Jon.

She panned her twitching eyes to him. He'd bested Gilles—and lived. The Crag were defeated.

Her heart swelled. She longed to embrace him, but her eyes darted to Leigh, who stood ready to cast, observing. Would he try to harm Jon, who'd walked on this... this betrayal? She couldn't let her guard down.

But as for the rite—she blinked and shook her head. The die had been cast. She had failed. And there was nothing Jon could do.

No need for violence. For *her* violence. "Leigh destroyed the only vial of king's blood."

They would solve this together. Solve it together, and *live.*

She curled her shoulders, retreating into herself. The flames receded; the glow of her skin faded.

It was over.

Jon stepped between her and Leigh. "Use my blood."

His blood?

King's blood—

Her mouth dropped open.

Leigh's eyes widened.

"I found out at Monas Amar," Jon said firmly, his gaze trained on Leigh.

"How?" She gaped at him.

"I can't let you do that," Leigh declared. "I don't want to hurt you, but I will stop you."

If he wanted to now, Leigh would stop her. But she wouldn't let him without a fight, even weakened as she was. He'd have to kill her.

The doors burst open.

Covered in blood and gore, Brennan threw himself at Leigh, seized his hands.

"Do what you need to do," he growled at her, trying to restrain Leigh beneath him. He wrapped his arm around Leigh's neck and head.

"Don't kill him." She lurched forward, but Jon grabbed her arm, held her.

"It's all right," he said, while Leigh stared at her, eyes fading. Dimming. Her fingers twitched. Her foot stepped forward. Her chest tightened, as did Jon's hold on her arm.

Finally, Brennan subdued Leigh, who lay unconscious but breathing. "He'll live."

"Use my blood." Jon turned her to face him.

What?

Her face went slack, and she shook her head.

Jon was king.

It had to be why she'd been ordered to escort him to Monas Amar. She'd been chosen to protect the new king, the last of the Farallan dynasty. It hadn't been a lowly escort mission.

She sucked in an epiphanous breath. The Proctor had known about the regicide. He'd kept it from her to ensure she'd accept the mission instead of going after Olivia. Her chest pounded.

The Heartseekers—they'd been searching among the paladins for the new king.

"I found out my parents were Queen Alexandrie and the king's younger brother, Prince James. I'm... the child of an affair." He dipped his head, blinking away a shadow of a thought.

Even Queen Alexandrie was rumored to have lovers. Gran's words rang in her mind.

"But they signed a document legitimizing me, so when the regicide happened, I... It's why I was discharged from the Order." He met her gaze squarely.

She looked at Jon, and she saw it now—the resemblance in his face that recalled Prince James. She and Jon had shared so much together, and she'd never even suspected.

But there was no time to think about it all. She needed to complete the rite. She clasped his hand in hers, and Jon met her look with a tentative smile.

Speechless, she pulled him behind her, tracing the sacred circle and the pentagram with rowan ash. Once she finished, she led him to the center and began to remove the armor covering his hand.

Steeling herself, she dropped the gauntlet and gazed above her. The moon was very close to filling the circular opening perfectly. The pouch of ash still in her hand, she tipped its contents over the center of the pentagram and the star-shaped opening.

The entire sigil beneath them, around them, glowed a ghostly white. One more ingredient.

The Veil was coming down. It was time.

She drew Jon's sword just enough and then held his unarmored hand to the sharp edge. Their eyes locked, he pressed his palm to the blade, then she slid the sword back into its sheath.

He clenched his hand into a fist.

As she looked up, the moon slowly moved from the circle.

His blood dripped from his palm onto the center of the pentagram, leaking into the crack in the middle, the final step of the rite and his royalty blooming between them. The ghostly glow of the sigil faded beneath them.

The reality flooded her memories and knowledge of the last several weeks, saturating every uncertainty with his revelation. All they hadn't known, all the questions—answered. It was all too much.

When she'd bared her soul to him in Melain, had he suspected? She'd had everything to lose by sharing her secrets with him, but she'd valued his love and trust more than the risks. Had he?

She pulled her hand free of his. "When did you suspect?"

He grabbed her shoulders. "It's not like that," he answered quickly, giving her a light squeeze. "I didn't know until they told me at Monas Amar. I promise." He brought his fingertips to his temple. "I can hardly believe I'm saying these words."

Neither could she. But faced with his strong, unwavering gaze, she believed him.

Here he was, fighting for his kingdom, for his people, not like the spoiled kings of the last few generations. A warrior king. A paladin king. He'd rule well.

But she remembered the bottle of immortelle, tucked away safely in her recondite pouch in her saddlebags. *Home,* he'd called it. With her.

A pang of sadness hit her. Divine irony. Jon, as the new king, could break her marriage contract with Brennan, but she—a mere noble, and disgraced at that—could never hope to marry him. A king wed for his kingdom's advantage. Jon would wed for his kingdom's advantage. Some princess. Not *her.* Never her.

Faced with his smile, she could barely meet his eyes. He didn't know yet. He didn't understand. And it would fall to her to tell him. To break his heart.

"Terra have mercy, say something, Rielle."

"I..." The life of a king's mistress was incomplete joy and complete misery. But this wasn't about her. There were bigger things happening. "You'll make a great king."

His gaze bored into her, a storm breaking in his sea-blue depths. It seemed her answer hadn't been what he'd wanted to hear.

He looked at her then with such a void; it demanded response—something, anything to fill the darkness.

She placed her palm over his, preparing to heal the wound, but her anima was too dim. Instead, she took his hand and reached out to him in resonance. He pulled back, and power flooded her like euphoria, forced into every corner of her being, so bright and alive, blinding, overwhelming—

She collapsed against him, against his arcanir, and the resonance broke. But his hand was still in hers, the feel of him still soothing warmth into her. Great Divine, she loved him.

He brushed her fingers with his. "Speak to me."

Her gaze never left his. She whispered the healing incantation over the sword slash in his skin and the wound in his shoulder.

If only their other problems could be repaired as easily. As king, he was going somewhere she couldn't follow. Their dreamy musings about being together after this battle could only ever be musings.

It hurt to breathe. "I'm going to the dungeon," she said softly, "to find Olivia."

He grasped her wrist, drew his eyebrows together. "Terra's troth, Rielle—"

"I'll come with you," Brennan interrupted, earning a scowl from Jon. "Trèstellan has a few arcanir cells, if I recall correctly." He slung an unconscious Leigh over his shoulders, holding his right arm and right leg securely. "We need to find out if Galvan was working with anyone."

The time to perform the rite had ended, for good or ill. Perhaps Jon's blood had hit the center of the pentagram before the moon had shifted. Whatever the Rift was, she had done all she could to prevent it. The rest was out of her hands.

A distant explosion sounded.

67

*R*ielle slipped her hand free of Jon's.

Brennan turned toward the door. "Movement." His nostrils flared. "Paladins."

One of them entered, his gaze flitting from each of them to the next until it rested on Jon. A squad followed.

"Your Majesty," the paladin commander said with a bow. "We've taken control of the upper levels. Paladin Grand Cordon Guérin—"

Jon held up a hand to the paladin commander, then lightly squeezed Rielle's wrist. His earnest eyes found hers. "It's not what we planned, exactly, but we can do all that we wished for in Melain... and more."

He grazed her cheek with loving fingers.

Her shoulders curled inward. "It's much more complicated than that now."

His hand firm on the small of her back, he pulled her in closer, raised her chin.

"It's very simple," he said with an abundance of conviction, his breath warm against her lips, seductive, making her melt against him. "Do you love me, Rielle?"

A shiver trembled through her as he inched closer to her mouth.

"Yes," she whispered, and his lips met hers, soft union giving way to firm demanding; he cupped her face with a gentle hand, rubbing her cheek.

The paladin commander cleared his throat. "Your Majesty—"

Jon broke away with a light parting kiss, the tip of his thumb trailing over her lips to her chin. He rested his head against hers. Without question, she loved him. What that meant for her future, she would have to learn.

But not now. Olivia needed her. Taking a deep breath, she pulled away.

"Return to me," Jon said, his eyes never leaving hers even as the paladin commander approached him. Several more paladins filed in.

"I will. Promise." She indulged the smile beneath the surface and nodded to him, the man she loved, her partner, her *home*, then tore herself away.

In the corridor, where a squad of paladins gathered the bodies of the Crag Company mercenaries, Brennan awaited.

"Pleased with yourself, aren't you?" he hissed in her ear as he hefted Leigh's weight. "A king to do your will."

Now was not the time. They could hiss and spit at each other later.

The sound of the explosion earlier had come from beyond the wall, where the flame-stone orb now rested. Olivia. Who knew what had exploded? They had to get to her as soon as possible.

She dispelled the orb, spreading its tiles over the corridor.

The wall behind it had newer masonry, like a doorway bricked over. Hoping it was stone, she tried to use earth magic to pull it apart.

Pieces ejected from the wall, spewing onto the ground with the remnants of the flame-stone orb and the Crag Company. She'd checked the map in Melain: the dungeons had been split from the Lunar Chamber by an unused, closed-off rectangular room.

Her anima was half-bright, but she cast a candlelight spell and proceeded through the arched doorway, Brennan close behind. The room's stagnant air mixed with that of the corridor and became breathable, if malodorous. Coffins decorated with ancient, winding vine scroll-work filled the room. An ancient sepulcher.

She spared the intricate designs only a fleeting glance as she made her way to the wall opposite the doorway she'd created. It, too, bore the same newer masonry. She spelled the newer stones free.

I'm on my way, Olivia. Just a little longer.

They entered the dungeon. After wandering down a tight, rib-vaulted hallway for some time, they located the first prisoners.

A man gripped the bars with gaunt, dirty fingers. "Did Nicolette send you?"

Others approached and studied them wide eyed through the bars.

"Yes." She glanced around. "Do you know who has the keys?"

The man tapped the bars. "The guard with the keys went downstairs when the explosion came."

"We'll find him and come back for you." Even if she didn't find the guard, she would try to break them out. Although she could blast the gates open, she didn't want to risk anyone getting hurt if the keys were available. "Have you seen a red-haired mage? A young woman?"

He drew his eyebrows together but nodded. "They brought in the Archmage the day it happened. Dragged her to a lower level."

Olivia. "Thank you. We'll have you freed on our way out. I promise."

The man squeezed the bars, and murmurs spread among the prisoners, but the man finally gave her a faint smile. "Goddess and Divine keep you both until then."

"And you." She headed for the stairs.

The lower level had flooded ankle deep. She and Brennan waded through until they reached a fork in the path. There, a guard slumped against the wall. She searched his body until she found two key rings, one iron and the other arcanir. She looked at Brennan, who jerked his head to the left.

"The arcanir cells are that way," he said, with a sigh, "but there are people down this way," he added, tipping his head toward the right.

She tilted her head. If the arcanir cells were somewhere else, why was Olivia imprisoned here? The only time Rielle had been imprisoned in iron was when she'd been gagged and her hands had been—

A chill shook her. She needed to get to Olivia *now*. She tossed Brennan the arcanir keys.

"Come find me when you've secured him." She nodded toward the unconscious Leigh.

Leigh's betrayal was still unbelievable. Perhaps she just hadn't wanted to believe him capable of it. But his unproven suspicions about the Divinity had pushed him this far.

Brennan nodded. "Shout if you need help, and I'll come running."

He waited until she acknowledged his comment before heading toward the arcanir dungeon.

Rising, she looked down the right corridor. There was still a chance that Brennan would find Olivia in the arcanir dungeon, but if the prisoners on the upper level were correct, Olivia would be here.

She proceeded toward the iron cells, freeing the few prisoners she found along the way.

"Olivia?" she called out, receiving no reply. She headed in deeper. "Olivia!"

A distant croak, followed by a cough, came as a reply.

BRENNAN HEFTED the mage on his shoulder as he made his way to the arcanir dungeon. The audacity. The Kamerish commoner had actually turned on Rielle.

Brennan shook his head. The mage had stolen her away all those years ago, allowed word of their affair to spread far and wide, claimed to have *loved* her, all for what? To betray her now? He couldn't be trusted. Ever again.

Commoner. Brennan's shoulders stiffened. Jonathan Ver had defied that label, hadn't he? Great Wolf, the commoner had turned out to be the gods-damned fucking king.

A snarl curled his lip. He should have seen it. The planes of his face, his coloring, the blue eyes so like those of the libertine Prince James. But royal bastards weren't cosseted away. They graced the court with heads held high, their mistress-mothers eager to take tarnished power over none.

This one, however, hadn't been born to any mere mistress. Prince James had plowed forbidden fields. The fucking queen. Brennan rubbed his face.

No king who purported to call himself a man would allow word of his cuckolding to spread. Even allowing the bastard to live had been an ill-conceived mercy granted by King Marcus. He'd ever be remembered now as the ineffectual cuckolded king succeeded by the lovechild of his queen and his brother. Fool.

But Jonathan Ver was now king.

A shudder rode Brennan's spine, and he cracked his neck. The darkness of the dungeon yawned into a long passage, but no hearts beat ahead. Only the ozone smell of arcanir awaited. He blew out a harsh breath.

Jonathan Ver was king; he could break the arranged marriage contract with ease but couldn't marry Rielle himself. A marriage from within the kingdom when Emaurria sorely needed aid? A king with a weak claim to the throne taking to wife a woman scorned by the Houses?

No. The Grands would never allow it. Parliament would never allow it. And the forsworn paladin, even full of desire, wouldn't set aside the needs of an entire kingdom. The Order didn't raise its orphans to choose them-selves over the greater good. And even if he wanted to, too many objections would confine him.

And Rielle would know that. She could share a king's bed but never a throne. She could break her betrothal but never marry a king. And when

Laurentine languished without its marquise, when the line of her father threatened to wither, she'd relent. She'd marry. And if she had to marry someone, why not the fiancé who'd found his conscience and had only treated her with remorse, kindness, respect, and affection since?

This path to victory was lengthy, but of them all, the least precarious. He'd waited this long; he could wait longer if it meant certain victory.

At last he arrived at the arcanir cells. He pulled out the keys, unlocked a cell door, and threw the mage inside, who landed with a thud and a cloud of dust. Brennan glanced around the space, his sight sharp even in pitch darkness. No food, no bed, no water. Not even a pot to piss in.

No less than he deserves.

He slammed the door and locked it. Soon, he'd be back for answers. But he had more pressing concerns now—returning to Rielle's side. Making sure that snarling little she-wolf didn't get herself killed.

No, he had greater plans for her.

What had the duchess said? *Rielle resists opening her heart to others, but it is not impenetrable.*

Not impenetrable...

If he could play the game of favor skillfully, he could penetrate the walls Rielle had erected between him and her heart. He could come in. She might finally love him. And the duchess might bind Jon's hands tightly enough to make it all possible.

As long as he remains king.

Father's ambitions must be smothered in the cradle.

After this, Father had to be made to see reason. The crown wasn't worth the trouble. Although Father had always been the political mastermind in the family, it was time to challenge him for that title.

The twelve steps to ascend the Emaurrian throne were perilous and bloody. If Jon had already ascended them, then Father put himself—and all the Marcels—under threat from the Order of Terra by continuing his attempt. Mother, Nora, Una, Caitlin. Nora's sons. Even Uncle Desmond and Uncle Aidan, their families, and Uncle Tor. And—Brennan cringed—himself. All their lives balanced on a blade's edge, vulnerable to the slightest breeze from wagging tongues.

What was so great about being a royal anyway? Royals were accountable. When the realm suffered, a king's head didn't rest securely on his shoulders. King Marcus had learned that firsthand.

There was no value in the sacrifice of happiness for the good of the kingdom. Brennan enjoyed pursuing his own pleasure, his own wealth, his own security. He didn't need to worry about millions of others. And he didn't need the Grands or Parliament compelling him to marry some foreign royal bitch for the sake of the kingdom when what he needed was Rielle. To be with her—that is, to break the curse.

No, Father had to see reason. Jon had to remain king. *And I need to keep currying favor.*

He made his way back through the dungeon toward Rielle.

68

*R*ielle ran toward the voice, lit the nearby torch with dwindling magic.

"Here," someone hoarsely called out. An old, tired voice from a dark corner.

She stopped and fumbled with the keys until she found the right one and jammed it into the lock.

"Don't worry. I'll get you out." She squinted into the darkness. Begrimed, mangled fingers shed the shadows. A misshapen hand. Another. Tattered, dirty rags that may have once been a dress. A wizened woman with hollow cheeks. Skin coated in dirt and dust.

Red hair—green eyes—

Rielle caught hold of the bars before her knees gave out.

"...Rielle?" Olivia asked, her voice a harsh rasp. Her dull eyes widened, and she straightened. "Don't... you're in danger..."

Rielle's heart thumped in her chest. Her best friend had been starved but was alive. *Alive.* She opened her mouth, but she had to try twice to find her voice. "The Crag are no more. Gilles is dead."

"Did you do it? The rite? Did you do the rite?"

"Yes." With trembling hands, Rielle unlocked the cell door, threw it open, and rushed to Olivia. She dropped to her knees and wrapped her arms around her, around her skeletal, small body. What she'd been through —what they'd done—

"Praise the Divine you're alive." She tightened her embrace, and Olivia rested her head on Rielle's shoulder.

"I knew you'd come," she croaked. "I knew."

Rielle pulled away, cupped Olivia's cheek in her hand, met her eyes. Brightened eyes. Olivia raised a hand to hers—Divine, her hand, it—

"You must be thirsty." Rielle unclipped the waterskin from her belt, opened it, and handed it over.

Olivia drank, pressing it between her wrists. Both of her hands had been broken. An arcanir collar circled her neck. She was barely more than skin and bones. Starved. Neglected. Beaten. Abused.

Gilles had lain dead outside the Lunar Chamber, and he'd deserved every second of agony he'd suffered. Hopefully his death had been long and painful, payment for what he'd done to Olivia, the Faralles, and all of Courdeval.

When Olivia finished, Rielle accepted the waterskin, eyeing every bruise, cut, and smudge, the pressure filling her chest to painful capacity.

"So you were the cause of all the screaming." Olivia managed to don a smile over a look of complete discomfort.

Rielle embraced her again, and Olivia's arms closed weakly around her in return.

Too long. She'd waited too long to come.

There had been only one chance to perform the rite—Spiritseve. It had needed to be tonight, with Nicolette's assistance, the diversion, and the help of Brennan, Jon, the paladins, and Leigh for that chance.

"So Gilles is dead." Olivia pressed her cheek against Rielle's shoulder. "He threw me in here, a bargaining chip to extract information from Prince James."

Prince James?

Jon's father.

Rielle straightened. "Is he still alive?"

Olivia shook her head and lowered her gaze. "Gilles then kept me here to trap you."

"Trap me?" Rielle smoothed a hand over Olivia's knotted curls. "Well, he's dead now. So is the Crag Company. I wish I had come sooner. Spiritseve—"

"But you came," Olivia whispered, her eyes watery. "That's what matters."

With a final squeeze, Olivia pulled back and looked at her. "There could be more prisoners. We should check."

"Let me heal you." At least her hands. It would be the last of her magic, but she'd found Olivia. The rite was performed. It was all over finally.

Although the arcanir collar prevented Olivia using her magic, it did not prevent magic being cast on any part of her not covered in arcanir. She held out her hands in offering until Olivia placed hers in them. The bones had already begun to heal incorrectly, an unfortunate circumstance.

"This will hurt, Olivia. I'm sorry."

Olivia braced herself and winced through the healing. She faltered, but Rielle caught her, slung Olivia's arm over her shoulder, and helped her to her feet.

"Can you stand?"

Olivia smiled, flexing her fingers and hands. "Yes." She blushed. "I'm fine, really. You don't need to fuss over me."

"Who else would I fuss over if not you?"

Olivia shook her head, doing a poor job of suppressing a grin. Watching her face for reassurance, Rielle slowly let her get to her feet on her own. Despite her current frail condition, Olivia was a person who could stand on willpower alone.

"Are there any others still jailed upstairs?" Olivia asked.

"Yes, but the keys were on this level."

"We still need to finish checking this dungeon corridor. And perhaps we can try to do something about this flooding."

Her point was valid. The leak causing the flooding could worsen, and there could still be prisoners farther in. Those on the upper level still needed to be freed.

Even one more spell will mean fureur. Her anima was dark. There would be no more spellcasting.

But it was questionable whether Olivia could endure the rest of the search. The sooner she saw a proper healer, the better.

"Maybe you could free the prisoners on the upper level and find help while I check the rest of this block?" The route to the upper level was clear —safe for Olivia. "Do you think you'll be all right on your own?"

When Olivia nodded, Rielle offered her the keys to the cells on the upper level—the ones that hadn't worked on this one. "Do you remember Brennan?"

"Who could forget?" Olivia narrowed her eyes. "You two are on good terms?"

"Better than they were. He should be coming from the arcanir dungeon and might be able to pick the lock on your collar, so you could use your magic again. Look for him," she said, receiving a nod in reply, "or a forsworn paladin by the name of Jon."

Not a forsworn paladin but a king. Once this night was over, she had a long talk with Jon ahead of her, and questions of what being a king's lover might entail. But her work here wasn't finished.

"I'll look for them," Olivia said, with a reassuring nod. "Be careful." She offered a small smile before pulling Rielle into a hug.

"You, too."

Olivia pulled away and backed up a few steps before heading toward the stairwell. Rielle jingled the keys, grabbed the torch from its holder, and strode down the corridor.

"Wait," Olivia called. She braced against the wall. "Did you cross paths with a group of bandits called the Black Mountain Brigands?"

Rielle frowned. How did Olivia know about that? "Yes," she called back, approaching. "They attacked us on the way here. We killed them."

Olivia staggered, pushing into the wall with quivering fingers. She hung her head, matted locks of red hair curtaining her face. "All of them?"

Had there been someone she'd cared about among the Brigands? Or had someone from the Brigands wronged her, and she wanted confirmation that justice had been done?

"All," Rielle replied, carefully observing. "Was there—"

Without raising her head, Olivia brought a hand to cover her mouth. Sorrow... or relief? Rielle had almost closed the distance between them when Olivia held up a hand.

"I'm all right," she said, her voice low and soft. She was far from all right. "Really."

What had happened with the Brigands? Whatever it was, it had been important. Important enough to affect Olivia deeply. "You're just going to lie to me?"

Olivia finally looked up. Tears welled in her eyes and streamed down her face. When Rielle stepped closer, Olivia held up her hand again. "Please, I can't right now. I don't have it in me." She smiled sadly. "If you let me rest my head on your shoulder right now, I'll never move again, and there are people who still need our help."

Her heart pounding, Rielle nodded. She didn't know what affected Olivia so deeply, but the possibility of being the cause was hollowing. "Are we—?"

Olivia smiled again, this time warmly. "Yes. We're fine." She swiped at her wet cheeks. "I'll tell you all about it tomorrow. We'll just lock ourselves in for the night, eat custard tarts, and talk, just like old times."

Rielle grinned. The nights they'd spent chatting and eating custard tarts she'd stashed from kitchen duty were treasured memories. "Deal."

With a final nod, Olivia turned toward the stairwell and made her way down the corridor. Rielle went the other way, growing the distance between them with every step.

But she'd done what she'd come here to do. Olivia was alive, and free. And would have a best friend for a tail, at least for a month or two. Rielle grinned. If the Divinity had a problem with that, the Proctor could send someone to drag her back to the Tower. Or rather, someone to *try*.

Cell after empty cell, no prisoners, until a long walk led her to the end of the corridor, with bare stone for walls. Perhaps an entrance into the catacombs. If only she could recall the maps of the lower levels with clarity. She headed toward the edge.

A corner and a narrow passage lay beyond. A soft sobbing echoed from within.

Another prisoner. Had the explosion come from in there? Where did it lead? Was someone hurt?

The glow from her torch reflected from the stone wall's harsh, wet edges as she entered. If the flooding originated here, perhaps the Crag had a mage working with them, attempting to inundate the corridor and kill the prisoners.

"Hello?" she called. "I'm here to help."

The narrow passage finally gave way to wooden planks. Ahead was a small boat in a massive cave, a shadowy cavern at the end of a small waterway. Someone had arrived by this waterway. Someone she hadn't yet found.

With the torch in hand, she was turning when a strike to the back of her head took her off her feet.

Dazed, she fell to the pier, landing face first onto the wood.

Pain surged from the base of her skull and her jaw. Then gave way to a light-headed weakness.

Managing to roll onto her side, she dumbly fidgeted with the Sodalis ring on her thumb. Her double vision focused just for a moment on the blade of the obsidian dagger, the glow of fire shimmering on its black surface from her fading torchlight.

Firelight on a serpentine edge like black glass. A soulblade.

She'd seen its like before. In Bournand.

And... nine years ago, at her brother Liam's throat.

69

*J*on left the paladins with orders, rejected all attempts at escort, and made his way through the ruins of an ancient crypt, passing sarcophagi inscribed with intricate vines beneath a thick layer of dust. They had lain untouched for centuries—perhaps longer—and only now, with the onset of battle, had returned to memory.

Battle... Gilles lay dead—and Bastien at last had justice.

A strange lightness freed his chest; the weight he'd carried for five years had seeped out, along with the general's blood. He could almost feel content, but not until he found Rielle.

They had planned on being together after the rite. After Courdeval. Of course, neither of them had planned on him being king. The reality still came as a shock; he'd been unprepared, and so had she.

But it didn't change the basic truth between them. She had said yes.

He navigated around some rubble. Stepping through the gaping hole on the far wall of the crypt, he found himself in what looked like the dungeon, a long corridor stretching ahead of him with sparse sconces lighting the way. A strange, cold sweat coated his skin. He couldn't shake the feeling of unease. He picked up the pace. She couldn't be far.

Voices sounded from farther in—prisoners calling for help.

"I hear you," he called back and approached.

The iron bars seemed secure, but he rattled them anyway, hoping to find any loosened by the explosion.

"A man carrying another man, along with a woman went down to the lower level for keys," one of the prisoners told him. It could only be Brennan bearing Leigh, with Rielle. "Did Nicolette send you?"

Nicolette. The Black Rose assassin who had held the southeastern gate with her troops before the paladins had entered.

"She's still fighting in the city. The Order of Terra has taken the palace. I'll look for the keys, and I will see you freed." Jon set off in pursuit. He headed to the end of the corridor and down the stairs to a split.

A disheveled red-headed woman trudged toward him, bracing herself along the walls.

Emaciated, she wore the torn and dirty remains of the clothes she'd probably been jailed in. She looked ready to collapse, but when she looked up at him, her green eyes were uncharacteristically bright.

"James...?" she murmured weakly. She blinked, then frowned and shook her head. "Oh, I..."

He looked her over and didn't recognize her, but she seemed about Rielle's age. "Olivia? Rielle's friend?" When she nodded, he walked up to her. "You're alive."

"Yes." She breathed an amused snort, blinking sluggishly. "Yes, I am."

He shook his head. "Forgive me, I'm not myself today. Rielle—"

"Freed me."

Then Rielle was not only all right but had found her best friend alive. He could only imagine the relief she'd felt.

Olivia held up a set of keys. "I'm on my way upstairs to free everyone else."

"Are you certain you're able?"

"Yes." She took a deep breath and smiled. "I'm stronger than I look, promise."

"Where's Rielle? Was she to follow you?" He glanced past her.

Footsteps approached from behind. He whirled.

Brennan neared them, holding a torch. His leathers were still torn and caked in drying blood, but he seemed the quintessence of health, a stark contrast to the gory tale his clothing told. When he caught up to them, he inclined his head to Olivia. "Good to see you again, bookworm."

"And you, Marquis Tregarde." She quirked an eyebrow at him. "I didn't think you had a savior complex."

"I don't." Brennan eyed Jon. "I just came here for the magic show."

Her eyes widened as she looked from him to Jon. "Then you both saw the rite performed?"

When they both nodded, she took a deep breath. Questions sparked to life in her inquisitive gaze. "When the sigil turned white, did a light then reach from the center to the lunar circle above?"

He frowned. The sigil had glowed white, but he didn't recall any light shining from the center. He and Brennan exchanged a look.

She frowned. "It was done before the moon moved from the lunar circle, correct?"

"It... it didn't quite go that way."

Her eyes went wide. "What do you mean..." She mumbled to herself, innumerable inquiries.

"The moon may have moved." Brennan shrugged.

"Or maybe I'm not who they think I am after all." Jon lowered his gaze to the floor, uncertain whether he'd be grateful or disappointed.

"You're definitely a Faralle." Brennan's firm tone left no room for argument. "You're the very image of your parents. I've met them. And, come to think of it, you're as self-righteous, hot-headed, and entitled as any of the Faralles."

Jon stiffened, narrowing his eyes at him. The werewolf knew how to deliver a compliment with a barb. Brennan shrugged and offered a sardonic grin. With the blood flaking on his skin, the grin was eerie.

"A Faralle." Olivia brightened anew and searched his eyes, her lower lip trembling. "I-I see it, but... how can that be?"

"I am the love child of Prince James and Queen Alexandrie, or so I am told." He heaved a defeated sigh. How many more times would he relay those words?

She gaped, her skin blanched to a sickly white. "James and... the queen?"

He nodded. "They signed some sort of legitimization document upon my birth and left it with Father Derric... He brought it to Monas Amar." Jonathan Dominic Armel Faralle. The name was a mouthful, with so much more weight than the name of an orphan. He was still unused to it; perhaps he always would be.

"Your eyes—the color of the Bay of Amar at twilight. Just like your father's." She stared a moment, then dropped her gaze to his feet. "The wren... Y-you are the king... Your Majesty." She bowed from the waist.

Jon frowned, reached out for her shoulders, and raised her. She could barely walk, and she was bowing for the likes of him? "Please... don't."

She raised an eyebrow and stared. Many of the paladins had given him the same look. He supposed he would be seeing it with overwhelming frequency in the coming weeks. But first—"About Rielle?"

Right away, Olivia turned and gestured to the corridor behind her. "She went to check the rest of the cells and look for the source of the flooding." She paused, then gave him a slow once-over that led to a smile. "She told me to look for you... Your Majesty."

Rielle had mentioned him? Judging by Olivia's face, at least it had been something good.

Brennan took a few steps toward the direction Olivia had indicated, clearly done socializing.

"Thank you," Jon said. "There are paladins upstairs, at the end of a hallway, through a crypt. They should have food, water, and medical care for everyone." He rested a reassuring hand on her shoulder. "Terra's blessings upon you."

"And upon you, Your Majesty." She was about to bow, then caught herself and only inclined her head.

JON RUSHED through the corridor with Brennan, splashing through the water flooding the ground.

"So, 'Your Majesty,' is it?" Brennan eyed him peripherally as they went deeper. "And to think, I forgot to bow when you arrived in the Coquelicot District."

"Considering you were lying supine in prostration, I think you can be forgiven." Jon held back a grin.

"You could have said something at the gate."

"I'd seen enough bows for one day." He looked straight ahead, thankful for a reprieve from the archers that had lined the city's enceinte. "At least ten for every arrow shot in my direction."

"Me, bowing to you?" Brennan huffed a laugh. "You were in no danger of that."

It was an odd day indeed when Brennan's attitude was refreshing.

They passed an open cell containing a box—Brennan opened it, said there was a head inside, and quickly closed it.

They continued deeper in, finding the block empty. After the open cell, there were no further signs of Rielle. Could she have gone all the way to the end to check for prisoners? If so, he and Brennan would find her.

At last, they reached the end of the corridor, its bars in disarray, damaged by a large chunk of stone from high up on the wall. Off to the side, around the corner, was an entrance to a dark tunnel.

Brennan stopped next to him and held out the torch toward the entrance. There was no light to signal an end. He breathed deeply. "She came this way, without a doubt."

Jon stared down the tunnel, into the darkness. If she'd come this way, there would be light—a torch, a candlelight spell, something. "Rielle!" he called down the tunnel. His voice echoed.

There was no reply. But there was nowhere else to go. "She must have entered."

He moved to follow into the dark tunnel when Brennan grabbed his shoulder.

"Allow me." Brennan raised the torch. Before Jon could object, he added, "Werewolf senses." He took a deep breath and led the way in, lighting their path.

Jon turned sideways to fit through the passage, ignoring the scrape of armor against stone. Misgivings swirled in his head—why hadn't Rielle answered? There seemed to be only one exit, so there was nowhere else for her to be but ahead. Was she hurt?

Time dragged on despite their hurried steps, on and on, until finally, they crossed what felt like a long wooden platform. A dock?

Brennan walked to its edge, holding up the torch. Off to the side, a large portion of stone had been blown away and opened to a waterway. Perhaps the explosion had caused the flooding—a wave that had surged through the stone passage and into the lowest level of the dungeon.

Another step, and something clinked against one of his sabatons. He dropped to a knee, and Brennan approached, holding the torch closer.

There, on the dock, lay a ring.

Jon threw off his gauntlet and picked it up—the ring of a Sodalis. None of the paladins had yet made it to the dungeon. And no paladin who would willingly part with his ring but he.

He closed his fingers over it.

"Rielle," he whispered, searching the dock for any sign of what could have happened. He peered over the edge at the black water.

Terra have mercy—

No. The ring on the dock had to have been deliberately placed; she wouldn't have tossed it while falling in, and she wouldn't have parted with it unless for good reason. She'd either left it as a message and departed, or she'd been taken and able to remove it in time to indicate her last whereabouts.

Brennan looked out over the water and its serene surface while Jon, filled with dread, traced the edge of the dock until he came upon a horn cleat with a rope tied to it. He slipped the ring onto his finger, crouched, and pulled up the rope to its frayed, hastily cut end, crushing it in his hand to numbness.

"She was taken." He held up the end of the rope. He stared at the opening to the waterway. "Where does it let out?" He raked his memory of the capital and couldn't come up with an answer. "We'll need a boat. We'll need to get it through the tunnel somehow." Which was easier said than done. But it was their only option. "How long will it take? And how long to follow? If she's not on the other end—"

Brennan stiffened and dropped the torch with a growl.

Jon grabbed the torch and lifted it. Brennan's eyes turned to amber as he began to shift form; he dropped to his knees, holding his head in his hands, doubling over. He pounded a fist onto a wood plank, sending a hairline crack from the point of impact.

When Jon lowered the torch, Brennan looked up for a moment, his face wolfish and monstrous.

"Why are you shifting?"

Curling up, Brennan made a sound not unlike a canine snarl.

"The full moon, and... my control is gone," he said in a deep, growling rumble. "Rielle... She's... out of magic and in fureur, or... nullified with arcanir, or... dead." An otherworldly cry punctuated his last word.

Dead. The word reverberated inside him, an echo shuddering through his every bone. His eyes drawn to the dark water, he tried not to wonder whether she'd drowned. "No."

He forced an obstinate shake of his head. "There was a boat here. Rielle's alive, and we'll find her."

A search with no leads?

No, he couldn't think that way.

Brennan grew still, his breaths coming slower, and looked up at him with wide eyes.

"Come on." Jon held out his hand; although Brennan could easily kill him instead, Rielle had trusted him, and he would, too. At least enough.

Brennan gaped at him and hesitated before extending his own hand, the strange animal claws retracting and disappearing as they clasped hands. Jon helped him up and, when Brennan faltered, supported him.

Slinging the werewolf's arm around his neck, Jon held out the torch and began to head back to the tunnel. He had to make it back to Captain Perrault and enlist the help of the paladins to find any departing boats and stop them.

As he braced Brennan, he entered the overwhelming darkness of the stone pass, bound for the paladin camp. On the way there, his mind raced.

If she'd been taken, he had precious little time to find her. No time to take a boat through the tunnel. It had to let out somewhere along the bay; a few spotters on horseback could at least indicate a direction.

At last, he exited the palace. A sea of torches illuminated the paladins, priests, and Courdevallans spread out in a makeshift camp in the palace's upper ward. It sprawled into the middle ward and the lower, too, as far as he could see. Beneath it, Courdeval still burned, raging bright-hot fire against the black night sky.

The black night sky... Spotters would be useless. He needed a new plan.

A squad of paladins strode by with a group of prisoners while several more patrolled the area. He searched for the medical tent and, once he spotted it, made his way there.

"Where are we going?" Brennan asked with a groan.

"To the medical tent," Jon answered, bearing him there. "You need to rest."

A few paladins acknowledged him with respect, and murmurs of his identity rippled through the camp, bending waists and knees in waves. Jon rolled away the stiffness in his shoulders and made for the tent.

"I'll be fine," Brennan said, but he didn't resist when Jon led him in.

The tent's large interior neared fullness; the injured occupied nearly every cot, tended by Monas Amar's priests. Unlike the paladins, they kept their focus on the wounded and hardly paid him any mind. Jon breathed his relief and set Brennan down on a cot, then strode to the nearby supply depository. He'd start searching for Rielle, but he needed water, flint—

"Your Majesty, what are you doing?"

Derric. Of course, the one priest who preferred to harness his diligence for persuasive rather than medical purposes.

Jon returned to gathering supplies. "Are you following me now?"

"Someone has to keep an eye on the king." Derric's tone—calm but pedagogic—was one Jon had grown up hearing. "What are you doing?"

Not today. It wouldn't work on him today. Shaking his head, he stuffed a knapsack. "Packing."

"Why?" Such an innocent question, but Derric's argument was sure to follow.

Jon grabbed some rations. "On the way to Monas Amar, I... fell in love with a woman. She's now missing." And he would find her.

To his credit, Derric worked through his surprise. "Do you know where she is? Where will you start your search?"

"I don't know," he replied through gritted teeth.

Derric exhaled a long breath behind him. "I taught you better than this.

Do I need to point out the futility of beginning a search with no information?"

No, he didn't.

With no indication of where she was or where she was bound, a search had little chance of success. But he had to try; it was all he could do.

Derric, however, had never been content to ignore damaging truths.

Jon stopped, letting the silence pervade while reality set in, clenching his fists. "What else is there to do? Nothing? Let her get taken? Let her suffer? Let her die?"

He threw his arm out, sweeping the knapsack and everything else off the table.

Bracing his hands on the wood, he wanted nothing more than to crush it to dust.

"I have to do something," he snarled. "She's out there, somewhere, probably hurt, needing help... *my* help—"

"The paladins can cover more ground." Derric's calm never broke. "They can look for her."

Jon clenched his teeth, his shoulders tense. "No. It needs to be me." She needed him, now more than ever, and he would not—refused to—let her down. " 'Let the heavens fall upon my head if I defend not the innocent, help not the weak, redeem not the suffering,' " he said, quoting a line from the Order's oath. "I haven't forgotten. Have you?"

Derric heaved a lengthy exhalation through his nose. "Perhaps you have. Paladin Grand Cordon Guérin can order an entire company of paladins to look for her if necessary, but only one man can lead this kingdom. Not just *one* woman, but a *nation* of women—and men, and children—are relying on their king. Those fires out there"—Derric waved his arm toward the city proper—"aren't just burning in buildings and streets, but in hearts of your people, consuming them as surely as wood and thatch. Will you abandon your land—your people—to chaos so that you can search for one woman?"

His land? His people? He'd been king only a few hours, only to one order of men who desperately wished it so, but he'd been a paladin nearly all his life, handling what kings and generals would have deemed inconsequential matters, wherein one or a couple or a few lives hung in the balance. Those lives mattered. Rielle mattered.

He slammed a frustrated palm on the table. Abandoning his new responsibility as king to go after Rielle? "Yes."

Derric exhaled a sigh behind him.

No, it wasn't how he'd been raised, but he could only live with one decision, and ignoring Rielle's disappearance wasn't it.

Footsteps caught his attention.

Brennan stood in the doorway, wincing, but his brow set in determination. "I think I may have a solution."

70

With some reluctance and a dull throbbing at the back of her head, Rielle opened her eyes, squinting to mitigate the harshness of the rising sun's blinding rays. Behind a golden cloak, the sky was a brightening coral. Bobbing with the grainy wooden planks beneath her, she blinked twice at the sight of a billowy indigo sail catching the wind, a design featuring two crossed cutlasses its sole decoration.

The mark of Kezani pirates.

"Surprise."

Rielle tried to raise her arm to cast, but no magic came. And her arm refused to cooperate. She rolled, trying to move her arms apart, the clink of chain links signaling the futility of her efforts.

Arcanir bonds.

The shadowmancer laughed, satisfied and loud. The woman who'd attacked Jon in Bournand. Shadow. She leaned against a crate, casually eating an orange, her ash-gray eyes serene. "No, Favrielle, I'm afraid not. Dangerous creatures are sold shackled."

Sold.

The word cut through her mind. Rielle tensed, trying to hold back the shudder that threatened to ripple through her. She turned her face away, leaning her back against the mast and gathering her legs under herself. Stubbornly, she looked out at the water.

No, Shadow would derive no more satisfaction from her.

"Nothing to say?" Shadow popped a segment of fruit into her mouth. "Or have you resigned yourself to the fate that awaits you?"

No need to acknowledge the questions. Her fate would reveal itself in time regardless; beyond being defeated by a single strike, she refused to humiliate herself any more.

She could have laughed—for all the long, exhausting battles she had fought and survived, she had at last fallen prey in an instant to nothing but a sneak attack.

It seemed that the Divine was not without a sense of irony.

"Are you not curious why you are here?" Shadow's harsh tone betrayed her growing impatience.

Of course she was curious. But silence was power.

By now, Brennan, Olivia, and Jon would be aware of her disappearance. Finding the cavern at the end of the dungeon was a certainty. She brushed her thumb against her index finger, assured that she had removed the Sodalis ring. If Jon found it, he would know what it meant.

Hope filling her chest, she stroked her bare thumb.

"You left something behind."

Rielle moved her hands out of view. But it didn't matter. It wasn't as though Shadow could go back for the Sodalis ring anyway.

"Perhaps you think your king will come for you," Shadow said, "but he will not."

Rielle turned away once more.

"No, you see, you left him a rather heartfelt letter insisting you can never be together, that he forget you while you put some distance between the two of you."

Letter? Shadow had... had left a forged letter?

"He may make some inquiries for a few days, but make no mistake—he will ascend the throne and forget you between the thighs of many women. Then, he will wed a queen or a princess as kings do." She laughed and tossed away the last bit of orange peel.

No, Jon would never just accept that and forget her.

"How long will he wait for you, believing you abandoned him, when every jewel in the Emaurrian court will vie for his favor?"

No, no—

She shook her head. He wouldn't. He wouldn't ever—

"You would do well to abandon your hopes. Your masters will not care about your desires, so you should resign yourself to serving theirs."

A seagull, the waves, the endless stretch of blue—

"You should steel yourself," Shadow teased, "and prepare to live the life you deserve."

Deserve?

Perhaps after all she'd done, everyone she'd killed in fureur, she did deserve this. Pain, confinement, retribution. Perhaps it pleased the grand scales of judgment. Justice.

But shackles, a life of punishment—it was too easy. Like Gran's offer to do nothing, it was far too simple to account for the lives she'd taken. At birth, she'd been given something. A power. But it did not belong to her alone; it belonged to every innocent life she'd ever taken, and to every innocent life that needed saving, and it roared with the deafening voice of the Divine—roared its demand of atonement.

That was her path. And neither Shadow, nor anyone else, would keep her from it. Not while she drew breath. She smiled.

Shadow pushed off from the crate she'd been leaning against and approached with all the menace of a mountain cat. She drew her hand up and slapped Rielle across her face.

"Damn you, demon. You have the audacity to *smile* after you killed my husband?" She drew the obsidian blade and brandished it. "This dagger is all that was left of him."

The soulblade. Rielle wriggled her ankle—the soulblade she'd tucked into her boot the morning she'd departed for Monas Amar was gone.

All that was left of him?

The soulblade had belonged to someone else, a man she'd killed? She stared at the blade, its shimmering black surface catching the light. Her inner barriers trembled. Weakened. She winced.

Firelight on a serpentine edge like black glass. Laurentine. Liam. She'd tried so hard to forget it that she almost had.

The man with the dagger, when she'd been thirteen, when Laurentine had been attacked—"You mean to avenge that man? That torturer? Death was too good for him."

Another strike to the face.

Rielle's cheek stung, but she steeled herself. "Your husband attacked my family and tortured them. His death is on his own hands."

Shadow crouched down to eye level, toying with the soulblade. "You burned him and his men, right along with your own family. Your father, mother, sisters, brothers, your household... On whose hands are their deaths?"

"It was an accident." An abrupt reply. Those words came too easily. Saying them anew brought back a shudder. "But the man who'd held that dagger, the man who'd intentionally captured and hurt my family, tortured my brother—he deserved far worse than death."

Shadow held the soulblade up to Rielle's neck, its sharp edge against her skin. "So do you. How many have you tortured and killed? You think intent matters to the dead?" Her words were no more than a growl. "I should kill you right now."

Rielle tensed, holding back a shudder. After all that this woman had orchestrated, after ignoring the opportunity to end it in the cavern, there was no way that mere killing would satisfy her now.

"Do it," Rielle challenged, "so that I won't have to listen to your wagging tongue any longer." She stuck out her chin, hoping against hope that she held still the tremble weaving through every inch of her.

Clenching her teeth, Shadow pressed the edge harder against her neck.

The sting of a cut. Divine, she'd miscalculated. Fatally. A cut from the sangremancy-cursed blade into the intended target's flesh would kill instantly.

Is this the end?

A loud exhalation and a Kezani expletive later, Shadow yanked the dagger away.

The wetness of blood trickled down Rielle's neck. *I'm cut.*

She held her breath; death would come, quick and certain.

But nothing happened.

She let herself exhale. A soulblade was enchanted so the shallowest of cuts would kill one target instantly and one target only. And she was still alive.

I'm not the intended target.

"No." Shadow shook her head vehemently. "You will suffer as I have suffered." She examined the serpentine blade, and sunlight glinted off its surface. "When I discovered your guilt, I resolved to exact the same price you took from me."

Rielle froze; she'd killed Shadow's husband, but didn't have one herself. "The same price...?"

Shadow leaned in and brandished the dagger. "I could have cursed you with this dagger, could have plunged this into your chest and felt the life leave your body, but that would have been too easy." She sheathed it. "No... With this dagger, I cursed the one you love above all others. You will be helpless and far from home, and I will kill him."

Jon. Rielle threw herself forward with all of her strength, cursing at the chains that stopped her short of Shadow, seething. Instinct had drawn upon her magic, but none came. The ache of emptiness throbbed in its place. The arcanir had fulfilled its purpose, nullifying her power.

Not that she had anima to spare.

Grimly, she realized that, along with her magic, Brennan's control of his Wolf had gone. Her capture had not only led to her own bleak circumstances but also a dangerous risk to him and those around him.

For a moment, Shadow just watched her, the corners of her mouth turning up.

Rielle stiffened; what secrets had her face betrayed that the woman before her mistook for defeat? "This isn't over."

"No, it's not over until your lover's life seeps from his body. Blood for blood." Shadow headed to the edge of the ship's deck. She kicked over the side in one smooth movement, grabbing hold of a rope ladder.

You will burn for this.

Shadow had enslaved her and threatened to kill Jon. It was circumstance alone—the arcanir chains—that kept Shadow breathing. If she hurt him in any way—

"I will destroy you," Rielle vowed.

Shadow laughed. "You will want to. More than you can fathom. And that brings me such satisfaction." With a final smile, she descended, the give of the rope ladder the only sign she'd landed on a waiting pinnace.

Rielle thumped her head against the mast. She'd escorted the last of the Faralles to Monas Amar, saved Olivia, and helped break the siege of Courdeval, but she couldn't do a damned thing to stop Shadow from killing Jon.

When she imagined Shadow bound for the palace, bound for Jon, she thrashed in her chains, her hands filling with quaking purpose. She yanked at them, drawing against them with all her strength, pushing against the mast with her feet, so hard the arcanir cuffs grated against her wrists. What she would give, what she would do to be free, only long enough to—

A moment later, darkness blotted out the sun.

A large boot smashed her shoulder against the mast. Gasping for breath, she followed the thick, leather-wrapped leg up to a tall man's bearded face beneath a wide-brimmed, decorated black hat.

"Cease your racket," he said, in a harshly accented voice. "You are bound for the market alive... but not unharmed."

She glared up at her captor, trying to discern the lines of his face under the shadow of his hat.

The boot connected with her face. She fell to the deck, the wind knocked from her lungs. Scrambling for breath. Trying to reach up to cover her pounding jaw only to be stopped by the chains.

"Looking into your betters' eyes like that will earn you lashes where you are bound." He stood over her while she breathed hard.

When he finally strolled away, she shifted closer to the mast, curling her legs up to her chest, trying to shut out the cold and unfeeling wind, the rocking of the ship beneath her, and the sunshine, cruel in its unabashedly bright cheer.

71

*B*rennan crumpled the message in his hand as he rode through the Azalée District of Courdeval. So someone had arrived at Victoire. His eldest sister, Nora, was in Vauquelin with her two sons, and the younger two, Caitlin and Una, were at Maerleth Tainn with Mother. That left one Marcel in his family.

Father.

And he had words for Father. Especially after recognizing Phantom and the map in Melain's smuggler tunnels, and after what the captured Black Mountain Brigand had said. Father's ill-advised coup d'état plans needed to be clipped before they could flower.

And if Father knew anything about Rielle, today he would answer.

Few people moved about the cobblestone roads. During the regicide, in addition to the Faralles, many of the courtiers had met their ends, which meant many empty villas in Azalée. The Order had secured the capital, and Courdevallans trickled back into their city, but few survivors, it seemed, called this district home.

The ample linden trees of the Azalée District now bore golden crowns, a macabre echo of the flames that had destroyed it. Indeed, heaviest among the district's scents were the choked stench of wet ash, the too-sweet smell of old death, the putrid complexity of varied viscera, and the rusted metal of dried blood.

Finally, Victoire came into view. Sided with stone and decorative half-timbering, it was the grandest and largest villa to be found in Azalée, the natural order of things for a Marcel's property. Its round stone center tower alone, topped by a conical roof, dwarfed the Alaire family villa nearby. Apt, as the Alaires had always been small men with small minds and small fortunes. At least compared to the Marcels.

As he rode up, a groom and a manservant, liveried in black and gold, ran out to greet him. The scrappy young groom bowed low and took his horse by the bridle.

"Lord Brennan," the elderly manservant—whatever his name was—stammered. "We weren't expecting you."

Of course not. With Trèstellan Palace so empty of courtiers and household staff, who would spy for Father? Without spies, word was scarce. And without word, so were expectations.

He scowled at the doddering manservant and dismounted. Fear. The oldster reeked of fear. Was Father in one of his moods?

Removing his riding gloves, Brennan narrowed his eyes. "I didn't realize I needed to provide notice to visit my own family's property." He shoved the gloves at the manservant.

The man accepted them and bowed lower. "Of course not, my lord! I wouldn't dare even suggest—"

Brennan waved him off, neatened his black brocade doublet, and stared down the entry doors. "Take me to my father."

The man bowed profusely, his bald pate shining in the afternoon sun. "Yes, my lord. Please, follow me."

Brennan followed him into the villa. The place had come out of the siege nigh unscathed, and inside, it appeared the same as it always had. No one would have dared loot property belonging to the Marcels—Father's memory was perfect. And long.

The hazel trees and leaves carved into the moldings, sconces, and banisters came to life as they never had. As he climbed the stairs, he closed his eyes and traced the simple, rounded, double-serrated hazel leaf pattern on the banister. The Lothaire villa, Couronne, had similar carvings, but of honeysuckle.

Rielle. He'd thought of little else for two days. Where was she?

Was she even alive?

He pulled his fingers away from the banister and curled them into a fist. The Crag prisoners he'd questioned had reported one ship in port, but no one knew its name, its colors, or where it made berth. Jon had provided him a squad of men to canvas the docks and question the returning Courdevallans, but it was the height of stupidity to rely on hope when action was available.

Tomorrow he'd question the mage. Jon had finally granted him permission to interrogate the man and elicit answers by any means necessary. Brennan's face hardened. He would ask questions, of course, but the primary purpose wouldn't be answers; it would be a lesson in consequences. The consequences of betraying the woman he—

He straightened his back.

The woman he planned to marry.

After he was through with Leigh Galvan, no one would dare move against her but with a lethal case of masochism.

And by the time he was done, he'd know the name of every accomplice, the specifics of every plan, and he'd give the mage no information with which to manipulate. It wasn't his first interrogation.

Any means necessary. He wouldn't leave Rielle in the hands of mercenaries, pirates, whatever lowlifes had dared abduct her. Every second she was gone, who could say what she suffered? If anyone threatened her, scared her, hurt a hair on her head, he would—

He hissed.

That is, if anyone deprived him of his means of control. Of his curse-breaking.

The manservant stopped in front of the study. "Just a moment," he said, turning to the ornately carved oak door and raising his knuckles to it.

Rolling his eyes, Brennan cut him off and threw the door open, leaving the manservant agog.

Inside, Father sat in a winged tufted leather armchair with a book. His coal-black hair, now dusted with shades of ash, was cropped short, and his black velvet doublet and wool trousers fit him well—he'd remained faithful to his training regimen, if to little else. Faolan Auvray Marcel could always be relied on to tend to himself, his fortune, and his women. His black leather boots, shined to high gloss, caught the late-afternoon sun from the window. His crisp white shirt contrasted starkly against his deep bronze skin, a shade darker than Brennan's.

"Father."

Serene, he didn't look up from his book. "To what do I owe the pleasure?"

The manservant shuffled in, but Father dismissed him with a hand. "Leave us, Preston."

"As you wish, Your Grace." The man bowed shakily and made his exit.

Brennan strolled deeper into the study and grazed a finger along the leather spines of a shelf of books. One lay on the edge; he picked it up and continued scanning the rest while he gathered his thoughts.

The siege had broken two days ago. Maerleth Tainn was at least a week away by carriage. And yet here Father was.

Brennan found an empty space among the shelved books and easily slipped into place the one he held.

To be here so soon after the siege broke, Father had to have been nearby. Invested. It all fit.

Brennan eyed the replaced book—one of a series of ledgers. "You made a play for the crown."

After a moment, he resumed his perusal of the tomes. He'd give Father the chance to catch his breath.

The old man must have supposed him completely ignorant. Brennan could have laughed. Father had chosen decidedly loose-lipped tools if he'd wanted discretion.

Brennan stopped at the spine of the latest *Court Duelist* and smiled. Every Marcel property stocked the series for him. Once upon a time, he and Rielle had read the first couple volumes together, to each other.

It was the court's worst-kept secret that the romantic duelist hero was based on Prince James. Jon's father. Jon's royal father.

Brennan repressed the urge to curse. He had no love for Rielle's royal paramour, but Jon served a necessary purpose in filling the throne—keeping Father off it. A play for the crown was dangerous, and royalty came with responsibilities Brennan would never want. Never in his life would he have thought he'd support Rielle's lover as king, but there it was.

When Father still didn't answer, Brennan turned to him. He'd come for information, and he wouldn't be so easily rebuffed. "No answer?"

"No question."

He could hear the smug smile in Father's voice. He grimaced. "I need to know where Rielle is."

Father closed his book, laced his fingers, and looked at Brennan with an amused glimmer. "What, she's not off dallying with another commoner?"

Brennan's stomach clenched, but he banked the outrage and strolled to the window. He wouldn't give Father such easy access to his emotions. It would be easier for the old man to irritate him and answer no questions, but he'd find no ease today.

Outside the window, beyond Azalée, the city was busy rebuilding. Men littered roofs, hung from walls, and ascended on ladders, repairing the siege's damage. Courdeval had suffered before and rebuilt. It would again.

"Did you have anything to do with her disappearance?" Brennan asked calmly but firmly.

Silence.

He listened for Father's heart, and it beat a little faster—realization.

"As part of a faction seeking what's best for the kingdom, did I hire Gilles?" Father dropped the book onto a table. "Yes." He rose and strode to the window to join Brennan. He scanned the horizon. "But I don't have your woman, and I don't know where she is."

No irregularity in Father's heart to suggest a lie. That was it, then. Father had hired Gilles. Endangered the whole family with his vain pursuit of the crown.

Brennan fought back a snarl.

But would he admit to treason and endangering the family, but lie about Rielle? It seemed unlikely. "And how much blood will your scheme cost us?"

"None." Father's voice was even. "I was careful."

Brennan could have laughed. If only Father knew how many loose ends he'd left. Fewer now, of course, thanks to Brennan.

He was about to ask whether Father would stop his machinations, but he glanced down through the glass at the courtyard, at the servants bustling about. One carried in a gown box. No doubt for a mistress.

"Which one's here? Gabrielle? Fleur?"

Father grinned. "Marie de Brignac." He breathed her name like a satisfied exhalation.

Brennan raised his eyebrows. He had seen the woman once, a strikingly beautiful maiden in her late twenties with hazelnut-brown hair, dark-blue eyes, and light-bronze skin. Mixed blood was rare among the Houses of Emaurria, flowing only among the Faralles, the Marcels, and whomever they deigned to bed or wed—and her mother was an Emaurrian maid of the Royal Household who'd been granted a small manor house—Brignac— not far from the capital.

The king hadn't elevated her to nobility, but the maid's daughter, Marie, was said to be King Marcus's bastard child. She certainly had his features.

For a mistress, the daughter of the king he had assassinated...

Many men held grudges; some men, however, buried them, buried them so deep in their hearts that to live was to grudge. Such a man was Faolan Auvray Marcel.

But Father hadn't come here for pleasure.

Brennan watched the servants bustling in the courtyard, their lives made hectic by their lord's stay. "Was it worth the coin? Killing him?"

Father exhaled another long breath. This one not satisfied but bored.

"I'm not sure what you mean. Our family was unable to collect on a loan, and we've suffered losses." He gave Brennan a shrewd look.

A clear lie. But alibis had to be secured. And this would work. A substantial sum to compensate a Free Company could have also been lost on a loan, if the right men were paid to produce the evidence.

"Now that Marcus is no longer standing in the way of progress, we'll earn it back soon enough."

"That's not an answer," Brennan pushed.

Father glanced out the north-facing window at the palace. "It's all I have."

The coup d'état had failed. He'd achieved the removal of King Marcus and other obstacles, but he hadn't won the crown.

And he wouldn't—not with the Order protecting their own so carefully. Any further plan was doomed to fail.

Brennan hadn't come here to discuss failures. "Do you know where Rielle is or not?"

Father peered down at Victoire's courtyard. "I didn't even know she was missing."

No irregularity.

Father turned to him. "You're going after her, I presume?"

Even the thought of leaving her to some wretched fate was unpalatable. Brennan nodded.

Father rested a hand on his shoulder. "Take as many knights and men-at-arms as you want, as much coin as you want—whatever you need."

Brennan eyed him. Father didn't care whether Rielle lived or died, of course; what he cared about was that someone had dared take what belonged to the Marcels. And such slights could not go unanswered.

"Yes, Father." He turned to take his leave and moved to the door.

"Brennan?" Father called from the window.

"Yes?"

"You are my only son," he said, turning around to lean against the window frame. "If the rumors from Melain are true, the king is in love with her. He is young and foolish... He'll break the marriage contract."

There was no question. Jon would free her of obligation, give her the power of choice.

Once upon a time, forcing her into marriage had seemed an attractive option.

But he didn't have it in him to force her into anything anymore.

It had been a game, toying with her and pushing her limits, hadn't it?

Trying to destroy her options had shown her his power, his worth, and the inevitability of their fate together—or it had, at one time.

Her determination, her resolve, the look on her face in Melain as she'd plunged the glass into her body now etched into his memory forever. Some nights, he lay awake, her resolute, powerful, broken face haunting him. And he'd been the one to push her so far, to corner her, to break her. His own hands might as well have been on that shard of glass.

Never again. He never wanted to see that broken face again. Not to marry her. Not even to break the curse. If the ghost of that face returned, he wasn't sure he could ever see the world again but through the haze of that anguished specter.

No, he could never—would never—hurt her like that again. He splayed his fingers and then clenched them tight.

Father studied him. "When you return, regardless of what happens with Favrielle, you need to marry."

Brennan nodded curtly and exited the study. He shut the door behind him, strode to the stairs, and gripped the banister.

To marry another woman would be to let the one he was destined for slip away. A contract, a love, and a curse had brought them together, three threads fate now stretched. The contract would soon be cut. But the love?

She'd loved him once. Of that he was certain. And he—he loved her, too. *Had* loved her.

Had? He ran his fingers over the engraved hazel leaves that he and Rielle used to admire together.

Could she still? Would she? Ever?

After all he'd done, could she ever love him again?

His breaths came slower, harder. He'd humiliated her. Hurt her. Abused her—physically, emotionally, psychologically. He'd been a vile, hateful monster, not worthy of love but a sword through the heart.

How could she still love him? She wouldn't. She would never.

Tension vibrated through his arms—he wanted to rip the banister from the wall, tear apart the house, everyone in it, himself.

Himself. He wanted to rip himself apart.

Instead, he pounded down the stairs, ignoring everything and everyone, shoving aside the doddering old man with his gloves, leaving his horse behind. He stormed out of Victoire and strode through the defeated streets of Azalée.

In Trèstellan, when he had no longer felt her through the bond—when he'd thought her dead, it hadn't been the thought of controlling the Wolf that had assailed him. It had been the thought of her, the concept of her removal from life itself, that unbearable notion.

She hated him, would never love him, for how could she? He'd destroyed all hope of that, hadn't he? And yet, that impossibility, despite its neat certainty, wove through him like a shard of glass.

The cold air he'd once been impervious to now bit, its chill wind meeting his wet eyes. The agony he'd so long repressed rose to the surface, refusing to be denied.

Great Wolf damn the wind.

A few hearts beat around him, some voices whispered, and he looked about, at the faces passing by in the street in the biting autumn air. Let them talk. He didn't care. Their words meant nothing—a lesson he should have learned years ago.

He rounded a corner and found a villa's gate hanging off its hinges. He slipped in and trudged through the brush, ripping shrubs out with their roots, tearing up a garden as he sought the dark corner. There, he pressed his back against the cool wall and slid to a crouch, dropping his head in his hands. His face tightened to bursting, eyes stinging, every muscle in his body hardening to painful rigidity, and his fingernails bit into his palms, spikes of pain blooming the wetness of blood. The darkness welcomed him, embraced him, invited him to explore greater depths.

Here, away from prying eyes, he could at last be himself. Not the Wolf. The man.

He wanted her to love him.

He surrendered to the dark, wept as he hadn't in years, letting the reality shred through him, cut its way out. He'd given her his love once, and she'd tossed it away. To live was to grudge. He'd crushed her mercilessly in turn, hurt her—how many times? And now, the cruel irony of it, he wanted her to love him.

It would be easier to crush that, too, to bury the grudge deeper in his heart. It was easier to hate than to hurt. That hatred could temper him to steel—sharpen him until he became only deadly edges. Like Father.

But it was delusion.

He hurt. Rielle had hurt him, and when he couldn't have her love, he'd taken her hate.

She hates me.

Her hate had been easier to stomach than her rejection, hadn't it? Having the upper hand had lessened the pain, hadn't it?

I love her.

To deny it, he'd broken her, pushed her nearly into her grave. And now she was gone, could even be—

He dropped his gaze to the shrubs he'd torn up and discarded, studying their leaves.

Honeysuckle.

A raw, hoarse laugh rent free of him, and he dragged a sleeve across his eyes.

Rielle had to be alive. She had to be alive because she hated him and he loved her and the gods loved irony.

But first, in order to ever love him, she'd need to forgive him. He'd find her, alive, and earn that forgiveness.

Love her. Love those she loves. Convince her you want to make amends, and convince yourself. Then make them.

Amends. Tomorrow, he and a blade would visit the mage, he'd meet with his squad of soldiers, and begin.

72

*D*rip.

Leigh watched as another droplet of blood rolled languidly down his arm all the way to the tip of his fifth finger and plummeted to the arcanir-coated stone floor.

Drip.

It had been over a decade since he had last seen the inside of a cell. Even then, it hadn't been for very long. With no word on an audience, caged in a prison built for mages and cuffed in arcanir, the future was decidedly bleak. Even for someone like him.

It was ridiculous.

There was no other word for it. He closed his eyes sluggishly, shook his head, and snarled. The Divinity. No one had wanted to see it, to understand, to realize that—with no fight at all—they were giving away their freedom to a power only too happy to take it. For over a thousand years, the Divinity of Magic had played in the shadows of global politics, offering means and support to what it had deemed just causes and just rulers, taking presence, influence, and respect in exchange.

Countries and their people gleefully accepted peace while closing their eyes to atrocities. The anarchic North became a mess of warlords and clans because its rulers had refused to send mages to a Tower and had thus refused the Divinity's so-called "aid." Mission after mission eliminated "dangerous" leaders in the North, anyone who might have united the clans and formed a nation independent of the Divinity's influence.

And yet countries like the Kezan Isles and Sonbahar, which dealt in piracy and slavery, gained the support of the Divinity easily, despite resisting any change to their brutal ways. The Kezan Isles did so by paying tribute and sending mage children across the Shining Sea to Magehold in Silen. Sonbahar did it by welcoming a Tower into its harsh land, without abolishing slavery. What did that speak of, if not the Divinity's cold pragmatism?

So many mages in the Divinity's service had dark pasts heavy with alienation and sorrow. While magic had always had its price, it had become markedly steeper since the Divinity had begun to centralize mages.

Drip.

Leigh rested his head against the cell wall. It had taken him years to realize the Divinity was to blame for his own heart-wrenching loss of his family. But he had seen it as a doyen, year after year, novices in his classroom wearing the somber expressions of orphanage and depression. Even the one who had once captured his heart.

But even she had refused to see the truth.

Rielle still hadn't come to see him yet, but her exacting monster of a fiancé certainly had. Leigh sighed and shook the blood from his hands, tired of the ceaseless dripping. The monster had come with a blade, a blade that had been insistent and relentless in its questioning—whom he was working with, what his plan consisted of, how he had planned to evade capture, and so on.

Its sharp edge was unsatisfied with the answer: the entirety of his "plan" had consisted of revealing the Divinity as unneeded, rallying three Archon lines—the so-called "heretics," and trusting his former apprentice to believe him and join him.

Yes, the blade had been unsatisfied. Very unsatisfied. And he had the injuries to prove it.

Light footsteps echoed from down the hall. Perhaps Rielle had finally deigned to visit. She never could be upset with him for long.

"Did you come for an apology, or did you just miss me?" he called out.

"Neither," was the answer, but its speaker was not Rielle: Olivia. "Someone told me you were down here. Leigh Galvan in chains had to be seen to be believed."

Clad in a green velvet gown with a high neck and long sleeves, she was vivid in her austere modesty. Always conservative. Always buttoned up, held in, restrained, as if she feared her body would flee her dominion if not for the constraints of fabric. But that had always been Olivia.

Fitted as it was, the dress illustrated the difficult conditions she had survived. Her flame-red hair, gathered in its large plaited bun at the nape of her neck, and her bright-green eyes made Olivia Sabeyon stand out anywhere.

"Deriding your former master?" He shook his shackles. "Forgive me for not kissing your hand."

Olivia clutched the bars, flinching at the arcanir. On her fifth finger, she bore the Ring of the Archmage, a large emerald intricately set in recondite. She squinted to view him in the dim light, then unhanded the bars and cast a healer's soothing light spell. "You look terrible."

Leigh supposed he must have looked the picture of gore. "Yes, well, we mustn't allow torture to get us down."

Olivia examined him with large, rapt eyes that soon glazed over. "He tortured you."

Leigh did not reply.

"Did you tell him where Rielle is?"

Leigh leaned forward. "She's missing?"

"Yes."

"Since when?"

"Spiritseve."

The chains clinked as he rose to his feet. "Tell me what happened."

Olivia's eyelids were heavy as she looked away. "Rielle freed me, then went deeper into the dungeon. I should have never agreed to let her go alone..."

"Olivia—"

She closed her eyes for a moment. "The king and Brennan went after her. They found a hidden dock, but Rielle was nowhere to be found, just some letter she'd allegedly left in my cell, bidding Jon goodbye."

He exhaled a sharp breath through his nose. "She'd have said it to his face. It's a forgery."

Olivia nodded. "I agree. But there's still no other explanation. I'd been in that cell all day and all night, Leigh, and no one but she had come. I have no answers."

He took a few steps back to lean against the wall and rapped it lightly with his fist. Damn it. Damn everything.

"You had nothing to do with it?"

"Olivia," he said, boring his eyes into hers. "You should know better than anyone that I would never hurt Rielle."

She held his gaze for a moment, then slowly nodded. "The only shred of evidence I have is that Shadow wanted her for something, but—"

"If Shadow's responsible, she's in the wind. We have a better chance of finding the Divine." He glanced down at her ring and sighed. "But we *can* find Rielle. She'll want to be found. If you're still the Archmage, then you have Jon's ear. Convince him to free me. I will find her."

She looked away when he said the name. "The priests have barely convinced His Majesty to stay in Courdeval for the stability of the kingdom, after the rite was completed too late. He's not in a state to hear much of mercy right now."

"It's not mercy. It's pragmatism. I can do what he can't." Testing the length of the chains, Leigh moved as close to the bars as he could manage. "Please."

Her mouth fell open. No doubt she was stunned to hear the word; in truth, he rarely said it.

"I will see what I can do." She reached for his hand, then gestured a healing spell, her soft moss-green presence entering him.

He closed his eyes and sighed. At least the dripping would finally cease.

But what had she said about—something about the rite and stability?

Finished, she withdrew. "There. Good as new."

"What does the stability of the kingdom have to do with the rite?" He flexed his fingers. Still stiff. "Wasn't it all just for show? The Divinity puffing up its own importance?"

Her mouth turned down, her shoulders slumped, even her eyes dulled.

To say that Olivia appeared devastated was a vast understatement.

He frowned. She weathered disaster well, and to see her in such a state...? No sound but the beating of his disquieted heart filled his ears.

"No." She lowered her gaze, a ruminative crease forming on her brow. "Only the ruling Faralles and their Archmages have been privy to this knowledge, but I suppose you'll see the consequences soon enough. Long, long ago, when the humans defeated the elves and conquered Emaurria, a primitive ritual was used to secure that victory. It was said that the elves were superior to humanity, that all the Immortals were, and that, alive, they would always pose a danger."

He knew those tales well. But that's all they were: tales.

"So mankind corrupted their ritual and used it against the elves—and every other race and species they deemed a threat. Left their bodies in stone, but their souls trapped beyond the Veil, the door between the Lone and our world. The annual Moonlit Rite maintains the Veil and prevents those souls from returning. Every performance of the rite since has kept that door sealed. Now the Rift has torn it open."

His mouth was so dry he couldn't swallow. "You're telling me that the Immortals—elves, fairies, werewolves, vampires, dragons, krakens, mermaids, and so on—are not only real but returning?" He backed up until he hit a slimy wall. "That... cannot be."

Drip. Far away this time.

"It is." Eyes shadowed, she drew in a deep breath. "There are already multiple reports of strange creatures coming in."

Drip.

He stared at her, at the blur she became, one with the darkness. He'd killed Kieran to thwart the rite's performance, even betrayed Rielle, all to undercut the Divinity.

Drip.

Oh, yes. He'd succeeded in making the Divinity look irresponsible and unneeded all right, but the success had an aftertaste so bitter it choked.

Drip.

Silent, Olivia gave him a piteous parting glance and turned to walk away. There had simply been no more words, nothing more that either of them could offer, when they both knew the dire truth.

He had opened the door for, and welcomed, the greatest atrocity in recent history.

Perhaps even the end of mankind.

73

*J*on tried to shrug off the middle-aged Keeper of the Seals and Minister of Justice, but the little man possessed a determination that belied his size.

"Your Majesty, with all due respect, you cannot garrison paladins in the palace," Jacques Fernand D'Ambray said over the commotion of voices in the bustling war room. One of the few officers left over from King Marcus's administration, D'Ambray had taken refuge in the nearby town of Sauveterre after fleeing the coup d'état.

Jon sighed at the complaint. The last four days had been full of them, even amid funerals for his family and other Courdevallan nobles. He'd had to shuffle the man out of his quarters after naming Valen Grand Chamberlain, one of the highest posts in the Emaurrian court. D'Ambray's shock at a commoner's appointment to the position wouldn't have lessened if he'd been struck by lightning.

The past few days had seen Jon do many things D'Ambray asserted he could not. "I did, so that must mean I can."

He signed off on a requisitions order presented to him. At least when he kept busy, his thoughts didn't settle on the one thing he actually wanted to do—the one thing duty and every officer in the Order wouldn't let him do. Even now, he waited on word from Brennan.

If anyone could find Rielle, it was the werewolf bonded to her, with his preternatural senses.

Jon wanted to be there himself, but that was the selfish desire of a man in love. What Rielle needed right now was not him, but to be found, for which—he begrudgingly admitted—Brennan was better equipped. But the truth salted his wounded heart.

He'd received correspondence supposedly from Rielle—a heartfelt goodbye—but even though it seemed to be written in her hand, with her words, it had to be false. There was no way she would've left such matters to a piece of parchment—

D'Ambray persisted. "None but the Royal Guard may—"

Tor arrived, eyeing all the activity uncomfortably, head and shoulders above most of the advisers, guards, servants, and subjects flitting about the room, but when Jon pulled him into an embrace, he relaxed.

"Tor," he greeted with relief. "It's good to see a familiar face."

"I am here to serve, Your Majesty," Tor said stiffly.

At Monas Amar, Tor had balked when he'd learned the truth, confessing he'd always known Jon was a bastard, but never a royal one. They'd shared a laugh over it.

"Please, to you of all people, it's Jon." He wouldn't have his mentor, who was family to him, hanging on ceremony.

Tor grinned. "Not in front of the others it isn't, sire."

"He is entirely correct, sire," D'Ambray interjected. "Formalities must be adhered to, lest your rule be considered weak."

When Jon scowled at him, D'Ambray bowed.

"Forgive my directness, sire," D'Ambray said. "I only wish to advise you in earnest."

Trusting any survivor of the coup, especially when the Crag Company's employer remained a mystery, was out of the question. Perhaps D'Ambray wanted nothing more than a secure position in a new regime, but he still had to be considered with caution.

"I know," Jon replied, "and for that, I thank you. But that'll be all, D'Ambray."

The man opened his mouth, but then he closed it, bowed, and made his exit. He wasn't the only Divinist noble to have made his discomfort known at the Order of Terra's new levels of presence and influence.

Jon turned to Tor. "You said you are here to serve?"

"Yes, my king," Tor replied, inclining his head.

"I hope I can hold you to that," Jon said, with a deep breath. "I would like to appoint you Constable of Emaurria."

The First Officer of the Crown and the highest officer of the Emaurrian army, it was not only a position of trust but of power. Born a noble of a distinguished House, Tor was an unobjectionable candidate. And one of the few people he trusted to find the traitor who'd seen the Faralles dead and the capital besieged.

"I am honored," Tor replied, his eyebrows pulling in, "but... a vassal may not serve two masters."

Therein lay the difficulty: in order to accept the position, Tor would have to renounce his oath as a paladin. A heavy favor. But if Jon planned to live until his coronation, he'd need to surround himself with those he trusted. "I know I'm asking a lot of you, but your country needs you. I need you."

One of his new clerks brought him a document announcing his rise and calling for a meeting of Parliament. Jon confirmed its contents, sending the clerk away to have copies delivered across the kingdom. He turned back to Tor, who looked downward, his brow creased.

"May I have until tomorrow to consider it?" he asked in a somber tone.

"I trust you will come to the correct decision," a voice said from behind them.

Tor turned around first. "Derric."

"Meet the new Grand Master of Emaurria," Jon said with a grin.

Wearing his new robes and chain of office, Derric was a pillar of white but for his clean-shaven head and ornate chain of office. He regarded Tor with warm brown eyes. "It's true. The king, however, will require more than a glorified priest as Master of Emaurria if he is to return this land to order," he added with a smile.

Derric, born a commoner, had resisted appointment to Master of Emaurria, but someone trustworthy had to direct the Royal Household, including the Royal Guard, and the domestic and religious branches. When it came to trust, Derric was at the top of the list.

"I will give the matter serious thought." Tor turned to Jon. "Your Majesty." He bowed before making his exit.

Jon raised his eyebrows and watched him leave. He closed his eyes for a moment and exhaled heavily.

And just when would he hear from Brennan? It had been all day, with no lead on Rielle forthcoming.

Derric approached, and Jon cracked an eye open. The line between Derric's eyebrows meant an unpleasant topic was at hand.

"Preparations for your coronation are under way," he said, "but we still need at least a token number of Parliament members to confirm the legitimization."

Unpleasant didn't even begin to cover where this was going. Returning to his work, he bent over a map of the region. Red markers indicated where pockets of the Crag Company were holed up. The paladins, for the moment at least, had them outnumbered—several times over.

More worrisome were the purple markers, indicating reports of strange animals killing and harming Emaurrians. The Immortals. The monsters whose spirits had crossed through the Rift. Paladin Grand Cordon Guérin had agreed to send troops to investigate.

Derric rested a hand on the map—over the Brise-Lames River, right where he'd been looking. "You need to secure your line. You need an heir. You need to marry."

Jon heaved a sigh and crossed his arms. It was not the first time in the last few days that Derric had raised the subject.

"No."

Undeterred, Derric leaned over the map with him. "Our strongest ally is Pryndon, from which your grandfather, King Frédéric Dominic El-Amin Faralle, married Princess Elizabeth, daughter of your great-grandfather, King Jonathan Breckenridge of Pryndon—and *Pryndon* is *all the way across the Shining Sea*, with King Jonathan and his children long dead and all but forgotten, just like his ties with Emaurria."

It was enough to make Jon's head spin.

"When Prince Basile was killed, his betrothal to Princess Melora of Morwen died along with him," Derric whispered. "The promise of that marriage secured an alliance between Morwen and Emaurria. Her father, King Odhrán, has already inquired whether *you* intend to honor the arrangement. Because your uncle, King Marcus, chose to marry from within the kingdom, Emaurria is incredibly weak unless you start building alliances."

Jon grimaced and looked away. "Prince Basile was *fifth* in the line of succession."

"Yes," Derric replied, "but you don't have the luxury of heirs to bargain away, do you?"

With Rielle missing, the last thing he wanted to hear about was marriage. He glared at Derric, then began the long walk to the palace kitchens.

Derric followed. "This isn't a problem you can ignore. Prince Robert—the Crown Prince—was married to Princess Giuliana of Silen. Had they lived, she would have been queen. King Macario has already sent an offer of marriage on behalf of his youngest daughter, Princess Alessandra, for which you should be immensely grateful. He could do far worse to the kingdom that failed to protect his daughter and grandchildren."

The smell of freshly baked bread grew stronger. At last, Jon had reached the kitchen, dodging a bevy of hanging dried herbs and smoked meats. He walked around wheels of cheese and crates of fruit and vegetables until he reached a large table covered in loaves.

"These are important matters you can't run away from," Derric added behind him. "And you don't have to go to the kitchen for food... There is a palace full of staff eager to serve your every request."

The cooks and servants jumped out of his way, asking how they could serve, but he waved them off. Spotting some fresh butter, he tore off a piece of partial rye, dusted flour off a nearby stool, sat, and buttered the bread.

As he bit into it, he wondered if Rielle had enough to eat. Or anything at all.

The bite turned to ashes in his mouth.

"Jon!" Derric exclaimed, earning gasps from the servants within earshot. "This kingdom will not survive *politics*, let alone the Rift, unless you start acting in its interest."

He paused, pinning Derric with a cold glare. "I'm here. Have I done anything but act in this kingdom's best interest, forsaking even my own?"

With a coarse exhalation, Derric sat. "I know you wanted to chase after that marquise, son. I know. You love her. But you're a king now, and that comes with certain obligations. A marriage to her would not only bring no alliances whatsoever but insult what fragile relations we *do* have, leaving this kingdom vulnerable, and it would fracture the Houses. You well know she's promised to Duke Faolan's heir."

Jon scowled. *I do know.*

Her betrothal to Brennan had weighed on his mind since he'd learned of it, and the added difficulties of his new position didn't help, but there had to be a way. No matter what Derric or anyone else said, there had to be a way.

The first Farallan king, Tristan Armand Marcel Faralle, had married a Lothaire. If the Blade could marry the pirate queen, Rosalie Vignon Lothaire, then there had to be a way for him and Rielle. He wouldn't let her slip through his fingers just because others deemed their union *inconvenient*.

"Despite all this, I know you still want to find her. But you have to leave the investigation to the paladins. Others can search for her, but only *you* can rule this land."

It was this argument and Brennan's oath to search for Rielle that kept him in Trèstellan Palace. Barely.

"The paladins are already spread thin securing the kingdom," Jon fought back, "and the single care I have as a man will not outweigh that task for them. Their duty is to the Order, first and always."

They'd already had the same argument multiple times since the night of her disappearance. At least he could count on the werewolf to find Rielle.

But the question of how to handle the marriage problem had weighed on his mind. There were agreements and alliances to be made, but the issue of betrothal was inescapable. Many lands would send suitresses and contingent offers of support. And to choose one would be to deny the others, perhaps inviting more than mere indifference from their lands.

His thoughts had returned to his days as a page at Monas Ver, and the rare book of tales that would arrive on Derric's order from time to time. Pages, squires, paladins, and priests alike would ply him with favors for the privilege of reading the new arrival after he finished. Cleverly, Derric accepted favor from all, but could only pass on the book to one.

"A quick marriage won't fix everything. Even if I were to do as you say, marrying a princess of one land to form an alliance will unmistakably turn away the others."

Derric nodded. "Then what do you propose?"

A way to keep marriage at bay and give himself room to breathe. "What this land needs is time—time to gather its composure, rebuild its government, replenish its army. And we can secure that time by entertaining alliances with not one but *many* countries."

Derric crossed his arms. "Are you suggesting that we... flaunt you as a prize to be won, leaving each country to believe it has a chance of supplying the future queen?" He knitted his eyebrows. "Keeping the kingdom protected from foreign threats long enough to regain its stability? It's... sensible."

Sensible. Disingenuous. Dishonorable. But the most practical of all his options.

Dusting his hands off, Jon rose from the stool and began the trek back to the war room.

Derric rose to follow. "The plan is sound, and it should keep the peace for some time, but how long until that time runs out? You will still need to marry."

Hopefully long enough to find Rielle.

He was no prize—illegitimate, raised as a peasant, and with a precarious hold on the throne—but many kings longed for their daughters to become queens, to gain some power in another country's affairs, to add to their own. And he would use whatever time the plan could earn him to see that Rielle was found.

From down the hall, a messenger hurried to him and handed off a roll of leather-wrapped parchment, which he opened and read as he walked. Not the word he'd been waiting for, but good news. "I am not entirely without allies."

"You do have the paladins on your side, but the Order of Terra cannot protect a kingdom on its own," Derric remarked.

The Order had been apolitical for a very long time, and its recent actions were anomalous. How long would Paladin Grand Cordon Guérin assist the Crown and allow Jon to recruit from his ranks?

"The Order isn't our only ally," Jon said, with a smile. "Three days ago, I sent a dove with a message offering Pons Olivier the position of Lord Chancellor of Emaurria. He just accepted." He handed off the message to Derric, who received it and read it wide eyed, his countenance brightening. The taut lines of his face softened.

It was true, then. When the Proctor had spoken of Derric, Jon had wondered about their relationship. And it was clear now, in Derric's face. After a long separation, they would be reunited. While a benefit to the kingdom at large, it was undoubtedly a personal boon for them both.

"I'm also retaining Olivia Sabeyon as Archmage of Emaurria," Jon added. "At the very least, we know the Divinity protects its hold on power. I've also sent word to Magehold asking for aid. I think that the Grand Divinus will happily acquiesce to offset the negativity surrounding the Moonlit Rite."

Quiet lingered for the brief period until they made it to the war room, still bustling with activity. He looked ahead to see Olivia striding toward him, a worried frown on her wan face.

"What is it?" he asked.

"Word from Bisclavret, Your Majesty," she said.

He knew Bisclavret as a march near the Marcellan Peaks.

"Strange creatures have been spotted there—massive giants radiating cold. They've been attacking flocks of livestock and scaring the surrounding villages. Some of the villages' militias are mobilizing and the marquis has sent some forces, but..."

Jon grabbed a nearby quill, dipped it in ink, and bent over a desk, hastily scrawling a note on some paper for a paladin captain. He folded it up, called over a nearby clerk to pour hot wax over it, and sealed it with a press of his royal signet ring. He blew on the wax to harden it before handing the note to Olivia.

"See what information you can uncover about them today," Jon said, "then take this to Captain Perrault and tell him what you know. He should send paladins."

Olivia brought the sealed note close to her chest, hesitating before her next words. "Your Majesty, there is one other matter... would it be possible to discuss it in private?"

Jon exhaled heavily. There were endless matters. His day was filled from before dawn until well after dusk with matters. But Olivia had been indispensable the last few days, and if she had a concern, he would hear it—as long as it wasn't about releasing Leigh again. That was not going to happen.

"I will call on you when I am done here," he said, ignoring a critical sniff from Derric behind him, "if that is all right."

She nodded and bowed before departing.

"Your Majesty," Derric scolded, his voice a hiss, "if you frequent a woman's quarters at night, you risk the appearance of impropriety."

There was no chance of impropriety. At all. And in times like this, practicality prevailed over appearances. "You do realize that *actual* impropriety requires neither night nor quarters?"

Derric's mouth dropped open.

It had been a long time since he'd dropped Derric's jaw like that. *That one's for you, Bastien.*

Jon stared into space, filled with the span of memories. "And I was a paladin for nearly a decade. To abandon my troth to Terra, it took falling in love with a woman who is... irreplaceable to me." He twirled the Sodalis ring he'd given her. It belonged not on his finger but hers. "Since meeting her, my heart threatens to crumble and burst all at once. The loss of her would be my undoing... And anyone who has known love could not imagine I would mark her disappearance by tumbling her best friend."

Before Derric could reply, another messenger came running and held out a note.

"From the Principal Secretary, Your Majesty," he said with a bow.

Brennan.

"Wait here." Jon cracked open the wax seal and read the contents, his heart racing. A lead—a ship seen departing the docks the night of Spiritseve.

He darted to the desk, scribbled two short notes, sealed them, and handed them off to the messenger.

"One for the Principal Secretary and one for the Captain of the HMS *Isabelle*," Jon said. "May Terra speed your steps."

The messenger nodded and sped off.

The chains of duty were invisible, but with Brennan doing what the man in Jon—and not the king—longed to do, they felt just as heavy. Jon stared after the messenger, shutting out the voices in the room for a moment, his eyes open until the world before him became a blur.

74

*T*he salt on the air was thick as Brennan boarded the carrack's gangplank. The HMS *Isabelle* was the only ship from the Royal Emaurrian Navy to have returned to the Bay of Amar since the loyalists had retaken Courdeval.

The waterway from the hidden cavern had let out to the bay. The *Siren*, an independent Kezani caravel, had been the only ship seen on the Bay of Amar by the militia fighting near the docks. If he could find where the *Siren* made berth, then perhaps he had a chance of finding Rielle. When he had sent Jon a note with this information, the king had offered the HMS *Isabelle* to him at once.

After Spiritseve, the full moon had brought suffering the likes of which Brennan had nearly forgotten, crippling nights from nearly a decade ago, but now he had about a month's time before he would be forced to Change again. Before then, he would be in Suguz, and he would find out what he needed to know by any means necessary. By naming him Principal Secretary, a mere formality, Jon had nevertheless given him carte blanche to reacquire Rielle.

And that was exactly what Brennan intended to do.

He pulled on his hood and descended below deck.

END OF BOOK ONE

Thanks for reading *Blade & Rose*! If you enjoyed the adventure, please consider sharing your thoughts on social media and leaving a review on Amazon or Goodreads. I can't overstate how important this is, especially for indie authors. You'd have my eternal gratitude!

Ready for the next installment in the Blade and Rose series? The next book in the series is called *By Dark Deeds*, available now!

AUTHOR'S NOTE

Thank you for reading *Blade & Rose*, the first book in the Blade and Rose series. If you'd like to find out about new releases, you can sign up for my newsletter at www.mirandahonfleur.com. As a thank-you gift, you will receive "Winter Wren," a prequel short story to the Blade and Rose series, featuring Rielle's first meeting with a certain paladin.

If you enjoyed this book and would like to see more, please consider sharing your thoughts about it on social media and leaving a review—it really helps me as an indie author to know whether people like my work and want to read more of it.

Rielle's journey continues in *By Dark Deeds*, the second volume in the six-book Blade and Rose series. Like its name, *By Dark Deeds* is a darker story in many ways, and when I set out to write this series, the vision of the other side beyond struggle and adversity, the dawn after a long night, was full in my heart. I hope you will find experiencing Rielle's journey—along with its ups and downs—as rewarding as I found writing it.

I have a lot of people to thank for this book. Firstly, my husband, Tony, whose encouragement to start writing again made this book possible and whose constant patience in entertaining my brainstorming is proof positive of his love. Thanks also go to my mom, who listened to my cockamamie plan to trade in law for writing fiction and had the grace to ask, "So what's your book about?"

And huge thanks go to my close friends at Enclave, whose feedback and enthusiasm have made this book a thousand times better—Ryan Muree,

Katherine Bennet, and Emily Gorman, I couldn't have done this without you, and there's no one else I'd rather be taking this journey with... all the way to the French castle and beyond. Thanks also to my friend, Gwynn White, who's guided me, been with this book since the early drafts, and given me the tough love that set me on the right path.

Thanks also go to Imogen Keeper, for ripping this manuscript to shreds, just like I asked. "Out of the hottest fire comes the strongest steel," and thanks to you, this steel is the strongest I could make it. Thanks also go to my critiquers and beta readers: Sue Seabury, Deborah Osborne, Zeta Lordes, Elkin Kennard, R.A. Winter, William MacBride, Ernesto Victorio, Ray Harmeyer, L.R. Todd, M. Lavena Murray, William Huffam, Susan Stuckey, Annie Perriment, Monalisa Foster, and Maria Arnt, whose feedback encouraged me to keep at it until I got it right.

I also never dreamed I'd have an audiobook published, but here we are! As of November 2018, *Blade & Rose* is available in audio on Audible, Amazon, and iTunes. A huge thank-you to the extremely talented Amanda Leigh Cobb for her superb job bringing the characters and the story to life. Thanks also to Patrycja Pakula and Lea Vickery for their hard work on getting it ready for release with me, and Lea—you know just how indispensable you are to me. Hiring you has been one of the best decisions I've made in this career, and I'm so grateful for all you do for me.

And you, my readers. I couldn't do this without you! I love hearing from you, so please feel free to drop me a line on: www.mirandahon fleur.com, Facebook, or Instagram. Thank you for reading!

Sincerely,
Miri

ABOUT THE AUTHOR

 Miranda Honfleur is a born-and-raised Chicagoan living in Indianapolis. She grew up on fantasy and science fiction novels, spending nearly as much time in Valdemar, Pern, Tortall, Narnia, and Middle Earth as in reality.

In another life, her J.D. and M.B.A. were meant to serve a career in law, but now she gets to live her dream job: writing speculative fiction starring fierce heroines and daring heroes who make difficult choices along their adventures and intrigues, all with a generous (over)dose of romance.

Her current series include Blade and Rose, a romantic epic fantasy spanning six books, and The Dark-Elves of Nightbloom, a series of fantasy romance standalones. With over 250,000 books sold, Miranda has been toying with readers' hearts and apologizing for crushing them since 2017.

When she's not snarking, writing, or reading her Kindle, she hangs out and watches Netflix with her husband, gets constantly tackled by her dogs Gizmo and Luna, and plays board games with her friends.

Reach her at:
www.mirandahonfleur.com
miri@mirandahonfleur.com

instagram.com/mirandahonfleur

amazon.com/author/mirandahonfleur

facebook.com/MirandaHonfleur

bookbub.com/authors/miranda-honfleur

goodreads.com/MirandaHonfleur

patreon.com/honfleur

tiktok.com/@mirandahonfleur

twitter.com/MirandaHonfleur

pinterest.com/mirandahonfleur

youtube.com/mirandahonfleur1